The Minerva Anthology of 20th Century Women's Fiction

Judy Cooke was born in Wiltshire in 1938 and educated at King's College, University of London. She lectured in modern literature in the Extra-Mural Department, University of London, and in the USA, and became Head of the English department at Richmond College, Surrey. In 1981 she founded *The Fiction Magazine* which she edited until its demise in 1987, when she published a collection of stories, essays and poems by its contributors, *The Best of the Fiction Magazine*. She is now a freelance editor and works in the literature department of the British Council. Together with Malcolm Bradbury she is editing *New Writing*, an annual British Council anthology. She writes critical articles, reviews fiction regularly for the *Guardian* and has published short stories and a novel, *New Road*.

The Minerva Anthology
of 20th Century Women's Fiction

Judy Cooke was born in Wiltshire in 1938 and educated at King's College, University of London. She lectured in modern literature in the Extra-Mural Department, University of London, and in the USA, and became Head of the English department at Richmond College, Surrey. In 1981 she founded The Fiction Magazine, which she edited until its demise in 1987, when she published a collection of stories, essays and poems by its contributors: The Best of the Fiction Magazine. She is now a freelance editor and works in the literature department of the British Council. Together with Malcolm Bradbury she is editing New Writing, an annual British Council anthology. She writes critical articles, reviews fiction regularly for the Guardian, and has published short stories and a novel, New Road.

The Minerva Anthology of 20th Century Women's Fiction

Edited by JUDY COOKE

Minerva

A Minerva Paperback
THE MINERVA ANTHOLOGY OF
20TH CENTURY WOMEN'S FICTION

First published in Great Britain 1991
by Lime Tree
This Minerva edition published 1992
by Mandarin Paperbacks
Michelin House, 81 Fulham Road, London SW3 6RB

Minerva is an imprint of the Octopus Publishing Group,
a division of Reed International Books Limited

Introduction, novel extract introductions, biographical
notes and selection copyright © Judy Cooke 1991
The authors have asserted their moral rights

A CIP catalogue record for this title
is available from the British Library
ISBN 0 7493 9943 0

Printed and bound in Great Britain by
BPCC Hazells Ltd

Member of BPCC Ltd

This book is sold subject to the condition
that it shall not, by way of trade or otherwise,
be lent, resold, hired out, or otherwise circulated
without the publisher's prior consent in any form
of binding or cover other than that in which
it is published and without a similar condition
including this condition being imposed
on the subsequent purchaser.

Contents

Acknowledgements	vii
Introduction	ix
Margaret Atwood *Cat's Eye*	1
Elizabeth Bowen *The Death of the Heart*	27
Anita Brookner *Latecomers*	51
Angela Carter *The Magic Toyshop*	75
Colette *The Cat*	95
Anita Desai *Clear Light of Day*	195
Margaret Drabble *The Millstone*	259
Daphne Du Maurier *The Birds*	275
Marguerite Duras *The Lover*	319
Buchi Emecheta *Second Class Citizen*	331
Zoë Fairbairns *Daddy's Girls*	361
Nadine Gordimer *Blinder*	389
Georgina Hammick *People for Lunch*	401
Patricia Highsmith *Something You Have To Live With*	431
Ruth Prawer Jhabvala *How I Became a Holy Mother*	453
Rosamond Lehmann *Invitation to the Waltz*	479
Doris Lessing *The New Man*	499
Olivia Manning *The Spoilt City*	511
Katherine Mansfield *Prelude*	555
Alice Munro *Miles City, Montana*	613
Iris Murdoch *The Bell*	643
Edna O'Brien *Girl With Green Eyes*	697
Kathy Page *The Ancient Siddanese*	733

Sylvia Plath *The Bell Jar*	757
Jean Rhys *Wide Sargasso Sea*	791
Françoise Sagan *Bonjour Tristesse*	819
Ntozake Shange *Sassafrass, Cypress & Indigo*	843
Elizabeth Smart *By Grand Central Station I Sat Down and Wept*	867
Amy Tan *The Joy Luck Club*	875
Alice Walker *Everyday Use*	897
Fay Weldon *The Hearts and Lives of Men*	911
Edith Wharton *Pomegranate Seed*	983
Jeanette Winterson *Sexing the Cherry*	1025
Virginia Woolf *To The Lighthouse*	1041
Biographical Notes	1113

Acknowledgements

The original publication details of the texts in this anthology are given below. Copyright material is reproduced by kind permission of the publishers and authors. Every effort has been made to trace copyright owners correctly and credit them accordingly. Apologies are made for any errors or omissions.

Margaret Atwood, *Cat's Eye*. First published 1989 by Bloomsbury Publishing Ltd; copyright © 1989 Margaret Atwood.

Elizabeth Bowen, *The Death of the Heart*. First published 1938 in Great Britain by Jonathan Cape Ltd. Copyright © Elizabeth Bowen 1966.

Anita Brookner, *Latecomers*. First published in Great Britain by Jonathan Cape Ltd; copyright © Anita Brookner 1988.

Angela Carter, *The Magic Toyshop*. First published 1967 in Great Britain by William Heinemann Ltd; copyright © Angela Carter 1967.

Colette, *The Cat*. First published 1933 as *La Chatte*. This translation from the *Fleuron* edition first published in England in 1953 by Martin Secker and Warburg Ltd. Reprinted by permission of Martin Secker and Warburg Ltd.

Anita Desai, *Clear Light of Day*. First published 1980 in Great Britain by William Heinemann Ltd; copyright © Anita Desai 1980. Reprinted by permission of William Heinemann Ltd.

Margaret Drabble, *The Millstone*. First published 1965 in Great Britain by Weidenfeld & Nicolson; copyright © Margaret Drabble 1965.

Daphne Du Maurier, *The Birds*. First published 1952 by Victor Gollancz Ltd, in *The Apple Tree and some stories*; © 1952 The Estate of Daphne Du Maurier. Acknowledgement is also made to Curtis Brown on behalf of the Estate of Daphne Du Maurier.

Marguerite Duras, *The Lover*. Translated from the French by Barbara Bray, Collins 1985. Originally published in France as *L'Amant* by Les Editions de Minuit. Copyright © 1984 Les Editions de Minuit. Translation copyright © 1985 by Random House Inc. and William Collins.

Buchi Emecheta, *Second Class Citizen*. First published 1976 by Allison & Busby; copyright © 1974 Buchi Emecheta.

Zoë Fairbairns, *Daddy's Girls*. First published 1991 in Great Britain by Methuen London; copyright © Zoë Fairbairns 1991.

Nadine Gordimer, *Blinder*. From the collection *Something Out There*, first published 1984 in Great Britain by Jonathan Cape Ltd; copyright © Nadine Gordimer 1984.

Georgina Hammick, *People for Lunch*. From the collection *People for Lunch*, first published 1987 in Great Britain by Methuen London; copyright © Georgina Hammick 1987.

Patricia Highsmith, *Something You Have to Live With*. First published in *Ellery Queen's Mystery Magazine*, July 1976. From the collection *Slowly, Slowly in the Wind*, published in Great Britain 1979 by William Heinemann Ltd. Copyright © 1979 Patricia Highsmith. Reprinted by permission of William Heinemann Ltd.

Ruth Prawer Jhabvala, *How I Became a Holy Mother*. From the collection *How I Became a Holy Mother*, John Murray, 1976. Copyright © 1976 Ruth Prawer Jhabvala.

Rosamond Lehmann, *Invitation to the Waltz*. First published 1947; copyright © The Albatross Ltd 1947. Acknowledgement is made to The Society of Authors as the literary representative of the Estate of Rosamond Lehmann.

Doris Lessing, *The New Man*. From the collection *A Man and Two Women*, first published 1958 in Great Britain by Michael Joseph; copyright © Doris Lessing 1958.

Olivia Manning, *The Spoilt City*. First published 1962 in Great Britain by William Heinemann Ltd; copyright © Olivia Manning 1962. Reprinted by permission of William Heinemann Ltd.

Katherine Mansfield, *Prelude*. From the collection *Katherine Mansfield Short Stories*, selected and introduced by Claire Tomalin, published in Everyman Paperback 1983. *Prelude* was first published by the Hogarth Press in 1918 © Katherine Mansfield.

Alice Munro, *Miles City, Montana*. From the collection *The Progress of Love*, first published 1987 in Great Britain by Chatto & Windus Ltd; copyright © Alice Munro 1985, 1986. Originally published in *The New Yorker*.

Iris Murdoch, *The Bell*. First published 1958 in Great Britain by Chatto & Windus Ltd; copyright © Iris Murdoch 1958.

Edna O'Brien, *Girl With Green Eyes*. First published as *The Lonely Girl* 1962 in Great Britain by Jonathan Cape Ltd; published as *Girl With Green Eyes* 1964 by Penguin Books; copyright © Edna O'Brien 1962.

Kathy Page, *The Ancient Siddanese*. From the collection *As In Music*, first published 1990 in Great Britain by Methuen London; copyright © Kathy Page 1990.

Sylvia Plath, *The Bell Jar*. First published 1963 in Great Britain by William Heinemann Ltd; copyright © Victoria Lucas 1963.

Jean Rhys, *Wide Sargasso Sea*. First published 1966 in Great Britain by Andre Deutsch Ltd; copyright © Jean Rhys 1966.

Françoise Sagan, *Bonjour Tristesse*. First published 1955 in Great Britain by John Murray (Publishers) Ltd. Translated by Irene Ash.

Ntozake Shange, *Sassafras, Cypress & Indigo*. First published 1983 in Great Britain by Methuen London; copyright © Ntozake Shange 1982.

Elizabeth Smart, *By Grand Central Station I Sat Down and Wept*. First published 1945 in Great Britain by Editions Poetry London (Nicholson & Watson); copyright © Elizabeth Smart 1966.

Amy Tan, *The Joy Luck Club*. First published 1989 in Great Britain by William Heinemann Ltd; copyright © Amy Tan 1989. Reprinted by permission of William Heinemann Ltd.

Alice Walker, *Everyday Use*. From the collection *In Love and Trouble*, first published 1984 in Great Britain by the Women's Press; copyright © Alice Walker 1984.

Fay Weldon, *The Hearts and Lives of Men*. First published 1987 in Great Britain by William Heinemann Ltd; copyright © Fay Weldon 1987. Reprinted by permission of William Heinemann Ltd.

Edith Wharton, *Pomegranate Seed*. From *The World Over*, first published 1936 by D. Appleton-Century Co. Inc. and Hearst Magazines Inc. Copyright © 1936 D. Appleton-Century Inc. and Hearst Magazines Inc.

Jeanette Winterson, *Sexing the Cherry*. First published 1989 in Great Britain by Bloomsbury Publishing Ltd; copyright © Jeanette Winterson 1989.

Virginia Woolf, *To The Lighthouse*. First published May 1927 in Great Britain by Hogarth Press; copyright © the Estate of Virginia Woolf 1927.

Introduction

This collection of fiction, twenty-two novel extracts and twelve short stories, begins and ends with a woman considering her situation as an artist, in each case using the analogy of painting as a way of discussing problems in writing. Virginia Woolf and Margaret Atwood are working at a distance of some sixty years, which affords us a perspective on several crucial issues informing their fiction and that of their contemporaries.

Society has changed enormously between 1927 and 1989, the dates of Woolf's *To The Lighthouse* and Atwood's *Cat's Eye*, but give or take World War Two, the contraceptive pill and the legal and economic advances brought about by feminism thus far, the two novelists show remarkable accord. They acknowledge and comment on the upheavals shaping public life but its priorities seem removed from the major preoccupations and achievements of their own best work. Woolf was fifty-five on publication day, Atwood, fifty.

The relationship between each novelist's sexuality and her creativity establishes itself as a focus in most questions of definition. 'The smell of blood on the wall,' is what Atwood's protagonist, Elaine Risley, values most in painting. By which she means the cost of exploring and discovering the truth about herself, as much as the pain she has inflicted on her subjects. Mrs Smeath, for instance, mother of Grace, a childhood companion, a churchgoer, a good influence: Mrs Smeath is now to be seen rendered in egg tempera, 'wearing nothing but her flowered one-breast bib apron ... reclining on her maroon velvet sofa, rising to heaven, which is full of rubber plants, while a moon shaped like a doily floats in the sky.'

'I caught some shit for that piece,' Elaine recalls. Her own sense of self depended upon a vehement rejection of the Mrs and Miss Smeaths of this world, their assumptions about morality, their half-conscious cruelties. Now she finds herself in Toronto again, her home town, attending a retrospective of her own work and as isolated as ever, patronised by a new generation of Miss Smeaths, up-front post-feminists, who want to claim her as a witness to sexual harassment, sexual discrimination. Elaine has her own views about the politics of the art world. ('Listen,' she tells her husband, 'You know how hard it is to get a retrospective anywhere, if you're female?') But no way is she going to share these reservations with Charna, a young interviewer who makes her feel 'as if I'm at the dentist, mouth gracelessly open while some stranger with a light and a mirror gazes down my throat at something I can't see.'

Women are the sex to beware, then, in Atwood's book. And in *To The Lighthouse*. Woolf's protagonist, Lily Briscoe, is famously oppressed by the widowed Mr Ramsay (a portrait of Leslie Stephens, Woolf's father) and his melancholia. 'She set her clean canvas firmly upon the easel, as a barrier, frail, but she hoped sufficiently substantial to ward off Mr Ramsay... He changed everything. She could not see the colour; she could not see the lines; even with his back turned towards her, she could only think, But he'll be down on me in a moment ...' She remembers, too, Charles Tansley's judgement, delivered when she was in her thirties: 'Women can't paint, can't write.' Now she is forty-five, facing another new blank canvas and it is, still, *not* Mr Ramsay but his wife with whom she most dreads a confrontation. Because Mrs Ramsay, who is dead, now, was Lily's toughest adversary as well as her closest friend. Mrs Ramsay wanted Lily to dedicate herself to a man in marriage rather than preserving her independence, let alone a dedication to art.

Lily Briscoe becomes reconciled to the difficult memories

surounding the resented, mourned Mrs Ramsay (a portrait of Julia Stephens, Woolf's mother). Whereas Atwood's artists paints caricature, Lily celebrates her old enemy and even adopts her recipe for happiness, 'Life stand still here,' as her aesthetic principle. 'Life stand still.' It's a lot less violent than Atwood's image of blood on the wall but there is a chilling absolutism about the principle invoked, a foreshadowing of Plath's saddest poem, *Edge*, in which she describes death as perfection. The sense of tension and acute ambivalence, so vividly expressed by Woolf and Atwood, runs though much of the writing by women which has been most prized this century.

Jane Austen can persuade us that it is a lack of self-knowledge, more than any other factor, which is to blame for her heroines' unhappiness. Emma takes a second look at Mr Knightley, and all's well. There is no such jackpot waiting up ahead for Rosamond Lehmann's seventeen-year-old Olivia, invited to waltz, nor for Edna O'Brien's green-eyed girl. Precisely because they kow who they are and what they feel, they are unable to compromise. Once off, the blinkers stay off. The initiation into love, and then the loss of it, has inspired some of the most original prose within these pages, from Elizabeth Bowen's *The Death of the Heart* to Jean Rhys's *The Wide Sargasso Sea*; from Marguerite Duras's portrayal of physical passion in *The Lover* to Elizabeth Smart's searing depiction of betrayal in *On Grand Central Station I Sat Down and Wept*.

Angela Carter's *The Magic Toyshop* strikes such a splendid note because it confronts this romantic agony head on. It is a spirited defence of an equally convincing point of view: that the pleasure principle will overcome any amount of Mrs Ramsays. The more Melanie wants Finn, the more she becomes herself. Carter's brilliant fable illuminates another major theme running through this anthology, that of children and childhood.

It is a commonplace that the artist may have suffered a lonely or unhappy childhood and retreated to an inner life of words and dreams. Men write about childhood, of course, but with a few honourable exceptions, such as J. G. Ballard's novel, *The Kindness of Women*, the topic is more fully stated, more deeply felt, by women. A child cannot be perfected, like a work of art. It continually challenges its mother's preconceptions about character, and education, and, ultimately, justice; about a son's or a daughter's future. Children are indeed a novel form and the responsibilities and exasperations involved in their upbringing have produced some heartbreakingly funny writing. Try Georgina Hammick's story *People to Lunch* or the extract from Fay Weldon's novel, *The Hearts and Minds of Men*.

Paradoxically, the burden of motherhood is often a liberation for the artist. Margaret Drabble's work has changed and developed in many ways since her first books were published but her description of childbirth in *The Millstone* (1965) remains for me one of the most moving and innovatory passages in modern fiction – a breakthrough. In Buchi Emecheta's novel, *Second Class Citizen*, the protagonist, Adah, is a Nigerian living in London who decides to break with tradition and go out to work, thus scandalising her husband. 'She would only be responsible for her children, their clothes, their nursery fees and anything else the children needed. But Francis would not know how much she earned and on what date.' This momentous decision leads to many more and it isn't long before, 'her old dream came popping up. Why not attempt writing. She had always wanted to write. Why not?'

Entertainment and escapism are two important requirements to be met when selecting five hundred pages of narrative. To be fixed by Edith Wharton's glittering eye, or that of Kathy Page or Daphne du Maurier or Patricia Highsmith and to gradually sense the outcome of their ghost story, fantasy, horror story and psychological thriller respectively – that is to be blissfully unaware of the immediate moment and its demands. And there are so many new worlds within these pages to enter and come to understand. Anita Desai's detailed family portrait, set in Delhi; Amy Tan's exquisitely told stories of Chinese/American culture; Olivia Manning's stylish evocation of wartime Bucharest.

But why select writing by one sex? It is arguable that the female experience is given a clearer shape, a fuller emphasis, in fiction by women. Women share their lives with other women in a way that men don't always choose to do with other men. The key texts in this collection highlight that particular attraction. Over a twenty-five year span of teaching, and then editing, fiction, these books have become my companions; books I have bought or borrowed for myself. I should perhaps add that, given one choice, Anthony Powell's *A Dance to the Music of Time* would have to be my own favourite modern novel; its humour has taken me through more than one re-reading. But if I wanted to reflect on what giving birth is like, or life with adolescent children, or first love – no, I wouldn't go to Powell, or even Ballard. For that sense of companionship, I would turn to the writers here.

Judy Cooke

The Minerva Anthology
of 20th Century Women's Fiction

Margaret Atwood

extract from

Cat's Eye

Elaine Risley is alone in Toronto, her home town, attending a retrospective of her work at an avant-garde gallery. She finds herself 'in the middle of my life', enjoying a successful career as a painter with two grown-up daughters from her first marriage and a second husband, Ben, whom she loves. 'He is not any kind of artist, for which I am grateful.' Setting that the memories evoked by the trip will challenge her in a number of ways, she is nevertheless unprepared for the vivid ambivalence of her feelings towards Cordelia and Grace, childhood companions, and that part of her past shared with them.

Margaret Atwood

extract from

Cat's Eye

Elaine Risley is alone in Toronto, her home town, attending a retrospective of her work at an avant-garde gallery. She finds herself 'in the middle of my life', enjoying a successful career as a painter with two grown-up daughters from her first marriage and a second husband, Ben, whom she loves. 'He is not any kind of artist, for which I am grateful.' Sensing that the memories evoked by the trip will challenge her in a number of ways, she is nevertheless unprepared for the vivid ambivalence of her feelings towards Cordelia and Grace, childhood companions, and that part of her past shared with them.

I walk along Queen Street, past used comic book stores, windows full of crystal eggs and seashells, a lot of sulky black clothing. I wish I were back in Vancouver, in front of the fireplace with Ben, looking out over the harbour, while the giant slugs munch away at the greenery in the back garden. Fireplaces, back gardens: I wasn't thinking about them when I used to come down here to visit Jon, over the wholesale luggage store. Around the corner was the Maple Leaf Tavern, where I drank draft beer in the dark, two stoplights away from the art school where I drew naked women and ate my heart out. The streetcars rattled the front windows. There are still streetcars.

'I don't want to go,' I said to Ben.

'You don't have to,' he said. 'Call it off. Come down to Mexico.'

'They've gone to all the trouble,' I said. 'Listen, you know how hard it is to get a retrospective anywhere, if you're female?'

'Why is it important?' he said. 'You sell anyway.'

'I have to go,' I said. 'It wouldn't be right.' I was brought up to say please and thank you.

'Okay,' he said. 'You know what you're doing.' He gave me a hug.

I wish it were true.

Here is Sub-Versions, between a restaurant-supply store and a tattoo parlour. Both of these will go, in time: once

3

places like Sub-Versions move in, the handwriting's on the wall.

I open the gallery door, walk in with that sinking feeling I always have in galleries. It's the carpets that do it to me, the hush, the sanctimoniousness of it all: galleries are too much like churches, there's too much reverence, you feel there should be some genuflecting going on. Also I don't like it that this is where paintings end up, on these neutral-toned walls with the track lighting, sterilized, rendered safe and acceptable. It's as if somebody's been around spraying the paintings with air freshener, to kill the smell. The smell of blood on the wall.

This gallery is not totally sterilized, there are touches of cutting edge: a heating pipe shows, one wall is black. I don't give a glance to what's still on the walls, I hate those neo-expressionist dirty greens and putrid oranges, post this, post that. Everything is post these days, as if we're all just a footnote to something earlier that was real enough to have a name of its own.

Several of my own paintings have been uncrated and are leaning against the wall. They've been tracked down, requested, gathered in from whoever owns them. Whoever owns them is not me; worse luck, I'd get a better price now. The owners' names will be on little white cards beside the paintings, along with mine, as if mere ownership is on a par with creation. Which they think it is.

If I cut off my ear, would the market value go up? Better still, stick my head in the oven, blow out my brains. What rich art collectors like to buy, among other things, is a little vicarious craziness.

Face-out is a piece I painted twenty years ago: Mrs Smeath, beautifully rendered in egg tempera, with her grey hairpin crown and her potato face and her spectacles, wearing nothing but her flowered one-breast bib apron. She's reclining on her maroon velvet sofa, rising to Heaven, which is full of rubber plants, while a moon shaped like a doily floats in the sky. *Rubber Plant: The*

Ascension, it's called. The angels around her are 1940s Christmas stickers, laundered little girls in white, with rag-set curly hair. The word *Heaven* is stencilled at the top of the painting with a child's school stencil set. I thought that was a nifty thing to do, at the time.

I caught some shit for that piece, as I recall. But not because of the stencil.

I don't look at this painting for very long, or at any of them. If I do I'll start finding things wrong with them. I'll want to take an Exacto knife to them, torch them, clear the walls. Begin again.

A woman strides towards me from the back, in a modified blonde porcupine haircut, a purple jumpsuit and green leather boots. I know immediately that I should not have worn this powder-blue jogging outfit. Powder-blue is lightweight. I should've worn nun black, Dracula black, like all proper female painters. I should have some clotted-neck vampire lipstick, instead of wimping out with Rose Perfection. But that really would make me look like Haggis McBaggis. At this age the complexion can't stand those grape-jelly reds, I'd look all white and wrinkly.

But I will tough out the jogging suit, I'll pretend I meant it. It could be iconoclasm, how do they know? A powder-blue jogging suit lacks pretensions. The good thing about being out of fashion is that you're never in fashion either, so you can never be last year's model. That's my excuse for my painting, too; or it was for years.

'Hi,' says the woman. 'You must be Elaine! You don't look much like your picture.' What does that mean, I think: better or worse? 'We've talked a lot on the phone. My name is Charna.' Toronto didn't used to have names like Charna. My hand gets crunched, this woman's got about ten heavy silver rings strung on to her fingers like knuckledusters. 'We were just wondering about the order.' There are two more women; each of them looks five times more artistic than I do. They have abstract-art ear-rings, hair arrangements. I am feeling dowdy.

They've got take-out gourmet sprout-and-avocado sandwiches and coffee with steamed milk, and we eat those and drink that while we discuss the arrangement of the pictures. I say I favour a chronological approach, but Charna has other ideas, she wants things to go together tonally and resonate and make statements that amplify one another. I get more nervous, this kind of talk makes me twitch. I'm putting some energy into silence, resisting the impulse to say I have a headache and want to go home. I should be grateful, these women are on my side, they planned this whole thing for me, they're doing me an honour, they like what I do. But still I feel outnumbered, as if they are a species of which I am not a member.

Jon comes back tomorrow, from Los Angeles and his chainsaw murder. I can hardly wait. We'll circumvent his wife, go out for lunch, both of us feeling sneaky. But it's merely a civilized thing to do, having lunch with an ex-husband in a comradely way: a good coda to all that smashed crockery and mayhem. We've known each other since the year dot; at my age, our age, that's becoming important. And from here he looks like relief.

Someone else comes in, another woman. 'Andrea!' says Charna, stalking over to her. 'You're late!' She gives Andrea a kiss on the cheek and walks her over to me, holding her arm. 'Andrea wants to do a piece on you,' she says. 'For the opening.'

'I wasn't told about this,' I say. I've been ambushed.

'It came up at the last minute,' says Charna. 'Lucky for us! I'll put you two in the back room, okay? I'll bring you some coffee. Getting the word out, they call it,' she adds, to me, with a wry smile. I allow myself to be herded down the corridor; I can still be bossed around by women like Charna.

'I thought you would be different,' says Andrea as we settle.
'Different how?' I ask.
'Bigger,' she says.
I smile at her. 'I am bigger.'

Andrea checks out my powder-blue jogging suit. She herself is wearing black, approved, glossy black, not early sixties holdover as mine would be. She has red hair out of a spray can and no apologies, cut into a cap like an acorn. She's upsettingly young; to me she doesn't look more than a teenager, though I know she must be in her twenties. Probably she thinks I'm a weird middle-aged frump, sort of like her high school teacher. Probably she's out to get me. Probably she'll succeed.

We sit across from each other at Charna's desk and Andrea sets down her camera and fiddles with her tape-recorder. Andrea writes for a newspaper. 'This is for the Living section,' she says. I know what that means, it used to be the Women's Pages. It's funny that they now call it Living, as if only women are alive and the other things, such as the Sports, are for the dead.

'Living, eh?' I say. 'I'm the mother of two. I bake cookies.' All true. Andrea gives me a dirty look and flicks on her machine.

'How do you handle fame?' she says.

'This isn't fame,' I say. 'Fame is Elizabeth Taylor's cleavage. This stuff is just a media pimple.'

She grins at that. 'Well, could you maybe say something about your generation of artists — your generation of woman artists — and their aspirations and goals?'

'Painters, you mean,' I say. 'What generation is that?'

'The seventies, I suppose,' she says. 'That's when the women's — that's when you started getting attention.'

'The seventies isn't my generation,' I say.

She smiles. 'Well,' she says, 'what is?'

'The forties.'

'The forties?' This is archaeology as far as she's concerned. 'But you couldn't have been ...'

'That was when I grew up,' I say.

'Oh right,' she says. 'You mean it was *formative*. Can you talk about the ways, how it reflects in your work?'

'The colours,' I say. 'A lot of my colours are forties colours.' I'm softening up. At least she doesn't say *like* and *you know* all the time. 'The war. There are people who remember the war and people who don't. There's a cut-off point, there's a difference.'

'You mean the Vietnam War?' she says.

'No,' I say coldly. 'The Second World War.' She looks a bit scared, as if I've just resurrected from the dead, and incompletely at that. She didn't know I was *that* old. 'So,' she says. 'What is the difference?'

'We have long attention spans,' I say. 'We eat everything on our plates. We save string. We make do.'

She looks puzzled. That's all I want to say about the forties. I'm beginning to sweat. I feel as if I'm at the dentist, mouth gracelessly open while some stranger with a light and mirror gazes down my throat at something I can't see.

Brightly and neatly she veers away from the war and back towards women, which was where she wanted to be in the first place. Is it harder for a woman, was I discriminated against, undervalued? What about having children? I give unhelpful replies: all painters feel undervalued. You can do it while they're at school. My husband's been terrific, he gives me a lot of support, some of which has been financial. I don't say which husband.

'So you don't feel it's sort of demeaning to be propped up by a man?' she says.

'Women prop up men all the time,' I say. 'What's wrong with a little reverse propping?'

What I have to say is not altogether what she wants to hear. She'd prefer stories of outrage, although she'd be unlikely to tell them about herself, she's too young. Still, people my age are supposed to have stories of outrage; at least insult, at least put-down. Male art teachers pinching your bum, calling you *baby*, asking you why there are no great female painters, that sort of thing. She would like me to be furious, and quaint.

'Did you have any female mentors?' she asks.

'Female what?'

'Like, teachers, or other woman painters you admired.'

'Shouldn't that be mentresses?' I say nastily. 'There weren't any. My teacher was a man.'

'Who was that?' she says.

'Josef Hrbik. He was very kind to me,' I add quickly. He'd fit the bill for her, but she won't hear that from me. 'He taught me to draw naked women.'

That startles her. 'Well, what about, you know, feminism?' she says. 'A lot of people call you a feminist painter.'

'What indeed,' I say. 'I hate party lines, I hate ghettoes. Anyway, I'm too old to have invented it and you're too young to understand it, so what's the point of discussing it at all?'

'So it's not a meaningful classification for you?' she says.

'I like it that women like my work. Why shouldn't I?'

'Do men like your work?' she asks slyly. She's been going through the back files, she's seen some of those witch-and-succubus pieces.

'Which men?' I say. 'Not everyone likes my work. It's not because I'm a woman. If they don't like a man's work it's not because he's a man. They just don't like it.' I am on dubious ground, and this enrages me. My voice is calm; the coffee seethes within me.

She frowns, diddles with the tape-recorder. 'Why do you paint all those women then?'

'What should I paint, men?' I say. 'I'm a painter. Painters paint women. Rubens painted women, Renoir painted women, Picasso painted women. Everyone paints women. Is there something wrong with painting women?'

'But not like that,' she says.

'Like what?' I say. 'Anyway, why should my women be the same as everyone else's women?' I catch myself picking at my fingers, and stop. In a minute my teeth will be chattering like those of cornered mice. Her voice is getting farther and farther away, I can hardly hear her. But I see her, very clearly: the ribbing on the neck of her sweater, the fine hairs of her cheek, the shine of a button. What I hear is what she isn't saying. *Your clothes are stupid. Your art is crap. Sit up straight and don't answer back*.

'Why do you paint?' she says, and I can hear her again as clear as anything. I hear her exasperation, with me and my refusals.

'Why does anyone do anything?' I say.

* * *

The light fades earlier; on the way home from school we walk through the smoke from burning leaves. It rains, and we have to play inside. We sit on the floor of Grace's room, being quiet because of Mrs Smeath's bad heart, and cut out rolling-pins and frying pans and paste them around our paper ladies.

But Cordelia makes short work of this game. She knows, instantly it seems, why Grace's house has so many Eaton's Catalogues in it. It's because the Smeaths get their clothes that way, the whole family – order them out of the Eaton's Catalogue. There in the Girls' Clothing section are the plaid dresses, the skirts with straps, the winter coats worn by Grace and her sisters, three colours of them, in lumpy, serviceable wool, with hoods: Kelly Green, Royal Blue, Maroon. Cordelia manages to convey that she herself would never wear a coat ordered from the

Eaton's Catalogue. She doesn't say this out loud though. Like the rest of us, she wants to stay on the good side of Grace.

She bypasses the cookware, flips through the pages. She turns to the brassieres, to the elaborately laced and gusseted corsets – foundation garments, they're called – and draws moustaches on the models, whose flesh looks as if it's been painted over with a thin coat of beige plaster. She pencils hair in, under their arms, and on their chests between the breasts. She reads out the descriptions, snorting with stifled laughter: '"Delightfully trimmed in dainty lace, with extra support for the mature figure." That means big bazooms. Look at this – *cup* sizes! Like teacups!'

Breasts fascinate Cordelia, and fill her with scorn. Both of her older sisters have them by now. Perdie and Mirrie sit in their room with its twin beds and sprigged-muslin flounces, filing their nails, laughing softly; or they heat brown wax in little pots in the kitchen and take it upstairs to spread on their legs. They look into their mirrors, making sad faces – 'I look like Haggis McBaggis! It's the curse!' Their wastebaskets smell of decaying flowers.

They tell Cordelia there are some things she's too young to understand, and then they tell these things to her anyway. Cordelia, her voice lowered, her eyes big, passes on the truth: the curse is when blood comes out between your legs. We don't believe her. She produces evidence: a sanitary pad, filched from Perdie's wastebasket. On it is a brown crust, like dried gravy. 'That's not blood,' Grace says with disgust, and she's right, it's nothing like when you cut your finger. Cordelia is indignant. But she can prove nothing.

I haven't thought much about grown-up women's bodies before. But now these bodies are revealed in their true, upsetting light: alien and bizarre, hairy, squashy, monstrous. We hang around outside the room where Perdie and Mirrie are peeling the wax off their legs while they utter yelps of pain, trying to see through the keyhole, giggling: they embarrass us, although we don't know why. They know they're being laughed at and come to the door to shoo us away. 'Cordelia, why don't you and your little friends bug off!' They smile a little ominously, as if they know already what is in store for us. 'Just wait and see,' they say.

This frightens us. Whatever has happened to them, bulging them, softening them, causing them to walk rather than run, as if there's some invisible leash around their necks, holding them in check – whatever it is, it may happen to us too. We look surreptitiously at the breasts of women on the street, of our teachers; though not of our mothers, that would be too close for comfort. We examine our legs and underarms for sprouting hairs, our chests for swellings. But nothing is happening: so far we are safe.

Cordelia turns to the back pages of the catalogue, where the pictures are in grey and black and there are crutches and trusses and prosthetic devices. 'Breast pumps,' she says. 'See this? It's for pumping your titties up bigger, like a bicycle pump.' And we don't know what to believe.

We can't ask our mothers. It's hard to imagine them without clothes, to think of them as having bodies at all, under their dresses. There's a great deal they don't say. Between us and them is a gulf, an abyss, that goes down and down. It's filled with wordlessness. They wrap up the garbage in several layers of newspaper and tie it with string, and even so it drips on to the freshly waxed floor. Their clothes-lines are strung with underpants, nighties, socks, a display of soiled intimacy, which they have washed and rinsed, plunging their hands into the grey curdled water. They know about toilet brushes, about toilet seats, about germs. The world is dirty, no matter how much they clean, and we know they will not welcome our grubby little questions. So instead a long whisper runs among us, from child to child, gathering horror.

Cat's Eye

Cordelia says that men have carrots, between their legs. They aren't really carrots but something worse. They're covered with hair. Seeds come out the end and get into women's stomachs and grow into babies, whether you want it or not. Some men have their carrots pierced and rings set into them as if they are ears.

Cordelia's unclear about how the seeds get out or what they're like. She says they're invisible, but I think this can't be so. If there are seeds at all they must be more like bird seeds, or carrot seeds, long and fine. Also she can't say how the carrot gets in, to plant the seeds. Belly buttons are the obvious choice, but there would have to be a cut, a tear. The whole story is questionable, and the idea that we ourselves could have been produced by such an act is an outrage. I think of beds, where all of this is supposed to take place: the twin beds at Carol's house, always so tidy, the elegant canopy bed at Cordelia's, the dark mahogany-coloured bed in Grace's house, heavily respectable with its crocheted spread and layers of woollen blankets. Such beds are a denial in themselves, a repudiation. I think of Carol's wry-mouthed mother, of Mrs Smeath with her hairpinned crown of greying braids. They would purse their lips, draw themselves up in a dignified manner. They would not permit it.

Grace says, 'God makes babies,' in that final way of hers which means there is nothing more to be discussed. She smiles her buttoned-up disdainful smile, and we are reassured. Better God than us.

But there are doubts. I know, for instance, a lot of things. I know that 'carrot' is not the right word. I've seen dragonflies and beetles, flying around, stuck together, one on the back of the other; I know it's called 'mating'. I know about ovipositors, for laying eggs, on leaves, on caterpillars, on the surface of the water; they're right out on the page, clearly labelled, on the diagrams of insects my father corrects at home. I know about queen ants, and about the female praying mantises eating the males. None of this is much help. I think of Mr and Mrs Smeath, stark naked, with Mr Smeath stuck to the back of Mrs Smeath. Such an image, even without the addition of flight, will not do.

I could ask my brother. But, although we've examined scabs and toe-jam under the microscope, although we aren't worried by pickled ox eyes and gutted fish and whatever can be found under dead logs, putting this question to him would be indelicate, perhaps hurtful. I think of JUPITER scrolled on the sand in his angular script, by his extra, dextrous finger. In Cordelia's version it will end up covered with hair. Maybe he doesn't know.

Cordelia says boys put their tongues in your mouth when they kiss you. Not any boys we know, older ones. She says this the same way my brother says 'slug juice' or 'snot' when Carol's around, and Carol does the same thing, the same wrinkle of the nose, the same wriggle. Grace says that Cordelia is being disgusting.

I think about the spit you sometimes see, downtown, on the sidewalk; or cow's tongues in butcher's shops. Why would they want to do such a thing, put their tongues in other people's mouths? Just to be repulsive, of course. Just to see what you would do.

* * *

I go up the cellar stairs, which have black rubber stair-treads nailed on to them. Mrs Smeath is standing at the kitchen sink in her bib apron. She's finished her nap and now she's upright, getting supper. She's peeling potatoes; she often peels things. The peel falls from her large knuckly hands in a long pale spiral. The paring knife she uses is worn so thin its blade is barely more than a crescent-moon sliver. The kitchen is steamy, and smells of marrow-fat and stewing bones.

Cat's Eye

Mrs Smeath turns and looks at me, a skinless potato in her left hand, the knife in her right. She smiles. 'Grace says your family don't go to church,' she says. 'Maybe you'd like to come with us. To our church.'

'Yes,' says Grace, who has come up the stairs behind me. And the idea is pleasing. I'll have Grace all to myself on Sunday mornings, without Carol or Cordelia. Grace is still the desirable one, the one we all want.

When I tell my parents about this plan they become anxious. 'Are you sure you really want to go?' my mother says. When she was young, she says, she had to go to church whether she liked it or not. Her father was very strict. She couldn't whistle on Sundays. 'Are you really sure?'

My father says he doesn't believe in brainwashing children. When you're grown up, then you can make up your own mind about religion, which has been responsible for a lot of wars and massacres in his opinion, as well as bigotry and intolerance. 'Every educated person should know the Bible,' he says. 'But she's only eight.'

'Almost nine,' I say.

'Well,' says my father. 'Don't believe everything you hear.'

On Sunday I put on the clothes my mother and I have picked out, a dress of dark-blue and green wool plaid, white ribbed stockings that attach with garters on to my stiff white cotton waist. I have more dresses than I once had, but I don't go shopping with my mother to help pick them out, the way Carol does. My mother hates shopping, nor does she sew. My girls' clothes are second-hand, donated by a distant friend of my mother's who has a larger daughter. None of these dresses fits me very well; the hems droop, or the sleeves bunch up under my arms. I think this is the norm, for dresses. The white stockings are new though, and even itchier than the brown ones I wear to school.

I take my blue cat's eye marble out of my red plastic purse and leave it in my bureau drawer, and put the nickel my mother's given me for the collection plate into my purse instead. I walk along the rutted streets towards Grace's house, in my shoes; it isn't time for boots yet. Grace opens her front door when I ring. She must have been waiting for me. She has a dress on too and white stockings, and navy-blue bows at the ends of her braids. She looks me over. 'She doesn't have a hat,' she says.

Mrs Smeath, standing in the hallway, considers me as if I'm an orphan left on her doorstep. She sends Grace upstairs to search for another hat, and Grace comes back down with an old one of dark-blue velvet with an elastic under the chin. It's too small for me but Mrs Smeath says it will do for now. 'We don't go into our church with our heads uncovered,' she says. She emphasizes *our*, as if there are other, inferior, bareheaded churches.

Mrs Smeath has a sister, who is going with us to church. Her name is Aunt Mildred. She's older and has been a missionary in China. She has the same knuckly red hands, the same metal-rimmed glasses, the same hair crown as Mrs Smeath, only hers is all grey, and the hairs on her face are grey too and more numerous. Both of them have hats that look like packages of felt carelessly done up, with several ends sticking into the air. I've seen such hats in the Eaton's Catalogues of several years back, worn by models with sleeked-back hair and high cheek-bones and dark-red, glossy mouths. On Mrs Smeath and her sister they don't have the same effect.

When all of the Smeaths have their coats and hats on we climb into their car: Mrs Smeath and Aunt Mildred in the front, me and Grace and her two little sisters in the back. Although I still worship Grace, this worship is not at all physical, and being squashed into the back seat of

Cat's Eye

her car, so close to her, embarrasses me. Right in front of my face Mr Smeath is driving. He is short and bald and hardly ever seen. It's the same with Carol's father, with Cordelia's: in the daily life of houses, fathers are largely invisible.

We drive through the nearly empty Sunday streets, following the streetcar tracks west. The air inside the car fills with the used breath of the Smeaths, a stale smell like dried saliva. The church is large and made of brick; on the top of it, instead of a cross, there's a thing that looks like an onion and goes around. I ask about this onion, which may mean something religious for all I know, but Grace says it's a ventilator.

Mr Smeath parks the car and we get out of it and go inside. We sit in a row, on a long bench made of dark shiny wood, which Grace says is a pew. This is the first time I've ever been inside a church. There's a high ceiling, with lights shaped like morning glories hanging down on chains, and a plain gold cross up at the front with a vase of white flowers. Behind that there are three stained-glass windows. The biggest, middle one has Jesus in white, with his hands held out sideways and a white bird hovering over his head. Underneath it says in thick black Bible-type letters with dots in between the words: THE·KINGDOM·OF·GOD·IS·WITHIN·YOU. On the left side is Jesus sitting down, sideways in pinky-red, with two children leaning on his knees. It says: SUFFER·THE·LITTLE·CHILDREN. Both of the Jesuses have haloes. On the other side is a woman in blue, with no halo and a white kerchief partly covering her face. She's carrying a basket and reaching down one hand. There's a man sitting down at her feet, with what looks like a bandage wound around his head. It says: THE·GREATEST·OF·THESE·IS·CHARITY. Around all these windows are borders, with vines twining around and bunches of grapes, and different flowers. The windows have light coming in behind them, which illuminates them. I can hardly take my eyes off them.

Then there's organ music and everyone stands up, and I become confused. I watch what Grace does, and stand up when she stands up, sit when she sits. During the songs she holds the hymn book open and points, but I don't know any of the tunes. After a while it's time for us to go to Sunday School, and so we file out with the other children in a line and go down into the church basement.

At the entrance to the Sunday School place there's a blackboard, where someone has printed, in coloured chalk: KILROY WAS HERE. Beside this is a drawing of a man's eyes and nose, looking over a fence.

Sunday School is in classes, like ordinary school. The teachers are younger though; ours is an older teenager with a light-blue hat and a veil. Our class is all girls. The teacher reads us a Bible story about Joseph and his coat of many colours. Then she listens as the girls recite things they're supposed to have memorized. I sit on my chair, dangling my legs. I haven't memorized anything. The teacher smiles at me and says she hopes I will come back every week.

After this all the different classes go into a large room with rows of grey wooden benches in it, like the benches we eat our lunches on at school. We sit on the benches, the lights are turned off, and coloured slides are projected on to the bare wall at the far end of the room. The slides aren't photographs but paintings. They look old-fashioned. The first one shows a knight riding through the forest, gazing upwards to where a shaft of light streams down through the trees. The skin of this knight is very white, his eyes are large like a girl's, and his hand is pressed to where his heart must be, under his armour, which looks like car fenders. Under his large, luminous face I can see the light-switches and the top boards of the wainscoting, and the corner of the small piano, where it juts out.

The next picture has the same knight only smaller, and

underneath him some words, which we sing to the heavy thumping of chords from the unseen piano:

> I would be true, for there are those who trust me,
> I would be pure, for there are those who care,
> I would be strong, for there is much to suffer,
> I would be brave, for there is much to dare.

Beside me, in the dark, I hear Grace's voice going up and up, thin and reedy, like a bird's. She knows all the words; she knew all the words to her memory passage from the Bible too. When we bend our heads to pray I feel suffused with goodness, I feel included, taken in. God loves me, whoever he is.

After Sunday School we go back into the regular church for the last part, and I put my nickel on the collection plate. Then there is something called the Doxology. Then we walk out of the church and stuff back into the Smeath's car, and Grace says carefully, 'Daddy, may we go and see the trains?' and the little girls, with a show of enthusiasm, say, 'Yes, yes.'

Mr Smeath says, 'Have you been good?' and the little girls say, 'Yes, yes,' again.

Mrs Smeath makes an indeterminate sound. 'Oh, all right,' says Mr Smeath to the little girls. He drives the car south through the empty streets, along the streetcar tracks, past a single streetcar like a gliding island, until finally we see the flat grey lake in the distance, and below us, over the edge of a sort of low cliff, a flat grey plain covered with train tracks. On this metal-covered plain several trains are shunting slowly back and forth. Because it is Sunday, and because this is evidently a routine after-church Sunday event for the Smeaths, I have the idea that the train tracks and the lethargic, ponderous trains have something to do with God. It is also clear to me that the person who really wants to see the trains is not Grace, or any of the little girls, but Mr Smeath himself.

We sit there in the parked car watching the trains until Mrs Smeath says that the dinner will be ruined. After that we drive back to Grace's house.

I am invited for Sunday dinner. It's the first time I've ever stayed for dinner at Grace's. Before dinner Grace takes me upstairs so we can wash our hands, and I learn a new thing about her house: you are only allowed four squares of toilet paper. The soap in the bathroom is black and rough. Grace says it's tar soap.

The dinner is baked ham and baked beans and baked potatoes and mashed squash. Mr Smeath carves the ham, Mrs Smeath adds the vegetables, the plates get passed around. Grace's little sisters look at me through their eyeglasses when I start to eat.

'We say grace in this house,' says Aunt Mildred, smiling firmly, and I don't know what she's talking about. I look at Grace: why do they want to say her name? But they all bend their heads and put their hands together and Grace says, 'For what we are about to receive may the Lord make us truly thankful, Amen,' and Mr Smeath says, 'Good food, good drink, good God, let's eat,' and winks at me. Mrs Smeath says, 'Lloyd,' and Mr Smeath gives a small, conspiratorial laugh.

After dinner Grace and I sit in the living-room, on the velvet chesterfield, the same one Mrs Smeath takes her naps on. I've never sat on it before and feel I'm sitting on something reserved, like a throne or a coffin. We read our Sunday School paper, which has the story of Joseph in it and a modern story about a boy who steals from the collection plate but repents and collects waste-paper and old bottles for the church, to make reparations. The pictures are black and white pen and ink drawings, but on the front is a coloured picture of Jesus, in pastel robes, surrounded by children, all of different colours, brown, yellow, white, clean and pretty, some holding his hand, others gazing up at him with large worshipful eyes. This Jesus does not have a halo.

Cat's Eye

Mr Smeath dozes in the maroon easy chair, his round belly swelling up. From the kitchen comes the clatter of silverware. Mrs Smeath and Aunt Mildred are doing the dishes.

I reach home in the late afternoon, with my red plastic purse and my Sunday School paper. 'Did you like it?' says my mother, still with the same air of anxiety.

'Did you learn anything?' says my father.

'I have to memorize a psalm,' I say importantly. The word *psalm* sounds like a secret password. I am a little resentful. There are things my parents have been keeping from me, things I need to know. The hats, for instance: how could my mother have forgotten about the hats? God is not an entirely new idea for me: they have him at school in the morning prayers, and even in 'God Save the King'. But it seems there is more to it, more things to be memorized, more songs to be sung, more nickels to be donated, before he can be truly appeased. I am worried about Heaven though. What age will I be when I get there? What if I'm old when I die? In Heaven I want to be the age I am.

I have a Bible, on loan from Grace, her second-best. I go to my room and begin to memorize: 'The heavens declare the glory of God; and the firmament sheweth his handywork. Day unto day uttereth speech, and night unto night sheweth knowledge.'

I still don't have any bedroom curtains. I look out the window, look up: there are the heavens, there are the stars, where they usually are. They no longer look cold and white and remote, like alcohol and enamel trays. Now they look watchful.

* * *

The girls stand in the schoolyard or up on top of the hill, in small clumps, whispering and whispering and doing spoolwork. It's now the fashion to have a spool with four nails pounded into one end, and a ball of wool. You loop the wool over each nail in turn, twice around, and use a fifth nail to hook the bottom loops over the top ones. Out of the other end of the spool dangles a round thick wool tail, which you're supposed to wind up like a flat snail-shell and sew into a mat to put the teapot on. I have such a spool, and so do Grace and Carol, and even Cordelia, although her wool is a snarl.

These clumps of whispering girls with their spools and coloured wool tails have to do with boys, with the separateness of boys. Each cluster of girls excludes some other girls, but all boys. The boys exclude us too, but their exclusion is active, they make a point of it. We don't need to.

Sometimes I still go into my brother's room and lie around on the floor reading comic books, but I never do this when any other girl is there. Alone I am tolerated, as part of a group of girls I would not be. This goes without saying.

Once I took boys for granted, I was used to them. But now I pay more attention, because boys are not the same. For example, they don't take baths as often as they're expected to. They smell of grubby flesh, of scalp, but also of leather, from the knee-patches on their breeks, and wool, from the breeks themselves, which come down only to below the knee, and lace up there like football pants. On the bottom parts of their legs they wear thick wool socks, which are usually damp and falling down. On their heads, outdoors, they wear leather helmets that strap under the chin. Their clothing is khaki, or navy-blue or grey, or forest green, colours that don't show the dirt as much. All of this has a military feel to it. Boys pride themselves on their drab clothing, their drooping socks, their smeared and inky skin: dirt, for them, is almost as good as wounds. They work at acting like boys. They call each other by their last names, draw attention to any extra departures from cleanliness. 'Hey, Robertson! Wipe off the snot!' 'Who farted?' They punch one another on the arm, saying, 'Got you!' 'Got you back!' There always seem to be more of them in the room than there actually are.

My brother punches arms and makes remarks about smells like the rest of them, but he has a secret. He would never tell it to these other boys, because of the way they would laugh.

The secret is that he has a girlfriend. This girlfriend is so secret she doesn't even know about it herself. I'm the only one he's told, and I have been double-sworn not to tell anyone else. Even when we're alone I'm not allowed to refer to her by her name, only by her initials, which are B.W. My brother will sometimes murmur these initials when there are other people around, my parents for instance. When he says them he stares at me, waiting for me to nod or give some sign that I have heard and understood. He writes me notes in code, which he leaves where I'll find them, under my pillow, tucked into my top bureau drawer. When I translate these notes they turn out to be so unlike him, so lacking in invention, so moronic in fact, that I can hardly believe it: 'Talked to B.W.' 'Saw HER today.' He writes these notes in coloured pencil, different colours, with exclamation marks. One night there's a freak early snowfall, and in the morning when I wake up and look out my bedroom window there are the supercharged initials, etched in pee on the white ground, already melting.

I can see that this girlfriend is causing him some anguish, as well as excitement, but I can't understand why. I know who she is. Her real name is Bertha Watson. She hangs around with the older girls, up on the hill under the stunted fir trees. She has straight brown hair with bangs and she's of ordinary size. There's no magic about her that I can see, or any abnormality. I'd like to know how she's done it, this trick with my brother that's turned him into a stupider, more nervous identical twin of himself.

Knowing this secret, being the only one chosen to know, makes me feel important in a way. But it's a negative importance, it's the importance of a blank sheet of paper. I can know because I don't count. I feel singled out, but also bereft. Also protective of him, because for the first time in my life I feel responsible for him. He is at risk, and I have power over him. It occurs to me that I could tell on him, lay him open to derision; I have that choice. He is at my mercy and I don't want it. I want him back the way he was, unchanged, invincible.

The girlfriend doesn't last long. After a while nothing more is heard of her. My brother makes fun of me again, or ignores me; he's back in charge. He gets a chemistry set and does experiments down in the basement. As an obsession I prefer the chemistry set to the girlfriend. There are things stewing, horrible stinks, little sulphurous explosions, amazing illusions. There's invisible writing that comes out when you hold the paper over a candle. You can make a hard-boiled egg rubbery so it will go into a milk bottle, although getting it out again is more difficult. *Turn Water to Blood*, the instructions say, *and Astound Your Friends*.

He still trades comic books, but effortlessly, absentmindedly. Because he cares less about them he makes better trades. The comic books pile up under his bed, stacks and stacks of them, but he seldom reads them any more when the other boys aren't around.

My brother exhausts the chemistry set. Now he has a star map, pinned to the wall of his room, and at night he turns out the lights and sits beside the darkened, open window, in the cold, with his maroon sweater pulled on over his pyjamas, gazing skyward. He has a pair of my father's binoculars, which he's allowed to use as long as he keeps the strap around his neck so he won't drop them. What he really wants next is a telescope.

When he allows me to join him, and when he feels like talking, he teaches me new names, charts the reference points: Orion, the Bear, the Dragon, the Swan. These are constellations. Every one of them is made up of a huge number of stars, hundreds of times bigger and hotter than our own sun. These stars are light-years away, he says. We aren't really seeing them at all, we're just seeing the light they sent out years, hundreds of years, thousands of years ago. The stars are like echoes. I sit there in my flannelette pyjamas, shivering, the back of my neck hurting from the upward tilt, squinting into the cold and the infinitely receding darkness, into the black cauldron where the fiery stars boil and boil. His stars are different from the ones in the Bible: they're wordless, they flame in an obliterating silence. I feel as if my body is dissolving and I am being drawn up and up, like thinning mist, into a vast emptying space.

'Arcturus,' my brother says. It's a foreign word, one I don't know, but I know the tone of his voice: recognition, completion, something added to a set. I think of his jars of marbles in the spring, the way he dropped the marbles into the jar, one by one, counting. My brother is collecting again; he's collecting stars.

Elizabeth Bowen

extract from

The Death of the Heart

It is London in the late 1930s and the sixteen-year-old orphan Portia is striving to hold her own in a coterie of rather grand early middle-aged people. She is especially in awe of her sister-in-law, Anna.

The Marx Brothers, that evening at the Empire, had no success with Portia. The screen threw its tricky light on her unrelaxed profile: she sat almost appalled. Anna took her eyes from the screen to complain once or twice to Thomas, 'She doesn't think this is funny.' Thomas, who had been giving unwilling snorts, relapsed into gloom, and said, 'Well, they are a lowering lot.' Anna leaned across him, 'You liked Sandy Macpherson, didn't you, Portia? – Thomas, do kick her and ask if she liked Sandy Macpherson?' The organist still loudly and firmly playing had gone down with his organ, through floodlit mimosa, into a bottomless pit, from which 'Parlez Moi d'Amour' kept on faintly coming up till someone down there shut a lid on him. Portia had no right to say that people were less brave now. . . . Now the Marx Brothers were over, the three Quaynes dived for their belongings and filed silently out – they missed the News in order to miss the Rush.

Anna and Portia, glum for opposing reasons, waited in the foyer while Thomas went for a taxi. For those minutes, in the mirror-refracted glare, they looked like workers with tomorrow ahead. Then someone looked hard at Anna, looked back, looked again, registered indecision, raised his hat and returned, extending a large anxious delighted hand. 'Miss *Fellowes*!'

'Major Brutt! How extraordinary this is!'

'To think of my running into *you*. It's extraordinary!'

'Especially as I am not even Miss Fellowes, now – I mean, I am Mrs Quayne.'

'Do excuse me –'

'How could you possibly know? ... I'm so glad we've met again.'

'It must be nine years plus. What a great evening we had – you and Pidgeon and I –' He stopped quickly: a look of doubt came into his eyes.

Portia stood by, meanwhile. 'You must meet my sister-in-law,' said Anna at once: 'Major Brutt – Miss Quayne.' She went on, not with quite so much assurance, 'I hope you enjoyed the Marx Brothers?'

'Well, to tell you the truth – I knew this place in the old days; I'd never heard of these chaps, but I thought I would drop in. I can't say I –'

'Oh, you find them lowering, too?'

'I dare say they're up-to-date, but they're not what I call funny.'

'Yes,' Anna said, 'they are up-to-date for a bit.' Major Brutt's eyes travelled from Anna's smiling and talking mouth, via the camellia fastened under her chin, to the upturned brim of Portia's hat – where it stayed. 'I hope', he said to Portia, '*you* have enjoyed yourself.'

Anna said, 'No, I don't think she did, much – Oh, look, my husband has got a taxi. Do come back with us: we must all have a drink. . . . Oh, Thomas, this is Major Brutt.'. . . As they walked out two-and two to the taxi, Anna said to Thomas out of the side of her mouth, 'Friend of Pidgeon's – we once had an evening with him.'

'*Did* we? I don't – When?'

'Not you and I, silly. I and Pidgeon. Years ago. But he really must have a drink.'

'Naturally,' said Thomas. Putting on no expression, he steered her by one elbow through the crowd at the door – for whenever you come out, you never avoid the Rush. In the taxi, infected by Major Brutt, Thomas sat bolt upright, looking hard at everything through the window in a military way. Whereas Major Brutt, beside him, kept glancing most timidly at the ladies' faces flowering on fur

The Death of the Heart

collars in the dark of the cab. He remarked once or twice, 'I must say, this is an amazing coincidence.' Portia sat twisted sideways, so that her knees should not annoy Thomas. Oh, the charm of this accident, this meeting in a sumptuous place – this was one of those polished encounters she and Irene spied on when they had peeped into a Palace Hotel. As the taxi crawled into Windsor Terrace, she exclaimed, all lit up, 'Oh, thank you for taking me!'

Thomas only said, 'Pity you didn't like it.'

'Oh, but I did like being there.'

Major Brutt said firmly, 'Those four chaps were a blot – This where we stop? Good.'

'Yes, we stop here,' Anna said, resignedly getting out.

The afternoon mist had frozen away to nothing; their house, footlit by terrace lamps, ran its pilasters up into glassy black night air. Portia shivered all down and put up her hands to her collar; Major Brutt's smart clatter struck a ring from the pavement; he slapped his coat, saying, 'Freezing like billy-o.'

'We can slide tomorrow,' said Thomas. 'That will be jolly.' He scooped out a handful of silver, stared at it, paid the taxi and felt round for his key. As though he heard himself challenged, or heard an echo, he looked sharply over his shoulder down the terrace – empty, stagy, E-shaped, with frigid pillars cut out on black shadow: a façade with no back. 'We're wonderfully quiet up here,' he told Major Brutt.

'Really more like the country.'

'For God's sake, let us in!' Anna exclaimed – Major Brutt looked at her with solicitude.

It was admirably hot and bright in the study – all the same, indoors the thing became too far-fetched. Major Brutt looked about unassumingly, as though he would like to say, 'What a nice place you've got here,' but was not sure if he knew them well enough. Anna switched lamps off with a strung-up air, while Thomas, having said, 'Scotch, Irish or brandy?' filled up the glasses on the tray. Anna could not speak – she thought of her closed years: seeing Robert Pidgeon, now, as a big fly in the amber of this decent man's memory. Her own memory was all blurs and seams. She started dreading the voice in which she could only say, 'Do you hear anything of him? How much do you see him, these days?' Or else, 'Where is he now, do you know?' Magnetism to that long-ago evening – on which Robert and she must have been perfect lovers – had made her bring back this man, this born third, to her home. Now Thomas, by removing himself to a different plane, made her feel she had done a thoroughly awkward thing. The pause was too long: it smote her to see Major Brutt look, uncertain, into his whisky, clearly feeling ought he not, then, to drink this? Ought he not to be here?

Otherwise he could wish for nothing better. The Quaynes had both seen how happy he was to come. He was the man from back somewhere, out of touch with London, dying to go on somewhere after a show. He would be glad to go on almost anywhere. But London, these nights, has a provincial meanness bright lights only expose. After dark, she is like a governess gone to the bad, in a Woolworth tiara, tarted up all wrong. But a glamour she may have had lives on in exiles' imaginations. Major Brutt was the sort of man who, like a ghost with no beat, hesitates round the West End about midnight – not wanting to buy a girl, not wanting to drink alone, not wanting to go back to Kensington, hoping something may happen. It grows less likely to happen – sooner or later he must be getting back. If he misses the last tube, he will have to run to a taxi; the taxi lightens his pocket and torments him, smelling of someone else's woman's scent. Like an empty room with no blinds his imagination gapes on the scene, and reflects what was never there. If this is to be all, he may as well catch the last tube. He may touch the hotel porter for a drink in the lounge

The Death of the Heart

– lights half-out, empty, with all the old women gone to bed. There is vice now, but you cannot be simply naughty.

'Well, here's luck,' Major Brutt said, pulling himself together, raising his glass boldly. He looked round at their three interesting faces. Portia replied with her glass of mild-and-soda: he bowed to her, she bowed to him and they drank. 'You live here, too?' he said.

'I'm staying here for a year.'

'That's a nice long visit. Can your people spare you?'

'Yes,' Portia said. 'They – I –'

Anna looked at Thomas as much as to say, check this, but Thomas was looking for the cigars. She saw Portia, kneeling down by the fire, look up at Major Brutt with a perfectly open face – her hands were tucked up the elbows of her short-sleeved dress. The picture upset Anna, who thought how much innocence she herself had corrupted in other people – yes, even in Robert: in him perhaps most of all. Meetings that ended with their most annihilating and bitter quarrels had begun with Robert unguarded, eager – like that. Watching Portia, she thought, is she a snake, or a rabbit? At all events, she thought, hardening, she has her own fun.

'Thanks very much, no: no, I never smoke them,' Major Brutt said, when Thomas at last found the cigars. Having lit his own, Thomas looked at the box suspiciously. 'These *are* going,' he said. 'I told you they were.'

'Then why don't you lock them up? It's Mrs Wayes, I expect; she has got a man friend and she's ever so good to him.'

'Has she been taking your cigarettes?'

'No, not lately; Matchett once caught her at it. Besides, she is far too busy reading my letters.'

'Why on earth not sack her?'

'Matchett says she is thorough. And thorough chars don't grow on every bush.'

Portia excitedly said, 'How funny bushes would look!'

'Ha-ha,' said Major Brutt. 'Did you ever hear the one about the shoe-tree?'

Anna swung her feet up on the sofa, a little back from the others, and looked removed and tired – she kept touching her hair back. Thomas squinted through his glass of drink at the light: now and then his face went lockjawed with a suppressed yawn. Major Brutt, having drunk two-thirds of his whisky, in his quiet way started dominating the scene. Portia's first animation was in the room somewhere, bobbing up near the ceiling like an escaped balloon. Thomas suddenly said, 'You knew Robert Pidgeon, I hear?'

'I should say so! An exceptional chap.'

'I never knew him, alas.'

'Oh, is he dead?' said Portia.

'*Dead?*' Major Brutt said. 'Oh, Lord, no – at least, I should think that is most unlikely. He had nine lives. I was with him most of the war.'

'No, I'm sure he wouldn't be dead,' Anna agreed. 'But do you know where he is?'

'I last had actual news of him in Colombo, last April – missed him there by about a week, which was bad. We are neither of us much of a hand at letters, but we keep in touch, on the whole, in the most astonishing way. Of course, Pidgeon is full of brain: the man could do anything. At the same time, he is one of those clever fellows who can get on with almost anyone. He is not a chap, of course, that I should ever have met if it hadn't been for the war. We both took it on the Somme, and I got to know him best after that, when we were on leave together.'

'Was he badly wounded?' said Portia.

'In the shoulder,' said Anna, seeing the pitted scar.

'Now Pidgeon was what you could call versatile. He could play the piano better than a professional – with more go, if you know what I mean. In France, he once smoked a plate and did a portrait of me on it – exactly like me, too; it really was. And then, of course, he wrote

The Death of the Heart

a whole lot of stuff. But there was absolutely no sort of side about him. I've never seen a man with so little side.'

'Yes,' Anna said, 'and what I always remember is that he could balance an orange on the rim of a plate.'

'Did he do that often?' said Portia.

'Very often indeed.'

Major Brutt, who had been given another drink, looked straight at Anna. 'You haven't seen him lately?'

'No, not very lately. No.'

Major Brutt quickly said, 'He was always a rare bird. You seldom hear of him twice in the same place. And I've been rolling round myself a good bit, since I left the Army, trying one thing and another.'

'That must have been interesting.'

'Yes, it is and it's not. It's a bit uncertain. I commuted my pension, then didn't do too well out in Malay. I'm back here for a bit, now, having a look round. I don't know, of course, that a great deal will come of it.'

'Oh, I don't see why not.'

Major Brutt, a good deal encouraged, said, 'Well, I've got two or three irons in the fire. Which means I shall have to stick around for a bit.'

Anna failed to reply, so it was Thomas who said, 'Yes, I'm sure you're right to do that.'

'I'll be seeing Pidgeon some time, I dare say. One never knows where he may or may not turn up. And I often run into people – well, look at tonight.'

'Well, do give him my love.'

'He'll be glad to hear how you are.'

'Tell him I'm very well.'

'Yes, tell him that,' Thomas said. 'That is, when you do see him again.'

'If you always live in hotels,' said Portia to Major Brutt, 'you get used to people always coming and going. They look as though they'd always be there, and then the next

35

moment you've no idea where they've gone, and they've gone for ever. It's funny, all the same.'

Anna looked at her watch. 'Portia,' she said, 'I don't want to spoil the party, but it's half-past twelve.'

Portia, when Anna looked straight at her, immediately looked away. This was, as a matter of fact, the first moment since they came in that there had been any question of looking straight at each other. But during the conversation about Pidgeon, Anna had felt those dark eyes with a determined innocence steal back again and again to her face. Anna, on the sofa in a Récamier attitude, had acted, among all she had had to act, a hardy imperviousness to this. Had the agitation she felt throughout her body sent out an aura with a quivering edge, Portia's eyes might be said to explore this line of quiver, round and along Anna's reclining form. Anna felt bound up with her fear, with her secret, by that enwrapping look of Portia's: she felt mummified. So she raised her voice when she said what time it was.

Portia had learnt one dare never look for long. She had those eyes that seem to be welcome nowhere, that learn shyness from the alarm they precipitate. Such eyes are always turning away or being humbly lowered – they dare come to rest nowhere but on a point in space; their homeless intentness makes them appear fanatical. They may move, they may affront, but they cannot communicate. You most often meet or, rather, avoid meeting such eyes in a child's face – what becomes of the child later you do not know.

At the same time, Portia had been enjoying what could be called a high time with Major Brutt. It is heady – when you are so young that there is no talk yet of the convention of love – to be singled out: you feel you enjoy human status. Major Brutt had met her eyes kindly, without a qualm. He remained standing: his two great feet were planted like rocks by her as she knelt on the rug, and from up there he kept bellowing down. When Anna

The Death of the Heart

looked at her watch, Portia's heart sank – she referred to the clock, but found this was too true. 'Half-past *twelve*,' she said. 'Golly!'

When she had said good night and gone, dropping a glove, Major Brutt said, 'That little kid must be great fun for you.'

* * *

Most mornings, Lilian waited for Portia in the old cemetery off Paddington Street: they liked to take this short cut on the way to lessons. The cemetery, overlooked by windows, has been out of touch with death for some time: it is at once a retreat and a thoroughfare not yet too well known. One or two weeping willows and tombs like stone pavilions give it a prettily solemn character, but the gravestones are all ranged round the walls like chairs before a dance, and halfway across the lawn a circular shelter looks like a bandstand. Paths run from gate to gate, and shrubs inside the paling seclude the place from the street – it is not sad, just cosily melancholic. Lilian enjoyed the melancholy; Portia felt that what was here was her secret every time she turned in at the gate. So they often went this way on their way to lessons.

They had to go to Cavendish Square. Miss Paullie, at her imposing address, organized classes for girls – delicate girls, girls who did not do well at school, girls putting in time before they went abroad, girls who were not to go abroad at all. She had room for about a dozen pupils like this. In the mornings, professors visited her house; in the afternoon there were expeditions to galleries, exhibitions, museums, concerts or classical *matinées*. A girl, by special arrangement, could even take lunch at Miss Paullie's house – this was the least of many special arrangements: her secretary lived on the telephone. All her arrangements, which were enterprising, worked out very well – accordingly Miss Paullie's fees were high. Though Thomas had rather jibbed at the expense, Anna convinced him of Miss Paullie's excellent value – she solved the problem of Portia during the day; what Portia learned might give her something to talk about, and there was always a chance she might make friends. So far, she had made only this one friend, Lilian, who lived not far away, in Nottingham Place.

Anna did not think Lilian very desirable, but this could not be helped. Lilian wore her hair forward over her shoulders in two long loose braids, like the Lily Maid. She wore a removed and mysterious expression; her rather big pretty developed figure already caught the eye of men in the street. She had had to be taken away from her boarding school because of falling in love with the cello mistress, which had made her quite unable to eat. Portia thought the world of the things Lilian could do – she was said, for instance, to dance and skate very well, and had at one time fenced. Otherwise, Lilian claimed to have few pleasures: she was at home as seldom as possible, and when at home was always washing her hair. She walked about with this rather fated expression you see in photographs of girls who have subsequently been murdered, but nothing had so far happened to her. . . . This morning, when she saw Portia coming, she signalled dreamily with a scarlet glove.

Portia came up with a rush. 'Oh dear, I'm afraid I have made us late. Come on, Lilian, we shall have to fly.'

'I don't want to run: I am not very well today.'

'Then we'd better take a 153.'

'If there is one,' said Lilian. (These buses are very rare.) 'Have I got blue rings under my eyes?'

'No. What did you do yesterday evening?'

'Oh, I had an awful evening. Did you?'

'No,' said Portia, rather apologetic. 'Because we went to the Empire. And imagine, quite by chance we met a man who knew someone Anna used once to know.

The Death of the Heart

Major Brutt, his name was – not the person she knew, the man.'

'Was your sister-in-law upset?'

'She was surprised, because he did not even know she was married.'

'I am often upset when I meet a person again.'

'Have you seen a person make an orange balance on the rim of a plate?'

'Oh, anyone could: you just need a steady hand.'

'All the people Anna always knows are clever.'

'Oh, you've brought your handbag with you today?'

'Matchett said I was such a silly not to.'

'You carry it in rather a queer way, if you don't mind my saying. I suppose you will get more used to it.'

'If I got too used, I might forget I had it, then I might forget and leave it somewhere. Show me, though, Lilian, how you carry yours.'

They had come out into Marylebone High Street, where they stood for a minute, patiently stamping, on chance of there being a 153 bus. The morning was colder than yesterday morning; there was a black frost that drove in. But they did not comment upon the weather, which seemed to them part of their private fate – brought on them by the act of waking up, like grown-up people's varying tempers, or the state, from day to day, of their own insides. A 153 did come lurching round the corner, but showed every sign of ignoring them, till Lilian, like a young offending goddess, stepped into its path, holding up a scarlet glove. When they were inside the bus, and had settled themselves, Lilian said reproachfully to Portia, 'You do look pleased today.'

She said, in some confusion, 'I do like things to happen.'

Miss Paullie's father was a successful doctor; her classes were held in a first-floor annexe, built for a billiard-room, at the back of his large house. In order that they might not incommode the patients, the pupils came and went by a basement door. Passers-by were surprised to see the trim little creatures, some of whom hopped out of limousines, disappear down the basement like so many cats. Once down there, they rang Miss Paullie's special bell, and were admitted to a fibre-carpeted passage. At the top of a flight of crooked staircase they hung their hats and coats in the annexe cloakroom, and queued up for the mirror, which was very small. Buff-and-blue tiles, marble, gilt-embossed wallpaper and a Turkey carpet were the note of the annexe. The cloakroom, which had a stained-glass window, smelt of fog and Vinolia, the billiard (or school) room of carpet, radiators and fog — this room had no windows: a big domed skylight told the state of the weather, went leaden with fog, crepitated when it was raining, or dropped a great square glare on to the table when the sun shone. At the end of the afternoon, in winter, a blue-black glazed blind was run across from a roller to cover the skylight, when the electric lights had been turned on. Ventilation was not the room's strong point — which may have been why Portia drooped like a plant the moment she got in. She was not a success here, for she failed to concentrate, or even to seem to concentrate like the other girls. She could not keep her thoughts at face-and-table level; they would go soaring up through the glass dome. One professor would stop, glare and drum the edge of the table; another would say, 'Miss Quayne, please, *please*. Are we here to look at the sky?' For sometimes her inattention reached the point of bad manners, or, which was worse, began to distract the others.

She was unused to learning, she had not learnt that one must learn: she seemed to have no place in which to house the most interesting fact. Anxious not to attract attention, not to annoy the professors, she *had* learned, however, after some weeks here, how to rivet, even to hypnotize the most angry professor by an unmoving regard — of his lips while he spoke, of the air over his head. . . .

The Death of the Heart

This morning's lecture on economics she received with an air of steady amazement. She brought her bag into lessons, and sat with it on her knee. At the end of the hour, the professor said good morning; the girls divided – some were to be taken round somebody's private gallery. The rest prepared to study; some got their fine pens out to draw maps; they hitched their heels up on the rungs of their chairs, looking glad they had not had to go out. Some distance away from the big table, Miss Paullie sat going through essays, in a gothic chair, at a table of her own. Because the day was dark, a swan-necked reading lamp bent light on to what Miss Paullie read. She kept turning pages, the girls fidgeted cautiously, now and then a gurgle came from a hot pipe – the tissue of small sounds that they called silence filled the room to the dome. Lilian stopped now and then to examine her mapping nib, or to brood over her delicate state. Portia pressed her diaphragm to the edge of the table, and kept feeling at her bag against her stomach. Everybody's attention to what they were doing hardened – optimistically, Portia now felt safe.

She leant back, looked round, bent forward and, as softly as possible, clicked open her bag. She took out a blue letter: this she spread on her knee below the table and started to read for the second time.

Dear Portia: What you did the other night was so sweet, I feel I must write and tell you how it cheered me up. I hope you won't mind – you won't, you will understand: I feel we are friends already. I was sad, going away, for various reasons, but one was that I thought you must have gone to bed by then, and that I should not see you again. So I cannot tell you what a surprise it was finding you there in the hall, holding my hat. I saw then that you must have been seeing how depressed I was, and that you wanted, you darling, to cheer me up. I cannot tell you what your suddenly being there like that in the hall, and

giving me my hat as I went away, meant. I know
I didn't behave well, up there in the drawing-room,
and I'm afraid I behaved even worse after you went
away, but that was not altogether my fault. You
know how I love Anna, as I'm sure you do too, but
when she starts to say to me 'Really, Eddie', I feel
like a wild animal, and behave accordingly. I am
much too influenced by people's manner towards me
– especially Anna's, I suppose. Directly people attack
me, I think they are right, and hate myself, and
then I hate them – the more I like them this is so.
So I went downstairs for my hat that night (Monday
night, wasn't it?) feeling perfectly black. When you
appeared in the hall and so sweetly gave me my hat,
everything calmed down. Not only your being there,
but the thought (is this presumptuous of me?) that
perhaps you had actually been waiting, made me feel
quite in heaven. I could not say so then, I thought
you might not like it, but I cannot help writing to say
so now.

Also, I once heard you say, in the natural way you
say things, that you did not very often get letters,
so I thought perhaps you might like to get this. You
and I are two rather alone people – with you that
is just chance, with me, I expect, it is partly my bad
nature. I am so difficult, you are so good and sweet.
I feel particularly alone tonight (I am in my flat,
which I do not like very much) because I tried just
now to telephone to Anna about something and she
was rather short, so I did not try any more. I expect
she gets bored with me, or finds me too difficult. Oh
Portia, I do wish you and I could be friends. Perhaps
we could sometimes go for walks in the park? I sit
here and think how nice it would be if –

'*Portia!*' said Miss Paullie.
Portia leaped as though she had been struck.

The Death of the Heart

'My dear child, don't sit hunched like that. Don't work under the table. Put your work *on* the table. What have you got there? Don't keep things on your knee.'

As Portia still did nothing, Miss Paullie pushed her own small table from in front of her chair, got up and came swiftly round to where Portia sat. All the girls stared.

Miss Paullie said, 'Surely that is not a letter? This is not the place or the time to read your letters, is it? I think you must notice that the other girls don't do that. And, wherever one is, one never does read a letter under the table: have you never been told? What else is that you have on your knee? Your bag? Why did you not leave your bag in the cloakroom? Nobody will take it here, you know. Now, put your letter away in your bag again, and leave them both in the cloakroom. To carry your bag about with your indoors is a hotel habit, you know.'

Miss Paullie may not have known what she was saying, but one or two of the girls, including Lilian, smiled. Portia got up, looking unsteady, went to the cloakroom and lodged her bag on a ledge under her coat – a ledge along which, as she saw now, all the other girls' bags had been put. But Eddie's letter, after a desperate moment, she slipped up inside her woollen directoire knickers. It stayed just inside the elastic band, under one knee.

Back in the billiard-room, the girls' brush-glossed heads were bent steadily over their books again. These silent sessions in Miss Paullie's presence were, in point of fact (and well most of them knew it), lessons in the deportment of staying still, of feeling yourself watched without turning a hair. Only Portia could have imagined for a moment that Miss Paullie's eye was off what any girl did. A little raised in her gothic chair, like a bishop, Miss Paullie's own rigid stillness quelled every young body, its nervous itches, its cooped-up pleasure in being itself, its awareness of the young body next door. Even Lilian, prone to finger her own plaits or to look at the voluptuous white insides of her arms, sat, during those hours with Miss Paullie, as though Lilian did not exist. Portia, still burning under her pale skin, pulled her book on the theory of architecture towards her, and stared at a plate of a Palladian façade.

But a sense of Portia's not being quite what was what had seeped, meanwhile, into the billiard-room. She almost felt something sniffing at the hem of her dress. For the most fatal thing about what Miss Paullie had said had been her manner of saying it – as though she did not say half of what she felt, as though she were mortified on Portia's behalf, in front of these better girls. No one had ever read a letter under this table; no one had even heard of such a thing being done. Miss Paullie was very particular what class of girl she took. *Sins* cut boldly up through every class in society, but mere misdemeanours show a certain level in life. So now, not only diligence, or caution, kept the girls' smooth heads bent, and made them not glance again at Irene's child. Irene herself – knowing that nine out of ten things you do direct from the heart are the wrong thing, and that she was not capable of doing anything better – would not have dared to cross the threshold of this room. For a moment, Portia felt herself stand with her mother in the doorway, looking at all this in here with a wild askance shrinking eye. The gilt-scrolled paper, the dome, the bishop's chair, the girls' smooth heads must have been fixed here always, where they safely belonged – while she and Irene, shady, had been skidding about in an out-of-season nowhere of railway stations and rocks, filing off wet third-class decks of lake steamers, choking over the bones of *loups de mer*, giggling into eiderdowns that smelled of the person-before-last. Untaught, they had walked arm-in-arm along city pavements, and at nights had pulled their beds close together or slept in the same bed – overcoming, as far as might be, the separation of birth. Seldom had they faced up to society – when they did, Irene did the wrong thing, then cried. How sweet, how sweetly exalted by her wrong act was Irene, when,

The Death of the Heart

stopping crying, she blew her nose and asked for a cup of tea. . . . Portia, relaxing a very little, moved on her chair: at once she felt Eddie's letter crackle under her knee. What would Eddie think of all this?

Miss Paullie, who had thought well of Anna, was sorry about Portia, and sorry for Anna. She was sorry Portia should have made no friend here but the more than doubtful Lilian, but she quite saw why this was, and it really could not be helped. She regretted that Mrs Quayne had not seen her way to go on sending someone to fetch Portia, as she had done for the first weeks. She had a strong feeling that Portia and Lilian loitered in the streets on the way home. Miss Paullie knew one must not be old-fashioned, but it gave better tone if the girls were fetched.

Any girls who stayed to lunch at Miss Paullie's lunched in a morning-room in the annexe basement: down here the light was almost always on. The proper dining-room of the house was a waiting-room, with sideboards like catafalques: where Dr Paullie himself lunched no one asked or knew.

The lunch given the girls was sufficient, simple and far from excellent – Lilian, sent to lunch here because of the servant shortage, always messed about at it with her fork. Miss Paullie, at the head of the table, encouraged the girls to talk to her about art. This Wednesday, this Wednesday of the letter, Portia seated herself as far away from Miss Paullie as she possibly could, whereupon Lilian seized the place next to Portia's with unusual zest.

'It really was awful for you,' Lilian said. 'I didn't know where to look. Why didn't you tell me you'd had a letter? I did think you were looking very mysterious. Why didn't you read it when you had your breakfast? Or is it the kind of letter one reads again and again? Excuse my asking, but who is it from?'

'It's from a friend of Anna's. Because I got him his hat.'

'Had he lost his hat?'

'No. I heard him coming downstairs, and his hat was there, so I gave it to him.'

'That doesn't seem a thing to write a letter about. Is he not a nice man, or is he very polite? What on earth were you doing in the hall?'

'I was in Thomas's study.'

'Well, that comes to the same thing. It comes to the same thing with the door open. You had been listening for him, I suppose?'

'I just was down there. You see, Anna was in the drawing-room.'

'You are extraordinary. What does he do?'

'He is in Thomas's office.'

'Could you really feel all that for a man? I'm never sure that I could.'

'He's quite different from St Quentin. Even Major Brutt is not at all like him.'

'Well, I do think you ought to be more careful, really. After all, you and I are only sixteen. Do you want redcurrant jelly with this awful mutton? I do. Do get it away from that pig.'

Portia slipped the dish of red-currant jelly away from Lucia Ames – who would soon be a débutante. 'I hope you are feeling better, Lilian?' she said.

'Well, I am, but I get a nervous craving for things.'

When the afternoon classes were over – at four o'clock today – Lilian invited Portia back to tea. 'I don't know,' said Portia. 'You see, Anna is out.'

'Well, my mother is out which is far better.'

'Matchett did say that I could have tea with her.'

'My goodness,' Lilian said, 'but couldn't you do that any day? And we don't often have my whole house to ourselves. We can take the gramophone up to the bathroom while I wash my hair; I've got three Stravinsky records. And you can show me your letter.'

Portia gulped, and looked wildly into a point in space. 'No, I can't do that, because I have torn it up.'

The Death of the Heart

'No, you can't have done that,' said Lilian firmly, 'because I should have seen you. Unless you did it when you were in the lavatory, and you didn't stay in there long enough. You do hurt my feelings: *I* don't want to intrude. But whatever Miss Paullie says, don't you leave your bag about.'

'It isn't in my bag,' said Portia unwarily.

So Portia went home to tea with Lilian and, in spite of a qualm, enjoyed herself very much. They ate crumpets on the rug in front of the drawing-room fire. Their cheeks scorched, but a draught crept under the door. Lilian, heaping coals of fire, brought down, untied from a ribbon, three letters the cello mistress had written to her during the holidays. She also told Portia how, one day at school when she had a headache, Miss Heber had rubbed with magnetic fingers Lilian's temples and the nape of her neck. 'When I have a headache I always think of her still.'

'If you've got a headache today, then ought you to wash your hair?'

'I ought not to, but I want it nice for tomorrow.'

'Tomorrow? What are you doing then?'

'Confidentially, Portia, I don't know what may happen.'

Lilian had all those mysterious tomorrows; yesterdays made her sigh, but were never accounted for. She belonged to a junior branch of emotional society, in which there is always a crisis due. Preoccupation with life was not, clearly, peculiar to Lilian: Portia could see it going on everywhere. She had watched life, since she came to London, with a sort of despair – motivated and busy always, always progressing: even people pausing on bridges seemed to pause with a purpose; no birds seemed to pursue a quite aimless flight. The spring of the works seemed unfound only by her: she could not doubt people knew what they were doing – everywhere she met alert cognisant eyes. She could not believe there was not a plan of the whole

47

set-up in every head but her own. Accordingly, so anxious was her research that every look, every movement, every object had a quite political seriousness for her: nothing was not weighed down by significance. In her home life (her new home life) with its puzzles, she saw dissimulation always on guard; she asked herself humbly for what reason people said what they did not mean, and did not say what they meant? She felt almost certain to find the clue when she felt the frenzy behind the clever remark.

Outdoors, the pattern was less involuted, very much simplified. She enjoyed being in the streets – unguarded smiles from strangers, the permitted frown of someone walking alone, lovers' looks, as though they had solved something, and the unsolitary air with which the old or the wretched seemed to carry sorrow made her feel people that at least knew each other, if they did not yet know her, if she did not yet know them. The closeness she felt to Eddie, since this morning (that closeness one most often feels in a dream), was a closeness to life she had only felt, so far, when she got a smile from a stranger across a bus. It seemed to her that while people were very happy, individual persons were surely damned. So, she shrank from that specious mystery the individual throws about himself, from Anna's smiles, from Lilian's tomorrows, from the shut-in room, the turned-in heart.

Portia turned over records and rewound the gramophone on the shut seat, and Stravinsky filled the bathroom while Lilian shampooed her hair. Lilian turbaned herself in a bath towel, and Portia carried the gramophone back to the fire again. Before Lilian's cascade of hair, turned inside out and scented in the heat, was quite dry, it had struck seven; Portia said she would have to be going home.

'Oh, they won't bother. You rang up Matchett, didn't you?'

'You said I could, but somehow I never did.'

The Death of the Heart

As Portia let herself into Windsor Terrace, she heard Anna's voice in the study, explaining something to Thomas. There came a pause while they listened to her step, then the voices went on. She stole over that white stone floor, with the chill always off, and made for the basement staircase. 'Matchett?' she called down, in a tense low voice. The door at the foot of the stairs was open: Matchett came out of the little room by the pantry and stood looking up at Portia, shading her eyes. She said, 'Oh, it's you!'

'I hope you didn't wonder.'

'I had your tea for you.'

'Lilian made me go back with her.'

'Well, that was nice for you,' said Matchett didactically. 'You haven't had your tea there for some time.'

'But part of the time I was miserable. I might have been having tea with you.'

'"Miserable!"' Matchett echoed, with her hardest inflection. 'That Lilian is someone your own age. However, you did ought to have telephoned. She's that one with the head of hair?'

'Yes. She was washing it.'

'I like to see a head of hair, these days.'

'But what I wanted was, to make toast with you.'

'Well, you can't do everything, can you?'

'Are they out for dinner? Could you talk to me while I have my supper, Matchett?'

'I shall have to see.'

Portia turned and went up. A little later, she heard Anna's bath running, and smelled bath essence coming upstairs. After Portia had shut her door, she heard the reluctant step of Thomas turn, cross the landing, into his dressing-room: he had got to put on a white tie.

Anita Brookner

extract from

Latecomers

Fibich and Hartmann have been business partners for more than twenty years but their friendship goes much further and deeper than their professional lives. They met as boys at an English boarding school and this shared childhood experience of being outsiders, refugees from Germany, has been as close a bond as their considerable success in later years. Happily married and enjoying a comfortable way of life, neither man has felt the necessity of exploring his past. Until Fibich makes a sudden decision.

At sixty-one Fibich grew old, perceptibly. No longer interested in his work, he put all his efforts into doing it, with fewer results. Because of his inherent meticulousness no one noticed this, but it seemed to him that the major exercise of the day was getting to the office, and then, after an aching interval, which he measured minute by minute, getting home again. He felt endangered by his absence from home, and, once home, was not much reassured. He begged Christine not to bother to devise meals for him; he would concentrate on trying to eat a little fish, which he would dismember with a tremulous knife and fork. He would discard his city clothes with a sigh of relief and put on his dressing-gown. Christine, trying to make a ceremony of this habit, which she saw as alarming, bought him a velvet smoking-jacket. He wore it once or twice to please her, and then relapsed into the dressing-gown. Once she saw him shuffling along from the bathroom, the cord tied loosely round his waist, and was thankful that Toto no longer lived at home to see his father in this condition. She wondered whether it was the prospect of Toto's imminent departure to Morocco, to make a film, and his absence for a projected six months, that had brought about this change. She even discussed this with Hartmann, since Fibich would say nothing. Hartmann, for once, was devoid of resource. 'The trip may have tired him,' said Hartmann. 'Let him rest. He'll be all right. We'll plan a holiday, take a house somewhere this summer. He will come round.'

So they let him rest. He slept voraciously, and sometimes dreamed. His dreams were not clear to him. In one he was being very kindly introduced by a companion to an aristocratic tailor who was to measure him for a suit. The fitting was to take place in Brighton, near the station. While he waited for the tailor to attend to him, which he never did, the scene abruptly changed to Copenhagen on a winter's morning. This was somehow significant. In the dream Fibich took photographs of Copenhagen which he later studied with the same companion who had introduced him to the tailor. But in one of the photographs the companion figured quite prominently, standing in front of a cottage in the grounds of a large mansion or hotel. There had been a displacement of some kind, a fobbing off, a lack of explanation. Fibich awoke from this dream with a sense of alarm, relieved to find himself in his own bed. The relief gave him a little energy with which to start the day, which he did with a factitious enthusiasm that he was forced to substitute for the real thing. At the office, where he still appeared to be effective, he sat for long periods at his desk, staring at his hands. 'He's a little tired,' explained Hartmann, who was thereby forced into regular attendance. Goodman, ever sympathetic, took most of the work off his shoulders.

It was Yvette's turn to appear with covered dishes. Turning bad into good, as was her habit, she regarded Fibich's malaise as a challenge to her psychological powers and excellent household management. Luxurious foods appeared, were discarded by Fibich as too elaborate, and were hastily eaten by Christine in order that feelings should not be hurt. 'Don't trouble yourself,' said Christine to Yvette, as a concoction of sole with mushrooms in a cream sauce was handed in. 'He has no appetite.' 'Then he needs building up,' said Yvette firmly. Her reassurance, though of a hollow nature, was balm to Christine's anxious spirit.

To Hartmann Yvette said, 'I don't think he eats enough.

Does he have a proper lunch?' 'He never has,' Hartmann informed her. 'Then you'd better see that he does. Take him to that place of yours. He'll eat if you're with him. After all, he is no longer young.' Hartmann was disgruntled, disturbed. He was the elder by five years, sixty-six to Fibich's sixty-one. Nobody remarked that he was no longer young. Of course he did not feel old. That, essentially, was the difference between Fibich and himself.

For the first time Hartmann was obliged to think about age, and about the future. He was not particularly inclined to make changes. Since his mother-in-law's revelations he no longer felt that France was a country to which he might wish to retire. This, he knew, was irrational. Nevertheless, he would wait a bit and see if the feeling passed. And if not, well, there were other places: Spain, Switzerland. And yet he had to confess that he had little taste for uprooting himself. Now that he was forced to acknowledge that he too got tired, that he was no longer eager to leave home in the mornings, that he always felt a sense of deliverance as the weekend approached, he thought it might be time to sell up, settle affairs, make arrangements, and then, perhaps, wait a little to see what everyone wanted to do. He would miss his little indulgences, his routines, but he was not without resource. By nature he was a man of pleasure, and he could see that there might be a voluptuous charm in simply filling the empty days as only he knew how: a morning of delicate shopping, a stroll, a decent lunch somewhere. Could it be that he was at last on the verge of that real, that ineluctable old age, in which he had never truly believed? If so, he thought, it had come suddenly and quickly. He pondered a moment in disbelief, looked around at Yvette's apricot walls, looked at Yvette herself, dressed in the bright colours she still loved, the hair an ever more ambitious gold, saw her, unconscious of his gaze, vigorously and importantly moving about her drawing-room, saw, in a flash, that he must stay alive for her sake, for she would never fare well as a widow. He felt an unaccustomed pang in the heart as he looked at her, never still, in her royal blue blouse and her black skirt, humming a little under her breath, beautifully concerned for his comfort and the perfection of his home. He sighed. Perhaps they would quietly remain here, and somehow carry on as they were. Perhaps Fibich would come out of his depression, if that was what it was, and resume his duties, bring his attention once more to bear on the present. Suddenly all that Hartmann required was to see smiles on the faces around him. It was, after all, what he had always required. In his own eyes he had changed very little, had always, even as a young man, had an adult sense of responsibility. He had always had the insight that if he organized the main structures of his life – work, home, marriage – in a satisfactory manner, then he was fully entitled to enjoy his liberty outside them. He had had an easy attitude to fidelity when first married, but now he realized that he had been faithful to his wife for so long that he would find anything else intolerable. He became aware that Yvette had made him happy. He looked at her, sitting at her little desk, making out her shopping list, her mouth firm with attention. She would never understand either *La Princesse de Clèves* or *Madame Bovary*, and he was glad of it. He went over to her and kissed her hair, put an arm around her thickening shoulders.

'You know,' he said gently. 'I think you have put on a little weight.'

'I may have filled out a bit,' she admitted. 'But no one could say that I haven't kept my figure.'

'No,' he agreed. 'No one could say that.'

He patted her arm, was suddenly reluctant to leave her. She was, however, as always, sublimely unconscious of his moods.

'Are you off?' she asked. 'Don't be late this evening. I might want to see Marianne.'

'What will you do today?' he asked her in his turn.

She looked at him in surprise. 'Oh, I have plenty to do, don't you worry about me. Are you all right, Hartmann? You're usually on your way by this time.'

'Yes,' he said. 'I'm all right. I'll see you later. Have a good day.'

But he hesitated by the door, looked back at her unrealistically golden head, bent once more over her list, and wondered suddenly what it would be like not to see her there. He shivered. But this was ridiculous! They were still young! This was the malaise that was afflicting Fibich: he must have caught it from him. He straightened his shoulders and left the room, took his hat and the cane he sometimes affected, decided to walk to the office to demonstrate how young and active he was. It was a clear day, mild but sunless: rain was forecast. The white sky reflected his mood, in which he detected a certain anxiety, and absence of joy. He put this down to the strain of Marianne's second pregnancy, which had worried him, but he was aware that this was not the only cause. If Fibich went . . . Again, he told himself, this was ridiculous. Because the man had had the absurd idea of going to Berlin and had understandably been shaken up by the experience, there was no need to regard him as endangered. He had always been nervous, and now he was just a little more nervous than he had been: it was as simple as that. And even if it were not simple, they had reached the stage in life in which matters had to be made simple if they themselves were to last out the course. How could Fibich have put them all at risk with his insane journey? And what had he proved? Striding up the tree-arching avenue in the park, Hartmann felt his heart expand with anger, and also with joy, as he recovered his normal equilibrium. Fibich must pull himself together. He must be told that he owed it to Christine, to his son, and to himself, Hartmann, to behave like a grown-up for once in his life. For that was the trouble with Fibich, he thought. Although recognizable as elderly, he had never grown up. Well now, he, Hartmann, would have to talk with Fibich, as man to man, not as the boys they had once been, would tell him about the sudden recognition of old age that he had had that morning, would remind him that they must make plans, settle affairs, and, most of all, preserve themselves so as to enjoy whatever future remained to them. Hartmann, gazing up proprietorially at the arching branches, the trees now in full leaf, felt his troubled thoughts leave him, and also his ill humour. This had always been his strength, he thought, his endless tolerance of idiosyncrasy in others. Nevertheless, he was determined to speak to Fibich quite firmly. He strode on, proud of his ability to cover the distance from Ashley Gardens to Spanish Place, at a steady pace, on this dull but cloudless May morning. And not even out of breath, he remarked to himself.

The morning passed without incident. Roger brought no news of Marianne's condition. She had been in the hospital for three weeks and now the baby was almost due. Hartmann felt a thrill of fear: if bad news were to come it would come from that quarter. It was only natural that his nerves were on edge, he thought. Perhaps if Fibich were to become a grandfather he might behave more sensibly, might realize that energies have to be reinvested in that new generation, not squandered on his own past. But he thought that Fibich might be denied the opportunity to see his grandchildren. He somehow knew that Toto would remain unmarried for a very long time, would indeed regard his youth, and in turn his youthfulness, as his stock in trade, and therefore remain professionally famous as a young man until at the very least in his late thirties. Hartmann realized with a shock that Toto was already twenty-nine, nearly thirty. Where had the time gone? Again with a shiver of disquiet he determined to bring Fibich to book, as if he alone were responsible for all this ageing, as if time had less purchase on Fibich than on the rest of them, as if it

Latecomers

devolved upon Fibich to bring them all safely through to the untroubled prospect that was, by now, surely theirs by right.

At half-past twelve he knocked on Fibich's door. Fibich, his hands folded and resting on top of an almost empty desk, looked up mildly. Hartmann resented his inactivity, as if this were proof of some private decision to abandon serious matters, until he saw that it was not inactivity at all: in the background, by the safe, was John Goodman, their all too devoted company secretary, whose eagerness was out of all proportion to what Hartmann and Fibich saw, still, as the frivolous nature of the enterprise. A small fortune built on flair, nothing but flair: how could they take credit for it? They had always had an amiable attitude towards work, the two of them, both knowing that in another life they would have done something more sensible, more serious, recognizing what they actually did do as appropriate to their uncertain position in every sort of hierarchy. Hartmann had the ideas and Fibich did the worrying: it suited them both perfectly. It was something of an effort for them to accommodate the personal career ambitions of both Myers and Goodman, young men on whom, Hartmann thought, youth was wasted, but fervid in their belief that what they did in this toy empire was important. Dark-suited, their rolled umbrellas a mark of *gravitas*, Myers and Goodman treated each other in a perfectly affable manner but with a lack of intimacy that entertained Hartmann profoundly. 'Such senators!' he had once remarked to Fibich. 'Such men of the cloth!' For he thought that work should be tackled exuberantly, light-heartedly, or not at all. Fibich was more tolerant, at least of Myers. Goodman worried him more. It was Goodman's assiduity he found hard to bear, his almost feminine desire to be necessary and wanted. And those extraordinary pleading eyes, the eyes of a harem favourite, quickly cast down, at the merest hint of reproof, into a double arc of dense, almost tangled lashes.

Fibich had devised many ways to outwit Goodman's sensibility, and had been forced to improvise many others, but that sensibility had never been exhausted. Trying to spare Goodman's feelings frequently brought on one of Fibich's migraine headaches. Hartmann treated him more teasingly and suffered from him accordingly less. Fibich could hardly bear to think about Goodman's life with his mother, in their little house in Putney, the news of the day faithfully served up to her over the evening meal. He saw them as himself and Aunt Marie Jessop, all those years ago. Nevertheless he continued to enquire after Mrs Goodman's health, although the radiant answers made him uneasy. Hartmann quite simply saw him as unawakened, waited for him to break out. In the meantime, since there were no signs of Goodman's ever breaking out, he would sportingly assume the existence of several girlfriends. 'Still out and about, John?' he would say. 'Still fancy free? Still tormenting the women?' Goodman would modestly lower his fabulous eyelashes, uncertain as to how to respond. At an admonitory shake of the head from Fibich, Hartmann would relent. 'Leave early today, John,' he would say. 'Give your mother a surprise. Everything seems to be taken care of. You do an excellent job.' Fibich often wished he had so light a touch. Goodman always appreciated Hartmann's sallies, but it was to Fibich that he looked for praise.

'Lunch,' said Hartmann firmly, determined to get down to the matter in hand. 'I am taking you out to lunch. All right, John, get some lunch yourself. And tell Tania to go too. We'll be back about two-thirty.'

Fibich looked at him in surprise. 'I am not hungry,' he said. 'Yes, John, finish up here later. I don't really want to eat.'

'I am taking you to lunch,' said Hartmann, handing him his hat. 'That is what is the matter with you, Fibich. You're neglecting yourself. And it's time we had a talk.'

In the street he looked about him with displeasure at

the prolonged sunlessness, the absence of good weather. Brave girls were dressed in flimsy garments, their bare legs white, their shoes inadequate. Harsh light came down unmediated from the colourless sky: rain still threatened but refused to materialize. Turning into the hotel dining-room, Hartmann was mildly put out to see nearly all the tables occupied. He stood majestically by the door, waiting to be ferried over to safe keeping. Reaching a table that was not his usual table, he flourished his white napkin, waved away the menu, and said, 'Sole. Grilled. Is that all right with you, Fibich? Fish is what you like, isn't it?'

'Thank you, thank you,' said Fibich. 'Sole, by all means.'

They sat in silence for a while, Fibich staring at his hands. Eventually Hartmann, who knew him so well, sighed.

'What happened there?' he asked. 'What did you find?'

Fibich looked up at him, still mildly.

'I found a foreign city that I did not remember,' he said. 'Rather a pleasant one. It meant nothing to me whatever.'

'And yet, since you came back you've been different. Changed. Something must have happened. What was it?'

Fibich smiled painfully. 'The only memory came last of all,' he said. 'Do you remember a commotion at Heathrow? A woman fainting?'

Hartmann nodded.

'The last sight of my mother,' said Fibich finally. 'She fainted when she said goodbye to me. I seemed to see her again. And since thinking about that moment, I find that I cannot endure . . .'

He dropped his head, made a helpless gesture with his hand, and knocked over a glass of water.

'Fibich!' said Hartmann warningly, summoning a waiter.

'I should have gone back,' whispered Fibich. 'I should not have left. I should have got off the train.'

'Is everything all right, gentlemen?' asked the head waiter, removing the wet tablecloth.

'Quite all right,' said Hartmann, rather too loudly. 'But I'm afraid we are in rather a hurry.'

'Your lunch is served, sir.' And the table was put to rights, hastily, while another waiter dealt with the fish, taking it off the bone and decorating it with lemon wedges and tartare sauce. 'A little wine, perhaps? If Mr Fibich is not feeling well?'

'No, no,' said Hartmann, again too loudly. 'That will be all.'

'Thank you,' said Fibich, in a voice slightly higher than normal, feigning enthusiasm. But his face was pale, and as the smell of fish rose from the plate in front of him his eyes filled with tears.

Hartmann stared at him in alarm. A collapse here, in Durrant's Hotel, where he lunched every day? A breakdown, the end of Fibich? He watched as Fibich tried to eat, raising and lowering his fork, disguising the untasted fragments beneath the sauce, the tears sliding down his face. He glanced round to see if anyone were watching. Conversation had ceased at the adjoining table.

'Come, Fibich,' he said. 'Thomas. You are safe. You are here. Try to eat. You have such a good appetite. Make an effort.' He was distractedly torn between anger and pity. But as the tears continued to fall he summoned the waiter again. 'On my account,' he said. 'We have to go.'

'Of course, sir. I understand.' They were outside in what seemed like record time, their passage shielded by waiters, their hats handed to them silently. Hartmann was aware of a momentary cessation of activity, a collective holding of breath, before they reached the blessed anonymity of the street.

Somehow he got Fibich back to the office, his coat hanging off his shoulders, his hat on the back of his head. Hartmann could not bear to put him to rights, simply drew his arm through his own, walked him like a child, aware of what they must look like, an upright bourgeois with his dissolute brother. Two girls, passing, giggled, taking Fibich to be drunk. As they reached their building, Fibich stumbled on the step. Then they were inside, safe from alien eyes. Hartmann guided Fibich to his room, to his chair, removed his hat, stood there while Fibich wept.

Goodman, returning, and thinking to find the room empty, went in to finish his work at the safe. He stopped at the sight of Fibich, whose tears were now spent, sitting with his head lowered to his clenched hands, still in his coat. Hartmann lifted his hand in warning, putting his finger to his lips. But Goodman, who was all too naturally of a filial nature, disappeared, came back with a glass of water, knelt by Fibich's desk, and took his hand.

'Mr Fibich,' he said gently. 'Would you like me to make you some coffee?'

Fibich raised his head, looked around him, and then looked down into Goodman's extravagant eyes, while Hartmann eased his coat from his shoulders.

'John,' he said presently, in an almost normal voice. 'I think I must have turned a little faint.'

'Drink this, sir,' said Goodman, proffering the glass.

Fibich drank slowly, shuddering as the icy water reached his stomach. 'That's better,' he said, his face still ghastly. 'Did you have lunch, John?'

'Oh, yes, sir,' Goodman's voice was devoid of embarrassment. Life at home, even at the age he was, must have conditioned him to work of this nature. Hartmann's opinion of him rose.

'And do you look after yourself properly, John?'

'Oh, yes, sir,' said Goodman again. 'My mother sees to that. We eat very healthfully. Mother sees to it that I eat a lot of salads.'

'That's good,' said Fibich. 'Take care of your mother,

John.' Hartmann turned away and looked out of the window. 'Is she in good health? Do you keep her company?'

Goodman did not appear to find these questions unusual. 'We've always been close,' he replied. 'My father left home when I was little, so there's just been the two of us. We do everything together.'

'And what will you do this weekend?' asked Fibich.

'I dare say we shall go over and visit my married sister,' said Goodman. 'I'm an uncle, you see. My sister has a small girl. We like to see her as often as we can.'

'That's good, John, very good.' Fibich's colour was returning, as if the contemplation of Goodman's home life were gradually filling him with reassurance.

'Perhaps a cup of coffee, Mr Fibich?'

'Why, yes, John, if you would be so kind.' At a nod from Hartmann Goodman left the room.

'Hartmann,' said Fibich. 'Something has happened.'

Hartmann stood behind him, his hands on Fibich's shoulders.

'Nothing has happened,' he said. 'You're still here. And so am I. Perhaps you did what you had to do, faced facts, did your grieving. Perhaps it is over for you now. I was lucky,' he went on, wiping the moisture from his eyes. 'I dismissed it all. And I was able to do this, somehow. I don't know how. I can't explain it, any of it. Perhaps you had to go through this to be free of it. A little crisis,' he said, blowing his nose. 'One might even say it was overdue. And all managed without the benefit of psychiatrists. Think of that!'

Fibich looked around him wonderingly. 'I feel better,' he said. But he did not look well, Hartmann thought. Nevertheless, his colour was nearly back to normal, and he drank the coffee that Goodman brought. Both watched him as he replaced the cup carefully in its saucer.

'Perhaps you should go home, sir, when you've had a rest.'

'Yes,' said Fibich. 'I should like to go home.'

Latecomers

'We will both go,' said Hartmann. 'And you too, John. Finish what you have to do and go home.'

'Buy your mother some flowers,' said Fibich. 'Give her a nice surprise.'

'I usually do, at the weekends,' said Goodman. 'We always enjoy our weekends.'

They both watched him as he collected the cups. Doomed, thought Hartmann. Saved, thought Fibich.

They took a taxi, leaving Fibich's car behind. They sat in the back, two elderly gentlemen, Hartmann resting his hands on his cane. They said nothing, simply marking the passage from danger back to normal life. The streets were empty: it seemed as if most people had left early for the weekend, despite the unpromising weather. Fibich appeared to have recovered from his attack, or whatever it was, thought Hartmann. He cautiously allowed himself to hope for the best. He resolved, at some point during the weekend, to speak to him about retirement. They would both retire, he thought, remembering his melancholy of the morning. It was time. And it was unthinkable, in any event, that he might carry on without Fibich. Their day was done, he now saw, although it terrified him to think that this might be so. Nothing too precipitate, of course: perhaps a year to wind things up, convert themselves into shareholders, make provision for the children. It could be done, he saw, and all in due season. There was no need to get out immediately, no need to frighten anybody. Everyone would understand. And their wives would be glad of their company. He thought back to Yvette, as he had seen her that morning. All in due season, he thought. All in due season.

Fibich thought of his home, of Christine, of his son. How painfully he had missed them, he thought: how wrongly he had spent his time, trying to re-establish a life before the only life he knew. He longed to reach his home, which was the only haven he would ever reach, and yet how temporary, how unstable even that now seemed to him. In any event he had always had an ambivalent attitude towards his home, for while the idea was sacred to him, the reality of it always proved fugitive. This was nothing to do with its physical location, or the fashion in which it was arranged: he even liked Christine's hazy muted colours, although he regarded the rooms as belonging entirely to her, with himself as a visitor, agreeably housed, but, it seemed to him, on a temporary basis. When in the office he would sometimes think lovingly of his home, yet as soon as he was back there he was afflicted with a restlessness which had him seizing his hat again and calling to Christine that he was going to get a bottle of wine, or post a letter, or simply take a walk in an attempt to dislodge the beginnings of a headache. He would wonder if he might feel better somewhere else, would search the Sunday newspapers, go with Hartmann to visit blocks of flats in St John's Wood, in South Kensington, in Highgate or Chiswick. Hartmann enjoyed these visits as simple excursions – he was in any event curious about other people's living arrangements – but to Fibich they were a matter of greater importance. Would he feel better if he received the evening sun, if he had a balcony, a patio, a roof terrace, if there were a caretaker on the premises, if the shops were near to hand, if there were three bathrooms instead of two, if he faced the other way? He did not know. He only knew that he felt a dismay amounting to anguish at the thought that he was already experiencing the maximum amount of comfort to be derived from the concept 'home'. He worried that it loomed so large, yet filled him with despair. Whatever brief moments of satisfaction he had felt in his life were always lessened by the idea of going home. He could be sitting comfortably in his own chair, in his own drawing-room, doing something entirely pleasant – reading, listening to music – when the idea of home would strike through him with a pang, as if home were somewhere else. Thus the homesickness that had afflicted him in Berlin had nothing to do with any

Latecomers

home that he had ever known, but rather as if his place were eternally elsewhere, and as if, displaced as he was, he was only safe when he was fast asleep.

Gliding down Park Lane in the taxi, with Hartmann silent beside him, he began again to wonder whether they should not all sell up and go to the sun. For surely he would feel safer in the sun, source of all life, all joy, drawing him out of that deathly sleep every morning, summoning him, challenging him, revivifying him? The white skies and the green leaves of London had never given him the comfort that burning heat and brilliant light would certainly supply. For ten months of the year he felt cold, and his longing for warmth, like his longing for home, seemed unconquerable. He was not like Hartmann, who had the gift of being able to enjoy everything, every change in the climate, every amusement in the working day, every prospect of a new life. Fibich wished only to be safe, and, once safe, to be free, and, once free, to be brave. He had always known this, but never so clearly, never so nakedly as he did in this taxi, which even now was at the bottom of Grosvenor Gardens, and was taking him home to his wife, who must not be told that he was gravely damaged, merely a little tired, a little overstressed and in need of a holiday. Hartmann would see to it. Hartmann would know what to do, what to say. For his part he felt quite calm, as if that shameful weeping had sedated him, leaving him devoid of resource, devoid too of his habitual nervousness, but cold, very cold.

They found Christine arranging pink and white tulips in a square glass vase. 'I'm so glad you're early,' she said. 'Toto is coming to dinner. You're eating with us, Hartmann. Does Yvette know you are home?'

'No,' he said, 'I haven't been upstairs yet.'

'You are more than welcome to stay,' she said. 'Will you have tea? Or did you have some at the office? You look cold, Fibich. Take your coat off. You'll soon get warm.'

She was too busy to pay them much attention. Fibich

watched her, patting her tulips, straightening a couple of books on a side table, twitching curtains into place.

'Toto coming to dinner?' he asked. This was almost unprecedented.

'Apparently he is off on Monday. The dates are being put forward. And we shan't see him for six months.'

She put her hand to her heart, as if registering the full impact of this news.

Fibich smiled, went over to her. 'Then we must see that he has a nice evening,' he said.

It appeared that nothing would be mentioned of the affair of Fibich's day, for which Fibich was grateful. He had not yet decided what to make of it. He now viewed his conduct with distaste, the distaste of a rational man. He felt quiet and empty, had no desire to return to that moment of – what had it been? revelation? – which he had experienced in the hotel dining-room. Whatever it had been, he had a sense of finality, as if the episode were done with. The partial easing of his feelings (for he knew there might be more to come) had been violently registered as a physical upheaval over which he had no control, and, as with any other illness, he was too glad to have got it over to investigate it further. Health, he supposed, was an absence of physical despair, and for the moment he felt none. Like a restored invalid he welcomed the warmth of the room, the flowers in the vase, the tea in his cup. Like an invalid he drank greedily, ate, with a careful and painful exactitude, the slice of iced apricot flan that Christine made so well. Hartmann lingered, turning to the window, his cup in his hand.

'You are very quiet, Hartmann,' said Christine. 'What are you thinking?'

'I was thinking of a housekeeper we had,' he said. 'In Munich. Her name was Frau Dimke. I have just remembered it. And my nurse was Frau Zarzicki.'

But Fibich waved a hand at him, as if to say, 'That life is over. Leave it alone. It has no place here. Remember not to remember, or you will be like me.' And Hartmann nodded, as if he understood what Fibich did not need to put into words, so present was it in both their minds.

Hartmann smiled. Such smiles they both had, thought Christine. That was what had bound her to them in the first place, their wonderful smiles, eager in Hartmann's case, tentative, like an English sun, in Fibich's. And from the joyless world of her youth she had retained a nostalgia for joy, although she herself was untrained for such emotion, and was awkward with it. Toto had it, that smile, although in his case it came too rarely, and when it did come could be perverted to do duty for feeling. Latterly, she thought, smiling herself, he had begun to look more like Fibich, tall, inwardly pondering, so that the smile, when it came, had a thoughtful reflective quality to it. In her eyes Fibich had changed little: it was Toto in whom all the major changes could be observed. Fibich, just today, when his hair was a little untidy and beginning to grow long again, might have been the man she married, tall and spare, absent-minded, with the same loping walk that she had often and secretly observed from behind the curtains of her father's flat in West End Lane. If anything it was Hartmann who had changed, grown pear-shaped, silver-haired. But his face, beneath the expensively barbered and flattened hair, was still the same, the face of an impudent boy impatient to grow into a fully fledged roué. It was all a matter of expression, she thought. He still cocked his head to one side, pursed his lips as if to kiss someone, anyone, widened his eyes at the thought of treats to come. And Fibich, too, had kept his original expression. He had a characteristic way of smiling and shaking his head at the same time that she had always found endearing. She saw that in time Toto might come to have that little mannerism, although in Toto the family likeness had taken a long time to come to the surface. She hoped that there was nothing of herself in Toto, although many people had remarked on his brilliant eyes, so unusual with dark hair, and, in rare moments of exaltation Christine did suppose that he might possibly have inherited them from her.

'What are you smiling at, Hartmann?' she asked.

'I am smiling at you smiling,' he said. 'One can see your boy is coming home.' He sighed. 'If only Marianne were here. Then we could all be together. No news, I suppose?'

'Nothing in the last hour. You had better ring the hospital and give them this number. Then you can relax this evening.'

'Yes,' he said. 'I must go and change. What time do you want us, Christine?'

'Toto is coming at seven-thirty,' she told him.

He smiled again. 'Then we will come at eight.'

When Toto came in, on the stroke of seven-thirty, with a carrier bag, she almost cried out at the resemblance to his father. He had let himself in with his key, and was deep in thought, going through his lines, she supposed, for she had no notion of how films were made. He straightened up, with a visible effort, and smiled at her. That smile again! From the bag he produced a bottle of wine and a pot plant, which she put in the place of honour on a small table, sweeping aside her tulips in order to do so.

'My dear boy,' she said. 'My dear boy.'

He flapped his hand at her. 'It's only a plant, Ma,' he said. 'The wine is for Dad. Drink it when I'm not here. You're very quiet, Dad. Daddy? Are you all right?'

'Never better,' said Fibich.

This was new, he thought, this noticing. But because he now wished to preserve his son from those quaking feelings of loss and regret which were his almost constant companions, he said little, put away his anxiety and his solicitude, the enquiries about Toto's health, sleep, exercise that he longed to make and habitually did make. Now it was appropriate, on the eve of Toto's departure, to treat him like a man, and in order to do so he must behave like a man himself. For he knew, somehow, that Toto, who was about to leave them (and who knew if he, Fibich, would ever see him again?) must feel some of that melancholy experienced by all those who leave their known worlds behind, and leave behind, too, those who love them, exchanging them for the more brutal attitudes of casual acquaintances, acquaintances who might see him as a novice who must undergo some rites of initiation if he were to be one of them. For whom could Toto trust, since he loved no one? He would be for ever dependent, whether he knew it or not, on those who loved him. And Fibich, in the clarity of this unusual day, could see that Toto was beginning to be aware of this, and to begin his own life, in which the mourning process would not be entirely absent.

The arrival of Yvette, in a blast of 'Joy' and a black and gold striped dress that made her look like a wasp, lightened the atmosphere. 'Hartmann is still telephoning,' she said disgustedly. 'He telephones every hour. He is driving them all mad. I told him I would *know* when the baby was born. "I am a mother," I said. "I will *know*." He takes no notice, of course. As if I were not concerned myself.'

'And of course Roger would let you know,' said Christine.

'Oh, Roger,' said Yvette, with surprise in her voice. 'I'd forgotten about Roger, to tell you the truth.'

Toto laughed. 'I adore you, Yvette.'

'Well, of course, darling,' she smiled. 'You always did. And how's our clever boy, then?'

They ate roast lamb, with tiny carrots and turnips, and a pudding that consisted of squares of shortbread floating on a sea of fruit. Toto ate swiftly, his eyes on his plate. 'There is plenty more,' observed Fibich mildly, almost amused to see his appetite duplicated so exactly. The day had brought revelations, he thought. *Life* brings revelations. He remembered some inkling of this having come to him in Berlin. He had felt then on the verge of a great discovery. But perhaps that was the discovery, quite simply that life brings revelations, supplies all the material we need. And if it does not supply it in the right order, then we must simply wait for more to come to light. He felt a coldness at the thought that more might be revealed to him, was no longer so anxious to bring it about, might even be content, he thought, to wait, and even to hope that nothing more would be vouchsafed to him this side of the grave. He glanced at his wife, whose eyes were all for Toto. Yet Fibich knew that in those last days, if he were granted the grace to be aware of them, Toto would be his, entirely his. For at the end he knew, even if Toto were not there (and he could not help wishing, selfishly, that he might be) he would, with his knowledge, die a happy man.

'There is cheese, if anyone wants it,' said Christine. Nobody did. She put a dish of chocolate-covered marzipan on the table, and went out to make coffee.

'Why do you never put on weight?' wondered Yvette. 'You both have such a sweet tooth. Hartmann was saying this morning that he thought I had filled out a little.'

'I was mistaken,' said Hartmann gravely. 'You look to me as you looked when I first saw you. Voluptuous, sensual, a woman of mystery. You maddened us with desire, back there in the Farringdon Road. I had to tie Fibich down to his desk. He was like a werewolf. A lycanthrope,' he added, taking the last of the marzipan. 'We imagined men fighting duels over you. Not much of a typist, though, as I remember.'

'Oh, Hartmann,' protested Yvette. 'You are always making fun of me.'

'I?' He put his hand to his breast. 'Would I do that?'

'I think I ran that office very competently,' she said.

'My darling, I can safely say without fear of contradiction that we have never had another secretary like you.'

The evening passed as if there were to be no birth, no departure. Fibich reflected that it might well be the last of such evenings. He felt a sense of completion, not devoid of sadness. They would never move, he could see that now. They would stay as they were, for whatever changes would take place would take place in their children, not in themselves. He supposed that he and Hartmann would continue to go to the office, do a little less, perhaps, then a great deal less, until they could do no more. Then they would take their rest. He did not know which of them would be left to take care of the others. For himself now it would simply be a matter of trying his best. He looked around him, at the faces at the table. Toto had wandered off to watch television. Christine was flushed, as she always was in moments of pleasure. Yvette – and he could see that she was now quite plump – sat with her hand through Hartmann's arm. And Hartmann looked quite old. But just the same, still the same bold young man that he had been on leaving the army, ready for anything. Fibich turned and looked at his son, who sat, long legs stretched out in front of him, in front of the television.

'Remind him to take something warm for the evenings,' he said to Christine.

'But it will be hot!' said Yvette. 'Marvellously hot. We should go to the sun ourselves this year. What do you say, Christine?'

'It would be better to wait until the winter,' she answered. 'I don't want to be away until Toto comes back.'

'And have you forgotten Marianne?' said Hartmann.

'Oh, God. Should I telephone again?'

'Not yet,' Yvette told him. 'You know what would be nice? If we took a house somewhere, and the children came too. Would you like that, Toto? Would you come?'

'Leave him alone,' said Fibich, smiling. 'He will come if he wants to. And if not, not.'

Toto leaned forward and switched off the television.

'Rubbish,' he commented. 'And he wasn't good. What was that, Daddy? A house? Oh, yes, I'll come. I'll come. If you really want me, that is.'

Angela Carter

extract from

The Magic Toyshop

Melanie, orphaned together with her younger brother and sister, has already fallen in love with her Irish 'aunt' Margaret (who cannot speak) and Margaret's brothers Finn and Francie. But the head of her new family, Uncle Philip, puppet master and creator of the magic toyshop, is a tyrant. Melanie is more frightened than flattered to be cast in the leading role for his Christmas show.

Melanie, orphaned together with her younger brother and sister, has already fallen in love with her Irish aunt Margaret (who cannot speak) and Margaret's brothers Finn and Francie. But the head of her new family, Uncle Philip, puppet master and creator of the magic toyshop, is a tyrant. Melanie is more frightened than flattered to be cast in the leading role for his Christmas show.

One night, her aunt drew a length of white chiffon out of a paper bag. The painted dog's eyes shone with white lights, reflecting it. She gestured Melanie over to her and draped the material around her shoulders. All at once, Melanie was back home and swathing herself in diaphanous veiling before a mirror. But the cuckoo clock poked out its head and called nine o'clock and there she was, in Uncle Philip's house.

'Your costume,' wrote Aunt Margaret on a pad, to save herself getting up. 'For the show.'

'What am I?' asked Melanie.

'Leda. He is making a swan. He is having trouble with it. He says Finn is trying to spoil it.'

This seemed very likely to Melanie.

'How big is the swan?'

Her aunt sketched a vague shape in the air.

'I don't think,' said Melanie, 'that I want to be Leda.'

'That is how he sees you. White chiffon and flowers in your hair. A very young girl.'

'What kind of flowers?'

Aunt Margaret drew out a handful of artificial daisies, yellow and white like fried eggs. Melanie would be a nymph crowned with daisies once again; he saw her as once she had seen herself. In spite of everything, she was flattered.

'Needs must,' she said. 'I suppose.' Her aunt's scissors flashed in the light like exclamation marks as she snipped into the flimsy stuff.

When the dress was roughly tacked together, Melanie had to put it on and go down and show it to Uncle Philip. She had to take all her clothes off and wear just the chiffon tunic with the white satin ribbons criss-crossed between her breasts (which, she observed with interest, seemed to have grown and the nipples to have got rather darker.) Aunt Margaret brushed her hair with the silver-backed brush which, like Winnie the Pooh, had survived the crash; she brushed and brushed until Melanie's black hair swirled like the Thames in flood, and then she floated all the daisies on it. She took a cigar box from a cupboard, opened it and displayed a number of sticks of greasepaint. Melanie's eyelids were painted blue and her lips coral. She felt greasy, basted with lard.

'Have you any nice jewellery?'

'Only confirmation pearls.' They, too, had survived. Aunt Margaret stroked them and adored them and fastened them round Melanie's neck. A few pins left in the chiffon tunic scratched Melanie's flesh. She wriggled.

'The pearls are the finishing touch. You look so pretty!'

'Well, I wish I could see myself. It is a long time since I dressed up.' Recollecting, she bit her lip.

'Go down, now.'

'By myself?'

Aunt Margaret nodded. Melanie slung her coat round her shoulders for the thin silky stuff hardly kept out the draughts and the house was freezing cold. Tea was long over and, downstairs, the evening's work was well under way. The curtains were open and Finn stood on the stage surrounded by cans of paint, open eyes of pure of colour, working on a blackcloth showing a sea with a blood-orange sunset, something like the background to the picture of the dog in the kitchen. Under the crude strip lighting, Uncle Philip squatted on the floor with a mound of feathers on a spread sheet before him. He was sorting the feathers into smaller piles. His moustache was lightly furred with down.

The Magic Toyshop

'Here I am,' said Melanie.

He stayed on his heels, resting his bulky hands on his dirty white overall knees. Tonight, his eyes were the no-colour of old newspapers.

'Why, his head is quite square!' thought Melanie. She had never noticed before. This evening, some disarrangement of the pale hair emphasized the corners. His head was a jack-in-a-box. A pin stuck in her armpit painfully.

'Take off that wrap,' he said.

She obeyed, shivering, for the basement was heated only by a miserly, inefficient little oil stove. Finn painted on. She heard the slap-slap of his brush as he filled in a large area of sky.

'You're well built, for fifteen.' His voice was flat and dead.

'Nearly sixteen.'

'It's all that free milk and orange juice that does it. Do you have your periods?'

'Yes,' she said, too shocked to do more than whisper.

He grunted, displeased.

'I wanted my Leda to be a little girl. Your tits are too big.'

Finn flung down his paintbrush.

'Don't talk to her like that!'

'Keep your mouth shut and mind your own business, Finn Jowle. I'll talk to her anyway I please. Who is it pays for her board?'

'I can talk how I like, as well as you!'

Uncle Philip stroked his moustache thoughtfully, not looking at Finn at all.

'Oh, no,' he said calmly. 'Oh, no, you can't. Get on painting. You haven't got all day.'

The discord jangled between them. Melanie's head ached.

'Finn,' she said. 'Please. I don't mind.'

'You see?' said Uncle Philip with a queer inflection of triumph. Finn shrugged and picked up his brush.

79

'And wipe out that paint mark you just made!'

Scowling, Finn scrubbed at the brush-mark on the floor with the elbow of his paint-stiffened overall.

'You'll do, then,' Uncle Philip said to her. 'I suppose you'll have to do. And you've got quite nice hair. And pretty legs.' But he was resenting her because she was not a puppet.

'Turn round.'

She turned round.

'Smile.'

She smiled.

'Not like that, you silly bitch. Show your teeth.'

She smiled, showing her teeth.

'You've got a bit of a look of your ma. Not much but a bit. None of your father, thank God. I never could abide your father. He thought 'isself too good for the Flowers by a long chalk, he did. A writer, he called 'isself. Soft bastard, he never got his hands dirty.'

'But he was awfully clever!' protested Melanie, stung with defiance at last.

'Not so clever he thought to put a bit by to take care of you lot when he'd gone,' Uncle Philip pointed out reasonably. 'And so I've got his precious kids all for my very own, haven't I? To make into little Flowers.'

He began to sort the feathers again. Jesus wants me for a sunbeam, Uncle Philip wants me for a little flower. The feathers moved about in the current of air that blew in under the door. Uncle Philip sighed heavily, the sigh of a man being thankful for exceedingly small mercies.

'You'll do,' he said. 'I suppose. Now piss off.'

Finn looked up angrily and Melanie ran upstairs before the sharp words and blows began. Why was Finn standing up for her, quixotically acting her champion like this? Because it was such an easy way of rousing her uncle? But did Finn care how much it upset her to see them so fierce with each other? He probably did not even notice. She took the flowers from her hair and carefully stepped

The Magic Toyshop

out of the tunic. She did not think she would like herself in it if she could see herself and she did not think she would like to see her face bright and thick with greasepaint.

'I wish the show was all over,' she said.

Her aunt nodded and her eyes strangely spilled over with quick tears. She thrust her fists into her eyes and her shoulders shook. She cried often, these days. The bull terrier at once left off lapping water from its baking dish and went and put its head on her knee. Melanie was again surprised at the quick, alert sympathy of the dog, how he combined the roles of guard dog and four-legged comforter. She wished she could act just as quietly, just as simply. She put her hand on the older woman's shoulder and Aunt Margaret blindly grasped it with her own bird-claw. They stayed together like this for a long time. Each time Aunt Margaret cried, she and her niece became closer.

Finn said: 'You must rehearse with me.' He did not raise his eyes to Melanie but stared at the backs of his hands. The chisel cut had left a broad, purple, crescent-shaped scar.

'What, on the stage?'

'Do you think he'd allow us on to his lovely stage? Never. We'll have to do it in my room.'

'Why with you and not the swan?'

'You're not to see the swan until the performance so that you will react to it spontaneously. But you've got to practise with me to get the movements right so I'm to stand in for the swan.'

His voice was softer than a goose's neck, almost inaudible, and he kept his eyes turned away.

'Are we to rehearse in costume?' she asked half apprehensively, thinking of the white chiffon and her own white flesh showing through like milk in white glass.

'What, you think I should feather myself?'

He looked like the petrol-soaked wreck of a swan come to grief in a polluted river. His trousers and shirt (an old-fashioned shirt of striped flannel which should have had a collar but did not) were motleyed with all sorts of paint and a welter of dirt and sweat. His bare feet were warty with dirt. There was a dark brown tidemark round his throat and heavy thumbprints of dirt under his ears. The fungus was on his chin again. He smelt sickening and stale, a sour-sweet stench as if he was going bad.

'You should take more care of yourself,' she said. 'Oh, Finn, wash yourself. And cut your hair, perhaps.' For orange tendrils of uncombed hair curled round the shoulders of his grimy shirt.

'Why should I?'

She could not answer that.

It was the becalmed middle of a Sunday afternoon. In the kitchen, Aunt Margaret sat in her grey dress and vicious collar, sewing at the Greek tunic with the finest of stitches. Tea was already laid in the dining-room, the calm white cloth laid with green-banded Sunday china, milk and sugar standing on tiptoe to be used in jug and bowl. Victoria napped in her cage beside the blossoming geranium. Jonathon made ships downstairs while Uncle Philip constructed his swan and planned how it should be strung. Francie had taken his fiddle and gone off about his own business in his Easter Rising trilby and mackintosh. The house rested.

'Come on, then,' said Finn.

They climbed the stairs together past all the closed doors of Bluebeard's castle. Finn's hoarse, snoring breathing echoed noisily. They went into his room and he kicked the door to behind him. His face was a picture of sulky boredom.

'Let's get this stupid game over with, then.'

She looked around her, disconcerted. The room was as bare as if all the brothers' possessions were packed up in trunks and cases and put away in preparation for imminent departure. On the wall which she had never seen because it was the one with the peephole in it was

The Magic Toyshop

a shelf with the only small and personal thing in the room standing on it, a single, faded photograph in a black, badly fitting frame. The photograph was of a woman with a broad face who looked the camera squarely in the eye without a smile. She wore a Galway shawl and there was a baby in the fold of it.

'Our mother,' said Finn, 'with Maggie in arms.'

Behind her head was a desolation of rocks.

'Back home,' said Finn and said no more.

Next to the photograph was the Anglepoise lamp coiled up ready to spring. But for the strip of mirror and the portrait of her aunt, the walls were empty. There was no sign of the St Sebastian triptych. He must have hidden it. By the shelf was a built-in cupboard but everything else she saw was familiar. She sat down on the roses-and-castles chair with a ludicrous sense of formality, as if paying a polite call in a tailored suit and a small, veiled hat.

'This is how it goes,' said Finn. He seemed to grudge every word he spoke. 'Leda walks by the shore, gathering shells.'

From his pocket, he took a convoluted shell, all milky mother-of-pearl. He set it down on the bit of rug.

'Night is coming on. She hears a beating of wings and sees the approach of the swan. She runs away but it bears down and casts her to the ground. Curtain.'

'Is that all?'

'It is only a vehicle for his handsome swan, after all.'

She rose and stooped for the shell. She moved badly because he was watching her.

'Make it more fluid,' he said wearily. 'Move from the hips.'

She stooped again, waggling her backside, which was the only way she could think of moving from her hips.

'For Chrissake, Melanie. Did they teach you hockey when you went to school?'

'Well, yes. They did.'

He sneered.

'Move – ah, like this.' He scooped up the shell. But he no longer moved like a wave of the sea. He creaked, indeed, like a puppet. He had forgotten his grace was all gone. He stopped short, fingering the shell.

'Anyway,' he said. 'Try again.'

She tried.

'Better, maybe. Now, do it again. I'm the swan.'

She walked by the shore, gathering shells. Finn stood on his toes. His hair was all over his face; she could hardly see him. He made swishing noises indicating the beating of wings.

'When you hear that, you worry. You run a few steps.'

She ran a few steps.

'Right.'

He ran after her. It was charades. She giggled.

'No, don't be silly! You're supposed to be a poor frightened girl.'

'I can't take it seriously.'

'But, Melanie, he'll turn you out if you can't work for him. And what would you do then?'

'He wouldn't,' she said wondering. 'He couldn't.'

'Yes, he could and would.' He was reasonable and serious. 'We could do nothing for you. You would starve.'

'I hate him,' she said. She had not meant to say this. Their eyes met and looked away again.

'Start from the beginning. Pretend. Act.'

This time, things went better. She screwed her eyes up and pretended she saw evening coming on. And pretended she could hear gulls mewing and the squeak of sand under the balls of her feet and the rhythm of wings. So it was easy to look frightened and to run a little way.

'You run and stumble and I bear you to the ground.' He concealed a yawn. 'Put the shell down and we'll go through it all.'

She obeyed him. The gulls mewed and the sand shifted and the swan hurtled down and it was easy. She sprang away from Finn and it was no longer a pretence –

The Magic Toyshop

she stumbled over the knotted fringe of the rug. Overbalancing, she clutched at Finn to save herself but pulled him over with her. Clinging to each other, Melanie laughing, they toppled in slow motion to the floor.

But Finn did not laugh. And Melanie's laughter trickled to nothing when she saw his pale, bony face half-hidden by hair and could see nothing there, no hint of a smile or inflection of tenderness which might mean she would be spared. He lay as close as a sheet to a blanket; and he smelt of decay, but that no longer mattered. Shuddering, she realized that this no longer mattered. She waited tensely for it to happen.

She was seized with a nervous, unlocalized excitement. They lay together on the bare, splintered boards. There was no time any more. And no Melanie, either. She was utterly subdued. She was changing, growing. All that was substantial to her was the boy whom she touched all down the length of her but did not touch. The moment was eternity, trembling like a dewdrop on a rose, endlessly about to fall. Grudgingly, slowly, reluctantly, he put his hand on her right breast. Time began with a jolt, their time. She let her breath out in a hissing rush. He closed his Atlantic eyes. He looked like a death-mask of himself. It was killing him to leave his isolation, but leave it he must.

'This is the start,' she said to herself, clearly. She heard her own voice, certain and distinct, inside her head. No more false starts, as in the pleasure gardens, but the real beginning of a deep mystery between them. What would he do to her, would he be kind? She looked down with a fear that was also a pleasure at his stained, scarred hand. His workman's hand, which was strong and cunning. The light seemed to die about her, leaving her to see by her senses only.

'No,' said Finn aloud. 'No!'

He leapt to his feet and sprinted across the room. He jumped into the cupboard and shut the door. From the cupboard came a muffled cry. 'No!' again.

The tension between them was destroyed with such wanton savagery that Melanie fell limply back and struggled with tears. She still felt his five fingertips, five red cinders, burning on her breast. But he was gone. She felt cold and ill.

'No!' more faintly.

'What have I done wrong?' she asked the door of the cupboard. No answer. 'Finn?'

Still no answer. She felt a fool, lying on the floor with her skirt rumpled over her knees. She could see under the beds, a pair of shoes standing harmlessly under each one in no dust. The room was very clean although Finn was not. Francie's shoes were brilliant with polish but Finn's were caked with mud – though where could he have been, had he been walking in the pleasure garden by himself, talking to the broken queen and patting the stone lioness on the head? His shoes were lopsided with walking.

'Maybe,' she thought, 'he wouldn't because I never polished his shoes.' Anything was possible, when he went to earth in a cupboard to get away from her.

From the keyhole of the cupboard issued a blue trail of smoke. She was horrified until she guessed he had lit a cigarette. Probably, in the close confinement, he would suffocate in his own smoke. Or set himself on fire like a Buddhist monk, but accidentally.

'Isn't he *silly*,' she thought. She felt very old, but not mature.

'Don't smoke in the cupboard,' she said.

A fresh puff of smoke answered her. Grumbling beneath her breath, she dragged herself upright and went and opened the door. The cupboard was just deep enough to hold him sitting cross-legged, his head concealed in the pin-striped folds of Francie's second-best suit, which hung on a hanger. There were also some ghostly white shirts there. On a shelf at the top of the cupboard were piled paintings of all shapes and sizes. Finn's hand, with a cigarette in it, poked out of the folds of clothing and

The Magic Toyshop

tapped ash on to the floor. He said nothing. She examined the crossed soles of his feet.

'Finn,' she said, 'there's a splinter in your left foot.'

'Go away,' he said.

'If you don't take the splinter out, it will fester. They will probably have to amputate your leg, in the end.'

'Please. Go away.'

'Why are you hiding in the cupboard, Finn?' she asked like a mother to an inexplicable child at the end of a hard day.

'Because there's room for me,' he said. The Lewis Carroll logic of this was too much for her; she ran up a white flag, acknowledging defeat.

'Oh, Finn, why did you run away from me?' And the words issued out on the wings of a wail.

'You are too young,' he said, 'to say things like that. You must have read it in a woman's magazine.' His voice was muffled in serge, dressed up for the Arctic in cap and muffler.

She pushed aside the clothing and revealed him, all small and disconsolate and shrivelled looking, knees drawn up under chin in a foetal position. He scowled with squinting ferocity, like a balked Siamese cat.

'You see,' he said, 'he wanted me to fuck you.'

She had only read the word before, in cold and aseptic print, never heard it spoken except in heat by rough farm-workers who did not realize she was walking by. She was deeply agitated. She had never connected the word with herself; her phantom bridegroom would never have fucked her. They would have made love. But Finn, she acknowledged with a sinking of her spirit, would have. She could tell by the way he ground out his cigarette on the floor.

'It was his fault,' he said. 'Suddenly I saw it all, when we were lying there. He's pulled our strings as if we were his puppets and there I was, all ready to touch you up just as he wanted. He told me to rehearse Leda and the swan with you. Somewhere private. Like in your room, he said. Go up and rehearse a rape with Melanie in your bedroom. Christ. He wanted me to do you and he set the scene. Ah, he's evil!'

Melanie kicked at a knot in the floorboards with the toe of her shoe. She noticed that the toe was scuffed and the shoes would need mending. Did the household have credit at a cobbler's shop? She tried to concentrate on this so as not to have to think about what Finn was saying.

'Well,' said Finn, parting the clothes in order to light a fresh cigarette, 'I'm not having any, see? I'm not going to do what he wants even if I do fancy you. So there.'

Melanie abandoned trying to think about cobbling.

'Oh, but Finn, why ever does he want you to—'

'To pull you down, Melanie. He couldn't stand your father and he can't stand you and the other kids being your father's children, though he doesn't mind you being your mother's. You represent the enemy to him, who use toilet paper and fish knives.'

'We never had fish knives,' said Melanie.

He disregarded this. He became distraught and incoherent.

'And you're so fresh and innocent, all of you, and so you're something to change and destroy. Well, Victoria is Maggie's baby, now, and he has Jonathon working all day and all night under his eye and there is only you left not accounted for. So he thinks I should do you because he despises me, too, and he thinks I'm God's scum. He does, really. A dirty beatnik and he'd turn me out if it wasn't for Maggie and if it wasn't for the painting, and I'd go, anyway, if it wasn't for Maggie. And so I should do you because you shave under your armpits and maybe you would have a baby and that would spite your father.'

'My father is dead.'

'He knows. All the same, it's all the same to him.'

'I don't shave under my armpits.'

The Magic Toyshop

'It's a manner of speaking.' His face twisted in a grimace of pain or pure disgust and he threw away his cigarette and buried his head in his arms. She shifted her weight from foot to foot, uncertain and bewildered. She hardly took in what he said. Without understanding, she said: 'And you don't want me, then?'

'That's got nothing to do with it,' he snapped. 'Besides, you're too young. I found that out in the pleasure garden. Later on, perhaps. But you're too young.'

'I know,' she said. 'It is my curse.'

'Isn't it terrible?' Finn said. 'This is a madhouse. He is making me mad.'

He hid himself with the clothes again, jerking them about on their hangers. Disturbed, the pile of paintings on the shelf slithered to the floor. Melanie picked them up wearily. She was exhausted with surprises. First the St Sebastian triptych, all finished, down to the last arrowhead and gobbet of blood. She made a face at it and thrust it away. Then she saw herself, and was touched.

She was taking off her chocolate sweater and was all twisted up, a rather thin but nicely made young girl with a delicate, withdrawn face, against a wall of dark red roses. Her wallpaper. She looked very scrubbed. She looked like a virgin who cleaned her teeth after every meal and delighted to take great bites from rosy apples. Her black hair exploded about her head in great Art Nouveau ripples. It looked as though Finn was trying his hand at curves. The picture was as flat and uncommunicative as all his pictures and seemed to be an asexual kind of pin-up. Round the bare upper part of her right arm was a black band. He did not see her precisely as she saw herself but it could have been very much worse.

'But why has he put in the mourning band?' she thought.

Nevertheless, she was pleased.

'Did you make sketches of me through the spy-hole when I was undressing?' she asked.

89

'Don't look at my pictures.'

'I'm only putting them away.'

Then she saw the horrible picture. It was a hell of leaping flames through which darted black figures. Uncle Philip was laid out on a charcoal grill like a barbecued pork chop. He was naked, gross and abhorrent. His flesh was beginning to crack and blister as his fat bubbled inside it. His white hair was budding in tiny flames. Beside him stood a devil in red tights with horns and a forked tail. He held a pair of red-hot tongs in his hands with which he was tweaking Uncle Philip's testicles. Uncle Philip's face was branded with a fiery hoofprint. His mouth was a black, screaming hole from which issued a banner with the words: 'Forgive me!' The devil had Finn's former, grinning face.

'So that is where his grin went,' thought Melanie. 'He wiped it off his face and slapped it on to the cardboard.' Finn would never grin again.

From Finn's painted lips, which were made of fire, came the one word: 'Never!' Over the top of the picture, in a white shield, was a title, also in Gothic script: 'In Hell, all wrongs are righted.' The inspiration of the whole was Hieronymus Bosch. Melanie dropped the picture with a sob.

'I told you not to look.'

'You are right. It is a mad house.' She began to cry. Finn crawled out of the cupboard on all fours and clasped her knees, burying his head between her thighs. She dug her fingers in his hair convulsively and said the words which floated on top of her mind, thoughtlessly; if she had thought about them, she would never have said them.

'I think I want to be in love with you but I don't know how.'

'There you go again, talking like a woman's magazine,' said Finn. 'What you feel is because of proximity, because I am here. Anyway, you are too young, we have been into that. And it would be a waste of your

The Magic Toyshop

time, for I'm going to make him murder me, aren't I?'

Then the gong sounded for tea, which somehow had to be endured, the shrimps shelled, the bread buttered, the milk and tea poured into the cups, Victoria's cake to be cut into fingers so that she could eat it all up. In the witch-ball, they all sat, monstrously swollen, eating at a warped white table that stretched for ever. Melanie kept her eyes on the witch-ball so as not to have to look at Uncle Philip.

The next day was Christmas Eve but it was no different to any other day except that the shop was very, very busy. It was crowded all through the day and Melanie and Aunt Margaret tottered on burning feet by the time they turned the sign on the door round to read 'closed'. The shelves were almost bare, the stock almost gone. Even the hobby horse and the toy puppets had gone from the windows, leaving only the plastic holly behind. Notes spilled out of the money drawer. They were down to the last roll of flowered wrapping paper. The shop had the look of a battlefield the morning after. On its perch, the parakeet drooped as if it, too, had been worked off its feet.

'Well,' wrote Aunt Margaret, 'at least we shall have a day of rest tomorrow.'

Although nothing more. Melanie wrestled with self-pity and memory as she sat in the kitchen with her book while her aunt sewed the last seams of the Greek tunic. No holly in the kitchen, no mistletoe over the lampshade. No Christmas tree with small coloured lights. Uncle Philip received Christmas cards and calendars from traders and wholesalers with whom he dealt but he destroyed them as soon as they arrived so there were no cards on the mantelpiece. Nothing. And the house was peculiarly cold. Perhaps it was freezing itself out of spite.

Melanie wondered if they would go to church, to Midnight Mass, because she, in a muddled way, thought they must be religious if they believed so firmly in Hell.

Angela Carter

But bedtime was at the usual time and, though Francie returned very late, he was slightly drunk so he could not have been to church. She heard his uncertain footsteps on the stairs and he was humming a hornpipe under his breath.

Finn must have been lying awake in the darkness, as she was, the wall separating them like Tristan's sword, for she could hear the soft murmur of him and Francie talking together for a little while, but she could not make out one word. Then a little light came through the uncovered spy-hole, a flickering, surreptitous light. And her nostrils caught the smell of charring wood. They were burning something. Guiltily, she got out of bed to look. Out of bed, it was colder than she would have thought possible, the temperature of Russia when nights are coldest there. The floorboards struck ice up through the unprotected soles of her feet. She felt gooseflesh rising up all over her.

The brothers' room was dim and shadowed; she made out their two shapes with difficulty. They were hunched together in the middle of the room. The strip of mirror suddenly flashed at a struck match. Francie's raincoat glimmered; he still wore his coat and hat. He knelt on the floor, steadying himself with one hand. In the other, he held upright a small, carved doll with a shock of yellowish white hair made from unravelled string. It had a small, dandyish white shirt with a bootlace tie. Aunt Margaret must have made the shirt, it was so small and fine. It must have been difficult to make it so small.

Finn was carefully applying matches to various parts of the doll. As soon as the clothing began to smoulder and glow, igniting the wood beneath, he pinched out the charred, burnt part and began again on another place. Both were quite silent and busy, absorbed. She saw the dog was also present, sitting watching them without blinking. When the matches shone out, its eyes were fluorescent raspberries. Its white fur looked unnatural, bleached on purpose, for a disguise. Finn put a match to the doll's trousered groin and he and Francie laughed very quietly. The Jowles were keeping Christmas in their own way.

Melanie went back to bed and pulled the covers over her head. But there was no warmth in the blankets and the stone hot-water-bottle had cooled in her absence. It was so cold she thought the mucus would freeze inside her nose and her brain congeal to a ridged knob of ice. She kept her head under the blankets so that she would not see the magic light.

Colette
The Cat

ONE

Towards ten o'clock, the family poker-players began to show signs of weariness. Camille was fighting against sleepiness as one does at nineteen. By starts she would become fresh and clear-eyed again; then she would yawn behind her clasped hands and reappear pale, her chin white and her cheeks a little black under their ochre-tinted powder, with two tiny tears in the corners of her eyes.

'Camille, you ought to be in bed!'

'At ten o'clock, Mummy, at ten o'clock! Who on earth goes to bed at ten o'clock?'

Her eyes appealed to her fiancé, who lay back, overcome, in the depths of an armchair.

'Leave them alone,' said another maternal voice. 'They've still seven days to wait for each other. They're a bit dazed at the moment. It's very natural.'

'Exactly. One hour more or less . . . Camille, you ought to go home to bed. So ought we.'

'Seven days!' cried Camille. 'But it's Monday today! And I hadn't given it a thought! Alain! Wake up! Alain!'

She threw her cigarette into the garden and lit a fresh one. Then she sorted out the scattered cards, shuffled them and laid them out as fortune-tellers do.

'To know whether we'll get the car, that marvellous baby roadster, before the ceremony! Look, Alain! I'm not cheating! It's coming out with a journey and an important piece of news!'

'What's that?'

'The roadster, of course!'

Without raising the nape of his neck from the chair, Alain turned his head towards the open french window, through which came the sweet smell of fresh spinach and new-mown hay. The grass had been shorn during the day, and the honeysuckle, which draped a tall dead tree, added the nectar of its first flowers to the scent of the cut grass. A crystalline tinkle announced the entrance of the ten o'clock tray of soft drinks and iced water, carried by old Emile's tremulous hands, and Camille got up to fill the glasses.

She served her fiancé last, offering him the misted tumbler with a smile of secret understanding. She watched him drink and felt a sudden pang of desire at the sight of his mouth pressing against the rim of the glass. But he felt so weary that he refused to share that pang and merely touched the white fingers with the red nails as they removed his empty tumbler.

'Are you coming to lunch tomorrow?' she asked him under her breath.

'Ask the cards.'

Camille drew back quickly, and began to act the clown a little over her fortune-telling.

'Never, never joke about twenty-four-hours! Doesn't matter so much about crossed knives, or pennies with holes in them, or the talkies, or God the Father . . .'

'Camille!'

'Sorry, Mummy. But one mustn't joke about twenty-four-hours! He's a good little chap, the knave of spades. A nice black express messenger, always in a hurry.'

'In a hurry to do what?'

'Why, to talk, of course! Just think, he brings the news of the next twenty-four hours, even of the next two days. If you put two more cards on his right and left, he foretells the coming week.'

She was talking fast, scratching at two little smudges of lipstick at the corners of her mouth with a pointed nail.

The Cat

Alain listened to her, not bored, but not indulgent either. He had known her for several years and classified her as a typical modern girl. He knew the way she drove a car, a little too fast and a little too well; her eye alert and her scarlet mouth always ready to swear violently at a taxi-driver. He knew that she lied unblushingly, as children and adolescents do; that she was capable of deceiving her parents so as to get out after dinner and meet him at a night-club. There they danced together, but they drank only orange-juice because Alain disliked alcohol.

Before their official engagement, she had yielded her discreetly wiped lips to him both by daylight and in the dark. She had also yielded her impersonal breasts, always imprisoned in a lace brassière, and her very lovely legs in the flawless stockings she bought in secret; stockings 'like Mistinguett's, you know. Mind my stockings, Alain!' Her stockings and her legs were the best things about her.

'She's pretty,' Alain thought dispassionately, 'because not one of her features is ugly, because she's an out-and-out brunette. Those lustrous eyes perfectly match that sleek, glossy, frequently washed hair that's the colour of a new piano.' He was also perfectly aware that she could be as violent and capricious as a mountain stream.

She was still talking about the roadster.

'No, Daddy, *no*! Absolutely no question of my letting Alain take the wheel while we're driving through Switzerland! He's too absent-minded. And besides, he doesn't really like driving. I know him!'

'She knows me,' Alain echoed in his own mind. 'Perhaps she really thinks she does. Over and over again, I've said to her too: "I know you, my girl." Saha knows her too. Where is that Saha?'

His eyes searched round for the cat. Then, starting limb by limb, first one shoulder, then the other, he unglued himself from the armchair and went lazily down the five steps into the garden.

The garden was very large and surrounded by other

gardens. It breathed out into the night the heavy smell of well-manured earth given over to producing flowers and constantly forced into fertility. Since Alain's birth, the house had hardly changed at all. 'An only son's house,' Camille said jeeringly. She did not hide her contempt for the high-pitched roof with the top-storey windows set in the slates and for certain modest mouldings which framed the french windows on the ground floor.

The garden, like Camille, also seemed to despise the house. Huge trees, which showered down the black, calcined twigs which fall from elms in their old age, protected it from neighbours and passers-by. A little farther on, in a property for sale and in the playground of a school, stood isolated pairs of similar old elms, relics of a princely avenue which had formed part of a park which the new Neuilly was fast destroying.

'Where are you, Alain?'

Camille was calling him from the top of the steps but, on an impulse, he refused to answer. Deliberately, he made for the safer refuge of the shadows, feeling his way along the edge of the shaven lawn with his foot. High in the sky a hazy moon held court, looking larger than usual through the mist of the first warm days. A single tree – a poplar with newly opened glossy leaves – caught the moonlight and trickled with as many sparkles as a waterfall. A silver shadow leapt out of a clump of bushes and glided like a fish against Alain's ankles.

'Ah! There you are, Saha! I was looking for you. Why didn't you appear at table tonight?'

'Me – rrou – wa,' answered the cat, 'me-rrou-wa.'

'What, me-rrou-wa? And why me-rrou-wa? Do you really mean it?'

'Me-rrou-wa,' insisted the cat, 'me-rrou-wa.'

He stroked her, tenderly groping his way down the long spine that was softer than a hare's fur. Then he felt under his hand the small, cold nostrils dilated by her violent purring. 'She's my cat. My very own cat.'

The Cat

'Me-rrou-wa,' said the cat very softly. 'R . . . rrou-wa.'

Camille called once more from the house and Saha vanished under a clipped euonymus hedge, black-green like the night.

'Alain! We're going!'

He ran to the steps, while Camille watched him with a welcoming smile.

'I can see your hair running,' she called out. 'It's crazy to be as fair as all that!'

He ran quicker still, strode up the five steps in one bound, and found Camille alone in the drawing-room.

'Where are the others?' he asked under his breath.

'Cloakroom,' she whispered back. 'Cloakroom and visit to "work in progress". General gloom. "It's not getting on! It'll never be finished!" What the hell do we care! If one was smart, one could hold on to Patrick's studio for keeps. Patrick could find himself another. I'll fix it, if you like.'

'But Patrick would only leave the "Wedge" as a special favour to please *you*.'

'Of course. One will take advantage of that.'

Her face sparkled with that peculiarly feminine unscrupulousness which Alain could not bring himself to accept as a matter of course. But he remonstrated only on her habit of saying 'one' for 'we', and she took this as a reproach.

'I'll soon get into the way of saying "we".'

So that he should want to kiss her, she turned out the ceiling light as if by accident. The one lamp left alight on a table threw a tall, sharply defined shadow behind the girl.

With her arms raised and her hands clasped on the nape of her neck, Camille gave him an inviting look. But he had eyes only for the shadow. 'How beautiful she is on the wall! Just fine-drawn enough, just as I should like her to be.'

He sat down to compare the one with the other. Flattered, Camille arched herself, thrusting out her breasts and her hips like a nautch-girl, but the shadow was better at that game than she was. Unclasping her hands, the girl walked across the room, preceded by the ideal shadow. Arrived at the open french window, the shadow leapt on one side and fled out into the garden along the pink gravel of a path, embracing the moon-spangled poplar between its two long arms as it went. 'What a pity!' sighed Alain. Then he feebly reproached himself for his inclination to love in Camille herself some perfected or motionless image of Camille. This shadow, for example, or a portrait or the vivid memory she left him of certain moments, certain dresses.

'What's the matter with you tonight? Come and help me put on my cape, at least.'

He was shocked at what that 'at least' secretly implied and also because Camille, as she passed before him through the door leading to the cloakroom and pantry, had almost imperceptibly shrugged her shoulders. 'She doesn't need to shrug her shoulders. Nature and habit do that for her anyway. When she's not careful, her neck makes her look dumpy. Ever, ever so slightly dumpy.'

In the cloakroom they found Alain's mother and Camille's parents stamping as if with cold and leaving footmarks the colour of dirty snow on the matting. The cat, seated on the window-sill outside, watched them inhospitably but with no animosity. Alain imitated her patience and endured the ritual of pessimistic lamentations.

'It's the same old thing.'

'It's hardly any farther on than it was a week ago.'

'My dear, if you want to know what *I* think, it won't be a fortnight, it'll be a month. What am I talking about, a month? More likely two months before their nest . . .'

At the word 'nest', Camille flung herself into the peaceful fray so shrilly that Alain and Saha closed their eyes.

'But since we've already decided what to do! And since we're actually frightfully *pleased* at having Patrick's place! And since it suits Patrick down to the ground

The Cat

because he hasn't a bean – hasn't any money – sorry, Mummy. We'll just take our suitcases and – Alley Oop! – straight up to heaven on the ninth floor! Won't we, Alain?'

He opened his eyes again, smiled into the void, and put her light cape round her shoulders. In the mirror opposite them he met Camille's black, reproachful look but it did not soften his heart. 'I didn't kiss her on the lips when we were alone. All right, very well then, I didn't kiss her on the lips. She hasn't had her full ration of kisses-on-the-lips today. She had the quarter-to-twelve one in the Bois, she had the two o'clock one after coffee, she had the half-past-six one in the garden, but she's missed tonight's. Well, if she's not satisfied, she's only got to put it down on the account . . . What's the matter with me? I'm so sleepy, I'm going mad. This life's idiotic; we're seeing far too much of each other and yet we never see each other properly. On Monday I'll definitely go down to the shop and . . .'

In imagination, the chemical acidity of the bales of new silk assailed his nostrils. But the inscrutable smile of M. Veuillet appeared to him as in a dream and, as in a dream, he heard words which, at twenty-four, he had still not learnt to hear without dread. 'No, no, my young friend. Will a new adding-machine that costs seventeen thousand francs pay back its initial outlay within the year? It all depends on that. Allow your poor father's oldest partner . . .' Catching sight again in the looking-glass of the vindictive image and handsome dark eyes which were watching him, he folded Camille in both his arms.

'Well, Alain?'

'Oh, my dear, let him alone! These poor infants . . .'

Camille blushed and disengaged herself. Then she held up her cheek to Alain in such a boyish brotherly grace that he nearly put his head on her shoulder. 'Oh, to lie down and go to sleep! Oh, good Lord! Just to lie down and sleep!'

From the garden came the voice of the cat.

'Me-rrou-wa . . . Rrr-rrouwa.'

'Hark at the cat! She must be hunting,' said Camille calmly. 'Saha! Saha!'

The cat was silent.

'Hunting?' protested Alain. 'Whatever makes you think that? To begin with, we're in May. And then she's saying: "Me-rrou-wa!"'

'So what?'

'She wouldn't be saying "Me-rrou-wa" if she were hunting! What she's saying there – and it's really rather strange – means a warning. It's almost the cry calling her little ones together.'

'Good Lord!' cried Camille, flinging up her arms. 'If Alain's going to start interpreting the cat, we shall be here all night!'

She ran down the steps and, at the touch of old Emile's shaking hand, two old-fashioned gas-globes, like huge mauve planets, illuminated the garden.

Alain walked ahead with Camille. At the entrance gate, he kissed her under her ear, breathed in, under a perfume too old for her, a good smell of bread and dark hair, and squeezed the girl's bare elbows under her cape. When she seated herself at the steering-wheel, with her parents in the back, he felt suddenly wide awake and gay.

'Saha! Saha!'

The cat sprang out of the shadow, almost under his feet. When he began to run, she ran too, leaping ahead of him with long bounds. He guessed she was there without seeing her; she burst before him into the hall and came back to wait for him at the top of the steps. With her frill standing out and her ears low, she watched him running towards her, urging him on with her yellow eyes. Those deep-set eyes were proud and suspicious, completely masters of themselves.

'Saha! Saha!'

Pronounced in a certain way, under his breath, with

The Cat

the 'h' strongly aspirated, her name sent her crazy. She lashed her tail, bounded into the middle of the poker-table and, with her two cat's hands spread wide open, she scattered the playing-cards.

'That cat, that cat!' said his mother's voice. 'She hasn't the faintest notion of hospitality! Look how delighted she is that our friends have gone!'

Alain let out a spurt of childish laughter, the laugh he kept for home and the close intimacy which did not extend beyond the screen of elms or the black, wrought-iron gate. Then he gave a frantic yawn.

'Good heavens, how tired you look! Is it possible to look as tired as that when one's happy? There's still some orangeade. No? We can go up then. Don't bother, Emile will turn out the lights.'

'Mother's talking to me as if I were getting over an illness or as if I were starting up paratyphoid again.'

'Saha! Saha! What a demon! Alain, you couldn't persuade that cat? . . .'

By a vertical path known to herself, marked on the worn brocade, the cat had almost reached the ceiling. One moment she imitated a grey lizard, flattening against the wall with her paws spread out; then she pretended to be giddy and tried an affected little cry of appeal. Alain obediently came and stood below and Saha slid down, glued to the wall like a raindrop sliding down a pane. She came to rest on Alain's shoulder and the two of them went up together to their bedroom.

A long hanging cluster of laburnum, black outside the open window, became a long pale yellow cluster when Alain turned on the ceiling light and the bedside lamp. He poured the cat off on to the bed by inclining his shoulder, then wandered aimlessly to and from between his room and the bathroom like a man who is too tired to go to bed.

He leaned out over the garden, looked with a hostile eye

for the white mass of the 'alterations'. Then he opened and shut several drawers and boxes in which reposed his real secrets: a gold dollar, a signet ring, an agate charm attached to his father's watch chain, some red and black seeds from an exotic canna plant, a First Communicant's mother-of-pearl rosary and a thin broken bracelet, the souvenir of a tempestuous young mistress who had passed swiftly and noisily out of his life. The rest of his worldly goods consisted merely of some paper-covered books he had had rebound and some letters and autographs.

Dreamily he turned over these little scraps of wreckage, bright and worthless as the coloured stones one finds in the nests of pilfering birds. 'Should I throw all this away ... or leave it here? It means nothing to me. Or does it mean something?' Being an only child, he was attached to everything which he had never shared with anyone else and for whose possession he had never had to fight.

He saw his face in the glass and became suddenly irritated with himself. 'Why can't you go to bed? You look a wreck. Positively disgraceful!' he said to the handsome fair young man. 'People only think me handsome because I'm fair. If I were dark, I'd be hideous.' For the hundredth time, he criticized his long cheeks and his slightly equine nose. But, for the hundredth time, he smiled so as to display his teeth to himself and admiringly touched the natural wave in his fair, over-thick hair. Once again he was pleased with the colour of his eyes, greenish-grey between dark lashes. Two dints hollowed his cheeks on either side of the smile, his eyes receded, circled with mauve shadows. He had shaved that morning but already a pale, stubbly bristle coarsened his upper lip. 'What a mug! I pity myself. No, I repel myself. Is *that* a face for a wedding night?' In the depths of the mirror, Saha gravely watched him from the distance.

'I'm coming, I'm coming.'

He flung himself on the cool expanse of the sheets, humouring the cat. Rapidly, he went through certain

The Cat

ritual litanies dedicated to the particular graces and virtues of a small, perfect, pure-bred Russian Blue.

'My little bear with the big cheeks. Exquisite, exquisite, exquisite cat. My blue pigeon. Pearl-coloured demon.'

As soon as he turned out the light, the cat began to trample delicately on her friend's chest. Each time she pressed down her feet, one single claw pierced the silk of the pyjamas, catching the skin just enough for Alain to feel an uneasy pleasure.

'Seven more days, Saha,' he sighed.

In seven days and seven nights he would begin a new life in new surroundings with an amorous and untamed young woman. He stroked the cat's fur, warm and cool at the same time and smelling of clipped box, thuya and lush grass. She was purring full-throatedly and, in the darkness, she gave him a cat's kiss, laying her damp nose for a second under Alain's nose between his nostrils and his lip. A swift, immaterial kiss which she rarely accorded him.

'Ah! Saha. Our nights . . .'

The headlights of a car in the nearest avenue pierced the leaves with two-revolving white beams. Over the wall of the room passed the enlarged shadow of the laburnum and of a tulip-tree which stood alone in the middle of a lawn. Above his own face Alain saw Saha's face illuminated for a moment. Before it was eclipsed again, he had seen that her eyes were hard.

'Don't frighten me!' he implored.

For, when Alain was sleepy, he became once more weak and fanciful, caught in the mesh of a sweet and interminable adolescence.

He shut his eyes while Saha kept vigil, watching all the invisible signs which hover over sleeping human beings when the light is put out.

He always dreamed a great deal and descended into his dreams by definite stages. When he woke up, he did not talk about his adventures of the night. He was jealous of a realm which had been enlarged by a delicate and ill-governed childhood; by long sojourns in bed during his swift growth into a tall frail slender boy.

He loved his dreams and cultivated them. Not for anything in the world would he have revealed the successive stages which awaited him. At the first stopping-place, while he could still hear the motor-horns in the avenue, he met an eddy of faces, familiar yet distorted, which he passed through as he might have passed through a friendly crowd, geeting one here and there. Eddying, bulbous, the faces approached Alain, growing larger and larger. Light against a dark background, they became lighter still as if they received their illumination from the sleeper himself. Each was furnished with one great eye and they circled round in an effortless gyration. But a submerged electric current shot them far away as soon as they touched an invisible barrier. In the humid gaze of a circular monster, in the eye of a plump moon or that of a wild archangel with rays of light for hair, Alain could recognize the same expression, the same intention which none of them had put into words and which Alain of the dream noted with a sense of security: 'They'll tell it me tomorrow.'

Sometimes they disappeared by exploding into scattered, faintly luminous fragments. At other times, they only continued as a hand, an arm, a forehead, an eyeball full of thoughts or as a starry dust of chins and noses. But always there remained that prominent, convex eye which, just at the moment of making itself clear, turned round and exposed only its other, black surface.

The sleeping Alain pursued, under Saha's watchful care, his nightly shipwreck. He passed beyond the world of convex faces and eyes and descended through a zone of darkness where he was conscious of nothing but a powerful, positive blackness, indescribably varied and, as it were, composed of submerged colours. On the confines of this, he launched into the real, complete, fully formed dream.

The Cat

He came up violently against a barrier which gave a great clang like the prolonged, splintering clash of a cymbal. And then he found himself in the dream city, among the passers-by, the inhabitants standing in their doorways, the gold-crowned guardians of the square and the stage crowd posted along the path of an Alain who was completely naked and armed with a walking-stick. This Alain was extremely lucid and sagacious: 'If I walk rather fast, after tying my tie in a special way, and particularly if I whistle, there's every chance that no one will notice I am naked.' So he tied his tie in a heart-shaped knot and whistled. 'That's not whistling, what I'm doing. It's purring. Whistling's like this . . .' But he still continued to purr. 'I'm not at the end of my tether yet. All I've got to do . . . it's perfectly simple . . . is to cross this sun-drenched open space and go round the bandstand where the military band is playing. Child's play. I run, making perilous jumps to distract attention, and I come out in the zone of shadow . . .'

But he was paralysed by the warm, dangerous look of a dark man in the stage crowd; a young man with a Greek profile perforated by a great eye like a carp's. 'The zone of shadow . . . the zone of *the* shadow . . .' Two long shadowy arms, graceful and rustling with poplar leaves, appeared at the word 'shadow' and carried Alain away. During the most ambiguous hour of the short night, he rested in that provisional tomb where the living exile sighs, weeps, fights, and succumbs, and from which he rises, unremembering, with the day.

TWO

THE high sun was edging the window when Alain awoke. The newly-opened cluster of laburnum hung, translucid, above the head of Saha; a blue, diurnal Saha, innocently engaged in washing herself.

'Saha!'

'Me-rrang!' answered the cat aggressively.

'Is it my fault if you're hungry? You only had to go downstairs and ask for your milk if you're in a hurry.'

She softened at her friend's voice and repeated the same word less emphatically, showing her red mouth planted with white teeth. That look of loyal and exclusive love alarmed Alain: 'Oh heavens, this cat! What to do with this cat? I'd forgotten I was getting married. And that we've got to live in Patrick's place.'

He turned towards the photograph in the chromium frame where Camille gleamed as if covered in oil; a great splash of reflected light on her hair, her painted mouth vitrified in inky black, her eyes enormous between two palisades of eyelashes.

'Fine piece of studio portraiture,' muttered Alain.

He had quite forgotten that he himself had chosen this photograph for his room; a photograph which bore no resemblance to Camille or to anyone at all. 'That eye . . . I've seen that eye.'

He took a pencil and lightly retouched the eye, toning down the excess of white. All he succeeded in doing was to spoil the print.

'Mouek, mouek, mouek. Ma-a-a-a . . . Ma-a-a-a,' said Saha, addressing a little moth imprisoned between the window-pane and the net curtain.

Her leonine chin was trembling; she coveted it so much that she stammered. Alain caught the moth with two fingers and offered it to the cat.

'Hors-d'oeuvre, Saha!'

In the garden, a rake was lazily combing the gravel. Alain could see in his mind the hand that guided the rake; the hand of an ageing woman; a mechanical, obstinate hand in a huge white glove like a policeman's.

'Good morning, Mother!' he called.

A distant voice answered him, a voice whose words he

The Cat

did not try to catch; the affectionate, insignificant murmur was all that he needed. He ran downstairs, the cat at his heels. In broad daylight, she knew how to change herself into a kind of blustering dog. She would hurtle noisily down the stairs and rush into the garden with tomboyish jumps that had no magic about them. She seated herself on the little breakfast table, among the medallions of sunlight, beside Alain's plate. The rake, which had stopped, slowly resumed its task.

Alain poured out Saha's milk, stirred a pinch of salt and a pinch of sugar into it, then gravely helped himself. When he breakfasted alone, he did not have to blush for certain gestures elaborated by the unconscious wishes of the maniac age between six and seven. He was free to blind all the 'eyes' in his bread with butter and to frown when the coffee in his cup rose above the water-line marked by a certain gilt arabesque. A second thin slice had to follow the first thick slice, whereas the second cup demanded an extra lump of sugar. In fact a very small Alain, hidden in the depths of a tall, fair, handsome young man, was impatiently waiting for breakfast to be over so that he could lick both sides of the honey spoon; an old ivory spoon, blackened and flexible with age.

'Camille, at this moment, is eating her breakfast standing up. She's biting at one and the same time into a slice of lean ham squeezed between two rusks and into an American apple. And she keeps putting down a cup of tea without sugar in it on various bits of furniture and forgetting it.'

He raised his eyes and contemplated his domain; the domain of a privileged child which he cherished and whose every inch he knew. Over his head the old, severely pollarded elms stirred only the tips of their young leaves. A cushiony mass of pink silene, fringed with forget-me-nots, dominated one lawn. Dangling like a scarf from the dead tree's scraggy elbow, a trail of polygonum intertwined with the four-petalled purple clematis fluttered in every breath of wind. One of the standard sprinklers spread a white peacock tail shot with a shifting rainbow as it revolved over the turf.

'Such a beautiful garden . . . such a beautiful garden,' said Alain under his breath. He stared disgustedly at the silent heaps of rubbish, timber, and bags of plaster which defaced the west side of the house. 'Ah! It's Sunday, so they're not working. It's been Sunday all the week for me.' Though young and capricious, and pampered, he now lived according to the commercial rhythm of a six-day week and felt Sunday in his bones.

A white pigeon moved furtively behind the weigela and the pink clusters of the deutzias. 'It's not a pigeon; it's mother's hand in her gardening glove.' The big white glove moved just above ground, raising a drooping stalk, weeding out the blades of grass that sprang up overnight. Two greenfinches came hopping along the gravel path to pick up the breakfast crumbs, and Saha followed them with her eye without getting excited. But a tomtit, hanging upside down in an elm above the table, chirped at the cat out of bravado. Sitting there with her paws folded, her head thrown back, and the frill of fur under her chin displayed like a pretty woman's jabot, Saha tried hard to restrain herself; but her cheeks swelled with fury and her little nostrils moistened.

'As beautiful as a fiend! More beautiful than a fiend!' Alain told her.

He wanted to stroke the broad skull in which lodged ferocious thoughts, and the cat bit him sharply to relieve her anger. He looked at the two little beads of blood on his palm with the irascibility of a man whose woman has bitten him at the height of her pleasure.

'Bad girl! Bad girl! Look what you've done to me!'

She lowered her head, sniffed the blood, and timidly questioned her friend's face. She knew how to amuse him and charm him back to good humour. She scooped

The Cat

up a rusk from the table and held it between her paws like a squirrel.

The May breeze passed over them, bending a yellow rose-bush which smelt of flowering reeds. Between the cat, the rose-bush, the pairs of tomtits, and the last cockchafers, Alain had one of those moments when he slipped out of time and felt the anguished illusion of being once more back in his childhood. The elms suddenly became enormous, the path grew wider and longer and vanished under the arches of a pergola that no longer existed. Like the hag-ridden dreamer who falls off a tower, Alain returned violently to the consciousness of being nearly twenty-four.

'I ought to have slept another hour. It's only half-past nine. It's Sunday. Yesterday was Sunday for me too. Too many Sundays. But tomorrow . . .'

He smiled at Saha as though she were an accomplice. 'Tomorrow, Saha, there's the final trying-on of the white dress. Without me. It's a surprise. Camille's dark enough to look her best in white. During that time, I'll go and look at the car. It's a bit cheese-paring, a bit mingy, as Camille would say, a roadster. That's what you get for being "such a young married couple".'

With a vertical bound, rising in the air like a fish leaping to the surface of the water, the cat caught a black-veined cabbage-white. She ate it, coughed, spat out one wing, and licked herself affectionately. The sun played on her fur, mauve and bluish like the breast of a woodpigeon.

'Saha!'

She turned her head and smiled at him.

'My little puma! Beloved cat! Creature of the tree-tops! How will you live if we're separated? Would you like us to enter an Order? Would you like? . . . oh, I don't know what . . .'

She listened to him, watching him with a tender, absent expression. But when the friendly voice began to tremble, she looked away.

113

'To begin with, you'll come with us. You don't hate cars. If we take the saloon instead of the roadster, behind the seats there's a ledge ...'

He broke off and became gloomy at the recent memory of a girl's vigorous voice, ideally pitched for shouting in the open air, trumpeting the numerous merits of the roadster. 'And then, when you put down the windscreen, Alain, its *mar*vellous. When she's all out, you can feel the skin of your cheeks shrinking right back to your *ears*.'

'Shrinking right back to your ears. Can you imagine anything more frightful, Saha?'

He compressed his lips and made a long face like an obstinate child planning to get its own way by guile.

'It's not settled yet. Suppose I prefer the saloon? I suppose I've got *some* say in the matter?'

He glared at the yellow rose-bush as if it were the young girl with the resonant voice. Promptly the path widened, the elms grew taller, and the non-existent pergola reappeared. Cowering among the skirts of two or three female relatives, a childish Alain surveyed another compact family among whose opaque block gleamed a very dark little girl whose big eyes and black ringlets rivalled each other in a hostile, jetty brilliance. 'Say "How d'you do ..." Why don't you want to say "How d'you do?"' It was a faint voice from other days, preserved through years of childhood, adolescence, college, the boredom of military service, false seriousness, false business competence. Camille did not want to say 'How d'you do?' She sucked the inside of her cheek and stiffly sketched the brief curtsey expected of little girls. 'Now she calls that a "twist-your-ankle" curtsey. But when she's in a temper, she still bites the inside of her cheek. It's a funny thing, but at those moments she doesn't look ugly.'

He smiled and felt an honest glow of warmth for his fiancée. After all, he was quite glad that she should be healthy and slightly commonplace in her sensuality. Defying the innocent morning, he called up images

The Cat

designed now to excite her vanity and impatience, now to engender anxiety, even confusion. Emerging from these disturbing fancies, he found the sun too white and the wind dry. The cat had disappeared but, as soon as he stood up, she was at his side and accompanied him, walking with a long, deer-like step and avoiding the round pebbles in the pinkish gravel. They went together as far as the 'alterations' and inspected with equal hostility the pile of rubbish, a new french window, devoid of panes, inserted in a wall, various bathroom appliances, and some porcelain tiles.

Equally offended, they calculated the damage done to their past and their present. An old yew had been torn up and was very slowly dying upside down, with its roots in the air. 'I ought never, never to have allowed that,' muttered Alain. 'It's a disgrace. You've only known it for three years, Saha, that yew. But I . . .'

At the bottom of the hole left by the yew, Saha sensed a mole whose image, or rather whose smell went to her head. For a minute she forgot herself to the point of frenzy, scratching like a fox-terrier and rolling over like a lizard. She jumped on all four paws like a frog, clutched a ball of earth between her thighs as a fieldmouse does with the egg it has stolen; escaped from the hole by a series of miracles, and found herself sitting on the grass, cold and prudish and recovering her breath.

Alain stood gravely by, not moving. He knew how to keep a straight face when Saha's demons possessed her beyond her control. The admiration and understanding of cats was innate in him. Those inborn rudiments made it easy for him, later on, to read Saha's thoughts. He had read her like some masterpiece from the day, when on his return from a cat-show, Alain had put down a little five-months old she-cat on the smooth lawn at Neuilly. He had brought her because of her perfect face, her precocious dignity, and her modesty that hoped for nothing behind the bars of a cage.

'Why didn't you buy a Persian instead?' asked Camille.

'That was long before we were engaged,' thought Alain. 'It wasn't only a little she-cat I bought. It was the nobility of all cats, their infinite disinterestedness, their knowledge of how to live, their affinities with the highest type of humans.' He blushed and mentally excused himself. 'The highest, Saha, is the one that understands *you* best.'

He had not yet got to the point of thinking 'likeness' instead of 'understanding' because he belonged to that class of human beings which refuses to recognize or even to imagine its animal affinities. But at the age when he might have coveted a car, a journey abroad, a rare binding, a pair of skis, Alain nevertheless remained the young-man-who-has-bought-a-little-cat. His narrow world resounded with it. The staff of Amparat et Fils in the Rue des Petits Champs were astonished and M. Veuillet inquired after the 'little beastie'.

'Before I chose you, Saha, I don't believe I'd ever realized that one *could* choose. As for all the rest ... My marriage pleases everyone, including Camille. There are moments when it pleases me too, but ...'

He got up from the green bench and assumed the important smile of the heir of Amparat Silks who is condescendingly marrying the daughter of Malmert Mangles, 'a girl who's not *quite* our type', as Mme Amparat said. But Alain was well aware that, when Malmert Mangles spoke about Amparat Silks among themselves, they did not forget to mention, sticking up their chins: 'The Amparats aren't in silk any more. The mother and son have only kept their shares in the business and the son's not the real director, only a figurehead.'

Cured of her madness, her eyes gentle and golden, the cat seemed to be waiting for the return of mental trust, of that telepathic murmur for which her silver-fringed ears were straining.

'You're not just a pure and sparkling spirit of a cat either,' went on Alain. 'What about your first seducer,

The Cat

the white tom without a tail? Do you remember that, my ugly one, my trollop in the rain, my shameless one?'

'What a bad mother your cat is!' exclaimed Camille indignantly. 'She doesn't even give a thought to her kittens, now they've been taken away from her.'

'But that was just what a young girl would say,' Alain went on defiantly. 'Young girls are always admirable mothers before they're married.'

The full, deep note of a bell sounded on the tranquil air. Alain leapt up with a guilty start at the sound of wheels crushing the gravel.

'Camille! It's half-past eleven . . . Good Heavens!'

He pulled his pyjama jacket together and retied the cord so hastily and nervously that he scolded himself. 'Come, come, what's the matter with me? I shall be seeing plenty more of them in a week. Saha, are you coming to meet them?'

But Saha had vanished and Camille was already stamping across the lawn with reckless heels. 'Ah! She really does look attractive.' His blood pulsed pleasurably in his throat and flushed his cheeks. He was entirely absorbed in the spectacle of Camille in white, with a little lock of well-tapered hair on either temple and a tiny red scarf which matched her lipstick. Made-up with skill and restraint, her youth was not obvious at the first glance. Then it revealed itself in the cheek that was white under the ochre powder; in the smooth, unwrinkled eyelids under the light dusting of beige powder round the great eyes that were almost black. The brand-new diamond on her left hand broke the light into a thousand coloured splinters.

'Oh!' she cried. 'You're not ready! On a lovely day like this!'

But she stopped at the sight of the rough, dishevelled fair hair, of the naked chest under the pyjamas and Alain's flushed confusion. Her young girl's face so clearly expressed a woman's warm indulgence that Alain no longer dared to give her the quarter-to-twelve kiss of the Bois.

'Kiss me,' she implored, very low, as if she were asking him for help.

Gauche, uneasy and ill-protected by his thin pyjamas, he made a gesture towards the pink flowering shrubs from whence came the sound of the shears and the rake. Camille did not dare throw herself on his neck. She lowered her eyes, plucked a leaf, and pulled her shining locks of hair forward on her cheeks. But, from the movement of her nostrils, Alain saw she was searching in the air, with a certain primitive wildness, for the fragrance of a fair-skinned, barely covered body. In his heart he secretly condemned her for not being sufficiently afraid of it.

THREE

WHEN he woke up, he did not sit up in bed at one bound. Haunted in his sleep by the unfamiliar room, he half-opened his eyes and realized that cunning and constraint had not entirely left him during his sleep, for his left arm, flung out across a desert of linen sheet, lay ready to recognize, but ready, also, to repel ... But all the wide expanse of bed to his left was empty and cool once more. If there had been nothing in front of the bed but the barely rounded corner of the triangular room and the unaccustomed green gloom, split by a rod of bright yellow light which separated two curtains of solid shadow, Alain would have gone to sleep again lulled by the sound of someone humming a little Negro song.

He turned his head cautiously and opened his eyes a trifle wider. He saw someone moving about, now white, now pale blue according to whether she was in the narrow strip of sunlight or the shadow. It was a naked young woman with a comb in her hand and a cigarette between her lips, wandering about the room and humming. 'What

The Cat

impudence,' he thought. 'Completely naked! Where does she think she is?'

He recognized the lovely legs with which he had long been familiar, but the stomach, shortened by a navel placed rather low, surprised him. An impersonal youthfulness justified the muscular buttocks and the breasts were small above the visible ribs. 'Has she got thinner, then?' The solidity of her back, which was as wide as her chest, shocked Alain. 'She's got a common back.' At that moment, Camille leaned her elbow on one of the windowsills, arched her back, and hunched up her shoulders. 'She's got a back like a charwoman.' But suddenly she stood upright again, took a couple of dancing steps and made a charming gesture of embracing the empty air. 'No, I'm wrong. She's beautiful. But what a ... what brazenness; Does she think I'm dead? Or does it seem perfectly natural to her to wander about stark naked? Oh, but that will change!'

As she turned towards the bed, he closed his eyes again. When he opened them, Camille had seated herself at the dressing-table they called the 'invisible dressing-table', a transparent sheet of beautiful thick glass laid on a black metal frame. She powdered her face, touched her cheeks and chin with the tips of her fingers, and suddenly smiled, turning her eyes from the glass with a gravity and a weariness which disarmed Alain. 'Is she happy then? Happy about what? *I* certainly don't deserve it. But why is she naked?'

'Camille,' he called out.

He thought she would rush towards the bathroom, hastily covering herself with some hastily snatched-up undergarment. Instead, she ran to the bed and bent over the young man who lay there, overwhelming him with her strong brunette's smell.

'Darling! Have you slept well?'

'Stark naked!' he scolded.

She opened her big eyes comically.

'What about you?'

Bare to his waist, he did not know what to reply. She paraded for him, so proudly and so completely devoid of modesty that he rather rudely flung her the crumpled pyjama-jacket which lay on the bed.

'Quick, put that on. Personally, I'm hungry.'

'Old mother Buque's at her post. Everything's in working order and functioning.'

She disappeared and Alain wanted to get up and dress and smooth his rumpled hair. But Camille returned, girded in a big bathrobe that was new and too long for her, and gaily carrying a loaded tray.

'What a mess, my dears! There's a kitchen bowl and a pyrex cup and the sugar's in the lid of a tin. I'll get it all straightened out in a day or two. My ham's dry. These anaemic peaches are left-overs from lunch. Mother Buque's a bit lost in her electric kitchen. I'll teach her how to manage the various switches. Then I've put some water in the ice compartments of the fridge. It's a good thing I'm here! Monsieur has his coffee very hot and his milk boiling and his butter hard. No, that's my tea, don't touch! What are you looking for?'

'Nothing.'

Because of the smell of coffee, he was looking for Saha.

'What's the time?'

'At last a tender word!' cried Camille. 'Very early, my husband. It was a quarter-past eight by the kitchen alarm-clock.'

As they ate, they laughed a good deal and spoke little. By the increasing smell of the green oilcloth curtains, Alain could guess the strength of the sun which warmed them. He could not take his mind off that sun outside, the unfamiliar horizon, the nine vertiginous storeys, and the bizarre architecture of the 'Wedge' which was their temporary home.

He listened to Camille as attentively as he could,

The Cat

touched at her pretending to have forgotten what had passed between them in the night. He was touched, too, by her pretending to be perfectly at home in their haphazard lodging and by her unselfconsciousness, as if she had been married at least a week. Now that she had something on, he tried to find a way of showing his gratitude. 'She doesn't resent either what I've done to her or what I haven't, poor child. After all, the most tiresome part is over. Is it always like this the first night? This bruised, unsatisfactory feeling? This half-success, half-disaster?'

He threw his arm cordially round her neck and kissed her.

'Oh! You're nice!'

She had said it so loud and with so much feeling that she blushed and he saw her eyes fill with tears. But she bravely fought down her emotion and jumped off the bed on the pretext of removing the tray. She ran towards the windows, tripped over her long bathrobe, let out a great oath, and hauled on a ship's rope. The oilcloth curtains slid back. Paris, with its suburbs, bluish and unbounded like the desert, dotted with still-fresh verdure and flashes of shining panes, entered at one bound into the triangular room which had only one cement wall, the other two being half glass.

'It's beautiful,' said Alain softly.

But he was half lying and his head sought the support of a young shoulder from which the bathrobe had slipped. 'It's not a place for human beings to live. All this horizon right on top of one, right in one's bed. And what about stormy days. Abandoned on the top of a lighthouse among the albatrosses.'

Camille was lying beside him on the bed now. Her arm was round his neck and she looked fearlessly, now at the giddy horizons of Paris, now at the fair, dishevelled head. This new pride of hers which seemed to draw strength ahead from the coming night and the days that would follow, was no doubt satisfied with her newly acquired rights. She was licensed to share his bed, to prop up a young man's naked body against her thigh and shoulder, to become acquainted with its colour and curves and defects. She was free to contemplate boldly and at length the small dry nipples, the loins she envied, and the strange design of the capricious sex.

They bit into the same tasteless peach and laughed, showing each other their splendid, glistening teeth and the gums which were a little pale, like tired children's.

'That day yesterday!' sighed Camille. 'When you think that there are people who get married so often!'

Her vanity returned and she added: 'All the same, it went off very well. Not a single hitch. It did go off well, didn't it?'

'Yes,' said Alain feebly.

'Oh, *you* . . . You're just like your mother. I mean, as long as your lawn isn't ruined and people don't throw cigarette-ends on your gravel, you think everything's fine. Isn't that a fact? All the same, our wedding would have been prettier at Neuilly. Only that would have disturbed the sacred cat! Tell me, you bad boy, what do you keep looking at all round you?'

'Nothing,' he said sincerely, 'because there's nothing to look at. I've seen the dressing-table. I've seen the chair – we've seen the bed . . .'

'Couldn't you live here? I'd love to. Just think . . . three rooms and three balconies! If only one could stay here!'

'Doesn't one say: "If only *we* could stay here"?'

'Then why do *you* say: "One says"? Yes, if only one could stay here, as *we* say.'

'But Patrick will be back from his cruise in three months.'

'Who cares? He'll come back. And we'll explain that we want to stay on. And we'll chuck him out.'

'Oh! You'd actually do that?'

She shook her black mop affirmatively, with a radiant, feminine assurance in dishonesty. Alain wanted to give

The Cat

her a severe look but, under his eyes, Camille changed and became as nervous as he felt himself. Hastily he kissed her on the mouth.

Silent and eager, she returned his kiss, feeling for the hollow of the bed with a movement of her loins. At the same time her free hand, which was holding a peachstone, groped in the air for an empty cup or ashtray.

Leaning over her, he caressed her lightly, waiting for her to open her eyes again.

She was pressing her eyelashes down over two small, glittering tears which she was trying to stop from flowing. He respected this restraint and this pride. They had done their best, the two of them, aided by the morning warmth and their two odorous, facile bodies.

Alain remembered Camille's quickened breathing and her warm docility. She had shown an untimely eagerness which was very charming. She reminded him of no other woman; in possessing her for the second time, he had thought only of the careful handling she deserved. She lay against him, her legs and arms relaxed, her hands half-closed, cat-like for the first time. 'Where is Saha?'

Mechanically he gave Camille the ghost of a caress 'for Saha', drawing his nails slowly and delicately all the way down her stomach. She cried out with shock and stiffened her arms. One of them hit Alain who nearly hit her back. She sat up, with her hair on end and her eyes hostile and threatening.

'Are you vicious, by any chance?'

He had expected nothing like this and burst out laughing.

'There's nothing to laugh about!' cried Camille. 'I've always been told that men who tickle women are vicious. They may even be sadists!'

He got off the bed so as to be able to laugh more freely, quite forgetting he was naked. Camille stopped talking so suddenly that he turned round and surprised her lit-up, dazed face staring at the body of the young man whom one night of marriage had made hers.

'D'you mind if I steal the bathroom for ten minutes?'

He opened the glass door let into one end of the longest wall which they called the hypotenuse.

'And then I'll go over to my mother's for a moment.'

'Yes ... Don't you want me to come with you?'

He looked shocked and she blushed for the first time that day.

'I'll see if the alterations ...'

'Oh! the alterations! Don't tell me you're interested in those alterations! Admit' – she folded her arms like a tragic actress – 'admit that you're going to see my rival!'

'Saha's not your rival,' said Alain simply.

'How can she be your rival,' he went on to himself. 'You can only have rivals in what's impure.'

'I don't need *such* a serious protestation, darling. Hurry up! You haven't forgotten that we're lunching together on our own at Père Léopold's? On our own at last, just the two of us! You'll come back soon? You haven't forgotten we're going for a drive? Are you taking in what I'm saying?'

What he took in very clearly was that the words 'come back' had acquired a new and preposterous significance and he looked at Camille askance. She was flaunting her newly married bride's tiredness, drawing his attention to the faint swelling of her lower lids under the corners of her great eyes. 'Will you always have such enormous eyes the moment you wake up, whatever time of day or night? Don't you know how to keep your eyes half-closed? It gives me a headache to see eyes as wide open as all that.'

He felt a dishonest pleasure, an evasive comfort in calling her to account in his mind. 'After all, it's less ungracious than being frank.' He hurried to reach the square bathroom, the hot water, and a solitude propitious to thought. But, as the glass door inserted in the hypotenuse reflected him from head to foot, Alain opened

The Cat

it with complacent slowness and was in no haste to shut it again.

When he was leaving the flat an hour later, he opened the wrong door on one of the balconies which ran along every side of the Wedge. Like the sharp down-stroke of a fan, the east wind which was turning Paris blue, blowing away the smoke and scouring the distant Sacré Coeur, caught him full in the face. On the cement parapet, five or six pots, put there by well-meaning hands, contained white roses and hydrangeas and lilies sullied by their pollen. 'Last night's dessert is never attractive.' Nevertheless, before he went down, he sheltered the ill-treated flowers from the wind.

FOUR

He stole into the garden like a boy in his teens who has stayed out all night. The air was full of the heady scent of beds being watered, of the secret exhalation of the filth which nourishes fleshy, expensive flowers and of spray blown on the breeze. In the very act of drawing a deep breath to inhale it all, he suddenly discovered he needed comforting.

'Saha! Saha!'

She did not come for a moment or two, and at first he did not recognize that bewildered, incredulous face which seemed clouded by a bad dream.

'Saha darling!'

He took her on his chest, smoothing the soft flanks which seemed to him a trifle hollow, and removed cobwebs, pine needles, and elm twigs from the neglected fur. She pulled herself together quickly and resumed her familiar expression and her cat's dignity. Her face, her pure golden eyes looked again as he had known them. Under his thumb, Alain could feel the palpitations of a hard, irregular little heart and also the beginnings of a faint, uncertain purr. He put her down on an iron table and stroked her head. But at the moment of thrusting her head into Alain's hand, wildly and as if for life in the way she had, she sniffed that hand and stepped back a pace.

His eyes sought the white pigeon, the gloved hand behind the pink flowering shrubs, behind the flaming rhododendrons. He rejoiced that yesterday's 'ceremony' had respected the beautiful garden and only ravaged Camille's home.

'Imagine those people here! And those four bridesmaids in pink paper! And the flowers they'd have picked, and the deutzias sacrificed to adorn fat women's bosoms! And Saha!'

He called in the direction of the house: 'Has Saha had anything to eat or drink? She looks awfully queer. I'm here, Mother.'

A heavy white shape appeared in the doorway of the hall and answered from the distance: 'No. Just fancy, she had no supper and wouldn't drink her milk this morning. I think she was waiting for you. Are you all right, dear?'

He stood at the foot of the steps, deferential in his mother's presence. He noticed that she did not offer him her cheek as usual and that she kept her hands clasped together at her waist. He understood and shared this motherly sense of decency with a mixture of embarrassment and gratitude. 'Saha hasn't kissed me either.'

'After all, the cat's often seen you go away. She made allowances for your going off sometimes.'

'But I didn't go so far,' he thought.

Near him, on the iron table, Saha drank her milk avidly like an animal that has walked far and slept little.

'Alain, wouldn't you like a cup of warm milk too? Some bread and butter?'

'I've had breakfast, Mother. *We've* had breakfast.'

The Cat

'Not much of a breakfast, I imagine. In such a gloryhole!'

With the eye of an exile, Alain contemplated the cup with the gilt arabesque beside Saha's saucer; then his mother's heavy face, amiable under the mass of wavy, prematurely white hair.

'I haven't asked you whether my new daughter is satisfied.' She was frightened he would misunderstand her and added hurriedly: 'I mean, whether she's in good health.'

'Excellent, Mother. We're going out to Rambouillet for lunch in the forest. I've got to run the car in.' He corrected himself: '*We've* got to run the car in, I mean.'

They remained alone together in the garden, he and Saha, both torpid with silence and weariness and overcome with longing to sleep.

The cat fell asleep suddenly on her side, her chin up and her teeth bared like a dead animal. Feathery panicles from the Venetian sumach and clematis petals rained down on her without her so much as twitching in the depths of the dream in which, no doubt, she was enjoying the security of her friend's inalienable presence. Her defeated attitude, the pale, drawn corners of her periwinkle-grey lips gave evidence of a night of miserable watching.

Above the withered stump draped with climbing plants, a flight of bees over the ivy-flowers gave out a solemn cymbal note, the identical note of so many summers. 'To go to sleep out here, on the grass, between the yellow rose-bush and the cat. Camille won't come till dinner-time, that will be very pleasant. And the cat, good heavens, the cat . . .' Over by the 'alterations' could be heard the rasp of a plane shaving a beam, the clang of an iron hammer on a metal girder, and Alain promptly embarked on a dream about a village peopled with mysterious blacksmiths. As eleven sounded from the belfry of the school near by, he got up and fled without daring to wake the cat.

127

Colette

FIVE

JUNE came with its longer days, its night skies devoid of mystery which the late glow of the sunset and the early glimmer of dawn over the east of Paris kept from being wholly dark. But June is cruel only to city-dwellers who have no car and are caged up in hot stone and forced to live elbow to elbow. A never-still breeze played round the Wedge, rippling the yellow awnings. It blew through the triangular room and the studio, broke against the prow of the building, and dried up the little hedges of privet that stood in boxes on the balconies. With the help of their daily drives, Alain and Camille lived pleasantly enough. The warm weather and their sensual life combined to make them drowsy and less exacting with each other.

'Why did I call her an untamed girl?' Alain asked himself in surprise. Camille swore less when she was driving the car and had lost certain crudities of speech. She had also lost her passion for night-clubs with female gipsy singers who had nostrils like horses.

She spent much time eating and sleeping, opened her now much gentler eyes very wide, gave up a dozen summer projects, and became interested in the 'alterations' which she visited daily. Often she lingered long in the garden at Neuilly, where Alain, when he came back from the dark offices of Amparat Fils in the Rue des Petits Champs, would find her idle, ready to prolong the afternoon and drive along the hot roads.

Then his mood would darken. He would listen to her giving orders to the singing painters and the distant electricians. She would question him in a general, peremptory way as if, as soon as he was there, it was her duty to renounce her new gentleness.

'Business going all right? Crisis still expected? Have you managed to put over the spotted foulard on the big dress-houses?'

She did not even respect old Emile, whom she shook

The Cat

until he let fall certain formulas pregnant with oracular imbecility.

'What do you think of our shanty, Emile? Have you ever seen the house looking so nice?'

Between his whiskers, the old butler muttered answers as shallow and colourless as himself.

'You wouldn't know the place any more. Had anyone told me, in the old days, that this house would be divided up into little compartments ... There's certainly a difference. It will be very nice being so near each other, very gay.'

Or else, drop by drop, he poured a stream of blessings over Alain, blessings in which there was an undercurrent of hostility.

'Monsieur Alain's young lady is beginning to look ever so well. What a fine voice she has. When she's speaking loud, the neighbours can hear every word. You can't deny she has a splendid voice but ... The young lady speaks her mind all right. She told the gardener that the bed of pink silene and forget-me-not looked cuckoo. I still have to laugh when I think of it.'

And he raised his pale, oyster-coloured eyes, which had never laughed in their life, to the pure sky. Alain did not laugh either. He was worried about Saha. She was getting thinner and seemed to have given up a hope; undoubtedly the hope of seeing Alain every day again – and alone. She no longer ran away when Camille arrived. But she did not escort Alain to the gate and, when he sat by her, she looked at him with a profound and bitter wisdom. 'Her look when she was a little cat behind the bars. The same, same look.' He called her very softly: 'Saha ... Saha ...' strongly aspirating the h's. But she did not jump or flatten her ears and it was days since she had given her insistent: 'Me-rrang'! or the 'Mouek-mouek-mouek' of good humour and greed.

One day, when he and Camille had been summoned to Neuilly to be informed that the enormous, heavy, new sunk bath would cave in the tiled platform supporting it, he heard his wife sigh: 'It'll never be finished!'

'But,' he said, surprised, 'I thought you really much preferred the Wedge with its petrels and cormorants.'

'Yes. But all the same . . . And after all it's your house here, your real house. *Our* house.'

She leaned on his arm, rather limp and unusually hesitant. The bluish whites of her eyes, almost as blue as her light summer dress; the unnecessary but admirable make-up of her cheeks and mouth and eyelids did not move him in the least.

Nevertheless, it seemed to him that, for the first time, she was asking his advice without speaking. 'Camille here with me. So soon! Camille in pyjamas under the rose trellis.' One of the oldest climbing roses carried its load of flowers, which faded as soon as they opened, as high as his head and their oriental scent dominated the garden in the evening; he could smell it where they stood by the steps. 'Camille in a bathrobe under the screen of elms. Wouldn't it be better, all things considered, to keep her shut away in the little gazebo of the Wedge? Not here, not here . . . not yet.'

The June evening, drenched with light, was reluctant to give way to darkness. Some empty glasses on a wicker table were still attracting the big orange bumble-bees but, under all the trees except the pines, an area of impalpable damp was growing, bringing a promise of coolness. Neither the rose geraniums, so prodigal of their southern scent upon the air, nor the fiery poppies suffered from the fierce onslaught of summer. 'Not here, not here,' Alain repeated to the rhythm of his own footsteps. He was looking for Saha and did not want to call her out loud. He found her lying on the little low wall which buttressed a blue knoll covered with lobelias. She was asleep, or appeared to be asleep, curled up in a ball. 'Curled up in a ball? At this time and in this weather? Sleeping curled up like that is a winter position!'

The Cat

'Saha darling!'

She did not quiver as he picked her up and held her in the air. She only opened two hollow eyes, very beautiful and almost indifferent.

'Heavens, how light you are! But you're ill, my little puma!'

He carried her off and ran back to his mother and Camille.

'But, Mother, Saha's ill! Her coat's shocking – she weighs next to nothing – and you never told me!'

'It's because she eats nothing,' said Mme Amparat. 'She refuses to eat.'

'She doesn't eat? And what else?'

He cradled the cat against his chest and Saha abandoned herself to him. Her breathing was shallow and her nostrils dry. Mme Amparat's eyes, under the thick white waves, glanced intelligently at Camille.

'Nothing else,' she said.

'She's bored with you,' said Camille. 'After all she's your cat, isn't she?'

He thought she was laughing at him and raised his head defiantly. But Camille's face had not changed and she was seriously examining Saha, who shut her eyes again as soon as touched by her.

'Feel her ears,' said Alain sharply. 'They're burning.'

In an instant, his mind was made up.

'Right. I'm taking her with me. Mother, get them to fetch me her basket, will you? And a sack of sand for the tray. We've got everything else she needs. You understand I simply couldn't bear . . . This cat believes . . .'

He broke off and turned belatedly to his wife.

'It won't worry you, Camille, if I take Saha while we're waiting to come back here?'

'What a question! But where do you propose to put her at night?' she added so naïvely that Alain blushed because of his mother's presence and answered acridly: 'That's for her to decide.'

131

They left in a little procession; Alain carrying Saha, mute in her travelling-basket. Old Emile was bowed under the sack full of sand and Camille brought up the rear, bearing an old frayed kasha travelling rug which Alain called the Kashasaha.

SIX

'No, I never thought a cat would get acclimatized so quickly.'

'A cat's merely a cat. But Saha's Saha.'

Alain was proudly doing the honours of Saha. He himself had never kept her so close at hand, imprisoned in twenty-five square metres and visible at all hours. For her feline meditation, for her craving for solitude and shadow, she was reduced to withdrawing under the giant armchairs scattered about the studio or into the miniature hall or into one of the built-in wardrobes camouflaged with mirrors.

But Saha was determined to triumph over all obstacles. She accepted the uncertain times of meals and of getting up and going to bed. She choose the bathroom with its cork-topped stool to sleep in and she explored the Wedge with no affectation of wildness or disgust. In the kitchen, she condescended to listen to the lazy voice of Mme Buque summoning 'the pussy' to raw liver. When Alain and Camille went out, she installed herself on the giddy parapet and gazed into the abysses of air, following the flying backs of swallows and sparrows below her with a calm, untroubled eye. Her impassiveness on the edge of a sheer drop of nine storeys and the habit she had of washing herself at length on the parapet, terrified Camille.

'Stop her,' she yelled to Alain. 'She makes my heart turn over and gives me cramp in my calves.'

Alain gave an unperturbed smile and admired his cat who had recovered her taste for food and life.

The Cat

It was not that she was blooming or particularly gay. She did not recover the iridescence of her fur that had gleamed like a pigeon's mauve plumage. But she was more alive; she waited for the dull 'poum' of the lift which brought up Alain and accepted extra attentions from Camille, such as a tiny saucer of milk at five o'clock or a small chicken bone offered high up, as if to a dog who was expected to jump for it.

'Not like that! Not like that!' scolded Alain.

And he would lay the bone on a bath-mat or simply on the thick-piled beige carpet.

'Really ... on Patrick's carpet!' Camille scolded in turn.

'But a cat can't eat a bone or any solid food on a polished surface. When a cat takes a bone off a plate and puts it down on the carpet before eating it, she's told she's dirty. But the cat needs to hold it down with her paw while she crunches and tears it and she can only do it on bare earth or on a carpet. People don't know that.'

Amazed, Camille broke in: 'And how do *you* know?'

He had never asked himself that and got out of it by a joke: 'Hush! It's because I'm extremely intelligent. Don't tell a soul. M. Veuillet hasn't a notion of it.'

He taught her all the ways and habits of the cat, like a foreign language over-rich in subtle shades of meaning. In spite of himself, he spoke with emphatic authority as he taught. Camille observed him narrowly and asked him any number of questions which he answered unreservedly.

'Why does the cat play with a piece of string when she's frightened of the big ship's rope?'

'Because the ship's rope is the snake. It's the thickness of a snake. She's afraid of snakes.'

'Has she ever seen a snake?'

Alain looked at his wife with the grey-green, black-lashed eyes she found so beautiful ... 'So treacherous' she said.

'No . . . certainly not. Where could she have seen one?'
'Well, then?'
'Well, then she invents one. She creates one. You'd be frightened of snakes too, even if you'd never seen one.'
'Yes, but I've been told about them. I've seen them in pictures. I know they exist.'
'So does Saha.'
'But how?'

He gave her a haughty smile.

'How? But by her birth, like persons of quality.'
'So I'm not a person of quality?'

He softened, but only out of compassion.

'Good Heavens, no. Console yourself: I'm not either. Don't you believe what I tell you?'

Camille, sitting at her husband's feet, contemplated him with her wildest eyes, the eyes of the little girl of other days who did not want to say 'How d'you do?'

'I'd better believe it,' she said gravely.

They took to dining at home nearly every night, because of the heat, said Alain, 'and because of Saha' insinuated Camille. One evening after dinner, Saha was sitting on her friend's knee.

'What about me?' said Camille.

'I've two knees,' Alain retorted.

Nevertheless, the cat did not use her privilege for long. Some mysterious warning made her return to the polished ebony table where she seated herself on her own bluish reflection immersed in a dusky pool. There was nothing unusual about her behaviour except the fixed attention she gave to the invisible things straight in front of her in the air.

'What's she looking at?' asked Camille.

She was pretty every evening at that particular hour; wearing white pyjamas, her hair half loosened on her forehead and her cheeks very brown under the layers of powder she had been superimposing since the morning. Alain sometimes kept on his summer suit, without a waistcoat, but Camille laid impatient hands on him, taking off his jacket and tie, opening his collar and rolling up his shirt-sleeves, seeking and displaying the bare skin. He treated her as a hussy, letting her do as she wished. She laughed a little unhappily as she contained her feelings. And it was he who lowered his eyes with an anxiety that was not entirely voluptuous. 'What ravages of desire on that face! Her mouth is quite distorted with it. A young wife who's so *very* young. Who taught her to forestall me like that?'

The round table, flanked by a little trolley on rubber wheels, gathered the three of them together at the entrance to the studio, near the open bay window. Three tall old poplars, relics of a beautiful garden that had been destroyed, waved their tops at the height of the balcony and the great setting sun of Paris, dark red and smothered in mists, was going down behind their lean heads from which the sap was retreating.

Mme Buque's dinner – she cooked food well and served it badly – enlivened the hour. Refreshed, Alain forgot his day and the Amparat office and the tutelage of M. Veuillet. His two captives in the glass tower made a fuss of him. 'Were you waiting for me?' he murmured in Saha's ear.

'I heard you coming!' cried Camille. 'One can hear every sound from here!'

'Have you been bored?' he asked her one evening, fearing that she was going to complain. But she shook her black mop in denial.

'Not the least bit in the world. I went over to Mummy's. She's presented me with the treasure.'

'What treasure?'

'The little woman who'll be my maid over there. Provided old Emile doesn't give her a baby. She's quite attractive.'

She laughed as she rolled up her white crêpe sleeves over her bare arms before she cut open the red-fleshed melon round which Saha was tiptoeing. But Alain did not laugh: he was too taken up with the horror of imagining a new maid in his house.

'Yes? But do you remember,' he brought out, 'my mother's never changed her servants since I was a child.'

'That's obvious,' said Camille trenchantly. 'What a museum of old crocks!'

She was biting into a crescent of melon as she spoke and laughing, with her face to the setting sun. Alain admired, in a detached way, how vivid a certain cannibal radiance could be in those glittering eyes and on the glittering teeth in the narrow mouth. There was something Italian about her regular features. He made one more effort to be considerate.

'You never see your girl friends nowadays, it seems to me. Mightn't you perhaps . . .'

She took him up fiercely.

'And what girl friends, may I ask? Is this your way of telling me I'm a burden on you? So that I shall give you a little breathing space. That's it, isn't it?'

He raised his eyebrows and clicked his tongue 'tst . . . tst'. She yielded at once with a plebeian respect for the man's disdain.

'It's quite true. I never had any friends when I was a little girl. And now . . . can you see me with a girl who's not married. Either I'd have to treat her as a child or I'd have to answer all her dirty questions: "And what does one do *here* and how does he do *that* to you!" Girls,' she explained with some bitterness, 'girls don't stick together decently. There's no solidarity. It's not like all you men.'

'Forgive me! I'm not one of "all-you-men"!'

'Oh, I know that all right,' she said sadly. 'Sometimes I wonder if I wouldn't rather . . .'

She was very rarely sad and, when she was, it was because of some secret reticence or some doubt that she did not express.

The Cat

'*You* haven't any friends either,' she went on. 'Except Patrick and he's away. And even Patrick, you don't really care a damn about him.'

She broke off at a gesture from Alain.

'Don't let's talk about these things,' she said intelligently. 'There'll only be a quarrel.'

The long-drawn-out cries of children rose from the ground level and blended with the airy whistling of the swallows. Saha's beautiful yellow eyes, in which the great nocturnal pupil was slowly invading the iris, stared into space, picking out moving, floating, invisible points.

'Tell me, whatever's the cat looking at? Are you sure there's nothing, over there where she's staring?'

'Nothing . . . for us.'

Alain evoked with regret the faint shiver, the seductive fear that his cat friend used to communicate to him in the days when she slept on his chest at night.

'She doesn't make you frightened, I hope?' he said condescendingly.

Camille burst out laughing, as if the insulting word were just what she had been waiting for.

'Frightened? There aren't many things that frighten *me*, you know!'

'That's the statement of a silly little fool,' said Alain angrily.

Let's say you're feeling the storm coming, shall we?' said Camille, shrugging her shoulders.

She pointed to the wall, purpled with clouds which were coming up with the night.

'And you're like Saha,' she added. 'You don't like storms.'

'No one like storms.'

'I don't hate them,' said Camille judicially. 'Anyway, I'm not the slightest bit afraid of them.'

'The whole world is afraid of storms,' said Alain, hostile.

'All right, I'm not the whole world, that's all.'

'You are for me,' he said with a sudden, artificial grace which did not deceive her.

'Oh!' she scolded under her breath. 'I shall hit you.'

He bent his fair head towards her over the table and showed his white teeth.

'All right, hit me!'

But she deprived herself of the pleasure of rumpling that golden hair and offering her bare arm to those shining teeth.

'You've got a crooked nose,' she flung at him fiercely.

'It's the storm,' he said, laughing.

This subtlety was not at all to Camille's taste, but the first low rumblings of the thunder distracted her attention. She threw down her napkin to run out on the balcony.

'Come along! There'll be some marvellous lightning.'

'No,' said Alain, without moving. 'Come along, yourself.'

'Where to?'

He jerked his chin in the direction of their room. Camille's face assumed the obstinate expression, the dull-witted greed he knew so well. Nevertheless, she hesitated.

'But couldn't we look at the lightning first?'

He made a sign of refusal.

'Why not, horrid?'

'Because *I'm* frightened of storms. Choose. The storm or . . . me.'

'What do you think!'

She ran to their room with an eagerness which flattered Alain's vanity. But, when he joined her there, he found she had deliberately lighted a luminous glass cube near the vast bed. He deliberately turned it out.

The rain came in through the open bay-windows as they lay calm again, warm and tingling, breathing in the ozone that filled the room with freshness. Lying in Alain's arms, Camille made him understand that, while the storm

The Cat

raged, she would have liked him once again to forget his terror of it with her. But he was nervously counting the great sheets of lightning and the tall dazzling trees silhouetted against the cloud and he moved away from Camille. She resigned herself, raised herself on her elbow and combed her husband's crackling hair with one hand. In the pulsations of the lightning-flashes their two blue plaster faces rose out of the night and were swallowed up in it again.

'We'll wait till the storm's over,' she consented.

'And *that*,' said Alain to himself, '*that's* what she finds to say after an encounter that really means something. She might at least have kept quiet. As Emile says, the young lady speaks her mind straight out.'

A flickering flash, long as a dream, was reflected in a blade of fire in the thick slab of glass on the invisible dressing-table. Camille clutched Alain against her bare leg.

'Is that to reassure me? We know you're not frightened of lightning.'

He raised his voice so as to be heard above the hollow rumbling and the rain cascading on the flat roof. He felt tired and on edge, tempted to be unjust yet frightened to say openly that nowadays he was never alone. In his mind he returned violently to his old room with its white wallpaper patterned with stiff conventional flowers, a room which no one had ever tried to make prettier or uglier. His longing for it was so fierce that the murmur of the inefficient old radiator came back with the memory of the pale flowers on the wallpaper. The wheezy mutter that came from the hollow space below its copper pipes seemed to be part of the murmurs of the whole house; of the whispering of the worn old servants, half-buried in their basement, who no longer cared to go out even into the garden. . . . 'They used to say "She" when they talked about my mother but I've been "Monsieur Alain" since I first went into knickerbockers.'

Colette

A dry crackle of thunder roused him from the brief doze into which he had fallen. His young wife, leaning over him, propped on her elbow, had not stirred.

'I like you so much when you're asleep,' she said. 'The storm's going off.'

He took this as a demand and sat up.

'I'm following its example,' he said. 'How hot and sticky it is! I'm going to sleep on the waiting-room bench.'

The 'waiting-room bench' was their name for the narrow divan which was the solitary piece of furniture in a tiny room, a mere strip of glass-walled passage which Patrick used for sunbathing.

'Oh, no! Oh, no!' implored Camille. 'Do stay.'

But he had already slipped out of the bed. The great flashes in the clouds revealed Camille's hard, offended face.

'Pooh! Baby boy!'

At this, which he was not expecting, she pulled his nose. With an instinctive reflex of his arm, which he could not control and did not regret, he beat down the disrespectful hand. A sudden lull in the wind and rain left them alone in the silence, as if struck dumb. Camille massaged her hand.

'But...' she said at last, 'But... you're a brute.'

'Possibly,' said Alain. 'I don't like having my face touched. Isn't the rest of me enough for you? Never touch my face.'

'But you *are* ... you really *are* a brute,' Camille repeated slowly.

'Don't keep on saying it. Apart from that, I've nothing against you. Just mind you don't do it again.'

He lifted his bare leg back on to the bed.

'You see that big grey square on the carpet? It's nearly daybreak. Shall we go to sleep?'

'Yes ... let's ...' said the same, hesitant voice.

'Come on, then!'

He stretched out his left arm so that she could rest

her head on it. She did so submissively and with a circumspect politeness. Pleased with himself, Alain gave her a friendly jostle and pulled her towards him by her shoulder. But he bent his knees a little to keep her at a safe distance and fell asleep almost at once. Camille lay awake, breathing carefully, and watched the grey patch on the carpet growing lighter. She listened to the sparrows celebrating the end of the storm in the three poplars whose rustling sounded like the faint continuation of the rain. When Alain, changing his position, withdrew his arm, he gave her an unconscious caress. Three times his hand slid lightly over her head as if accustomed to stroking fur that was even softer than her soft black hair.

SEVEN

It was towards the end of June that incompatibility became established between them like a new season of the year. Like a season, it had its surprises and even its pleasures. To Alain, it was like a harsh, chilly spring inserted in the heart of summer. He was incessantly and increasingly aware of his repugnance at the idea of making a place for this young woman, this outsider, in his own home. He nursed this resentment and fed it with secret soliloquies and the sullen contemplation of their new dwelling. Camille, exhausted with the heat, called out from the high and now windless balcony: 'Oh, let's chuck everything. Let's take the old scooter and go somewhere where we can bathe. Shall we, Alain?'

'All right by me,' he answered with wily promptitude. 'Where shall we go?'

There was a peaceful interlude while Camille enumerated beaches and names of hotels. With his eye on Saha who lay flat and prostrated, Alain had the leisure to think and to conclude: 'I don't want to go away with her I . . .

I daren't. I'm quite willing to go for a drive, as we used to, and come back in the evening or late at night. But that's all. I don't want evenings in hotels and nights in a casino, evenings of ...' He shuddered: 'I need time. I realize that I take a long time to get used to things, that I'm a difficult character, that ... But I don't want to go off with *her*.' He felt a pang of shame as he realized that he had mentally said '*her*' just like Emile and Adèle when they were discussing 'Madame' in undertones.

Camille bought road-maps and they played at travelling through a France spread in quarters over the polished ebony table which reflected their two blurred, inverted faces.

They added up the mileage, ran down their car, cursed each other affably and felt revived, even rehabilitated by a comradeship they had forgotten. But tropical showers unaccompanied by gales drowned the last days of June and the balconies of the Wedge. Sheltering behind the closed panes, Saha watched the level rivulets, which Camille mopped up by stamping on table-napkins, winding across the inlaid tiles. The horizon; the city; the shower itself; all took on the colour of clouds loaded with inexhaustible rain.

'Would you rather we took the train?' suggested Alain suavely.

He had foreseen that Camille would fly out at the detested word. Fly out she did indeed — and blasphemously.

'I'm afraid,' he went on, 'that you're getting bored. All those trips we'd promised ourselves.'

'All those summer hotels. All those restaurants full of flies. All those seas full of people bathing,' she railed plaintively. 'Look here, you and I are quite used to driving around. But what we're good at is just going for drives. We're quite lost when it comes to a real journey.'

He saw that she was slightly depressed and gave her a brotherly kiss. But she turned round and bit him on his mouth and under his ear. Once again, they fell into the diversion which shortens the hours and makes the body attain its pleasure easily. It was beginning to make Alain tired. When he dined at his mother's with Camille and had to stifle his yawns, Mme Amparat lowered her eyes and Camille invariably gave a little, swaggering laugh. For she was proudly conscious of the habit Alain had acquired of making love to her hurriedly and almost peevishly, flinging her away the moment it was over to return to the cool side of the uncovered bed.

Ingenuously, she would rejoin him there and he did not forgive her for that although, silently, he would yield again. After that he felt at liberty to probe at leisure into the sources of what he called their incompatibility. He was wise enough to put these outside their frequent love-making. Clear-headed, helped by the very fact of his sexual exhaustion, he returned to those retreats where the hostility of man to woman keeps its unageing freshness. Sometimes she revealed herself to him in some commonplace realm where she slept in broad sunshine, like an innocent creature. Sometimes he was astonished, even scandalized, that she should be so dark. Lying in bed behind her, he surveyed the short hairs on her shaved neck, ranged like the prickles of a sea-urchin and drawn on the skin like the hatching on a map. The shortest of them were blue and visible under the fine skin before each one emerged through a small blackened pore.

'Have I never really had a dark woman?' he wondered. 'Two or three little black-haired things haven't left me any impression of *such* darkness.' And he held his own arm up to the light. It was yellowish-white; a typical fair man's arm with green-gold down and jade-coloured veins. His own hair seemed to him like a forest with violet shadows, whereas Camille's showed the strange whiteness of the skin between the exotic abundance of those ranks of black, slightly crinkled stalks.

The sight of a fine, very black hair stuck to the side of a

basin made him feel sick. Then the little neurosis changed and, abandoning the detail, he concentrated on her whole body. Holding that young, appeased body in his arms in the night which hid its contours he began to be annoyed that a creative spirit, in moulding Camille, had shown a strict reasonableness like that of his English nurse. 'Not more prunes than rice, my boy,' she used to say. 'Not more rice than chicken.' That spirit had modelled Camille adequately but with no concessions to lavishness or fantasy. He carried his annoyances and regrets into the antechamber of his dreams during that incalculable moment reserved for the black landscape peopled with bulbous eyes, fish with Greek noses, moons and chins. There he desired a big-hipped charmer of the 1900 type, liberally developed above a tiny waist, to compensate for the acid smallness of Camille's breasts. At other times, half asleep, he compromised and preferred a top-heavy bosom; two quivering, monstrous hillocks of flesh with sensitive tips. Such feverish desires, which were born of the sexual act and survived it, never affronted the light of day nor even complete wakefulness. They merely peopled a narrow isthmus between nightmare and voluptuous dream.

When the flesh was warm, the 'foreigner' smelt of wood licked by tongues of flame; birch, violets ... a whole bouquet of sweet, dark tenacious scents which clung long to the palms. These fragrances produced in Alain a kind of perverse excitement but did not always arouse his desire.

'You're like the smell of roses,' he said one day to Camille, 'you take away one's appetite.'

She looked at him dubiously and assumed the slightly gauche, downcast expression with which she received double-edged compliments.

'How awfully eighteen-thirty you are,' she murmured.

'You're much more so,' replied Alain. 'Oh, ever so much more so. I know who you're like.'

'Marie Dubas, the actress. I've been told that before.'

'Hopelessly wrong, my girl! Minus the bandeau, you're like all those girls who weep on the tops of towers on the works of Loïsa Puget. You can see them weeping on the cover of his romantic songs, with *your* great, prominent Greek eyes and those thick rims to the lower lid that makes the tears jump down on to the cheeks . . .'

One after another, Alain's senses took advantage of him to condemn Camille. He had to admit, at least, that she stood up admirably to certain remarks he fired her point-blank. They were provocative rather than grateful remarks that burst out of him at the times when, lying on the floor, he measured her with narrowed eyes and appraised her new merits without indulgence or regard for her feelings. He judged her particular aptitudes; he noted how that sensual ardour of hers, that slightly monotonous passion, had already developed an enlightened self-interest remarkable in so young a married woman. Those were moments of frankness and certainty and Camille did all she could to prolong their half-silent atmosphere of conflict; their tension like that of a tightrope on which balance was precarious and dangerous.

Having no deep-seated malice in herself, Camille never suspected that Alain was only half taken in by deliberate challenges, pathetic appeals and even by a cool Polynesian cynicism, and that each time he possessed his wife, he meant it to be the last. He mastered her as he might have put a hand on her mouth to stop her from screaming or as he might have murdered her.

When she was dressed again and sitting upright beside him in their roadster, he could look at her closely without rediscovering what it was that had made her his worst enemy. As soon as he regained his breath, listening to his decreasing heartbeats, he ceased to be the dramatic young man who stripped himself naked before wrestling with his companion and overthrowing her. The brief routine of pleasure; the controlled expert movements, the real or stimulated gratitude were relegated to the ranks of what is over, of what will probably never happen again. Then his greatest preoccupation would return, the one which he accepted as natural and honourable, the question which reassumed the first place it had so long deserved: 'How to stop Camille from living in *my* house?'

Once this period of hostility towards the 'alterations' had passed, he had genuinely put his faith in the return to the home of his childhood, in the tranquillizing influence of a life on ground level; a life in contact with the earth and everything the earth brings forth. 'Here, I'm suffering from living up in the air. Oh, to see branches and birds from *underneath* again!' he sighed. But he concluded severely, 'Pastoral life is no solution,' and once more had recourse to his indispensable ally, the lie.

On a blazing afternoon which melted the asphalt he went to his domain. All about it, Neuilly was a desert of the empty roads and empty tramways of July; the gardens were abandoned except for a few yawning dogs. Before leaving Camille, he had installed Saha on the coolest balcony of the Wedge. He was vaguely worried every time he left his two females alone together.

The garden and the house were asleep and the little iron gate did not creak as he opened it. Overblown roses, red poppies, the first ruby-throated Canna lilies and dark snapdragons burned in isolated clumps on the lawns. At the side of the house gaped the new doorway and two new windows in a freshly painted little one-storey building. 'It's all finished,' Alain realized. He walked carefully, as he did in his dreams, and trod only on the grass.

Hearing the murmur of a voice rising from the basement, he stopped and absent-mindedly listened. It was only the old well-known voices of servility and ritual grumbling, the old voices of which used to say 'She' and 'Monsieur Alain'. Once upon a time they had flattered the

The Cat

fragile, fair-haired little boy and his childish pride . . . 'I was a king, once,' Alain said to himself, smiling sadly.

'Well, so *she'll* soon be coming to sleep here, I suppose?' one of the old voices asked audibly.

'That's Adèle,' thought Alain. Leaning against the wall, he listened without the least scruple.

'Of course she will,' bleated Emile. 'That flat's shockingly badly built.

The housemaid, a greying Basque woman with a hairy face, broke in: 'You're right there. From their bathroom you can hear everything that goes on in the water-closet. Monsieur Alain won't like *that*.'

'*She* said, the last time *she* came that *she* didn't need curtains in her little drawing-room because there are no neighbours on the garden side.'

'No neighbours? What about us when we go to the wash-house? What's one going to see when *she's* with Monsieur Alain?'

Alain could guess the smothered laughter and the ancient Emile continued: 'Oh, perhaps one won't see as much as all *that*. *She*'ll be put in her place, all right. Monsieur Alain's not the sort to let himself go on a sofa at any time of day or night.'

There was a silence during which Alain could hear nothing but the sound of a knife on the grindstone. But he stayed listening, with his back against the hot wall and his eyes vaguely searching between a flaming geranium and the acid green of the turf as if he half-expected to see Saha's moonstone-coloured fur.

'As for me,' said Adèle, 'I think it's oppressive, that scent *she* puts on.'

'And her frocks,' supplemented Juliette, the Basque woman. 'The way she dresses isn't really good style. *She* looks more like an actress. Behaves like one too, with that brazen way of hers. And now what's she going to land us with in the way of a lady's maid? Some creature out of an orphanage, I believe, or worse.'

A fanlight slammed and the voices were cut off. Alain felt weak and trembling. He breathed like a man who has just been spared by a gang of murderers. He was neither surprised nor indignant. There was not much difference between his own opinion of Camille and that of the harsh judges in the basement. But his heart was beating fast because he had meanly eavesdropped without being punished for it and because he had been listening to prejudiced witnesses and unsought accomplices. He wiped his face and took a deep breath as if inhaling this gust of misogyny, this pagan incense offered exclusively to the male principle, had anaesthetized him. His mother, who had just wakened from her siesta and was putting back the shutters of her room, saw him standing there, with his cheek still leant against the wall.

She called softly, like a wise mother.

'Ah! my boy ... Is anything the matter?'

He took her hands over the window-sill, like a lover.

'Nothing at all. I was out for a walk and just thought I'd look in.'

'A very good idea.'

She did not believe him but they smiled at each other, perfectly aware that neither was telling the truth.

'Mother, could I ask you to do me a little favour?'

'A little favour in the way of money, isn't that it? I know you're none too well off this year, my poor children.'

'No, Mother. Please, would you mind not telling Camille that I came here today? As I didn't come here for any special reason, I mean with no special reason except just to look in and give you a kiss. I'd rather .... Actually, that's not all. I want you to give me some advice. Strictly between the two of us, you know.'

Mme Amparat lowered her eyes, ran her hand through her wavy white hair, and tried to avert the confidence.

'I'm not much of a talker, as you know. You've caught me all untidy. I look like an old gipsy. Won't you come inside into the cool?'

The Cat

'No, Mother. Do you think there's any way . . . it's an idea I can't get out of my head . . . a polite way, of course . . . something that wouldn't offend anyone . . . but some way of stopping Camille from living here?'

He seized his mother's hands, expecting them to tremble or to draw away. But they stayed, cold and soft, between his own.

'These are just a young husband's ideas,' she said, embarrassed.

'What do you mean?'

'With young married couples, things go too well or they go too badly. I don't know which works out best in the end. But they never go straightforwardly, just of their own accord.'

'But, Mother, that's not what I'm asking you. I'm asking you whether there isn't any way . . .'

For the first time, he was unable to look his mother in the face. She gave him no help and he turned away irritably.

'You're talking like a child. You run about the streets in this frightful heat and you come to me after a quarrel and ask me impossible questions. *I* don't know. Questions whose only answer is divorce. Or moving house. Or heaven knows what.'

She got breathless whenever she talked and Alain only reproached himself for making her flush and pant even at saying so little. 'That's enough for today,' he thought prudently.

'We haven't had a quarrel, Mother. It's only I who can't get used to the idea . . . who doesn't want to see . . .'

With a wide, embarrassed gesture, he indicated the garden that surrounded them: the green lake of the lawn; the bed of fallen petals under the rose arches; a swarm of bees over the flowering ivy; the ugly, revered house.

The hand he had kept in one of his clenched and hardened into a little fist and he suddenly kissed that sensitive hand: 'Enough, that's enough for today.'

149

'I'm off now, Mother. Monsieur Veuillet's telephoning you at eight tomorrow about this business of the shares going down. Do I look better now, Mother?'

He raised his eyes that looked greener in the shade of the tulip-tree and threw back his face which from habit, affection and diplomacy he had forced into his old childish expression. A flutter of the lids to brighten the eye, the seductive smile, a little pout of the lips. His mother's hand unclenched again and reached over the sill to feel Alain's well-known weak spots; his shoulder-blades, his Adam's apple, the top of his arm. She did all this before replying.

'A little better. Yes, really, quite a lot better.'

'I've pleased her by asking her to keep something secret from Camille.' At the remembrance of his mother's last caress, he tightened his belt under his jacket. 'I've got thinner, I'm getting thinner. No more physical culture – no physical culture other than making love.'

He went off with a light step, in his summer clothes, and the cooling breeze dried his sweat and blew the acrid smell of it ahead of him. He left his native castle inviolate, his subterranean cohort intact, and the rest of the day would pass easily enough. Until midnight, no doubt, sitting in the car beside an inoffensive Camille, he would drink in the evening air, now sylvan as they drove between oak plantations edged with muddy ditches, now dry and smelling of wheatstraw. 'And I'll bring back some fresh couch-grass for Saha.'

Vehemently, he reproached himself for the lot of his cat who lived so soundlessly at the top of their glass tower. 'She's like her own chrysalis, and it's my fault.' At the hour of their conjugal games she banished herself so rigorously that Alain had never seen her in the triangular room. She ate just sufficient to keep alive; she had lost her varied language and given up all her demands, seeming to prefer her long waiting to everything else.

The Cat

'Once again, she's waiting behind bars. She's waiting for me.'

Camille's shattering voice came through the closed door as he reached the landing.

'It's that filthy bloody swine of an animal! I wish it were dead! What? No, Madame Buque, I don't care what you say. To hell with it! To hell with it!'

He made out a few more violent expressions. Very softly he turned the key in the lock but, once over his own threshold, he could not consent to listen without being seen. 'A filthy bloody swine of an animal? But what animal? An animal in the house?'

In the studio Camille, wearing a little sleeveless pullover and a knitted beret miraculously balanced on her skull, was furiously pulling a pair of gauntlet gloves over her bare hands. She seemed stupefied at the sight of her husband.

'It's you! Where have you sprung from?'

'I haven't sprung from anywhere. I've simply arrived home. Who are you so furious with?'

She avoided the trap and neatly turned the attack on Alain.

'You're very cutting, the first time you get home punctually. *I'm* ready. I've been waiting for you.'

'You haven't been waiting for me since I'm punctual to the minute. Who were you so angry with? I heard "filthy bloody swine of an animal?" What animal?'

She squinted very slightly but sustained Alain's look.

'The dog!' she cried. 'That damned dog downstairs, the dog that barks morning, noon and night. It's started again! Can't you hear it barking? Listen!'

She raised her finger to make him keep quiet and Alain had time to notice that the gloved finger was shaking. He yielded to a naïve need to make sure.

'Just fancy, I thought you were talking about Saha.'

'Me?' cried Camille. 'Me speak about Saha in that tone?

Why I wouldn't dare! The heavens would fall if I did! For goodness' sake, are you coming?'

'Go and get the car out, I'll join you down below. I've just got to get a handkerchief and a pullover.'

His first thought was to find the cat. On the coolest balcony, near the deck-chair in which Camille occasionally slept in the afternoon, he could see nothing but some fragments of broken glass. He stared at them blankly.

'The cat's with me, Monsieur,' came the fluting voice of Mme Buque. 'She's very fond of my wicker stool. She sharpens her claws on it.'

'In the kitchen,' thought Alain painfully. 'My little puma, my cat of the garden, my cat of the lilacs and the butterflies, in the kitchen! Ah! All that's going to change!'

He kissed Saha on the forehead and chanted some ritual praises, very low. He promised her couch-grass and sweet acacia flowers. But he found both the cat and Mme Buque artificial and constrained; Mme Buque in particular.

'We may be back to dinner and we may not, Madame Buque. Has the cat everything she needs?'

'Yes, Monsieur. Oh yes, indeed, Monsieur,' said Mme Buque hurriedly. 'I do everything I possibly can, really I do, Monsieur!'

The big, fat woman was red in the face and seemed on the verge of tears. She ran a friendly, clumsy hand over the cat's back. Saha arched her back and proffered a little 'm'hain', the mew of a poor timid cat which made her friend's heart swell with sadness.

The drive was more peaceful than he had hoped. Sitting at the wheel, her eyes alert, her feet and hands perfectly synchronized, Camille drove him as far as the slope of Montfort-l'Amaurey.

'Shall we have dinner out of doors, Alain? Shall we, Alain, darling?'

She smiled at him in profile, beautiful as she always

The Cat

was in the twilight; her cheek brown and transparent, her teeth and the corner of her eye the same glittering white. In the forest of Rambouillet, she put down the windscreen and the wind filled Alain's ears with a sound of leaves and running water.

'A little rabbit! . . .' cried Camille. 'A pheasant!'

'It's still a rabbit . . . One moment more and I . . .'

'He doesn't know his luck, that chap!'

'You've got a dimple in your cheek like you have in your photos as a child,' said Alain, beginning to come to life.

'Don't talk about it! I'm getting enormous!' she said, shaking her shoulders.

He watched for the return of the laugh and the dimple, and his eyes wandered down to the robust neck, free of any trace of the 'girdle of Venus', the round, inflexible neck of a handsome white Negress. 'Yes, she really has got fatter. And in the most seductive way. For her breasts, those too . . .' He withdrew into himself once more and came up, morosely, against the age-old male grievance. 'She's getting fat from making love. She's battening on *me*.' He slipped a jealous hand under his jacket, felt his ribs, and ceased to admire the childish dimple in her cheeks.

But he felt a certain gratified vanity when they sat down a little later at a famous inn and the neighbouring diners stopped talking and eating to stare at Camille. And he exchanged with his wife the smiles, the movements of the chin and all the rituals of coquetry suitable to a 'handsome couple'.

However, it was only for him that Camille lowered her voice and displayed a certain languor and certain charming attentions which were not in the least for show. In revenge, Alain snatched out of her hand the dish of raw tomatoes and the basket of strawberries, insisted that she ate chicken with a cream sauce, and poured her out a wine which she did not care for but which she drank fast.

'You know perfectly well I don't like wine,' she repeated each time she emptied her glass.

The sun had set but the sky was still almost white, dappled with small deep-pink clouds. But night and coolness seemed to be rising as one from the forest which loomed, massive, beyond the tables of the inn. Camille laid her hand on Alain's.

'What is it? What is it? What's the matter?' he said in terror.

Astonished, she withdrew her hand. The little wine she had drunk gleamed gaily in her eyes in which shone the tiny, quivering image of the pink balloons hung from the pergola.

'Nothing's the matter, silly. You're as nervous as a cat! Is it forbidden for me to put my hand on yours?'

'I thought,' he admitted weakly, 'I thought you wanted to tell me something . . . something serious . . . I thought,' he burst out with it, 'you were going to tell me you were pregnant.'

Camille's shrill little laugh attracted the attention of the men at the near-by tables.

'And you were as overcome as all that? With joy or . . . fed-up-ness?'

'I don't exactly know. What about you? Would you be pleased or not pleased? We've hardly thought about it . . . at least, *I* haven't. But what are you laughing at?'

'Your face! All of a sudden, a face as if you were just going to be hanged. It's too funny. You'll make my eye-black come unstuck.'

With her two forefingers, she lifted up either eyelid.

'It isn't funny, it's serious,' said Alain, glad to put her in the wrong. 'But why was I so terrified?' he thought.

'It's only serious,' said Camille, 'for people who've got nowhere to live or who've only got two rooms. But people like us . . .'

Serene, lulled into optimism by the treacherous wine,

The Cat

she smoked and talked as if she were by herself, her thigh against the table and her legs crossed.

'Pull down your skirt, Camille.'

She did not hear him and went on: 'We've got all the essentials a child needs. A garden – and what a garden! And a dream of a room with its own bathroom.'

'A room?'

'Your old room. We'd have it repainted. And it would be very nice of you not to insist on a frieze of little ducks and fir trees on a sky-blue background. That would ruin the taste of our offspring.'

He restrained himself from stopping her. She was talking at random, her cheeks flushed, as she stared into the distance, seeing all she was building up. He had never seen her so beautiful. He was fascinated by the base of her neck, like the smooth unwrinkled bole of a tree, and by the nostrils which were blowing out smoke. 'When I give her pleasure and she tightens her lips, she opens her nostrils like a little horse as she breathes.

He heard such crazy predictions fall from the reddened scornful lips that they ceased to alarm him: Camille was calmly proceeding with her woman's life among the wreckage of Alain's past. 'Good Lord,' he thought. 'How she's got it all organized. I'm certainly learning something!' A tennis-court was to replace the great, useless lawn. The kitchen and the pantries . . .

'Haven't you ever realized how inconvenient they are? And think of all that wasted space. It's like the garage. I'm only saying all this, darling, so as you should know I think a lot about our real setting up house. Above all, we must be tactful with your mother. She's so awfully sweet . . . we mustn't do anything she wouldn't approve of. Must we?'

He put in haphazard 'Yesses' and 'Noes' as he picked up some wild strawberries scattered on the cloth. After hearing her say 'your old room', he had been immunized by a provisional calm, a foretaste of indifference.

'Only one thing may make things awkward for us,' Camille went on. 'Patrick's last postcard dated from the Balearic Isles. Do pay attention! It'll take less time for Patrick to get back from the Balearics than for our decorator to get everything finished. I hope he comes to a violent end, that son of Penelope by a male tortoise! But I shall put on my siren voice: "Patrick, my pet . . ." You know my siren voice makes a tremendous impression on Patrick.'

'From the Balearic Isles . . .' broke in Alain thoughtfully. 'From the Balearic Isles.'

'Otherwise practically from next door. Where are you off to? Do you want us to go? It was so nice here.'

Her brief intoxication was over. She stood up shivering and yawning with sleepiness.

'I'll drive,' said Alain. 'Put on the old coat that's under the cushion. And go to sleep.'

A flak of flying insects, bright silver moths and stag-beetles hard as pebbles, whirled in front of the headlights and the car drove back the wing-laden air like a wave. Camille did indeed go to sleep, sitting perfectly upright. She was trained not to encumber the driver's arm and shoulder, even in her sleep. She merely gave a little forward jerk of her head at every jolt in the road.

'From the Balearic Isles,' Alain kept repeating to himself. The dark air, the white fires which caught and repulsed and decimated the flying creatures took him back to the populous threshold of his dreams; the sky with its stardust of exploded faces, the great hostile eyes which put off till tomorrow a reckoning, a password or a significant figure. He was so deep in that world that he forgot to take the short cut between Pontchartrain and the Versailles toll-gate and Camille scolded him in her sleep. 'Bravo!' applauded Alain. 'Good reflex action! Good little faithful, vigilant senses. Ah, how much I like you, how well we get on, when you're asleep and I'm awake.'

*

The Cat

Their sleeves and their unprotected hair were wet with dew when they set foot in their newly built street, empty in the moonlight. Alain looked up; nine storeys up, in the middle of the almost round moon, the little horned shadow of a cat was leaning forward, waiting.

'Look! Look how she's waiting!'

'You've got good eyes,' said Camille, yawning.

'If she were to fall! Whatever you do, don't call her!'

'You needn't worry,' said Camille. 'If I did call her, she wouldn't come.'

'For good reason,' said Alain unpleasantly.

As soon as he had said it, he was angry with himself. 'Too soon, too soon! And what a bad moment to choose!' Camille dropped the hand that was just about to push the bell.

'For good reason? For what good reason? Come on, out with it. I've been lacking in respect to the sacred animal again? The cat's complained of me?'

'I've gone too far,' thought Alain, as he closed the garage door. He crossed the street again and rejoined his wife who was waiting for him in battle order. 'Either I give in for the sake of a quiet night, or I stop the discussion by giving her a good, hard slap . . . or . . . It's too soon.'

'Well! I'm talking to you!'

'Let's go up first,' said Alain.

They did not speak as they went up, squeezed side by side in the narrow lift. As soon as they reached the studio, Camille tore off her beret and gloves and threw them across the room as if to show she had not given up the quarrel. Alain busied himself with Saha, inviting her to quit her perilous post. Patient, determined not to displease him, the cat followed him into the bathroom.

'If it's because of what you heard before dinner, when you came in,' began Camille shrilly the moment he reappeared.

Alain had decided on his line and interrupted her wearily: 'My dear, what are we going to say to each other?

Nothing that we don't know already. That you can't bear the cat, that you blew up Mother Buque because the cat broke a vase – or a glass – I saw the pieces. I shall answer that I'm extremely fond of Saha and that you'd be just as jealous if I'd kept a warm affection for some friend of my childhood. And so it'll go on all night. I'd prefer to sleep, thanks very much. Look here, the next time, I advise you to take the initiative and have a little dog.'

Startled, embarrassed by having nothing for her temper to fasten on, Camille stared at him with raised eyebrows.

'The next time? What next time? What do you mean? What initiative?'

As Alain merely shrugged his shoulders, she flushed, her face suddenly became very young again and the extreme brightness of her eyes presaged tears. 'Oh, how bored I am!' groaned Alain inwardly. 'She's going to admit it. She's going to tell me I was right. How boring!'

'Listen, Alain.'

With an effort, he feigned anger and assumed a false air of authority.

'No, my dear. No, no, no! You're not going to force me to finish off this charming evening with a barren discussion. You're not going to make a drama out of a piece of childish nonsense any more than you're going to stop me being fond of animals.'

A kind of bitter gaiety came into Camille's eyes but she said nothing. 'Perhaps I was a little hard. "Childish nonsense," was unnecessary. And as to being fond of animals, what do I know about that?' A small, shadowy blue shape, outlined like a cloud with a hem of silver, sitting on the dizzy edge of the night, absorbed his thoughts and removed him from that soulless place where, inch by inch, he was defending his chance of solitude, his egotism, his poetry . . .

'Come along, my little enemy,' he said with disloyal charm, 'let's go and rest.'

The Cat

She opened the door of the bathroom where Saha, installed for the night on the cork-seated stool, appeared to take only the faintest notice of her.

'But why, but why? Why did you say "the next time"?'

The noise of running water drowned Camille's voice. Alain did not attempt to answer. When he rejoined her in the huge bed, he wished her good-night and kissed her carelessly on her unpowdered nose, while Camille's mouth clung to his chin with a small greedy sound.

Waking early, he went off quietly to lie down on the 'waiting-room bench', the narrow divan squeezed between two walls of glass panes.

It was there that, during the following nights, he finished off his sleep. He closed the opaque oilcloth curtains on either side; they were almost new but already half destroyed by the sun. He breathed on his body the very perfume of his solitude, the sharp feline smell of restharrow and flowering box. One arm extended, the other folded on his chest, he resumed the relaxed, lordly attitude of his childhood sleep. Suspended from the narrow top of the three-cornered house, he encouraged with all his might the return of his old dreams which the lover's exhaustion had dispersed.

He escaped more easily than Camille could have wished, constrained as he was to fly on the very spot. Escape no longer meant a staircase descended on tiptoe, the slamming of a taxi door, a brief farewell note. None of his mistresses had prepared him for Camille and her young girl's eagerness; Camille and her reckless desire. Neither had they prepared him for Camille's stoical behaviour as an offended partner. She made it a point of honour not to complain.

Having escaped and lain down again on the waiting-room bench, Alain strained an uneasy ear toward the room he had just left, as his head felt for the hard little cushion he preferred to all the others. But Camille never reopened the door. Left alone, she pulled the crumpled sheet and the silk eiderdown over her, gnawed her bent finger in resentful regret, and snapped off the chromium strip-light which threw a narrow white beam across the bed. Alain never knew whether she had slept in the empty bed or whether she was learning so young that a solitary night imposes an armed vigil. It was impossible to tell, since she reappeared fresh and rather carefully dressed instead of in the bathrobe and pyjamas of the night before. But she could not understand that a man's sensuality is brief and seasonal and that its unpredictable return is never a new beginning.

Lying alone, bathed in the night air, measuring the height and the silence of his tower-top by the faintness of the hoots from the boats on the near-by Seine, the unfaithful husband delayed going to sleep till the apparition of Saha. She came to him, a shadow bluer than the shadows, along the ledge outside the open glass pane. There she stayed on the watch and would not come down on to Alain's chest although he implored her with the words that she knew: 'Come, my little puma, come along ... My cat of the tree-tops, my cat of the lilacs. Saha, Saha, Saha.'

She resisted, sitting there above him on the window-sill. He could see nothing of her but her cat's shape against the sky, her chin down and her ears passionately orientated towards him. He could never catch the expression of her look.

Sometimes the dry dawn, the dawn before the wind got up, found the two of them sitting on the east side balcony. Cheek by cheek they watched the sky pale and the flight of white pigeons leaving the beautiful cedar of the Folie-Saint-James one by one. Together they felt the same surprise at being so high above the earth, so alone and so far from being happy. With the ardent, sinuous movement of a huntress, Saha followed the pigeons' flight and uttered an occasional 'ek ... ek ...' the faint echo

The Cat

of the 'mouek . . . mouek . . .' of excitement, greed and violent games.

'Our room,' Alain said in her ear. 'Our garden, our house.'

She was getting thin again and Alain found her light and enchanting. But he suffered at seeing her so gentle and patient. Her patience was that of all those who are wearied out and sustained by a promise.

Sleep overcame Alain again as soon as daylight had begun to shorten the shadows. Rayless at first and looming larger through the mist of Paris, the sun swiftly shrank and lightened. As it rose, already burning hot, it awoke a twittering of sparrows in the gardens. The growing light revealed all the untidiness of a hot night on balconies and window-sills and in little yards where captive shrubs languished – a garment forgotten on a deck-chair, empty glasses on a metal table, a pair of sandals. Alain hated the indecency of small dwellings oppressed by summer and regained his bed with one bound through a yawning panel in the glass. At the foot of the nine-storeyed building, a gardener lifted his head and saw this white young man leap through the transparent wall like a burglar.

Saha did not follow him. Sometimes she strained her ears in the direction of the triangular room; sometimes she dispassionately watched the awakening of the distant world on ground level. Someone let out a dog from a small decrepit house. The dog leapt forward without a bark, rushed round and round the tiny garden, and did not recover its voice until it had finished its aimless run. Women appeared at the windows; a maid furiously slammed doors and shook out orange cushions on a flat roof; men, waking regretfully, lit the first bitter cigarette. At last, in the fireless kitchen of the Wedge, the automatic, whistling coffee-pot and the electric teapot clashed against each other; through the porthole window of the bathroom there emerged Camille's perfume and her noisy yawning. Saha resignedly folded her paws beneath her and pretended to sleep.

EIGHT

ONE evening in July, when the two of them were waiting for Alain's return, Camille and the cat were resting on the same parapet; the cat crouched on all four paws, Camille leaning on her folded arms. Camille did not like this balcony-terrace, reserved for the cat and shut in by two cement partitions which cut off both the wind and all communication with the balcony on the prow.

They exchanged a glance of sheer mutual investigation and Camille did not say a word to Saha. Propped on her elbows, she leant over as if to count the storeys by the orange awnings that flapped from top to bottom of the dizzy façade, she brushed against the cat who got up to make room for her, stretched, and lay down a little farther off.

When Camille was alone, she looked very much like the little girl who did not want to say 'how d'you do?' Her face returned to childhood because it wore that expression of inhuman innocence, of angelic hardness which ennobles children's faces. Her gaze wandered over Paris, over the sky from which the light drained a little earlier each day, with an impartial severity which possibly condemned nothing. She yawned nervously, stood upright, and took a few absent-minded steps. Then she leant over again, forcing the cat to jump down. Saha stalked away with dignity and would have preferred to go back into the room. But the door in the hypotenuse had been shut and Saha patiently sat down. The next moment she had to get out of Camille's way for she was pacing from one partition to the other with long, jerky strides. The cat jumped back on to the parapet. As if in play, Camille dislodged her as she leant on

The Cat

her elbows and once again Saha took refuge against the closed door.

Motionless, her eyes far away, Camille stood with her back to her. Nevertheless the cat was looking at Camille's back and her breath came faster. She got up, turned two or three times on her own axis and looked questioningly at the closed door. Camille had not moved. Saha inflated her nostrils and showed a distress which was almost like nausea. A long, desolate mew escaped from her, the wretched reply to a silent imminent threat. Camille faced round abruptly.

She was a trifle pale; that is to say, her rouge stood out in two oval moons on her cheeks. She affected an air of absent-mindedness as she would if a human eye had been staring at her. She even began to sing under her breath and resumed her pacing from one partition to the other, pacing to the rhythm of her song, but her voice failed her. She forced the cat, whom her foot was about to kick, to regain her narrow observation post with one bound, then to flatten herself against the door.

Saha had regained her self-control and would have died rather than utter a second cry. Tracking the cat down, without appearing to see her, Camille paced to and fro in silence. Saha did not jump on the parapet till Camille's feet were right on top of her and she only leapt down again on to the floor of the balcony to avoid the outstretched arm which would have hurled her from the height of the nine storeys.

She fled methodically and jumped carefully, keeping her eyes fixed on her adversary and condescending neither to fury nor to supplication. The most violent emotion of all, the terror of dying, soaked the sensitive soles of her paws with sweat so that they left flower-like prints on the stucco balcony.

Camille seemed the first to weaken and to lose her criminal strength. She made the mistake of noticing that the sun was going down, gave a glance at her wrist watch, and was aware of the clink of glasses inside. A moment or two more and her resolution would have deserted her as sleep deserts the somnambulist, leaving her guiltless and exhausted. Saha felt her enemy's firmness waver, hesitated on the parapet and Camille, stretching out both arms, pushed her into space.

She had time to hear the grating of claws on the rough-cast wall, to see Saha's blue body, twisted into an S, clutching the air with the force of a rising trout; then she shrank away, with her back to the wall.

She felt no temptation to look down into the little kitchen garden edged with new rubble. Back in the room, she put her hands over her ears, withdrew them, and shook her head as if she could hear the hum of a mosquito. Then she sat down and nearly fell asleep. But the oncoming night brought her to her feet again. She drove away the twilight by lighting up glass bricks, luminous tubes and blinding mushrooms of lamps. She also lit up the long chromium eye which poured the opaline beam of its glance across the bed.

She walked about with supple movements, handling objects with light, adroit, dreaming hands.

'It's as if I'd got thinner,' she said out loud.

She changed her clothes and dressed herself in white.

'My fly in the milk,' she said, imitating Alain's voice. Her cheeks regained their colour at a sudden sensual memory which brought her back to reality and she waited for Alain's arrival.

She bent her head in the direction of the buzzing lift and shivered at every noise; those dull knockings, those metallic clangs, those sounds as of a boat grinding at anchor, those muffled bursts of music, which echo the discordant life of a new block of flats. But she was not surprised when the hollow tinkle of the bell in the hall replaced the fumbling of a key in the lock. She ran and opened the door herself.

'Shut the door,' Alain ordered. 'I must see first of all

The Cat

whether she hasn't hurt herself. Come and hold the lamp for me.'

He carried Saha alive in his arms. He went straight to the bedroom, pushed aside the things on the invisible dressing-table, and gently put the cat on the slab of glass. She held herself upright and firm on her paws but her deep-set eyes wandered all about her as they would have done in a strange house.

'Saha!' called Alain in a whisper. 'If there's nothing the matter with her, it's a miracle. Saha!'

She raised her head, as if to reassure her friend, and leant her cheek against his hand.

'Walk a little, Saha. Look, she's walking! Good Lord! Falling six storeys. It was the awning of the chap on the second floor that broke the fall. From there she bounced off on to the concierge's little lawn – the concierge saw her pass in the air. He said: "I thought it was an umbrella falling." What's she got on her ear? No, it's some white off the wall. Wait till I listen to her heart.'

He laid the cat on her side and listened to the beating ribs, the tiny disordered mechanism. With his fair hair spread out and his eyes closed, he seemed to be sleeping on Saha's flank and to wake with a sigh only to see Camille standing there silent and apart, watching the close-knit group they made.

'Can you believe it? There's nothing wrong. At least I can't find anything wrong with her except a terribly agitated heart. But a cat's heart is usually agitated. But however could it have happened! I'm asking you as if you could possibly know, my poor pet! She fell from this side,' he said, looking at the open french window. 'Jump down on the ground, Saha, if you can.'

After hesitating, she jumped but lay down again on the carpet. She was breathing fast and went on looking all round the room with the same uncertain look.

'I think I'll phone Chéron. Still, look, she's washing

herself. She wouldn't wash herself if she'd been injured internally. Oh, good Lord!'

He stretched, threw his jacket on the bed, and came over to Camille.

'What a fright. How pretty you look, all in white. Kiss me, my fly in the milk!'

She let herself fall into the arms which had remembered her at last and could not hold back some broken sobs.

'No? You're actually crying?'

He was upset himself and hid his forehead in the soft, black hair.

'I . . . I didn't know that you were kind.'

She had the courage not to draw away from him at that. However, Alain quickly returned to Saha whom he wanted to take out on the balcony because of the heat. But the cat resisted and contented herself with lying near the open door, turned towards the evening, blue as herself. From time to time, she gave a brief shudder and looked anxiously into the triangular room behind her.

'It's the shock,' explained Alain. 'I wanted her to go and sit outside.'

'Leave her alone,' said Camille faintly, 'since she doesn't want to.'

'Her wishes are orders. Today, of all days! Is there likely to be anything eatable left over at this hour? It's half-past nine!'

Mother Buque wheeled the table out on to the balcony and they dined looking over the east side of Paris where the most lights glimmered. Alain talked a lot, drank water with a little wine in it, and accused Saha of clumsiness, impudence, and 'cat's sins'.

'"Cat's sins" are the kind of playful mistakes and lapses of judgement which can be put down to their having been civilized and domesticated. They've nothing in common with the clumsiness and carelessness that are almost deliberate.'

The Cat

But Camille no longer asked him: 'How do you know that?' After dinner, he carried Saha and drew Camille into the studio where the cat consented to drink the milk she had refused. As she drank, she shivered all over as cats do when they are given something too cold to drink.

'It's the shock,' Alain repeated. 'All the same, I shall ask Chéron to look in and see her tomorrow morning. Oh, I'm forgetting everything!' he cried gaily. 'Will you phone the concierge? I've left that roll of plans down in his lodge. The one that Massart, our precious furnishing chap, deposited there.'

Camille obeyed while Alain, tired and relaxed after the strain, dropped into one of the scattered armchairs and closed his eyes.

'Hallo!' said Camille at the telephone. 'Yes . . . That must be it. A big roll . . . Thanks so much.'

He laughed with his eyes still closed. She had returned to his side and stood there, watching him laugh.

'That absurd little voice you put on! What is this new little voice? "A big roll . . . Thanks so much",' he mimicked. 'Do you keep that extremely small voice for the concierge? Come here, it needs the two of us to face Massart's latest creations.'

He unrolled a sheet of thick drawing-paper, on the ebony table. Saha, who loved all kinds of paper, promptly leapt on the tinted drawing.

'Isn't she sweet!' exclaimed Alain. 'It's to show me she's not in the least hurt. O my miraculously escaped one! Hasn't she a bump on her head? Camille, feel her head. No, she hasn't a bump. Feel her head all the same, Camille.'

A poor little murderess meekly tried to emerge from her banishment, stretched out her hand, and touched the cat's head with humble hatred.

Her gesture was received with the most savage snarl, a scream and an epileptic leap. Camille shrieked 'Ha!' as

167

if she had been burned. Standing on the unrolled drawing the cat covered the young woman with a flaming stare of accusation, the fur on her back erect, her teeth bared and the dry red of her open jaw showing.

Alain had sprang up, ready to protect Saha and Camille from each other.

'Take care! She's . . . perhaps she's mad . . . Saha!'

She stared at him angrily but with a lucidity that proved she had not lost her reason.

'What happened? Where did you touch her?'

'I didn't touch her at all.'

They were both speaking low, hardly moving their lips.

'Then, why this?' said Alain. 'I don't understand. Put your hand out again.'

'No, I don't want to!' protested Camille. 'Perhaps she's gone wild,' she added.

Alain took the risk of stroking Saha. She flattened her erect fur and yielded to the friendly palm but glared once more at Camille with brilliant, accusing eyes.

'Why *this*?' Alain repeated slowly. 'Look, she's got a scratch on her nose. I hadn't seen it. It's dried blood. Saha, Saha, good now,' he said, seeing the fury growing in the yellow eyes.

Because her cheeks were swelled out and her whiskers stiffly thrust forward as if she were hunting, the furious cat seemed to be laughing. The joy of battle stretched the mauve corners of her mouth and tautened the mobile, muscular chin. The whole of her feline face was striving towards a universal language, towards a word forgotten by men.

'Whatever's *that*?' said Alain suddenly.

'Whatever's *what*?'

Under the cat's stare Camille was recovering her courage and the instinct of self-defence. Leaning over the drawing, Alain could make out damp prints in groups of four little spots round a central, irregular patch.

The Cat

'Her paws . . . wet?' muttered Alain.

'She must have walked in some water,' said Camille. 'You're making a fuss about nothing.'

Alain raised her head towards the dry blue night.

'In water? What water?'

He turned again to his wife. He looked at her with round eyes which made him look suddenly extraordinarily ugly. 'Don't you know what those footprints mean?' he said harshly. 'No, *you* wouldn't know. Fear, d'you understand, *fear*. The sweat of fear. Cat's sweat, the only time cats *do* sweat. So she was frightened.'

Delicately, he lifted one of Saha's front paws and dried the sweat on the fleshy pad. Then he pulled back the living white sheath into which the claws had been drawn back.

'She's got all her claws broken,' he said, talking to himself. 'She must have held on . . . clutching. She scratched the stone trying to save herself. She . . .'

He broke off his monologue and, without another word, took the cat under his arm and carried her off to the bathroom.

Alone, unmoving, Camille strained her ears. She kept her hands knotted together; free as she was, she seemed to be loaded with fetters.

'Madame Buque,' said Alain's voice, 'have you any milk?'

'Yes, Monsieur. In the fridge.'

'Then it's ice-cold?'

'But I can warm it on the stove. It won't take a second. It is for the cat? She's not ill, is she?'

'No, she's . . .'

Alain's voice stopped short and changed its tone: 'She's a little off meat in this heat. Thank you, Madame Buque. Yes, you can go now. See you in the morning.'

Camille heard her husband moving to and fro and turning on a tap. She knew that he was giving the cat food and fresh water. A diffused shadow, above the metal lampshade, came up as high as her face which was as still as a mask except for the slow movement of the great eyes.

Alain returned, carelessly tightening his leather belt, and sat down again at the ebony table. But he did not summon Camille back to sit beside him and she was forced to speak first.

'You've sent old Mother Buque off?'

'Yes. Shouldn't I have?'

He lit a cigarette and squinted at the flame of the lighter.

'I wanted her to bring something tomorrow morning.'

'Oh, it doesn't matter a bit . . . don't apologize.'

'But I'm not apologizing. Though, actually, I ought to.'

He went over to the open bay window, drawn by the blue of the night. He was studying a certain tremor in himself, a tremor which did not come from his recent emotion, but which was more like the tremolo of an orchestra, muffled and foreboding. From the Folie-Saint-James a rocket shot up, burst into luminous petals that withered one by one as they fell, and the blue of the night recovered its peace and its powdery depth. In the amusement park, a grotto, a colonnade, and a waterfall were suddenly lit up with incandescent white; Camille came nearer to him.

'Are they having a gala night? Let's wait for the fireworks. Do you hear the guitars?'

Absorbed in his inner tremor, he did not answer her. His wrists and hands were tingling, his loins were weak and felt as if a thousand insects were crawling over them. His state reminded him of the hateful lassitude, the fatigue he used to feel after the school sports. After running and rowing he would emerge vindictive, throbbing and exhausted and equally contemptuous of his victory or defeat. Now, he was at peace only in that part of himself which was no longer anxious about Saha. For several minutes – or perhaps for very few – ever since the

The Cat

discovery of the broken claws, ever since Saha's furious terror, he had lost all sense of time.

'It's not fireworks,' he said. 'Probably just some dances.'

From the movement Camille made beside him in the shadow, he realized that she had given up expecting him to answer her. He felt her coming closer without apprehension. He saw the outline of the white dress; a bare arm; a half face lit by the yellow light from the lamps indoors and a half face that shadowed blue in the clear night. The two halves were divided by the small straight nose and each was provided with a large, almost unblinking eye.

'Yes, of course, it's dances,' she agreed. 'They're mandolines, not guitars. Listen ... "*Les donneurs ... de sé-é-réna ... des, Et les bel-les é-écou-teu ...*'

Her voice cracked on the highest note and she coughed to excuse her failure.

'But what a tiny voice ...' thought Alain, astonished. 'What has she done with her voice that's as big and open as her eyes?' She's singing in a little girl's voice. Hoarse, too.'

The mandolines stopped and the breeze brought a faint human noise of clapping and applause. A moment later, a rocket shot up, burst into an umbrella of mauve rays in which hung tears of living fire.

'Oh!' cried Camille.

Both of them had emerged from the darkness like two statues; Camille in lilac marble; Alain whiter, with his hair greenish and his eyes almost colourless. When the rocket had gone out, Camille sighed.

'It never lasts long enough,' she said plaintively.

The distant music started again. But the capricious wind deadened the sound of the stringed instruments into a vague shrill buzzing and carried the blasts of the accompanying brass, on two notes, loudly and insistently right into their ears.

'What a shame,' said Camille. 'They've probably got

a frightfully good jazz band. That's "Love in the Night" they're playing.'

She hummed the tune in a high, shaky, almost inaudible voice, as if she had just been crying. This new voice of hers acutely increased Alain's disquiet. It induced in him a need for revelation, a desire to break down whatever it was that – a long time ago or only a moment ago? – had risen between himself and Camille. It was something to which he could not yet give a name but which was growing fast; something which prevented him from putting his arm round her neck like a boy; something which kept him motionless at her side, alert and expectant, against the wall still warm from the heat of the day. Turning impatient, he said, 'Go on singing.'

A long red, white, and blue shower, falling like the branches of a weeping willow, streaked the sky over the park and showed Alain a Camille startled and already defiant: 'Singing what?'

'"Love in the Night" or anything else. It doesn't matter what.'

She hesitated, then refused.

'Let me listen to the jazz . . . even from here you can hear it's simply marvellous.'

He did not insist. He restrained his impatience and mastered the tingling which had now spread over his entire body.

A swarm of gay little suns, revolving brightly against the darkness, took flight. Alain secretly confronted them with the constellations of his favourite dreams.

'Those are the ones to remember. I'll try and take them with me down there,' he noted gravely. 'I've neglected my dreams too much.' At last, in the sky over the Folie, there rose and expanded a kind of straying pink and yellow dawn which burst into vermilion discs and fiery ferns and ribbons of blinding metal.

The shouts of children on the lower balconies greeted this miraculous display. By its light, Alain saw Camille

The Cat

absent and remote, absorbed in other lights in her own mind.

As soon as the night closed in again, his hesitation vanished and he slipped his own bare arm under Camille's. As he touched that bare arm, he fancied he could see it; its whiteness hardly tinged by the summer and clothed in a fine down that lay flat on the skin, reddish-brown on the forearm, paler near the shoulder.

'You're cold,' he murmured. 'You're not feeling ill?'

She began to cry very quietly and so promptly that Alain suspected she had been preparing her tears.

'No. It's you. It's you who . . . who don't love me.'

He leant back against the wall and drew Camille against his hip. He could feel her trembling, and cold from her shoulders to her knees, bare above her rolled stockings. She clung to him faithfully, leaning all her weight on him.

'Aha, so I don't love you. Right! Is this another jealousy scene on account of Saha?'

He felt a muscular tremor run through the whole of the body he was supporting, a renewal of energy and self-defence. Encouraged by the moment, by a kind of indescribable opportunism, he insisted: 'Instead of adopting this charming animal, like me. Are we the only young couple who have a cat or a dog? Would you like a parrot or a marmoset – a pair of doves – a dog, to make me very jealous in my turn?'

She shook her shoulders, protesting with annoyance through closed lips. With his head high, Alain carefully controlled his own voice and egged himself on. 'Go on, a few more bits of nonsense; fill her up and we'll get somewhere. She's like a jar that I've got to turn upside down to empty. Go on. Go on.'

'Would you like a little lion . . . or a baby crocodile of barely fifty? No? Come on, you'd much better adopt Saha. If you'd just take the least bit of trouble, you'd soon see . . .'

Camille wrenched herself out of his arms so violently that he staggered.

'No!' she cried. '*That*, never! Do you hear me? *Never*!'

'Ah, now we've got it!' Alain said to himself with delight. He pushed Camille into the room, pulled down the outer blind, lit up the rectangle of glass in the ceiling, and shut the window. With an animal movement, Camille rushed over to the window and Alain opened it again.

'On condition you don't scream,' he said.

He wheeled the only armchair up to Camille and sat astride on the solitary chair at the foot of the wide, turned-down bed with its new, clean sheets. The oilcloth curtains, drawn for the night, gave a greenish cast to Camille's pale face and her creased white dress.

'Well?' began Alain. 'No compromise possible? Appalling story? Either her or me?'

She answered with a brief nod and Alain realized that he must drop his bantering tone.

'What do you want me to say?' he went on, after a silence. 'The only thing I don't want to say to you? You know very well I'll never give up this cat. I should be ashamed to. Ashamed in myself and ashamed before her.'

'I know,' said Camille.

'And before you,' Alan finished.

'Oh, *me*!' said Camille, raising her hand.

'You count too,' said Alain hardly. 'Tell me. Is it only me you've anything against? You've no reproach against Saha except her affection for me?'

She answered only with a troubled, hesitant look and he was irritated at having to go on questioning her. He had thought that a short violent scene would force all the issues; he had relied on this easy way out. But, after her one cry, Camille had stiffened defensively and was furnishing no fuel for a quarrel. He resorted to patience: 'Tell me, my dear. What is it? Mustn't I call you my dear? Tell me, if it were a question of another cat and not Saha, would you be so intolerant?'

The Cat

'Of course I wouldn't,' she said very quickly. 'You wouldn't love it as much as that one.'

'Quite true,' said Alain with loyal accuracy.

'Even a woman,' went on Camille, beginning to get heated, 'you probably wouldn't love a *woman* as much as that.'

'Quite true,' said Alain.

'You're not like most people who are fond of animals. No, you're *not*. Patrick's fond of animals. He takes big dogs by the scruff of their necks and rolls them over. He imitates cats to see the faces they make – he whistles to the birds.'

'Quite. In other words, he's not difficult,' said Alain.

'But you're quite different. You *love* Saha.'

'I've never pretended not to. But I wasn't lying to you, either, when I said to you: "Saha's not your rival."'

He broke off and lowered his eyelids over his secret which was a secret of purity.

'There are rivals *and* rivals,' said Camille sarcastically.

Suddenly she reddened. Flushed with sudden intoxication, she advanced to Alain.

'I saw the two of you!' she almost shrieked. 'In the morning, when you spend the night on your little divan. Before daybreak. I've seen you, both of you.'

She pointed a shaking hand towards the balcony.

'Sitting there, the two of you . . . you didn't even hear me! You were like that, cheek to cheek.'

She went over to the window, recovered her breath and marched down on Alain again.

'It's for you to say honestly whether I'm wrong in being jealous of this cat and wrong in suffering.'

He kept silence so long that she became angry again.

'Do speak! Do *say* something! At the point we've got to . . . What are you waiting for?'

'The sequel,' said Alain. 'The rest.'

He stood up quietly, bent over his wife, and lowered

175

his voice as he indicated the french window: 'It was you, wasn't it? You threw her over?'

With a swift movement she put the bed between herself and him but she did not deny it. He watched her escape with a kind of smile: 'You threw her over,' he said dreamily. 'I felt very definitely that you'd changed everything between us. You threw her over . . . she broke her claws trying to clutch on to the wall.'

He lowered his head, imagining the attempted murder.

'But *how* did you throw her over? By holding her by the skin of her neck? By taking advantage of her being asleep on the parapet? Had you been planning this for a long time? You hadn't had a fight with each other first?'

He raised his head and stared at Camille's hands and arms.

'No, you've no marks. She accused you well and truly, didn't she, when I made you touch her. She was magnificent.'

His eyes left Camille and embraced the night, the dust of stars, the tops of the three poplars which the lights in the room lit up.

'Very well,' he said simply, 'I'm going away.'

'Oh listen . . . do *listen* . . .' Camille implored wildly, almost in a whisper.

Nevertheless, she let him go out of the room. He opened cupboards, talked to the cat in the bathroom. The sound of his footsteps warned Camille that he had changed into his outdoor shoes and she looked, automatically, at the time. He came in again, carrying Saha in a bulging basket which Mme Buque used for shopping. Hurriedly dressed, with his hair dishevelled and a scarf round his neck, his untidiness so much suggested that of a lover that Camille's eyelids pricked. But she heard Saha moving in the basket and tightened her lips.

'As you see, I'm going away,' repeated Alain. He lowered his eyes, lifted the basket a trifle, and corrected himself with calculated cruelty. '*We're* going away.'

The Cat

He secured the wicker lid, explaining as he did so: 'This was all I could find in the kitchen.'

'You're going to your home?' inquired Camille, forcing herself to imitate Alain's calm.

'But of course.'

'Are you . . . can I count on seeing you during the next few days?'

'Why, certainly.'

Surprise made her weaken again. She had to make an immense effort not to plead, not to weep.

'What about you?' said Alain. 'Will you stay here alone tonight? You won't be frightened? If you insisted, I'd stay, but . . .'

He turned his head towards the balcony.

'But, frankly, I'm not keen on it. What do you propose to say to your family?'

Hurt at his sending her, by implication, home to her people, Camille pulled herself together.

'I've nothing to say to them. These are things which only concern *me*, I presume. I've no inclination for family councils.'

'I entirely agree with you . . . provisionally.'

'Anyway, we can decide as from tomorrow.'

He raised his free hand to ward off this threat of a future.

'No. Not tomorrow. Today there isn't any tomorrow.'

In the doorway, he turned back.

'In the bathroom, you'll find my key and all the money we've got here.'

She interrupted with irony: 'Why not a hamper of provisions and a compass?'

She was putting on a brave act and surveyed him with one hand on her hip and her head erect on her handsome neck. 'She's building up my exit,' thought Alain. He wanted to reply with some similar last-minute coquetry, to toss his hair over his forehead and give her that narrowed look between his lashes which seemed to disdain what it rested on. But he renounced a pantomime which would look absurd when he was carrying a shopping-basket and confined himself to a vague bow in Camille's direction.

She kept up her expression of bravado and her theatrical stance. But before he went out, he could see more clearly, at a distance, the dark circles round her eyes and the moisture which covered her temples and her smooth, unlined neck.

Downstairs, he crossed the street automatically, the key of the garage in his hand. 'I can't do that,' he thought and he retraced his steps towards the avenue some way off where cruising taxis could be picked up at night. Saha mewed two or three times and he calmed her with his voice. 'I can't do that. But it really would be much pleasanter to take the car. Neuilly is impossible at night.' He was surprised, having counted on a blessed sense of release, to find himself losing his composure as soon as he was alone. Walking did not restore his calm. When, at last, he found a stray taxi, the five-minute drive seemed almost interminable.

He shivered in the warm night under the gas-jet, waiting for the gate to be opened. Saha, who had recognized the smell of the garden, was giving short sharp mews in the basket which he had put down on the pavement.

The scent of the wistarias in their second flowering came across the air and Alain shivered more violently, stamping from one foot to the other as if it were bitterly cold. He rang again but the house gave no sign of life in spite of the solemn, scandalous clamour of the big bell. At last a light appeared in the little buildings by the garage and he heard old Emile's dragging feet on the gravel.

'It's me, Emile,' he said when the colourless face of the old valet peered through the bars.

The Cat

'Monsieur Alain?' said Emile, exaggerating his quavering voice. 'Monsieur Alain's young lady isn't indisposed? The summer is so treacherous. Monsieur Alain has some luggage, I see.'

'No, it's Saha. Leave her, I'll carry her. No, don't turn up the gas-lamps, the light might wake Madame. Just open the front door for me and go back to bed.'

'Madame is awake – it was she who rang for me. I hadn't heard the big bell. In my first sleep, you see.'

Alain hurried ahead to escape Emile's chatter and the sound of his shaky footsteps following him. He did not stumble at the turnings of the paths though there was no moon that night. The great lawn, paler than the flower-beds, guided him. The dead, draped tree in the middle of the grass looked like a huge standing man with his coat over his arm. The smell of watered geraniums made Alain's throat tighten and he stopped. He bent down, opened the basket with groping fingers, and released the cat.

'Saha, our garden.'

He felt her glide out of the basket and, from pure tenderness, took no more notice of her. Like an offering, he gave her back the night, her liberty, the soft spongy earth, the wakeful insects, and the sleeping birds.

Behind the shutters on the ground floor, a lighted lamp was waiting and Alain's spirits fell again. 'To have to talk again, to have to explain to my mother . . . explain what? It's so simple. It's so difficult.'

All he longed for was silence, the room with the faded flowers on the wallpaper, his bed, and, above all, for vehement tears; great sobs as raucous as coughs that would be his secret, guilty compensation.

'Come in, darling, come in.'

He seldom went into his mother's room. His selfish aversion to medicine bottles and droppers, boxes of digitalis pills and homoeopathic remedies dated from childhood and was as acute as ever. But he could not resist the sight of the narrow, unadorned bed and of the woman with the thick white hair who was heaving herself up on her wrists.

'You know, Mother, there's nothing extraordinary about all this.'

He accompanied this idiotic statement with a smile of which he was promptly ashamed; a horizontal, stiff-cheeked smile. His tiredness had overwhelmed him in the sudden rush, making him do and say the exact opposite of what he meant to. He sat down by his mother's bedside and loosened his scarf.

'Forgive my appearance. I came just as I was. I arrive at preposterous times without giving you warning.'

'But you did give me warning,' said Mme Amparat.

She glanced at Alain's dusty shoes.

'Your shoes look like a tramp's.'

'I've only come from my place, Mother. But it was a long time before I could find a taxi. I was carrying the cat.'

'Ah,' said Mme Amparat, with an understanding look. 'You've brought back the cat?'

'Yes, of course. If you knew . . .'

He stopped, restrained by an odd discretion. 'These are things one doesn't tell. These stories aren't for parents.'

'Camille's not very fond of Saha, Mother.'

'I know,' said Mme Amparat.

She forced herself to smile and shook her wavy hair.

'That's extremely serious!'

'Yes. For Camille,' said Alain spitefully.

He got up and paced about among the furniture. It had white covers on it for the summer like the furniture in houses in the provinces. Having made up his mind not to denounce Camille, he could find nothing more to say.

'You know, Mother, there haven't been any screams or smashing of crockery. The glass dressing-table's still intact and the neighbours haven't come rushing up. Only I just need a little . . . a little time to be by myself . . . to rest. I won't hide it from you. I'm at the end of my tether,' he said, seating himself on the bed.

'No. You don't hide it from me,' said Mme Amparat. She laid a hand on Alain's forehead, turning up the young face, on which the pale stubble was beginning to show, towards the light. He complained, turning his changeable eyes away, and succeeded in holding off a little longer the storm of tears he had promised himself.

'If there aren't any sheets on my old bed, Mother, I'll wrap myself up in any old thing.'

'There are sheets on your bed,' said Mme Amparat.

At that, he threw his arms round his mother and kissed her blindly on her eyes and cheeks and hair. He thrust his face into her neck, stammered 'Good-night' and went out of the room, sniffing.

In the hall, he pulled himself together and did not go upstairs at once. The night which was ending called to him and so did Saha. But he did not go far. The steps down into the garden were far enough. He sat down on one of them in the darkness and his outstretched hand encountered the fur, the sensitive antennae-like whiskers and the cool nostrils of Saha.

She turned round and round on one spot according to the ritual of wild creatures when they caress. She seemed very small to him and light as a kitten. Because he was hungry himself, he thought she must be needing food.

'We'll eat tomorrow . . . quite soon now . . . it's almost daylight.'

Already she smelt of mint and geranium and box. He held her there, trusting and perishable, promised, perhaps, ten years of life. And he suffered at the thought of the briefness of so great a love.

'After you, probably anyone can have me who wants me. A woman, many women. But never another cat.'

A blackbird whistled four notes that rang through the whole garden. But the sparrows had heard it and answered. On the lawn and the massed flowerbeds, faint ghosts of colour began to appear. Alain could make out a sickly white, a dull red more melancholy than black itself, a yellow smeared on the surrounding green, a round yellow flower which began to revolve and become more yellow and was followed by eyes and moons. Staggering, dropping with sleep, Alain reached his room, threw off his clothes, uncovered the bed, and was unconscious almost as soon as he had slipped between the cool sheets.

Lying on his back with one arm flung out and the cat, silent and concentrated, kneading his shoulder, he was falling straight like a plummet into the very depths of sleep when a start brought him back to the daylight, the swaying of the awakened trees, and the blessed clanging of the distant trams.

'What's the matter with me? I wanted . . . Ah, yes! I wanted to cry.' He smiled and fell asleep again.

His sleep was feverish and crowded with dreams. Two or three times he thought he had woken up and was becoming conscious of where he was, but each time he was undeceived by the expression of the walls of his room. They were angrily watching the fluttering of a winged eye.

'But I'm asleep . . . of course, I'm asleep.'

'I'm asleep . . .' he answered again to the crunching gravel. 'I'm asleep, I tell you,' he called to two dragging feet that brushed against the door. The feet went away and the sleeper congratulated himself in his dream. But the dream had come to a head under the repeated solicitings and Alain opened his eyes.

The sun he had left on the window-sill in May had become an August sun and reached no farther than the satiny trunk of the tulip-tree opposite the house. 'How the summer has aged,' Alain said to himself. He got up, naked, looked for something to wear and found some pyjamas, too short and too tight in the sleeves and a faded dressing-gown which he joyfully pulled on. The

The Cat

window summoned him but he was stopped by Camille's photograph which he had left, forgotten, by his bed. Curiously, he examined the inaccurate, retouched little portrait; whitened here, blackened there. 'It's more like her than I supposed,' he thought. 'How was it I didn't notice it? Four months ago I used to say "Oh, she's entirely different from that. Much more subtle, not nearly so hard." But I was wrong.'

The long, steady breeze ran through the trees with a murmur like a river's. Dazed and quite painfully hungry, Alain lay back on his pillows. 'How delightful it is, a convalescence.' To complete the illusion a knuckle tapped on the door and the bearded Basque woman entered, carrying a tray.

'But I'd have had breakfast in the garden, Juliette!'

A kind of smile appeared among the grey hairs on her face.

'I thought as much. Would Monsieur Alain like me to take the tray down?'

'No, no, I'm too hungry. Leave that there. Saha'll come in by the window.'

He called the cat who rose from some invisible retreat as if she had come into existence at his call. She bounded up the vertical path of climbing plants and fell back again – she had forgotten her broken claws.

'Wait, I'm coming!'

He brought her back in his arms and they gorged themselves, she on milk and rusks, he on slices of bread and butter and scalding hot coffee. On one corner of the tray, a little rose adorned the lid of the honey-pot.

'It's not one of my mother's roses,' Alain decided. It was an ill-made, stunted little rose, picked from a low branch, that gave out the queer smell of a yellow rose. 'It's a little homage from the Basque.'

Saha, radiant, seemed to have grown plumper overnight. Her shirt-frill erect, her four darker stripes well marked between her ears, she stared at the garden with the eyes of a happy despot.

'How simple it all is, isn't it, Saha? For you, at any rate.'

Old Emile entered in his turn and insisted on removing Alain's shoes.

'There's one of the laces got very worn. Monsieur Alain hasn't another? It doesn't matter, I'll put one of my own laces in,' he bleated with emotion.

'Decidedly, it's my gala-day,' said Alain to himself. The word drove him back by contrast to all the things that only yesterday had been daily bothers; time to get up and dress, time to go to the Amparat office, time to come back to lunch with Camille.

'But I've nothing on earth to put on!' he cried.

In the bathroom he recognized the slightly rusty razor, the worn cake of pink soap and the old toothbrush, and used them with the delight of a man who has got shipwrecked for fun. But he had to come down in the outgrown pyjamas as the Basque woman had carried off his clothes.

'Come Saha, Saha.'

She went ahead and he ran after her uncertainly in a pair of frayed raffia sandals that kept threatening to slip off. He stretched out his shoulders to feel the cape of the mild sun fall on them and half closed his eyes that had grown unaccustomed to the green reverberations of the lawns and the hot colours which blazed above a serried block of crimson love-lies-bleeding and a tuft of red salvias bordered with heliotrope.

'Oh, the same, the very same salvias!'

Alain had always known that little heart-shaped bed as red and invariably bordered with heliotrope. It was shaded by a lean, ancient cherry-tree which occasionally produced a few cherries in September.

'I can see six . . . seven. Seven green cherries!'

He was talking to the cat who, with empty, golden

The Cat

eyes, had her mouth half open, almost overcome by the excessive scent of the heliotropes. Her face had the look of almost sickened ecstasy animals assume when confronted with an overpowering smell.

She ate a blade of grass to recover herself, listened to various voices, and rubbed her nose against the hard twigs of the privet hedge. But she did not display any exuberance, any irresponsible gaiety and she walked nobly, surrounded by the tiny silver halo which outlined all her body.

'Thrown, from a height of nine storeys,' Alain thought as he watched her. 'Grabbed ... or pushed. Perhaps she defended herself ... perhaps she escaped to be caught again and thrown over. Assassinated.'

He tried by such conjectures to arouse his just anger, but he did not succeed. 'If I truly, deeply loved Camille, how furious I should be.' Around him shone his kingdom, threatened like all kingdoms. 'My mother assures me that in less than twenty years no one will be able to keep on houses and gardens like this. She's probably right. I'm quite willing to lose them. I don't want to let *them* come into them.'

He was shaken by the sound of a telephone ringing in the house. 'Come, come now! I'm not frightened, am I? Camille's not so stupid as to telephone me. To do her justice, I've never known a young woman so restrained in using that instrument.'

But he could not stop himself from running awkwardly towards the house, losing his sandals and tripping over pebbles, and calling out: 'Mother! Who's that on the phone?'

The thick white dressing-gown appeared on the steps and Alain felt ashamed of having called out.

'How I love your big white dressing-gown, Mother! Always the same, always the same.'

'Thank you very much on behalf of my dressing-gown,' said Mme Amparat.

She kept Alain waiting a moment before she said: 'It was Monsieur Veuillet. It's half-past nine. Have you forgotten the ways of the house?'

She combed her son's hair with her fingers and buttoned up the too-tight pyjama jacket.

'You're a pretty sight. I suppose you don't intend to spend the rest of your life as a ragamuffin?'

Alain was grateful to her for questioning him so adroitly.

'No question of that, Mother. In a moment, I'll get busy about all that.'

Mme Amparat tenderly interrupted his vague, wide gesture.

'Tonight . . . where will you be?'

'Here!' he cried, and the tears welled up in his eyes.

'Good gracious, what a child!' said Mme Amparat and he took up the word with the earnestness of a boy scout.

'Perhaps I am a child, Mother. That's why I want to think over what I ought to do to get out of this childishness.'

'Get out of it how? By a divorce? That's a door that makes a lot of noise.'

'But which lets in some air,' he dared to retort sharply.

'Wouldn't a separation . . . a temporary one, give just as good results? What about a thorough rest or a little travel, perhaps?'

He threw up his arms indignantly.

'My poor dear Mother, you've no idea. You're a thousand miles from imagining.'

He was going to bring it all out and tell her about the attempted murder.

'Very well then, leave me a thousand miles! Such things don't concern me. Have a little . . . a little reserve,' said Mme Amparat hastily and Alain took advantage of a misunderstanding which was due to her innate modesty.

The Cat

'Now, Mother, there's still all the tiresome side to be thought of. I mean the family point of view which is all mixed up with the business side. From the Malmerts' point of view, my divorce will be quite indefensible, no matter how much Camille may be partly responsible. A bride of three and a half months! I can hear it all.'

'Where do you get the idea that there's a business side involved? You and the little Malmert girl aren't running a firm together. A married couple is not a pair of business partners.'

'I know, Mother. But if things turn out as I expect, there's bound to be a horrible period of formalities and interviews and so on. It's never as simple as everyone says, a divorce.'

She listened to her son with gentle forbearance. She knew that certain causes produce unexpected results and that, all through his life, a man has to be born many times with no other assistance than that of chance, of bruises, of mistakes.

'It's never simple to leave anything we've wanted to attach to ourselves,' said Mme Amparat. 'She's not so bad, that little Malmert. A little . . . coarse, a little lacking in manners. No, not so bad. At least, that's my way of seeing it. I don't want to impose it on you. We've plenty of time to think it over.'

'I've taken care of that,' said Alain with harsh politeness. 'And, at the moment, I prefer to keep a certain story to myself.'

His face suddenly lit up in a laugh that restored it to childhood. Standing up on her hind legs, Saha, using her paw as a spoon, was fishing drowned ants out of a brimming watering-can.

'Look at her, Mother! Isn't she a miraculous cat?'

'Yes,' sighed Mme Amparat. 'She's your chimera.'

He was always surprised when his mother employed an unusual word. He greeted this one with a kiss on her prematurely aged hand with its swollen veins and the little brown flecks which Juliette lugubriously called 'earth-stains'.

At the sound of the bell ringing at the gate, he jerked himself upright.

'Run and hide,' said Mme Amparat. 'We're right in the way of the tradesmen. Go and dress yourself. Do you want the butcher's little boy to catch you in that extraordinary get-up?'

But they both knew perfectly well that it was not the butcher's little boy ringing at the visitor's gate. Mme Amparat had already turned her back and was hurrying up the steps, holding up her dressing-gown in both hands. Behind the clipped hedge Alain could see the Basque woman retreating in disorder, her black silk apron flying in the wind, while a slither of slippers on the gravel announced the flight of old Emile. Alain cut off his escape.

'You have at least opened the gate?'

'Yes, Monsieur Alain. The young lady's behind her car.'

He lifted terrified eyes to the sky, hunched up his shoulders, as if he were in a hailstorm, and vanished.

'Well, that's certainly something like a picnic! I wish I'd had time to get dressed. Gracious, she's got a new suit!'

Camille had seen him and came straight up to him without overmuch haste. In one of those moments of almost hilarious anxiety that crop up on dramatic occasions, he thought confusedly: 'Perhaps she's come to lunch.'

Carefully and lightly made-up as she was, armed with black lashes and beautiful parted lips and shining teeth, she seemed all the same to lose her self-assurance when Alain came forward to meet her. For he was approaching without breaking away from the shelter of his protective atmosphere. He was treading his native lawn under the rich patronage of the trees, and Camille looked at him with the eyes of a poor person.

The Cat

'Forgive me, I look like a schoolboy who's suddenly shot up out of all knowledge. We didn't arrange to meet this morning, did we?'

'No. I've brought you your big suitcase. It's packed full.'

'But you shouldn't have done that!' he expostulated. 'I'd have sent Emile round today to fetch it.'

'Don't talk to me about Emile. I wanted to give him your case but the old idiot rushed off as if I'd got the plague. The case is down there by the gate.'

She flushed with humiliation, biting the inside of her cheek. 'It's beginning well,' said Alain to himself.

'I'm terribly sorry. You know what Emile's like. Listen,' he decided, 'let's go on the lawn inside the yew hedges. We'll be quieter there than in the house.'

He promptly repented his choice, for that clearing, enclosed in clipped yews and furnished with wicker chairs, had been the scene of their secret kisses in the old days.

'Wait while I dust the twigs off. You mustn't spoil the pretty suit. Incidentally, I don't know it, do I?'

'It's new,' said Camille in a tone of profound sadness, as if she had said: 'It's dead.'

She sat sideways, looking about her. Two arched arcades, one opposite the other, broke the circle of greenery. Alain remembered something Camille had once confided to him: 'You've no idea how your beautiful garden used to frighten me. I used to come here like the little girl from the village who comes to play with the son of the grand people at the château, in their park. And yet, when you come to think of it . . .' She had spoiled everything by that last remark. That 'when you come to think of it' implied the prosperity of Malmert Mangles compared with the declining house of Amparat.

He observed that Camille kept her gloves on. 'That's a precaution that defeats its own ends. Without those gloves it's possible I mightn't have thought about her

189

hands, about what they've done. Ah, at last a little ... just a little anger,' he said to himself, listening to his heartbeats. 'I've taken enough time about it.'

'Well,' said Camille sadly, 'well, what are you going to do? Perhaps you haven't decided yet.'

'Oh yes. I've decided,' said Alain.

'Ah!'

'Yes. I can't come back.'

'I quite understand that there's no question of your coming back today.'

'I don't want to come back.'

'Not at all? Ever?'

He shrugged his shoulders:

'What does that mean, ever? I don't want to come back. Not now. I don't want to.'

She watched him closely, trying to distinguish the false from the true, the deliberate irritation from the authentic shudder. He returned her suspicion for suspicion. 'She's small, this morning. She looks rather like a pretty shopgirl. She's lost in all this green. We've already exchanged a fair number of useless remarks.'

In the distance, through one of the arched arcades, Camille caught sight of traces of the 'alterations' on one side of the face of the house; a new window, some freshly painted shutters. Bravely she threw herself into the path of danger: 'Suppose I'd said nothing yesterday?' she suggested abruptly. 'Suppose you'd known nothing?'

'What a superb woman's idea,' he sneered. 'It does you honour.'

'Oh,' said Camille, shaking her head. 'Honour, honour. It wouldn't be the first time that the happiness of two married people depended on something that couldn't be owned up to ... or wasn't owned up to. But I've got the idea that by *not* telling you, I'd only have made things worse than ever for myself. I didn't feel you were ... I don't know how to put it.'

Hunting for the word, she mimed it by clenching her

The Cat

hands together. 'She's wrong to draw attention to her hands.' thought Alain vindictively. 'Those hands that have sent someone to their death.'

'After all, you're so awfully little on my side,' said Camille. 'That's true, isn't it?'

That struck him. He had to admit, mentally, that she was right. He said nothing and Camille insisted plaintively in a voice he knew all too well.

'Isn't it true, you hateful man?'

'But, good God!' he burst out. 'That's not the question. The only thing that can possibly interest me – interest me in *you* – is to know whether you regret what you've done, whether you can't stop thinking about it, whether it makes you sick to think of it. Remorse, good heavens, remorse! There does exist such a thing as remorse!'

Carried away he got up and strode round the circular lawn, wiping his brow on his sleeve.

'Ah!' said Camille with a contrite, affected expression. 'Naturally, of course. I'd a million times rather *not* have done it. I must have lost my head.'

'You're lying,' he cried, trying not to shout. 'All you regret is that you didn't bring it off! One's only got to listen to you, to look at you with your little hat on one side and your gloves and your new suit – everything you've so carefully arranged to charm me. If you really had any regret, I'd see it in your face. I'd feel it!'

He was shouting now, in a low grating voice, and was no longer quite master of the rage he had fostered. The worn stuff of his pyjamas burst at the elbow and he tore off nearly the whole of his sleeve and flung it on a bush.

At first Camille had eyes only for the gesticulating arm, extraordinarily white against the dark block of the yew hedge.

He put his hands over his eyes and forced himself to speak lower.

'A little blameless creature, blue as the loveliest dreams.

A little soul. Faithful, capable of quietly, delicately dying if what she has chosen fails her. You held *that* in your hands, over empty space . . . and you opened your hands. You're a monster. I don't wish to live with a monster.'

He uncovered his damp face and came nearer to Camille, trying to find words which would overwhelm her. Her breath came short and her eyes went from the white naked arm to the bloodless face which was no less white.

'An animal!' she cried indignantly. 'You're sacrificing me to an animal. I'm your wife, all the same! You're leaving me for an animal!'

'An animal? Yes, an animal.'

Apparently calm now, he hid behind a mysteriously informed smile. 'I'm perfectly willing to admit that Saha's an animal. If she's really one, what is there higher than this animal and how can I make Camille understand that? She makes me laugh, this barefaced little criminal, all virtue and indignation, who pretends to know what an animal is.' He was prevented from going further by the sound of Camille's voice.

'*You're* the monster!'

'Pardon?'

'Yes, you. Unfortunately I can't exactly explain why. But I assure you I'm right. *I* wanted to get rid of Saha. That wasn't at all admirable. But to kill something that gets in her way, that makes her suffer – it's the first idea that comes into a woman's head, especially a jealous woman's. It's perfectly normal. What's abnormal, what's monstrous, is you. It's . . .'

She was struggling to make herself understood and, at the same time, pointing to certain accidental things about Alain which did indeed suggest a kind of delirium: the torn-off sleeve; the trembling, insulting mouth; the cheek from which all the blood had retreated; the wild crest of dishevelled fair hair. He made no protest and did not deign to defend himself. He seemed lost in some exploration from which there was no return.

The Cat

'If I'd killed . . . or wanted to kill . . . a woman out of jealousy, you'd probably forgive me. But since I raised my hand against the cat, you're through with me. And yet you don't want me to treat you as a monster.'

'Have I said I didn't want you to?' he broke in haughtily.

She looked at him with terrified eyes and made a gesture of impotence. Sombre and detached, he watched the young, execrable gloved hand every time it moved.

'Now for the future, what are we going to do? What's going to happen to us, Alain?'

He was so brimming over with intolerance that he nearly groaned. He wanted to cry out: 'We separate, we keep silent, we sleep, we breathe without the other always there! I'll withdraw far, far away – under this cherry-tree for example, under the wing of that magpie. Or into the peacock tail of the hose-jet. Or into my cold room under the protection of a little golden dollar, a handful of relics and a Russian Blue cat.'

He mastered himself and deliberately lied:

'But nothing, at the moment. It's too soon to make a . . . a decision. Later on, we'll see.'

This final effort to be reasonable and sociable exhausted him. He tottered as soon as he took the first steps when he got up to accompany Camille. She accepted this vague conciliation with hungry hope.

'Yes, of course. It's much too soon. A little later on. Stay where you are, don't bother to come with me to the gate. With your sleeve, people will think we've been fighting. Listen, perhaps I'll go and get a little swimming at Ploumanach with Patrick's brother and sister-in-law. Because the mere idea of living with my family at this moment . . .'

'Yes, do that. Take the roadster,' proposed Alain.

She flushed and thanked him too effusively.

'I'll give it you back, you know, the minute I get back to Paris. You may need it. Don't hesitate to ask me for it back. Anyway, I'll let you know when I'm going and when I get back.'

'Already she's organizing it all. Already she's throwing out the strands of her web, throwing out bridges. Already she's picking up the fabric, darning it, weaving the threads together again. It's horrifying. Is that what my mother admires in her? Perhaps, after all, it's very fine. I don't feel any more capable of understanding her than of making things up with her. How completely at ease she is in everything I find insupportable. If she'd only go now, if she'd only go away!'

She was going away, carefully avoiding holding out her hand to him. But, under the arcade of clipped trees, she dared vainly to brush against him with her ripening breasts. Left alone, he collapsed into a chair and near him, on the wicker table, suddenly, like a miracle, appeared the cat.

A bend in the path and a gap in the leaves allowed Camille to see Alain and the cat once more from the distance. She stopped short and made a movement as if to retrace her steps. But she swayed only for an instant and then walked away faster than ever. For a while Saha, on guard, was following Camille's departure as intently as a human being. Alain was half-lying on his side, ignoring it. With one hand hollowed into a paw, he was playing deftly with the first green, prickly August chestnuts.

Anita Desai

extract from

Clear Light of Day

Tara returns from abroad to a family reunion in Delhi and finds that old antagonisms between herself and her sister are still unresolved.

Tara returns from abroad to a family reunion in Delhi and finds that old antagonisms between herself and her sister are still unresolved.

The koels began to call before daylight. Their voices rang out from the dark trees like an arrangement of bells, calling and echoing each other's calls, mocking and enticing each other into ever higher and shriller calls. More and more joined in as the sun rose and when Tara could no longer bear the querulous demand in their voices, she got up and went out on to the veranda to find the blank white glare of the summer sun thrusting in between the round pillars and the purple bougainvillaea. Wincing, she shielded her eyes as she searched for the birds that had clamoured for her appearance, but saw nothing. The cane chairs on the veranda stood empty. A silent line of ants filed past her feet and down the steps into the garden. Then she saw her sister's figure in white, slowly meandering along what as children they had called 'the rose walk'.

Dropping her hands to pick up the hem of her long nightdress, Tara ran down the steps, bowing her head to the morning sun that came slicing down like a blade of steel on to the back of her neck, and crossed the dry crackling grass of the lawn to join her sister, who stood watching, smiling.

The rose walk was a strip of grass, still streaked green and grey, between two long beds of roses at the far end of the lawn where a line of trees fringed the garden – fig and silver oak, mulberry and eucalyptus. Here there was still shade and, it seemed to Tara, the only bit of cultivation left; everything else, even the papaya and lemon trees, the bushes of hibiscus and oleander, the beds of canna lilies, seemed abandoned to dust and neglect, to struggle as they could against the heat and sun of summer.

But the rose walk had been maintained almost as it was. Or had it? It seemed to Tara that there had been far more roses in it when she was a child – luscious shaggy pink ones, small crisp white ones tinged with green, silky yellow ones that smelt of tea – and not just these small negligible crimson heads that lolled weakly on their thin stems. Tara had grown to know them on those mornings when she had trailed up and down after her mother, who was expecting her youngest child and had been advised by her doctor to take some exercise. Her mother had not liked exercise, perhaps not the new baby either, and had paced up and down with her arms folded and her head sunk in thought while the koels mocked and screamed and dive-bombed the trees. Tara had danced and skipped after her, chattering, till she spied something flashing from under a pile of fallen rose petals – a pearl, or a silver ring? – and swooped upon it with a cry that broke into her mother's reverie and made her stop and frown. Tara had excitedly swept aside the petals and uncovered – a small, blanched snail. Her face wrinkling with disgust, her mother turned and paced on without a word, leaving Tara on her knees to contemplate the quality of disillusion.

But here was Bim. Bim, grey and heavy now and not so unlike their mother in appearance, only awake, watchful, gazing at her with her fullest attention and appraisal. Bim laughed when she saw Tara panting slightly in her eagerness.

Tara laughed back. 'Bim, the old rose walk is still here.'

'Of course,' said Bim, 'only the roses grow smaller and sicker every year,' and she bent to shake a long spindly branch from which a fully bloomed rose dangled. It came apart instantly, revealing a small naked centre and a few pathetic stamens clinging to the bald

Clear Light of Day

head while the petals fell in a bunch to the chocolate earth below.

Tara's mouth opened in dismay at the destruction of a rose in full bloom – she would never have done what Bim did – and then she saw the petals that had clung together in a bunch in their fall part and scatter themselves. As she stared, a petal rose and tumbled on to its back and she saw uncovered the gleam of a – a pearl? a silver ring? Something that gleamed, something that flashed, then flowed – and she saw it was her childhood snail slowly, resignedly making its way from under the flower up a clod of earth only to tumble off the top on to its side – an eternal, miniature Sisyphus. She brought her hands together in a clap and cried, 'Look, a snail!'

Bim watched her sister in surprise and amusement. Was Tara, grown woman, mother of grown daughters, still child enough to play with a snail? Would she go down on her knees to scoop it up on a leaf and watch it draw its albuminous trail, lift its tiny antennae, gaze about it with protruding eyes and then, the instant before the leaf dipped and it slid downwards, draw itself into its pale pod?

As Tara performed the rites of childhood over the handy creature, Bim stood with lowered head, tugging at the hair that hung loosely about her face as she had done when she had sat beside her brother's bed that summer that he was ill, with her forehead lowered to the wooden edge of the bed, a book of poetry open on her lap, reading aloud the lines:

> Now sleeps the crimson petal, now the white;
> Nor waves the cypress in the palace walk;
> Nor winks the gold fin in the porphyry font:
> The firefly wakens . . .

Her lips moved to the lines she had forgotten she remembered till she saw the crimson petals fall in a heap on the snail in the mud, but she would not say them aloud to

Tara. She had no wish to use the lines as an incantation to revive that year, that summer when he had been ill and she had nursed him and so much had happened in a rush. To bury it all again, she put out her toe and scattered the petals evenly over the damp soil.

Now Tara's hand trembled, the leaf she held dipped and the doomed creature slid soundlessly back to earth.

They both stood staring as it lay there, shocked and still.

Tara murmured, 'You looked so like Mama from a distance, Bim – I mean, it's so – the sun –' for she realized at once that Bim would not like the comparison.

But Bim did not seem to hear, or care. 'Did you sleep at all?' she asked instead, for last night on arriving from the airport Tara had laughed and chattered and claimed to be too excited to sleep.

'How could I?' cried Tara, laughing, and talked of the koels in the morning, and the dog barking in the night, and the mosquitoes singing and stinging in the dark, as they walked together up the grassy path, Tara in her elegant pale blue nylon nightgown and elegant silver slippers and Bim in a curious shapeless hand-made garment that Tara could see she had fashioned out of an old cotton sari by sewing it up at both sides, leaving enough room for her arms to come through and cutting out a wide scoop for her neck. At the feet a border of blue and green peacocks redeemed the dress from total shabbiness and was – Tara laughed lightly – original. 'How he barks,' she repeated. 'Don't the neighbours complain?'

'I think they've grown used to him at last, or else they've realized it does no good to complain – I never will chain him up and, as I tell them when they do protest, he has such a beautiful voice, it's a pleasure to hear him. Not like the yipping and yapping of other people's little lap dogs,' she said with a toss of her grey head.

Although they spoke softly, no louder than a pair of birds to each other, the dog must have heard his name

Clear Light of Day

or realized he was being discussed. When Tara had come out on to the veranda he had been asleep under the wooden divan, hidden from her by the striped cotton rug with which it was covered, and he had only twitched his whiskers when he heard her pass by. Now he was suddenly out there on the grass walk with them, standing with his four legs very wide apart, his nose diving down into the clods of earth where the snail still lay futilely struggling to upright itself. As it finally flipped on to its edge, he gave a thunderous sneeze.

'Badshah!' cried Bim, delighted with his theatrical performance, and his one eye gleamed at the approval in her voice while the other followed the snail. But it disappeared under the rose petals once more and he came lolloping towards them, stubbed his moist nose into their legs, scuffed his dirty claws into their heels, salivated over their feet and then rushed past them in a show of leadership.

'He does like to be first always,' Bim explained.

'Is he nine now, Bim, or ten?'

'Twelve,' exclaimed Bim. 'See his old whiskers all white,' she said, diving forwards at his head and catching him by the ears, making him stand still with his head against her thigh. He closed his eyes and smiled a foolish smile of pleasure at her attention, then drew away with a long line of saliva dribbling from his jaws on to the grass, more copious and irregular than the fluent snail's. 'He is Begum's son, you know, and she lived to be – fourteen?'

Tara lifted her hair from the back of her neck and let it fall again, luxuriantly, with a sigh. 'How everything goes on and on here, and never changes,' she said. 'I used to think about it all,' and she waved her arm in a circular swoop to encompass the dripping tap at the end of the grass walk, the trees that quivered and shook with birds, the loping dog, the roses – 'and it is all exactly the same, whenever we come home.'

'Does that disappoint you?' Bim asked drily, giving her

a quick sideways look. 'Would you like to come back and find it changed?'

Tara's face was suddenly wound up tightly in a frown as if such a thought had never struck her before and she found it confusing. 'Changed? How? You mean the house newly painted, the garden newly planted, new people coming and going? Oh no, how could I, Bim?' and she seemed truly shocked by the possibility.

'But you wouldn't want to return to life as it used to be, would you?' Bim continued to tease her in that dry voice. 'All that dullness, boredom, waiting. Would you care to live that over again? Of course not. Do you know anyone who would – secretly, sincerely, in his innermost self – *really* prefer to return to childhood?'

Still frowning, Tara murmured meaninglessly, 'Prefer to what?'

'Oh, to going on – to growing up – leaving – going away – into the world – something wider, freer – brighter,' Bim laughed. 'Brighter! Brighter!' she called, shading her eyes against the brightness.

Tara's head sank low, her frown deepened. She could not trust Bim to be quite serious: in her experience, the elder sister did not take the younger seriously – and so all she said was a murmured, 'But you didn't, Bim.'

'I?' said Bim flatly, with her eyes still shaded against the light that streamed across the parched lawn and pressed against the trees at the fringe. 'Oh, I never go anywhere. It must seem strange to you and Bakul who have travelled so much – to come back and find people like Baba and me who have never travelled at all. And if we still had Mira-*masi* with us, wouldn't that complete the picture? This faded old picture in its petrified frame?' She stopped to pluck the dead heads off a rose bush dusted grey with disease. 'Mira-*masi* swigging secretly from her brandy bottle. Baba winding up his gramophone. And Raja, if Raja were here, playing Lord Byron on his death-bed. I, reading to him. That is what you might have come back to, Tara. How would you have liked that?'

Tara stood staring at her silver toes, at the clods of upturned earth in the beds and the scattered dead heads, and felt a prickle of distrust in Bim. Was Bim being cruel again? There could be no other motive. There could be no reply. She made none and Bim swung away and marched on, striding beside Badshah.

'That is the risk of coming home to Old Delhi,' she announced in the hard voice that had started up the prickle of distrust that ran over the tips of the hairs on Tara's arms, rippling them. 'Old Delhi does not change. It only decays. My students tell me it is a great cemetery, every house a tomb. Nothing but sleeping graves. Now *New* Delhi, they say is different. That is where things happen. The way they describe it, it sounds like a nest of fleas. So much happens there, it must be a jumping place. I never go. Baba never goes. And here, here nothing happens at all. Whatever happened, happened long ago – in the time of the Tughlaqs, the Khiljis, the Sultanate, the Moghuls – that lot.' She snapped her fingers in time to her words, smartly. 'And then the British built New Delhi and moved everything out. Here we are left rocking on the backwaters, getting duller and greyer, I suppose. Anyone who isn't dull and grey goes away – to New Delhi, to England, to Canada, the Middle East. They don't come back.'

'I must be peculiar then,' Tara's voice rose bravely. 'I keep coming back. And Bakul.'

'They pay your fare, don't they?' her sister said.

'But we *like* to come, Bim. We *must* come – if we are not to lose touch, I with all of you, with home, and he with the country. He's been planning this trip for months. When the girls arrive, and we go to Hyderabad for the wedding, Bakul wants to go on from there and do a tour of the whole country. He did it ten years ago and he says it is time to do it again, to make sure –'

'Of what?'

The question was sarcastic but Tara gave her head a toss of assurance and pride. Her voice too had taken on the strength and sureness that Bim noticed it usually did when she spoke of her husband. She told Bim evenly, 'That he hasn't forgotten, or lost touch with the way things are here. If you lose touch, then you can't represent your country, can you?' she ended, on an artificial note.

Bim of course detected that. She grunted, 'Hmph. I don't know. If that is what they tell you in the diplomatic service then that is what you must say.'

'But it's true,' Tara exclaimed, immediately dropping artificiality and sounding earnest. 'One has to come back, every few years, to find out and make sure again. I'd like to travel with him really. But there's the wedding in Raja's house, I suppose that will be enough to keep us busy. Are you coming, Bim? You and Baba? Couldn't we all go together? Then it will be a proper family reunion. Say you'll come! You have your summer vacation now. What will you do alone in Delhi, in the heat? Say you'll come!'

Bim said nothing. In the small silence a flock of mynahs suddenly burst out of the green domes of the trees and, in a loud commotion of yellow beaks and brown wings, disappeared into the sun. While their shrieks and cackles still rang in the air, they heard another sound, one that made Bim stop and stare and the dog lift his head, prick up his ears and then charge madly across to the eucalyptus trees that grew in a cluster by the wall. Rearing up on his hind legs, he tore long strips of blue and mauve bark off the silken pink tree-trunks and, throwing back his head, bellowed in that magnificent voice that Bim admired so much and that soured – or spiced – her relations with the neighbours.

'What is it?' called Tara as Bim ran forwards, lifting the peacock-edged nightie in order to hurry.

It was her cat, crouched in the fork of the blue and pink

tree, black and bitter at being stranded where she could not make her way down. Discovered first by the mynahs and then by Badshah, she felt disgraced.

Bim stood below her, stretching out her arms and calling, imploring her to jump. Badshah warned her not to do anything of the sort in a series of excited barks and whines. Tara waited, laughing, while the cat turned her angry face from one to the other, wondering whom to trust. At last Bim coaxed her down and she came slithering along the satiny bark, growling and grumbling with petulance and complaint at her undignified descent. Then she was in Bim's arms, safely cradled and shielded from Badshah's boisterous bumps and jumps, cuddled and cushioned and petted with such an extravagance of affection that Tara could not help raising her eyebrows in embarrassment and wonder.

Although Bim was rubbing her chin on the cat's flat-topped head and kissing the cold tips of her ears, she seemed to notice Tara's expression. 'I know what you're thinking,' she said. 'You're thinking how old spinsters go ga-ga over their pets because they haven't children. Children are the *real* thing, you think.'

Tara's look of surprise changed to guilt. 'What makes you say that? Actually, I was thinking about the girls. I was wondering —'

'Exactly. That's what I said. You think animals take the place of babies for us love-starved spinsters,' Bim said with a certain satisfaction and lowered the rumpled cat to the gravel walk as they came up to the house. 'But you're wrong,' she said, striding across the sun-slashed drive. 'You can't possibly feel for them what I do about these wretched animals of mine.'

'Oh Bim,' protested Tara, recognizing the moment when Bim went too far with which all their encounters had ended throughout their childhood, but she was prevented from explaining herself by the approach of a monstrous body of noise that seemed to be pushing its way out through a tight tunnel, rustily grinding through, and then emerged into full brassy volume, making the pigeons that lived on the ledge under the veranda ceiling throw up their wings and depart as if at a shot. It was not Bakul who was responsible for the cacophony. He was sitting – flabbily, flaccidly – in one of the cane chairs on the veranda with the tea tray in front of him, waiting for someone to come and pour. The noise beat and thrummed in one of the curtained rooms behind him. 'Sm-o-oke gets in your eyes,' moaned an agonized voice, and Tara sighed, and her shoulders drooped by a visible inch or two.

'Baba still plays the same old records?' she asked as they went slowly up the wide stairs between the massed pots of spider lilies and asparagus fern to the veranda.

'He never stops,' said Bim, smiling. 'Not for a day.'

'Don't you mind the noise?'

'Not any more,' said Bim, the lightness of her tone carefully contrived. 'I don't hear it any more.'

'It's loud,' complained Tara in a distressed voice. 'I used to look for records to send Baba – I thought he'd like some new ones – but they don't make 78s any more.'

'Oh he doesn't want any new records,' said Bim. 'He wouldn't play them. He loves his old ones.'

'Isn't it strange,' said Tara, wincing at the unmodulated roar that swept across the still, shady veranda in an almost visible onslaught of destruction.

'We *are* strange, I *told* you,' laughed Bim, striding across the tiled floor to the cane chairs and the tea tray. 'Oh, Bakul – *bhai*, you're up. Did you sleep?' she asked carelessly, sitting down in front of the tray. But instead of pouring out the tea she only lifted the milk jug and, bending down, filled a saucer for the cat who crouched before it and began to lap even before Bim had finished pouring so that some drops fell on her ears and on her whiskers, a sight that made Bim laugh as she held the jug, waiting for the cat to finish the milk. Then she bent and refilled the saucer. Tara, who had poured out a cup of tea for Bakul, waited for her to surrender the milk jug. When she did, there was very little left in it for Bakul's tea. Tara shook it to bring out a few reluctant drops.

'Is that enough?' she asked uneasily, even guiltily, handing the cup to Bakul.

He shrugged, making no reply, his lower lip thrust out in the beginning of a sulk. It may not have been the lack of milk, though, it might have been the din that stood about them like sheets of corrugated iron, making conversation impossible. As he stirred his tea thoughtfully with a little spoon, the song rose to its raucous crescendo as though the singer had a dagger plunged into his breast and were letting fly the heartfelt notes of his last plaint on earth. Then at last the rusty needle ground to a halt in the felt-embedded groove of the antique record and they all sighed, simultaneously, and sank back in their chairs, exhausted.

The pigeons that had retreated to the roof came fluttering back to their nests and settled down with small complaining sounds, guttural and comfortable. The bamboo screen in the doorway lifted and Baba came out for his tea.

He did not look as if he could be held responsible for any degree of noise whatsoever. Coming out into the veranda, he blinked as if the sun surprised him. He was in his pyjamas – an old pair with frayed ends, over which he wore a grey bush-shirt worn and washed almost to translucency. His face, too, was blanched, like a plant grown underground or in deepest shade, and his hair was quite white, giving his young, fine face a ghostly look that made people start whenever he appeared.

But no one on the veranda started. Instead, they turned on him their most careful smiles, trying to make their smiles express feelings that were comforting, reassuring, not startling.

Then Bim began to bustle. Now she called out for more

milk and a freshly refilled jug appeared from the pantry, full to the brim, before Bakul's widened eyes. Baba's cup was filled not with tea at all but with milk that had seemed so short a moment ago. Then, to top it, a spoonful of sugar was poured in as well and all stirred up with a tremendous clatter and handed, generously slopping, to Baba who took it without any expression of distaste or embarrassment and sat down on his little cane stool to sip it. Even the cat was transfixed by the spectacle and sat back on her haunches, staring at him with eyes that were circles of sharp green glass.

Only Bim seemed to notice nothing odd. Nor did she seem to think it necessary to speak to or be spoken to by Baba. She said, 'Look at her. You'd think I had given her enough but no, if we take any ourselves, she feels it's come out of her share.'

After a minute Tara realized she was speaking of the cat. Tara had lost the childhood habit of including animals in the family once she had married and begun the perpetual travels and moves that precluded the keeping of pets. It was with a small effort that she tore her eyes away from her brother and regarded the reproachful cat.

'She's too fat,' she said, thinking pet-owners generally liked such remarks. It was not a truthful one: the cat was thin as a string.

Bim put out her toe and scratched the creature under her ear but the cat turned angrily away, refusing such advances, and kept her eyes riveted on Baba till he had sipped the last drop of milk and put the cup back on the saucer with an unmistakably empty ring. Then she dropped sulkily on to the tiles and lay there noisily tearing at her fur with a sandpapered tongue of an angry red.

While the two women sat upright and tense and seethed with unspoken speech, the two men seemed dehydrated, emptied out, with not a word to say about anything. Only the pigeons cooed on and on, too lazy even to open their

Clear Light of Day

beaks, content to mutter in their throats rather than sing or call. The dog, stretched out at Bim's feet, writhed and coiled, now catching his tail between his teeth, now scrabbling with his paws, then bit at fleas and chewed his hair, weaving a thick mat of sound together with the cat who was busy with herself.

Bakul could bear it no longer. When his expression had grown so thin and so sour that it was about to split, he said, in a voice meant to be sonorous, 'Our first morning in Delhi.' To Bim's wonder and astonishment, Tara smiled at this radiantly as though he had made a profound remark on which he was to be congratulated. He gave her a small, confidential smile in return. 'What shall we do with it?'

Bim suddenly scratched her head as if the dog had started up something there. 'I don't know about you,' she said, 'but I have some of my students coming over this morning.'

'Students? But Bim, I thought your summer vacation had begun.'

'Yes, yes, but I wanted to give them some reading lists so they don't waste all their time walking up and down the Mall in Simla or going to the pictures. Then they reminded me I had missed a tutorial and had to see some of their papers. You see, it isn't just I who make them work – they make me work, too. So I asked them to come down here – they love to come, I don't know why. I'll go and get ready – I'm late. And you? You two? What will you do?'

Tara gazed at her husband for answer till he finally lowered his eyes by careful inches from the plaster moulding under the ceiling where the pigeons strutted and squatted and puffed themselves, and said, 'Perhaps I could ask my uncle to send us a car. Then we could go and call on some of my relations in New Delhi. They will be expecting us.'

'I'll get ready,' said Tara, instantly getting to her feet as if in relief.

Bim, who remembered her as a languid little girl, listless, a dawdler, noted her quick movements, her efficient briskness, with some surprise, but said nothing. Instead, she turned to Baba and drawled, slowly, 'And Baba,' as she bent forward and started stacking the cups on to the wooden tray. The others got up and stretched and walked about the veranda except for Baba, who sat calmly with his long white hands dangling loosely on either side of him. When Bim said 'Baba' again, he smiled gently at the floor. 'Baba,' she said again in a very low voice so that Bakul, standing on the steps and scrutinizing the bougainvillaea at the pillars, would not hear her, 'do you think you might go to the office today?'

Tara, who was at the door at the end of the veranda, about to lift the bamboo curtain and go in, paused. Somehow she had heard. Even in her rush to get dressed and be ready for anything her husband might suggest, she paused in shock to find that Bim still made attempts to send Baba to the office. Considering their futility, she thought they must have been given up long ago. She could not help stopping and turning round to see Bim piling up the tea tray and Baba seated on his small child's stool, smiling, his hands helplessly dangling, the busy dog licking, scratching, while the morning took another stride forward and stood with its feet planted on the tiled floor.

'Won't you go today, Baba?' Bim asked softly, not looking at him, looking at the tea cups. 'Do go. You could catch a bus. It'll make a change. We'll all be busy. Then come home to lunch. Or stay if you find it interesting.'

Baba smiled at the bare tiles. His hands swung as if loose in their sockets, as if in a light breeze. But there was no breeze: the heat dropped out of the sky and stood before them like a sheet of foil.

Then Bim got up and lifted the tray and went barefoot down the other end of the veranda to the pantry. Tara

Clear Light of Day

could hear her talking to the cook in her normal speaking voice. She turned and went into the room herself, unable to face the sight of Baba alone and hopeless on the veranda. But Baba did not stay either. He must have gone back to his room, too, for in another minute or two she heard that ominous roar pushing its way through the tunnel and emerging as the maudlin clamour of 'Lilli Marlene'.

'Now this is precisely what I told you,' Bakul said, bustling into the bedroom after making his phone call. 'I pointed out to you how much more convenient it would be to stay with my uncle and aunt, right in the centre of town, on Aurangzeb Road, how it would save us all the trouble of finding a car to travel up and down in . . .'

Tara, who was bending over the bed, laying out his clothes, straightened and said in a strained voice, 'But I had not meant to go anywhere. I only wanted to stay at home.'

He flicked his silk dressing gown open and said impatiently, 'You know you can't do that when there's so much to do – relations to visit, colleagues to look up, all that shopping you had planned to do –'

'I'll wait till the girls come. I'll go shopping with them,' said Tara with an unaccustomed stubbornness. She held up a cluster of ties and waited, a bit sullenly, for him to choose one.

He put out his hand and picked one of broadly striped raw silk and said, 'You surely don't mean that. You can't just sit about with your brother and sister all day, doing nothing.'

'But it's what I want – just to be at home again, with them. And of course there are the neighbours – I'll see them. But I don't want to go anywhere today, and I don't want to go to New Delhi at all.'

'Of course you will come,' Bakul said quite sharply,

going towards the bathroom with an immense towel he had picked up. 'There's no question about that.'

When the bathroom door had shut, Tara went out on to the veranda again. The veranda ran all around the house and every room opened out on to it. This room had been hers and Bim's when they were girls. It opened on to the dense grove of guava trees that separated the back of the house from the row of servants' quarters. Bright morning sounds of activity came from them – a water tap running, a child crying, a cock crowing, a bicycle bell ringing – but the house was separated from them by the thick screen of low, dusty guava trees in which invisible parrots screamed and quarrelled over the fruit. Now and then one fell to the ground with a soft thud. Tara could see some lying in the dust with chunks bitten out by the parrots. If she had been younger – no, if she had been sure Bakul would not look out and see – she would have run down the veranda steps and searched for one that was whole. Her mouth tingled with longing to bite into that hard astringent flesh under the green rind. She wondered if her girls would do it when they arrived to spend their holidays here. No, they would not. Much travelled, brought up in embassies, fluent in several languages, they were far too sophisticated for such rustic pleasures, she knew, and felt guilty over her own lack of that desirable quality. She had fooled Bakul into believing that she had acquired it, that he had shown her how to acquire it. But it was all just dust thrown into his eyes, dust.

Further up the veranda was Baba's room and from behind the light bamboo curtain that hung in the doorway came the guttural rattling of 'Don't Fence Me In'. For a while Tara leant her head against a pillar, listening. It was not unfamiliar, yet it disturbed.

A part of her was sinking languidly down into the passive pleasure of having returned to the familiar – like a pebble, she had been picked up and hurled back

Clear Light of Day

into the pond, and sunk down through the layer of green scum, through the secret cool depths to the soft rich mud at the bottom, sending up a line of bubbles of relief and joy. A part of her twitched, stirred like a fin in resentment: why was the pond so muddy and stagnant? Why had nothing changed? She had changed – why did it not keep up with her?

Why did Bim allow nothing to change? Surely Baba ought to begin to grow and develop at last, to unfold and reach out and stretch. But whenever she saw them, at intervals of three or five years, all was exactly as before.

Drawing away from the pillar, she moved towards his room, propelled by her disturbance, by her resentment at this petrified state in which her family lived. Bakul was right to criticize it, disapprove of it. Yes, he was right, she told herself and, lifting the dusty bamboo curtain, slipped into Baba's room.

He was sitting on his bed, a string cot spread with a cotton rug and an old sheet, that stood in the centre of the room under the slowly revolving electric fan. He was crouched low, listening raptly to the last of 'Don't Fence Me In' unwinding itself on the old HMV gramophone on a small bamboo table beside his bed. The records, not so very many of them – there must have been breakages after all – were stacked on a shelf beneath the table in their tattered yellow sleeves. The string cot, the table, the HMV gramophone, a canvas chair and a wardrobe – nothing else. It was a large room and looked bare. Once it had been Aunt Mira's room, and crowded. Baba looked up at her.

Tara stood staring, made speechless by his fine, serene face, the shapeliness of his long fingers, his hands that either moved lightly as if in a breeze or rested calmly at his sides. He was an angel, she told herself, catching her lip between her teeth – an angel descended to earth, unsoiled by any of it.

213

But then why did he spend his days and years listening to this appalling noise? Her daughters could not live through a day without their record-player either; they, too, kept it heaped with records that slipped down on to the turntable in a regular sequence, keeping them supplied with an almost uninterrupted flow of music to which they worked and danced with equal ease. But, she wanted to explain to him, theirs was an ever-growing, ever-changing collection, their interest in it was lively, fresh, developing all the time. Also, she knew they would outgrow their need of it. Already Maya had friends who took her to concerts from which she returned with a sheen of uplifting pleasure spread across her face and talked of learning to play the flute. Soon it would be behind her – this need for an elemental, primitive rhythm automatically supplied. But Baba would never leave his behind, he would never move on.

Her anguish and impatience made her say, very quickly and loudly, as the record ground to a halt and before Baba could turn it over, 'Are you going out this morning, Baba? We've sent for a car – can we give you a lift?'

Baba lifted the smoothly curving metal arm off the record and sat with his hand resting on it, protectively. It was clear he would have liked to turn over the record but he hesitated, politely, his eyes cast down, flickering slightly as if with fear or guilt.

Tara too began to squirm with guilt at having caused him this panic. 'Are you, Baba?'

He glanced at her very quickly, with a kind of pleading, and then looked away and shook his head very slightly.

This made her cry out, 'But don't you go to the office in the mornings?'

He kept his head lowered, smiling slightly, sadly.

'Never?'

The room rang with her voice, then with silence. In the shaded darkness, silence had the quality of a looming dragon. It seemed to roar and the roar to reverberate,

Clear Light of Day

to dominate. To escape from it would require a burst of recklessness, even cruelty. Was it to keep it at bay that Baba played those records so endlessly, so obsessively? But it was not right. She herself had been taught, by her husband and by her daughters, to answer questions, to make statements, to be frank and to be precise. They would have none of these silences and shadows. Here things were left unsaid and undone. It was what they called 'Old Delhi decadence'. She knotted her fingers together in an effort to break it.

'Do you think you will go to the office today?' she persisted, beads of perspiration welling out of her upper lip.

Now Baba took his hand off the gramophone arm, relinquishing it sadly, and his hands hung loosely at his sides, as helplessly as a dead man's. His head, too, sank lower and lower.

Tara was furious with herself for causing him this shame, this distress. She hated her probing, her questioning with which she was punishing him. Punishing him for what? For his birth – and for that he was not responsible. Yet it was wrong to leave things as they were – she knew Bakul would say so, and her girls, too. It was all quite lunatic. Yet there was no alternative, no solution. Surely they would see there was none. Sighing, she said in a tone of defeat, 'I'll ask Bim.'

She had said the right thing at last. Quite inadvertently, even out of cowardice. It made Baba raise his head and smile, sweetly and gently as he used to do. He even nodded, faintly, in agreement. Yes, Bim, he seemed to say, Bim will decide. Bim can, Bim will. Go to Bim. Tara could not help smiling back at his look of relief, his happy dependence. She turned to leave the room and heard him lift the record and turn it over. As she escaped down the veranda she heard Bing Crosby's voice bloating luxuriantly out into 'Ah-h'm dream-in'' of a wha-ite Christmas . . .'

*

But now something had gone wrong. The needle stuck in a groove. 'Dream-in', dream-in', dream-in" hacked the singer, his voice growing more and more officious. Shocked, Baba's long hands moved with speed to release it from the imprisoning groove. Then he found the needle grown so blunt and rusty that, as he peered at it from every angle and turned it over and over with a melancholy finger, he accepted it would do no longer. He sighed and dropped it into the little compartment that slid out of the green leather side of the gramophone and the sight of all the other obsolete needles that lay in that concealed grave seemed to place a weight on his heart. He felt defeated and infinitely depressed. Too depressed to open the little one-inch square tin with the picture of the dog on it, and pick out a clean needle to insert in the metal head. It remained empty, toothless. The music had come to a halt. Out in the garden a koel called its wild, brazen call. It was not answered so it repeated the call, more demandingly.

For a while Baba paced about the room, his head hanging so low that one would have thought it unnatural, physically impossible. Now and then he lifted his hands to his head and ran his long bony fingers nervously through his white hair so that it was grooved and furrowed like the lines of an aged face. The silence of the room, usually so loud with the rollicking music of the forties, seemed to admit those other sounds that did not soothe or protect him but, on the contrary, startled him and drove him into a panic – the koel calling, calling out in the tall trees, a child crying in the servants' quarters, a bicycle dashing past, its bell jangling. Baba began to pace up and down faster and faster as if he were running away from it. Then, when he could bear it no longer, he went to the cupboard and pulled open its door, searched frantically for clothes to wear, pulled out whatever seemed to him appropriate, and began to dress hurriedly, dropping his pyjamas on to the floor, flinging others on to the sagging

Clear Light of Day

canvas chair by the bed, hurriedly buttoning and lacing and pulling on and off till he felt sufficiently clothed.

Without a glance into the mirror on the cupboard door or an attempt to tidy the room, he fled from it.

Tara, still sitting on the steps with an arm around the veranda pillar, waiting for Bakul to emerge so that she could go in and dress, saw a pale elongated shape lurching and blundering down the veranda and on to the drive, bent almost double as if in pain or in fear – or perhaps because of the sun beating down with white-hot blows. She stood up in fright and it took her a minute to realize it was Baba.

By then he was already at the gate and had turned out of it into the road. Tara hurried down the steps on to the drive, shading her eyes, her mouth open to call him, but she stopped herself. How old was Baba now? If he wanted to go out, ought he at his age to be called back and asked to explain?

If she had, Baba would have been grateful. If anything, anyone had stopped him now, he would have collapsed with relief and come crawling home like a thirsty dog to its water bowl. Once, when he had ventured out, a bicycle had dashed against him as he stood hesitating at the edge of the road, wondering whether to cross. The bicyclist had fallen and cursed him, his voice rising to a shrill peak and then breaking on Baba's head like eggs, or slivers of glass. Another time, he had walked as far as the bus stop but when the bus had arrived there was such a scuffle between those trying to get off and those trying to get on that people were pushed and bumped and shoved and when one man was somehow expelled from the knotted mob, Baba saw his sleeve torn off his shirt, hanging limply as if he had no arm, were an amputee. Baba thought of the man's face, of the ruined shirt. He heard all those shouts again, the shouts that had been flung at his head, knocking into him till he was giddy with blows.

He was small. He was standing on the dunes. There was nothing here but the silver sand and the grey river and the white sky. But out of that lunar stillness a man loomed up, military in a khaki uniform and towering scarlet turban, and roughly pushed past him shouting *'Hato! Hato!'* to make way for a white horse that plunged up out of the dunes and galloped past Baba, crouching on his knees in the sand, the terror of the horse hooves beating through his head, the sand flying back into his face and the voice still commanding *'Hato! Hato!'*

His knees trembled in anticipation, knowing he would be forced down, or flung down if he continued down the road. But it was as if Tara had given him a push down a steep incline. She had said he was to go. Bim had said he was to go. Bim and Tara, both of them, wanted him to go. He was going.

His feet in their unfastened sandals scuffed through the dust of Bela Road. Sharp gravel kept slipping into them, prodding him. His arms swung wildly, propelling him along. His head bobbed, his white hair flopped. His eyes strained and saw black instead of white. Was he going to faint? Would he fall? Should he stop? Could he? Or would they drive him on? *'Hato! Hato!'*

Then he heard the crash he knew would come. Instantly he flinched and flung up his arm to protect his face. But it was not he who had crashed. It was a cart carrying a load of planks that had tipped forwards as the horse that drew it fell first on to its knees, then on to its nose and lay squirming in the middle of the road. Baba shrank back, against the wall, and held his arm before his eyes but still he saw what happened: the driver, a dark man with a red rag tied about his head, leapt down from the mound of planks and raised his arm, and a switch or a whip, and brought it down with all his force on the horse's back. The horse gave a neighing scream, reared up its head with the wet, wringing mane streaming from it, and then stretched out on the stones, a shiver running up and down its legs

Clear Light of Day

so that it twitched and shook. Again the man raised the whip, again it came down on the horse's back, neck, head, legs – again and again. Baba heard screams but it was the man who screamed as he whipped and slashed and beat, screamed abuse at the animal who did not move but seemed to sink lower and lower into the dust. 'Swine! Son of a swine!' the man panted, red eyes straining out of the dark face. *'Suar! Sala! Suar ka bachcha!'* All the time his arm rose up in the air and came down, cutting and slashing the horse's flesh til black stuff oozed on to the white dust and ran and spread, black and thick, out of the horse.

Baba raise both his arms, wrapped them about his head, his ears and eyes, tightly, and, blind, turned and stumbled, almost fell but ran on back up the road to the house, to the gate. His shoulder hit the white gate-post so that he lurched and fell to his knees, then he rose and stumbled, his arms still doubled over his eyes so that he should not see and about his ears so that he should not hear.

Tara saw him as he came climbing up the steps on his knees and ran forwards to help him to his feet. Tugging at his arms to drag them away from his face, she cried, 'Are you hurt? Baba, Baba, say – are you hurt? Has someone hurt you?' Pulling his arms away, she uncovered his face and saw his eyes rolling in their sockets like a wild horse's, his lips drawn back from his teeth as if he were racing, and the blue-black shadows that always lay under his eyes spreading over his face like a bruise, wet with his tears. Then she stopped demanding that he should speak, and helped him to his room, on to his bed, rushed out and down the veranda in search of Bim, in search of water. There was no one on the veranda or in the kitchen. The cook had gone out to market. She tilted the earthen water jar to fill a tumbler and hurried back with it, her legs cutting into her nightgown and the water spilling in splashes on to the tiles as she hurried, thinking of Baba's face. She lifted his head to help him drink but most of it ran down his chin into his shirt. When she lowered his head, he shrank into a heap, shivering, and she stayed a while, smoothing his hair and patting his cheek till she thought he was quieter, nearly asleep, then went to find Bim.

But Bakul stepped out of their room, his tie in one hand and his shoes in another, to ask, 'Aren't you getting ready, Tara? We'll be late. The car will be here any minute and you know Uncle is very punctual. We mustn't keep him waiting.' He went back to finish dressing without having seen Tara's face or anything there to stop him.

He noticed nothing – a missing shoe-horn and frayed laces having presented him with a problem meanwhile – till she came in, her shoulders sloping, her hair hanging, and sat down on the foot of the bed instead of going in to dress. Then he spoke more sharply. 'Why aren't you getting ready?'

'I don't think I'll come after all,' she mumbled. She always mumbled when she was afraid, as if she hoped not to be heard.

She expected him to explode of course. But even for Bakul it was too hot, the atmosphere of the old house too turgid and heavy to push or manipulate. Bending down to tie two perfect bows, he merely sighed, 'So, I only have to bring you home for a day, Tara, and you go back to being the hopeless person you were before I married you.'

'Yes,' she muttered, 'hopeless.' Like Baba's, her face looked bruised.

'And you won't let me help you. I thought I had taught you a different life, a different way of living. Taught you to execute your will. Be strong. Face challenges. Be decisive. But no, the day you enter your old home, you are as weak-willed and helpless and defeatist as ever.' He stood up and looked down to see if his shoes were bright enough to reflect his face. Nothing less would do. Yes,

yes. He shrugged his shoulders inside his shirtsleeves. 'What should I do with you? I ought to take you away immediately. Let us go and stay with my uncle in New Delhi.'

'No.' She shook her head. 'Leave me here.'

'You're not happy here,' he said, and the unexpectedness of these words made her look up at him, questioning. 'Look at your face – so sad, so worried.' He even came close to her and touched her cheek, very lightly, as if he could hardly bear the unpleasant contact but forced himself to do it out of compassion. 'If only you would come with me, I would show you how to be happy. How to be active and busy – and then you would be happy. If you came.'

But she shook her head. She felt she had followed him enough, it had been such an enormous strain, always pushing against her grain, it had drained her of too much strength, now she could only collapse, inevitably collapse.

Bakul had married her when she was eighteen. He knew her. He left her, saying, 'Then I'll tell Uncle you are busy with your own family and will come another time,' and went out to wait for the car.

He passed Bim as he went through the drawing room. Bim was holding court there – seated on the divan with her legs drawn up under her – like Tara, she had not dressed yet and was still in her nightdress – and on the carpet below sat the students, a brightly coloured bunch of young girls in jeans and in *salwar-kameez*, laughing and eyeing each other and him as he went through. He raised his eyebrows at Bim and gave her a significant look as if to say, '*This* – your history lesson?'

Bim nodded and laughed and wriggled her toes and waggled her pencil, completely at ease and without the least sense of guilt. 'No, no, you won't,' he heard her say as he went out on to the veranda, 'you won't get me started on the empress Razia – nor on the empress

Nur Jehan. I refuse. We must be serious. We are going to discuss the war between Shivaji and Aurangzeb – no empresses.'

The girls groaned exaggeratedly. 'Please, miss,' he heard them beg as he sat down on a creaking cane chair to wait, 'please let's talk about something interesting, miss. You will enjoy it too, miss.'

'Enjoy? You rascals, I haven't asked you here to enjoy yourselves. Come on, Keya, please begin – I'm listening –' and then there was some semblance of order and of a tutorial going on that Bakul could almost recognize and approve. He wondered, placing one leg over the other reflectively, as he had sometimes wondered when he had first started coming to this house, as a young man who had just entered the foreign service and was in a position to look around for a suitable wife, if Bim were not, for all her plainness and brusqueness, the superior of the two sisters, if she had not those qualities – decision, firmness, resolve – that he admired and tried to instil in his wife who lacked them so deplorably. If only Bim had not that rather coarse laugh and way of sitting with her legs up . . . now Tara would never . . . and if her nose were not so large unlike Tara's which was small . . . and Tara was gentler, more tender . . . He sighed a bit, shifting his bottom on the broken rattan seat of the chair. Things were as they were and had to be made the most of, he always said. At least in this country, he sighed, and just then his uncle's car appeared at the gate, slowly turned in, its windshield flooded by the sun, and came up the drive to park beneath the bougainvillea.

Bim did get Tara to smile before the morning was over, however. Tara was leaning against the veranda pillar, watching the parrots quarrel in the guava trees, listening for a sound from Baba's room, hoping to hear a record played, when Bim came out with her band of girls

Clear Light of Day

and suddenly shouted, 'Ice-cream! Caryhom Ice-cream-wallah!' and, before Tara's startled eyes, a bicycle with a small painted van attached to it that had been rolling down the empty, blazing road stopped and turned in at the gate with its Sikh driver beaming broadly at the laughing girls and their professor.

Seeing Tara, Bim called out, 'Look at these babies, Tara. When they hear the Caryhom ice-cream man going by they just stop paying any attention to my lecture. I can't do anything till I've handed each of them a cone. I suppose strawberry cones are what you all want, you babies? Strawberry cones for all of them, *Sardar-ji*,' she ordered and stood laughing on the steps as she watched him fill the cones with large helpings of pink ice-cream and hand them to the girls, who were giggling, Tara realized, as much at their professor as at this childish diversion.

Bim noticed nothing. Swinging her arms about, she saw to it that each girl got her cone and then had one of them, a pretty child dressed in *salwar-kameez* patterned with pink and green parrots, carry a dripping cone down the veranda to Tara. 'Tara,' she called, 'that's for you. *Sardar-ji* made it specially for you,' she laughed, smiling at the ice-cream man who had a slightly embarrassed look, Tara thought. Embarrassed herself, she took the slopping cone from the girl and licked it to please Bim, her tongue recoiling at the synthetic sweetness. 'Oh Bim, if my daughters were to see me now – or Bakul,' she murmured, as Bim walked past holding like a cornucopia a specially heaped and specially pink ice-cream cone into Baba's room. Tara stopped licking, stared, trying to probe the bamboo screen into the room where there had been silence and shadows all morning. She heard Bim's voice, loud and gay, and although Baba made no audible answer, she saw Bim come out without the cone and knew Baba was eating it, perhaps quite happily. There was something magnetic about the icy pink sweetness, the synthetic sweet pinkness, she reflected, licking.

Now Bim let out a shout and began to scold. One of the girls had tipped the remains of her cone on to the veranda steps for the dog to lick – she had seen him standing by, watching, his tongue lolling and leaking. 'You silly, don't you know dogs shouldn't eat anything sweet? His hair will fall out – he'll get worms – it'll be your fault – he'll be spoilt – he won't eat his bread and soup now.'

'Let him enjoy himself, miss,' said the girl, smirking at the others because they all knew perfectly well how pleased Bim was to see them spoil her dog.

Tara narrowed her eyes at the spectacle of Bim scolding her students and smiling with pleasure because of the attention they had paid her dog, who had now licked up all the ice-cream and was continuing to lick and lick the floor as if it might have absorbed some of the delicious stuff. Remembering how Bim used to scold her for not disciplining her little daughters and making them eat up everything on their plates or go to bed on time, she shook her head slightly.

But the ice-cream did have, she had to admit, a beneficial effect all round: in a little while, as the students began to leave the house, prettily covering their heads against the sun with coloured veils and squealing as the heat of the earth burnt through their slippers, the gramophone in Baba's room stirred and rumbled into life again. Tara was grateful for it. She wished Bakul could see them now – her family.

When Bakul did come, late in the afternoon, almost comatose from the heat and the heavy lunch he had eaten, to fall on to his bed and sleep, this passage of lightness was over, or overcome again by the spirit of the house.

Tara, upright in a chair, tried first to write a letter to her daughters, then decided it was too soon, she would wait till she had more to say to them, and put the letter

Clear Light of Day

away in her case and tried to read instead, a book from the drawing-room bookshelf that had been there even when she was a child – Jawaharlal Nehru's *Letters To A Daughter* in a green cloth binding – and sitting on the stuffed chair, spongy and clammy to touch, she felt that heavy spirit come and weigh down her eyelids and the back of her neck so that she was pinned down under it, motionless.

It seemed to her that the dullness and the boredom of her childhood, her youth, were stored here in the room under the worn dusty red rugs, in the bloated brassware, amongst the dried grasses in the swollen vases, behind the yellowed photographs in the oval frames – everything, everything that she had so hated as a child and that was still preserved here as if this were the store-room of some dull, uninviting provincial museum.

She stared sullenly, without lifting her head, at a watercolour above the plaster mantelpiece – red cannas painted with some watery fluid that had trickled weakly down the brown paper: who could have painted that? Why was it hung here? How could Bim bear to look at it for all of her life? Had she developed no taste of her own, no likings that made her wish to sweep the old house of all its rubbish and place in it things of her own choice? Tara thought with longing of the neat, china-white flat in Washington, its cleanliness, its floweriness. She wished she had the will to get to her feet and escape from this room – where to? Even the veranda would be better, with the pigeons cooing soothingly, expressing their individual genius for combining complaint and contentment in one tone, and the spiky bougainvillaeas scraping the outer walls and scattering their papery magenta flowers in the hot, sulphur-yellow wind. She actually got up and went to the door and lifted the bamboo screen that hung there, but the blank white glare of afternoon slanted in and slashed at her with its flashing knives so that she quickly dropped the screen. It creaked into place, releasing a noseful of dust. On the wall a gecko clucked loudly and disapprovingly at this untoward disturbance. She went back to the chair. If she could sleep, she might forget where she was, but it was not possible to sleep with the sweat trickling down one's face in rivulets and the heat enclosing one in its ring of fire.

Bakul said one could rise above the climate, that one could ignore it if one filled one's mind with so many thoughts and activities that there was no room for it. 'Look at me,' he had said the winter that they froze in Moscow. 'I don't let the cold immobilize me, do I?' and she and the girls, swaddled in all their warm clothing and the quilts and blankets off their beds, had had to agree that he did not. And gradually he had trained her and made her into an active, organized woman who looked up her engagement book every morning, made plans and programmes for the day ahead and then walked her way through them to retire to her room at night, tired with the triumphant tiredness of the virtuous and the dutiful. Now the engagement book lay at the bottom of her trunk. Bim had said nothing of engagements and, really, she could not bear to have any in this heat. The day stretched out like a sheet of glass that reflected the sun – too bare, too exposed to be faced.

Out in the garden only the coppersmiths were awake, clinging to the tree-trunks, beating out their mechanical call – tonk-tonk-tonk. Tonk-tonk-tonk.

Here in the house it was not just the empty, hopeless atmosphere of childhood, but the very spirits of her parents that brooded on – here they still sat, crouched about the little green baize folding table that was now shoved into a corner with a pile of old *Illustrated Weeklies* and a brass pot full of red and yellow spotted canna lilies on it as if to hold it firmly down, keep it from opening up with a snap and spilling out those stacks of cards, those long note-books and thin pencils with which her parents had sat, day after day and year after year till their deaths,

Clear Light of Day

playing bridge with friends like themselves, mostly silent, heads bent so that the knobs in their necks protruded, soft stained hands shuffling the cards, now and then speaking those names and numbers that remained a mystery to the children, who were not allowed within the room while a game was in progress, who had sometimes folded themselves into the dusty curtains and stood peeping out, wondering at this strange, all-absorbing occupation that kept their parents sucked down into the silent centre of a deep, shadowy vortex while they floated on the surface, staring down into the underworld, their eyes popping with incomprehension.

Raja used to swear that one day he would leap up on to the table in a lion-mask, brandishing a torch, and set fire to this paper-world of theirs, while Bim flashed her sewing scissors in the sunlight and declared she would creep in secretly at night and snip all the cards into bits. But Tara simply sucked her finger and retreated down the veranda to Aunt Mira's room where she could always tuck herself up in the plum-coloured quilt that smelt so comfortingly of the aged relation and her ginger cat, lay her head down beside that purring creature and feel such a warmth, such a softness of comfort and protection as not to feel the need to wreck her parents' occupation or divert their attention. It would have frightened her a bit if they had come away, followed her and tried to communicate with her.

And now she stirred uneasily in her chair although it held her damply as if with suckers, almost afraid that they would rise from their seats, drop their cards on the table and come towards her with papery faces, softly shuffling fingers, smoky breath, and welcome her back, welcome her home.

Once her father had risen, padded quietly to her mother's bedroom behind that closed door, and Tara had slipped in behind him, folded herself silently into the faded curtain and watched. She had seen him lean over her mother's bed and quickly, smoothly press a little shining syringe into her mother's arm that lay crookedly on the blue cover, press it in very hard so that she tilted her head back with a quick gasp of shock, or pain – Tara saw her chin rising up into the air and the grey head sinking back into the pillow and heard a long, whimpering sigh like an air-bag minutely punctured so that Tara had fled, trembling, because she was sure she had seen her father kill her mother.

All her life Tara had experienced that fear – her father had killed her mother. Even after Aunt Mira and Bim and Raja had explained to her what it was he did, what he kept on doing daily, Tara could not rid herself of the feel of that original stab of suspicion. Sometimes, edging up close to her mother, she would study the flabby, floury skin punctured with a hundred minute needle-holes, and catch her breath in an effort not to cry out. Surely these were the signs of death, she felt, not of healing?

Now she stared fixedly at the door in the wall, varnished a bright hideous brown with the varnish swelling into blisters or cracking into spidery patterns in the heat, and felt the same morbid, uncontrollable fear of it opening and death stalking out in the form of a pair of dreadfully familiar ghosts that gave out a sound of paper and filled her nostrils with white insidious dust.

In the sleeping garden the coppersmiths beat on and on monotonously like mechanics at work on a metal sheet – tonk-tonk-tonk. Tonk-tonk-tonk.

To look at Bim one would not think she had lived through the same childhood, the same experiences as Tara. She led the way so briskly up the stairs on the outside of the house to the flat rooftop where, as children, they had flown kites and hidden secrets, that it was clear she feared no ghosts to meet her there. Now they leant upon the stucco balustrade and looked down at the garden patterned with the light and shade of early evening. The

Clear Light of Day

heat of the day and the heavy dust were being sluiced and washed away by the garden hose as the gardener trained it now on the jasmines, now on the palms, bringing out the green scent of watered earth and refreshed plants. Flocks of parrots came winging in, a lurid, shrieking green, to settle on the sunflowers and rip their black-seeded centres to bits, while mynahs hopped up and down on the lawn, quarrelling over insects. Bim's cat, jet-black, picked her way carefully between the puddles left by the gardener's generously splashing, spraying hose, and twitched her whiskers and went 'meh-meh-meh' with annoyance when the mynahs shrieked at the sight of her and came to swoop over and dive-bomb her till she retreated under the hedge. A pair of hoopoes promenaded sedately up and down the lawn, furling and unfurling the striped fans on their heads. A scent of spider lilies rose from the flowerpots massed on the veranda steps as soon as they were watered, like ladies newly bathed, powdered and scented for the evening.

On either side of their garden were more gardens, neighbours' houses, as still and faded and shabby as theirs, the gardens as overgrown and neglected and teeming with wild, uncontrolled life. From the rooftop they could see the pink and yellow and grey stucco walls, peeling and spotted, or an occasional *gol mohur* tree scarlet with summer blossom.

Outside the sagging garden gate the road led down to the Jumna river. It had shrunk now to a mere rivulet of mud that Tara could barely make out in the huge flat expanse of sand that stretched out to the furry yellow horizon like some sleeping lion, shabby and old. There were no boats on the river except for a flat-bottomed ferry boat that idled slowly back and forth. There was no sign of life beyond an occasional washerman picking his washing off the sand dunes and loading it on to his donkey, and a few hairless *pai* dogs that slunk about the mud flats, nosing about for a dead fish or a frog to devour. A fisherman strode out into the river, flung out his net with a wave of his wrists and then drew in an empty net.

Tara could tell it was empty because he did not bend to pick up anything. There was nothing. 'Imagine,' she said, with wonder, for she could not believe the long-remembered, always-remembered childhood had had a backdrop as drab as this, 'we used to *like* playing there – in that dust and mud. What could we have seen in it – in that muddy little trickle? Why, it's hardly a river – it's nothing, just nothing.'

'Now Tara, your travels have made you very snobbish,' Bim protested, but lazily, good-naturedly. She was leaning heavily on her elbows, letting her grey-streaked hair tumble in whatever bit of breeze came off the river up to them, and now she turned to lean back against the balustrade and look up at the sky that was no longer flat and white-hot but patterned and wrinkled with pale brush-strokes of blue and grey and mauve. A flock of white egrets rose from the river bed and stitched their way slowly and evenly across this faded cloth. 'Nothing?' she repeated Tara's judgement. 'The holy river Jumna? On whose banks Krishna played his flute and Radha danced?'

'Oh Bim, it is nothing of the sort,' Tara dared to say, sure she was being teased. 'It's a little trickle of mud with banks of dust on either side.

'It's where my ashes will be thrown after I am dead and burnt,' Bim said unexpectedly and abruptly. 'It is where Mira-*masi*'s ashes were thrown. Then they go down into the sea.' Seeing Tara start and quiver, she added more lightly, 'It's where we played as children – ran races on the dunes and dug holes to bury ourselves in and bullied the ferryman into giving us free rides to the melon fields. Don't you remember the melons baking in the hot sand and splitting them open and eating them all warm and red and pouring with pink juice?'

Clear Light of Day

'That was you and Raja,' Tara reminded her. 'I never dared get into that boat, and of course Baba stayed at home. It was you and Raja who used to play there, Bim.'

'I and Raja,' Bim mused, continuing to look up at the sky till the egrets pierced through the soft cloth of it and disappeared into the dusk like so many needles lost. 'I and Raja,' she said, 'I and Raja.' Then, 'And the white horse and Hyder Ali Sahib going for his evening ride?' she asked Tara almost roughly, trying to shake out of her some corroboration as if she were unsure if this image were real or only imagined. It had the making of a legend, with the merest seed of truth. 'Can you remember playing on the sand late in the evening and the white horse riding by, Hyder Ali Sahib up on it, high above us, and his peon running in front of him, shouting, and his dog behind him, barking?' She laughed quite excitedly, seeing it again, this half-remembered picture. 'We stood up to watch them go past and he wouldn't even look at us. The peon shouted to us to get out of the way. I think Hyder Ali Sahib used to think of himself as some kind of prince, a nawab. And Raja *loved* that.' Her eyes gleamed as much with malice as with remembrance. 'Raja stood up straight and stared and stared and I'm sure he longed to ride on a white horse with a dog to run behind him just as old Hyder Ali did. Hyder Ali Sahib was always Raja's ideal, wasn't he?' she ended up.

Her words had cut a deep furrow through Tara's forehead. She too pressed down on her elbows, feeling the balustrade cut into her flesh as she tried to remember. Did she really remember or was it only Bim's picture that she saw, in shades of white and black and scarlet, out there on the shadowy sand-bank? To cover up a confusion she failed to resolve, she said 'Yes, and d'you remember Raja marching up and down here on the roof, swinging his arms and reciting his poems to us while we sat here on the balustrade, swinging our legs and listening? I used to feel like crying, it was so beautiful – those poems about death, and love, and wine, and flames.'

'They weren't. They were terrible,' Bim said icily, tossing her head with a stubborn air, like a bad-tempered mare's. '*Terrible* verses he wrote.'

'Oh Bim,' Tara exclaimed in dismay, widening her eyes in horror at such sacrilege. It was a family dictum that Raja was a poet and wrote great poetry. Now Bim, his favourite sister, was denying this doctrine. What had happened?

'Of course it was, Tara – terrible, terrible,' Bim insisted. 'We're not fifteen and ten years old any more – you and I. Have you tried reading it recently? It's *nauseating*. Can you remember any two lines of it that wouldn't make you sick with embarrassment now?'

Tara was too astounded, and too stricken to speak. Throughout her childhood, she had always stood on the outside of that enclosed world of love and admiration in which Bim and Raja moved, watching them, sucking her finger, excluded. Now here was Bim, cruelly and wilfully smashing up that charmed world with her cynicism, her criticism. She stood dismayed.

Bim was fierce. She no longer leant on the balustrade, drooping with reminiscences. She walked up and down agitatedly, swinging her arms in agitation, as Raja had done when quoting poetry in those days when he was a poet, at least to them. 'If you'll just come to my room,' she said, suddenly stopping, 'I'll show you some of those poems – I think they must be still lying around although I don't know why I haven't torn them all up.'

'Of course you wouldn't!' Tara exclaimed.

'Why not?' Bim flung at her. 'Come and see, tell me if you think it worth keeping,' and she swept down the stairs with a martial step, looking back once to shout at Tara, '*And*, apart from poetry recitals, Tara, this terrace is where I cut your hair for you and made you cry. What an uproar there was.' She gave her head a quick, jerky

Clear Light of Day

toss. 'And here you are, with your hair grown long again, and it's mine that's cut short. Only no one cared when I cut *mine*.'

Tara hung back. She had been perfectly content to pace the terrace in the faint breeze, watch the evening darken, wait for the stars to come out and talk about the old days. Even if it was about the haircut, painful as that had been. But Bim was clattering down the stone stairs, the bells of the pink-spired temple at the bend of the river were suddenly clanging loudly and discordantly, the sky had turned a deep green with a wide purple channel through it for the night to come flowing in, and there was nothing for it but to follow Bim down the stairs, into the house, now unbearably warm and stuffy after the freshness and cool of the terrace, and then into Bim's cluttered, untidy room.

It had been their father's office room and the furniture in it was still office furniture – steel cupboards to hold safes and files, metal slotted shelves piled with registers and books, and the roll-top desk towards which Bim marched as Tara hesitated unwillingly by the door. Throwing down the lid, Bim started pulling out papers from the pigeon-holes and opening drawers and rifling through files and tutorial papers and college registers. Out of this mass of paper she separated some sheets and held them out to Tara with an absent-minded air.

Tara, glancing down at them, saw that they were in Urdu, a language she had not learnt. It was quite useless her holding these sheets in her hand and pretending to read the verses that Raja had once recited to them and that had thrilled her then with their Persian glamour. But Bim did not notice her predicament, she was still occupied with the contents of the rifled desk. Finally she found what she was looking for and handed that, too, to Tara with a grim set of her mouth that made Tara quake.

'What is this, Bim?' she asked, looking down and seeing it was in Raja's English handwriting.

'A letter Raja wrote – read it. Read it,' she repeated as Tara hesitated, and walked across to the window and stood there staring out silently, compelling Tara to read while she tensely waited.

Tara read – unwillingly, unbelievingly.

Raja had written it years ago, she saw, and tried to link the written date with some event in their family history that might provide it with a context.

> You will have got our wire with the news of Hyder Ali Sahib's death. I know you will have been as saddened by it as we are. Perhaps you are also a bit worried about the future. But you must remember that when I left you, I promised I would always look after you, Bim. When Hyder Ali Sahib was ill and making out his will, Benazir herself spoke to him about the house and asked him to allow you to keep it at the same rent we used to pay him when father and mother were alive. He agreed – you know he never cared for money, only for friendship – and I want to assure you that now that he is dead and has left all his property to us, you may continue to have it at the same rent, I shall never think of raising it or of selling the house as long as you and Baba need it. If you have any worries, Bim, you have only to tell
> – Raja.

It took Tara some minutes to think out all the implications of this letter. To begin with, she studied the date and tried to recall when Hyder Ali had died. Instead a series of pictures of the Hyder Ali family flickered in the half-dark of the room. There was Hyder Ali, once their neighbour and their landlord, as handsome and stately as a commissioned oil painting hung over a mantelpiece, all in silver and grey and scarlet as he had been on the white horse on

Clear Light of Day

which he rode along the river bank in the evenings while the children stood and watched. He had cultivated the best roses in Old Delhi and given parties to which poets and musicians came. Their parents were not amongst his friends. Then there was his daughter Benazir, a very young girl, plump and pretty, a veil thrown over her head as she hurried into the closed carriage that took her to school, and the Begum whom they seldom saw, she lived in the closed quarters of the house, but at Id sent them, and their other tenant-neighbours, rich sweets covered with fine silver foil on a tray decked with embroidered napkins. They had lived in the tall stucco house across the road, distinguished from all the others by its wealth of decorative touches like the coloured fanlight above the front door, the china tiles along the veranda walls and the coloured glass chandeliers and lamps. They had owned half the houses on that road. When they left Delhi during the partition riots of 1947, they sold most of these houses to their Hindu tenants for a song – all except for Bim's house which she did not try to buy and which he continued to let to her at the same rent as before. It was to this that Raja, his only son-in-law and inheritor of his considerable property, referred in his letter. It was a very old letter.

Still confused, she said slowly, 'But, Bim, it's a very old letter – years old.'

'But I still have it,' Bim said sharply, staring out of the window as if she too saw pictures in the dark. 'I still keep it in my desk – to remind me. Whenever I begin to wish to see Raja again or wish he would come and see us, then I take out that letter and read it again. Oh, I can tell you, I could write him such an answer, he wouldn't forget it for many years either!' She gave a short laugh and ended it with a kind of a choke, saying, 'You say I should come to Hyderabad with you for his daughter's wedding. How can I? How can I enter his house – my landlord's house? I, such a poor tenant? Because of me, he can't raise the

235

rent or sell the house and make a profit – imagine that. The sacrifice!'

'Oh Bim,' Tara said helplessly. Whenever she saw a tangle, an emotional tangle of this kind, rise up before her, she wanted only to turn and flee into that neat, sanitary, disinfected land in which she lived with Bakul, with its set of rules and regulations, its neatness and orderliness. And seemliness too – seemliness. She sat down weakly on the edge of Bim's bed, putting the letter down on the bedside table beside a pile of history books. She turned the pages of Sir Mortimer Wheeler's *Early India and Pakistan* and thought how relevant such a title was to the situation in their family, their brother's marriage to Hyder Ali's daughter. She wished she dared lighten the atmosphere by suggesting this to Bim, but Bim stood with her back arched, martial and defiant. 'Why let this go on and on?' she sighed instead. 'Why not end it now by going to Moyna's wedding, and then forget it all?'

'I have ended it already,' Bim said stubbornly, 'by not going to see them and not having them here either. It is ended. But I don't forget, no.'

'I wouldn't ever have believed – no one would ever have believed that you and Raja who were so close – so close – could be against each other ever. It's just unbelievable, Bim, and so – unnecessary, too,' she ended in a wail.

'Yes?' said Bim with scorn, turning around to stare at her sister. 'I don't think so. I don't think it is unnecessary to take offence when you are insulted. What was he trying to say to me? Was he trying to make me thank him – go down on my knees and thank him for this house in which we all grew up? Was he trying to threaten me with eviction and warn me what might happen if I ever stopped praising him and admiring him?'

'Of course not, Bim. How silly. He simply didn't know quite what he was writing. I suppose he was in a state – his father-in-law having just died, and you know how

Clear Light of Day

he always felt about him – and then having to take over Benazir's family business and all that. He just didn't know what he was writing.'

'A poet – not knowing what he was writing?' Bim laughed sarcastically as she came and picked up the letter and put it back in the desk. It seemed to have a pigeon-hole all to itself as if it were a holy relic like fingernails or a crooked yellow tooth.

'Do tear it up,' cried Tara, jumping up. 'Don't put it back there to take out and look at and hold against Raja. Tear it up, Bim, throw it away,' she urged.

Bim put the lid up with a harsh set to her mouth. 'I will keep it. I must look at it and remind myself every now and then. Whenever you come here and ask why I don't go to Hyderabad and visit him and see my little nieces and nephews – well then, I feel I have to explain to you, prove to you . . .' She stammered a bit and faltered to a stop.

'*Why*, Bim?'

But Bim would not tell her why she needed this bitterness and insult and anger. She picked up an old grey hairbrush that had lost half its bristles and was so matted with tangles of hair that Tara shuddered at the sight of it, and began to brush her hair with short, hard strokes. 'Come, let's go and visit the Misras. They've been asking about you, they want to see you. Ask Bakul to come, too – he must be getting bored. And he knows the Misras. You *met* him at their house – I'd nearly forgotten,' she laughed, a bit distractedly.

Tara followed her out, relieved to be in the open again, out of the dense musty web of Bim's room, Bim's entanglements, and to see the evening light and the garden. A bush of green flowers beside the veranda shook out its night scent as they came out and covered them with its powdery billows. Badshah rushed up, whining with expectation.

The sound of a 1940s foxtrot on Baba's gramophone

followed them down the drive to the gate as if a mechanical bird had replaced the koels and pigeons of daylight. Here Bim stopped and told Badshah firmly to sit. They stood watching, waiting for him to obey. He made protesting sounds, turned around in circles, pawed Bim's feet with his claws, even whined a bit under his breath. Finally he yawned in resignation and sank on to his haunches. Then they turned out of the gate and ceased to hear the tinny rattle of the wartime foxtrot.

Walking up the Misras' driveway, they could hear instead the sounds of the music and dance lessons that the Misra sisters gave in the evenings after their little nursery school had closed for the day, for it seemed that they never ceased to toil and the pursuit of a living was unending. Out on the dusty lawn cane chairs were set in a circle and here the Misra brothers sat taking their rest – which they also never ceased to do – dressed in summer clothes of fine muslin, drinking iced drinks and discussing the day, which meant very little since the day for them had been as blank and unblemished as an empty glass.

They immediately rose to welcome their neighbours but Bim stood apart, feeling a half-malicious desire to go into the house and watch the two grey-haired, spectacled, middle-aged women – once married but both rejected by their husbands soon after their marriage – giving themselves up to demonstrations of ecstatic song and dance, the songs always Radha's in praise of Krishna, the dance always of Radha pining for Krishna. She hadn't the heart after all and instead of joining the men on the lawn, she went up the steps to the veranda where the old father half-sat, half-reclined against the bolsters on a wooden divan, a glass of soda water in his hand, looking out and listening to his sons and occasionally shouting a command at them that went unheard, then sadly, meditatively burping. Tara and Bakul sat down with the brothers on the lawn and talked and listened to the voices of pupils and teachers mournfully rising

Clear Light of Day

and falling down the scales played on a lugubrious harmonium and tried, while talking of Delhi and Washington, politics and travel, to imagine the improbable scene indoors. Eventually the little pupils came out, drooping and perspiring, and rushed off down the drive to the gate where their ayahs waited for them, chatting and chewing betel leaves. After a while, the teachers, too, emerged on to the veranda. They too drooped and perspired and were grey with fatigue. There was nothing remotely amusing about them.

'Bim, Bim, why must you sit here with Papa? Come into the garden and have a drink,' they cried at once, together.

But Bim would not listen. She tucked up her feet under her to make it plain she was not getting up. 'No, no, I want to listen to Uncle,' she said, not wishing to add that she had no liking for his sons' company. 'Uncle is telling me how he was sent to England to study law but somehow landed up in Burma and made a fortune instead. I want to hear the whole story. And you must go and meet Tara and Bakul. They've come.'

'Tara and Bakul?' cried the two sisters and, straightening their spectacles and smoothing down their hair and their saris, they rushed down into the garden while Bim stayed by the sick old man.

'But Uncle, is it a true story?' she teased him. 'I never know with you.'

'Can't you see the proof?' he asked, waving his glass of soda water so that it spilt and frothed and sizzled down his arm. 'Now if I had gone north and had to work in a cold climate, learnt to wear a tie and button a jacket and keep my shoes laced and polished, I would have returned a proper person, a disciplined man. Instead, as you see, I went east, in order to fulfil a *swami's* prophecy, and there I could make money without working, and had to undress to keep cool, and sleep all afternoon, and drink all evening – and so I came back with money and no discipline and no degree,' he laughed, deliberately spilling some more soda water as if in a gesture of fatalism.

'What, all to satisfy a *swami*?'

'Yes, yes, it is true, Bimla. My father used to go to this *swami-ji*, no great man, just one of those common little *swamis* who sit outside the railway station and catch those people who come from the village to make their fortunes in the city. "*Swami-ji, swami-ji*, will I have luck?" they ask, and he puts his hand on their heads in blessing and says, "Yes, son, if you first put five rupees in my pocket." That sort of man. My father went to him to buy a blessing for me – I was leaving for England next day. My trunk was packed, my passage booked, my mother was already weeping. But perhaps my father didn't give the *swami-ji* enough money. He said, "Your son go to England? To Vilayat? Certainly not. He will never go north. He will go east." "No, no," said my father, "his passage is already booked on a P & O boat, he is leaving for Bombay tomorrow to catch it, he is going to study law in a great college in England." But *swami-ji* only shook his head and refused to say another word. So, as my father was walking home, very slowly and thoughtfully, who should bump into him, outside the Kashmere Gate post office, but an old friend of his who had been in school with him and then gone to Burma to set up in the teak business. And this man, this scoundrel, may he perish – oh, I forgot! He perished long ago, Bimla, leaving me all his money – he clasped my father in his arms and said, "You are like a brother to me. Your son is my son. Send him to me, let him work for me and I will make a man of him." And so my passage was cancelled, I gave up my studies and went east, to Burma.' He gulped down half a glass of soda water suddenly, thirstily. 'That *swami-ji*,' he burped.

'And do you think if the *swami-ji* had not made that prophecy, your father would not have accepted his friend's offer?' asked Bim, filled with curiosity.

'Who can tell?' groaned the old man, shifting about in search of a more comfortable position. 'Fate – they talk about Fate. What is it?' He struck his head dramatically. 'This fate?'

'What is it, uncle? Does it pain?' Bim asked because his face, normally as smooth and bland as butter was furrowed and gleaming with sweat.

He sank back, sighing, 'Nothing, nothing, Bimla, my daughter, it is only old age. Just fate and old age and none of us escapes from either. You won't. You don't know, you don't think – and then suddenly it is there, it has come. When it comes, you too will know.'

Bim laughed, helping herself to some of the betel leaves in the silver box at his side. As she smeared them with lime and sprinkled them with aniseed and cardamoms, she said, 'You think one doesn't know pain when one is young, uncle? You should sit down some day with ninety examination papers to correct and try and make out ninety different kinds of handwriting, all illegible, and see that your class has presented you with ninety different versions of what you taught them – all wrong!' She laughed and rolled up the betel leaf and packed it into her mouth. 'That is what I have been doing all day and it has given me a fine pain, too.' She grasped her head theatrically and the old man laughed. Bim had always made him laugh, even when she was a little girl and did tricks on her bicycle going round the drive while his two daughters screamed, 'Bim, you'll fall!'

'You work too hard,' he said. 'You don't know how to enjoy life. You and my two girls – you are too alike – you work and let the brothers enjoy. Look at my sons there –' he waved his arm at them, the muslin sleeve of his shirt falling back to reveal an amulet tied to his arm with a black thread running through the thick growth of white hair. 'Look at them – fat, lazy slobs, drinking whisky. Drinking whisky all day that their sisters have to pay for – did you ever hear of such a thing? In my day, our sisters used to tie coloured threads on our wrists on Rakhibandhan day, begging for our protection, and we gave them gifts and promised to protect them and take care of them, and even if it was only a custom, an annual festival, we at least meant it. When my sister's husband died, I brought her to live here with us. She has lived here for years, she and her children. Perhaps she is still here, I don't know, I haven't seen her,' he trailed off vaguely, then ended up with a forceful, 'but *they* – they let their sisters do the same ceremony, and they just don't care what it means as long as they can get their whisky and have the time to sit on their backsides, drinking it. Useless rubbish, my sons. Everything they ever did has failed . . .'

'What, not the new business as well? The real estate business that Brij started? Has that failed already?'

'Of course,' cried the old man, almost with delight. 'Of course it has. Can it succeed when Brij, the manager, cannot go to the office because he thinks it is degrading and refuses to speak to his clients because they are Punjabis, from Pakistan, and don't belong to the old families of Delhi? What is one to do with a fool like that? Am I to kick him out of the house and flog him down the road to the office? And look at Mulk – our great musician – all he does is wave his hand in the air and look at the stars in the daytime sky, and sing. Sing! He only wants to sing. Why? For whom? Who asked him to sing? Nobody. He just wants to, that is all. He doesn't think anyone should ask him to work or earn money – they should only ask him to sing.'

Out on the lawn there was a burst of laughter.

'And what about the old business they ran – the ice factory and soda water business? They had a good manager to run that.'

'Good manager – ho, yes! Very good manager. Had them eating out of his hand. They thought he was an angel on earth – a *farishtha* – slaving for their sakes,

Clear Light of Day

to fill their coffers with gold – till one day they went to the office to open the coffer for some gold – they must have needed it for those Grant Road women they go to, those song-and-dance women – and they found it empty, and the money gone.'

'And the manager?'

'Gone! He took care of money – the money went – he went with it.' The old man roared, slapping his thigh so that a fold of his *dhoti* fell aside, revealing the grey-haired stretch of old, slack flesh. Straightening it casually, he added, 'What did they think? Someone else will work so that they can eat?'

'I didn't know about that,' said Bim, concerned. She had thought the Misras had at least one secure business behind them, as her own family still had their father's insurance business that still existed quietly and unspectacularly without their aid and kept them housed and fed. If the manager made more money than he ought to, Bim did not grudge him that. She earned her own living to supplement that unearned income, and it was really only Baba who needed to be supported. But the Misra boys – fat, hairy brutes – why should others look after them? The poor Misra girls, so grey and bony and needle-faced, still prancing through their Radha-Krishna dances and impersonating lovelorn maidens in order to earn their living . . . Bim shook her head.

'Fools,' the old man was still muttering as he fumbled about, looking for something under the pillows and bolsters and not finding it. Bim knew it was the hookah he was no longer allowed to smoke. 'Ugh,' he cried, the corners of his mouth turned down as though he were about to cry, like a baby. 'Not even my hookah any more. The doctor has said no, and the girls listen to the doctor, not to their father. What it is to be a father, to live without a smoke, or drink . . .'

Out on the lawn they were laughing again, their laughter spiralling up, up in the dark, as light as smoke.

'Laugh, laugh,' said the old man. 'Yes, laugh now – before it is all up with you and you are like me – washed up. But never mind, never mind,' he said to Bim, straightening his head and folding his arms so that he looked composed again, like a piece of stone sculpture. 'When I was young, when I was their age – do you think I was any better?' He winked suddenly at the surprised Bim. 'Was *I* a saint?' he laughed. 'I can tell you, I was just as fat, as greedy, as stupid, as wicked as *any* of them,' he suddenly roared, flinging out an arm as if to push them out of his way in contempt. 'A boozer, a womanizer, a bankrupt – running after drink, women, money – that was all I did, just like them, *worse* than them, any of them . . .' he chuckled and now his head wobbled on his neck as if something had come loose. '*Much* worse than any of them,' he repeated with desperate pride.

Bim, red-faced in the dark shadows, let down her feet cautiously and searched for her slippers.

And here was Jaya coming up the steps to fetch her. 'Bim, come and join us,' she called. 'Tara is telling us about Washington – it is such fun – and Papa should eat his dinner and go to sleep. Papa, I'm sending the cook with your dinner –' and she rushed off towards the kitchen while Bim went down the steps into the garden. The old man had sunk back against the bolsters and shut his eyes. She even thought he might have fallen asleep, he was so still, but a little later she heard him call, 'The pickle, Jaya – don't forget the black lemon pickle – let me have a little of it, will you?'

Out on the lawn the talk was more sober, more predictable in spite of the whisky that accompanied it. Someone brought Bim a tall glass that chattered with ice. Could it be from their factory, Bim wondered, sipping, stretching her bare feet in the grass and feeling its dry tickle.

'Bakul-*bhai*, tell me,' said the older brother, rolling the ice cubes around in his glass, 'as a diplomat in an Indian

Clear Light of Day

embassy, how do you explain the situation to foreigners? Now when the foreign press asks you, perhaps you just say "No comment", but when you meet friends at a party, and they ask you what is going on here – how can a Prime Minister behave as ours does – how can ministers get away with all they do here – what is being done about the problems of this country – who is going to solve them – how, why is it like this? – then what do you say to them, Bakul-*bhai*?'

Bim, who was lighting herself a cigarette, stopped to watch her brother-in-law cope with this interrogation. It was quite dark on the lawn and although a light had been switched on in the veranda so that the old father could see to eat his dinner, it only threw a pale rectangle of light across the beds of cannas close to the house, and did not illuminate Bakul's face. He kept them all waiting in silence as he considered and then began his measured and diplomatic reply.

Elegantly holding his cigarette in its holder at arm's length, Bakul told them in his ripest, roundest tones, 'What I feel is my duty, my vocation, when I am abroad, is to be my country's ambassador. All of us abroad are, in varying degrees, ambassadors. I refuse to talk about famine or drought or caste wars or – or political disputes. I refuse – I *refuse* to discuss such things. "No comment" is the answer if I am asked. I can discuss such things here, with you, but not with foreigners, not in a foreign land. There I am an ambassador and I choose to show them and inform them only of the best, the finest.'

'The Taj Mahal?' asked Bim, blowing out a spume of smoke that wavered in the darkness, and avoiding Tara's eye, watchful and wary.

'Yes, exactly,' said Bakul promptly. 'The Taj Mahal – the Bhagavad Gita – Indian philosophy – music – art – the great, immortal values of ancient India. But why talk of local politics, party disputes, election malpractices, Nehru, his daughter, his grandson – such matters as will soon pass into oblivion? *These* aren't important when compared with India, eternal India —'

'Yes, it does help to live abroad if you feel that way,' mused Bim, while her foot played with the hem of her sari and she looked carefully away from Tara who watched. 'If you lived here, and particularly if you served the Government here, I think you would be obliged to notice such things: you would see their importance. I'm not sure if you could ignore bribery and corruption, red-tapism, famine, caste warfare and all that. In fact, living here, working here, you might easily forget the Taj Mahal and the message of the Gita —'

'Never,' interrupted Bakul firmly, ripely. 'A part of me lives here, the deepest part of me, always —'

'Ah,' Bim in turn interrupted him. 'Then it is definitely important to live abroad. In all the comfort and luxury of the embassy, it must be much easier, *very* easy to concentrate on the Taj, or the Emperor Akbar. Over here I'm afraid you would be too busy queueing up for your rations and juggling with your budget, making ends meet —'

'Oh Bim,' Tara burst out in protest, 'you *do* exaggerate. I don't see you queueing up for your rations — or even for a *bus!*'

Bim burst out laughing, delighted at having provoked Tara, and agreed there was some exaggeration in what she said. This annoyed Bakul, who had taken it all so perfectly seriously, and he tapped his cigarette holder on the arm of his chair with the air of a judge tapping a gavel at a meeting grown unruly.

Tara cast her eyes around, looking for an escape. But Bim had thrown back her head in laughter, all the men beside her were laughing. Then she leant forward, a cigarette in her mouth, and Bakul leant towards her to light it. Seeing the match flare, the cigarette catch fire with a little throb, Tara was pricked with the realization that although it was she who was the pretty sister, had always

Clear Light of Day

been, so that in their youth the young men had come flocking about her like inquisitive, hopeful, sanguine bees in search of some nectar that they sniffed on the air, it was Bim who was attractive. Bim who, when young, had been too tall and square-shouldered to be thought pretty, now that she was grey – and a good deal grey, observed Tara – had arrived at an age when she could be called handsome. All the men seemed to acknowledge this and to respond. There was that little sensual quiver in the air as they laughed at what she said, and a kind of quiet triumph in the way in which she drew in her cheeks to make the cigarette catch fire and then threw herself back into her chair, giving her head a toss and holding the cigarette away so that a curl of smoke circled languidly about her hand. Tara thought how attractive a woman who smokes is: there is some link formed between the man who leans forward with a match and the woman who bends her head towards that light, as Bakul and Bim did.

Tara did not smoke and no one offered her a light. Or was it just that Tara, having married, had rescinded the right to flirt, while Bim, who had not married, had not rescinded? No, it was not, for Bim could not be said to flirt. Slapping hard at a mosquito that had lighted on her arm, she was saying to Manu who had offered to fetch a Flit-gun, 'That's too much of a bother – don't.' Bim never bothered.

The Misra brothers and sisters were not interested in the subtleties underlying such exchanges. One brother wanted to know, 'What is the price of good whisky in Washington? Not that terrible thing called bourbon but scotch – can you get scotch?' and the sisters asked Tara where she had bought her chiffon sari and her leather bag, and for how much. Bim listened to Tara giving them shoppers' information glibly but a little too fast, making her sound unreliable. It amused Bim to see, through a haze of cigarette smoke, Tara's not quite assimilated cosmopolitanism that sat on her oddly, as if a child had dressed up in its mother's high-heeled shoes – taller, certainly, but wobbling. Then the sisters' heads drew closer still to Tara, their voices dropped an octave, and they murmured, one from the left and one from the right, 'But how much longer can you keep your girls abroad? Mustn't they come home to marry now?'

Tara cowered back in her basket chair. 'They are only sixteen and seventeen,' she said plaintively.

'Time to marry – better to marry – time, time,' they cried, and Tara rubbed her mosquito-bitten toe in the grass in pained embarrassment, and Bim, overhearing them, lifted her eyebrows in horror and turned to Mulk, the younger brother who was silent, for sympathy.

Mulk had already drunk more glasses of whisky than anyone could count and sat ignoring the company, beating one hand on his knee, singing in little snatches in his hoarse, cracked voice, swaying his head joyfully to music that was audible only to him. Even since she had last seen him, he seemed to have deteriorated – his jaws prickled with several days' growth of beard, he wore a shirt with several buttons missing and a sleeve irremediably stained with betel juice, the slippers on his unwashed feet needed mending. He rolled his eyes in their sockets like a dog howling at the moon and hummed to himself. '*Zindagi*, O *Zindagi*,' he sang, tunelessly, and refreshed himself with another gulp of whisky.

Then suddenly the scene split, with a tearing sound. It was only whisky pouring out of an overturned glass and Mulk struggling to get out of the canvas chair, too tight for his heavy frame. As they all stopped talking to stare at him, he gestured widely and shouted dramatically, 'Where is my *tabla*-player? My harmonium player? My accompanists? Where are they? *Chotu-mia! Bare-mia!*' Standing, swaying on his thick legs, he roared at the lighted house and the scurrying figures on the veranda.

Clear Light of Day

'Shh, Mulk-*bhai*,' cried Jaya and Sarla, their faces shrinking into small dark knots. 'You will wake Papa. Why are you shouting? You know they aren't there.'

'Yes, I know they aren't there,' he blasted them, turning around and staggering towards them so that Bim and Tara had to hastily draw up their feet or he would have tripped over them. 'I know who turned them out – you two – you two turned them out –'

'Mulk, Mulk,' murmured his brothers.

Suddenly Mulk was clutching his hands to his chest like two puffy little birds and his voice rose in shrill, grotesque mimicry. '"It is a waste of money. How can we afford to keep them? We have to feed ourselves. Tell them to go, they must go – go – go –"' and he pushed out the two birds so that they fluttered away and fell at his sides. 'That is all I hear from them – these two –'

'Mulk, Mulk,' rose the pacifying croon from the pigeons in the chairs.

Mulk swung around to face Bim and Tara and Bakul now. 'They have got rid of my musicians,' he nearly wept. 'Sent them away. How am I to sing without accompaniment?'

'Mulk-*bhai*, we only pointed out that we haven't the money to pay them and we could not keep feeding them on kebabs and pilaos and kormas as you expected us to. Is it our fault if they went away once we stopped serving such food?'

'Food! It wasn't food they wanted. You are insulting them. You are insulting my *guru*. He does not want food, or money. He wants respect. Regard. That is what we must pay to a *guru*. But you have no respect, no regard. You think only of money – money – money. That is what you think about, you two –'

'Mulk, Mul-lk.'

'They have minds full of money, *dirty* minds. They don't understand the artist, how the artist lives for his art. They don't know how it is only music –' here he clasped

249

his chest with a moist, sweating paw – 'only music that keeps me alive. Not food. Not money. Music: what can it mean to those who only think of money? If I say, "I must have accompaniment for my singing," they say, "Oh there is no money!" If I say, "I want my friends to come tonight so I can sing for them, cook dinner for them please," they cry, "Oh we have no money!" Do you need money to make music?' he roared, lifting his arm so that the torn sleeve showed his armpit and the bush of grey hair in it. He stood, swaying, with the arm uplifted, the torn sleeve drooping, as he faced his visitors. 'Do you?' he roared, and they could see spit flying from his mouth and spraying them where they sat, helpless. 'Tell me – do you?'

The visitors were frozen. The family seethed. Then the sisters cracked like old dry pods from which the black seeds of protest and indignation spilt, infertile. Money, they were both saying, where were they to find money to pay for concerts and dinners?

'Don't I give you money?' shouted Mulk, lowering his head and swaying it from side to side threateningly. 'Where is all the money I give you – hey? Tell me. Tell me. Where is that five hundred rupee note I gave you – hey? Where is it? Show it to me. I want to see it. I want it.'

He began to plunge his legs up and down in the grass like a beast going methodically out of control. One of the small bamboo tables was knocked down, a glass spilt. Now at last Bakul acted. Rising to his feet casually, elegantly, he took Mulk by the arm, murmured to him in his most discreet voice, began to lead him away towards the house. They heard Mulk crying something about 'My *guru* – his birthday – I want to give – they won't let me – for my *guru* –' and then some sobbing intakes of breath, gasps for reason and control, and then only the flow of Bakul's voice, slipping and spreading as smoothly and evenly as oil, and then silence in which

Clear Light of Day

they became aware of Badshah barking fiercely out on the road.

Bim rose at last, brushing her sari as if there were crumbs, saying, 'Listen to Badshah – he's saying we must get back. Come, Tara, if we don't go home at once, the cook will fall asleep and we'll have no dinner and Baba will go to bed without any.'

Now the Misra sisters too were released from their shell-shocked postures and rose gratefully, chattering once more. 'But why don't you stay to dinner, Bim?' 'Tara, have pot luck with us. We can't throw a dinner party as we would have in the old days – but pot luck . . .' and the brothers shouted, 'Let's call Baba. Tell him we'll have music that will make him forget that rubbish he listens to – we'll get Mulk to sing!' Strangely enough, and much to Bim's and Tara's astonishment, Brij and Manu began to laugh, thumping each other like schoolboys. One even wiped his eyes of tears as he repeated 'Get Mulk to sing – Mulk to sing for us –' as if it were a family joke that only needed to be mentioned to set them off uncontrollably.

The sisters, a little more circumspect, edged closer to Tara, saying, 'Mulk gets that way when he has had too much to drink. He doesn't mean it – he will forget about it – we'll give him his dinner – and, oh stay for pot luck, Tara!'

But Bim would not listen. The last time she had accepted an invitation to 'pot luck' she had been distressed to see the two Misra sisters halving and sharing a *chapati* between them, and jars of pickles had had to be opened to make up for the lack of meat and vegetables. It would not do. 'No, that won't do,' she said firmly. 'Can you hear Badshah calling? Listen to that bark – he'll have all the neighbours up, and your father, too,' and she swept up the veranda to say good night to the old man who lay supine on the divan, his two white, knobbed feet sticking out at the end of the sheet that covered him, saw that he was asleep and then went down to herd Tara and Bakul down the drive.

The sisters came to the gate with them, lingering by the jasmine bush to pick some for Tara. Giving her a handful, Jaya said, 'Oh, Tara, these flowers make me think of that picnic – so many years ago now – do you remember, too? It was springtime – the flowers in Lodi Gardens –'

'And bees!' cried Sarla suddenly, catching Tara by the wrist so that a few of the jasmines fell. 'How those bees attacked Bim – oh don't you remember?'

But Tara withdrew her hand, dropping the remaining jasmine as she did so. She shook her head, refusing to remember any more. Bim, smiling faintly, covered up her ears with her hands and said, 'How that dog barks – he has a voice like a trumpet,' and led Tara and Bakul across the road to their own gate where Badshah waited.

As they crossed the dusty road, Bakul cast a look at the tall dark house behind the hedge and asked, 'What has happened to the Hyder Alis' house? Doesn't anyone live there?'

'No. I mean, only a poor relation of theirs. He must have been a nuisance to Raja in Hyderabad so they sent him here as caretaker. He takes opium – he just lies around – and the house is falling down about his ears. No one's replaced a brick or painted a wall there for years.'

'Oh what a shame – it was a lovely house, you know, Bakul,' said Tara.

Badshah's barks grew so urgent they could not speak to each other any more.

Baba was already asleep on his bed in the veranda when the sisters slipped quietly past, only glancing to see him lying on his side, one leg stretched out and the other slightly bent at the knee as if he were running, half-flying through the sky, one hand folded under his chin and the other uncurled beside it, palm upwards

Clear Light of Day

and fingers curved in – a finely composed piece of sculpture in white. Marble. Or milk. Or less: a spider's web, faint and shadowy, or just some moonlight spilt across the bed. There was something unsubstantial about his long slimness in the light white clothes, such a total absence of being, of character, of clamouring traits and characteristics. He was no more and no less than a white flower or harmless garden spider, the sisters thought, as if, when he was born, his parents, late in their lives, had no vitality and no personality left to hand down to him, having given it away in thoughtless handfuls to the children born earlier. Lying there in the dark, dressed in white, breathing quite imperceptibly, he might have been a creature without blood in his veins, without flesh on his bones, the sisters thought as they tiptoed past him, down the steps to the lawn to stroll.

The whole neighbourhood was silent now, asleep. The sound of traffic on the highway was distant, smothered by dust and darkness. At last one became aware of the presence of stars, the scent of night-flowering plants. The sisters, sleepless, rustled through the grass, up and down beside the long hedge. The black cat, pacing sedately beside them to begin with, suddenly leapt up into the air, darted sideways and disappeared.

Hands behind her back as she paced, Bim murmured, 'Do you know, for a long time after Mira-*masi* died – for a long, long time – I used to keep seeing her, just here by the hedge –'

'Bim,' Tara cried incredulously.

'Yes, yes, I used to *feel* I was seeing her – just out of the corner of my eye, never directly before me, you know – just slipping past this hedge here –' she put out her hand and touched the white-flowering *chandni* – 'quite white and naked, as she was when she – when she –'

'Then – at that time,' Tara helped, pained.

'– small, like a thin little dog, a white one, just slipping

253

along quietly – I felt as if towards the well at the back – that well –'

'That the cow drowned in?'

'And she used to say she would drown herself in but because she didn't, because she died, after all, in bed, I felt she was still trying to get there. A person needs to choose his death. But if I turned my head very quickly – then she would vanish – just disappear into the hedge –' and Bim touched it again, to remember, and had the back of her hand scratched by a thorn and heard some small creature skitter away into the leaves. 'I felt like one of those Antarctic explorers T.S. Eliot wrote about in his notes to *The Waste Land*, to that verse, do you know it, Tara?

Who is the third who walks always beside you?
When I count, there are only you and I together
But when I look ahead up the white road
There is always another one walking beside you
Gliding wrapt in a brown mantle, hooded
I do not know whether a man or a woman
– But who is that on the other side of you?

They were silent as they scraped through the catching grasses at their feet, and had their heads bowed, not looking. Tara gave a small sigh that she disguised as a yawn: she had listened so often to Bim and Raja quoting poetry – the two of them had always had so much poetry that they carried in their heads. As a little girl, tongue-tied and shy, too diffident to attempt reciting or even memorizing a poem – there had been that wretched episode in school when she was made to stand up and recite 'The Boy Stood On the Burning Deck' and it was found she could not proceed beyond the title – Tara was always struck dumb with wonder at their ability to memorize and quote. It was another of those games they shared and she did not. She felt herself shrink into that small miserable wretch

Clear Light of Day

of twenty years ago, both admiring and resenting her tall, striding sister who was acquainted with Byron, with Iqbal, even with T.S. Eliot.

Bim was calmly unaware of any of her sister's agonies, past or present. 'Only I was not at any extremity like those explorers in the icy wastes who used to see ghost figures,' she continued. 'I was not frozen or hungry or mad. Or even quite alone. I had Baba. After you married, and Raja went to Hyderabad, and Mira-*masi* died, I still had Baba. And that summer I got my job at the college and felt so pleased to be earning my living –'

She stopped abruptly as though there were a stone in the grass that she had stumbled on. Tara walked on, distracted, till she noticed Bim was not with her, then stopped to look back, fearfully. But Bim did not revive her tirade against Raja although Tara had feared they were beginning to slip into it again.

'Really, I was not mad in the least,' said Bim, strolling on. 'So then I thought there might be something in what the Tibetans say about the dead – how their souls linger on on earth and don't really leave till the forty-ninth day when a big feast is given and the last prayers are said and a final farewell given to the departed. It takes forty-nine days, they say in their Bardol Thodol, to travel through the three Bardos of death and all their stages. I felt Mira-*masi* was lingering on, in the garden, not able to leave because she hadn't been seen through all the stages with the relevant prayers and ceremonies. But then, who is?' Bim said more loudly, tossing her head, 'except for the Buddhist monks and nuns who die peacefully in their monasteries in the Himalayas? *We* were anything but peaceful that summer.'

'Yes, *what* a summer,' Tara murmured.

'Isn't it strange how life won't *flow*, like a river, but moves in jumps, as if it were held back by locks that are opened now and then to let it jump forwards in a kind of flood? There are these long still stretches –

nothing happens – each day is exactly like the other – plodding, uneventful – and then suddenly there is a crash – mighty deeds take place – momentous events – even if one doesn't know it at the time – and then life subsides again into the backwaters till the next push, the next flood? That summer was certainly one of them – the summer of '47 –'

'For everyone in India,' Tara reminded primly. 'For every Hindu and Muslim. In India and in Pakistan.'

Bim laughed. 'Sometimes you sound exactly like Bakul.'

Tara stopped, hurt. Bim had always had this faculty of cutting her short, hurting her, and not even knowing.

But this time, it seemed, she did know. She touched Tara's elbow lightly. 'Of course you must – occasionally – when you've been married so long,' she explained good-humouredly and even apologetically.

'But wouldn't you agree?' Tara said coldly.

'Yes, yes, you are perfectly right, Tara – it was so for all of us – for the whole family, and for everyone we knew, here in this neighbourhood. Nineteen forty-seven. That summer. We could see the fires burning in the city every night –'

Tara shuddered. 'I hate to think about it.'

'Why? It was the great event of our lives – of our youth. What would our youth have been without it to round it off in such a definite and dramatic way?'

'I was glad when it was over,' Tara's voice trembled with the passion she was always obliged to conceal. 'I'm so glad it is over and we can never be young again.'

'Young?' said Bim wonderingly, and as they were now near the veranda, she sank down on the steps where the quisqualis creeper threw its bunches of inky shadow on the white-washed steps, and sat there hugging her knees. Tara leaned against the pillar beside her, staring out and up at the stars that seemed to be swinging lower and lower as the night grew stiller. They made her deeply uneasy – they seemed so many milestones to mark the long distances, the dark distances that stretched and stretched beyond human knowledge and beyond human imagination. She huddled against the pillar, hugging it with one arm, like a child.

'Youth?' said Bim, her head sinking as if with sleep, or sorrow. 'Yes, I am glad, too, it is over – I never wish it back. Terrible, what it does to one – what it did to us – and one is too young to know how to cope, how to deal with that first terrible flood of life. One just goes under – it sweeps one along – and how many years and years it is before one can stand up to it, make a stand against it –' she shook her head sleepily. 'I never wish it back. I would never be young again for anything.'

An invisible cricket by her feet at that moment began to weep inconsolably.

Margaret Drabble

extract from

The Millstone

Rosamund Stacey, Cambridge arts graduate in her twenties, has surveyed the distant hostilities of her family, the demands of her predatory flat-mate and the attentions of Roger and George, neither of whom she really loves. Then the unexpected happens. She discovers that she is pregnant and allows her deepest emotions to surface for the first time.

Rosamund Stacey, Cambridge arts graduate in her twenties, has survived the distant hostilities of her family, the demands of her predatory flat-mate and the attentions of Roger and George, neither of whom she really loves. Then the unexpected happens. She discovers that she is pregnant and allows her deepest emotions to surface for the first time.

My baby was due in early March: I amused myself by trying to finish my thesis before my baby. It was in fact somewhat of a hopeless task, as I was not even expected to finish it before the following Christmas, but I have always been a quick worker and now I had very little else to distract me. As the winter wore on, and spring set in, I felt less and less like going out, even as far as to the British Museum, and I organized myself so that I could do a good deal of work at home. It was less entertaining than working in the library, but I could at least get on with it. It was all shaping up quite nicely: my director of studies, a don in Cambridge, had approved my synopsis, rough draft, first chapter, and other indications of the final product, and had been most encouraging. I felt happy about it; I had got it all into shape in my head and knew more or less exactly what I was going to say and what ground I had to cover. Then, towards the end of January, I began to flag. Although I would not admit it, I felt at times too tired to read. I ate more and more iron pills but they did not seem to have much effect. In the end I decided that I had merely got stale through too much concentration on too few things, and that I ought to branch out a little. It was, however, impossible to find anything amusing to do; I did not enjoy walking any more, public transport was a continual trial, I could not sit comfortably through a full-length picture, and I could not eat anything interesting without suffering for it afterwards. I felt thoroughly annoyed; I could understand, in this condition, why women are, as they certainly are, such perpetual complaining bores. I was discussing my problem with Lydia one evening; she suggested all sorts of occupations, like knitting, or rug-making, or basket-work, or weaving, but I rejected all these pseudo-useful employments with contempt. Then she said, finally, why don't you do jigsaw puzzles; and they were what I took up.

One can, if one tries, buy extremely complicated jigsaw puzzles with a thousand interlocking pieces, and pictures by old masters, or of ships at sea, and heaven knows what: also puzzles in the shape of maps of Europe, square puzzles, circular puzzles, star-shaped puzzles, reversible puzzles, anything one can imagine in the way of puzzles. I became addicted and would spend hours over them; it was a soothing, time-consuming process, and when I went to bed I would dream not of George, nor of babies locked away from me where I couldn't feed them, nor even of childbirth, but of pieces of blue sky edged with bits of tree, or small blue irregular shapes composing the cloak of the Virgin Mary. Lydia had an irritating habit of coming in at the end of an evening, just when I had mastered the most difficult part of a puzzle, and putting in all the easy obvious middle pieces; I got very annoyed with her. As a therapy, it worked extremely well; I found I could write my book and do a puzzle for alternate hours without getting unduly bored by either.

I suppose the end of anyone's first pregnancy is frightening. I cannot quite remember how frightened I was, because it is one of the horrible tricks of nature to make one forget instantly after childbirth all that one had feared and suffered, presumably so that one will carry on gaily with the next. In the same way one will protect with the utmost care an unborn child which one does not want and would prefer to lose, and which indeed as in my case may even have taken some steps, however feeble and ill-informed, towards losing; in January, after a party, I slipped on the stairs going down from a friend's flat and

The Millstone

would certainly have fallen had I been in anything like my normal state of balance: but as it was I clutched and hung on to the banisters like grim death and got away with a mere twisted ankle. And thus, unwillingly, I have forgotten how worried I must have been, because it now seems so long ago and to have so little importance. I was worried partly through ignorance, as I had deliberately found nothing out about the subject at all, and had steered clear of all natural childbirth classes, film strips of deliveries, and helpful diagrams, convinced that I had only to go near a natural childbirth class in order to call down upon myself the most phenomenally unnatural birth of all time. There was no point in tempting providence, I thought; one might as well expect the worst as one would probably get it anyway.

I remember, however, the night before it was born with some clarity. It was not due for another week so I was not particularly worried; I boiled myself a couple of eggs, then went to eat them in the sitting-room at about half past eight, and got out my typewriter at the same time in order to read over the last page of thesis that I had left inside it. When I opened the typewriter, however, it was not a page of discussion on Drayton's use of irony that met my eyes, but a page of something quite different, and not written by me at all. I knocked the top off my egg and started to read it, assuming, and rightly, that it was something of Lydia's; she had been complaining for weeks that her machine was going wrong. It was indeed something of Lydia's; it was a page from her next novel, which she had started shortly after moving in with me and which she had been working on, intermittently, ever since. I read the page with fascinated alarm; it was in the first person, and it was about a girl having an illegitimate baby. When I had finished the page, I abandoned my eggs and went into Lydia's bedroom to look for more. I found it, in a heap of loose leaves by her bed, and carried it back with me and sat down on the settee and started to read it.

I read the whole lot straight off, or what there was of it; it was not finished. It was nothing more nor less than my life story, with a few minor alterations here and there, and a few interesting false assumptions amongst the alterations. Clearly Lydia, for instance, had always assumed that Joe was the father of the child; there was an interesting though cleverly concealed portrait of Joe, and an absorbing scene in which the character that was me quarrelled violently with him and left him for ever. Her motives for this I thought a little far-fetched; she had apparently discovered that he was still sleeping with his mislaid wife, whom she had had the privilege of meeting, which was more than I had. This discovery had enraged her to such an extent that she had broken with him and refused any financial assistance from him. She had been planning to have the child only on the assumption that she and the Joe-character would live together and bring it up between them. Far-fetched as the theory seemed with regard to me, who did not know what the word jealousy meant, and indeed suffered from its opposite, if it has one, it certainly explained a possible line of conduct: it amused me to think of Lydia sitting there racking her brains trying to work out why I was having the child, and why I hadn't got rid of it. She had been inefficient enough on that score herself, by her own account, but then one never suspects that others share one's own degree of incompetence in such matters.

At first, for the first few chapters, I flattered myself that I emerged rather well – independent, strong-willed, and very worldly and *au fait* with sexual problems. An attractive girl, I thought. But then, as the chapters wore on, I began to have my doubts. Like myself, the character was engaged in academic research, an activity which Lydia appeared to regard with thorough contempt: she had invented for me a peculiarly meaningless and abstruse research subject, in fact none less than the ill-famed Henryson. I remembered I had told Lydia about my

264

The Millstone

Indian in some detail and she had laughed with me about him. I could not, however, be too indignant as I have always been aware that the Elizabethans, except for Shakespeare, are somewhat of a luxury subject, unlike nineteenth-century novelists or prolific Augustan poets. However, I did object very strongly to the way, subtle enough technically, that she hinted that the Rosamund character's obsession with scholarly detail and discovery was nothing more nor less than an escape route, an attempt to evade the personal crises of her life and the realities of life in general. She drew a very persuasive picture of the academic ivory tower; whenever anything unpleasant happened to this character, as in the course of the extant ten chapters was too frequently the case, she would retire to bed or the British Museum with a pile of books, as others retire perhaps with a bottle of gin. There was also a long discussion on this very topic between the girl and a friend of hers, who presumably represented vitality, modernity, honesty and so on; I was not malicious enough to consider this a self-portrait of Lydia, for it clearly was not, as the girlfriend in question was not like anyone I have ever met. She accused the me-character of having a jigsaw puzzle mind, a nasty crack in the circumstances I thought; she herself was busy frittering her life away in vital pursuits like serving in a theatre bar, working on a magazine, and having an affair with a television producer.

All in all, by the time I had finished this work I was both annoyed and upset. I did not think this view of scholarship at all justifiable; I could not produce my reasons for believing in its value, but in a way I was all the surer for that, for I knew it for a fact. Scholarship is a skill and I am good at it, and even if one rated it no higher than that it is still worth doing. Whether I used it as an escape or not was a different matter, and did not seem to me to be as relevant. It was work, and I did it, and reasons did not come into it; *il faut cultiver notre jardin*, as Voltaire so admirably said. Apart, however, from being annoyed by this attack on my livelihood, I was also very annoyed by the thought that Lydia had been living in my house for nothing and writing all this about me without saying a word. She had compared herself once to a spider, an image not wholly new, drawing material from its own entrails, but this seemed to me to be a somewhat more parasitic pursuit.

After re-reading certain passages, I put the whole lot back by her bed, including the sheet that had been in my typewriter; I had no intention of saying anything to her but I thought it possible she might remember where she had left it and suffer from her own conclusions. Then I went back and sat down by the fire and switched on the radio, just in time to hear George talking about next Sunday's concert. I thought how odd it was that I had bumped into Clare at Selfridge's but had not even set eyes in the last eight months on George. I switched off again when he had finished announcing as my thoughts kept reverting to Lydia, with decreasing anger. After all, I thought, she had been making herself very useful recently, doing all the heavy shopping, even the odd few minutes' Hoovering, and had, moreover, acquired through a friend of hers a woman who had volunteered to come in and mind the baby two days a week when I was well enough to go out. In fact, lately I had even come to think myself slightly in her debt, despite the disadvantageous rent situation: and here, at least, in those pages of typescript had been proof that I was still the donor, she still the recipient. More than ever now I had the upper hand; she had got her money's worth out of me. Do not think I resented this: on the contrary, looking at our relationship in this light, I felt much happier, for I saw that we had maintained a basis of mutual profit. Having arrived at this conclusion, I thought I would go to bed, and when I got up I found I was suffering from distinct pains in the back.

Once I noticed that I was feeling them, I realized that

The Millstone

I had been feeling them for quite a long time without paying them much attention. I instantly took them to be what, in fact, they were and was overcome with panic as it seemed such an inconvenient time to have to disturb hospital and ambulance men. It was a quarter past eleven, a time for all good citizens to be asleep. I was in a dilemma: the pains were not yet at all bad and I could clearly hang on at home for some time, but on the other hand the longer I waited the more inconvenient would grow the hour and the more irritable the nurses, midwives and ambulance people that I would have to encounter. I went to the bedroom and got out my little leaflet of instructions which told me to time the contractions and to ring the hospital when they became regular and more frequent than once every quarter of an hour. So I started to time them, and found to my alarm that they were perfectly regular and occurring once every three minutes. At half past eleven I rang the hospital, who told me to take an aspirin or two and ring the ambulance. So I did. Then I got out my suitcase, prepacked to order, put on my coat and waited. The men arrived within ten minutes, at exactly the same moment as Lydia who was returning home rather gay after a party. When she discovered my state and destination, she flung her arms around me, kissed me several times, and accompanied me downstairs in the lift, telling me en route about the party and how she had met Joe Hurt there, and how they had talked about me, and he had yet another book finished, and how fond of me he was, and how concerned, and how perhaps she quite liked him after all, and she would let him know instantly about the baby, whatever it turned out to be: the ambulance men and I listened to her story in solid quiet, but I was glad to have her there to stop my having to say things like It's a fine night, isn't it, or Sorry to disturb you at this hour, to these two silent men. Lydia looked rather weird, as her hair was coming down and she had lipstick all over one cheek: also she was wearing a strange long green lace dress and over it her usual grey mackintosh. She had no other coat. Her preoccupation with the subject of Joe I found illuminating, and I was glad to be able to put together, on new evidence, an attitude of hers that I had never understood.

I was glad too to be going from so good an address. I felt that by it alone I had bought a little deference and, sure enough, at the bottom of the stairs one of the men turned to Lydia and said, 'Would you like to come along, Miss, to see your friend in?' He was rather taken by her, I could see, and her eyes too lit up at the prospect of so strange an excursion, but I said firmly that I would be better off on my own, it was only just down the road, I couldn't dream of disturbing her; what she needed was a good sleep. I did not fancy the idea of the details of my labour becoming available to her professional curiosity: she could have a baby herself, I thought, if she really wanted to know what it was like. She stood on the pavement and waved goodbye, shouting good luck after me as the ambulance drew away; she was an odd and charming sight in her strangely tiered garments.

On the way to the hospital I thought how unnerving it is, suddenly to see oneself for a moment as others see one, like a glimpse of unexpected profile in an unfamiliar combination of mirrors. I think I know myself better than anyone can know me, and I think this even in cold blood, for too much knowing is my vice; and yet one cannot account for the angles of others. Once at a party I met a boy whom I had known at school, and not seen since; we both had known that the other would be present and I had recognized him at once, but when we met and talked he confessed that when looking out for me he had taken another girl to be me. I asked him which, and he had pointed through the crowd at a tall, skinny girl with too-neat hair and a shut, frightened face: I was amazed and oddly hurt by his near-mistake, for she was so utterly unlike me, so devoid of any of my qualities or defects. And yet she was the same height, the same colouring, and, looking back, I could see that there was enough in me at sixteen that could have developed that way and that in six years sixteen-year-old Rosamund Stacey might well have been her and not me.

When we arrived at the hospital, I thought with some relief that this would be my last visit, and that at the least the clinic was over with all its eroding grind. I climbed out of the ambulance and started off down the corridor, but one of the men stopped me and said that I had to go in a wheelchair. What do you mean, I said, I can walk.

'You're not allowed to walk,' he said.

'Why ever not?' I asked, not because I objected to going in a wheelchair, but because I couldn't see why not. 'I walked at the other end,' I said.

'Ah yes,' said the man, 'but at this end you're not allowed to. Come along now, you're our responsibility now, we can't allow you to walk, I'm afraid.'

So I sat down, succumbing to his threat that he would lose his job if I didn't, and they wheeled me off down countless corridors, up in a lift, down a floor in another one, and into a large room where I was told to get up and go and sign a list. Here, it seemed, I was allowed to walk. I had been expecting to see a few familiar faces, such as the thin little Yorkshire nurse, the fat Irish one, or even the smart red-haired midwife; I had, luckily in the event, no grandiose expectations of seeing any doctors or gynaecologists. But there was not a face I recognized in sight: a whole new army of people appeared to have taken over, who presumably came out only at night. I was a little disappointed; the other faces had become almost endeared by familiarity. I signed my name on the relevant register; the nurse in charge of it looked up and said, 'Well, you're the only one in tonight, we *were* having a quiet night,' and I smiled feebly, unsure whether she was expressing pleasure or annoyance at having something to do.

Margaret Drabble

Then they took me off to another room and took away all my clothes and put me in a hospital nightgown and asked me how often my contractions were. When I told them, they said Nonsense, but when they investigated they naturally enough found me to be right. Then they did various other unpleasant and compulsory things, found me my book when I asked for it, and left me to it, telling me to ring if I wanted anything. I lay there on this hard high bed for half an hour, trying to read, and then I rang the bell and asked if they couldn't do something about it. Not yet, they said, and off they went. I lay there for another ten minutes and then a quite different nurse came in and said I had to move, somebody else had to have my bed. I lay there and looked at her and said how. Don't you feel like walking, she said, and I said Oh, all right, as she seemed to expect me to, and I heaved myself down off this mountainously high iron bedstead and followed her down a corridor and into another room, where she helped me on to an equally high identical bed. Then I asked once more, politely, if they couldn't do something about it, and she said Oh yes, of course, wasn't it time I had some pethidine, and she would go and find someone to give me an injection.

A quarter of an hour later about five nurses arrived with the pethidine, which they administered; then they all sat in a row in the corridor outside and started to talk about their boyfriends. I listened to their conversation, trying to distract myself from sensations that did not seem quite reasonable or endurable, and after a while the drug began to work: the pain did not diminish but my resistance to it disappeared, and every two minutes regularly it flowed through me as though I were some other person, and as though I myself, what was left of me, was watching this swell and ebb from many miles away. It was no longer personal and therefore bearable; I just lay there and let it happen, and the voices of the five girls came to me very clearly and purely, the syntax

The Millstone

and connections of their dialogue illuminated by a strange pale warm light. One of them started off by telling the others about some character called Frank, against whom the others had apparently been warning her for some time, for when she described the way in which he had squeezed her knee in the cinema, the others began to exclaim with predestined admiring indignation.

'Honestly, I *told* you what he was like,' one of them said. 'I *told* you what he'd be up to, didn't I? You should have heard what Elaine said about him after the Christmas Ball.'

'Elaine asks for it,' said another voice, and they all giggled, and somebody else said, 'Well, you don't exactly go out of your way to avoid it yourself, do you? I mean to say, what *about* that dress you had on the other day? If that wasn't a topless dress, I'd like to know what is.'

'Do you know *what*,' said the owner of the dress, 'happened to me last time I was wearing it? I had to dash home, it was a Thursday and I hadn't got a late leave, and I *just* got to the corner of Charles Street at eleven-thirty, and I had to run like anything, and anyway I just got to the door as Bessie was locking up and I got in all right, but who do you think I met on the other side but Mrs Sammy Spillikins, all in her dressing-gown and slippers, and she gave me such a look and said in that voice of hers, you know what she sounds like, Well, well, well, Miss Ellis, she said, you do cut things rather fine, don't you? Are you in the habit of leaving things to the last moment like this? Mean old cow, I'd like to know what it's got to do with her. And she said she wanted a word, and she followed me all the way up to my room, just on the pretext of asking me some question about what Dr Cohen asked Gillian to do about the new radiator in the waiting room, and she stayed so long I had to take my coat off, and she kept looking and looking at me, and when she left do you know what she said? She said, In my day, with a dress like that, we used to wear modesty vests.'

Once more they all giggled merrily, and then someone volunteered the information that however old Sammy Spillikins looked, she was really only forty-two, which she had on the best of authority, and somebody else described, though as a matter of fact inaccurately, what a modesty vest was, when one of the gathering claimed not to know.

'How *disgusting*,' the ignorant one said vehemently when enlightened.

They then told some more anecdotes about their evidently circumscribed love lives before moving on to discuss their trade. They began mildly enough by inquiring how many had been born the night before, and what had happened to the little premature one that was failing earlier in the evening, but after a while the tone really became too extreme for my possible comfort; they described cases of women who had lain in labour for unbelievable lengths of time, of one who had screamed solidly for three hours, of a black woman who had scratched a nurse's face when she tried to give her an enema, of a white woman who had sworn at one of the black nurses and told her to get out, she wasn't having her filthy hands on her nice clean new baby. One of them said *en passant*, 'I'll be really glad to get out of this ward. I don't really mind the babies, but the mothers are enough to give anyone the creeps.' Then one of them started to recount in vivid detail the story of a woman whose labour she had attended a month earlier, who had died because they discovered at the last moment that this that and the other hadn't been properly dealt with; 'it was awful,' this girl said, 'the way they kept on telling her it was all fine, and I could see them getting bluer and bluer, you know how they look when anything really bad starts up.' At this I could take it no longer, and I heard my voice yell, from a long way away, 'Oh, for God's sake, pack it in, can't you?'

I don't think they caught what I said despite my

The Millstone

unnatural loudness of tone, but two of them came bustling in and said, 'What was that, did you call, how are you getting on?'

'I think this drug thing must be wearing off,' I said mildly, 'because it seems to be getting worse and worse, can you give me something else please, quick?'

'Oh no!' they said, 'not yet, you've a long time to go yet, we have to leave something to give you later on.'

'Oh,' I said feebly, 'what a pity.'

'Never mind,' they said, 'you're coming along nicely,' and they turned and went back to their row of seats outside and had just resumed their conversation, though in more muffled tones, when I heard myself start to moan rather violently, and they all came rushing back and within five minutes my child was born.

Right up to the very last minute, through sensations which though unbelievably violent were now no longer painful but indeed almost a promise of pleasure, I could hear them arguing among themselves, all of them; one had been dispatched for the midwife, one was looking for the gas and air, one was asking the others why they hadn't believed what I said, and another, while delivering the baby, had taken upon herself the task of calmer and soother of my nerves.

'That's all right,' she kept saying, 'that's fine, you're coming along fine. Oh, do try not to push.'

There was more panic in her smooth tones than in me; I felt all right now, I felt fine. The child was born in a great rush and hurry, quite uncontrolled and undelivered; they told me afterwards that they only just caught her, and I felt her fall from me and instantly sat up and opened my eyes, and they said, 'It's a girl, it's a lovely little girl.'

They told me to lie down again, and I lay down, asking if the baby was all right, expecting suddenly I don't know what, missing arms and fingers, and they said she was all right; so I lay there, happy that it was over, not expecting they would let me see her, and then I heard her cry,

Margaret Drabble

a strange loud sobbing cry. The midwife had by now arrived, all smiles and starch, and actually apologized for not having been there. 'It was quite a case,' she said, 'of too many cooks spoil the broth, you know, but you certainly managed to do all right without me, didn't you?' All the nurses too were suddenly humanized; they clustered round, helping to wash me and straighten me out, and telling me how unbelievably quick I'd been, and how I should have made more fuss, and that it was only half past two, and what was I going to call the baby. This last question was hastily silenced by the midwife, who presumably assumed the child would not be mine for long, but I did not care. I felt remarkably well, a usual reaction I believe on such occasions, and I could have got up and walked away. After ten minutes or so, when I had been returned to my own nightdress, a garment covered in Mexican embroidery which Beatrice had sent specially for the occasion, and which drew screams of admiration from the girls, the midwife asked me if I would like to see the child. 'Please,' I said gratefully, and she went away and came back with my daughter wrapped up in a small grey bloodstained blanket, and with a ticket saying Stacey round her ankle. She put her in my arms and I sat there looking at her, and her great wide blue eyes looked at me with seeming recognition, and what I felt it is pointless to try to describe. Love, I suppose one might call it, and the first of my life.

Daphne Du Maurier
The Birds

On December the third the wind changed overnight and it was winter. Until then the autumn had been mellow, soft. The leaves had lingered on the trees, golden red, and the hedgerows were still green. The earth was rich where the plough had turned it.

Nat Hocken, because of a wartime disability, had a pension and did not work full-time at the farm. He worked three days a week, and they gave him the lighter jobs: hedging, thatching, repairs to the farm buildings.

Although he was married, with children, his was a solitary disposition; he liked best to work alone. It pleased him when he was given a bank to build up, or a gate to mend at the far end of the peninsula, where the sea surrounded the farm land on either side. Then, at midday, he would pause and eat the pasty that his wife had baked for him, and sitting on the cliff's edge would watch the birds. Autumn was best for this, better than spring. In spring the birds flew inland, purposeful, intent; they knew where they were bound, the rhythm and ritual of their life brooked no delay. In autumn those that had not migrated overseas but remained to pass the winter were caught up in the same driving urge, but because migration was denied them followed a pattern of their own. Great flocks of them came to the peninsula, restless, uneasy, spending themselves in motion; now wheeling, circling in the sky, now settling to feed on the rich new-turned soil, but even when they fed it was as though they did so without hunger, without desire. Restlessness drove them to the skies again.

Black and white, jackdaw and gull, mingled in strange partnership, seeking some sort of liberation, never satisfied, never still. Flocks of starlings, rustling like silk, flew to fresh pasture, driven by the same necessity of movement, and the smaller birds, the finches and the larks, scattered from tree to hedge as if compelled.

Nat watched them, and he watched the sea-birds too. Down in the bay they waited for the tide. They had more patience. Oyster-catchers, redshank, sanderling and curlew watched by the water's edge; as the slow sea sucked at the shore and then withdrew, leaving the strip of seaweed bare and the shingle churned, the sea-birds raced and ran upon the beaches. Then that same impulse to flight seized upon them too. Crying, whistling, calling, they skimmed the placid sea and left the shore. Make haste, make speed, hurry and begone; yet where, and to what purpose? The restless urge of autumn, unsatisfying, sad, had put a spell upon them and they must flock, and wheel, and cry; they must spill themselves of motion before winter came.

Perhaps, thought Nat, munching his pasty by the cliff's edge, a message comes to the birds in autumn, like a warning. Winter is coming. Many of them perish. And like people who, apprehensive of death before their time, drive themselves to work or folly, the birds do likewise.

The birds had been more restless than ever this fall of the year, the agitation more marked because the days were still. As the tractor traced its path up and down the western hills, the figure of the farmer silhouetted on the driving-seat, the whole machine and the man upon it would be lost momentarily in the great cloud of wheeling, crying birds. There were many more than usual, Nat was sure of this. Always, in autumn, they followed the plough, but not in great flocks like these, nor with such clamour.

Nat remarked upon it, when hedging was finished for

The Birds

the day. 'Yes,' said the farmer, 'there are more birds about than usual; I've noticed it too. And daring some of them, taking no notice of the tractor. One or two gulls came so close to my head this afternoon I thought they'd knock my cap off! As it was, I could scarcely see what I was doing, when they were overhead and I had the sun in my eyes. I have a notion the weather will change. It will be a hard winter. That's why the birds are restless.'

Nat, tramping home across the fields and down the lane to his cottage, saw the birds still flocking over the western hills, in the last glow of the sun. No wind, and the grey sea calm and full. Campion in bloom yet in the hedges, and the air mild. The farmer was right, though, and it was that night the weather turned. Nat's bedroom faced east. He woke just after two and heard the wind in the chimney. Not the storm and bluster of a sou' westerly gale, bringing the rain, but east wind, cold and dry. It sounded hollow in the chimney, and a loose slate rattled on the roof. Nat listened, and he could hear the sea roaring in the bay. Even the air in the small bedroom had turned chill: a draught came under the skirting of the door, blowing upon the bed. Nat drew the blanket round him, leant closer to the back of his sleeping wife, and stayed wakeful, watchful, aware of misgiving without cause.

Then he heard the tapping on the window. There was no creeper on the cottage walls to break loose and scratch upon the pane. He listened, and the tapping continued until, irritated by the sound, Nat got out of bed and went to the window. He opened it, and as he did so something brushed his hand, jabbing at his knuckles, grazing the skin. Then he saw the flutter of the wings and it was gone, over the roof, behind the cottage.

It was a bird, what kind of bird he could not tell. The wind must have driven it to shelter on the sill.

He shut the window and went back to bed, but feeling his knuckles wet put his mouth to the scratch. The bird had drawn blood. Frightened, he supposed, and bewildered, the bird, seeking shelter, had stabbed at him in the darkness. Once more he settled himself to sleep.

Presently the tapping came again, this time more forceful, more insistent, and now his wife woke at the sound, and turning in the bed said to him, 'See to the window, Nat, it's rattling.'

'I've already seen to it,' he told her, 'there's some bird there, trying to get in. Can't you hear the wind? It's blowing from the east, driving the birds to shelter.'

'Send them away,' she said, 'I can't sleep with that noise.'

He went to the window for the second time, and now when he opened it there was not one bird upon the sill but half a dozen; they flew straight into his face, attacking him.

He shouted, striking out at them with his arms, scattering them; like the first one, they flew over the roof and disappeared. Quickly he let the window fall and latched it.

'Did you hear that?' he said. 'They went for me. Tried to peck my eyes.' He stood by the window, peering into the darkness, and could see nothing. His wife, heavy with sleep, murmured from the bed.

'I'm not making it up,' he said, angry at her suggestion. 'I tell you the birds were on the sill, trying to get into the room.'

Suddenly a frightened cry came from the room across the passage where the children slept.

'It's Jill,' said his wife, roused at the sound, sitting up in bed. 'Go to her, see what's the matter.'

Nat lit the candle, but when he opened the bedroom door to cross the passage the draught blew out the flame.

There came a second cry of terror, this time from both children, and stumbling into their room he felt the beating of wings about him in the darkness. The window was wide open. Through it came the birds, hitting first the

The Birds

ceiling and the walls, then swerving in mid-flight, turning to the children in their beds.

'It's all right, I'm here,' shouted Nat, and the children flung themselves, screaming, upon him, while in the darkness the birds rose and dived and came for him again.

'What is it, Nat, what's happened?' his wife called from the further bedroom, and swiftly he pushed the children through the door to the passage and shut it upon them, so that he was alone now, in their bedroom, with the birds.

He seized a blanket from the nearest bed, and using it as a weapon flung it to right and left about him in the air. He felt the thud of bodies, heard the fluttering of wings, but they were not yet defeated, for again and again they returned to the assault, jabbing his hands, his head, the little stabbing beaks sharp as a pointed fork. The blanket became a weapon of defence; he wound it about his head, and then in greater darkness beat at the birds with his bare hands. He dared not stumble to the door and open it, lest in doing so the birds should follow him.

How long he fought with them in the darkness he could not tell, but at last the beating of the wings about him lessened and then withdrew, and through the density of the blanket he was aware of light. He waited, listened; there was no sound except the fretful crying of one of the children from the bedroom beyond. The fluttering, the whirring of the wings had ceased.

He took the blanket from his head and stared about him. The cold grey morning light exposed the room. Dawn, and the open window, had called the living birds; the dead lay on the floor. Nat gazed at the little corpses, shocked and horrified. They were all small birds, none of any size; there must have been fifty of them lying there upon the floor. There were robins, finches, sparrows, blue tits, larks and bramblings, birds that by nature's law kept to their own flock and their own territory, and now, joining one with another in their urge for battle, had destroyed themselves against the bedroom walls, or in the strife had been destroyed by him. Some had lost feathers in the fight, others had blood, his blood, upon their beaks.

Sickened, Nat went to the window and stared out across his patch of garden to the fields.

It was bitter cold, and the ground had all the hard black look of frost. Not white frost, to shine in the morning sun, but the black frost that the east wind brings. The sea, fiercer now with the turning tide, white-capped and steep, broke harshly in the bay. Of the birds there was no sign. Not a sparrow chattered in the hedge beyond the garden gate, no early missel-thrush or blackbird pecked on the grass for worms. There was no sound at all but the east wind and the sea.

Nat shut the window and the door of the small bedroom, and went back across the passage to his own. His wife sat up in bed, one child asleep beside her, the smaller in her arms, his face bandaged. The curtains were tightly drawn across the window, the candles lit. Her face looked garish in the yellow light. She shook her head for silence.

'He's sleeping now,' she whispered, 'but only just. Something must have cut him, there was blood at the corner of his eyes. Jill said it was the birds. She said she woke up, and the birds were in the room.'

His wife looked up at Nat, searching his face for confirmation. She looked terrified, bewildered, and he did not want her to know that he was also shaken, dazed almost, by the events of the past few hours.

'There are birds in there,' he said, 'dead birds, nearly fifty of them. Robins, wrens, all the little birds from hereabouts. It's as though a madness seized them, with the east wind.' He sat down on the bed beside his wife, and held her hand. 'It's the weather,' he said, 'it must be that, it's the hard weather. They aren't the birds, maybe, from here around. They've been driven down, from up country.'

'But Nat,' whispered his wife, 'it's only this night that

The Birds

the weather turned. There's been no snow to drive them. And they can't be hungry yet. There's food for them, out there, in the fields.'

'It's the weather,' repeated Nat. 'I tell you, it's the weather.'

His face too was drawn and tired, like hers. They stared at one another for a while without speaking.

'I'll go downstairs and make a cup of tea,' he said.

The sight of the kitchen reassured him. The cups and saucers, neatly stacked upon the dresser, the table and chairs, his wife's roll of knitting on her basket chair, the children's toys in a corner cupboard.

He knelt down, raked out the old embers and relit the fire. The glowing sticks brought normality, the steaming kettle and the brown teapot comfort and security. He drank his tea, carried a cup up to his wife. Then he washed in the scullery, and, putting on his boots, opened the back door.

The sky was hard and leaden, and the brown hills that had gleamed in the sun the day before looked dark and bare. The east wind, like a razor, stripped the trees, and the leaves, crackling and dry, shivered and scattered with the wind's blast. Nat stubbed the earth with his boot. It was frozen hard. He had never known a change so swift and sudden. Black winter had descended in a single night.

The children were awake now. Jill was chattering upstairs and young Johnny crying once again. Nat heard his wife's voice, soothing, comforting. Presently they came down. He had breakfast ready for them, and the routine of the day began.

'Did you drive away the birds?' asked Jill, restored to calm because of the kitchen fire, because of day, because of breakfast.

'Yes, they've all gone now,' said Nat. 'It was the east wind brought them in. They were frightened and lost, they wanted shelter.'

'They tried to peck us,' said Jill. 'They went for Johnny's eyes.'

'Fright made them do that,' said Nat. 'They didn't know where they were, in the dark bedroom.'

'I hope they won't come again,' said Jill. 'Perhaps if we put bread for them outside the window they will eat that and fly away.'

She finished her breakfast and then went for her coat and hood, her school books and her satchel. Nat said nothing, but his wife looked at him across the table. A silent message passed between them.

'I'll walk with her to the bus,' he said. 'I don't go to the farm today.'

And while the child was washing in the scullery he said to his wife, 'Keep all the windows closed, and the doors too. Just to be on the safe side. I'll go to the farm. Find out if they heard anything in the night.' Then he walked with his small daughter up the lane. She seemed to have forgotten her experience of the night before. She danced ahead of him, chasing the leaves, her face whipped with the cold and rosy under the pixie hood.

'Is it going to snow, Dad?' she said. 'It's cold enough.'

He glanced up at the bleak sky, felt the wind tear at his shoulders.

'No,' he said, 'it's not going to snow. This is a black winter, not a white one.'

All the while he searched the hedgerows for the birds, glanced over the top of them to the fields beyond, looked to the small wood above the farm where the rooks and jackdaws gathered. He saw none.

The other children waited by the bus stop, muffled, hooded like Jill, the faces white and pinched with cold.

Jill ran to them, waving. 'My dad says it won't snow,' she called, 'it's going to be a black winter.'

She said nothing of the birds. She began to push and struggle with another little girl. The bus came ambling up the hill. Nat saw her on to it, then turned and walked

The Birds

back towards the farm. It was not his day for work, but he wanted to satisfy himself that all was well. Jim, the cowman, was clattering in the yard.

'Boss around?' asked Nat.

'Gone to market,' said Jim. 'It's Tuesday, isn't it?'

He clumped off round the corner of a shed. He had no time for Nat. Nat was said to be superior. Read books, and the like. Nat had forgotten it was Tuesday. This showed how the events of the preceding night had shaken him. He went to the back door of the farmhouse and heard Mrs Trigg singing in the kitchen, the wireless making a background to her song.

'Are you there, missus?' called out Nat.

She came to the door, beaming, broad, a good-tempered woman.

'Hullo, Mr Hocken,' she said. 'Can you tell me where this cold is coming from? Is it Russia? I've never seen such a change. And it's going on, the wireless says. Something to do with the Arctic circle.'

'We didn't turn on the wireless this morning,' said Nat. 'Fact is, we had trouble in the night.'

'Kiddies poorly?'

'No . . .' He hardly knew how to explain it. Now, in daylight, the battle of the birds would sound absurd.

He tried to tell Mrs Trigg what had happened, but he could see from her eyes that she thought his story was the result of a nightmare.

'Sure they were real birds,' she said, smiling, 'with proper feathers and all? Not the funny-shaped kind, that the men see after closing hours on a Saturday night?'

'Mrs Trigg,' he said, 'there are fifty dead birds, robins, wrens and such, lying low on the floor of the children's bedroom. They went for me; they tried to go for young Johnny's eyes.'

Mrs Trigg stared at him doubtfully.

'Well there, now,' she answered, 'I suppose the weather brought them. Once in the bedroom, they wouldn't know

285

Daphne Du Maurier

where they were to. Foreign birds maybe, from that Arctic circle.'

'No,' said Nat, 'they were the birds you see about here every day.'

'Funny thing,' said Mrs Trigg, 'no explaining it, really. You ought to write up and ask the *Guardian*. They'd have some answer for it. Well, I must be getting on.'

She nodded, smiled, and went back into the kitchen.

Nat, dissatisfied, turned to the farm-gate. Had it not been for those corpses on the bedroom floor, which he must now collect and bury somewhere, he would have considered the tale exaggeration too.

Jim was standing by the gate.

'Had any trouble with the birds?' asked Nat.

'Birds? What birds?'

'We got them up our place last night. Scores of them, came in the children's bedroom. Quite savage they were.'

'Oh?' It took time for anything to penetrate Jim's head. 'Never heard of birds acting savage,' he said at length. 'They get tame, like, sometimes. I've seen them come to the windows for crumbs.'

'These birds last night weren't tame.'

'No? Cold maybe. Hungry. You put out some crumbs.'

Jim was no more interested than Mrs Trigg had been. It was, Nat thought, like air-raids in the war. No one down this end of the country knew what the Plymouth folk had seen and suffered. You had to endure something yourself before it touched you. He walked back along the lane and crossed the stile to his cottage. He found his wife in the kitchen with young Johnnie.

'See anyone?' she asked.

'Mrs Trigg and Jim,' he answered. 'I don't think they believed me. Anyway, nothing wrong up there.'

'You might take the birds away,' she said. 'I daren't go into the room to make the beds until you do. I'm scared.'

'Nothing to scare you now,' said Nat. 'They're dead, aren't they?'

The Birds

He went up with a sack and dropped the stiff bodies into it, one by one. Yes, there were fifty of them, all told. Just the ordinary common birds of the hedgerow, nothing as large even as a thrush. It must have been fright that made them act the way they did. Blue tits, wrens, it was incredible to think of the power of their small beaks, jabbing at his face and hands the night before. He took the sack out into the garden and was faced now with a fresh problem. The ground was too hard to dig. It was frozen solid, yet no snow had fallen, nothing had happened in the past hours but the coming of the east wind. It was unnatural, queer. The weather prophets must be right. The change was something connected with the Arctic circle.

The wind seemed to cut him to the bone as he stood there, uncertainly, holding the sack. He could see the white-capped seas breaking down under in the bay. He decided to take the birds to the shore and bury them.

When he reached the beach below the headland he could scarcely stand, the force of the east wind was so strong. It hurt to draw breath, and his bare hands were blue. Never had he known such cold, not in all the bad winters he could remember. It was low tide. He crunched his way over the shingle to the softer sand and then, his back to the wind, ground a pit in the sand with his heel. He meant to drop the birds into it, but as he opened up the sack the force of the wind carried them, lifted them, as though in flight again, and they were blown away from him along the beach, tossed like feathers, spread and scattered, the bodies of the fifty frozen birds. There was something ugly in the sight. He did not like it. The dead birds were swept away from him by the wind.

'The tide will take them when it turns,' he said to himself.

He looked out to sea and watched the crested breakers, combing green. They rose stiffly, curled, and broke again, and because it was ebb tide the roar was distant, more remote, lacking the sound and thunder of the flood.

Then he saw them. The gulls. Out there, riding the seas.

What he had thought at first to be the white caps of the waves were gulls. Hundreds, thousands, tens of thousands ... They rose and fell in the trough of the seas, heads to the wind, like a mighty fleet at anchor, waiting on the tide. To eastward, and to the west, the gulls were there. They stretched as far as his eye could reach, in close formation, line upon line. Had the sea been still they would have covered the bay like a white cloud, head to head, body packed to body. Only the east wind, whipping the sea to breakers, hid them from the shore.

Nat turned, and leaving the beach climbed the steep path home. Someone should know of this. Someone should be told. Something was happening, because of the east wind and the weather, that he did not understand. He wondered if he should go to the call box by the bus stop and ring up the police. Yet what could they do? What could anyone do? Tens and thousands of gulls riding the sea there, in the bay, because of the storm, because of hunger. The police would think him mad, or drunk, or take the statement from him with great calm. 'Thank you. Yes, the matter has already been reported. The hard weather is driving the birds inland in great numbers.' Nat looked about him. Still no sign of any other bird. Perhaps the cold had sent them all from up country? As he drew near to the cottage his wife came to meet him, at the door. She called to him, excited. 'Nat,' she said, 'it's on the wireless. They've just read out a special news bulletin. I've written it down.'

'What's on the wireless?' he said.

'About the birds,' she said. 'It's not only here, it's everywhere. In London, all over the country. Something has happened to the birds.'

Together they went into the kitchen. He read the piece of paper lying on the table.

'Statement from the Home Office at eleven a.m. today.

The Birds

Reports from all over the country are coming in hourly about the vast quantity of birds flocking above towns, villages and outlying districts, causing obstruction and damage and even attacking individuals. It is thought that the Arctic air stream, at present covering the British Isles, is causing birds to migrate south in immense numbers, and that intense hunger may drive these birds to attack human beings. Householders are warned to see to their windows, doors and chimneys, and to take reasonable precautions for the safety of their children. A further statement will be issued later.'

A kind of excitement seized Nat; he looked at his wife in triumph.

'There you are,' he said, 'let's hope they'll hear that at the farm. Mrs Trigg will know it wasn't any story. It's true. All over the country. I've been telling myself all morning there's something wrong. And just now, down on the beach, I looked out to sea and there are gulls, thousands of them, tens of thousands, you couldn't put a pin between their heads, and they're all out there, riding on the sea, waiting.'

'What are they waiting for, Nat?' she asked.

He stared at her, then looked down again at the piece of paper.

'I don't know,' he said slowly. 'It says here the birds are hungry.'

He went over to the drawer where he kept his hammer and tools.

'What are you going to do, Nat?'

'See to the windows and the chimneys too, like they tell you.'

'You think they would break in, with the windows shut? Those sparrows and robins and such? Why, how could they?'

He did not answer. He was not thinking of the robins and the sparrows. He was thinking of the gulls . . .

He went upstairs and worked there the rest of the

morning, boarding the windows of the bedrooms, filling up the chimney bases. Good job it was his free day and he was not working at the farm. It reminded him of the old days, at the beginning of the war. He was not married then, and he had made all the blackout boards for his mother's house in Plymouth. Made the shelter too. Not that it had been of any use, when the moment came. He wondered if they would take these precautions up at the farm. He doubted it. Too easy-going, Harry Trigg and his missus. Maybe they'd laugh at the whole thing. Go off to a dance or a whist drive.

'Dinner's ready.' She called him, from the kitchen.

'All right. Coming down.'

He was pleased with his handiwork. The frames fitted nicely over the little panes and at the base of the chimneys.

When dinner was over and his wife was washing up, Nat switched on the one o'clock news. The same announcement was repeated, the one which she had taken down during the morning, but the news bulletin enlarged upon it. 'The flocks of birds have caused dislocation in all areas,' read the announcer, 'and in London the sky was so dense at ten o'clock this morning that it seemed as if the city was covered by a vast black cloud.

'The birds settled on rooftops, on window ledges and on chimneys. The species included blackbird, thrush, the common house-sparrow, and, as might be expected in the metropolis, a vast quantity of pigeons and starlings, and that frequenter of the London river, the black-headed gull. The sight has been so unusual that traffic came to a standstill in many thoroughfares, work was abandoned in shops and offices, and the streets and pavements were crowded with people standing about to watch the birds.'

Various incidents were recounted, the suspected reason of cold and hunger stated again, and warnings to householders repeated. The announcer's voice was smooth and

The Birds

suave. Nat had the impression that this man, in particular, treated the whole business as he would an elaborate joke. There would be others like him, hundreds of them, who did not know what it was to struggle in darkness with a flock of birds. There would be parties tonight in London, like the ones they gave on election nights. People standing about, shouting and laughing, getting drunk. 'Come and watch the birds!'

Nat switched off the wireless. He got up and started work on the kitchen windows. His wife watched him, young Johnny at her heels.

'What, boards for down here too?' she said. 'Why, I'll have to light up before three o'clock. I see no call for boards down here.'

'Better be sure than sorry,' answered Nat. 'I'm not going to take any chances.'

'What they ought to do,' she said, 'is to call the army out and shoot the birds. That would soon scare them off.'

'Let them try,' said Nat. 'How'd they set about it?'

'They have the army to the docks,' she answered, 'when the dockers strike. The soldiers go down and unload the ships.'

'Yes,' said Nat, 'and the population of London is eight million or more. Think of all the buildings, all the flats, and houses. Do you think they've enough soldiers to go round shooting birds from every roof?'

'I don't know. But something should be done. They ought to do something.'

Nat thought to himself that 'they' were no doubt considering the problem at that very moment, but whatever 'they' decided to do in London and the big cities would not help the people here, three hundred miles away. Each householder must look after his own.

'How are we off for food?' he said.

'Now, Nat, whatever next?'

'Never mind. What have you got in the larder?'

'It's shopping day tomorrow, you know that. I don't keep uncooked food hanging about, it goes off. Butcher doesn't call till the day after. But I can bring back something when I go in tomorrow.'

Nat did not want to scare her. He thought it possible that she might not go to town tomorrow. He looked in the larder for himself, and in the cupboard where she kept her tins. They would do, for a couple of days. Bread was low.

'What about the baker?'

'He comes tomorrow too.'

He saw she had flour. If the baker did not call she had enough to bake one loaf.

'We'd be better off in old days,' he said, 'when the women baked twice a week, and had pilchards salted, and there was food for a family to last a siege, if need be.'

'I've tried the children with tinned fish, they don't like it,' she said.

Nat went on hammering the boards across the kitchen windows. Candles. They were low in candles too. That must be another thing she meant to buy tomorrow. Well, it could not be helped. They must go early to bed tonight. That was, if . . .

He got up and went out of the back door and stood in the garden, looking down towards the sea. There had been no sun all day, and now, at barely three o'clock, a kind of darkness had already come, the sky sullen, heavy, colourless like salt. He could hear the vicious sea drumming on the rocks. He walked down the path, half-way to the beach. And then he stopped. He could see the tide had turned. The rock that had shown in mid-morning was now covered, but it was not the sea that held his eyes. The gulls had risen. They were circling, hundreds of them, thousands of them, lifting their wings against the wind. It was the gulls that made the darkening of the sky. And they were silent. They made not a sound. They

The Birds

just went on soaring and circling, rising, falling, trying their strength against the wind.

Nat turned. He ran up the path, back to the cottage.

'I'm going for Jill,' he said. 'I'll wait for her, at the bus stop.'

'What's the matter?' asked his wife. 'You've gone quite white.'

'Keep Johnny inside,' he said. 'Keep the door shut. Light up now, and draw the curtains.'

'It's only just gone three,' she said.

'Never mind. Do what I tell you.'

He looked inside the toolshed, outside the back door. Nothing there of much use. A spade was too heavy, and a fork no good. He took the hoe. It was the only possible tool, and light enough to carry.

He started walking up the lane to the bus stop, and now and again glanced back over his shoulder.

The gulls had risen higher now, their circles were broader, wider, they were spreading out in huge formation across the sky.

He hurried on; although he knew the bus would not come to the top of the hill before four o'clock he had to hurry. He passed no one on the way. He was glad of this. No time to stop and chatter.

At the top of the hill he waited. He was much too soon. There was half an hour still to go. The east wind came whipping across the fields from the higher ground. He stamped his feet and blew upon his hands. In the distance he could see the clay hills, white and clean, against the heavy pallor of the sky. Something black rose from behind them, like a smudge at first, then widening, becoming deeper, and the smudge became a cloud, and the cloud divided again into five other clouds, spreading north, east, south and west, and they were not clouds at all; they were birds. He watched them travel across the sky, and as one section passed overhead, within two or three hundred feet of him, he knew, from their speed, they were bound inland, up country, they had no business with the people here on the peninsula. They were rooks, crows, jackdaws, magpies, jays, all birds that usually preyed upon the smaller species; but this afternoon they were bound on some other mission.

'They've been given the towns,' thought Nat, 'they know what they have to do. We don't matter so much here. The gulls will serve for us. The others go to the towns.'

He went to the call-box, stepped inside and lifted the receiver. The exchange would do. They would pass the message on.

'I'm speaking from Highway,' he said, 'by the bus stop. I want to report large formations of birds travelling up country. The gulls are also forming in the bay.'

'All right,' answered the voice, laconic, weary.

'You'll be sure and pass this message on to the proper quarter?'

'Yes . . . yes . . .' Impatient now, fed-up. The buzzing note resumed.

'She's another,' thought Nat, 'she doesn't care. Maybe she's had to answer calls all day. She hopes to go to the pictures tonight. She'll squeeze some fellow's hand, and point up at the sky, "Look at all them birds!" She doesn't care.'

The bus came lumbering up the hill. Jill climbed out and three or four other children. The bus went on towards the town.

'What's the hoe for, Dad?'

They crowded around him, laughing, pointing.

'I just brought it along,' he said. 'Come on now, let's get home. It's cold, no hanging about. Here, you. I'll watch you across the fields, see how fast you can run.'

He was speaking to Jill's companions who came from different families, living in the council houses. A short cut would take them to the cottages.

'We want to play a bit in the lane,' said one of them.

The Birds

'No, you don't. You go off home, or I'll tell your mammy.'

They whispered to one another, round-eyed, then scuttled off across the fields. Jill stared at her father, her mouth sullen.

'We always play in the lane,' she said.

'Not tonight, you don't,' he said. 'Come on now, no dawdling.'

He could see the gulls now, circling the fields, coming in towards the land. Still silent. Still no sound.

'Look, Dad, look over there, look at all the gulls.'

'Yes. Hurry, now.'

'Where are they flying to? Where are they going?'

'Up country, I dare say. Where it's warmer.'

He seized her hand and dragged her after him along the lane.

'Don't go so fast. I can't keep up.'

The gulls were copying the rooks and crows. They were spreading out in formation across the sky. They headed, in bands of thousands, to the four compass points.

'Dad, what is it? What are the gulls doing?'

They were not intent upon their flight, as the crows, as the jackdaws had been. They still circled overhead. Nor did they fly so high. It was as though they waited upon some signal. As though some decision had yet to be given. The order was not clear.

'Do you want me to carry you, Jill? Here, come pick-a-back.'

This way he might put on speed; but he was wrong. Jill was heavy. She kept slipping. And she was crying too. His sense of urgency, of fear, had communicated itself to the child.

'I wish the gulls would go away. I don't like them. They're coming closer to the lane.'

He put her down again. He started running, swinging Jill after him. As they went past the farm turning he saw the farmer backing his car out of the garage. Nat called to him.

'Can you give us a lift?' he said.

'What's that?'

Mr Trigg turned in the driving seat and stared at them. Then a smile came to his cheerful, rubicund face.

'It looks as though we're in for some fun,' he said. 'Have you seen the gulls? Jim and I are going to take a crack at them. Everyone's gone bird crazy, talking of nothing else. I hear you were troubled in the night. Want a gun?'

Nat shook his head.

The small car was packed. There was just room for Jill, if she crouched on top of petrol tins on the back seat.

'I don't want a gun,' said Nat, 'but I'd be obliged if you'd run Jill home. She's scared of the birds.'

He spoke briefly. He did not want to talk in front of Jill.

'O.K.,' said the farmer, 'I'll take her home. Why don't you stop behind and join the shooting match? We'll make the feathers fly.'

Jill climbed in, and turning the car the driver sped up the lane. Nat followed after. Trigg must be crazy. What use was a gun against a sky of birds?

Now Nat was not responsible for Jill he had time to look about him. The birds were circling still, above the fields. Mostly herring gull, but the black-backed gull amongst them. Usually they kept apart. Now they were united. Some bond had brought them together. It was the black-backed gull that attacked the smaller birds, and even new-born lambs, so he'd heard. He'd never seen it done. He remembered this now, though, looking above him in the sky. They were coming in towards the farm. They were circling lower in the sky, and the black-backed gulls were to the front, the black-backed gulls were leading. The farm, then, was their target. They were making for the farm.

Nat increased his pace towards his own cottage. He saw the farmer's car turn and come back along the lane. It drew up beside him with a jerk.

The Birds

'The kid has run inside,' said the farmer. 'Your wife was watching for her. Well, what do you make of it? They're saying in town the Russians have done it. The Russians have poisoned the birds.'

'How could they do that?' asked Nat.

'Don't ask me. You know how stories get around. Will you join my shooting match?'

'No, I'll get along home. The wife will be worried else.'

'My missus says if you could eat gull, there'd be some sense in it,' said Trigg, 'we'd have roast gull, baked gull, and pickle 'em into the bargain. You wait until I let off a few barrels into the brutes. That'll scare 'em.'

'Have you boarded your windows?' asked Nat.

'No. Lot of nonsense. They like to scare you on the wireless. I've had more to do today than to go round boarding up my windows.'

'I'd board them now, if I were you.'

'Garn. You're windy. Like to come to our place to sleep?'

'No, thanks all the same.'

'All right. See you in the morning. Give you a gull breakfast.'

The farmer grinned and turned his car to the farm entrance.

Nat hurried on. Past the little wood, past the old barn, and then across the stile to the remaining field.

As he jumped the stile he heard the whirr of wings. A black-backed gull dived down at him from the sky, missed, swerved in flight, and rose to dive again. In a moment it was joined by others, six, seven, a dozen, black-backed and herring mixed. Nat dropped his hoe. The hoe was useless. Covering his head with his arms he ran towards the cottage. They kept coming at him from the air, silent save for the beating wings. The terrible, fluttering wings. He could feel the blood on his hands, his wrists, his neck. Each stab of a swooping beak tore his flesh. If only he could keep them from his eyes. Nothing else mattered. He must keep them from his eyes. They had not learnt yet how to cling to a shoulder, how to rip clothing, how to dive in mass upon the head, upon the body. But with each dive, with each attack, they became bolder. And they had no thought for themselves. When they dived low and missed, they crashed, bruised and broken, on the ground. As Nat ran he stumbled, kicking their spent bodies in front of him.

He found the door, he hammered upon it with his bleeding hands. Because of the boarded windows no light shone. Everything was dark.

'Let me in,' he shouted, 'it's Nat. Let me in.'

He shouted loud to make himself heard above the whirr of the gull's wings.

Then he saw the gannet, poised for the dive, above him in the sky. The gulls circled, retired, soared, one with another, against the wind. Only the gannet remained. One single gannet, above him in the sky. The wings folded suddenly to its body. It dropped, like a stone. Nat screamed, and the door opened. He stumbled across the threshold, and his wife threw her weight against the door.

They heard the thud of the gannet as it fell.

His wife dressed his wounds. They were not deep. The backs of his hands had suffered most, and his wrists. Had he not worn a cap they would have reached his head. As to the gannet . . . the gannet could have split his skull.

The children were crying, of course. They had seen the blood on their father's hands.

'It's all right now,' he told them. 'I'm not hurt. Just a few scratches. You play with Johnny, Jill. Mammy will wash these cuts.'

He half shut the door to the scullery, so that they could not see. His wife was ashen. She began running water from the sink.

The Birds

'I saw them overhead,' she whispered. 'They began collecting just as Jill ran in with Mr Trigg. I shut the door fast, and it jammed. That's why I couldn't open it at once, when you came.'

'Thank God they waited for me,' he said. 'Jill would have fallen at once. One bird alone would have done it.'

Furtively, so as not to alarm the children, they whispered together, as she bandaged his hands and the back of his neck.

'They're flying inland,' he said, 'thousands of them. Rooks, crows, all the bigger birds. I saw them from the bus stop. They're making for the towns.'

'But what can they do, Nat?'

'They'll attack. Go for everyone out in the streets. Then they'll try the windows, the chimneys.'

'Why don't the authorities do something? Why don't they get the army, get machine guns, anything?'

'There's been no time. Nobody's prepared. We'll hear what they have to say on the six o'clock news.'

Nat went back into the kitchen, followed by his wife. Johnny was playing quietly on the floor. Only Jill looked anxious.

'I can hear the birds,' she said. 'Listen, Dad.'

Nat listened. Muffled sounds came from the windows, from the door. Wings brushing the surface, sliding, scraping, seeking a way of entry. The sound of many bodies, pressed together, shuffling on the sills. Now and again came a thud, a crash, as some bird dived and fell. 'Some of them will kill themselves that way,' he thought, 'but not enough. Never enough.'

'All right,' he said aloud, 'I've got boards over the windows, Jill. The birds can't get in.'

He went and examined all the windows. His work had been thorough. Every gap was closed. He would make extra certain, however. He found wedges, pieces of old tin, strips of wood and metal, and fastened them at the sides to reinforce the boards. His hammering helped to deafen the sound of the birds, the shuffling, the tapping, and more ominous – he did not want his wife or the children to hear it – the splinter of cracked glass.

'Turn on the wireless,' he said, 'let's have the wireless.'

This would drown the sound also. He went upstairs to the bedrooms and reinforced the windows there. Now he could hear the birds on the roof, the scraping of claws, a sliding, jostling sound.

He decided they must sleep in the kitchen, keep up the fire, bring down the mattresses and lay them out on the floor. He was afraid of the bedroom chimneys. The boards he had placed at the chimney bases might give way. In the kitchen they would be safe, because of the fire. He would have to make a joke of it. Pretend to the children they were playing at camp. If the worst happened, and the birds forced an entry down the bedroom chimneys, it would be hours, days perhaps, before they could break down the doors. The birds would be imprisoned in the bedrooms. They could do no harm there. Crowded together, they would stifle and die.

He began to bring the mattresses downstairs. At sight of them his wife's eyes widened in apprehension. She thought the birds had already broken in upstairs.

'All right,' he said cheerfully, 'we'll all sleep together in the kitchen tonight. More cosy here by the fire. Then we shan't be worried by those silly old birds tapping at the windows.'

He made the children help him rearrange the furniture, and he took the precaution of moving the dresser, with his wife's help, across the window. It fitted well. It was an added safeguard. The mattresses could now be lain, one beside the other, against the wall where the dresser had stood.

'We're safe enough now,' he thought, 'we're snug and tight, like an air-raid shelter. We can hold out. It's just the food that worries me. Food, and coal for the fire.

The Birds

We've enough for two or three days, not more. By that time...'

No use thinking ahead as far as that. And they'd be giving directions on the wireless. People would be told what to do. And now, in the midst of many problems, he realized that it was dance music only coming over the air. Not Children's Hour, as it should have been. He glanced at the dial. Yes, they were on the Home Service all right. Dance records. He switched to the Light programme. He knew the reason. The usual programmes had been abandoned. This only happened at exceptional times. Elections, and such. He tried to remember if it had happened in the war, during the heavy raids on London. But of course. The BBC was not stationed in London during the war. The programmes were broadcast from other, temporary quarters. 'We're better off here,' he thought, 'we're better off here in the kitchen, with the windows and the doors boarded, than they are up in the towns. Thank God we're not in the towns.'

At six o'clock the records ceased. The time signal was given. No matter if it scared the children, he must hear the news. There was a pause after the pips. Then the announcer spoke. His voice was solemn, grave. Quite different from midday.

'This is London,' he said. 'A National Emergency was proclaimed at four o'clock this afternoon. Measures are being taken to safeguard the lives and property of the population, but it must be understood that these are not easy to effect immediately, owing to the unforeseen and unparalleled nature of the present crisis. Every householder must take precautions to his own building, and where several people live together, as in flats and apartments, they must unite to do the utmost they can to prevent entry. It is absolutely imperative that every individual stays indoors tonight, and that no one at all remains on the streets, or roads, or anywhere without doors. The birds, in vast numbers, are attacking anyone on sight, and have already begun an assault upon buildings; but these, with due care, should be impenetrable. The population is asked to remain calm, and not to panic. Owing to the exceptional nature of the emergency, there will be no further transmission from any broadcasting station until seven a.m. tomorrow.'

They played the National Anthem. Nothing more happened. Nat switched off the set. He looked at his wife. She stared back at him.

'What's it mean?' said Jill. 'What did the news say?'

'There won't be any more programmes tonight,' said Nat. 'There's been a breakdown at the BBC.'

'Is it the birds?' asked Jill. 'Have the birds done it?'

'No,' said Nat, 'it's just that everyone's very busy, and then of course they have to get rid of the birds, messing everything up, in the towns. Well, we can manage without the wireless for one evening.'

'I wish we had a gramophone,' said Jill, 'that would be better than nothing.'

She had her face turned to the dresser, backed against the windows. Try as they did to ignore it, they were all aware of the shuffling, the stabbing, the persistent beating and sweeping of wings.

'We'll have supper early,' suggested Nat, 'something for a treat. Ask Mammy. Toasted cheese, eh? Something we all like?'

He winked and nodded at his wife. He wanted the look of dread, of apprehension, to go from Jill's face.

He helped with the supper, whistling, singing, making as much clatter as he could, and it seemed to him that the shuffling and the tapping were not so intense as they had been at first. Presently he went up to the bedrooms and listened, and he no longer heard the jostling for place upon the roof.

'They've got reasoning powers,' he thought, 'they know it's hard to break in here. They'll try elsewhere. They won't waste their time with us.'

The Birds

Supper passed without incident, and then, when they were clearing away, they heard a new sound, droning, familiar, a sound they all knew and understood.

His wife looked up at him, her face alight. 'It's planes,' she said, 'they're sending out planes after the birds. That's what I said they ought to do, all along. That will get them. Isn't that gun-fire? Can't you hear guns?'

It might be gun-fire, out at sea. Nat could not tell. Big naval guns might have an effect upon the gulls out at sea, but the gulls were inland now. The guns couldn't shell the shore, because of the population.

'It's good, isn't it,' said his wife, 'to hear the planes?' And Jill, catching her enthusiasm, jumped up and down with Johnny. 'The planes will get the birds. The planes will shoot them.'

Just then they heard a crash about two miles distant, followed by a second, then a third. The droning became more distant, passed away out to sea.

'What was that?' asked his wife. 'Were they dropping bombs on the birds?'

'I don't know,' answered Nat, 'I don't think so.'

He did not want to tell her that the sound they had heard was the crashing of aircraft. It was, he had no doubt, a venture on the part of the authorities to send out reconnaissance forces, but they might have known the venture was suicidal. What could aircraft do against birds that flung themselves to death against propeller and fuselage, but hurtle to the ground themselves? This was being tried now, he supposed, over the whole country. And at a cost. Someone high up had lost his head.

'Where have the planes gone, Dad?' asked Jill.

'Back to base,' he said. 'Come on, now, time to tuck down for bed.'

It kept his wife occupied, undressing the children before the fire, seeing to the bedding, one thing and another, while he went round the cottage again, making sure that nothing had worked loose. There was no further drone of aircraft, and the naval guns had ceased. 'Waste of life and effort,' Nat said to himself. 'We can't destroy enough of them that way. Cost too heavy. There's always gas. Maybe they'll try spraying with gas, mustard gas. We'll be warned first, of course, if they do. There's one thing, the best brains of the country will be on to it tonight.'

Somehow the thought reassured him. He had a picture of scientists, naturalists, technicians, and all those chaps they called the back-room boys, summoned to a council; they'd be working on the problem now. This was not a job for the government, for the chiefs-of-staff – they would merely carry out the orders of the scientists.

'They'll have to be ruthless,' he thought. 'Where the trouble's worst they'll have to risk more lives, if they use gas. All the livestock, to, and the soil – all contaminated. As long as everyone doesn't panic. That's the trouble. People panicking, losing their heads. The BBC was right to warn us of that.'

Upstairs in the bedrooms all was quiet. No further scraping and stabbing at the windows. A lull in battle. Forces regrouping. Wasn't that what they called it, in the old wartime bulletins? The wind hadn't dropped, though. He could still hear it, roaring in the chimneys. And the sea breaking down on the shore. Then he remembered the tide. The tide would be on the turn. Maybe the lull in battle was because of the tide. There was some law the birds obeyed, and it was all to do with the east wind and the tide.

He glanced at his watch. Nearly eight o'clock. It must have gone high water an hour ago. That explained the lull: the birds attacked with the flood tide. It might not work that way inland, up country, but it seemed as if it was so this way on the coast. He reckoned the time limit in his head. They had six hours to go, without attack. When the tide turned again, around one-twenty in the morning, the birds would come back . . .

There were two things he could do. The first to rest,

The Birds

with his wife and the children, and all of them snatch what sleep they could, until the small hours. The second to go out, see how they were faring at the farm, see if the telephone was still working there, so that they might get news from the exchange.

He called softly to his wife, who had just settled the children. She came halfway up the stairs and he whispered to her.

'You're not to go,' she said at once, 'you're not to go and leave me alone with the children. I can't stand it.'

Her voice rose hysterically. He hushed her, calmed her.

'All right,' he said, 'all right. I'll wait till morning. And we'll get the wireless bulletin then too, at seven. But in the morning, when the tide ebbs again, I'll try for the farm, and they may let us have bread and potatoes, and milk too.'

His mind was busy again, planning against emergency. They would not have milked, of course, this evening. The cows would be standing by the gate, waiting in the yard, with the household inside, battened behind boards, as they were here at the cottage. That is, if they had time to take precautions. He thought of the farmer, Trigg, smiling at him from the car. There would have been no shooting party, not tonight.

The children were asleep. His wife, still clothed, was sitting on her mattress. She watched him, her eyes nervous.

'What are you going to do?' she whispered.

He shook his head for silence. Softly, stealthily, he opened the back door and looked outside.

It was pitch dark. The wind was blowing harder than ever, coming in steady gusts, icy, from the sea. He kicked at the step outside the door. It was heaped with birds. There were dead birds everywhere. Under the windows, against the walls. These were the suicides, the divers, the ones with broken necks. Wherever he looked he saw dead birds. No trace of the living. The living had flown seaward with the turn of the tide. The gulls would be riding the seas now, as they had done in the forenoon.

In the far distance, on the hill where the tractor had been two days before, something was burning. One of the aircraft that had crashed; the fire, fanned by the wind, had set light to a stack.

He looked at the bodies of the birds, and he had a notion that if he heaped them, one upon the other, on the window sills they would make added protection for the next attack. Not much, perhaps, but something. The bodies would have to be clawed at, pecked, and dragged aside, before the living birds gained purchase on the sills and attacked the panes. He set to work in the darkness. It was queer; he hated touching them. The bodies were still warm and bloody. The blood matted their feathers. He felt his stomach turn, but he went on with his work. He noticed, grimly, that every window-pane was shattered. Only the boards had kept the birds from breaking in. He stuffed the cracked panes with the bleeding bodies of the birds.

When he had finished he went back into the cottage. He barricaded the kitchen door, made it doubly secure. He took off his bandages, sticky with the birds' blood, not with his own cuts, and put on fresh plaster.

His wife had made him cocoa and he drank it thirstily. He was very tired.

'All right,' he said, smiling, 'don't worry. We'll get through.'

He lay down on his mattress and closed his eyes. He slept at once. He dreamt uneasily, because through his dreams there ran a thread of something forgotten. Some piece of work, neglected, that he should have done. Some precaution that he had known well but had not taken, and he could not put a name to it in his dreams. It was connected in some way with the burning aircraft and

The Birds

the stack upon the hill. He went on sleeping, though; he did not awake. It was his wife shaking his shoulder that awoke him finally.

'They've begun,' she sobbed, 'they've started this last hour, I can't listen to it any longer, alone. There's something smelling bad too, something burning.'

Then he remembered. He had forgotten to make up the fire. It was smouldering, nearly out. He got up swiftly and lit the lamp. The hammering had started at the windows and the doors, but it was not that he minded now. It was the smell of singed feathers. The smell filled the kitchen. He knew at once what it was. The birds were coming down the chimney, squeezing their way down to the kitchen range.

He got sticks and paper and put them on the embers, then reached for the can of paraffin.

'Stand back,' he shouted to his wife, 'we've got to risk this.'

He threw the paraffin on to the fire. The flame roared up the pipe, and down upon the fire fell the scorched, blackened bodies of the birds.

The children woke, crying. 'What is it?' said Jill. 'What's happened?'

Nat had no time to answer. He was raking the bodies from the chimney, clawing them out on to the floor. The flames still roared, and the danger of the chimney catching fire was one he had to take. The flames would send away the living birds from the chimney top. The lower joint was the difficulty, though. This was choked with the smouldering helpless bodies of the birds caught by fire. He scarcely heeded the attack on the windows and the door: let them beat their wings, break their beaks, lose their lives, in the attempt to force an entry into his home. They would not break in. He thanked God he had one of the old cottages, with small windows, stout walls. Not like the new council houses. Heaven help them up the lane, in the new council houses.

'Stop crying,' he called to the children. 'There's nothing to be afraid of, stop crying.'

He went on raking at the burning, smouldering bodies as they fell into the fire.

'This'll fetch them,' he said to himself, 'the draught and the flames together. We're all right, as long as the chimney doesn't catch. I ought to be shot for this. It's all my fault. Last thing I should have made up the fire. I knew there was something.'

Amid the scratching and tearing at the window boards came the sudden homely striking of the kitchen clock. Three a.m. A little more than four hours yet to go. He could not be sure of the exact time of high water. He reckoned it would not turn much before half-past seven, twenty to eight.

'Light up the primus,' he said to his wife. 'Make us some tea, and the kids some cocoa. No use sitting around doing nothing.'

That was the line. Keep her busy, and the children too. Move about, eat, drink; always best to be on the go.

He waited by the range. The flames were dying. But no more blackened bodies fell from the chimney. He thrust his poker up as far as it could go and found nothing. It was clear. The chimney was clear. He wiped the sweat from his forehead.

'Come on now, Jill,' he said, 'bring me some more sticks. We'll have a good fire going directly.' She wouldn't come near him, though. She was staring at the heaped singed bodies of the birds.

'Never mind them,' he said, 'we'll put those in the passage when I've got the fire steady.'

The danger of the chimney was over. It could not happen again, not if the fire was kept burning day and night.

'I'll have to get more fuel from the farm tomorrow,' he thought. 'This will never last. I'll manage, though. I can do all that with the ebb tide. It can be worked, fetching

The Birds

what we need, when the tide's turned. We've just got to adapt ourselves, that's all.'

They drank tea and cocoa and ate slices of bread and Bovril. Only half a loaf left, Nat noticed. Never mind though, they'd get by.

'Stop it,' said young Johnny, pointing to the windows with his spoon, 'stop it, you old birds.'

'That's right,' said Nat, smiling, 'we don't want the old beggars, do we? Had enough of 'em.'

They began to cheer when they heard the thud of the suicide birds.

'There's another, Dad,' cried Jill, 'he's done for.'

'He's had it,' said Nat, 'there he goes, the blighter.'

This was the way to face up to it. This was the spirit. If they could keep this up, hang on like this until seven, when the first news bulletin came through, they would not have done too badly.

'Give us a fag,' he said to his wife. 'A bit of a smoke will clear away the smell of the scorched feathers.'

'There's only two left in the packet,' she said. 'I was going to buy you some from the Co-op.'

'I'll have one,' he said, 't'other will keep for a rainy day.'

No sense trying to make the children rest. There was no rest to be got while the tapping and the scratching went on at the windows. He sat with one arm round his wife and the other round Jill, with Johnny on his mother's lap and the blankets heaped about them on the mattress.

'You can't help admiring the beggars,' he said, 'they've got persistence. You'd think they'd tire of the game, but not a bit of it.'

Admiration was hard to sustain. The tapping went on and on and a new rasping note struck Nat's ear, as though a sharper beak than any hitherto had come to take over from its fellows. He tried to remember the names of birds, he tried to think which species would go for this particular job. It was not the tap of the woodpecker. That would be light and frequent. This was more serious, because if it continued long the wood would splinter as the glass had done. Then he remembered the hawks. Could the hawks have taken over from the gulls? Were there buzzards now upon the sills, using talons as well as beaks? Hawks, buzzards, kestrels, falcons – he had forgotten the birds of prey. He had forgotten the gripping power of the birds of prey. Three hours to go, and while they waited the sound of the splintering wood, the talons tearing at the wood.

Nat looked about him, seeing what furniture he could destroy to fortify the door. The windows were safe, because of the dresser. He was not certain of the door. He went upstairs, but when he reached the landing he paused and listened. There was a soft patter on the floor of the children's bedroom. The birds had broken through . . . He put his ear to the door. No mistake. He could hear the rustle of wings, and the light patter as they searched the floor. The other bedroom was still clear. He went into it and began bringing out the furniture, to pile at the head of the stairs should the door of the children's bedroom go. It was a preparation. It might never be needed. He could not stack the furniture against the door, because it opened inward. The only possible thing was to have it at the top of the stairs.

'Come down, Nat, what are you doing?' called his wife.

'I won't be long,' he shouted. 'Just making everything shipshape up here.'

He did not want her to come; he did not want her to hear the pattering of the feet in the children's bedroom, the brushing of those wings against the door.

At five-thirty he suggested breakfast, bacon and fried bread, if only to stop the growing look of panic in his wife's eyes and to calm the fretful children. She did not know about the birds upstairs. The bedroom, luckily, was not over the kitchen. Had it been so she could not have failed to hear the sound of them, up there, tapping the

The Birds

boards. And the silly, senseless thud of the suicide birds, the death and glory boys, who flew into the bedroom, smashing their heads against the walls. He knew them of old, the herring gulls. They had no brains. The blackbacks were different, they knew what they were doing. So did the buzzards, the hawks . . .

He found himself watching the clock, gazing at the hands that went so slowly round the dial. If his theory was not correct, if the attack did not cease with the turn of the tide, he knew they were beaten. They could not continue through the long day without air, without rest, without more fuel without . . . his mind raced. He knew there were so many things they needed to withstand siege. They were not fully prepared. They were not ready. It might be that it would be safer in the towns after all. If he could get a message through, on the farm telephone, to his cousin, only a short journey by train up country, they might be able to hire a car. That would be quicker – hire a car between tides . . .

His wife's voice, calling his name, drove away the sudden, desperate desire for sleep.

'What is it? What now?' he said sharply.

'The wireless,' said his wife. 'I've been watching the clock. It's nearly seven.'

'Don't twist the knob,' he said, impatient for the first time, 'it's on the Home where it is. They'll speak from the Home.'

They waited. The kitchen clock struck seven. There was no sound. No chimes, no music. They waited until a quarter past, switching to the Light. The result was the same. No news bulletin came through.

'We've heard wrong,' he said, 'they won't be broadcasting until eight o'clock.'

They left it switched on, and Nat thought of the battery, wondered how much power was left in it. It was generally recharged when his wife went shopping in the town. If the battery failed they would not hear the instructions.

'It's getting light,' whispered his wife. 'I can't see it, but I can feel it. And the birds aren't hammering so loud.'

She was right. The rasping, tearing sound grew fainter every moment. So did the shuffling, the jostling for place upon the step, upon the sills. The tide was on the turn. By eight there was no sound at all. Only the wind. The children, lulled at last by the stillness, fell asleep. At half-past eight Nat switched the wireless off.

'What are you doing? We'll miss the news,' said his wife.

'There isn't going to be any news,' said Nat. 'We've got to depend upon ourselves.'

He went to the door and slowly pulled away the barricades. He drew the bolts, and kicking the bodies from the step outside the door breathed the cold air. He had six working hours before him, and he knew he must reserve his strength for the right things, not waste it in any way. Food, and light, and fuel; these were the necessary things. If he could get them in sufficiency, they could endure another night.

He stepped into the garden, and as he did so he saw the living birds. The gulls had gone to ride the sea, as they had done before; they sought sea food, and the buoyancy of the tide, before they returned to the attack. Not so the land birds. They waited and watched. Nat saw them, on the hedge-rows, on the soil, crowded in the trees, outside in the field, line upon line of birds, all still, doing nothing.

He went to the end of his small garden. The birds did not move. They went on watching him.

'I've got to get food,' said Nat to himself. 'I've got to go to the farm to find food.'

He went back to the cottage. He saw to the windows and the doors. He went upstairs and opened the children's bedroom. It was empty, except for the dead birds on the floor. The living were out there, in the garden, in the fields. He went downstairs.

The Birds

'I'm going to the farm,' he said.

His wife clung to him. She had seen the living birds from the open door.

'Take us with you,' she begged, 'we can't stay here alone. I'd rather die than stay here alone.'

He considered the matter. He nodded.

'Come on, then,' he said, 'bring baskets, and Johnny's pram. We can load up the pram.'

They dressed against the biting wind, wore gloves and scarves. His wife put Johnny in the pram. Nat took Jill's hand.

'The birds,' she whimpered, 'they're all out there, in the fields.'

'They won't hurt us,' he said, 'not in the light.'

They started walking across the field towards the stile, and the birds did not move. They waited, their heads turned to the wind.

When they reached the turning to the farm, Nat stopped and told his wife to wait in the shelter of the hedge with the two children.

'But I want to see Mrs Trigg,' she protested. 'There are lots of things we can borrow, if they went to market yesterday; not only bread, and . . .'

'Wait here,' Nat interrupted. 'I'll be back in a moment.'

The cows were lowing, moving restlessly in the yard, and he could see a gap in the fence where the sheep had knocked their way through, to roam unchecked in the front garden before the farm-house. No smoke came from the chimneys. He was filled with misgiving. He did not want his wife or the children to go down to the farm.

'Don't gib now,' said Nat, harshly, 'do what I say.'

She withdrew with the pram into the hedge, screening herself and the children from the wind.

He went down alone to the farm. He pushed his way through the herd of bellowing cows, which turned this way and that, distressed, their udders full. He saw the

313

car standing by the gate, not put away in the garage. The windows of the farm-house were smashed. There were many dead gulls lying in the yard and around the house. The living birds perched on the group of trees behind the farm and on the roof of the house. They were quite still. They watched him.

Jim's body lay in the yard . . . what was left of it. When the birds had finished, the cows had trampled him. His gun was beside him. The door of the house was shut and bolted, but as the windows were smashed it was easy to lift them and climb through. Trigg's body was close to the telephone. He must have been trying to get through to the exchange when the birds came for him. The receiver was hanging loose, the instrument torn from the wall. No sign of Mrs Trigg. She would be upstairs. Was it any use going up? Sickened, Nat knew what he would find.

'Thank God,' he said to himself, 'there were no children.'

He forced himself to climb the stairs, but halfway he turned and descended again. He could see her legs, protruding from the open bedroom door. Beside her were the bodies of the black-backed gulls, and an umbrella, broken.

'It's no use,' thought Nat, 'doing anything. I've only got five hours, less than that. The Triggs would understand. I must load up with what I can find.'

He tramped back to his wife and children.

'I'm going to fill up the car with stuff,' he said. 'I'll put coal in it, and paraffin for the primus. We'll take it home and return for a fresh load.'

'What about the Triggs?' asked his wife.

'They must have gone to friends,' he said.

'Shall I come and help you, then?'

'No; there's a mess down there. Cows and sheep all over the place. Wait, I'll get the car. You can sit in it.'

Clumsily he backed the car out of the yard and into the

The Birds

lane. His wife and the children could not see Jim's body from there.

'Stay here,' he said, 'never mind the pram. The pram can be fetched later. I'm going to load the car.'

Her eyes watched his all the time. He believed she understood, otherwise she would have suggested helping him to find the bread and groceries.

They made three journeys altogether, backwards and forwards between their cottage and the farm, before he was satisfied they had everything they needed. It was surprising, once he started thinking, how many things were necessary. Almost the most important of all was planking for the windows. He had to go round searching for timber. He wanted to renew the boards on all the windows at the cottage. Candles, paraffin, nails, tinned stuff; the list was endless. Besides all that, he milked three of the cows. The rest, poor brutes, would have to go on bellowing.

On the final journey he drove the car to the bus stop, got out, and went to the telephone box. He waited a few minutes, jangling the receiver. No good, though. The line was dead. He climbed on to a bank and looked over the countryside, but there was no sign of life at all, nothing in the fields but the waiting, watching birds. Some of them slept — he could see the beaks tucked into the feathers.

'You'd think they'd be feeding,' he said to himself, 'not just standing in that way.'

Then he remembered. They were gorged with food. They had eaten their fill during the night. That was why they did not move this morning . . .

No smoke came from the chimneys of the council houses. He thought of the children who had run across the fields the night before.

'I should have known,' he thought. 'I ought to have taken them home with me.'

He lifted his face to the sky. It was colourless and grey. The bare trees on the landscape looked bent and blackened by the east wind. The cold did not affect the living birds, waiting out there in the fields.

'This is the time they ought to get them,' said Nat, 'they're a sitting target now. They must be doing this all over the country. Why don't our aircraft take off now and spray them with mustard gas? What are all our chaps doing? They must know, they must see for themselves.'

He went back to the car and got into the driver's seat.

'Go quickly past that second gate,' whispered his wife. 'The postman's lying there. I don't want Jill to see.'

He accelerated. The little Morris bumped and rattled along the lane. The children shrieked with laughter.

'Up-a-down, up-a-down,' shouted young Johnny.

It was a quarter to one by the time they reached the cottage. Only an hour to go.

'Better have cold dinner,' said Nat. 'Hot up something for yourself and the children, some of that soup. I've no time to eat now. I've got to unload all this stuff.'

He got everything inside the cottage. It could be sorted later. Give them all something to do during the long hours ahead. First he must see to the windows and the doors.

He went round the cottage methodically, testing every window, every door. He climbed on to the roof also, and fixed boards across every chimney, except the kitchen. The cold was so intense he could hardly bear it, but the job had to be done. Now and again he would look up, searching the sky for aircraft. None came. As he worked he cursed the inefficiency of the authorities.

'It's always the same,' he muttered, 'they always let us down. Muddle, muddle, from the start. No plan, no real organization. And we don't matter, down here. That's what it is. The people up country have priority. They're using gas up there, no doubt, and all the aircraft. We've got to wait and take what comes.'

He paused, his work on the bedroom chimney finished, and looked out to sea. Something was moving out there. Something grey and white amongst the breakers.

The Birds

'Good old Navy,' he said, 'they never let us down. They're coming down channel, they're turning in the bay.'

He waited, straining, his eyes watering in the wind, towards the sea. He was wrong, though. It was not ships. The Navy was not there. The gulls were rising from the sea. The massed flocks in the fields, with ruffled feathers, rose in formation from the ground, and wing to wing soared upwards to the sky.

The tide had turned again.

Nat climbed down the ladder and went inside the kitchen. The family were at dinner. It was a little after two. He bolted the door, put up the barricade, and lit the lamp.

'It's night-time,' said young Johnny.

His wife had switched on the wireless once again, but no sound came from it.

'I've been all round the dial,' she said, 'foreign stations, and that lot. I can't get anything.'

'Maybe they have the same trouble,' he said, 'maybe it's the same right through Europe.'

She poured out a plateful of the Triggs' soup, cut him a large slice of the Triggs' bread, and spread their dripping upon it.

They ate in silence. A piece of the dripping ran down young Johnny's chin and fell on to the table.

'Manners, Johnny,' said Jill, 'you should learn to wipe your mouth.'

The tapping began at the windows, at the door. The rustling, the jostling, the pushing for position on the sills. The first thud of the suicide gulls upon the step.

'Won't America do something?' said his wife. 'They've always been our allies, haven't they? Surely America will do something?'

Nat did not answer. The boards were strong against the windows, and on the chimneys too. The cottage was filled with stores, with fuel, with all they needed for the next few days. When he had finished dinner he would put the stuff away, stack it neatly, get everything shipshape, handy-like. His wife could help him, and the children too. They'd tire themselves out, between now and a quarter to nine, when the tide would ebb; then he'd tuck them down on their mattresses, see that they slept good and sound until three in the morning.

He had a new scheme for the windows, which was to fix barbed wire in front of the boards. He had brought a great roll of it from the farm. The nuisance was, he'd have to work at this in the dark, when the lull came between nine and three. Pity he had not thought of it before. Still, as long as the wife slept, and the kids, that was the main thing.

The smaller birds were at the window now. He recognized the light tap-tapping of their beaks, and the soft brush of their wings. The hawks ignored the windows. They concentrated their attack upon the door. Nat listened to the tearing sound of splintering wood, and wondered how many million years of memory were stored in those little brains, behind the stabbing beaks, the piercing eyes, now giving them this instinct to destroy mankind with all the deft precision of machines.

'I'll smoke that last fag,' he said to his wife. 'Stupid of me, it was the one thing I forgot to bring back from the farm.'

He reached for it, switched on the silent wireless. He threw the empty packet on the fire, and watched it burn.

Marguerite Duras

extract from

The Lover

In her sixteenth year, the narrator finds herself responsible for acquiring money to help her impoverished mother. Dressed like a child prostitute, she journeys to school across her city, Saigon, a headmistress's daughter who nevertheless is up for sale. She quickly attracts an elegant Chinese lover, a rich man's son, and the intensity of their erotic exploration remains the central experience in both their lives.

In her sixteenth year, the narrator finds herself responsible for acquiring money to help her impoverished mother. Dressed like a child prostitute, she journeys to school across her city, Saigon, a headmistress's daughter who is, nevertheless, up for sale. She quickly attracts an elegant Chinese lover, a rich man's son, and the intensity of their erotic exploration remains the central experience in both their lives.

So you see it wasn't in the bar at Réam, as I wrote, that I met the rich man with the black limousine, it was after we left the concession, two or three years after, on the ferry, the day I'm telling you about, in that light of haze and heat.

It's a year and a half after that meeting that my mother takes us back to France. She'll sell all her furniture. Then go one last time to the dyke. She'll sit on the veranda facing the setting sun, look towards Siam one last time as she never will again, not even when she leaves France again, changes her mind again and comes back once more to Indo-China and retires to Saigon. Never again will she go and see that mountain, that green and yellow sky above that forest.

Yes, I tell you, when she was already quite old she did it again. She opened a French language school, the Nouvelle Ecole Française, which made enough for her to help me with my studies and to provide for her elder son as long as she lived.

My younger brother died in three days, of bronchial pneumonia. His heart gave out. It was then that I left my mother. It was during the Japanese occupation. Everything came to an end that day. I never asked her any more questions about our childhood, about herself. She died, for me, of my younger brother's death. So did my elder brother. I never got over the horror they inspired in me then. They don't mean anything to me any more. I don't know any more about them since that day. I don't even know how she managed to pay off her debts to the *chettys*, the Indian moneylenders. One day they stopped coming. I can see them now. They're sitting in the little parlour in Sadec wearing white sarongs, they sit there without saying a word, for months, years. My mother can be heard weeping and insulting them, she's in her room and won't come out, she calls out to them to leave her alone, they're deaf, calm, smiling, they stay where they are. And then one day, gone. They're dead now, my mother and my two brothers. For memories too it's too late. Now I don't love them any more. I don't remember if I ever did. I've left them. In my head I no longer have the scent of her skin, nor in my eyes the colour of her eyes. I can't remember her voice, except sometimes when it grew soft with the weariness of evening. Her laughter I can't hear any more – neither her laughter nor her cries. It's over, I don't remember. That's why I can write about her so easily now, so long, so fully. She's become just something you write without difficulty, cursive writing.

She must have stayed on in Saigon from 1932 until 1949. It was in December 1942 that my younger brother died. She couldn't move any more. She stayed on – to be near the grave, she said. Then finally she came back to France. My son was two years old when we met again. It was too late for us to be reunited. We knew it at first glance. There was nothing left to reunite. Except for the elder son, all the rest was over. She went to live, and die, in the department of Loir-et-Cher, in the sham Louis XIV château. She lived there with Dô. She was still afraid at night. She bought a gun. Dô kept watch in the attics on the top floor. She also bought a place for her elder son near Amboise. With woods. He cut them down. Then went and gambled the money away in a baccarat club in Paris. The woods were lost in one night. The point at which my memory suddenly softens, and perhaps my brother brings tears to my eyes, is after the loss of the money from the woods. I know he's found lying in his car in Montparnasse, outside the Coupole, and that he wants to die. After that, I forget. What she did, my mother, with that château of hers, is simply unimaginable, still all for the sake of the elder son, the child of fifty incapable of earning any money. She buys some electric incubators and instals them in the main drawing-room. Suddenly she's got six hundred chicks, forty square metres of them. But she made a mistake with the infra-red rays, and none of the chicks can eat, all six hundred of them have beaks that don't meet or won't close, they all starve to death and she gives up. I came to the château while the chicks were hatching, there were great rejoicings. Afterwards the stench of the dead chicks and their food was so awful I couldn't eat in my mother's château without throwing up.

She died between Dô and him she called her child, in her big bedroom on the first floor, where during heavy frosts she used to put the sheep to sleep, five or six sheep all around her bed, for several winters, her last.

It's there, in that last house, the one on the Loire, when she finally gives up her ceaseless to-ing and fro-ing, that I see the madness clearly for the first time. I see my mother is clearly mad. I see that Dô and my brother have always had access to that madness. But that I, no, I've never seen it before. Never seen my mother in the state of being mad. Which she was. From birth. In the blood. She wasn't ill with it, for her it was like health, flanked by Dô and her elder son. No one else but they realized. She always had lots of friends, she kept the same friends for years and years and was always making new ones, often very young, among the officials from up-country, or later on among the people in Touraine, where there were some who'd retired from the French colonies. She always had people around her, all her life, because of what they called her lively intelligence, her cheerfulness, and her peerless, indefatigable poise.

I don't know who took the photo with the despair. The one in the courtyard of the house in Hanoi. Perhaps my father, one last time. A few months later he'd be sent back to France because of his health. Before that he'd go to a new job, in Phnom Penh. He was only there a few weeks. He died in less than a year. My mother wouldn't go back with him to France, she stayed where she was, stuck there. In Phnom Penh. In the fine house overlooking the Mekong, once the palace of the king of Cambodia, in the midst of those terrifying grounds, acres of them, where my mother's afraid. At night she makes us afraid too. All four of us sleep in the same bed. She says she's afraid of the dark. It's in this house she'll hear of my father's death. She'll know about it before the telegram comes, the night before, because of a sign only she saw and could understand, because of the bird that called in the middle of the night, frightened and lost in the office in the north front of the palace, my father's office. It's there, too, a few days after her husband's death, that my mother finds herself face to face with her own father. She switches the light on. There he is, standing by the table in the big octagonal drawing-room. Looking at her. I remember a shriek, a call. She woke us up, told us what had happened, how he was dressed, in his Sunday best, grey, how he stood, how he looked at her, straight at her. She said: I wasn't afraid. She ran towards the vanished image. Both of them died on the day and at the time of the bird or the image. Hence, no doubt, our admiration for our mother's knowledge, about everything, including all that had to do with death.

*

The Lover

The elegant man has got out of the limousine and is smoking an English cigarette. He looks at the girl in the man's fedora and the gold shoes. He slowly comes over to her. He's obviously nervous. He doesn't smile to begin with. To begin with he offers her a cigarette. His hand's trembling. There's the difference of race, he's not white, he has to get the better of it, that's why he's trembling. She says she doesn't smoke, no thanks. She doesn't say anything else, doesn't say Leave me alone. So he's less afraid. He tells her he must be dreaming. She doesn't answer. There's no point in answering, what would she say? She waits. So he asks, But where did you spring from? She says she's the daughter of the headmistress of the girls' school in Sadec. He thinks for a moment, then says he's heard of the lady, her mother, of her bad luck with the concession they say she bought in Cambodia, is that right? Yes, that's right.

He says again how strange it is to see her on this ferry. So early in the morning, a pretty girl like that, you don't realize, it's very surprising, a white girl on a native bus.

He says the hat suits her, suits her extremely well, that it's very . . . original . . . a man's hat, and why not? She's so pretty she can do anything she likes.

She looks at him. Asks him who he is. He says he's just back from Paris where he was a student, that he lives in Sadec too, on this same river, the big house with the big terraces with blue-tiled balustrades. She asks him what he is. He says he's Chinese, that his family's from North China, from Fushun. Will you allow me to drive you where you want to go in Saigon? She says she will. He tells the chauffeur to get the girl's luggage off the bus and put it in the black car.

Chinese. He belongs to the small group of financiers of Chinese origin who own all the working-class housing in the colony. He's the one who was crossing the Mekong that day in the direction of Saigon.

*

She gets into the black car. The door shuts. A barely discernible distress suddenly seizes her, a weariness, the light over the river dims, but only slightly. Everywhere, too, there's a very slight deafness, or fog.

Never again shall I travel in a native bus. From now on I'll have a limousine to take me to the high school and back from there to the boarding school. I shall dine in the most elegant places in town. And I'll always have regrets for everything I do, everything I've gained, everything I've lost, good and bad, the bus, the bus-driver I used to laugh with, the old women chewing betel in the back seats, the children on the luggage racks, the family in Sadec, the awfulness of the family in Sadec, its inspired silence.

He talked. Said he missed Paris, the marvellous girls there, the riotous living, the binges, ooh là là, the Coupole, the Rotonde, personally I prefer the Rotonde, the nightclubs, the 'wonderful' life he'd led for two years. She listened, watching out for anything to do with his wealth, for indications as to how many millions he had. He went on. His own mother was dead, he was an only child. All he had left was his father, the one who owned the money. But you know how it is, for the last ten years he's been sitting staring at the river, glued to his opium pipe, he manages his money from his little iron cot. She says she sees.

He won't let his son marry the little white whore from Sadec.

The image starts long before he's come up to the white child by the rails, it starts when he got out of the black car, when he began to approach her, and when she knew, knew he was afraid.

From the first moment she knows more or less, knows

The Lover

he's at her mercy. And therefore that others beside him may be at her mercy too if the occasion arises. She knows something else too, that the time has now probably come when she can no longer escape certain duties toward herself. And that her mother will know nothing of this, nor her brothers. She knows this now too. As soon as she got into the black car she knew: she's excluded from the family for the first time and for ever. From now on they will no longer know what becomes of her. Whether she's taken away from them, carried off, wounded, spoiled, they will no longer know. Neither her mother nor her brothers. That is their fate henceforth. It's already enough to make you weep, here in the black limousine.

Now the child will have to reckon only with this man, the first, the one who introduced himself on the ferry.

It happened very quickly that day, a Thursday. He'd come every day to pick her up at the high school and drive her back to the boarding school. Then one Thursday afternoon, the weekly half-holiday, he came to the boarding school and drove off with her in the black car.

It's in Cholon. Opposite the boulevards linking the Chinese part of the city to the centre of Saigon, the great American-style streets full of trams, rickshaws and buses. It's early in the afternoon. She's got out of the compulsory outing with the other girls.

It's a native housing estate to the south of the city. His place is modern, hastily furnished from the look of it, with furniture supposed to be ultra-modern. He says: I didn't choose the furniture. It's dark in the studio, but she doesn't ask him to open the shutters. She doesn't feel anything in particular, no hate, no repugnance either, so probably it's already desire. But she doesn't know it. She agreed to come as soon as he asked her the previous evening. She's where she has to be, placed here. She feels a tinge of fear. It's as if this must be not only what she expects, but also what had to happen especially to her.

She pays close attention to externals, to the light, to the noise of the city in which the room is immersed. He's trembling. At first he looks at her as though he expects her to speak, but she doesn't. So he doesn't do anything either, doesn't undress her, says he loves her madly, says it very softly. Then is silent. She doesn't answer. She could say she doesn't love him. She says nothing. Suddenly, all at once, she knows, knows that he doesn't understand her, that he never will, that he lacks the power to understand such perverseness. And that he can never move fast enough to catch her. It's up to her to know. And she does. Because of his ignorance she suddenly knows: she was attracted to him already on the ferry. She was attracted to him. It depended on her alone.

She says: I'd rather you didn't love me. But if you do, I'd like you to do as you usually do with women. He looks at her in horror, asks, Is that what you want? She says it is. He's started to suffer here in this room, for the first time, he's no longer lying about it. He says he knows already she'll never love him. She lets him say it. At first she says she doesn't know. Then she lets him say it.

He says he's lonely, horribly lonely because of this love he feels for her. She says she's lonely too. She doesn't say why. He says: You've come here with me as you might have gone anywhere with anyone. She says she can't say, so far she's never gone into a bedroom with anyone. She tells him she doesn't want him to talk, what she wants is for him to do as he usually does with the women he brings to his flat. She begs him to do that.

He's torn off the dress, he throws it down. He's torn off her little white cotton panties and carries her over like that, naked, to the bed. And there he turns away and weeps. And she, slow, patient, draws him to her and starts to undress him. With her eyes shut. Slowly. He makes as if

The Lover

to help her. She tells him to keep still. Let me do it. She says she wants to do it. And she does. Undresses him. When she tells him to, he moves his body in the bed, but carefully, gently, as if not to wake her.

The skin's sumptuously soft. The body. The body's thin, lacking in strength, in muscle, he may have been ill, may be convalescent, he's hairless, nothing masculine about him but his sex, he's weak, probably a helpless prey to insult, vulnerable. She doesn't look him in the face. Doesn't look at him at all. She touches him. Touches the softness of his sex, his skin, caresses his goldenness, the strange novelty. He moans, weeps. In dreadful love.

And, weeping, he makes love. At first, pain. And then the pain is possessed in its turn, changed, slowly drawn away, borne towards pleasure, clasped to it.

The sea, formless, simply beyond compare.

Buchi Emecheta

extract from

Second Class Citizen

Adah leaves her parents in Nigeria to live in London's Rented Town. She finds her husband's traditional picture of what a wife should be up easier to bear in a society which may have many disadvantages but also facilitates a degree of freedom.

Adah leaves her parents in Nigeria to live in London's Kentish Town. She finds her husband's traditional views of what a wife should be are easier to bear in a society which may have many disadvantages but also facilitates a degree of freedom.

POPULATION CONTROL

The snow melted from the pavements, from the gardens and from the roofs of houses. Spring was in the air and everything sprung up as if injected with new life by the gods. Even in a dark street, as dark as Willes Road in Kentish Town, one could hear the birds sing.

One Monday morning, when her family were still asleep, Adah got together her wash things to have her bath. There was no bathroom in the house in which they lived so she paid visits to the public baths in Prince of Wales Road several times in the week. It was on one of these visits, on a Monday, that she saw this bird; grey, small, solitary but contented in its solitude. Adah stood still on the other side of the road watching this grey bird, singing, singing, hopping from one window ledge to another, happy in its lonely freedom. Adah was intrigued by the creature. Fancy being moved this early in the morning by such a small thing as this grey bird, when less than a year before she had seen wilder birds, all gaudy in their colours, all wild in their songs. She never took notice of birds then, in the back yards of Lagos houses. Then she thought to herself: suppose there was never any winter, when every living thing seems to disappear from the face of the earth, the birds would always be around, they would become an everyday thing, and she wouldn't have noticed and admired it and listened to its watery song. Was that not what we need in Africa, to have a long, long winter, when there would be no sunshine, no birds, no wild flowers and no warmth?

That would make us a nation of introverts, maybe, and when eventually spring came, then we would be able to appreciate the songs of birds. What does that mean? Has Nature been too merciful to us, robbing us of the ability to wake ourselves up from our tropical slumber to know that a simple thing like the song of a grey bird on a wet Monday morning in spring can be inspiring? Was that why the early Europeans who came to Africa thought the black man was lazy because of his over-abundant environment which robbed him of the ability to think for himself? Well, Adah concluded, to cheer herself up, that may be so, but that happened years and years ago, before the birth of her Pa.

She was different. Her children were going to be different. They were all going to be black, they were going to enjoy being black, be proud of being black, a black of a different breed. That's what they were going to be. Had she not now learned to listen to the songs of birds? Was that not one of the natural happenings that inspired her favourite poet, Wordsworth? She might never be a famous poet like Wordsworth, because he was too great, but Adah was going to train herself to admire the songs of birds however riotous, to appreciate the beauty of flowers however extravagant their scent. She jolted herself to, reminding herself that she was the mother of three babies, and that she was supposed to be rushing for her Monday morning bath.

The women who cleaned the baths greeted her like an old friend. They knew she was always the first customer on Monday mornings, because Saturdays were usually too busy, and the baths too crowded. She preferred Mondays, when most people had gone to work and the ladies working at the baths would not have to hurry her up. The only snag was that on Monday mornings she seldom got very hot water, because the boiler, or whatever heated the water, had to be turned off over the weekend. It usually took a long time to heat up, but Adah did not mind the lukewarmness of the water, because that was the price she was paying for a long, quiet bath.

Her bath that Monday morning was particularly important, because she was going to the Family Planning Clinic. She had attended the week before and had been loaded with masses of literature. She had read about the jelly, the Pill, the cap and so many other things. She told Francis she was going, but Francis told her not to go because men knew how to control themselves better, the way it was done in the Bible. You hold the child and you don't give it to the woman, you pour it away. Adah considered this. It was not because she had stopped trusting her husband, but her husband could hurt her without meaning to, for wasn't that the way he had been brought up? She knelt and prayed to God to forgive her for making other plans behind her husband's back.

When it was time to take Bubu to the clinic to be weighed, she saw a motherly-looking nurse and told her, 'Please, could I have the Pill? You see, I am not twenty-one yet and if I had another child it would be my fourth, and I originally came here to study and bring up the two babies I brought from home. Can you help me? I need the Pill.'

The woman smiled and tickled Bubu on the cheek. They had a Family Planning Clinic in the evenings on Mondays. She would get the literature for Adah to read and she could decide with her husband which would suit them best. Well, how was Adah to tell the woman that Francis said that the best way to control the population was to pour it on the floor? Adah could not bring herself to tell the nurse that. The last nail in the coffin was when the woman brought a form which Adah's husband was supposed to sign to tell them that he was all for it, that he wanted his wife equipped with birth-control gear. There was going to be trouble over that, for Francis would never sign a thing like that, and he would raise hell if he realized that Adah got the literature without his permission. What was Adah going to do? Why was it necessary to have a husband brought into an issue like that? Could not the woman be given the opportunity of exercising her own will? Whatever happened, she was not going to have any more children. She did not care which way she achieved this, but she was having no more children. Two boys and a girl were enough for any mother-in-law. If her mother-in-law wanted another one, she could get her son another wife. Adah was not going to have any more. It was not going to be easy for her to forget the experience she had had recently having Bubu. That was a warning. She might not be so lucky next time.

Francis announced that he had read his two chapters scheduled for the day and that he was tired of reading and that he was going down to the Nobles to watch their television. Adah encouraged him to go. She wanted to read the birth-control literature in detail. Adah fished the now rumpled leaflets out from under Bubu's cot where she had hidden them. She read them again and again. Three facts stuck. One was that the Pill is the one you swallow just like aspirin. Secondly, the jelly is the one you allow to melt inside. The cap, which was the third thing, was the one you fitted in. Adah chuckled and was amused at it all. Fancy making a special cap for your other end instead of for your head. Well, these Europeans would stop at nothing. She was not going to choose the cap though, as it would be too messy, messing around with one's insides. No, she would go for the Pill, that was less complicated. The jelly? No, Francis would notice and ask questions.

But how was she to make Francis sign the form? The thought came to her that she could sign it for him. But that would be forgery. She imagined herself at a court and the magistrate sending her to jail for seven years for forging her husband's signature. But at the end of it she would be alive, and once alive, she might be allowed to look after her children. But if she did not forge the

Second Class Citizen

signature it might mean another child, another traumatic birth, another mouth to feed; and she was still not getting anywhere with her studies. The price she would have to pay for being an obedient and loyal wife would be too much. She forged the signature. She saved and scraped from the housekeeping money to pay for the first lot of pills. The money had been saved, the form signed, and, to add to her joy, she now had another library job waiting for her at the Chalk Farm Library. She was going to keep this job, no matter what. She was not going to allow herself to get pregnant again. Never.

But first she had to have this Monday bath, in case she had to strip herself to be examined or something. She had told Francis that Bubu was such a big baby, gaining weight every day, that the people at the clinic would like his photograph taken that Monday evening. It pained her, having to resort to the very method she had always used when she was little. That horrible tendency to twist the facts. But what else was there for her to do? She prayed to God again and again to forgive her.

She had to take Bubu with her, because if she had not, Francis would have said, 'I thought you told me that the people at the clinic were going to take his photo, because he was such a beautiful baby?' So she took Bubu with her.

At the clinic, she was shown into a waiting-room, where there were other women waiting. Two were undressed with their stockings rolled down round their ankles, just as you are when you are expecting, and the doctor wants to examine you. They reminded Adah of the pre-natal clinics. She was now used to that sort of thing – stripping yourself naked to be examined. It did not bother her any more. She asked herself, why should it worry me? I've only got what you've got. Why should I be ashamed of my body? It did not matter any more.

Three screens were set up in the middle of the square room. Women were to undress behind the screen and then sit down and wait to be called one by one into the doctor's room to be equipped with birth-control gear.

Adah saw a young West Indian mother and purposely went and sat down beside her. She wanted to be on home ground because she was frightened and because the young girl was the only woman there holding a baby. Adah could look after her baby for her when she went in to be equipped, and she could look after Adah's. That would be fair. With such noble thoughts in her mind, she greeted the West Indian girl with a friendly smile. The girl smiled back showing a golden tooth wedged in between her ordinary teeth.

They soon started to talk. She, the West Indian girl, was going to be trained as a nurse, so she needed some form of birth-control during her training. Her husband did not mind. So, months before, she was given the Pill. But, she cried to Adah, see what the Pill had done to her. She pulled up her sleeves and showed Adah a very fine rash. The rash was all over her face and neck. Even her skinny wrists had not been spared. She was covered with the kind of rash that reminded Adah of the rash caused by prickly heat in Africa.

'Do they make you scratch? I mean, do you feel scratchy all the time?'

'Yeah, man. That's the trouble now. I don't mind the appearance. But they itch all the time.'

Adah looked at her face again, and as she did so the girl started to scratch the back of her skirt. She was trying to hide it from the other women, trying to hide the fact that her bottom was itching. God have mercy! thought Adah. Her bottom as well? Then she asked the girl, 'Have you got the itch down there as well?'

The girl nodded. She had it all over her. Adah called to God to have mercy on her again. What was she to do now? She was not going on the Pill if she was going to end up looking like somebody with chicken-pox, or scratching like this girl as if she was covered with yaws. No, she

Second Class Citizen

was not going to have the Pill, and she was not going home empty-handed with no birth-control. She thought about the jelly and knew that it would only work when husband and wife are in agreement, for he would have to wait until it melted before coming on. So the jelly was out of the question for her. She could only go for the cap. That almighty cap which is specially made for one's inside. She had to think quickly. Francis might not know. The business was always done in the dark anyway. But suppose he felt it? Supposing he saw her fixing the cap in their one-room apartment with no bathroom and with the toilet as filthy as a rubbish dump? She could not fix the cap in the toilet, for what would happen if the cap fell? It would have collected enough germs to send her to her Maker in no time with cancer of the bottom. Adah was sure you could get cancer easily from under there. What was she going to do now? If only Francis would be reasonable. Whatever happened, she was going to risk it. A cap was better than nothing.

It came to her turn to go and see the doctor and the midwife who fixed you up with your own special size of cap. It was a messy job. They kept trying this and that and kept scolding Adah to relax otherwise she would go home with the wrong cap that would not fit her properly and *that* would mean another child. The fear of what Francis would say and what he would write to his mother and her relations loomed, full of doom, in her subconscious. Only she could feel it. The other two females, who were now tut-tutting at her and growing impatient and telling her to relax her legs, could not see the same picture that Adah was seeing. It was the picture of her mother-in-law when she heard that Adah went behind her husband's back to equip herself with something that would allow her to sleep around and not have any more children. She was sure they would interpret it that way, knowing the psychology of her people. The shame of it would kill her. Her children's name would be smeared as well. God, don't let Francis find out. In desperation, the two women, the doctor and the midwife gave her a size of cap that they thought should fit. If it did not fit, it was not their fault, because Adah did not help them at all because she was feeling so guilty of what she was doing. First she had forged her husband's signature, now she had got a cap which she was sure was going to cause a row if he found out. But suppose he did not find out and suppose it worked? That would mean no children and she would keep her new job and finish her course in librarianship. With that happy thought, she put the new equipment in Bubu's pram and went home.

But when she got home, she was faced with another problem. How was she to know what was going to happen on a particular night? Must she then wear the cap every night? That was the safest thing, but the cap was not very comfortable and Adah knew that it wobbled and she had to walk funnily to keep it in. And of course Francis would know. Oh, God, if only they had an extra room, then Francis would not have to see and watch and to make irritating remarks about her every move!

She ran down to their backyard toilet that had no electric light and fitted herself with her new cap. She could hear Titi and Vicky having their usual fight, and soon Francis would start calling for her to come and quieten her children. She fitted the cap in a hurry, almost going sick at the thought of it all. At that moment she felt really sorry for doctors and nurses. The amount of messing they have to do with people's insides! She dashed up, for Francis was already calling her and asking her what the hell it was she was doing down there in the toilet. Was she having another baby in there? Adah looked blank and said nothing. The fact that she was quiet made Francis suspicious. He then asked her what the matter was. Adah said that nothing was the matter.

He looked at her again and asked, 'Have you got a boil or something?'

Adah turned round from where she was tucking the kids into bed and asked, 'What boil?'

And Francis, still looking intensely at her, replied: 'Boil in the leg. You walk funny.'

Adah smiled, a wobbly, uncertain sort of smile, for her heart was beating so fast and so loudly, the noise was like a Nigerian housewife pounding yams in her *Odo*. Her heart was going 'gbim, gbim, gbim,' just like that. She was surprised and shocked to realize that Francis could not hear the guilty beating of that heart of hers. She thought everybody could hear it because it was so loud to her that it hurt her chest, making it difficult to breathe. But she managed a smile, that sort of lying smile. And it worked wonders.

Then she said, just to press home another point, 'You were calling me so loudly when I was down there in the backyard, that I ran up the stairs, and I bumped my toe on one of them, and it hurts a bit.'

Francis arched his brows but said nothing.

Soon it was midnight, and the row which Adah had dreaded flared up. Francis got the whole truth out of her. So, she a married woman, married in the name of God and again married in the name of the Oboshi, the goddess of Ibuza, came to London and became clever enough within a year to go behind his back and equip herself with a cap which he, Francis, was sure had been invented for harlots and single women. Did Adah not know the gravity of what she had done? It meant she could take other men behind his back, because how was he to know that she was not going to do just that if she could go and get the gear behind his back? Francis called all the other tenants to come and see and hear about this great issue – how the innocent Adah who came to London only a year previously had become so clever. Adah was happy when Pa Noble came, because at least it made Francis stop hitting her. She was dizzy with pain and her head throbbed. Her mouth was bleeding. And once or twice during the proceeding she felt tempted to run out and call the police. But she thought better of it. Where would she go after that? She had no friends and she had no relations in London.

Francis made it clear that he was writing to his mother and father. Adah was not surprised at this. But she was frightened, for despite everything she still respected her mother-in-law. But her son Francis was severing the ties of friendship that existed between Adah and his family. She knew that, after that, things were not going to be the same any more. She cried then. She was lonely again, just as she was when Pa died and Ma married again and she had to live in a relative's house.

Her marriage with Francis? It was finished as soon as Francis called in the Nobles and the other tenants. She told herself that she could not live with such a man. Now everybody knew she was being knocked about, only a few weeks after she had come out of hospital. Everybody now knew that the man she was working for and supporting was not only a fool, but that he was too much of a fool to know that he was acting foolishly. Pa Noble reminded Francis of Adah's health and God bless the old man, he sent all the inquisitive tenants away. There was nothing bad in Adah getting birth-control gear, Pa Noble said, but she should have told her husband.

What was the point of Adah telling them that she had told her husband and he had said you could control children by pouring them on the floor? But it did not matter. She was almost twenty-one. And, among her people, a girl of twenty-one was no longer a girl, but a woman who could make decisions. Let Francis write to her people and his people. If she liked, she would read their letters, if she did not she could throw them into the fire. The only person that mattered was her brother. She would write and tell him the truth. Boy had never liked Francis anyway. He knew even before Adah found out that Francis looked like those men who could live off women because of his good looks. Adah had just left school and was full of the religious idea that you could change anybody by your own personal example and by prayers. She was wrong and Boy her brother was right.

A few weeks later, Francis had his examination result, and it was another failure. Of course the fault was Adah's, especially as she managed to scrape through a part of her library examination. To explain his failures Francis wrote to his parents about the cap. But by the time their reply came, Adah was being eaten up by another problem. She was pregnant again.

THE COLLAPSE

Yes, Adah was pregnant again. This time she did not cry, she did not wring her hands, but behaved philosophically. If this pattern was going to be her lot in life she would do all she could do change it, but what was she going to do if all her efforts failed?

She went to her Indian doctor. She told him her whole story and that she wanted the pregnancy terminated. The Indian doctor was not a young man at all, but he had a certain way of saying things and was so small that one could easily take him for a young man. He had made good in London and had two sons who were both up at Cambridge; he had married a woman doctor he met when he was a student himself. He was very popular among the blacks living in that part of Kentish Town at the time. Adah guessed that if she appealed to him, being Indian and once a student in London, he would understand her predicament.

He understood, shook his head, sympathized and said, 'You should have come to us for the cap. The ones sold at the clinic are cheap ones and they go loose quickly. You should have told me about it.'

That was very nice. That was what Adah ought to have done if she had known. But how was she supposed to know? Smell it out like a witch doctor? Had he and his wife not put a notice in the waiting-room about the danger of smoking? Could they not have had a similar notice to say that birth control was available for the asking? It was too late now. She was pregnant, she knew it, but the doctor told her that it was too early for confirmation. He would give her some white pills. Adah was to take them and they would work.

Adah wondered what those pills were meant to do for her. But in her state of apathetic resignation, she did not ask questions. The pills were going to terminate the pregnancy. If the pregnancy was going to be terminated, what was the point of telling Francis? How did she know he would not misunderstand? Even if he did understand, how could she be sure he was not going to repeat it to the Nobles, to his parents and to everybody? Could she tell Francis and say, 'Look, I am telling you this under the seal of the confessional. You must not repeat it.' That would be impossible.

She now saw this situation as a challenge, a new challenge. When she was little and alone, the challenge had been that of educating herself, existing through it all, alone, all by herself. She had hoped that in marriage she could get herself involved in her man's life and he would share the same involvement in hers. She had gambled with marriage, just like most people, but she had gambled unluckily and had lost. Now she was alone again with this new challenge that included her children as well. She was going to live, to survive, to exist through it all. Some day, help would come from somewhere. She had been groping for that help as if she were in the dark. Some day her fingers would touch something solid that would help her pull herself out. She was becoming aware of that Presence again – the Presence that had directed her through childhood. She went nearer to It in her prayers. She never knelt down to pray in the orthodox way. But she talked to Him while stirring peppery African soup on

Second Class Citizen

her cooker; she talked to Him when she woke up in the morning; she talked to Him all the time, and Adah felt that He was always there.

There was no time to go to church and pray. Not in England. It took her years to erase the image of the Nigerian church which usually had a festive air. In England, especially in London, 'church' was a big grey building with stained-glass windows, high ornamental ceilings, very cold, full of rows and rows of empty chairs, with the voice of the vicar droning from the distant pulpit, crying like the voice of John the Baptist lost in the wilderness. In London, churches were cheerless.

She could not then go to any of them because it made her cry to see such beautiful places of worship empty when, in Nigeria, you could hardly get a seat if you came in late. You had to stand outside and follow the service through a microphone. But you were happy through it all, you were encouraged to bellow out the songs – that bellowing took away some of your sorrows. Because most of the hymns seem to be written by psychologists. One was always sure of singing or hearing something that would come near to the problem you had in mind before coming to church. In England you were robbed of such comfort.

London, having thus killed Adah's congregational God, created instead a personal God who loomed large and really alive. She did not have to go to church to see this One. He was always there, when she was shelving books in the library, when she was tucking her babies up to sleep, when she was doing anything. She grew nearer to Him, to the people with whom she worked, but away from Francis. The gulf between them which had grown with her stay in the hospital had been made deeper by the cap incident, and now this new child would make it greater still. But she was not going to tell Francis and she did not feel guilty about it. Francis would not be of any help.

She concentrated on working and enjoying her new job.

It was at the Chalk Farm Library that she met Peggy, the Irish girl with a funny hair style, who was heartbroken because her Italian summer-holiday boyfriend did not fulfil his promises. Peggy had gone on holiday the summer before, just to enjoy the Italian sun and the Roman scenery. She got involved with this handsome Italian youth, surprisingly tall for an Italian, but Peggy said he was Italian. It was love at first sight, and many promises were made. Peggy was a library assistant and the young man was reading Engineering in a university, the name of which Adah had forgotten. The young man seemed to have forgotten the promises he had made Peggy, and she was threatening to go to the address he gave her to find him and give him a piece of her mind. The talk was always of this young man and what Peggy was going to do to him, and how she was going to get her own back. Peggy never really told Adah what it was she had given him that pained her so much. But she let Adah know that she gave so much that she would regret it all her life. She was twenty-three, not very beautiful but small and fun to be with.

Then there was the big boss, Mr Barking. He was thin and bad-tempered, but without a touch of malice. His daughter had married a worthless fellow and he was determined to squash that marriage if it cost him his life. That daughter was ill because of the mental cruelty being inflicted on her by this no-good husband. Mr Barking never talked about his wife; he had got so used to her being there, in his home, that she was never discussed. That wife of his made good chicken sandwiches. Adah had seen Mr Barking munching and munching away at lots of chicken sandwiches in the staff room, and sometimes they made her feel like having one.

Bill was a big handsome Canadian; Adah did not know why he had come to England in the first place, because he looked down on anything English. He used the word 'Britisher' for the English, just like the Americans do.

Even his Christmas cake was flown out from Canada. His mother sent him clothes, food, everything. He would not study for the British Library Association Examinations because he did not trust the British system of education. He had married the children's librarian the year before. Her name was Eileen and she was tall and beautiful, a more perfect match you could never imagine. But Bill knew a little about everything. He liked black writers. Adah did not know any black writers apart from the few Nigerian ones, like Chinua Achebe and Flora Nwapa, and she did not know that there were any other black writers. Bill tut-tutted at her and told her what a shame it was that an intelligent black girl like her should know so little about her own black people. Adah thought about it and realized that Bill was right. He was an intelligent man, that Canadian, and Adah liked him a lot. During the staff break he would talk and expand about authors and their new books. He would then request it and the Camden Borough would buy it, and he would read it first; then he would pass it on to Adah and she would pass it to Peggy. Peggy would pass it to any other members of the staff who were in the mood to read books. It was through Bill that Adah knew of James Baldwin. She came to believe, through reading Baldwin, that black was beautiful. She asked Bill about it and he said, did she not know that black was beautiful.

Bill was the first real friend she had had outside her family. She had a tendency to trust men more because her Pa never let her down. She had already cultivated the taste for wide reading, and Bill, whose wife was expecting a second child within two years of their marriage, was always in the mood for literary talk. Adah was fascinated. She even started reading Marx and was often quoting to herself that if the worst came to the very worst she would leave Francis with her children since she had nothing to lose but her chains.

She got into the light-hearted atmosphere in which the

library staff did their work. There was another girl, a half-caste West Indian, one of the people who found it difficult to claim to be black. She liked Adah because Adah was at that stage forcing everybody to like her. The people at that library made her forget her troubles. Everybody seemed to have troubles then. Bill's wife was having another baby and their flat was very small. He was toying with the idea of going back to his old job, for he had been a radio news-caster in Canada. Why did he come here in the first place? Adah had wondered. He gave the hint, very tentatively, that he was running away from his mother who seemed to have organized a girl she wanted him to marry. He came to England to escape, but then he had met Eileen. Poor man, he was too handsome to be left alone. He was a six footer. Peggy's problem was money to take her to Italy, where she hoped to get a working holiday in order to look for the young Italian who had lied to her. Mr Barking seldom joined in their light-hearted talk, but they all knew he was thinking of his daughter. Fay did not like to associate herself with the black people because she was too white, a mulatto. So, to press home this point, when she qualified as a librarian, she got engaged to this English man who was away in Cambridge reading Law. Adah never saw this man, but she saw Fay's car which was so smashed that it was going to cost Fay a fortune to repair. Fay said her boyfriend had smashed it. Adah was sorry for her, particularly as, although she was very beautiful in a film-star type of way with smooth, glossy skin, a perfect figure and thick beautiful hair, she was at least thirty. And thirty seemed an enormous age to Adah at the time. A woman of thirty and not married was to her an outrage then.

When everybody started talking about their problems, Adah would start laughing.

Peggy would say, 'What the bloody hell are you laughing for?'

Then Bill would reply for her: 'She has no problems.

She's happily married to a brilliant husband who is reading to be a Cost and Works accountant, and she is already going through all her library examinations . . .'

Adah would not contradict him. Was the world not too full of sadness? What was the point of telling them all her woes. Yes, they all believed she had no problems because she wanted them all to believe that.

Three months passed speedily in this way and she knew that the pills the doctor had given her had not worked. She told herself not to panic. Women had been caught in worse situations before. Francis would only laugh and say: 'I thought you were being clever, getting the cap behind my back.' She had been through the worst. Even his beatings and slappings did not move her any more. She did not know where she got her courage from, but she was beginning to hit him back, even biting him when need be. If that was the language he wanted, well, she would use it. Was she not the greatest biter in her school? Francis threatened to break all her teeth for her, and grew his nails as long as those of a tiger, so whenever Adah opened her mouth to bite, Francis would dig his tiger nails into her flesh, almost choking her. Then the thought struck her that she could be killed and the world would think it was an accident. Just a husband and wife fighting. She still hit back occasionally when she knew she was near the door or out of danger, but she gave in to his demands for the sake of peace. They were like the demands of a wicked child who enjoys torturing a live animal given to him as a pet.

Adah wanted to know the truth from the doctor before she started looking for a room for herself and her children. Mr Noble was fed up with their fights and had asked them to move. To cap it all, the women in the house wrote Adah an open petition begging her to control her husband, because he was chasing them all. The letter was posted unsealed, and sent to the wrong branch of the library. So other library assistants could read it if they liked. Adah was not worried, she was going anyway.

She waited patiently for her turn at the surgery, then went in. The doctor greeted her and asked her how she was and she said, 'The child is sitting there pretty. It did not come out as you made me believe it was going to.' Her voice was low and panicky for the first time.

The look the doctor gave her was terrible. It seemed to chill her blood. His dark Indian skin seemed to have gone a shade darker. He was making an effort to speak but the anger inside him was choking him so that he gobbled feebly just like a kettle on the boil . . . then just like a kettle he spluttered: 'I did not give you the pills to abort the child.'

Adah recoiled like a frightened snake, but again, like a snake, she was gathering all her inner energy ready to attack this frightened little man. What did he mean? Adah asked with a voice that had a tinge of brutal harshness in it. She felt like digging her teeth into those eyes that were popping out like a dead fish's.

'All right, so I am having the baby. But I'll tell you this, the pills you gave me were abortive and you know it and I know it, because I carry the child and know what happened the first few weeks you gave them to me. If my child is imperfect in any way, you are responsible. You know that.'

She walked out of the surgery, not to her own home, but to a park near Gospel Oak village and then sat down, thinking. She had suspected something like this would happen, but to have it confirmed this way made her feel a traitor. She cried for herself, she cried for her children, and she cried for the unborn child. Suppose the child was born imperfect, just like those unfortunate thalidomide babies, what was she going to do then? Her thoughts went to her brother, Boy, who had sent her all his savings, asking her to leave Francis and his children and come back to Nigeria where her work at the Consulate would be waiting for her. Boy,

Second Class Citizen

poor Boy, he was very much annoyed over the cap issue which Francis had written to his parents about. This child would give them another song to sing. They would ask why, if she was on birth-control, which she went and got herself, did she then become pregnant? They would say the child was not her husband's, that it'd probably be a white child. You know, like the people who fitted the cap. And then everybody would laugh. Her own people would cover their faces in shame. She found herself being grateful that her parents were dead. This would have killed them. She had raised everybody's hopes when she was at the Methodist Girls' High School, she had raised their hopes higher when she got strings of 'A' levels by taking correspondence courses, and the hopes were being realized when she was in a good job at the American Consulate. If only she had stopped then. She could have passed the rest of her examinations by correspondence. After all, was Ibadan University not a branch of the great *London* University she was so mad about?

But would her children have been in this kind of nursery school where they were then? She got confused. Had it all been worth it?

Then a hand touched her shoulder. The hand was a black man's. Adah jumped. Sitting there, thinking and shedding silent tears, she had not heard the man cross the park. He was an African, a Nigerian. And when he spoke, Adah knew he was Ibo.

'You've had a fight with your husband?'

Adah did not answer. Then the man went on: 'My name is Okpara, and I know you are Ibo because of the marks on your face. I don't want to hear anything. Let's go and beg his forgiveness. He would let you in.' Typical Ibo psychology; men never do wrong, only the women; they have to beg for forgiveness, because they are bought, paid for and must remain like that, silent obedient slaves.

Adah showed him the way to her house. Had not the magic pass word 'Ibo' been uttered? The man talked all the way about this and that. He had a wife, too, with a baby boy, and he had read Law. They had been here some time and were getting ready to go home in about four months. His wife was a secretary and he worked in the Civil Service here. He had now finished his studies. But, he told Adah, they still quarrelled, though he would never beat his wife. He had outgrown that, but they still quarrelled. These quarrels did not mean the end of marriage. He reminded Adah of an old Ibo saying.

'Don't you remember, or have you forgotten, the saying of our people, that a husband and his wife always build their home for many things but particularly for quarrels? A home is where you quarrel in.' Adah nodded, she did remember.

She should have asked Mr Okpara whether the old people lived in one room, whether the men gave babies to their wives in such quick succession. Had not her Ma told her that during her time they used to nurse and breast-feed a child for at least three years? At least those men, the men of the time Mr Okpara was talking about, had other amusements. They had their tribal dances, they had their age-group meetings from which they arrived too drunk with palm-wine to have the energy to ask for their wives. Superstition played a big role in the lives of those people; if you slept with your wife when she was nursing a child, the child would die, so husbands abstained from their nursing wives for a period of three years. Many men were polygamous for this reason. They would build a separate hut for the nursing wife, pension her off for that long period and take in a childless one. These people could afford to build a house in which to quarrel.

But not in London, where her Francis sat all week in the same room by the same kitchen table turning the pages of this book and that book, getting up only to eat or go down to the Nobles to watch their television. Francis could never have a mind as healthy as those men. Again it struck her that their plan had failed, and that it had all

Second Class Citizen

been her fault. She should not have agreed to work all the time. She should have encouraged Francis to work, just like this man's wife, whom she had not seen, had encouraged her husband to work. Francis would have met other men, like this one, and he would have copied them. It was not too late, she consoled herself. That was what she was going to try to do. It might even still save the marriage. After all had not Mr Okpara studied privately in the evenings and still gained a certificate instead of going to watch the television from six o'clock to close-down?

To Mr Okpara she said nothing because she still maintained to herself that failure to make her marriage work was her own affair. She did not mind listening to the story of a successful one, and maybe getting some tips on how to make hers work, but she was not letting this stranger know. Why did she allow Mr Okpara to come home with her? Adah herself did not know the answer. She did not tell the man anything, even though her mind was crying for someone to listen to her, to understand her. Yet she felt that by talking to this stranger, although he was kind and an Ibo like herself, she would be betraying her husband, her family, her children. You don't tell people your troubles when you are still in the midst of them, otherwise it makes them bigger, more insoluble. You tell people when it's all over, then others can learn from your mistakes, and then you can afford to laugh over it. Because by then they have stopped hurting, you have passed them all, have graduated from them.

They got into their room. The scene that met their eyes was comical, and that was an understatement. Vicky was sitting on the settee, waving his wet nappy in the air like a flag. Titi was perched on the bed, looking thoughtfully at Vicky and their father. Bubu was lying flat on his back in the cot, listening to the songs Francis was singing to his children from the Jehovah's Witnesses handbook, looking as untidy as ever. His unshaved face became more noticeable now that Mr Okpara was in the room.

The latter was darker than Francis; he was not tall, about five foot eight, the same height as Francis, but he was immaculate. His white shirt was dazzling, and the fact that he was very black pronounced the whiteness still further. He was wearing a black three-piece suit, and his black shoes shone. His black briefcase added to his dignity somehow and the black rolled umbrella he was carrying completed the image – a black clerk in Britain coming home from the city.

As for Francis, to Adah he did not look like the image of anything. He was just himself, just Francis Obi, and Adah saw then that if she was going to model him on the image of this Mr Okpara, she was going to have a big fight ahead of her. Francis was Francis, not ashamed of being Francis, and was not going to change, even if Adah brought two hundred successful Ibo students to show him. He was proud to be what he was and Adah had better start getting used to him that way or move out.

Francis swore to Mr Okpara that he did not touch Adah. 'She simply went out. I did not know where, but I knew she would come back because she can't bear to leave her children for long. I did not beat her. Did she say that?'

Okpara was not daunted. They were not happy, Adah was not happy and this country was a dangerous place to be unhappy in, because you have nobody to pour out your troubles to, so that was why most lonely African students usually had emotional breakdowns because they had no one to share their troubles with. Did Francis want *his* wife to have such a breakdown? Okpara asked. Would that not be a drain on his purse?

This startled Francis and Adah. She did not know that people still lived like that, the husband paying for the doctor's bills. Even in Nigeria, whenever it was necessary for a private doctor to be called, she had always paid. She could not remember Francis ever paying for anything like that. Okpara was out of touch with the problem at hand, and Francis, now confused with anger, shame and disappointment, resented this intrusion into his family life. Adah hurried to make coffee.

She did not know that Francis had come to such a situation that he had told himself subconsciously that he would never pass his examinations. He had as it were told himself that his ever becoming a Cost and Works accountant in this world was a dream. She did not know that for this reason he would do everything to make Adah a failure like himself. He could not help it, it was human nature. He was not a bitter man.

He lashed his tongue at Okpara, told him to go back home and mind his own business. It was then that Adah realized that Okpara was English only on the surface. An English person would have felt insulted and would leave. But not Okpara. He was Ibo, an this was an Ibo family in trouble, and he was not going to leave until he had made them promise to pay a visit, so that they would see how the Okparas lived. He asked Adah if she had relations in London. Could they not intervene for her?

Adah thought this over. She had no close relatives in London, and the few distant ones would simply laugh. They would say: 'We thought she was the educated lady who knew all the answers. Did we not warn her against marrying that man? Did she not make her own bed? Well, let her sleep in it!' So Adah shook her head and said she had nobody.

After coffee, Okpara talked and advised Francis to be a man. Staying at home, and singing to his children from the hymn book of the Jehovah's Witnesses would not feed and clothe his family, to say nothing of his old parents at home. So he must get a job and study in the evenings. After all, the subjects were not completely new to him any more. Otherwise he would lose his manhood, and these children that he was singing to would soon realize that it was their mother that bought them clothes and food.

Francis stared at him as he said this, because it was a great humiliation to an African not to be respected by his own children. Okpara noticed that he had touched a soft spot for he then banged at the kitchen table, just to emphasize his point. He went on and said did Francis not know that the children born in this country get clever right from their mother's stomach? They know and they can remember what goes on around them. So if Francis wanted to hold the respect of his two sons, he'd better know what he was doing. Okpara did not mention Titi, she was only a girl, a second-class human being; it did not matter whether she respected her father or not. She was going to grow into an ordinary woman not a complete human like a man.

In the weeks and months that followed Okpara and his pretty little wife did their best but Francis would always be Francis. He had been used to being worked for, by a woman whom he knew belonged to him by right. Adah could not escape because of the children or so Francis thought.

When she told him she was expecting another child, the laughter that greeted this announcement was like a mad monkey's in the zoo. It was so animal-like, so inhuman, so mirthless, and yet so brutal. Adah was sure she was five months gone before she told him. She had first got over the pain in her own mind, but was still anxious about the perfection of the baby. She worried about that sometimes, but one thing she had learnt from Bubu's confinement was that she was not going to that hospital as a poor nigger woman. Her baby was going to arrive in style. She knitted and sewed, and this time her maternity grant was not going to Francis. She was buying a brand-new pram, a new shawl and a new outfit for herself for when she came out of the hospital. She met a West Indian girl who had had a baby girl by a Nigerian; but the man had not married her because, according to him, the child was not his. It was this girl who showed Adah that you could live on what was called the Assistance until your children grew up and you could get a job. Adah had heard of this Assistance before, in Nigeria; she learnt about it in her Social History lessons. She did not know that she could still claim it. If only she had known, she would have left Francis earlier. But she did not know.

She addressed twenty greeting cards to herself, gave three pounds to Irene, the girl, and told her to post three cards a day after the baby was born. Two big bunches of flowers were to be sent to her, one on her arrival, with Francis's name attached to it with sentimental words. The other one was to arrive at the hospital after her safe delivery. But if she did not survive the birth, Irene was to put Adah's children's names on it and make it into a wreath. Irene got sentimental and started to cry; Adah told her not to, because we all have to die some time. She was sure that if she was going to be operated upon like before, she did not have much chance. But the Indian doctor, now sorry for what he had done, had become Adah's strongest ally. The chances of her not being operated upon were fifty-fifty. Adah knew that if there was one single chance of her not being cut up, she was going to take that one chance. Her body had a way of rejecting anything foreign, she had known that too. So instead of handing over her pay packet to Francis to dole out the two pounds for housekeeping to her she would buy everything the doctors and the midwives told her to eat. Francis raised many rows, but Adah had a more important thing to worry about – her unborn child. It was so small she could hardly feel it. Her figure did not get big like it did when she was having the others. But she kept strictly to the diet prescribed.

It was then that she was introduced to the modern way of relaxation birth. Adah attended all the classes. It all seemed so easy that she regretted the unnecessary pain she had experienced with the other children. She did not lie about the date of her confinement and she was determined to have her four weeks' rest before going into hospital.

The money was not enough to go round and she told Francis, 'From now on, fend for yourself. I know the children are mine, because they need to be fed. You must go out and work. If not, I shall only cater for my children.'

Francis told her that she could not do it. Adah said nothing, but carried out her plans. He must go out to work. She cared about his studies and all that, but the children were growing both in size and in number. They came first. They had a right to happiness as well, not just Francis. He told her to write down the statement that she would not feed him any more. Adah wrote it without any hesitation. If the world was going to blame her for not feeding her able-bodied husband, let it go ahead. She did not care any more. She had three children to think about and soon there would be four.

They were sorry at the Chalk Farm Library that she was going. She was sorry too, but there, in that library, she discovered a hidden talent which she did not know she had before – the uninhibited ability to make friends easily. People had a way of trusting her easily because she was always trying to laugh however bad the situation. She learned to avoid gloomy people; they made her unhappy. So, since she could not avoid seeing Francis and his sad face, she shut him off from her mind's eye. She saw him but her mind did not register him any more. She heard him say that he had reported her to a Ministry or Board or something because she had signed that she would not feed him any more. Adah waited for the Law to come for her, but the Law did not.

He came with her to the hospital in the ambulance, though. On the second morning of her stay, her big bunch of flowers arrived. Her table was gay with cards even before Dada arrived. She came that night, small, but painless, and perfect. Adah was sure that the child arrived in the world smiling and laughing. She was so small, less than five pounds in weight, but beautiful, just like a black doll – and a girl. Adah was thankful for this child, so perfect and so beautiful that she nicknamed her 'Sunshine'.

She came home by herself in a taxi, and did it in style. She made everybody believe that she had wanted it so, to surprise her husband. She did not tell them that Francis had refused to come for her. They would start to pity her, and she could do without that. She tipped the nurses generously and they all laughed and thanked her. When she got home, she wrote a very nice letter to them all thanking them and she could hear them in her mind's ear saying what a nice happy African woman she was. She had no troubles in the world. Because of this attitude her problems became insignificant. They were all part of her life.

Hunger drove Francis to work as a clerical officer in the post office. Adah's hopes rose. This might save the marriage after all. But she was disappointed. Francis would pay the rent and still gave her only two pounds for the six of them and nothing more. Adah did not know how much he was earning or when he was paid. She warned him, though, that she was going into the Civil Service herself, and that she was going to do the same thing. She would not pay the rent, because it was a man's job to do that, she would not contribute to the food budget, because was she not his wife? She would only be responsible for her children, their clothes, the nursery fees and anything else the children needed. But Francis would not know how much she earned or on what date, because he had started it. He told her that she could not do that because she was his wife. He could refuse to allow her to go out to work. Then Adah retorted saying:

'This is England, not Nigeria. I don't need your signature to secure a job for me.'

But Adah hoped and prayed that this new sense of awareness and of pride in himself would continue. He bought himself a suit and shirts, he bought a small transistor radio, which Adah and the children were not allowed to touch and which he carried with him wherever he went, to work and even to the toilet. Adah laughed inside herself, and said how like a small boy Francis could be. She paid for her own food and the children's from the little savings she had collected from her superannuation pay. For the roof over their heads, she paid by being a wife to Francis at night, and by washing his endless shirts.

Her baby grew stronger, and she paid off her conscience by breast-feeding her. She was not going to bottle-feed this one. She had read somewhere that breast-fed babies were more intelligent, and grew stronger, than those fed from the bottle. She learned, too, that there was less likelihood of the mother becoming pregnant again if she did that. So she breast-fed her child.

Things seemed to be working out well, but Adah's money was running short, and the children needed new clothes. She worked out a timetable, and found that she could manage to have three hours of quiet each afternoon. Then her old dream came popping up. Why not attempt writing? She had always wanted to write. Why not? She ran to Foyle's and bought herself a copy of *Teach Yourself to Write* and sat down throughout all those months when she was nursing Dada and wrote the manuscript of a book she was going to call *The Bride Price*.

Zoë Fairbairns

extract from

Daddy's Girls

Christine is a child of the sixties. The elder sister of Janet, she struggles to develop independence in a family where her parents are at war. Her own initiation into sex reflects the emotional chaos of her upbringing.

'I'm very clever,' said my mother. 'He doesn't suspect.'

It was Friday evening. We were at Bleswick Junction, waiting for the train. I was giving myself a sight-test. I chose a single railway line and followed it into the gleaming silver tangle of rails outside the station.

'A wife who suspected wouldn't go off like this, would she?'

My railway line got lost among the other dazzling lines. I shaded my eyes against the early evening sunlight and squinted into the glare.

'A suspicious, nagging wife will drive a man away, Christine. The home should be a haven of peace.'

I couldn't find my railway line. I hoped that didn't mean I was going to need glasses. I would look horrible in glasses. I squinted at the lines till my eyes watered. Through the water a train came into view.

The announcer said, 'Oxford train. Change at Oxford for Birmingham.'

My mother said, 'I met Daddy in Oxford once.'

'Did you?'

'*My* Daddy. He and Mummy were home on leave. They got leave every three years, it was quite good. Lots of people didn't get nearly as much as that. He had to do some research at the Bodleian, so they took furnished rooms. Miss Dolby put me on the train at the end of term and Daddy and Mummy met me at Oxford. I ran the whole length of the platform and he picked me up.'

That seemed to be the end of the story. I followed her on

to the train. It was crowded with people going home from work. They looked tired and fed up. They fidgeted with copies of the *Evening Standard* and the *Evening News*, ran fingers round the insides of grimy shirt collars, and looked out of the window with bleakness in their eyes.

I wanted them to know that tomorrow I was going to see my long lost boyfriend. I was wearing a new dress with red roses because my mother had insisted that I look respectable for her friend Billy. I would have preferred to be wearing something a bit more CND-ish but at least I felt fresh and romantic.

'When he comes to his senses,' whispered my mother at the top of her voice, 'he won't hear a word of reproach from me.'

I begged her with my eyes to be quiet but she said, 'It's not his fault. It's not even her fault. She's a very, very sick girl. I pity her.' As the train picked up speed, so did my mother's pity for Pam. 'There's a certain type of girl, Christine. You can spot them at children's parties. Adorable little things. Rosebuds, with maggots inside. They make up to the little boys and they make up to the Daddies and they get extra pieces of cake. They get everything they want. It's a pity they can't be spotted at birth because that's when they should be strangled.'

'Shall I go and see if there's a buffet?'

'There should be institutions for keeping them out of harm's way. What do you want a buffet for, you're not hungry or thirsty. Nothing'll happen while Janet's around, will it? He wouldn't want to upset Janet, would he?'

'No.'

'I want him to have his fill of her. Have her till he's sick of her.'

'Janet?'

'*Pam*. The novelty'll wear off. He'll see her, warts and all.'

Daddy's Girls

I wished she would lower her voice at least. To set an example I lowered mine. 'She hasn't got warts.'

'She probably has, and a great deal else besides,' said my mother with a mean snigger.

The tired-looking people in the carriage were perking up and listening hard. A man hid behind his *Evening News*, and shook.

I turned my face to the window and pretended to go to sleep. I stared at the gold insides of my eyelids. Silence fell over the carriage. I peeped at her through my eyelashes and saw her writing in her *Household Memoranda* book. I was glad she had stopped talking but there was something embarrassing about the way she chewed her pencil, stared into space and frowned with concentration, like a child doing homework.

I shut my eyes again. I tried to picture Adam's face. We were to meet at nine o'clock tomorrow morning at the headquarters of Construction Not Destruction. I hoped I would recognize him. I couldn't quite remember what he looked like.

'I'm not going to reproach him.' My mother's foot brushed my ankle. The train was slowing down. 'When he comes to his senses he won't hear one word of reproach from me.' We were arriving at Oxford and she was saying what she had been saying shortly before I fell asleep. I looked nervously at the other passengers and wondered if she had been doing Continuous Performances.

'Why should I reproach him? I don't know anything.' We got our things together. Beyond the window the towers and domes of Oxford glowed in the sunset. 'I don't know anything and I never have known anything. That's what's so clever about me.' We got off the train. 'The dreaming spires,' she said. 'I hope Janet will get into Oxford. I don't want her to end up like me.'

'Getting married, you mean? Who'd want her?'

We sat on a bench to wait for our connection. She said,

'Of course I didn't mean not to get married. I'd marry Daddy again ten times over.' Her voice was warm with love. I felt like puking.

'What did you mean then?'

'Nothing really.'

'What did you mean? Why don't you want Janet to end up like you?'

'I don't want either of you to. I want you to fulfil your potential, as I never did.'

'Why didn't you? Why don't you now? Why don't you go back to nursing?'

'Because Daddy —'

'Why don't you go to evening classes?'

'It's not as simple as that.'

'Why? Why isn't it?'

'There you go again. Christine Toms QC for the prosecution.' She opened her handbag and took a photograph out of her wallet. 'Billy,' she said, 'will meet with your approval. She got her SRN *and* her Midwifery. You'll be able to have a long talk with her about how hopeless *I* am.'

The picture showed my mother dressed in wartime nurse's uniform with another nurse at her side. The other one was a head taller than my mother and had a gawky arm round her shoulder. She had wispy hair, thick spectacles and a distinct look of Dilly Dreem the Lovable Duffer.

The platform was filling up. The Birmingham train was announced. My mother said, 'I'd better give you your ticket in case we get separated.' People started to push forward. 'Have I given you any pocket money for the weekend?' She stuffed bits of paper into one of my hands and the handle of my suitcase into the other. She said, 'I'm not the beast of burden.' We ran for the train. I seemed to be losing her in the crush but she mouthed, 'It's all right.' She signalled that she would go to the back of the train and I should go to the front. This doubled the chances of finding at least one seat. I found one, squashed between a nun and a city gent.

Daddy's Girls

The train moved off. I felt uneasy without my mother, though there was no reason. This was normal drill. If my mother didn't find a seat, she would come looking for me and we would share mine. If she had found one she would sit in it and meet me at Birmingham.

The air in the compartment was sweet and stuffy. The nun's habit was touching my clothes. Nuns gave me the creeps. Sharp pain bit into my hand and I wondered if I might be getting a stigmata. What would she think of that? I realized what the trouble was. I was clutching my ticket so tightly that the corner of the cardboard was cutting into my palm. I loosened my hand and saw what else I was holding. I had the photograph of Billy, a pound note and piece of *Household Memoranda* paper with my mother's handwriting on it.

Dear Christine,
  I have decided to go home and catch them in the act as all this uncertainty is bad for our family life. Tell Billy and Frank that I have had to have a tooth out unexpectedly but we really must get together soon. From Billy and Frank's house phone home and tell Janet or Daddy or even the Slut if she has the temerity to answer our phone that we have arrived safely. They can settle in for the night all nice and cosy and never imagine that I am nearby waiting for my chance. Sorry for this note but I knew that if I told you what I was going to do you would argue and cross-examine me like the barrister you are at heart and could be if only you would apply yourself and go to university as I never did!
Lots of love from Mummy.

* * *

The sun set. The sky went purple. The train pushed on and on through the countryside. Lights came on in snug farmhouses. The train carried me past them. Towns poked their fingers out into the fields. We went past bomb sites, building sites, gasworks and factories. Floodlights shed their pinkish–yellow glare over acres of gleaming, identical cars with no number plates.

At Snow Hill Station a woman approached me. I recognized her from the photograph but I was surprised at how much older than my mother she seemed. She had lost her gawkiness and looked like a grown woman who might also be a nurse. She said, 'You must be Christine Toms,' and a man tried to take my suitcase.

I snatched it back. The woman said, 'Where's your mother? I'd have known you anywhere. You're her image.'

'I'm not.' I pushed past her. 'You've made a mistake.' I headed towards the exit and the dark city.

'Are you sure?' she cried, and I realized she was as silly as my father had said she was. I looked over my shoulder. She was looking over hers. Frank was looking too, and so was their daughter. I assumed it was their daughter. She had a surly expression. I liked that. If I had been dragged out at ten o'clock at night to meet and make friends with a total stranger just because her mother and my mother were nurses together once, I'd have had a surly expression.

I wanted to reassure her. *It's all right. You won't have to share your room. I'm not here.*

They were still looking at me so I hurried out of the station and found a phone box. I phoned Billy's home and was answered by a girl who I guessed was either another daughter or a babysitter. There was no danger that she would know my voice or my mother's, but I shrieked a bit to be on the safe side. I told her that I and my daughter Christine couldn't come after all because Christine wasn't very well. I tried to make it sound as if what Christine had wrong with her was something to do with her periods, so that the girl wouldn't ask for details. She didn't. She just said, 'They've gone to the station to meet you.'

Daddy's Girls

I said, 'I'm so sorry for the inconvenience. We *must* get together soon.'

Opposite the station was a row of bus stops in front of a huge dark church with white gravestones. I looked at the timetables on the bus stops, but none of them mentioned the road where Construction Not Destruction was.

I took a taxi. We seemed to travel a long way through the shadowy city but it was hard to tell whether we were actually getting anywhere. We kept being diverted past roadworks and along one-way streets. I didn't blame my father for not wanting to come to Birmingham, it was all being dug up. Cranes and scaffolding towered above cement mixers and heaps of bricks on bomb sites. The square white beginnings of modern buildings peeped out of the rubble like the tips of new teeth.

We turned down a narrow street. The light from the few lamp posts was dim and greenish yellow. We could hardly read the numbers on the houses, which were small and huddled together in terraces. Their front doors faced straight on to the street. My father would have called them 'omes for the workers.

Some of the houses were boarded up. There were gaps in the terraces. The houses on each side of the gaps were propped up by wooden struts shaped like lopsided letter A's.

One of the gaps had frames in it with dangling ropes. They looked as if they would come in handy for public executions. A sign read 'CONSTRUCTION NOT DESTRUCTION ADVENTURE PLAYGROUND'.

I got out of the cab and waited for the driver to turn into Birmingham's answer to PC Tutsworth and say he wasn't going to leave a nice young girl like me in a place like this. But once he'd taken all my money he drove off at high speed, as if what he really wanted to be was Birmingham's answer to Stirling Moss. He left a smell of petrol in the warm night air where it mixed with soot and dog's muck and a faint hint of flowers.

Nailed to a tree in front of the adventure playground was a sign advertising a CND Poetry and Jazz evening, with today's date and the name of a pub, but no address. I thought that must mean the pub was nearby, and locals would know where it was. All I had to do was find some locals. I peered into the darkness around me but saw no one. I heard running footsteps and a shout of drunken laughter but they were some way off.

I chose a house with a light on. I knocked. A snarling dog hurled itself against the other side of the front door, shaking it till I thought it would give way. I ran.

I heard more drunken voices, and went towards them. I wandered a bit and found the pub. Everyone seemed to be leaving. I ducked into the Saloon Bar where the barmaids were collecting glasses and telling people to drink up. Their accents reminded me of Beryl Reid in *Educating Archie*. I made for the Ladies.

It was half-way up a flight of stairs. From the top of the stairs came the sound of jazz, tantalizing waves of music. I walked towards the waves and they engulfed me, making me tingle.

Smoke curled round a half open door. I peered in. The room was hot, and dark except for a spotlight on three jazz players with embroidered waistcoats and gleaming instruments. Cigarette tips glowed around them.

When the players got to the end of their music, a man wearing a bowler hat over long beatnik hair stood up to read his poem. He spent a lot of time shuffling pieces of paper, but when he got to the poem he seemed to be making it up as he went along. He sounded quite angry and kept saying 'fuck'.

He finished his poem and everybody clapped wildly, which he liked. He was a show-off. He reminded me of Janet. He looked as if he wanted to read us another poem but one of the barmen came up from downstairs

Daddy's Girls

and put the lights on. 'Thanks very much, ladies and gents.'

People stretched their limbs and rubbed their eyes as if they were coming out of hibernation. Adam was only a few feet away from me. I recognized him at once, even though his hair was longer than I remembered it and seemed to have gone grey.

He was wearing a frayed jersey and corduroy trousers with paint stains on them. His glasses looked different. The frames were thinner. He was talking to a group of people. Some of them were girls. One of the girls passed a packet of cigarettes. Everyone took one, including Adam. Someone brought out a lighter. They passed it round. Somebody said something that made them laugh. I didn't hear the joke, I just heard the laughter. I felt left out. The sound of the laughter told me that if Adam didn't recognize me I would walk out into the night and never be seen again. If he wasn't pleased to see me I would die. I wouldn't commit suicide, I wouldn't need to, I would simply disappear and die of natural causes.

It must have been a good joke because the laughter went on and on. He rolled his head around. His eyes met mine, went away and came back. He rushed over and hugged me. I hugged him. I didn't care who saw, I was so happy and relieved. He felt small after Miguel, but hard and strong, perhaps from all his building work. Suddenly I was shy. I tried to make the hug go on and on so that I wouldn't have to say anything, or look at him.

His hair smelt of sawdust and paint which explained the greyness and made me sneeze. He said, 'Bless you,' for the sneeze and then looked puzzled. 'I thought you weren't coming till tomorrow.'

'I'll go back then. If you don't want me.'

'Of course I want – but what about you mother and Bertie?'

'*Billy*. Can I have a cigarette?'

'Don't you buy your own yet?'

I took his cigarette and smoked it. He called, 'Jane, have you got a fag?' The girl tossed him one and he lit it from mine.

He said, 'Where's your mother?'

'If I'd known you wanted her, I'd have sent her instead.' I looked as sexy as I could and it worked. He smiled and shrugged and kissed me.

The room was emptying. The barman said, 'Thanks very much, ladies and gents,' put one hand on my back and another on Adam's, and pushed us towards the door.

Adam took my suitcase and we went down the stairs. We had a kiss on each stair. The barman rammed us in the ribs with a tray of glasses. 'Thanks very much, ladies and gents.' Outside the pub, other Poetry and Jazz people were kissing under lamp posts. I looked for Jane but I couldn't see her. Adam walked me into a shadowy corner and we kissed as if we had been starving and had found food. Every time he tried to stop I started another kiss because I didn't want him going after Jane.

* * *

The church hall was near the adventure playground. It reminded me of my father's rugby club, except that the people wandering about inside it looked as if they had brains. Student-type girls and men with beards came and went from the kitchen with mugs of coffee. Paper arrows on the wall showed where males and females were supposed to be sleeping, but no one was going to sleep. They sat on rucksacks, rolled their own cigarettes and had fierce arguments about the Labour Party. Two men were discussing something technical about one of their guitars. They passed the guitar backwards and forwards and strummed a few notes to make their points.

A fussy priest in jeans looked at me, looked at his clip board and looked at me again. 'Hullo! Who's this?'

Adam said, 'It's Chris, she's just arrived. Chris, this is Keith.'

'Pleased to meet you.'

'Chris what? Is she staying?'

'Toms,' I said. 'And yes.'

'The girls sleep up that end.' Keith bustled off.

Adam looked at my dress and my suitcase. 'You have brought a sleeping bag?'

'No.'

'Didn't I say to bring one?'

'I haven't got one.'

He looked at me. 'Has something happened?'

'Billy's children have got scarlet fever.'

'Scarlet —?'

'The whole family's in quarantine. No one's allowed in or out. It's awful.'

He sighed. 'We'd better get you some bedding.' He took me up a flight of stairs to a store-room full of broken pews and boxes of prayer books. On a shelf was a pile of grey blankets and grey pillows. He let go of my hand and scooped up an armful of the bedding. He looked as if he meant to take it downstairs but he stopped, changed his mind and dropped it on the floor.

He held out his arms to me and said, 'Please tell me why you're here.'

'If you don't want me, I'll go away again.'

'I do want you.'

We leaned against a broken pew, kissing. He tasted of paint and smelled of sweat but I didn't mind. I didn't mind my back getting uncomfortable either, but I pretended to. The more uncomfortable I seemed to be, the more he comforted me, and I needed a bit of comforting.

He admired my dress. I let him undo the zip.

Music and talk drifted up from downstairs. He took off my bra. He smiled as if someone had given him a present. He kissed the tip of my left nipple, then my right. They tingled and went hard. They were so hard they hurt. He soothed them. He ran his hands between my breasts and up and down the sides. They felt as if they wanted me to cry, because in all that time with Miguel they had never been properly appreciated and now they were being appreciated again.

He took off his glasses and his jersey. He pressed his hard, skinny chest against my soft, full one. *You'd never think we were the same species*. We were the same species now.

The door opened. A man and a girl stood there looking disappointed. They said, 'Oh, sorry.'

'Don't mention it,' said Adam into my neck.

The girl said, 'You might have put the sign on the door.'

There was a square skylight in the roof. Against its faint glow I could see the blank outline of his head. I couldn't see his features. He could have been anybody.

Anybody at all could have been unhooking my suspenders and rolling my stockings down. He didn't even smell right. Any paint-covered workman could have his hand inside my knickers.

I couldn't believe I was going to do this but I didn't think I was going to stop.

My eyes got used to the darkness. His face was white and devilish. Pews surrounded us like the bars of a cage but we weren't in a cage. We were free. We could do whatever we wanted. I knew what he wanted to do. I knew I was supposed to stop him. He wouldn't stop of his own free will, it was up to me.

He fiddled with the buckle of his belt. It sounded dangerous.

'Don't.'

'You mean I've got to keep my trousers on? What a rotter you are.' He left the buckle alone.

I don't know who's there, I thought.

'It's only me,' he said

I must be safe with him if he can read my mind.

Daddy's Girls

The talking and strumming from downstairs faded into silence. In the silence several hearts thumped. One was Adam's. The others were mine. My main heart had sent little hearts to different parts of my body to thump there. One was in my head. Another was in my stomach. A third thumped in the wetness between my legs.

It retreated from Adam's fingers and went on thumping in safety, deep inside, out of reach.

He said, 'Do you believe I can undo my belt and take my trousers down without using my hands?'

'No.'

'You're right, I can't.' He put his hands on the insides of my thighs. 'So if you can feel my hands, you know I've still got my trousers on.' He opened my thighs and put his face there.

I thought he was going to kiss me, which would have been bad enough. Bad enough for him. I didn't mind it. In fact I quite liked it. I thought he must be hating it, but he sort of settled down, as if he were about to have a good long drink from a river. A swamp was more like it. How could he? I was getting warmer and warmer down there, and up here my breaths were coming fast with little moans at the end of them. I didn't mean to let out those moaning sounds, but there they were. I was embarrassed by the moans and embarrassed by the disgusting thing Adam was doing. He didn't seem to have realised how disgusting it was but he soon would. And when he did he would move away.

I didn't think I could bear that so I moved away first. I got hold of the sides of his head and pushed.

He looked anxious. 'Aren't I doing it right?'

'What?'

His eyes and teeth glowed up towards me. 'Why did you stop me?'

'Well.'

'Are you sufficiently aroused?'

He seemed to want an answer.

I tried out some in my head.

What if I said *yes* and I was wrong?

What if I said *no* and he got angry?

I didn't want to say *no*. I wanted his tongue back. I put my fingers where his tongue had been. They weren't as good as his tongue, but they weren't bad.

He threw his trousers and his underpants over a pew and lay on top of me. I tasted the dust in his hair and felt his penis. My fingers got out of its way, like pedestrians in front of a lorry. I still couldn't believe I was doing this.

He prodded me and made me flinch. That prod spoiled everything. I didn't want to do it after all.

I moved away. He came after me and gave me a long, deep kiss before trying again. He was trembling and gasping. I moved away again. He stopped me. 'I think you're supposed to come towards me. Sort of like this.' He moved his hips about.

'Why?'

'It says in *Modern Woman and* – '

'Why should I hurt myself?'

'If you want to – '

'I don't'.

'Oh.' He looked as if he couldn't believe it. He looked as if he were going to rape me. 'You mean not now? Or never?'

'How should I know?'

He turned away furiously and lit a cigarette. He didn't offer me one. The cigarette calmed him down and he said quietly, 'Either you do this with me now or you'll do it some other time with someone else or you'll be a virgin for the rest of your life. Do you accept my reasoning so far?'

Pompous git, I thought. I nearly said, *Save it for your clever girlfriends at Oxford*, but I didn't want him to save it for them.

He said, 'Is there anyone else you'd prefer?'

'No.'

'And do you want to be a virgin for –'

'No.'

'Well then.' He propped himself up on his elbows again and reared above me. I thought, *This is it*, but he stopped and said, 'There is another possibility. I think you can go to a doctor and have it done under local anaesthetic. Fancy that?'

'Not much.'

He leaned forward and my body gave way.

It hurt a bit but it wasn't nearly as bad as I'd been led to expect by the authoress of *The Second Sex*. Adam seemed to be having a much worse time than I was having. He heaved about, groaned and flopped on top of me as if he had just died.

The French authoress must have been unlucky with her defloration. Whoever had done it, it certainly wasn't Adam. He lit two cigarettes and gave me one. 'Best cigarette in the world,' he said.

I took a few puffs and agreed with him. I watched my smoke-stream mingle with his until there was only one. I could remember a time when I hadn't liked smoking very much and I wondered if sex was like that and you had to get used to it.

As if he had read my mind again, he said, 'Sorry.'

'It's all right, it was nothing.'

He sighed.

'It was lovely,' I lied. 'Especially before.'

'I should have kept going. I hope I'm not doomed to be a premature ejaculator for ever.'

'What's a premature −?'

'Some men can go on for hours.'

I was glad he wasn't one of them but I didn't say anything.

* * *

He fell asleep. I lay with my eyes wide open. I had pins and needles, I felt sore and sticky between my legs, and I was wondering what had happened to my family.

I imagined my mother talking to herself on the train and getting out at Bleswick. She scurried home and hid in the garden. I wondered if she knew that the lilac bush provided the best hiding place. It had a good view of the house and gave off a nice smell.

She waited for darkness. The moon came out. She probably got a bit chilly. She watched to see which lights came on in which windows.

Janet's bedroom light came on first. Janet's going-to-bed routine took about half an hour. She folded her clothes, checked to see that I hadn't been interfering with any of her collections (as if I would), wrote a novel or two and said a thank you prayer for her day's achievements. She got into bed and turned out the light.

Which light would have gone on next? Or lights? If two lights went on – one in the double bedroom and the one in the spare – everything could still be perfectly innocent. But I had a feeling that only the double bedroom light had gone on. The window of the spare room stayed dark.

That would have settled it. I imagined my mother breathing faster and faster. In the window of her own bedroom, the light went out. She gasped with bitterness. They were nice and cosy. She was outside, alone with her jealous rage.

It would have been a rage to scorch the lilac leaves. It would have been a worse rage than any I had ever seen, and I had seen a few. It would be wilder than her Christmas rages, more furious than her slimming rages, or her rages when the boiler wouldn't light, or she couldn't find her handbag, madder than the frenzies in which she begged me to pretend not to know what I knew about my father.

There could be no more pretence after this. But what was *this*? What would she have done? Would she have climbed up the ladder to the bedroom window and caught them in the act?

The act. Adam lay with his head against my beautiful

Daddy's Girls

breasts. It was *our* act. I thought how lucky I was to have him, now that my home was about to become a broken home. If my mother had murdered my father and Pam, or burned the house down or something like that, Janet would probably be put into an orphanage, but I would stay here with Adam.

I woke by myself, itching from the blankets. I could smell bacon frying. I stood up. Wetness trickled like tears between my legs. I ran my hands through my tangled hair and over my face to feel whether it had changed. The skin felt dry but strangely soft. I walked round the store-room, picking my scattered clothes off the pews.

I wanted a full-length mirror to look in, and a bath. I wanted Adam. I put my dress on over my naked body. I pretended it was a négligée. I took my sponge bag out of my case and opened the door of the store-room. At the bottom of the stairs people milled about, rubbing their eyes and clearing up. They wore dungarees and paint-stained overalls which looked as if they had slept in them. I felt rather glamorous. Under my dress I was naked and I knew things. I would know those things for ever, whatever happened.

I followed the smell of bacon into the main hall. The sleeping bags had been cleared away and piled on the stage. There was a trolley with a tea urn and cups. Folding tables and chairs had been set out.

Each table had a catering pack of cornflakes, a pile of bowls and a big metal jug of milk. Through the hatch, I could see Adam in the kitchen with Jane. They both had badges on with the word ORGANIZER, and chefs' hats with CND symbols cut out of them. She wore a pretty apron of purple gingham over tight trousers and a big grey home-knitted jersey. She was frying bacon. He was spreading margarine on slices of Wonderloaf.

I watched them for a long time but they didn't see me. I went to the Ladies. Girls wearing jeans and men's shirts were washing their faces and cleaning their teeth. They stared at me in my dress through eyes that hadn't had enough sleep.

I hadn't had enough sleep either but I had a reason. I had done it. Whatever happened for the rest of my life, I had done *it*. I looked into the eyes of the girl students and guessed which ones had done it and which ones hadn't done anything.

There was no bath so I held my face flannel under a tap, squeezed it out and took it into a cubicle to wipe between my legs. I wondered whether any of the girls had guessed what I was doing and why. I wondered if they disapproved. I didn't care if they did. I wanted them to.

Still barefoot and dressed like a woman of the streets, I went to the kitchen. I said loudly, 'Can I help?'

Adam jumped as if he had been doing something wrong. This made me even more suspicious that he had been. 'Good morning, Chris!'

'Morning.' I picked up a knife.

Jane said, 'You're a weekend volunteer, aren't you? You've got your own rotas.' She was pretending to be friendly but she was looking at the knife and she seemed nervous.

'It's all right.' I spread some margarine. 'I don't mind helping.'

'You don't have to, honestly,' said Adam. 'Have some breakfast. And er –' he smiled – 'get dressed.' He said it as if he didn't want me to think he was ordering me about but he wanted me to do what he said.

Without a word I went back to the store-room and put on jeans and a jersey. If he wanted me to look like everybody else, then I would look like everybody else. Last night he hadn't thought I was like everybody else. As I came back down the stairs I swung my hips in a sexy, automatic sort of way that I seemed to have learnt.

As I queued for breakfast, I felt empty and sad. Why

Daddy's Girls

should I queue up for him? I wanted him to be mine, as I was his. I looked at all the men. I wondered if they realized. I wondered if they were jealous of Adam. I tried to decide which ones I liked. There was one with black hair and a black beard and black curls peeping between his shirt buttons. I wondered what it would be like with somebody like him who was hairy and coarse.

I reached the front of the queue. You had to help yourself to slices of bread and hold them apart while Adam put bacon between them. He did mine very sexily. He gave me an extra rasher and a big smile. I thought he was going to say something but he turned to the next person in the queue.

I got myself some tea and sat with it and my bacon sandwich at one of the tables. The other people at the table were quite nice; they asked where I had come from and when I said Bleswick they pretended to have heard of it. But I couldn't take my eyes off Adam and Jane in the kitchen beyond the hatch.

My sadness had a sickly, familiar feeling. I seemed to know that this always happened after a girl lost her virginity, and it served her right.

I seemed to have done it dozens of times. I seemed to know what to expect. He had lost respect for me and I had lost him.

The priest from last night, who was wearing one of the ORGANIZER badges, banged the side of one of the metal jugs with a spoon. He said, 'I'm not going to preach a sermon,' and the long-termers cheered. He said, 'Thank you. Remember that the whole point of Construction Not Destruction is to provide an answer to the challenge that is so often put to those of us who are against the bomb. What are you *for*? What is your alternative? This weekend, *you* are the alternative.

'Don't ram politics down people's throats. Some of them aren't interested in politics, and that's their privilege. Some of them oppose us, and that's their privilege too. Some of them think ban-the-bombers are sex-crazed drug addicts.' The long-termers cheered again, and Adam winked at me from the kitchen. Keith wasn't laughing. 'This is a serious matter. They've read it in the *Daily Express*, so it must be true. Once again, it's their privilege to suspect what they want, but it is not yours to confirm their suspicions. Remember, you are the ambassadors of the peace movement, and behave accordingly. If our personal behaviour turns people against us, we're wasting our time as far as building our movement is concerned.'

Adam was looking very, very solemn. I was sure I was going to giggle. I kept snorting and blowing my nose. Keith said, 'I'm not saying don't enjoy yourselves. I'm not a killjoy, God knows. But –'

'Make sure no one finds out about it, eh, Keith?' someone suggested.

'Make sure *I* don't find out.' He looked as if the joke had gone far enough.

* * *

I was down on the rota to do Slum Renovation with four strangers. I said to Adam, 'Why can't I be with you?'

'You will be.' He kissed me, but he was in a rush. 'Tonight.' He wasn't my lover any more, he was an Organizer, a long-term volunteer, a big shot.

'Why not today?'

'I'm staying here,' he said. 'Cleaning and catering.'

'I could do that.'

'Housework? You?'

I pointed at the rota. 'I don't know these people.'

He was completely unsympathetic. 'Get to know them. You're a big girl now.'

'You sound like my mother.'

'Which reminds me,' he said.

'What?' I edged away.

'Where is she?'

'Stop going on about that.'

'You still haven't told me why you changed your plans.'

'Look, do you want me to go on this rota or not?'

The others in my group were a fierce-faced Italian girl called Marcella who had a red hammer-and-sickle badge with Russian lettering pinned to her blue pullover, an engaged couple from Sussex University called Tim and Rachel, and Lawrence who was in charge.

Lawrence turned out to be the hairy one from the breakfast queue. He gave the orders while the rest of us loaded stepladders, dust sheets, rolls of wallpaper and tins of paint into a van. We climbed in after them.

Lawrence drove and talked to us over his shoulder. 'We're going to see the Trentons. They're a problem family.'

Marcella said, 'It is the capitalist system that is the problem.'

'Yes, love. Have any of you done any painting or decorating before?'

'Of course.' Marcella sounded as if she thought Lawrence ought to know that she was an expert.

Rachel said, 'We've done a bit, haven't we, Tim? Only I wasn't very good.'

'What about you, Chris? Have you had any experience?'

I didn't answer. I was thinking about my own problem family, and how pleased my mother would be if a team of volunteers were to turn up and decorate 79 Manor Road, Bleswick. If she hadn't burned it down, that was.

Lawrence said, 'I don't think Chris is going to tell us whether she's had any experience or not. I think she prefers to keep quiet about it.' He chuckled into his beard and his eyes glittered at me in the driving mirror. He stopped the van, came round the back and opened the doors. He offered his hand to Marcella, who ignored it and jumped down by herself. I tried to do the same but he got hold of me round my waist and held on for much longer than he had to. Rachel was helped down by Tim.

We were parked in front of a terrace of sooty little houses in a windy street. Lawrence knocked at one of the doors, *bang-tiddy-bang-bang, bang-bang*, and a fat woman with bad teeth and lots of children let us in.

We carried our equipment into the house. The air smelt of nappies, fish and BO. The furniture was odd and old and broken, and frayed bits of carpet were sticky underfoot.

Lawrence showed us the work that had been done so far. Construction Not Destruction had put in a bathroom and an inside toilet, and had re-plastered one of the bedrooms. The bedroom now needed painting and wallpapering. Lawrence put Tim and Marcella in charge of this because they had experience. Rachel didn't look at all pleased about Tim being on his own in the bedroom with Marcella, even if the beds were covered with dust sheets. Lawrence said, 'Rachel and Chris can make a start on the kitchen,' and Rachel looked at me with dislike in her eyes.

'What do we do?' I asked him.

'Strip,' he said meaningfully. 'Rub down and make good.' The kitchen looked as if it would take all day to clear up, never mind decorate. Mrs Trenton said to Lawrence, 'I'm sorry, love, I'm all behind this morning.'

'We're here to help, Mrs T,' he said. 'You get your feet up.' He put his hand under her elbow and gallantly took her out of the room.

The sink and the draining board were covered with empty tins. Rachel carried them out to the bin in the yard. I started clearing dirty plates off the table.

'There's not much point in doing that,' said Rachel, with her hands full of tins. 'There's nowhere to put anything.'

'What shall I do then?'

She gave me the usual look of women who got exasperated when I didn't know what housework to do, but who weren't prepared to tell me. 'Can't you *see*?'

Daddy's Girls

Stuck to the greasy wallpaper were picture postcards, family snaps and portraits of the Queen and President Kennedy cut out of magazines. I started to take them down, peeling back the sellotape. I thought that was one job I couldn't mess up.

I was wrong. A piece of sellotape brought a long strip of the soggy wallpaper away with it. I went on pulling and part of the wall came too, with stones and dust and chunks of plaster. Rachel said, 'You should have put dust sheets down before you started that. Why don't you help me with the washing-up?'

I would have loved to, but I didn't dare let go of the paper. If I didn't keep it pressed against the wall, the avalanche started again. I almost wished my father would walk in. He knew about walls.

'Help,' I said.

'Oh, honestly,' said Rachel. *'Lawrence!'*

He grinned at me. He said, 'You *haven't* done it before, have you?' He stood close behind me and took the wallpaper out of my hand. He didn't exactly stop the avalanche so much as leave it to subside. At least I wasn't responsible for it any more. I felt his breath on my neck.

Mrs Trenton looked in to see how we were getting on. The dust made her cough, and she stared in alarm at the hole in her wall. The wallpaper hung off it like skin round a wound. I thought she was probably thinking that it was all very well for us to spend a weekend smashing up her house when we had homes of our own to go to at the end of it.

The trouble was, I didn't know whether I had.

I said, 'Please, Mrs Trenton, can I use your phone?'

'What phone?' she replied, and Lawrence looked as if I should have known and shouldn't have asked. He said, 'Is it something urgent?'

'No.'

Mrs Trenton said, 'There's a call box at the shop.'

Lawrence said, 'I've got a better idea. My lodgings are just round the corner. There's a phone there.'

'It's all right. It doesn't matter.'

'Come on, love.' He put his hand on my shoulder. 'I'll take you.'

Rachel called after us, 'That's right, leave me to do everything.'

His room was at the back and the top of a tall house. It had a steep fire escape with missing steps. We had to keep stopping for breath.

'Home sweet home,' he said. He nodded at the phone. 'Help yourself.' I thought he might leave me to make my phone call in peace but there was nowhere for him to go. It didn't matter. There was nothing to listen to. The phone rang and rang in Bleswick but there was no reply. I got the operator to check the line. He said it was all right.

I waited and waited and gave up. I wished I hadn't tried. I wanted to go back to the Trentons and knock walls down. I wished I had the kind of face that didn't show things. I wished I could be casual, but I couldn't. I was in a panic, and Lawrence saw. He came over to where I was sitting. He took my hands in his hard, dirty ones and raised me to my feet. His arms went round me in a lovely strong restful hug. I supposed I shouldn't really be letting him hug me, but no one else seemed to be sympathetic. Adam was too busy with his precious Jane.

Lawrence sat me down on the bed. He kissed me fiercely, biting my lips. His breath was stale and his beard tasted of alcohol but I let him run it all over my face until I couldn't see anything except black hairy darkness.

I couldn't see what was happening so nothing could be. When he started to unzip my jeans, he didn't do it seductively or gently or mischievously as Adam would have done it, he did it casually as if they were his own jeans. Perhaps they were his. I didn't feel as if I had any right to tell him what he could or couldn't do with them.

His breath came in fast, sour, hissing gasps. He left my zip for a moment and fumbled with his fly buttons. This

Daddy's Girls

gave me a chance to start pulling my zip back up but he stopped me. 'You know you want it, love.' It sounded like a favour he was about to do me. I would be ungrateful to refuse. He opened the front of his trousers and let his penis out. It was the first one I had ever seen in daylight. I was astonished at how painful it looked, even for him, never mind what it would do to me while I was still sore.

I tried to move away. He said, 'You can't get out of it now.' It had stopped being a favour. It was a punishment, though I didn't know what for.

Outside, the fire escape was clanging as if an athlete or some other very energetic person were racing up it. A shadow appeared against the glass top of the outside door. I would have recognized the shape of the shadow even if I hadn't heard the vigorous footsteps. Lawrence said, 'Fuck,' and let go of me. I did up my clothes and opened the door to my mother.

Nadine Gordimer
Blinder

Rose lives in the backyard. She has lived there from the time when she washed the napkins of the children in the house, who are now university students. Her husband had disappeared before she took the job. Her lover, Ephraim, who works for Cerberus Security Guards, has lived with her in the yard for as long as anyone in the house can remember. He used to be night watchman at a parking garage, and the children, leaving for school in the morning after Rose had cooked breakfast for them, would meet 'Rose's husband' in his khaki drill uniform, wheeling his bicycle through the gateway as he came off shift. His earlobes were loops that must once have been filled by ornamental plugs, his smile was sweetened by splayed front teeth about which, being what he was, who he was, he was quite unselfconscious.

That is what they remember, the day they hear that he is dead. The news comes by word-of-mouth, as all news seems to in the backyards of the suburb; who is in jail, caught without a pass, and must be bailed out, who has been told to leave a job and backyard at the end of the month, who has heard of the birth of a child, fathered on annual leave, away in the country. There is a howling and keening in the laundry and the lady of the house thinks Rose is off on a blinder again. In her forties Rose began to have what the family and their friends call a drinking problem. Nothing, in the end, has been done about it. The lady of the house thought it might be menopausal, and had Rose examined by her own doctor. He found she had high blood pressure and treated her for that, telling her employer the drinking absolutely must be stopped, it exacerbated hypertension. The lady of the house made enquiries, heard of a Methodist Church that ran a non-racial Alcoholics Anonymous as part of its community programme, and delivered Rose by car to the weekly meetings in a church hall. Rose calls the AA euphemistically 'my club' and is no longer sloshed and juggling dishes by the family's dinner-hour every night, but she still goes off every two months or so on a week's blinder. There is nothing to be done about it; the lady of the house – the family, the grown children for whom Rose is the innocence of childhood – can't throw her out on the street. She has nowhere to go. If dismissed, what kind of reference can be given her? One can't perjure oneself on the most important of the three requirements of prospective employers: honesty, industry, sobriety.

Over the years, Ephraim has been drawn into discussions about Rose's drinking. Of course, if anyone is able to help her, it should be he, her lover. Though to talk of those two as lovers ... The men always must have a woman, the women always seem to find a man; if it's not one, then another will do. The lady of the house is the authority who has gone out to the yard from time to time to speak to Ephraim. The man of the house has no time or tact for domestic matters.

Ephraim, what are we going to do about Rose?

I know, madam.

Can't you get her to stop? Can't you see to it that she doesn't keep any of the stuff in the room?

(It is a small room; with two large people living there, Rose and Ephraim, there can't be much space left to hide brandy and beer bottles.)

But she goes round the corner.

(Of course. Shebeens in every lane.)

So what can we do, Ephraim? Can't you talk to her?

Blinder

What I can do? I talk. Myself, I'm not drinking. The madam ever see me I'm drunk?

I know, Ephraim.

And now Ephraim is dead, they say, and Rose is weeping and gasping in the laundry. The lady of the house does not know whether Rose was in the laundry when one of Ephraim's brothers (as Rose says, meaning his fellow workers) from Cerberus Security Guards came with the news, or whether the laundry, that dank place of greasy slivers of soap, wire coat-hangers and cobwebs, was her place to run to, as everyone has a place in which the package of misery is to be unpacked alone, after it is delivered. Rose sits on an upturned bucket and the water from her eyes and nose makes papier mâché heads, in her fist, out of the Floral Bouquet paper handkerchiefs she helps herself to (after such a long service, one can't call it stealing) in the lady of the house's bathroom. Ephraim has been dead a week, although the news comes only now. He went home last week on leave to his village near Umzimkulu. The bus in which he was travelling overturned and he was among those killed. His bicycle, a chain and padlock on the back wheel, is there where he stored it safely against his return, propped beside the washing machine with its murky submarine eye.

It is a delicate matter to know how to deal with Rose. The ordinarily humane thing to do – tell her not to come back into the house to prepare dinner, take off a few days, recover from the shock – is not the humane thing to do, for her. Under that bed of hers on its brick stilts there quickly will be a crate of bottles supplied by willing 'friends'; it is quite natural that someone with her history will turn to drink. So the lady of the house makes a pot of tea and gently calls Rose to their only common ground, the kitchen, and sits with her a while, drinking tea with her on this rare occasion, just as she will go to visit a friend she hasn't seen for years, if he is dying, or will put in a duty appearance at a wedding in some branch of kin from which she has distanced herself in social status, tastes and interests.

Flesh and tears seem to fuse naturally on Rose's face; it is a sight that causes the face itself to be seen afresh, dissolved of so long a familiarity, here in the kitchen, drunk and sober, cooking a leg of lamb as only she can, or grovelling awfully, little plaited horns of dull hair sticking out under the respectability of her maid's cap fallen askew as she so far forgets herself, in embarrassing alcoholic remorse, to try to kiss the hand of the lady of the house. That face – Rose's face – has changed, the lady of the house notices, just as she daily examines the ageing of her own. The fat smooth brown cheeks have resting upon them beneath the eyes two hollowed stains, the colour of a banana skin gone bad. The drinking has stored its poison there, its fatigue and useless repentance. The body is what the sea recently has been discovered to be: an entity into which no abuse can be thrown away, only cast up again.

Rose doesn't ask, what's for dinner? – not tonight. She is scrubbing potatoes, she has taken the T-bone steaks out of the refrigerator, as if this provides a ritual in place of mourning. It is best to leave her to it, the calm of her daily task. The grown children, when they arrive at different intervals later in the afternoon or evening, go one by one back to childhood to put their arms around Rose, this once, again, in the kitchen, and there are tears again from her. They talk about Ephraim, coming home to the backyard early in the morning, just as they were leaving for school, and she actually laughs, a spluttery sob, saying: I used to fry for him some bread and eggs in the fat left from your bacon! – A collusion between the children and the servant over something the lady of the house didn't know, or pretended never to have known. The grown children also recall for Rose how one or other of them, riding a motorcycle or driving a car, passed him only the other day, where he singled himself out, waving and calling a greeting from the uniformed corps in the Cerberus

Blinder

Security Guards transport vehicle. The daughter of the house recently happened to enter the headquarters of a mining corporation, where he was on duty in the glassy foyer with his shabby wolf of a guard dog slumped beside him. She had said, poor thing, put out a hand to stroke it, and Ephraim had expertly jerked the dog away to a safe distance, laughing, while it came to life in a snarl. He's very good with those dogs, Rose says, that dog won't let anyone come near him, *any*one . . .

But it is over. Ephraim has been buried already; it's all over. She has heard about his death only after he has been buried because she is not the one to be informed officially. He has – had, always had – a wife and children there where he came from, where he was going back to, when he was killed. Oh yes. Rose knows about that. The lady of the house, the family, know about that; it was the usual thing, a young man comes to work in a city, he spends his whole life there away from his home because he has to earn money to send home, and so – the family in the house privately reasoned – his home really is the backyard where his town woman lives? As a socio-political concept the life is a paradigm (the grown child who is studying social science knows) of the break-up of families as a result of the migratory labour system. And that system (the one studying political science knows) ensures that blacks function as units of labour instead of living as men, with the right to bring their families to live in town with them.

But Ephraim deluded himself, apparently, that this backyard where he was so much at home was not his home, and Rose, apparently, accepted his delusion. This was not the first time he had gone home to his wife and children of course. Sometimes the family in the house hadn't noticed his absence at all, until he came back. Rose would be cooking up a strange mess, in the kitchen: Ephraim had brought a chunk of some slaughtered beast for her; she nibbled his gift of sugar-cane, spitting out the fibre. Poor old Rose. No wonder she took to drink (yes, the lady of the

395

house had thought of that, privately) made a convenience of by a man who lived on her and sent his earnings to a wife and children. Now the man dies and Rose is nothing. Nobody. The wife buries him, the wife mourns him. Her children get the bicycle; one of his brothers from Cerberus Security Guards comes to take it from the laundry and bandage it in brown paper and string, foraged from the kitchen, for transport by rail to Umzimkulu.

When the bus flung Ephraim out and he rolled down and died in the brilliant sugar-cane field, he was going home because there was trouble over the land. What land? His father's land, his brothers' land, his land. Rose gives a garbled version anyone from that house, where at least two newspapers a day are read, can interpret: the long-service employee of Cerberus Security Guards was to be spokesman for his family in a dispute over ancestral land granted them by their local chief. Boundary lines have been drawn by government surveyors, on one side there has been a new flag run up, new uniforms put on, speeches made – the portion of the local chief's territory that falls on that side is no longer part of South Africa. The portion that remains on the other side now belongs to the South African government and will be sold to white farmers – Ephraim's father's land, his brothers' land, his land. They are to get some compensation – money, that disappears in school fees and food, not land, that lasts for ever.

The lady of the house never does get to hear what happened, now that Ephraim is dead. Rose doesn't say; isn't asked; probably is never told. She appears to get over Ephraim's death very quickly, as these people do, after the first burst of emotion – perhaps it would be better to assume she has to take it philosophically. People whose lives are not easy, poor people, to whom things happen but who don't have the resources to make things happen, don't have the means, either, to extricate themselves from what has happened. Of the remedies of a change of scene, a different job, another man, only the possibility of another man is open

Blinder

to her, and she's no beauty any longer, Rose, even by tolerant black standards. That other remedy – drink – one couldn't say she turns to that, either. Since Ephraim has disappeared from the backyard she drinks neither more nor less. The lady of the house, refurbishing it, thinks of offering an old club armchair to Rose. She asks if there is place in her room, and Rose says, Oh yes! Plenty place.

There is the space that was occupied by Ephraim, his thick spread of legs in khaki drill, his back in braces, his Primus stove and big chromium-fronted radio. Rose spends the whole afternoon cleaning the upholstery with carbon tetrachloride, before getting one of the grown children to help her move the chair across the yard. The lady of the house smiles; there was never any attempt to clean the chair while this was part of the duty of cleaning the house.

On Saturdays, occasionally, all members of the family are home for lunch, as they never are on other days. There is white wine this Saturday, as a treat. Rose has baked a fish dish with a covering of mashed potato corrugated by strokes of a fork and browned crisp along the ridges – it is delicious, the kind of food promoted to luxury class by the everyday norm of cafeterias and fast-food counters. In the middle of the meal, Rose appears in the dining-room. The clump of feet that has preceded her gives away that there is someone behind her, out of sight in the passage. The dark hollows under Rose's eyes are wrinkled up with excitement, she shows off: Look who I've got to see you! Look who is here!

The lady of the house is taking good, indulgent, suspicious stock of her, she knows her so well she can tell at once whether or not she's been at the bottle. No – the lady of the house signals with her eyes to the others – Rose is not drunk. Everyone stops eating. Rose is cajoling, high, in her own language, and gesturing back into the passage, her heavy lifted arm showing a shaking jowl of flesh through the tear in her overall – Rose can never be persuaded to mend anything, like the drinking, there is nothing to be done . . .

Nadine Gordimer

She loses patience – making a quick, conniving face for the eyes of the family – and goes back into the passage to fetch whoever it is. Heads at table return to plates, hands go out for bread or salt. Wine goes to a mouth. Rose shushes and pushes into the room a little group captured and corralled, bringing with them – a draught from another place and time suddenly blowing through the door – odours that have never been in the house before. Hair ruffles along the small dog's back; one of the grown children quickly and secretly puts a hand on its collar. Smell of wood-smoke, of blankets and clothes stored on mud floors between mud walls that live with the seasons, shedding dust and exuding damp that makes things hatch and sprout; smell of condensed milk, of ashes, of rags saved, of wadded newspapers salvaged, of burning paraffin, of thatch, fowl droppings, leaching red soap, of warm skin and fur, cold earth: the family round the table pause over their meal, its flavour and savour are blown away, the utensils they've been eating with remain in their hands, the presence of a strangeness is out of all proportion to the sight of the black countrywoman and her children, one close beside her, one on her back. The woman never takes her eyes off Rose, who has set her down there. The baby under the blanket closed over her breast with a giant safety-pin cannot be seen except for a green wool bonnet. Only the small child looks round and round the room; the faces, the table, dishes, glasses, flowers, wine bottle; and seems not to breathe. The dog rumbles and its collar is jerked.

Rose is leaning towards the woman, smiling, hands on the sides of her stomach, and encourages her in their language. She displays her to the assembly caught at table. You know who this is, madam? You don't know? She's from Umzimkulu. It's Ephraim's wife. (She swoops up the small child, stiff in her hands.) Ephraim's children. Youngest and second youngest. Look – the baby; it's a little girl. – And she giggles, for the woman who won't respond, can't respond to what is being said about her.

The lady of the house has got up from her chair. She's

waiting for Rose to stop jabbering so that she can greet the woman. She goes over to her and puts out her hand, but the woman draws her own palms together and claps them faintly, swaying politely on her feet, which are wearing a pair of men's shoes below thick beaded anklets. So the lady of the house puts a hand on the woman's back, on the blanket that holds the lump of baby, and says to Rose, Tell her I'm very glad to meet her.

As if they were children again, the young people at the table recite the ragged mumble of a greeting, smiling, the males half-rising. The man of the house draws his eyebrows together and nods absently.

She's here about the pension, Rose says, they say she can get a pension from Cerberus Security Guards.

She laughs at the daring, or simpleton trust? – she doesn't know. But the heads around the table know about such things. The children have grown up so clever.

The lady of the house has always been spokesman and diplomat: Did she get anything?

Not yet, they didn't give . . . But they'll write a letter, maybe next month, Rose says, and – this time the performance is surely for the benefit of the country woman instead of the family – leans across to the fruit bowl on a side table and twists off a bunch of grapes which she then pokes at the belly of the small child, who is too immobilized by force of impressions to grasp it. Rose encourages him, coyly, in their language, setting him down on his feet.

Rose, says the lady of the house, give them something to eat, mmh? There's cold meat . . . or if you want to take eggs . . .

Rose says, thank you, mam – procedurally, as if the kitchen were not hers to dispense from, anyway.

The woman has been got in, now there is the manoeuvre of getting her out; she stands as if she would stand for ever, with her baby on her back and her child holding a bunch of grapes that he is afraid to look at, while nobody knows whether to go on eating or wait till Rose takes her away.

The lady of the house is used to making things easy for others: Tell her — thank her for coming to see us.

Rose says something in their language and, after a pause, the woman suddenly begins to speak, turned to Rose but obviously addressing the faces at table through her, through the medium, the mediator of that beer-bloated body, that face ennobled with the bottle's mimesis of the lines and shadings of worldly wisdom. Rose follows with agreeing movements of lips and head, reverberating hum of punctuation. She says: She thanks you. She says goodbye.

Hardly has Rose removed her little troupe when she is back again. Perhaps she remembers the family is eating lunch, has come to ask if they'll want coffee? But no. With exaggerated self-effacement, not looking at anyone else, she asks whether she can talk to the madam a moment?

Now?

Yes, please, now.

The lady of the house follows her into the passage.

Can you borrow me ten rands, please madam.

(This will be an advance on her monthly wages.)

Right away?

Please, mam.

So, interrupting her family meal, the lady of the house goes upstairs and fetches two five rand notes from her purse. She sees Rose, as she comes back down the stairs, waiting in the passage like one of the strangers whose knock at the front door Rose herself will answer but whom she does not let into the living-rooms and keeps standing while she goes to call the lady of the house.

Two fives all right? The lady of the house holds out the notes.

Thank you, thanks very much; Rose pushes the money into her overall pocket, that is ripped away at one corner.

For the bus, Rose says, by way of apology for the urgency. Because she's going back there, now, to that place, Umzimkulu.

Georgina Hammick
People for Lunch

'I must get up,' Mrs Nightingale said, but did not move. During the night she had worked her way down the bed so that her feet were now resting on the brass rail at its end. Two years ago today it had been Edward's feet striking this same brass rail with peculiar force that had woken her. 'I don't feel well,' he'd said, and she'd replied – sleepily? sharply? – she needed to know but could not remember – 'Then you'd better not go to work today.' When he'd gone on, haltingly, to murmur: 'No. I can't,' she'd sat up, wide awake and afraid. For Edward was a workaholic. Nothing prevented him going to the office. She'd leant over him and seen that his face and neck were beaded with sweat. She'd touched his forehead and found it as cold and green as marble. 'I've got a pain,' he said, 'in my chest.' Each word was a single, concentrated effort. 'I can't breathe.' Stumbling to the telephone which lived on Edward's side of the bed, she'd started to panic. How could she explain to the doctor, probably still in bed and asleep, how serious it was with Edward lying beside her listening? It was then that she'd begun to shake, and her teeth to rattle in her jaw like pebbles in a bag. She'd knocked the telephone directory on to the floor and misdialled the number half a dozen times. (It was not true that anxious, panicky people proved themselves level-headed, under fire.) 'Be calm, Fanny. Go at it slowly,' Edward had said, lying still, his eyes unfocussed on the ceiling.

*

A shuddering sigh on Mrs Nightingale's left made her turn her head. Lying close on the adjoining pillow was the face of Bone. The dog's small body was concealed by the duvet, as was Mrs Nightingale's own. Mrs Nightingale stared at Bone's black nose, at the white whiskers that sprouted from her muzzle and chin, at her short sandy eyelashes. Bone's eyes were shut, but the left ear was open, its flap splayed on the pillow to reveal an intricacy of shiny and waxy pink coils. Mrs Nightingale leant across and blew gently in this ear. Bone opened one eye and shut it again. Mrs Nightingale put her arms round Bone and laid her head against the dog's neck. It smelt faintly of chicken soup. Bone jerked her head away and stretched her legs so that her claws lodged themselves in Mrs Nightingale's stomach. Mrs Nightingale kissed Bone on the muzzle just above the black, shiny lip. Bone opened her jaws wide in a foetid yawn and stretched again and went back to sleep. Mrs Nightingale got out of bed and left Bone, still covered to her neck by the duvet, sleeping peacefully.

Bone was not allowed in beds, only on them, and she reminded the dog of this. 'I don't like dogs,' she added untruthfully. The house was very quiet. Mrs Nightingale walked out bare-footed on to the uncarpeted landing and stood for a moment listening to the inharmonious ticking of the clocks downstairs. There was no sound from her children's bedrooms and their doors were uninvitingly shut. 'I hate being a widow,' she said aloud.

The bathroom door was blocked by a wrinkled dustbin sack full to overflowing with clothes intended for a jumble sale. She dragged it out of the way. From its torn side hung the yellowing arm of a Viyella cricket shirt. From its top protruded a brown Harris tweed skirt. Liza's name was still stitched to the tiny waistband. Had she ever really been that size? Mrs Nightingale had meant, before the move, to unpick the nametape from Liza's old uniform and take it back to the school for resale, but there had never been the time. This black sack was one of many about the house. Before moving she'd labelled them as to contents, but on examination recently they all contained the same things: out-grown clothes, single football boots, curtains originally made for Georgian sash windows that would not fit the small casements here, curtain hooks, picture hooks, bent wire coat hangers.

Lying motionless in the bath Mrs Nightingale saw Edward on the stretcher being carried into the ambulance. He had joked with the ambulance men. She would never forgive him for that. It had been his joking, and the doctor saying on arrival, just before he'd sent her out of the room: 'If you move, Edward, you're a dead man. If you lie still and do exactly what I say, you'll be all right,' that had given her hope. She could see Edward now, calling out from the stretcher to the twins, shivering in their night things on the front door step: 'Be good, monkeys. I'll be back soon.' And she could see herself, wrapped in his dressing gown, bending down to kiss his cold cheek before the ambulance doors closed. She'd wanted to go with him, she'd needed to go with him, but had had to wait for her mother to come and look after the twins.

The bath water was by now tepid and Mrs Nightingale's finger ends were white and shrunk. As she lay there, unable to move, the church bells began a faint tolling through the shut window and at once the image of the ambulance with its frenetic blue light turning out of the drive was replaced by a picture of dead tulips and lilac in the vase beneath the lectern. She'd seen these on Friday when she'd gone to the church to check the Flower Rota List and found her name down for this Sunday. She forced herself out of the bath and pounded down the passage to Liza's room. She shook the mound of bedclothes.

'Liza – did you remember to do the church flowers yesterday?'

Liza was gliding through a dark lake on the back of a

sea-serpent. She opened blank blue eyes for a second and then shut them again.

'Did you do the church flowers?'

The eyes opened again, flickered and then closed. Waking was a trial for Liza.

'Liza –'

'No. I didn't. Sorry.'

'You're the absolute end.' Mrs Nightingale was furious. 'You asked what you could do to help and I said –'

'Sorry, Mum.'

'You're not asked to do much. And you're eighteen, not six.'

'Don't flap,' – Liza's voice sounded as though it had been dredged from the bottom of a deep lake – 'the congregation's geriatric. No one will notice if the flowers are dead.' She yawned. 'You're sopping wet,' she said incuriously to her mother.

'I need your help,' Mrs Nightingale cried. 'Get up at once, now, before you fall asleep again.' She stood for a moment awaiting results, but as there were none, left the room banging the door behind her.

Mrs Nightingale visited the twins' room next. They were fast asleep on their backs. Lily, on the camp bed they took turns for, was snoring.

'Wake up, both of you,' Mrs Nightingale said. She trampled over their discarded clothes. 'Wake up now.' They sat up slowly, looking hurt and puzzled. 'It's late,' Mrs Nightingale said, 'Nine o'clock. They'll be here by half past twelve and there's a lot to do. You must get up. Now.'

'Who'll be here?' Poppy asked.

'Nine o'clock isn't late, it's early,' Lily said. 'It's Sunday.'

'Now,' Mrs Nightingale said and left the room.

When Mrs Nightingale opened Dave's door he was propped on one elbow, reading. His hair, which had been recently cut by a fellow student using blunt nail

People for Lunch

scissors, stuck out in stiff tufts. Here and there patches of scalp were visible. They'd had a row about the hair when he arrived. Usually Mrs Nightingale cut Dave's hair, and when she did he looked very nice. This present cut, which he'd admitted he wasn't that keen on himself, was an example of the perversity her son was given to and that Mrs Nightingale found exasperating and incomprehensible. He glanced up at her as she came in.

'Hallo, Mamma. How are you, darlin'?'

The question took Mrs Nightingale off-guard. Suddenly, she wanted to tell him. She wanted to say: 'Daddy died two years ago today.' She wanted to collapse on Dave's bed and howl, perhaps all day, perhaps for ever. Instead she stayed in the middle of the room and stared at the row of hats that hung from hooks above Dave's bed and which, together with the accents – foreign, regional – he adopted, formed part of her son's disguise kit.

'If you're awake, why aren't you up?' Mrs Nightingale heard herself say.

'Stay cool,' Dave said. 'I'm just tucking into Elizabeth Bishop.' He waved a paperback in the air that his mother recognised as her own and removed from its shelf without permission.

'How do you rate her? Compared to Lowell. . .?'

'Get up, please,' Mrs Nightingale said.

'Okay, Marlene. Tuck in.'

Marlene, the second syllable of which was pronounced to rhyme with Jean, was not Mrs Nightingale's name, which was Frances. Marlene, which sometimes became Marlena, second syllable to rhyme with Gina, was the name Dave had bestowed on his mother some years ago when she'd started regularly cutting his hair. 'I'm due for a visit to Marlene's salon,' he'd say, ringing her from Leeds. 'Is the head stylist available?'

Mrs Nightingale moved backwards to Dave's door and fell over the bicycle wheel she'd noted on her way in and taken care to avoid.

'Shit. And your room's in shit, Dave.'

'Cool it.'

'Look, it is in shit and it smells. Do you have to sleep with the window shut? Why are you wearing that tee-shirt in bed?'

'I haven't any pyjamas, that's why,' Dave said reasonably.

'I know if I leave now you'll just go on reading –' Mrs Nightingale was getting desperate '– so get out now, while I'm here.'

'I will as soon as you go. I've got nothing on below this tee-shirt, and the sight of my amazing, user-friendly equipment might unsettle you for the day. Tuck in, Marlene.' He yawned, showing a white tongue and all his fillings, and stretched his huge arms above his head.

Mrs Nightingale returned to her bedroom and dressed herself in scruffy, everyday clothes. Then she pulled Bone out of the bed and swept the bottom sheet with her hands. Being white, Bone's hairs did not show up well against the sheet but Mrs Nightingale knew they were there, and sure enough they flew around the room and settled on the floorboards like snowflakes in a paperweight snowstorm. Mrs Nightingale straightened the duvet and banged the pillows while Bone sat on her haunches, sorrowfully watching. As soon as the lace cover was on Bone leapt back on the bed and made herself comfortable among the cushions. Mrs Nightingale looked at her watch. This time two years ago she had just arrived at the hospital having driven at ninety most of the way. There'd been nowhere to park so she'd parked in one of the doctors' spaces. 'You can't park there,' an old man planting out geraniums by the hospital steps had told her, having watched her manoeuvre. Three floors up, on Harnham Ward, Sister had looked up from her notes and said: 'The specialist has examined your husband and would like to see you now.' Mrs Nightingale suddenly remembered the specialist's nose, aquiline and messily freckled. She'd stared at it as

People for Lunch

they sat opposite each other, divided by a desk. 'He's on the edge of a precipice,' the specialist had said. 'It was an almost total infarct – that means the supply of blood and oxygen to the heart has been severely reduced. A large part of the heart muscle is already dead. The next forty-eight hours will be crucial. If he survives, and I can give you no assurances, the dead muscle will be replaced in time by scar tissue, which is very tough and can do the same sort of job –'

I hate doctors, Mrs Nightingale thought as she went downstairs. Hate them. She took one look at the kitchen, then shut the door and went into the drawing-room, a room too poky to deserve the title that, from the habit of a lifetime, she had given it. It smelled of soot and damp and cigarettes, and of something indefinable that might have been the previous owners. Mrs Nightingale got down on her knees in front of the fireplace and swept the wood ash and cigarette stubs she found there into a dome. She stuck a firelighter on top of this, but the log baskets were empty except for two pieces of bark and several families of woodlice, so she got up again and started to punch the sofa cushions into shape. Dave came in while she was doing this. He was still wearing the tee-shirt but to his lower half he'd now added an Indian tablecloth which he'd wrapped twice round himself and tucked in at the waist.

'You left a filthy mess in the kitchen last night,' Mrs Nightingale said, remembering the slag heap of coffee grounds decorated by a rusty Brillo pad on the kitchen table. 'I thought you were going to get dressed.'

'Liza's in the bathroom.' Dave scratched his armpit, then sat down heavily on the sofa cushions and rested his head on his knees.

'Dave, I've just done that sofa. We've got people for lunch –'

'Yup. Sure thing. Sorry. What can I do?' He stayed where he was and Mrs Nightingale stared, mesmerized, at his large yellow feet. The toenails were black and torn. Black wire sprouted from his big toes. The same wire twined his calves, visible beneath the tablecloth. It stopped at the ankles, but continued, Mrs Nightingale knew, beyond his knees to his thighs, where it no longer twined, but curled. It was impossible that this huge male person had ever been inside her body. 'Well, the log baskets are empty, as you see,' Mrs Nightingale said, 'so when you're dressed –'

'Sure, sure.'

'I did ask you, you know,' Mrs Nightingale bravely continued, 'when you arrived, if you'd be responsible for getting the wood in, and you said –'

'Yeah. Yeah. Sure. Yup. Tuck in.' He sat for a moment longer and then got up, hitching the tablecloth which had slipped a little. He looked round the room. 'I like your little house, Marlene.'

'It isn't *my* house.' Mrs Nightingale was hurt by Dave's choice of possessive adjective. 'It's *our* house. It's home.'

'Yup.'

'No chance, I suppose,' she said as he padded to the door, 'of your wearing your contact lenses at lunch?' Dave stopped dead in his tracks and turned sharply. 'What's wrong with my specs?' He whipped them off and examined them myopically, close to his nose. They were bright scarlet with butterfly sides, the sort typists wore in the fifties. One arm was attached to the frame by a grubby selotape bandage.

'Nothing's wrong with them. It's just that you look nicer without them. You're quite nice looking, so it seems a shame –'

'Oh Christ,' Dave said and then hit his head on the beam above the door. 'Fuck. I hit my head everywhere I go in this fucking house. Cottage. Hen coop. Hovel.'

By the time Mrs Nightingale had finished scrubbing the potatoes they were all down in the kitchen with her. The

People for Lunch

kitchen was too small for five people comfortably to be in at one time. She had once, when they were all tripping over each other, made this observation and had received a long lecture from Dave on the living conditions of the average farm-labourer and his family in the latter part of the nineteenth century. Her son was nothing if not inconsistent, Mrs Nightingale thought, remembering the hen coop remark.

'Who's finished the Shreddies?' Poppy was on her knees on the brick floor, peering in a cupboard.

'Dave had them last night – don't you remember?' Liza said, sawing at a grapefruit with the bread knife. A pool of cloudy juice and pips spread over the table, soaking an unpaid telephone bill. Mrs Nightingale snatched it up.

'Here, have this' – Liza plonked the grapefruit halves into bowls and handed one of them to Poppy. 'This is better for you. You're too fat for cereal.'

'Speak for yourself, you great spotty oaf. At least I haven't got suppurating zits all over my face –'

'You will soon,' Dave interrupted cheerfully. 'You're into a pubescent exploding-hormone situation. Tuck in.'

'If you had, they might detract from your nose which, by the way' – Liza glanced at it casually – 'is one big blackhead.'

There was a skirmish. Mrs Nightingale caught the milk bottle as it leapt from the table.

'Cool it, girls.' Dave had seen his mother's face. 'Marlene's trying to get organized. Aren't you, Marlene?' He was propped against the Rayburn, dressed now in one of his father's city shirts and scarlet trousers, the bottoms of which were tucked into old school games stockings, one brilliantly striped, the other grey, and shovelling Weetabix into his mouth from a bowl held within an inch of his face. Each time the spoon went in it banged horribly against his teeth. 'Is the Rayburn *meant* to be off?' he asked, mock-innocently, between mouthfuls.

Mrs Nightingale was about to burst into tears.

'What? Out of my way please.' She pushed the red legs to one side, and knelt on the dog bed in front of the stove. Inside an erratic flame flickered. She turned the thermostat as high as it would go.

'Why's the heat gone down?'

'How the fuck should I know? The wind, probably –'

'Don't swear, Mummy,' Poppy said, grabbing a banana from the fruit bowl and stripping it.

'Put that banana back! It's for lunch.'

'We've got rhubarb crumble for lunch. I made it yesterday, remember.' Poppy took a bite out of the banana, folded the skin over the end and replaced it in the fruit bowl on top of a shrivelled orange.

'Look,' Mrs Nightingale said, 'we'll never be ready at this rate. Couldn't you all just –'

'Keep calm, Mamma. Sit down a moment and drink this.' Liza handed her mother a mug of coffee. 'There's nothing to do. Really. They won't be here till one at the earliest. All we've got to do is get the joint in –'

'Are we eating animals? Yuk. Unreal. Animals are people –'

'Shut up, Lily. – Do the spuds and the veg and lay the table and light the fire and pick some flowers – five minutes at the most.'

'The whole house is in chaos,' Mrs Nightingale said, 'it's composed of nothing but tea chests and plastic bags.'

'They're not coming to see the house. They know we've only just moved. They're coming to see *you*.'

'Actually, they're coming to inspect our reduced circumstances,' Dave said in a prissy voice. He picked up a piece of toast and stretched for the marmalade. Mrs Nightingale pushed it out of his reach. 'No, you've had enough.'

'Daddy couldn't bear them,' Lily said, staring into space.

'Couldn't bear who?' Poppy paused at the door.

'The Hendersons, stupid.'

'The Hendersons? Are *they* coming to lunch? Unreal.'

People for Lunch

'Where do you think you're going to, Poppy? You haven't cleared up your breakfast things –'

'I'm going to the lav, if you must know. I'm coming back.'

'While you're up there, Fatso, take some of the gunge off your face!' Dave shouted at her.

'Have you got the logs in?' Mrs Nightingale asked Dave, knowing that he hadn't.

'I'm just about to. We shouldn't *need* a fire in May,' he said, resentfully as though his mother were to blame for the weather. 'Right, Marlena.' He rubbed his hands. 'Here we go-o,' he added in the manner of an air hostess about to deposit a snack on the knees of a passenger. He sat down on Poppy's chair and pulled a pair of canvas boots from under the table. A lace snapped as he put them on.

'Are you going to shave before they arrive?' Mrs Nightingale asked, eyeing him.

'Dunno. Oi moigh' – Dave rubbed his chin so that it rasped – 'an' yere agine oi moigh 'na'. Don't you like me looking manly and virile?' Mrs Nightingale said No, she didn't much. No.

'Mrs Henderson will, though. She's got a yen for me. She'll really tuck in.'

'Oh ha ha,' Liza snorted from the sink.

'Mr Henderson has too. He's always putting his arm round my shoulder. Squeezing me. Kissing –'

'I don't suppose he's that desperate to get herpes. He hasn't seen you since you were about ten –'

'Do something for me, Lil, would you,' Mrs Nightingale said, as Dave minced from the room flexing his biceps. Lily sighed. Did she know what today was? Mrs Nightingale thought perhaps she did. It was impossible to get near Lily at the moment. She resented everything her mother said and did, prefacing her argument with 'Daddy always said' or 'Daddy would have agreed with me that . . .' She'd been in a sulk since the move because the cottage was thatched, i.e. spooky, witchy, bug-infested – and because her father had never been in it. 'Wake up, there,' – Mrs Nightingale waved her hand slowly up and down in front of Lily's face. Lily managed not to blink.

'Go and get Bone off my bed and put her out. She hasn't had a pee yet.' Lily went on sitting there, expressionless. Then all of a sudden she leapt up, scraping back her chair, and ran out of the room.

'Bone, Bone, my darling one, I'm coming.' They could hear her clattering up the stairs, calling 'Bone, beloved angel, Bone –'

'She's mad,' Liza said, stacking plates in the rack. 'All my family's mad. And Dave is completely off the wall.' Mrs Nightingale kissed Liza's spotty face, pink and damp with steam. 'I love you, Lize,' she said.

As Mrs Nightingale rootled in the kitchen drawer looking for enough knives to lay the dining-room table with, Dave's face appeared at the window above the sink. He flattened his nose against the pane and drummed on it with his fingers. 'Open up! Open up!' he shouted. Liza leaned across the taps and biffed the window. It opened in a rush. Dave's face disappeared for a second, and then reappeared half in the window. 'Ladies,' he said with a South London inflexion and in confidential tones, holding up what looked like a piece of string and dangling it from between his fingers and thumb, 'do your hubbies' jock-straps pass the window test? If not –' he leered and let go of the jock-strap which fell across the sill and draped itself over the hot tap, and then held up a packet of something: 'Try new Weedol! Fast-acting, rainproof and guaranteed to eradicate all biological stains for an entire season. Just one sa*chette*' – he paused to consult the packet – 'treats 160 yards, or – if you ladies prefer a more up-to-date terminology – 135 square metres, of normally soiled jock-straps.' He backed away from the window, creased with laughter, and tripped over a flower pot.

People for Lunch

'Pathetic,' Liza said, tugging at the window catch, 'quite pathetic.'

'Logs!' Mrs Nightingale shouted at him, just before the window jerked to, scattering them with raindrops, 'Logs, logs, logs!'

Mrs Nightingale did her best with the dining-room which, not being a room they had so far needed to use, had become a dumping ground. There were ten full tea chests stacked in one corner, her husband's golf clubs in a khaki bag, a clothes horse, innumerable lampshades and a depressed-looking cockatoo under a glass dome. Beneath the window precariously stacked books awaited the bookshelves Dave had promised to put up in the summer holidays. Everything in the room, including a dining-table much too large for it, was deep in dust. Mrs Nightingale looked at her watch. This time two years ago she'd sat beside Edward, who'd lain on his back without pillows, his chest and arms wired to a machine. Attached to the machine was a cardiograph that measured and recorded his heartbeat. The signal had gone all over the place, sometimes shooting to the top of the screen, and the bleeps, at each beat, had been similarly erratic – six, say, in succession followed by a silence which, each time it occurred, she'd felt would never be broken. 'The heroin was delicious,' Ed had murmured in a moment of consciousness, 'it took all the pain away, but they won't let me have any more in case I get hooked.' Why couldn't you have died at once, Mrs Nightingale thought, remembering her agony watching the nurse adjusting the drip, which had kept getting stuck, and checking the leads on Ed's chest which, because he rolled around a lot, were in constant danger of coming loose. This had happened once, when there'd been no nurse in the room. She'd been on the edge of her chair, her eyes alternately on Ed, and on the screen, when suddenly the bleeps had stopped and the signal had flattened into a straight, horizontal line.

A red light had come on at the side of the machine and with it a whine like the unobtainable tone when you dial. He's dead, she'd thought. Sister had rushed in at once and checked Ed's pulse and then the leads and after a minute or two the crazy signal was back and the bleeps. 'Try not to worry, dear,' Sister had said. 'Worrying doesn't help.'

Mrs Nightingale forced herself out of her chair and went in search of a duster.

'The joint's in the oven,' Liza said. She had an apron on which bore the message I Hate Cooking, and was standing at the stove stirring a saucepan. 'I'm making onion sauce.' She looked up. 'Are you okay, Ma?' By way of an answer Mrs Nightingale enquired if anyone had seen the silver anywhere. Poppy knew. She and Lily were scraping carrots and glaring at each other across the kitchen table. She got up and helped her mother drag the despatch box from under the sink in the washroom. Back in the dining-room she stood and watched her mother dust the table.

'Mum – can I have a friend to stay – Julia, I mean, in the holidays?'

'Maybe. If we're straighter by then.' Mrs Nightingale didn't like Julia. On the child's last visit Mrs Nightingale had caught her in her clothes cupboard, examining the labels and checking to see how many pairs of Gucci shoes Mrs Nightingale owned, which was none. Mrs Nightingale didn't own a Gucci watch, either, and evidently wasn't worth speaking to: Julia hadn't addressed one word to her in five days. She'd managed a few indirect hits, though, as when at breakfast one morning, having accepted without comment the plate of scrambled eggs Mrs Nightingale had handed her, she'd leaned on one elbow to enquire of Poppy: 'Presumably your mother will be racing at Goodwood next week?' Mrs Nightingale was damned if she'd have Julia to stay again.

'I get bored without a friend,' Poppy moaned on. Mrs Nightingale wasn't having any of that. 'You can't

People for Lunch

be bored,' she said, 'and you've got Lily.' She unwrapped a yellowing candlestick from a piece of yellowing newspaper. 'Here, take this.'

'We don't get on,' Poppy said. 'We've got nothing in common.' That was rubbish, Mrs Nightingale told her.

'It isn't rubbish. She's so moody. She never speaks – just sits and stares.'

Since the truth of this could not be denied, Mrs Nightingale changed tack. 'As a matter of fact you don't deserve to have a friend to stay.'

Poppy put down the spoon she'd been tentatively rubbing with a duster and stared at her mother with her mouth open.

'Your half-term report is the worst yet,' Mrs Nightingale continued, 'and we ought to discuss it. Not now. I don't mean now. Later. This evening, perhaps, when they've gone.'

'Miss Ansell doesn't like me. It's not my fault.'

'It isn't just Miss Ansell,' Mrs Nightingale said, more in sorrow than in anger. 'No one, no one – apart from Miss Whatsername – you know, games mistress – had a good word to say about you. You won't get a single "O" Level at this rate. Lily, on the other hand –'

'*Don't* compare me with her. She's quite different to me.'

'Different *from* me. Yes. She knows how to work, for one thing. And she reads. You never open a book.'

'I do.'

'The Beano annual. And you're *thirteen*.'

Poppy grinned sheepishly at that. 'Oh, Muzkin,' she said, and sidled up to her mother and put her arms round her waist.

'Muzkin nothing,' Mrs Nightingale said, disentangling herself. For it really was worrying. Poppy never did open a book. If ever she happened by some mischance to pick one up, she'd drop it again as soon as she'd realized her mistake. As a result of this her ignorance went wide and deep. Mrs Nightingale spent sleepless nights discussing the problem with Bone.

Liza's head appeared round the dining-room door.

'Bone's eaten the Brie, I'm afraid,' Liza said, 'so there's only mousetrap for lunch.'

'Where is she? I'll kill her!' Mrs Nightingale cried preparing to do so.

'I've already beaten her,' Liza said. 'It's my business, she's my dog.'

Not when it comes to spending millions of pounds a year on Chum and Butch and Winalot and vet's bills, Mrs Nightingale thought. Not when it comes to clearing up mountains of dog sick and dog shit. Then she's my dog. She followed Liza back to the kitchen. 'Where's Dave?' she asked crossly. 'Where's the wood?'

'He's gone to get some milk and the papers,' Liza said, knowing what her mother's reaction would be.

'*What?*'

'I asked him to go because we're out of milk and you'll want the papers so that the Hendersons can read them after lunch.'

'Has he taken my car?' Mrs Nightingale was beside herself.

'Of course he's taken your car. How else would he go?'

Mrs Nightingale hated Dave taking her car. She hated him taking it because being stuck up a track with rusty bicycles the only means of escape made her feel a prisoner. She hated him taking it because he hadn't asked permission and because she didn't trust him not to drive like a racing driver – i.e. a maniac. It was her car. She hated Dave too because he ought to have remembered what the day was. There was something wrong with him that he hadn't. Something very wrong indeed.

'He has no business to take my car,' she said, 'he'll be gone for hours.'

People for Lunch

Liza was taking glasses out of a cupboard. 'Don't be stupid,' she said briskly. 'He'll be back in a minute. He's only gone for the papers, for God's sake. He was *trying* to be helpful.' She held a glass up to the light. 'These glasses are filthy. I'd better wash them.'

'Get up, Lily,' Mrs Nightingale was now in a state of rage and panic. Lily was lying in the dog bed on top of Bone, kissing Bone's ears. 'Get up! Have you made your bed and tidied your room?'

'You can't make a camp bed.' Lily got up reluctantly, her navy angora jersey now covered with dog hairs.

'Answer that, would you, on your way,' Mrs Nightingale snapped as the telephone rang from the drawing-room. Lily returned almost at once.

'It's Granny. She wants to talk to *you*.'

'Fuck,' Mrs Nightingale said. 'Didn't you tell her we've got people for lunch?' Lily shrugged. 'Well, go back and tell her I'm frantic –'

'I'll say,' murmured Liza, putting glasses on a tray. 'These glasses are gross – did you get them from the garage?'

'– and that I'll ring her after tea. Go *on*. Hurry.'

'Granny sounded a bit hurt,' Lily said when she came back, 'She said to tell you she was thinking about you today.'

'What for?' Liza said.

What for, Mrs Nightingale repeated to herself, what for –? 'What can Dave be doing?' she said, 'He's been gone for hours.' She opened the oven door. The joint seemed to be sizzling satisfactorily.

'Stop flapping,' Liza said.

'Did you put garlic on the joint? And rosemary? I couldn't see any.'

'Of course. Stop flapping.'

'Poppy, you're *soaked*! Couldn't you have worn a mac?' Poppy squelched into the kitchen and dumped a collection of sodden wild flowers on the table.

419

'*I* was going to do the flowers,' Liza said.

'God, the gratitude you get in this place,' Poppy fingered the limp cluster. 'What are these?'

'Ladies' smocks. *Must* you do that in here?' Liza said as Poppy found an assortment of jugs and lined them up on the table. 'I'm trying to get lunch. You can't put wallflowers in with that lot,' she added in disgust.

'Why can't I?' Poppy wanted to know.

'Because they're orange, stupid.'

'Piss off. I like them. I like the *smell*.'

Mrs Nightingale left her daughters to it and took the tray of glasses into the dining-room. Perhaps Dave *had* had an accident. Perhaps, at this very moment, firemen were fighting to cut his lifeless body from the wreckage. That was all she needed. It was typical of him to put her in this position of anxiety today of all days. 'If he's alive I'll kill him,' she thought aloud, knowing that when – please God – he did walk in she'd feel nothing but relief. As she went back into the kitchen he came in by the other door, accompanied by a smell of deep frying. The Sunday papers and two cartons of long-life milk were crushed against his chest. He uncrossed his arms and unloaded their contents into the watery mess of broken stems and leaves on the kitchen table.

'Hey – mind my flowers,' Poppy said. She sniffed. 'I can smell chips.'

'Whoops. Sorry.' Dave straightened up and caught sight of his mother. 'Hi there, Marlene.' He licked his fingers, slowly and deliberately. 'Finger fuckin' good,' he said when he'd finished. There was a silence, succeeded by a snort of laughter from Liza, succeeded by another silence.

'Dave, could I have a word with you, please –' Mrs Nightingale spoke through clenched teeth. She jerked her thumb towards the door. 'Outside.'

'Righto, Marlena.' He snatched up the *Observer* and followed his mother into the hall.

People for Lunch

'Watch out, Dave,' Poppy sang out after him. 'You're in deep trouble, Boyo.'

'What are you so screwed-up about?' Dave asked when Mrs Nightingale, determined that they shouldn't be overheard, had shut the drawing-room door. Dave plonked himself into the nearest arm chair.

'Get up out of that chair! Put that newspaper down!' Dave got up, very slowly. 'Take that smirk off your face!' Mrs Nightingale shouted. He towered above her, shifting from one foot to the other, while his eyes examined the ceiling with interest. 'I've had you,' Mrs Nightingale went on, her voice shaking. 'I wish you weren't here. You're twenty years old. You're the only so-called man in this house. I should be able to look to you for help and support. You had no business to take my car without asking –'

'Liza said we were out of milk –'

'It's not her car. It's *mine*. And *I*'d asked you to get the wood in. That's *all* I asked you to do. All all *all*!'

'Oh come *on* –'

'I won't come on.' Mrs Nightingale's voice rose. 'You were gone for hours while everyone else was working. Did you really eat chips, by the way?'

'I was hungry, I'm a big boy,' Dave said, perhaps hoping to appeal to that need (he supposed all women had) to mother and protect huge grown men as though they were babies.

'You didn't have breakfast till ten. And it'll be lunchtime any minute. You can't have been hungry.' Dave said nothing. He was bored with this interview and showed it by jiggling his knee. 'That finger business wasn't funny,' Mrs Nightingale said. 'It was disgusting. How could you, in front of Lily and Poppy?'

'Lily wasn't in the kitchen, actually,' Dave said. He started to pace about with his head down, a sure sign that he was losing his temper.

'Don't be pedantic with me, Dave.' Dave stopped pacing

and swung round and pointed his finger at his mother in a threatening fashion.

'Fuck *you*,' he said. 'You're a complete hypocrite. No one in this house uses filthier language than you. It's "shit this" and "bugger that" all fucking day. We took the words in with your milk –' There was a pause, during which Mrs Nightingale considered reminding him that the twins, at least, had been bottle-fed, but Dave was quite capable of turning this fact to his advantage, so she said nothing. 'Well, I'm sick of your dramas and panics,' he continued, warming to his theme of self-justification. 'I can't stand the atmosphere in this place. I can't *work* here. I'm going back to Leeds. My tutor didn't want me to take time off to help you, and I've missed two important lectures already.' He made for the door.

'Typical,' Mrs Nightingale said, taking care not to say 'fucking well typical' as she would normally have done. 'You can't take any sort of criticism, ever. You just shout abuse and then walk out – it's too easy. What's more, you haven't been any help to me at all. You haven't lifted a finger –'

'Mum' – Liza's head appeared round the door as Dave reached it. He took two steps backwards – 'shouldn't you be putting your face on? It's after twelve.'

'Go away,' Mrs Nightingale said, 'I'm talking to Dave.'

'Sounds like it. Poor Dave.' Liza's head withdrew. The door banged shut.

Mrs Nightingale and her son stood in silence, both waiting for something. Dave stared at the floor and at the front page of the *Observer* which lay at his feet. He pushed at it with the toe of one green canvas boot.

'Sorry I was rude,' he said at last without looking up.

Mrs Nightingale gave a sigh. Dave was good at apologies – much better than she was – and sometimes indulged in them for days after a particularly bloody row, castigating himself and telling anyone who'd listen what a shit he'd been. The trouble was, the apologies changed

People for Lunch

nothing, as Mrs Nightingale had learned. They never prevented his being rude and aggressive (and unfair, she thought, *unfair*) next time round. She didn't want his apologies. She wanted him to stop the behaviour that made them necessary. She watched him now get down on his knees and take off his specs and rub them on a dirty red-and-white spotted handkerchief and put them back on his nose. He picked up the *Observer* with his left hand and then struck at it with the fist of his right.

'I'm going to kill Mrs Thatcher,' he said, 'listen to this –' Oh dear, thought Mrs Nightingale.

Dave and newspapers did not mix. Cruise missiles, violence in inner cities, child abuse, drug abuse, vivisection, famine, rape, murder, abortion, multiple births, divorce rate, pollution, terrorism, persecution of Blacks and homosexuals, sex discrimination, unemployment, pornography, police brutality, rate capping – the stuff that newspapers were made of – were a daily cross he bore alone. 'You can't take the whole burden of the world on your shoulders,' she'd tell him when he rang from a Leeds call box desperate over the destruction of South American rain forests, or the plight of the latest hijack victims. 'The world has always been a terrible place,' she'd say, 'we just know more about it now because of the media. Horror used to be more *local*.' Then – since it seemed important to end on a positive note – she'd go on to remind him of ways in which the world had changed for the better, instancing the huge advances made in medicine this century (T.B. and polio virtually wiped out, infant mortality and death in childbirth negligible, etc.) and reminding him that there were salmon in the Thames these days, and that people could fall into the river and swallow whole bucketfuls of its waters and not die. 'Try and get a sense of proportion,' she'd say, something she'd never managed herself. She knew that when she lectured Dave it was herself she was trying to comfort. The world was a far nastier place than it had been when she was a child, even though there'd been a world war going on for some of that time. Far nastier.

Thinking about all this she was spared hearing Mrs Thatcher's latest pronouncement, although it was impossible to miss the passion in Dave's recital of the same. She came to when he stopped in mid-sentence, and put the paper down.

'It's the twenty-third today,' he said, 'Did you realise?'

'I know,' Mrs Nightingale said.

'Oh, Mum, I'm sorry. Why didn't you say?'

Dave, on his knees, began to rock backwards and forwards, his arms folded across his stomach. 'Poor old Dad, poor old Dad,' he said. Then he burst into tears. Mrs Nightingale got down on her knees beside her son. She put her arm round his shoulders which reeked of wet wool and chipped potatoes. She sensed that he did not want her arms round him but did not know how to extricate himself. After several minutes he blew his nose on the red-spotted handkerchief and licked at the tears which were running down his chin.

'I must get the wood in and light the fire.' He disengaged himself and got up. 'Then I'll shave. Sorry, Mum.' He gave her a pale smile. At the door he turned, and said in a sharper tone: 'But I still don't understand why you didn't *say*. And why didn't we go to church this morning – or did you, before we were up?'

'No,' Mrs Nightingale said.

'And why are the fucking Hendersons coming to lunch? You don't like them and Pa couldn't stand them. None of it makes sense.' He shook his head, spraying the room with water like a wet dog.

'Look, Dave,' Mrs Nightingale began. She explained that she hadn't asked the Hendersons, they'd asked themselves. She couldn't put them off for ever. Also she'd thought that having people to lunch might make the day easier in some way. And as for church – well, he didn't like Rite A any more than she did. It always put them into a rage, so there was no point, was there, in going.

'True,' Dave said.

It *was* true, she told him. But what she thought they might do, once they'd got rid of the Hendersons, was drive up to the churchyard and take Poppy's flowers perhaps, and put them on Daddy's grave.

Dave's eyes started to fill again. '. . . and then go to Evensong in the Cathedral, if there's time. It'll be a proper service with proper singing and anthems and sung responses.'

'Yup. Cool.'

'All right, sweetheart?' Dave nodded and fiddled with his watchstrap, a thin piece of canvas, once red-and-white striped. 'I suppose you realize,' Mrs Nightingale lied, 'that when I asked you to give me a hand this week, it was just an excuse for wanting you here today. I needed you.' But perhaps it was not a lie, she thought. Perhaps, subconsciously, she had needed him.

'I'm getting the wood now,' Dave said. He peered out of a dismal mullioned window, against which a yew branch flapped in the gale. 'I think the rain's stopping.'

The kitchen when Mrs Nightingale entered it was clean and tidy, everything washed up and put away. Liza was taking off her apron.

'All done,' she said.

She was a wonder, Mrs Nightingale told her, a real star.

'Mum, you must get changed, they'll be here –'

Mrs Nightingale stopped in the doorway. 'Liz – do you know what today is?'

'It's the day Daddy died,' Liza said. 'Go on, Mum, I'll come and talk to you when I've done the ice.'

The back door banged as Mrs Nightingale climbed the

stairs. She could hear Dave's grunts as he humped the log baskets into the hall. It was a relief to be on her own for five minutes. She needed to be alone with Edward who – she stood on the dark landing and peered at her watch – this time two years ago had been about to leave her. Suddenly, without warning and without saying goodbye. Not even a look. Not even a pressure of the hand. She'd hated him for this, until it had dawned on her that it was inevitable. He'd been hopeless at partings. The number of times she'd driven him to Heathrow and been rewarded not with hugs and the 'I'll miss you, darlings' and 'take care of your precious selves' other people seemed to get, but with a preoccupied peck and then his back view disappearing through the barrier. 'Turn round and wave, you bugger,' she used to will him, but he never did.

'You two ready?' she called, in hopeless competition with Madness, through the twins' bedroom door. Then she opened her own. The room looked as though burglars had visited it. The drawers of both clothes chests had been wrenched out; garments spilled from them on to the floor. A brassière, its strap looped round a wooden drawer knob, trailed greyly to the rug where two leather belts lay like coiled springs. Mrs Nightingale turned her gaze to the dressing-table. Here unnumbered treasures drooped from every drawer and orifice. The surface of the table was littered with screws of cotton wool and with unstoppered scent bottles, from which all London, Paris and New York disagreeably breathed. A cylinder of moisturizing lotion lay on its side oozing cucumber extract into the contents of her jewel case which sat, open and empty, on the stool. Three cotton wool buds, their ends clotted with ear wax, had been placed in the china tray which normally housed Mrs Nightingale's lipsticks. Only two lipsticks remained in the tray; the rest, which had been torn apart and abandoned with their tongues protruding, were jumbled up with beads and cotton wool. Mrs Nightingale recognized her daughter Poppy's hand in

People for Lunch

all this. She opened her mouth wide in anger and despair, but no sound came. Instead, the telephone screamed from the table by her bed. When after the eighth ring no one had answered downstairs, Mrs Nightingale picked up the receiver.

'Mrs Nightingale? Mr Selby-Willis here.'

'Oh hallo, Jerry,' Mrs Nightingale said. (Fuck fuck fuck fuck fuck.) 'How are you?'

'How are *you*?' Jerry Selby-Willis asked, in his best bedroom drawl.

'Well if you must know, I'm frantic. I've got people arriving for lunch any minute.'

'One normally does on a Sunday. Grania's just gone off to the station to meet our lot. I can't imagine *you* being frantic about anything —'

'It just goes to show how little —'

'When are you going to have luncheon with me?' Jerry Selby-Willis interrupted her. 'Or dinner?'

'Jerry, I've only *just* moved house —' Mrs Nightingale began. She had accepted none of his invitations. 'Then you're in need of a nice, relaxing dinner. Tuesday. Have you got your diary there?'

'No. Look, I'm afraid I must go. I haven't got my face on —'

'I'll ring you tomorrow, from the office.'

She must remember to leave the telephone off the hook tomorrow, Mrs Nightingale thought, as she wrenched garments from hangers, tried them on, examined the result in the looking glass, and tore them off again. Or else get the children to answer the telephone and say she was out.

'I've got nothing to wear!' she wailed, as Liza came into the room.

'That looks fine,' Liza said. 'Where's your hairbrush?'

While Liza brushed her mother's hair, Mrs Nightingale perched on the dressing-table stool and searched for her blue beads.

Georgina Hammick

'I can't find my blue beads,' she said, turning out another drawer.

'Poppy's wearing them,' Liza said. 'She said you said she could. Time you dyed your hair, I think, or else made with the *Grecian 2000*,' she said kindly, putting the brush down.

'I think I heard a car,' Mrs Nightingale said, 'do you think you could round everyone up and go down and tell the Hendersons I'm coming. Give them a drink.'

Alone, Mrs Nightingale looked at her watch. It was ten past one. Edward was dead. He'd been dead a full quarter of an hour. At five to one, no doubt when she'd been fending off Jerry Selby-Willis, the signal on the cardiograph had flattened into a straight line for real this time, and the bleeps had ceased. She had not kept vigil; she had not been with him, holding his hand. She sat on the stool, twisting her wedding ring round and round her finger, for comfort. When at last she lifted her head she caught her reflection in the glass and was dismayed to see how pinched and wary and closed her face had become. 'Things have got to get better,' she said aloud. 'I must make them better.' There was a little moisturizer left in the bottle. She squeezed some into her palm and rubbed it into her forehead and cheeks, into the slack skin under her chin, into her crêpey neck. 'I am alive,' she said, 'I am not old. I am a young woman. I could live for another forty years yet.' She fumbled for the blusher, and worked it into her cheeks. 'I am a *person*,' she said threateningly into the glass. 'I am me, Frances.'

There was a thundering on the stairs, followed by Dave, out of breath at the door.

'Hi, folks, it's Lamborghini time,' he hissed. 'The Hendersons are in an arriving situation.' He had not shaved, after all, but on the other hand he was not wearing his red secretary spectacles either. You could not have everything, Mrs Nightingale supposed.

People for Lunch

'Hurry up, Marlene,' he said. 'You can't leave us alone with them.' He vanished, and then immediately reappeared. 'You should know that Mrs H. is wearing a salmon two-piece, with turquoise accessories. Tuck in.'

Mrs Nightingale grabbed a lipstick from the table and stretched her mouth into the grimace that, with her, always preceded its application. At the first pressure the lipstick, which had been broken by Poppy earlier and stuck back by her into its case, toppled and fell, grazing Mrs Nightingale's chin as it did so with a long gash of *Wicked Rose*.

Patricia Highsmith

Something You Have to Live With

'Don't forget to lock all the doors,' Stan said. 'Someone might think because the car's gone, nobody's home.'

'All the doors? You mean two. You haven't asked me anything – aesthetic, such as how the place looks now.'

Stan laughed. 'I suppose the pictures are all hung and the books are in the shelves.'

'Well, not quite, but your shirts and sweaters – and the kitchen. It looks – I'm happy, Stan. So is Cassie. She's walking all around the place purring. See you tomorrow morning then. Around eleven, you said?'

'Around eleven. I'll bring stuff for lunch, don't worry.'

'Love to your mom. I'm glad she's better.'

'Thanks, darling.' Stan hung up.

Cassie, their ginger-and-white cat aged four, sat looking at Ginnie as if she had never seen a telephone before. Purring again. Dazed by all the space, Ginnie thought. Cassie began kneading the rug in an ecstasy of contentment, and Ginnie laughed.

Ginnie and Stan Brixton had bought a house in Connecticut after six years of New York apartments. Their furniture had been here for a week while they wound things up in New York, and yesterday had been the final move of smaller things like silverware, some dishes, a few pictures, suitcases, kitchen items and the cat. Stan had taken their son Freddie this morning to spend the night in New Hope, Pennsylvania, where Stan's mother lived. His mother had had a second heart attack and was recuperating at home. 'Every time I see her, I think it may be the last. You don't mind if I go, do you, Ginnie? It'll keep Freddie out of the way while you're fiddling around.' Ginnie hadn't minded.

Fiddling around was Stan's term for organizing and even cleaning. Ginnie thought she had done a good job since Stan and Freddie had taken off this morning. The lovely French blue-and-white vase which reminded Ginnie of Monet's paintings stood on the living room bookcase now, even bearing red roses from the garden. Ginnie had made headway in the kitchen, installing things the way she wanted them, the way they would remain. Cassie had her litter pan ('What a euphemism, litter ought to mean a bed,' Stan said) in the downstairs john corner. They now had an upstairs bathroom also. The house was on a hill with no other houses around it for nearly a mile, not that they owned all the land around, but the land around was farmland. When she and Stan had seen the place in June, sheep and goats had been grazing not far away. They had both fallen in love with the house.

Stanley Brixton was a novelist and fiction critic, and Ginnie wrote articles and was now half through her second novel. Her first had been published but had had only modest success. You couldn't expect a smash hit with a first novel, Stan said, unless the publicity was extraordinary. Water under the bridge. Ginnie was more interested in her novel-in-progress. They had a mortgage on the house, and with her and Stan's freelance work they thought they could be independent of New York, at least independent of nine-to-five jobs. Stan had already published three books, adventure stories with a political slant. He was thirty-two and for three years had been overseas correspondent for a newspaper syndicate.

Ginnie picked up a piece of heavy twine from the living room rug, and realized that her back hurt a little from the day's exertions. She had thought of switching on the TV, but the news was just over, she saw from her watch, and

Something You Have to Live With

it might be better to go straight to bed and get up earlyish in the morning.

'Cassie?'

Cassie replied with a courteous, sustained, 'M-wah-h?'

'Hungry?' Cassie knew the word. 'No, you've had enough. Do you know you're getting middle-aged spread? Come on. Going up to bed with me?' Ginnie went to the front door, which was already locked by its automatic lock, but she put the chain on also. Yawning, she turned out the downstairs lights and climbed the stairs. Cassie followed her.

Ginnie had a quick bath, second of the day, pulled on a nightgown, brushed her teeth and got into bed. She at once realized she was too tired to pick up one of the English weeklies, political and Stan's favourites, which she had dropped by the bed to look at. She put out the lamp. *Home*. She and Stan had spent one night here last weekend during the big move. This was the first night she had been alone in the house, which still had no name. *Something like White Elephant maybe*, Stan had said. *You think of something*. Ginnie tried to think, an activity which made her instantly sleepier.

She was awakened by a crunching sound, like that of car tyres on gravel. She raised up a little in bed. Had she heard it? Their driveway hadn't any gravel to speak of, just unpaved earth. But –

Wasn't that a *click*? From somewhere. Front, back? Or had it been a twig falling on the roof?

She had locked the doors, hadn't she?

Ginnie suddenly realized that she had not locked the back door. For another minute, as Ginnie listened, everything was silent. What a bore to go downstairs again! But she thought she had better do it, so she could honestly tell Stan that she had. Ginnie found the lamp switch and got out of bed.

By now she was thinking that any noise she had

heard had been imaginary, something out of a dream. But Cassie followed her in a brisk, anxious way, Ginnie noticed.

The glow from the staircase light enabled Ginnie to find her way to the kitchen, where she switched on the strong ceiling light. She went at once to the back door and turned the Yale bolt. Then she listened. All was silent. The big kitchen looked exactly the same with its half modern, half old-fashioned furnishings – electric stove, big white wooden cupboard with drawers below, shelves above, double sink, a huge new fridge.

Ginnie went back upstairs, Cassie still following. Cassie was short for Cassandra, a name Stan had given her when she had been a kitten, because she had looked gloomy, unshakeably pessimistic. Ginnie was drifting off to sleep again, when she heard a bump downstairs, as if someone had staggered slightly. She switched on the bedside lamp again, and a thrust of fear went through her when she saw Cassie rigidly crouched on the bed with her eyes fixed on the open bedroom door.

Now there was another bump from downstairs, and the unmistakable rustle of a drawer being slid out, and it could be only the dining-room drawer where the silver was.

She had locked someone in with her!

Her first thought was to reach for the telephone and get the police, but the telephone was downstairs in the living-room.

Go down and face it and threaten him with something – or them, she told herself. Maybe it was an adolescent kid, just a local kid who'd be glad to get off unreported, if she scared him a little. Ginnie jumped out of bed, put on Stan's bathrobe, a sturdy blue flannel thing, and tied the belt firmly. She descended the stairs. By now she heard more noises.

'Who's *there*?' she shouted boldly.

'Hum-hum. Just me, lady,' said a rather deep voice.

Something You Have to Live With

The living-room lights, the dining-room lights were full on.

In the dining-room Ginnie was confronted by a stocking-hooded figure in what she thought of as motorcycle gear: black trousers, black boots, black plastic jacket. The stocking had slits cut in it for the eyes. And the figure carried a dirty canvas bag like a railway mailbag, and plainly into this the silverware had already gone, because the dining-room drawer gaped, empty. He must have been hiding in a corner of the dining-room, Ginnie thought, when she had come down to lock the back door. The hooded figure shoved the drawer to carelessly, and it didn't quite close.

'Keep your mouth shut, and you won't get hurt. All right?' The voice sounded like that of a man of at least twenty-five.

Ginnie didn't see any gun or knife. 'Just what do you think you're doing?'

'What does it look like I'm doing?' And the man got on with his business. The two candlesticks from the dining-room table went into the bag. So did the silver table lighter.

Was there anyone else with him? Ginnie glanced towards the kitchen, but didn't see anyone, and no sound came from there. 'I'm going to call the police,' she said, and started for the living-room telephone.

'Phone's cut, lady. You better keep quiet, because no one can hear you around here, even if you scream.'

Was that true? Unfortunately it was true. Ginnie for a few seconds concentrated on memorizing the man's appearance: about five feet eight, medium build, maybe a bit slender, broad hands – but since the hands were in blue rubber gloves, were they broad? – rather big feet. Blond or brunette she couldn't tell, because of the stocking mask. Robbers like this usually bound and gagged people. Ginnie wanted to avoid that, if she could.

'If you're looking for money, there's not much in the

437

house just now,' Ginnie said, 'except what's in my handbag upstairs, about thirty dollars. Go ahead and take it.'

'I'll get around to it,' he said laughing, prowling the living-room now. He took the letter-opener from the coffee table, then Freddie's photograph from the piano, because the photograph was in a silver frame.

Ginnie thought of banging him on the head with – with what? She saw nothing heavy enough, portable, except one of the dining-room chairs. And if she failed to knock him out with the first swat? Was the telephone really cut? She moved towards the telephone in the corner.

'Don't go near the door. Stay in sight!'

'Ma-wow-wow-*wow*!' This from Cassie, a high-pitched wail that to Ginnie meant Cassie was on the brink of throwing up, but now the situation was different. Cassie looked ready to attack the man.

'Go back, Cassie, take it easy,' Ginnie said.

'I don't like cats,' the hooded man said over his shoulder.

There was not much else he could take from the living-room, Ginnie thought. The pictures on the walls were too big. And what burglar was interested in pictures, at least pictures like these which were a few oils done by their painter friends, two or three watercolours – Was this really happening? Was a stranger picking up her mother's old sewing basket, looking inside, banging it down again? Taking the French vase, tossing the water and roses towards the fireplace? The vase went into the sack.

'What's upstairs?' The ugly head turned towards her. 'Let's go upstairs.'

'There's *nothing* upstairs!' Ginnie shrieked. She darted towards the telephone, knowing it would be cut, but wanting to see it with her own eyes – cut – though her hand was outstretched to use it. She saw the abruptly

Something You Have to Live With

stopped wire on the floor, cut some four feet from the telephone.

The hood chuckled. 'Told you.'

A red flashlight stuck out of the back pocket of his trousers. He was going into the hall now, ready to take the stairs. The staircase light was on, but he pulled the flashlight from his pocket.

'Nothing *up* there, I tell you!' Ginnie found herself following him like a ninny, holding up the hem of Stan's dressing-gown so she wouldn't trip on the stairs.

'Cosy little nook!' said the hood, entering the bedroom. 'And what have we here? Anything of interest?'

The silver-backed brush and comb on the dresser were of interest, also the hand mirror, and these went into the bag, which was now dragging the floor.

'Aha! I like that thing!' He had spotted the heavy wooden box with brass corners which Stan used for cufflinks and handkerchiefs and a few white ties, but its size was apparently daunting the man in the hood, because he swayed in front of it and said, 'Be back for that.' He looked around for lighter objects, and in went Ginnie's black leather jewellery box, her Dunhill lighter from the bedside table. 'Ought to be glad I'm not raping you. Haven't the time.' The tone was jocular.

My God, Ginnie thought, you'd think Stan and I were rich! She had never considered herself and Stan rich, or thought that they had anything worth invading a house for. No doubt in New York they'd been lucky for six years – no robberies at all – because even a typewriter was valuable to a drug addict. No, they weren't rich, but he was taking all they had, all the *nice* things they'd tried over the years to accumulate. Ginnie watched him open her handbag, lift the dollar bills from her billfold. That was the least of it.

'If you think for one minute you're going to get away with this,' Ginnie said. 'In a small community like *this*?

You haven't a prayer. If you don't leave those things here tonight, I'll report you so quick –'

'Oh, shut up, lady. Where's the other rooms here?'

Cassie snarled. She had followed them both up the stairs.

A black boot struck out sideways and caught the cat sharply in the ribs.

'Don't touch that cat!' Ginnie cried out.

Cassie sprang growling on to the man's boot top, at his knee.

Ginnie was astounded – and proud of Cassie – for a second.

'Pain in the ass!' said the hood, and with a gloved hand caught the cat by the loose skin on her back and flung her against a wall with a backhand swing. The cat dropped, panting, and the man stomped on her side and kicked her on the head.

'You *bastard!*' Ginnie screamed.

'So much for your stinking – yowlers!' said the beige hood, and kicked the cat once again. His voice had been husky with rage, and now he stalked with his flashlight into the hall, in quest of other rooms.

Dazed, stiff, Ginnie followed him.

The guest-room had only a chest of drawers in it, empty, but the man slid out a couple of drawers anyway to have a look. Freddie's room had nothing but a bed and table. The hood wasted no time there.

From the hall, Ginnie looked into the bedroom at her cat. The cat twitched and was still. One foot had twitched. Ginnie stood rigid as a column of stone. She had just seen Cassie die, she realized.

'Back in a flash,' said the hooded man, briskly descending the stairs with his sack which was now so heavy he had to carry it on one shoulder.

Ginnie moved at last, in jerks, like someone awakening from an anaesthetic. Her body and mind seemed not to be connected. Her hand reached for the stair rail and missed

Something You Have to Live With

it. She was no longer afraid at all, though she did not consciously realize this. She simply kept following the hooded figure, her enemy, and would have kept on, even if he had pointed a gun at her. By the time she reached the kitchen, he was out of sight. The kitchen door was open, and a cool breeze blew in. Ginnie continued across the kitchen, looked left into the driveway, and saw a flashlight's beam swing as the man heaved the bag into a car. She heard the hum of two male voices. So he had a pal waiting for him!

And here he came back.

With sudden swiftness, Ginnie picked up a kitchen stool which had a square formica top and chromium legs. As soon as the hooded figure stepped on to the threshold of the kitchen, Ginnie swung the stool and hit him full on the forehead with the edge of the stool's seat.

Momentum carried the man forward, but he stooped, staggering, and Ginnie cracked him again on the top of the head with all her strength. She held two legs of the stool in her hands. He fell with a great thump and clatter on to the linoleum floor. Another whack for good measure on the back of the stockinged head. She felt pleased and relieved to see blood coming through the beige material.

'Frankie? – You okay? – *Frankie!*'

The voice came from the car outside.

Poised now, not at all afraid, Ginnie stood braced for the next arrival. She held a leg of the stool in her right hand, and her left supported the seat. She awaited, barely two feet from the open door, the sound of boots in the driveway, another figure in the doorway.

Instead, she heard a car motor start, saw a glow of its lights through the door. The car was backing down the drive.

Finally Ginnie set the stool down. The house was silent again. The man on the floor was not moving. Was he dead?

I don't care. I simply don't give a damn, Ginnie said inside herself.

But she did care. What if he woke up? What if he needed a doctor, a hospital right away? And there was no telephone. The nearest house was nearly a mile away, the village a good mile. Ginnie would have to walk it with a flashlight. Of course if she encountered a car, a car might stop and ask what was the matter, and then she could tell someone to fetch a doctor or an ambulance. These thoughts went through Ginnie's head in seconds, and then she returned to the facts. The fact was, he *might* be dead. Killed by her.

So was Cassie dead. Ginnie turned towards the living-room. Cassie's death was more real, more important than the body at her feet which only might be dead. Ginnie drew a glass of water for herself at the kitchen sink.

Everything was silent outside. Now Ginnie was calm enough to realize that the robber's chum had thought it best to make a getaway. He probably wasn't coming back, not even with reinforcements. After all, he had the loot in his car – silverware, her jewellery box, all the nice things.

Ginnie stared at the long black figure on her kitchen floor. He hadn't moved at all. The right hand lay under him, the left arm was outstretched, upward. The stockinged head was turned slightly towards her, one slit showing. She couldn't see what was going on behind that crazy slit.

'Are you *awake*?' Ginnie said, rather loudly.

She waited.

She knew she would have to face it. Best to feel the pulse in the wrist, she thought, and at once forced herself to do this. She pulled the rubber glove down a bit, and gripped a blondish-haired wrist which seemed to her of astonishing breadth, much wider than Stan's wrist, anyway. She couldn't feel any pulse. She altered the place

Something You Have to Live With

where she had put her thumb, and tried again. There was no pulse.

So she had murdered someone. The fact did not sink in.

Two thoughts danced in her mind: she would have to remove Cassie, put a towel or something around her, and she was not going to be able to sleep or even remain in this house with a corpse lying on the kitchen floor.

Ginnie got a dishtowel, a folded clean one from a stack on a shelf, took a second one, went to the hall and climbed the stairs. Cassie was now bleeding. Rather, she had bled. The blood on the carpet looked dark. One of Cassie's eyes projected from the socket. Ginnie gathered her as gently as if she were still alive and only injured, gathered up some intestines which had been pushed out, and enfolded her in a towel, opened the second towel and put that around her too. Then she carried Cassie down to the living-room, hesitated, then laid the cat's body to one side of the fireplace on the floor. By accident, a red rose lay beside Cassie.

Tackle the blood now, she told herself. She got a plastic bowl from the kitchen, drew some cold water and took a sponge. Upstairs, she went to work on hands and knees, changing the water in the bathroom. The task was soothing, as she had known it would be.

Next job: clothes on and find the nearest telephone. Ginnie kept moving, barely aware of what she was doing, and suddenly she was standing in the kitchen in blue jeans, sneakers, sweater and jacket with her billfold in a pocket. Empty billfold, she remembered. She had her house keys in her left hand. For no good reason, she decided to leave the kitchen light on. The front door was still locked, she realized. She found she had the flashlight in a jacket pocket too, and supposed she had taken it from the front hall table when she came down the stairs.

She went out, locked the kitchen door from the outside with a key, and made her way to the road.

No moon at all. She walked with the aid of the flashlight along the left side of the road towards the village, shone the torch once on her watch and saw that it was twenty past one. By starlight, by a bit of flashlight, she saw one house far to the left in a field, quite dark and so far away, Ginnie thought she might do better to keep on.

She kept on. Dark road. Trudging. Did *everybody* go to bed early around here?

In the distance she saw two or three white streetlights, the lights of the village. Surely there'd be a car before the village.

There wasn't a car. Ginnie was still trudging as she entered the village proper, whose boundary was marked by a neat white sign on either side of the road saying EAST KINDALE.

My God, Ginnie thought. *Is this true? Is this what I'm doing, what I'm going to say?*

Not a light showed in any of the neat, mostly white houses. There was not even a light at the Connecticut Yankee Inn, the only functioning hostelry and bar in town, Stan had remarked once. Nevertheless, Ginnie marched up the steps and knocked on the door. Then with her flashlight, she saw a brass knocker on the white door, and availed herself of that.

Rap-rap-rap!

Minutes passed. *Be patient*, Ginnie told herself. *You're over-wrought*.

But she felt compelled to rap again.

'Who's there?' a man's voice called.

'A neighbour! There's been an accident!'

Ginnie fairly collapsed against the figure who opened the door. It was a man in a plaid woollen bathrobe and pyjamas. She might have collapsed also against a woman or a child.

Then she was sitting on a straight chair in a sort of living-room. She had blurted out the story.

'We'll – we'll get the police right away, ma'am. Or an

Something You Have to Live With

ambulance, as you say. But from what you say –' The man talking was in his sixties, and sleepy.

His wife, more efficient looking, had joined him to listen. She wore a dressing-gown and pink slippers. 'Police, Jake. Man sounds dead from what the lady says. Even if he isn't, the police'll know what to do.'

'Hello, Ethel! That you?' the man said into the telephone. 'Listen, we need the police right away. You know the old Hardwick place? . . . Tell 'em to go there . . . No, *not* on fire. Can't explain now. But somebody'll be there to open the door in – in about five minutes.'

The woman pushed a glass of something into Ginnie's hand. Ginnie realized that her teeth were chattering. She was cold, though it wasn't cold outside. It was early September, she remembered.

'They're going to want to speak with you.' The man who had been in the plaid robe was now in trousers and a belted sports jacket. 'You'll have to tell them the time it happened and all that.'

Ginnie realized. She thanked the woman and went with the man to his car. It was an ordinary four-door, and Ginnie noticed a discarded Cracker Jack box on the floor of the passenger's seat as she got in.

A police car was in the drive. Someone was knocking on the back door, and Ginnie saw that she'd left the kitchen light on.

'Hya, Jake! What's up?' called a second policeman, getting out of the black car in the driveway.

'Lady had a house robbery,' the man with Ginnie explained. 'She thinks – Well, you've got the keys, haven't you, Mrs Brixton?'

'Oh yes, yes.' Ginnie fumbled for them. She was gasping again, and reminded herself that it was a time to keep calm, to answer questions accurately. She opened the kitchen door.

A policeman stooped beside the prone figure. 'Dead,' he said.

'The – Mrs Brixton said she hit him with the kitchen stool. That one, ma'am?' The man called Jake pointed to the yellow formica stool.

'Yes. He was coming *back*, you see. You see –' Ginnie choked and gave up, for the moment.

Jake cleared his throat and said, 'Mrs Brixton and her husband just moved in. Husband isn't here tonight. She'd left the kitchen door unlocked and two – well, one fellow came in, this one. He went out with a bag of stuff he'd taken, put it in a waiting car, then came back to get more, and that's when Mrs Brixton hit him.'

'Um-*hum*,' said the policeman, still stooped on his heels. 'Can't touch the body till the detective gets here. Can I use your phone, Mrs Brixton?'

'They cut the phone,' Jake said. 'That's why she had to walk to my place.'

The other policeman went out to telephone from his car. The policeman who remained put on water for coffee (or had he said tea?), and chatted with Jake about tourists, about someone they both knew who had just got married – as if they had known each other for years. Ginnie was sitting on one of the dining-room chairs. The policeman asked where the instant coffee was, if she had any, and Ginnie got up to show him the coffee jar which she had put on a cabinet shelf beside the stove.

'Terrible introduction to a new house,' the policeman remarked, holding his steaming cup. 'But we all sure hope –' Suddenly his words seemed to dry up. His eyes flickered and looked away from Ginnie's face.

A couple of men in plainclothes arrived. Photographs were taken of the dead man. Ginnie went over the house with one of the men, who made notes of the items Ginnie said were stolen. No, she hadn't seen the colour of the car, much less the licence plate. The body on the floor was wrapped and carried out on a stretcher. Ginnie had only a glimpse of that, from which the detective even tried to

Something You Have to Live With

shield her. Ginnie was in the dining-room then, reckoning up the missing silver.

'I didn't mean to kill him!' Ginnie cried out suddenly, interrupting the detective. 'Not *kill* him, honestly!'

Stan arrived very early, about 8 a.m., with Freddie, and went to the Inn to fetch Ginnie. Ginnie had spent the night there, and someone had telephoned Stan at the number Ginnie had given.

'She's had a shock,' Jake said to Stan.

Stan looked bewildered. But at least he had heard what happened, and Ginnie didn't have to go over it.

'All the nice things we had,' Ginnie said. 'And the cat –'

'The police might get our stuff back, Ginnie. If not, we'll buy more. We're all safe, at least.' Stan set his firm jaw, but he smiled. He glanced at Freddie who stood in the doorway, looking a little pale from lack of sleep. 'Come on. We're going home.'

He took Ginnie's hand. His hand felt warm, and she realized her own hands were cold again.

They tried to keep the identity of the dead man from her, Ginnie knew, but on the second day she happened to see it printed – on a folded newspaper which lay on the counter in the grocery store. There was a photograph of him too, a blondish fellow with curly hair and a rather defiant expression. *Frank Collins, 24, of Hartford* . . .

Stan felt that they ought to go on living in the house, gradually buy the 'nice things' again that Ginnie kept talking about. Stan said she ought to get back to work on her novel.

'I don't want any nice things any more. Not again.' That was true, but that was only part of it. The worst was that she had killed someone, stopped a life. She couldn't fully realize it, therefore couldn't believe it somehow, or understand it.

'At least we could get another cat.'

'Not yet,' she said.

People said to her (like Mrs Durham, Gladys, who lived a mile or so out of East Kindale on the opposite side from the Brixtons), 'You mustn't reproach yourself. You did it in defence of your house. Don't you think a lot of us wish we had the courage, if someone comes barging in intending to rob you . . .'

'I wouldn't hesitate – to do what you did!' That was from perky Georgia Hamilton, a young married woman with black curly hair, active in local politics, who lived in East Kindale proper. She came especially to call on Ginnie and to make acquaintance with her and Stan. 'These hoodlums from miles away – Hartford! – they come to rob us, just because they think we still have some family silver and a few *nice* things . . .'

There was the phrase again, the *nice* things.

Stan came home one day with a pair of silver candlesticks for the dining-room table. 'Less than a hundred dollars, and we can afford them,' Stan said.

To Ginnie they looked like bait for another robbery. They were pretty, yes. Georgian. Modern copy, but still beautiful. She could not take any aesthetic pleasure from them.

'Did you take a swat at your book this afternoon?' Stan asked cheerfully. He had been out of the house nearly three hours that afternoon. He had made sure the doors were locked, for Ginnie's sake, before he left. He had also bought a metal wheelbarrow for use in the garden, and it was still strapped to the roof of the car.

'No,' Ginnie said. 'But I suppose I'm making progress. I have to get back to a state of concentration, you know.'

'Of course I know,' Stan said. 'I'm a writer too.'

The police had never recovered the silverware, or Ginnie's leather box which had held her engagement ring (it had become too small and she hadn't got around to having it enlarged), and her grandmother's gold necklace and so forth. Stan told Ginnie they had checked all

Something You Have to Live With

the known pals of the man who had invaded the house, but hadn't come up with anything. The police thought the dead man might have struck up acquaintance with his chum very recently, possibly the same night as the robbery.

'Darling,' Stan said, 'do you think we should *move* from this house? I'm willing – if it'd make you feel – less –'

Ginnie shook her head. It wasn't the house. She didn't any longer (after two months) even think of the corpse on the floor when she went into the kitchen. It was something inside her. 'No,' Ginnie said.

'Well – I think you ought to talk to a psychiatrist. Just one visit even,' Stan added, interrupting a protest from Ginnie. 'It isn't enough for neighbours to say you did the natural thing. Maybe you need a professional to tell you.' Stan chuckled. He was in tennis shoes and old clothes, and had had a good day at the typewriter.

Ginnie agreed, to please Stan.

The psychiatrist was in Hartford, a man recommended to Stan by a local medical doctor. Stan drove Ginnie there, and waited for her in the car. It was to be an hour's session, but Ginnie reappeared after about forty minutes.

'He gave me some pills to take,' Ginnie said.

'Is *that* all? – But what did he say?'

'Oh.' Ginnie shrugged. 'The same as they all say, that – nobody blames me, the police didn't make a fuss, so what –' She shrugged again, glanced at Stan and saw the terrible disappointment in his face as he looked from her into the distance through the windshield.

Ginnie knew he was thinking again about 'guilt' and abandoning it, abandoning the word again. She had said no, she didn't feel guilty, that wasn't the trouble, that would have been too simple. She felt disturbed, she had said many times, and she couldn't do anything about it.

'You really ought to write a book about it, a novel,' Stan said – this for at least the fourth time.

'And how can I, if I can't come to terms with it myself, if I can't even analyse it first?' This Ginnie said for at least the third time and possibly the fourth. It was as if she had an unsolvable mystery within her. 'You can't write a book just stammering around on paper.'

Stan then started the car.

The pills were mild sedatives combined with some kind of mild picker-uppers. They didn't make a change in Ginnie.

Two more months passed. Ginnie resisted buying any 'nice things', so they had nothing but the nice candlesticks. They ate with stainless steel. Freddie pulled out of his period of tension and suppressed excitement (he knew quite well what had happened in the kitchen), and in Ginnie's eyes became quite normal again, whatever normal was. Ginnie got back to work on the book she had started before moving to the house. She didn't ever dream about the murder, or manslaughter, in fact she often thought it might be better if she did dream about it.

But among people – and it was a surprisingly friendly region, they had all the social life they could wish – she felt compelled to say sometimes, when there was a lull in the conversation, 'Did you know, by the way, I once killed a man?'

Everyone would look at her, except of course those who had heard her say this before, maybe three times before.

Stan would grow tense and blank-minded, having failed once more to spring in in time before Ginnie got launched. He was jittery at social gatherings, trying like a fencer to dart in with something, anything to say, before Ginnie made her big thrust. *It's just something they, he and Ginnie, had to live with*, Stan told himself.

And it probably would go on and on, even maybe when Freddie was twelve and even twenty. It had, in fact, half-ruined their marriage. But it was emphatically not worth divorcing for. He still loved Ginnie. She was still

Something You Have to Live With

Ginnie after all. She was just somehow different. Even Ginnie had said that about herself.

'It's something I just have to live with,' Stan murmured to himself.

'What?' It was Georgia Hamilton on his left, asking him what he had said. 'Oh, I know, I know.' She smiled understandingly. 'But maybe it does her good.'

Ginnie was in the middle of her story. At least she always made it short, and even managed to laugh in a couple of places.

Ruth Prawer Jhabvala

*How I Became
a Holy Mother*

On my twenty-third birthday when I was fed up with London and all the rest of it – boyfriends, marriages (two), jobs (modelling), best friends that are suddenly your best enemies – I had this letter from my girl friend Sophie who was finding peace in an ashram in South India:

> ... oh Katie you wouldn't know me I'm such a changed person. I get up at 5 – *a.m.*!!! I am an absolute vegetarian let alone no meat no eggs either and am making fabulous progress with my meditation. I have a special mantra of my own that Swamiji gave me at a special ceremony and I say it over and over in my mind. The sky here is blue all day long and I sit by the sea and watch the waves and have good thoughts ...

But by the time I got there Sophie had left – under a cloud, it seemed, though when I asked what she had done, they wouldn't tell me but only pursed their lips and looked sorrowful. I didn't stay long in that place. I didn't like the bitchy atmosphere, and that Swamiji was a big fraud, anyone could see that. I couldn't understand how a girl as sharp as Sophie had ever let herself be fooled by such a type. But I suppose if you want to be fooled you are. I found that out in some of the other ashrams I went to. There were some quite intelligent people in all of them but the way they just shut their eyes to certain things, it was incredible. It is not my role in life to criticize others so

I kept quiet and went on to the next place. I went to quite a few of them. These ashrams are a cheap way to live in India and there is always company and it isn't bad for a few days provided you don't get involved in their power politics. I was amazed to come across quite a few people I had known over the years and would never have expected to meet here. It is a shock when you see someone you had last met on the beach at St Tropez now all dressed up in a saffron robe and meditating in some very dusty ashram in Madhya Pradesh. But really I could see their point because they were all as tired as I was of everything we had been doing and this certainly was different.

I enjoyed myself going from one ashram to the other and travelling all over India. Trains and buses are very crowded – I went third class, I had to be careful with my savings – but Indians can tell when you want to be left alone. They are very sensitive that way. I looked out of the window and thought my thoughts. After a time I became quite calm and rested. I hadn't brought too much stuff with me, but bit by bit I discarded most of that too till I had only a few things left that I could easily carry myself. I didn't even mind when my watch was pinched off me one night in a railway rest-room (so-called). I felt myself to be a changed person. Once, at the beginning of my travels, there was a man sitting next to me on a bus who said he was an astrologer. He was a very sensitive and philosophical person – and I must say I was impressed by how many such one meets in India, quite ordinary people travelling third class. After we had been talking for a time and he had told me the future of India for the next forty years, suddenly out of the blue he said to me, 'Madam, you have a very sad soul.' It was true. I thought about it for days afterwards and cried a bit to myself. I did feel sad inside myself and heavy like with a stone. But as time went on and I kept going round India – the sky always blue like Sophie had said, and lots of rivers and fields as well as desert – just quietly travelling and

How I Became a Holy Mother

looking, I stopped feeling like that. Now I was as a matter of fact quite light inside as if that stone had gone.

Then I stopped travelling and stayed in this one place instead. I liked it better than any of the other ashrams for several reasons. One of them was that the scenery was very picturesque. This cannot be said of all ashrams as many of them seem to be in sort of dust bowls, or in the dirtier parts of very dirty holy cities or even cities that aren't holy at all but just dirty. But this ashram was built on the slope of a mountain, and behind it there were all the other mountains stretching right up to the snow-capped peaks of the Himalayas; and on the other side it ran down to the river which I will not say can have been very clean (with all those pilgrims dipping in it) but certainly looked clean from up above and not only clean but as clear and green as the sky was clear and blue. Also along the bank of the river there were many little pink temples with pink cones and they certainly made a pretty scene. Inside the ashram also the atmosphere was good which again cannot be said of all of them, far from it. But the reason the atmosphere was good here was because of the head of this ashram who was called Master. They are always called something like that – if not Swamiji then Maharaj-ji or Babaji or Maharishiji or Guruji; but this one was just called plain Master, in English.

He was full of pep and go. Early in the morning he would say, 'Well what shall we do today!' and then plan some treat like all of us going for a swim in the river with a picnic lunch to follow. He didn't want anyone to have a dull moment or to fall into a depression which I suppose many there were apt to do, left to their own devices. In some ways he reminded me of those big business types that sometimes (in other days!) took me out to dinner. They too had that kind of superhuman energy and seemed to be stronger than other people. I forgot to say that Master was a big burly man, and as he didn't wear all that many clothes – usually only a loincloth –

you could see just how big and burly he was. His head was large too and it was completely shaven so that it looked even larger. He wasn't ugly, not at all. Or perhaps if he was one forgot about it very soon because of all that dynamism.

As I said, the ashram was built on the slope of a mountain. I don't think it was planned at all but had just grown: there was one little room next to the other and the Meditation Hall and the dining hall and Master's quarters – whatever was needed was added and it all ran higgledy-piggledy down the mountain. I had one of the little rooms to myself and made myself very snug in there. The only furniture provided by the ashram was one string bed, but I bought a handloom rug from the Lepers Rehabilitation Centre and I also put up some pictures, like a Tibetan Mandala which was very colourful. Everyone liked my room and wanted to come and spend time there, but I was a bit cagey about that as I needed my privacy. I always had lots to do, like writing letters or washing my hair and I was also learning to play the flute. So I was quite happy and independent and didn't really need company though there was plenty of it, if and when needed.

There were Master's Indian disciples who were all learning to be swamis. They wanted to renounce the world and had shaved their heads and wore an orange sort of toga thing. When they were ready, Master was going to make them into full swamis. Most of these junior swamis were very young – just boys, some of them – but even those that weren't all that young were certainly so at heart. Sometimes they reminded me of a lot of school kids, they were so full of tricks and fun. But I think basically they were very serious – they couldn't not be, considering how they were renouncing and were supposed to be studying all sorts of very difficult things. The one I liked the best was called Vishwa. I liked him not only because he was the best looking, which he undoubtedly was, but I

How I Became a Holy Mother

felt he had a lot going for him. Others said so too – in fact, they all said that Vishwa was the most advanced and was next in line for full initiation. I always let him come and talk to me in my room whenever he wanted to, and we had some interesting conversations.

Then there were Master's foreign disciples. They weren't so different from the other Europeans and Americans I had met in other ashrams except that the atmosphere here was so much better and that made them better too. They didn't have to fight with each other over Master's favours – I'm afraid that was very much the scene in some of the other ashrams which were like harems, the way they were all vying for the favour of their guru. But Master never encouraged that sort of relationship, and although of course many of them did have very strong attachments to him, he managed to keep them all healthy. And that's really saying something because, like in all the other ashrams, many of them were not healthy people; through no fault of their own quite often, they had just had a bad time and were trying to get over it.

Once Master said to me, 'What about you, Katie?' This was when I was alone with him in his room. He had called me in for some dictation – we were all given little jobs to do for him from time to time, to keep us busy and happy I suppose. Just let me say a few words about his room and get it over with. It was *awful*. It had linoleum on the floor of the nastiest pattern, and green strip lighting, and the walls were painted green too and had been decorated with calendars and pictures of what were supposed to be gods and saints but might as well have been Bombay film stars, they were so fat and gaudy. Master and all the junior swamis were terribly proud of this room. Whenever he acquired anything new – like some plastic flowers in a hideous vase – he would call everyone to admire and was so pleased and complacent that really it was not possible to say anything except, 'Yes very nice.'

When he said, 'What about you, Katie?' I knew at once

what he meant. That was another thing about him – he would suddenly come out with something as if there had already been a long talk between you on this subject. So when he asked me that, it was like the end of a conversation, and all I had to do was think for a moment and then I said, 'I'm okay.' Because that was what he had asked: was I okay? Did I want anything, any help or anything? And I didn't. I really was okay now. I hadn't always been but I got so travelling around on my own and then being in this nice place here with him.

This was before the Countess came. Once she was there, everything was rather different. For weeks before her arrival people started talking about her: she was an important figure there, and no wonder since she was very rich and did a lot for the ashram and for Master when he went abroad on his lecture tours. I wondered what she was like. When I asked Vishwa about her, he said, 'She is a great spiritual lady.'

We were both sitting outside my room. There was a little open space round which several other rooms were grouped. One of these – the biggest, at the corner – was being got ready for the Countess. It was the one that was always kept for her. People were vigorously sweeping in there and scrubbing the floor with soap and water.

'She is rich and from very aristocratic family,' Vishwa said, 'but when she met Master she was ready to give up everything.' He pointed to the room which was being scrubbed: 'This is where she stays. And see – not even a bed – she sleeps on the floor like a holy person. Oh Katie, when someone like me gives up the world, what is there? It is not such a great thing. But when *she* does it –' His face glowed. He had very bright eyes and a lovely complexion. He always looked very pure, owing no doubt to the very pure life he led.

Of course I got more and more curious about her, but when she came I was disappointed. I had expected her to be very special, but the only special thing about her was that I should meet her *here*. Otherwise she was a type I had often come across at posh parties and in the salons where I used to model. And the way she walked towards me and said, 'Welcome!' – she might as well have been walking across a carpet in a salon. She had a full-blown, middle-aged figure (she must have been in her fifties) but very thin legs on which she took long strides with her toes turned out. She gave me a deep searching look – and that too I was used to from someone like her because very worldly people always do that: to find out who you are and how usable. But in her case now I suppose it was to search down into my soul and see what that was like.

I don't know what her conclusion was, but I must have passed because she was always kind to me and even asked for my company quite often. Perhaps this was partly because we lived across from each other and she suffered from insomnia and needed someone to talk to at night. I'm a sound sleeper myself and wasn't always very keen when she came to wake me. But she would nag me till I got up. 'Come on, Katie, be a sport,' she would say. She used many English expressions like that: she spoke English very fluently though with a funny accent. I heard her speak to the French and Italian and German people in the ashram very fluently in their languages too. I don't know what nationality she herself was – a sort of mixture I think – but of course people like her have been everywhere, not to mention their assorted governesses when young.

She always made me come into her room. She said mine was too *luxurious*, she didn't feel right in it as she had given up all that. Hers certainly wasn't luxurious. Like Vishwa had said, there wasn't a stick of furniture in it and she slept on the floor on a mat. As the electricity supply in the ashram was very fitful, we usually sat by candlelight. It was queer sitting like that with her on the floor with a stub of candle between us. I didn't have to do much talking as she did it all. She used her arms a lot, in sweeping gestures, and I can still see them weaving around there by candlelight as if she was doing a dance with them; and her eyes which were big and baby-blue were stretched wide open in wonder at everything she was telling me. Her life was like a fairy-tale, she said. She gave me all the details though I can't recall them as I kept dropping off to sleep (naturally at two in the morning). From time to time she'd stop and say sharply, 'Are you asleep, Katie?' and then she would poke me till I said no I wasn't. She told me how she first met Master at a lecture he had come to give in Paris. At the end of the lecture she went up to him – she said she had to elbow her way through a crowd of women all trying to get near him – and simply bowed down at his feet. No words spoken. There had been no need. It had been predestined.

She was also very fond of Vishwa. It seemed all three of them – i.e. her, Master, and Vishwa – had been closely related to each other in several previous incarnations. I think they had been either her sons or her husbands or fathers, I can't remember which exactly but it was very close so it was no wonder she felt about them the way she did. She had big plans for Vishwa. He was to go abroad and be a spiritual leader. She and Master often talked about it, and it was fascinating listening to them, but there was one thing I couldn't understand and that was why did it have to be Vishwa and not Master who was to be a spiritual leader in the West? I'd have thought Master himself had terrific qualifications for it.

Once I asked them. We were sitting in Master's room and the two of them were talking about Vishwa's future. When I asked, 'What about Master?' she gave a dramatic laugh and pointed at him like she was accusing him: 'Ask him! Why don't you ask him!'

He gave a guilty smile and shifted around a bit on his throne. I say throne – it really was that: he received everyone in this room so a sort of dais had been fixed up at one end and a deer-skin spread on it for him to sit on; loving disciples had painted an arched back to the dais and decorated it with stars and symbols stuck on in silver paper (hideous!).

When she saw him smile like that, she really got exasperated. 'If you knew, Katie,' she said, 'how I have argued with him, how I have fought, how I have begged and pleaded on my *knees*. But he is as stubborn as – as –'

'A mule,' he kindly helped her out.

'Forgive me,' she said (because you can't call your guru names, that just isn't done!); though next moment she had worked herself up again. 'Do you know,' she asked me, 'how many people were waiting for him at the airport last time he went to New York? Do you know how many came to his lectures? That they had to be turned away from the *door* till we took a bigger hall! And not to speak of those who came to enrol for the special three-week Meditation-via-Contemplation course.'

'She is right,' he said. 'They are very kind to me.'

'Kind! They want him – need him – are crazy with love and devotion –'

'It's all true,' he said. 'But the trouble is, you see, I'm a very, very lazy person.' And as he said this, he gave a big yawn and stretched himself to prove how lazy he was: but he didn't look it – on the contrary, when he stretched like that, pushing out his big chest, he looked like he was humming with energy.

That evening he asked me to go for a stroll with him. We walked by the river which was very busy with people dipping in it for religious reasons. The temples were also busy – whenever we passed one, they seemed to be bursting in there with hymns, and cymbals, and little bells.

Master said, 'It is true that everyone is very kind to me in the West. Oh they make a big fuss when I come. They have even made a song for me – it goes – wait, let me see –'

He stopped still and several people took the opportunity to come up to ask for his blessing. There were many other holy men walking about but somehow Master stood out. Some of the holy men also came up to be blessed by him.

'Yes it goes: *"He's here! Our Masterji is here Jai jai Master! Jai jai He!"* They stand waiting for me at the airport, and when I come out of the customs they burst into song. They carry big banners and also have drums and flutes. What a noise they make! Some of them begin to dance there and then on the spot, they are so happy. And everyone stares and looks at me, all the respectable people at the airport, and they wonder, "Now who is this ruffian?"'

He had to stop again because a shopkeeper came running out of his stall to crouch at Master's feet. He was the grocer – everyone knew he used false weights – as well as the local moneylender and the biggest rogue in town, but when Master blessed him I could see tears come in his eyes, he felt so good.

'A car has been bought for my use,' Master said when we walked on again. 'Also a lease has been taken on a beautiful residence in New Hampshire. Now they wish to buy an aeroplane to enable me to fly from coast to coast.' He sighed. 'She is right to be angry with me. But what am I to do? I stand in the middle of Times Square or Piccadilly, London, and I look up and there are all the beautiful beautiful buildings stretching so high up into heaven: yes I look at them but it is not them I see at all, Katie! Not them at all!'

He looked up and I with him, and I understood that what he saw in Times Square and Piccadilly was what we saw now – all those mountains growing higher and higher above the river, and some of them so high that you couldn't make out whether it was them with snow on top or the sky with clouds in it.

Before the Countess's arrival, everything had been very easy-going. We usually did our meditation, but if we happened to miss out, it never mattered too much. Also there was a lot of sitting around gossiping or trips to the bazaar for eats. But the Countess put us on a stricter régime. Now we all had a timetable to follow, and there were gongs and bells going off all day to remind us. This started at 5 a.m. when it was meditation time, followed by purificatory bathing time, and study time, and discussion time, and hymn time, and so on till lights-out time. Throughout the day disciples could be seen making their way up or down the mountainside as they passed from one group activity to the other. If there was any delay in the schedule, the Countess got impatient and clapped her hands and chivied people along. The way she herself clambered up and down the mountain was just simply amazing for someone her age. Sometimes she went right to the top of the ashram where there was a pink plaster pillar inscribed with Golden Rules for Golden Living (a sort of Indian Ten Commandments): from here she could look all round, survey her domain as it were. When she wanted to summon everyone, she climbed up there with a pair of cymbals and how she beat them together! Boom! Bang! She must have had military blood in her veins, probably German.

She had drawn up a very strict timetable for Vishwa to cover every aspect of his education. He had to learn all sorts of things; not only English and a bit of French and German, but also how to use a knife and fork and even how to address people by their proper titles in case ambassadors and big church people and such were drawn into the movement as was fully expected. Because I'd been a model, I was put in charge of his deportment. I was supposed to teach him how to walk and sit nicely. He had to come to my room for lessons in the afternoons, and it was quite fun though I really didn't know what to teach him. As far as I was concerned, he was more graceful than anyone I'd ever seen. I loved the way he sat on the floor with his legs tucked under him; he could sit like that without moving for hours and hours. Or he might lie full-length on the floor with his head supported on one hand and his ascetic's robe falling in folds around him so that he looked like a piece of sculpture you might see in a museum. I forgot to say that the Countess had decided he wasn't to shave his hair any more like the other junior swamis but was to grow it and have long curls. It wasn't long yet but it was certainly curly and framed his face very prettily.

After the first few days we gave up having lessons and just talked and spent our time together. He sat on the rug and I on the bed. He told me the story of his life and I told him mine. But his was much better than mine. His father had been the station master at some very small junction, and the family lived in a little railway house near enough the tracks to run and put the signals up or down as required. Vishwa had plenty of brothers and sisters to play with, and friends at the little school he went to at the other end of town; but quite often he felt like not being with anyone. He would set off to school with his copies and pencils like everyone else, but half way he would change his mind and take another turning that led out of town into some open fields. Here he would lie down under a tree and look at patches of sky through the leaves of the tree, and the leaves moving ever so gently if there was a breeze or some birds shook their wings in there. He would stay all day and in the evening go home and not tell anyone. His mother was a religious person who regularly visited the temple and sometimes he went with her but he never felt anything special. Then Master came to town and gave a lecture in a tent that was put up for him on the Parade Ground. Vishwa went with his mother to hear him, again not expecting anything special, but the moment he saw Master something very peculiar happened: he couldn't quite describe it, but he said it was like when there is a wedding on a dark night and the fireworks start and there are those that shoot up into the sky and then burst into a huge white fountain of light scattering sparks all over so that you are blinded and dazzled with it. It was like that, Vishwa said. Then he just went away with Master. His family were sad at first to lose him, but they were proud too like all families are when one of them renounces the world to become a holy man.

Those were good afternoons we had, and we usually took the precaution of locking the door so no one could interrupt us. If we heard the Countess coming – one good thing about her, you could always *hear* her a mile off, she never moved an inch without shouting instructions to someone – the moment we heard her we'd jump up and unlock the door and fling it wide open: so when she looked in, she could see us having our lesson – Vishwa walking up and down with a book on his head, or sitting like on a dais to give a lecture and me showing him what to do with his hands.

When I told him the story of *my* life, we both cried. Especially when I told him about my first marriage when I was only sixteen and Danny just twenty. He was a bass player in a group and he was really good and would have got somewhere if he hadn't freaked out. It was terrible seeing him do that, and the way he treated me after those first six months we had together which were out of this world. I never had anything like that with anyone ever again, though I got involved with many people afterwards. Everything just got worse and worse till I reached an all-time low with my second marriage which was to a company director (so-called, though don't ask me what sort of company) and a very smooth operator indeed besides being a sadist. Vishwa couldn't stand it when I came to that part of my story. He begged me not to go on, he put his hands over his ears. We weren't in my room that time but on top of the ashram by the Pillar of the Golden Rules. The view from here was fantastic, and it was so high up that you felt you might as well be in heaven, especially at this hour of the evening when the sky was turning all sorts of colours though mostly gold from the sun setting in it. Everything I was telling Vishwa seemed very far away. I can't say it was as if it had never happened, but it seemed like it had happened in someone else's life. There were tears on Vishwa's lashes, and I couldn't help myself, I had to kiss them away. After which we kissed properly. His mouth was as soft as a flower and his breath as sweet; of course he had never tasted meat nor eaten anything except the purest food such as a lamb might eat.

The door of my room was not the only one that was locked during those hot afternoons. Quite a few of the foreign disciples locked theirs for purposes I never cared to enquire into. At first I used to pretend to myself they were sleeping, and afterwards I didn't care what they were doing. I mean, even if they weren't sleeping, I felt there was something just as good and innocent about what they actually *were* doing. And after a while – when we had told each other the story of our respective lives and had run out of conversation – Vishwa and I began to do it too. This was about the time when preparations were going on for his final Renunciation and Initiation ceremony. It's considered the most important day in the life of a junior swami, when he ceases to be junior and becomes a senior or proper swami. It's a very solemn ceremony. A funeral pyre is lit and his junior robe and his caste thread are burned on it. All this is symbolic – it means he's dead to the world but resurrected to the spiritual life. In Vishwa's case, his resurrection was a bit different from the usual. He wasn't fitted out in the standard senior swami outfit – which is a piece of orange cloth and a begging bowl – but instead the Countess dressed him up in the clothes he was to wear in the West. She had herself designed a white silk robe for him, together with accessories like beads, sandals, the deer-skin he was to sit on, and an embroidered shawl.

How I Became a Holy Mother

Getting all this ready meant many trips to the bazaar, and often she made Vishwa and me go with her. She swept through the bazaar the same way she did through the ashram, and the shopkeepers leaned eagerly out of their stalls to offer their salaams which she returned or not as they happened to be standing in her books. She was pretty strict with all of them – but most of all with the tailor whose job it was to stitch Vishwa's new silk robes. We spent hours in his little shop while Vishwa had to stand there and be fitted. The tailor crouched at his feet, stitching and restitching the hem to the Countess's instructions. She and I would stand back and look at Vishwa with our heads to one side while the tailor waited anxiously for her verdict. Ten to one she would say, 'No! Again!'

But once she said not to the tailor but to me, 'Vishwa stands very well now. He has a good pose.'

'Not bad,' I said, continuing to look critically at Vishwa and in such a way that he had a job not to laugh.

What she said next however killed all desire for laughter: 'I think we could end the deportment lessons now,' and then she shouted at the tailor: 'What is this! What are you doing! What sort of monkey-work do you call that!'

I managed to persuade her that I hadn't finished with Vishwa yet and there were still a few tricks of the trade I had to teach him. But I knew it was a short reprieve and that soon our lessons would have to end. Also plans were now afoot for Vishwa's departure. He was to go with the Countess when she returned to Europe in a few weeks' time; and she was already very busy corresponding with her contacts in various places, and all sorts of lectures and meetings were being arranged. But that wasn't the only thing worrying me: what was even worse was the change I felt taking place in Vishwa himself, especially after his Renunciation and Initiation ceremony. I think he was getting quite impressed with himself. The Countess made a point of treating him as if he were a guru already, and she bowed to him the same way she did to Master. And of course whatever she did everyone else followed suit, specially the foreign disciples. I might just say that they're always keen on things like that – I mean, bowing down and touching feet – I don't know what kick they get out of it but they do, the Countess along with the rest. Most of them do it very clumsily – not like Indians who are *born* to it – so sometimes you feel like laughing when you look at them. But they're always very solemn about it and afterwards, when they stumble up again, there's a sort of holy glow on their faces. Vishwa looked down at them with a benign expression and he also got into the habit of blessing them the way Master did.

Now I stayed alone in the afternoons, feeling very miserable, specially when I thought of what was going on in some of the other rooms and how happy people were in there. After a few days of this I couldn't stand being on my own and started wandering around looking for company. But the only person up and doing at that time of day was the Countess who I didn't particularly want to be with. So I went and sat in Master's room where the door was always open in case any of us needed him any time. Like everybody else, he was often asleep that time of afternoon but it didn't matter. Just being in his presence was good. I sat on one of the green plastic benches that were ranged round his room and looked at him sleeping which he did sitting upright on his throne. Quite suddenly he would open his eyes and look straight at me and say, 'Ah Katie,' as if he'd known all along that I was sitting there.

One day there was an awful commotion outside. Master woke up as the Countess came in with two foreign disciples, a boy and a girl, who stood hanging their heads while she told us what she had caught them doing. They were two very young disciples; I think the boy didn't even have to shave yet. One couldn't imagine them doing anything really evil, and Master didn't seem to think so.

How I Became a Holy Mother

He just told them to go away and have their afternoon rest. But because the Countess was very upset he tried to comfort her which he did by telling about his early life in the world when he was a married man. It had been an arranged marriage of course, and his wife had been very young, just out of school. Being married for them had been like a game, specially the cooking and housekeeping part which she had enjoyed very much. Every Sunday she had dressed up in a spangled sari and high-heeled shoes and he had escorted her on the bus to the cinema where they stood in a queue for the one-rupee seats. He had loved her more than he had ever loved anyone or anything in all his life and had not thought it possible to love so much. But it only lasted two years at the end of which time she died of a miscarriage. He left his home then and wandered about for many years, doing all sorts of different jobs. He worked as a motor mechanic, and a salesman for medical supplies, and had even been in films for a while on the distribution side. But not finding rest anywhere, he finally decided to give up the world. He explained to us that it had been the only logical thing to do. Having learned during his two years of marriage how happy it was possible for a human being to be, he was never again satisfied to settle for anything less; but also seeing how it couldn't last on a worldly plane, he had decided to look for it elsewhere and help other people to do so with him.

I liked what he said, but I don't think the Countess took much of it in. She was more in her own thoughts. She was silent and gloomy which was *very* unusual for her. When she woke me that night for her midnight confessions, she seemed quite a different person: and now she didn't talk about her fairy-tale life or her wonderful plans for the future but on the contrary about all the terrible things she had suffered in the past. She went right back to the time she was in her teens and had eloped with and married an old man, a friend of her father's, and from there on it was all just one long terrible story of bad marriages and unhappy love affairs and other sufferings that I wished I didn't have to listen to. But I couldn't leave her in the state she was in. She was crying and sobbing and lying face down on the ground. It was eerie in that bare cell of hers with the one piece of candle flickering in the wind which was very strong, and the rain beating down like fists on the tin roof.

The monsoon had started, and when you looked up now, there weren't any mountains left, only clouds hanging down very heavily; and when you looked down, the river was also heavy and full. Every day there were stories of pilgrims drowning in it, and one night it washed over one bank and swept away a little colony of huts that the lepers had built for themselves. Now they no longer sat sunning themselves on the bridge but were carted away to the infectious diseases hospital. The rains came gushing down the mountain right into the ashram so that we were all wading ankle-deep in mud and water. Many rooms were flooded and their occupants had to move into other people's rooms resulting in personality clashes. Everyone bore grudges and took sides so that it became rather like the other ashrams I had visited and not liked.

The person who changed the most was the Countess. Although she was still dashing up and down the mountain, it was no longer to get the place in running order. Now she tucked up her skirts to wade from room to room to peer through chinks and see what people were up to. She didn't trust anyone but appointed herself as a one-man spying organization. She even suspected Master and me! At least me – she asked me what I went to his room for in the afternoon and sniffed at my reply in a way I didn't care for. After that one awful outburst she had, she didn't call me at night any more but she was certainly after me during the day.

She guarded Vishwa like a dragon. She wouldn't even let me pass his room, and if she saw me going anywhere in that direction, she'd come running to tell me to take the other way round. I wasn't invited any more to accompany them to the bazaar but only she and Vishwa set off, with her holding a big black umbrella over them both. If they happened to pass me on the way, she would tilt the umbrella so he wouldn't be able to see me. Not that this was necessary as he never seemed to see me anyway. His eyes were always lowered and the expression on his face very serious. He had stopped joking around with the junior swamis, which I suppose was only fitting now he was a senior swami as well as about to become a spiritual leader. The Countess had fixed up a throne for him at the end of Master's room so he wouldn't have to sit on the floor and the benches along with the rest of us. When we all got together in there, Master would be at one end on his throne and Vishwa at the other on his. At Master's end there was always lots going on – everyone laughing and Master making jokes and having his fun – but Vishwa just sat very straight in the lotus pose and never looked at anyone or spoke, and only when the Countess pushed people to go and touch his feet, he'd raise a hand to bless them.

With the rains came flies and mosquitoes, and people began to fall sick with all sorts of mysterious fevers. The Countess – who was terrified of germs and had had herself pumped full of every kind of injection before coming to India – was now in a great hurry to be off with Vishwa. But before they could leave, he too came down with one of those fevers. She took him at once into her own room and kept him isolated in there with everything shut tight. She wouldn't let any of us near him. But I peeped in through the chinks, not caring whether she saw me or not. I even pleaded with her to let me come in, and once she let me but only to look at him from the door while she stood guard by his pillow. His eyes were shut and he was breathing heavily and moaning in an awful way. The Countess said I could go now, but instead I rushed up to Vishwa's bed. She tried to get between us but I pushed her out of the way and got down by the bed and held him where he lay moaning with his eyes shut. The Countess shrieked and pulled at me to get me away. I was shrieking too. We must have sounded and looked like a couple of madwomen. Vishwa opened his eyes and when he saw me there and moreover found that he was in my arms, *he* began to shriek too, as if he was frightened of me and that perhaps I was the very person he was having those terrible fever dreams about that made him groan.

It may have been this accidental shock treatment but that night Vishwa's fever came down and he began to get better. Master announced that there was going to be a Yagna or prayer-meet to give thanks for Vishwa's recovery. It was to be a really big show. Hordes of helpers came up from the town, all eager to take part in this event so as to benefit from the spiritual virtue it was expected to generate. The Meditation Hall was repainted salmon pink and the huge holy *OM* sign at one end of it was lit up all round with coloured bulbs that flashed on and off. Everyone worked with a will, and apparently good was already beginning to be generated because the rains stopped, the mud lanes in the ashram dried up, and the river flowed back into its banks. The disciples stopped quarrelling which may have been partly due to the fact that everyone could move back into their own rooms.

The Countess and Vishwa kept going down into the town to finish off with the tailors and embroiderers. They also went to the printer who was making large posters to be sent abroad to advertise Vishwa's arrival. The Countess often asked me to go with them: she was really a good-natured person and did not want me to feel left out. Especially now that she was sure there wasn't a dangerous situation working up between me and Vishwa. There she was right. I wasn't in the least interested in him and felt that the less I saw of him the better. I couldn't forget the way he had shrieked that night in the Countess's room as if I was something

How I Became a Holy Mother

impure and dreadful. But on the contrary to me it seemed that it had been *he* who was impure and dreadful with his fever dreams. I didn't even like to think what went on in them.

The Great Yagna began and it really was great. The Meditation Hall was packed and was terribly hot not only with all the people there but also because of the sacrificial flames that sizzled as more and more clarified butter was poured on them amid incantations. Everyone was smiling and singing and sweating. Master was terrific – he was right by the fire stark naked except for the tiniest bit of loincloth. His chest glistened with oil and seemed to reflect the flames leaping about. Sometimes he jumped up on his throne and waved his arms to make everyone join in louder; and when they did, he got so happy he did a little jig standing up there. Vishwa was on the other side of the Hall also on a throne. He was half reclining in his spotless white robe; he did not seem to feel the heat at all but lay there as if made out of cool marble. He reminded me of the god Shiva resting on top of his snowy mountain. The Countess sat near him, and I saw how she tried to talk to him once or twice but he took no notice of her. After a while she got up and went out which was not surprising for it really was not her scene, all that noise and singing and the neon lights and decorations.

It went on all night. No one seemed to get tired – they just got more and more worked up and the singing got louder and the fire hotter. Other people too began to do little jigs like Master's. I left the Hall and walked around by myself. It was a fantastic night, the sky sprinkled all over with stars and a moon like a melon. When I passed the Countess's door, she called me in. She was lying on her mat on the floor and said she had a migraine. No wonder, with all that noise. I liked it myself but I knew that, though she was very much attracted to Eastern religions, her taste in music was more for the Western classical type (she loved string quartets and had had a long *affaire* with a cellist). She confessed to me that she was very anxious to leave now and get Vishwa started on his career. I think she would have liked to confess more things, but I had to get on. I made my way uphill past all the different buildings till I had reached the top of the ashram and the Pillar of the Golden Rules. Here I stood and looked down.

I saw the doors of the Meditation Hall open and Master and Vishwa come out. They were lit up by the lights from the Hall. Master was big and black and naked except for his triangle of orange cloth, and Vishwa was shining in white. I saw Master raise his arm and point it up, up to the top of the ashram. The two of them reminded me of a painting I've seen of I think it was an angel pointing out a path to a pilgrim. And like a pilgrim Vishwa began to climb up the path that Master had shown him. I stood by the Pillar of the Golden Rules and waited for him. When he got to me, we didn't have to speak one word. He was like a charged dynamo; I'd never known him like that. It was more like it might have been with Master instead of Vishwa. The drums and hymns down in the Meditation Hall also reached their crescendo just then. Of course Vishwa was too taken up with what he was doing to notice anything going on round him, so it was only me that saw the Countess come uphill. She was walking quite slowly and I suppose I could have warned Vishwa in time but it seemed a pity to interrupt him, so I just let her come on up and find us.

Master finally settled everything to everyone's satisfaction. He said Vishwa and I were to be a couple, and whereas Vishwa was to be the Guru, I was to embody the Mother principle (which is also very important). Once she caught on to the idea, the Countess rather liked it. She designed an outfit for me too – a sort of flowing white silk robe, really quite becoming. You might have seen posters of Vishwa and me together, both of us in

How I Became a Holy Mother

these white robes, his hair black and curly, mine blonde and straight. I suppose we do make a good couple – anyway, people seem to like us and to get something out of us. We do our best. It's not very hard; mostly we just have to sit there and radiate. The results are quite satisfactory – I mean the effect we seem to have on people who need it. The person who really has to work hard is the Countess because she has to look after all the business and organizational end. We have a strenuous tour programme. Sometimes it's like being on a one-night stand and doing your turn and then packing up in a hurry to get to the next one. Some of the places we stay in aren't too good – motels where you have to pay in advance in case you flit – and when she is very tired, the Countess wrings her hands and says, 'My God, what am I doing here?' It must be strange for her who's been used to all the grand hotels everywhere, but of course really she likes it. It's her life's fulfilment. But for Vishwa and me it's just a job we do, and all the time we want to be somewhere else and are thinking of that other place. I often remember what Master told me, what happened to him when he looked up in Times Square and Piccadilly, and it's beginning to happen to me too. I seem to *see* those mountains and the river and temples; and then I long to be there.

Rosamond Lehmann

extract from

Invitation to the Waltz

Olivia, just past her seventeenth birthday, is longing for the evening when she can accompany her older sister, Kate, to a grown-up party for the first time. This is 1920 and the major event in the social life of the village where the girls live is the annual dance given by Lady Spencer at Meldon Towers. It proves to be an education for Olivia.

The elderly gentleman with the thick white wavy hair approached her. She had noticed him before, dancing with the youngest girls in the room one after the other; the girls drooping a little, pressed to his paunch.

'Would you be so very very kind as to spare a dance for an old fogy?'

'Oh yes, of course I will.'

'What? You will? Oh, how kind!'

He clasped her to him and set off with slow, rather laboured but elegant strides.

He repeated, 'How kind to spare a dance for old Methuselah.'

'Oh, but you're not old.'

She gave him an encouraging smile. His skin was puckered and wrinkled, tortoise-like, under the chin, his cheeks puffy and veined with purple, his eyes a bit glazed and bloodshot. Otherwise he didn't look bad. His hair was beautiful.

'What? Oh, come now – you're trying to flatter me – aren't you . . . Not that I feel my age. Not a bit of it. Far from it.'

'It's what you feel that matters, isn't it?'

'Ah, very true, very true. What a clever little lady. You've hit the nail on the head this time. It's what you feel that matters. I feel as young as ever, and that's a fact. If the heart stays young, why, then *you* stay young, whatever the calendar has to say about it – eh?'

'Yes, of course.'

Gathering impetus from this reflection, he crushed her to him and swung heavily, vigorously round on a corner... 'Shall I tell you a secret? Eh?'

'Yes, do.'

She beamed at him, all attention.

'I only took up dancing again two years ago. Before that – ah, well – circumstances were different. I'd have said my dancing days were done... over and done...' He blew a gusty sigh down her neck.

'Oh, really?' After a few more steps, she added, 'And now you've started again?'

'I have,' he said gravely. 'The ladies are very kind to me – especially the young ladies. They don't seem to mind dancing with me. They don't object.'

'I should think not,' she said warmly.

He must have had a Great Sorrow, and put it behind him. His voice was brave and ringing.

'I must confess I had my qualms at first. I thought the old machinery might creak a bit. Ha! Ha! Ha!' He swung again, quite wildly, to show how well the old machinery was working. 'As a matter of fact I took a few lessons on the quiet, just to get the hang of this jazz, you know. I was very lucky in my teacher. Doreen Delaval her name was. A thoroughly cheery soul – you know, a real jolly girl, as keen as mustard – pretty girl, too – a lady, of course. Belonged to an old county family. Fell on bad times, had to sell their place up. This little girl Doreen, she'd always had a turn for dancing, so she pulled up her socks and took to it for a living. Plucky thing to do.'

'Does she manage to – to make a living all right?'

'What? M'yes, yes. She's all right. She's doing well.'

He was beginning to breathe a trifle heavily. She ventured, 'Just say when you'd like to stop.'

'Stop? Do you want to stop?'

'Oh no, rather not. I just thought perhaps you might like to.'

Invitation to the Waltz

'Not a bit of it. I can dance all night and feel the better for it. And that's a fact.'

'Can you really?'

She looked up at him admiringly, for he was still a bit put out, suspicious.

'Yes, and I don't lie abed next morning. I don't coddle myself – never have. That's what's kept me fit. But of course if you want a rest . . .'

'Oh *no*. I'd much rather go on.'

'Afraid I don't know many of these new-fangled steps. I don't get much practice.'

'Oh, I don't mind. I'm not a bit well up in them either.'

But this wasn't the right answer. A silence ensued, and she amended, 'As a matter of fact, you dance beautifully. You're so frightfully easy to dance with.'

'What? Do you think so? Ah, I'm afraid you're a flatterer. What? Aren't you?'

'Not at all.'

Curious: he had a sort of family likeness to Major Skinner; but – owing perhaps to the loftier moral tone – he was somehow more cloying, more slippery; and far more uneasy and exacting.

'Ah, well, I dare say some folk would call me an old fool.'

'Why should they?'

'What? Undignified, you know. Making myself ridiculous.'

'How absurd. I'm sure nobody could think so.'

'What? D'you think it's absurd? Well, so do I. But folk are apt to get in a groove as they grow older, you know. They lose their resilience, their elasticity. Their horizons contract.'

'I expect they forget they were young themselves once.'

'Ah, that's it.' He was delighted. 'They forget. They get narrow-minded.'

'Narrow-minded people are such a bore. I don't think

it matters what they say. They're not worth bothering about. Where I live I shock some of the old frumps dreadfully because I go for walks without my hat on.'

'Oh, so you're unconventional too, are you? Then you and I'll get on like a house afire. I thought we should. We've got a lot in common. I felt it directly I saw you.' He pressed her to him, sighed richly. 'The gods were good to me, little lady. They granted me a spirit that can never grow old. Whatever they denied me, they granted me that. I suppose that's why you young folk don't seem to mind my company.' He paused, but this time she failed him and remained silent, and soon he added with another, thinner sigh, 'All the same, one feels lonely sometimes.'

'I hope you're not lonely,' she said politely.

'What? Lonely? Ah well, I can't complain. Life can be very rich in spite of everything. One can be alone and yet not lonely, can't one? One has one's philosophy.'

She tried to give him a look of bright interest, but it was getting harder. He does need so much bolstering up.

'All the same, there are times when one longs for real companionship – for the touch of a vanished hand...' He lowered his voice to add, 'I lost my dear wife three years ago. We were everything to each other.'

What was it in the way he said this that froze the springs of sympathy? Perhaps the way he dropped his voice; or a sort of glibness, as if there were a crack, an unsound place concealed... But of course it must have been a terrible grief.

'I'm so sorry. How awful for you.'

'Thank you. I knew you were sympathetic. Your voice told me so. Gentle and low, an excellent thing in woman.' He pressed her again. 'Ah, sympathy's a wonderful gift.'

The band stopped. He released her, clapped enthusiastically, mopped his face. He was perspiring freely.

Invitation to the Waltz

'Ah, that was splendid – splendid. Now what about an ice? Eh?' He looked at her roguishly. 'That 'ud slip down nicely, wouldn't it? Come on now. Let's see how many we can account for. I'll take you on!'

She followed him, wanly simpering. His schoolboy spirits weren't infectious.

* * *

Tony said, 'Look here, don't you ever ride?'

'No,' said Kate. 'I never do. When I was very small we had a pony. But the truth is – since the war we haven't been able to afford anything much.'

'How sickening for you. You would so love it.'

'I'm sure I would. It's always been one of the things I wanted most – to have a horse of my own.'

He said with his quick engaging diffidence, 'You'd look corking on a horse. You're simply made for it.'

'Am I?'

She smiled, looking over his shoulders with shining unseeing eyes.

'I could teach you in no time.'

'Do you think you could?'

'I know I could.' He continued eagerly, 'And I could mount you too. I've got the very horse for a beginner. An old mare of my father's, as comfortable and quiet as anything. . . . Why not?'

'Well, for one thing I haven't any clothes.'

'Oh, bother clothes. We'll find you a pair of breeches.'

'All right. I'd love to.'

'I'll take you a few times round our big field for a start, and then as soon as you've got confidence we could go up on to the downs.'

'Oh, how glorious!'

They looked at one another, radiant.

485

Rosamond Lehmann

* * *

Dance after dance with an old fogy. Three running now, pressed to his paunch. It seemed as if it might go on for ever. Not even Reggie to the rescue. Reggie must be at the buffet with the Martins. Neither he nor they had appeared upon the floor for a considerable time. No hope, no help. Programme a blank right on till Number 19, and that seemed now distant and improbable as a dream.

His name was Mr Verity. He spoke of the little shack he had recently acquired in the vicinity; of the wonder of the sunsets viewed from his study window. He mentioned his best friends, his books, and quoted more than once from the Poet. Gather ye rosebuds, he said. Also, Then come kiss me sweet and twenty. Also, Si joonesse savvy. He asked her if she would take tea one day with a lonely old man; his housekeeper, dear devoted old soul, would make her welcome. He talked a good deal too about people with titles whom he fished and shot with.

Her senses shrank away from him. They seemed to shout their frantic distaste into his heedless, his leathery ear. I don't like you. I don't like touching you. I hate dancing with you. I can't bear you. She gave up smiling; almost gave up answering. Her face set stiffly, in utter dejection. Next dance I'll say I'm booked and go and hide in the cloakroom. But he'll know it's an excuse. It'll hurt his feelings. He'll go away and think, I'm a lonely old man. Oh, help! help! Will no one help?

As she accompanied him for the fourth time towards the ballroom, Marigold appeared suddenly from nowhere, caught at her arm; whisked her aside, drew her far away without a word to him or a backward look.

'I thought you needed rescuing.'

'Oh, I *did*! You angel!'

She clasped Marigold's hand in pure relief and gratitude.

'I thought sudden tactics would be the most effictitious ... You did look down-hearted.'

'I thought I'd never get away from him.'

'I know what he's like – the old octopus ...' Her voice was harsh with contempt. 'He fished and fished for an invitation to this. He's our neighbour, worse luck. He's taken that cottage by the south gate. He tells everyone Daddy and he were lads together at Cambridge, and that Daddy begged him to come and settle near him. I call him Johnny Walker. Did he ask you to tea?'

'Yes. He did.'

'I thought as much. He's always trying that on. Mum thinks he's harmless, but of course he's not likely to be up to any of his tricks with her. They talk politics and county together, and he butters her up, and she thinks he's so sensible and so fond of young people and so picturesque and old-world with his white hair. In fact she was quite umbrageous with me when I called him a dirty old man. But of course Mum's hopeless. She thinks virgins are sacred to all men – you know, all the Tennyson flower stuff. Of course he's the most infernal snob too, but she can't see that. Still, I must admit he's quite different with the elderly ones. You wouldn't know him. It's the young ones that rouse him – especially the ones in their teens.'

'How queer ... Have you been to tea with him?'

'Catch me. He did try it on once, but I said could I bring my governess, so he changed the subject.'

'What d'you suppose he'd do?'

'Oh, fumble about a bit, I expect – you know, feel your muscle and mess about with your hands pretending he's a fortune-teller, and measure how tall you were against him – that sort of feeble pawing. It's a sort of disease old men get, I believe.'

'Yes, I think it must be.'

'They go native. Honestly it's a warning. Did he tell you he'd got a grown-up son and daughter?'

'No, he didn't. He kept on hinting he was all alone in the world.'

'He would. But he's got two children, and they won't live with him. Mum thinks it's this modern selfishness, but I bet the trouble was he was too sprightly for them. Fancy having a lasciverous old father prodding and stroking every girl you brought into the house. Mine's not like that – not yet, anyway. Is yours?'

'Oh no. Not in the least.'

Dad prodding young girls . . . Olivia giggled.

'Though he adores a mild flirt with the pretty ones.'

'I don't think mine even does that,' said Olivia, after reflection.

She saw Johnny Walker standing alone by the ballroom door, pretending not to watch them out of the corner of his eye. He knows we're talking about him. How was it that Marigold, so sheltered, so well brought up, knew so much, in such a shrewd cynical, coarse-grained way, about the facts of life? – had on the tip of her tongue the best sort of snub for a tiresome old man, so that he knew it was no go, so that he feared her? Whereas oneself, one would never know what to say, one never spotted hidden motives, swallowed any story, trusted everybody, would very likely land oneself in a mess one day . . . Even now, seeing him furtively watch Marigold's pert expressive face, feeling him brood sheepishly over the ungracious, the wanton, flouting way they'd left him in the lurch, yet not dare to approach them, feeling the sickly collapse of his self-esteem, even now she was tempted to reassure him somehow, apologise, show him she was sorry. For it was Major Skinner all over again – the painfulness of seeing an old white-haired person humiliated before youth, ashamed of wanting the thing he wanted. He'd never get it. It was too late. He was old and done for. How his heart must ache . . . Oh dear! I wish I could want to comfort you . . . She saw the faintly stricken expression on his face. He stood there

Invitation to the Waltz

representing the pathos, the indignity of being old; of the dancing days being done. Oh, maidens! he cried in vain. He wouldn't dare ask any more of them to dance tonight. Soon he would creep off home. And Marigold had done this to him without an instant's compunction or compassion ... out of kindness to, pity for, oneself? ... out of pure malice and scorn for him? A strange impulse, a curious action – one of Marigold's. Why, whence, out of her new estrangement and excitement, had she noticed, and darted?

'There's Rex waiting for me. I must fly. Are you enjoying yourself? Have you had lots of partners?'

'I haven't got very much more booked,' admitted Olivia. 'Only Number nineteen.'

'Oh, you must fill up or he'll pounce again.' She gave a chuckle. 'Who d'you fancy? Oh, there's Timmy Douglas. He's so sweet. He's my favourite man – almost – no, quite. He's sure not to be full up, poor darling. When his wife's dancing with someone else, he mostly just stands and waits. Come on, I'll introduce you.'

She saw, against the wall inside the ballroom, a young man, tall, pale, standing and waiting. He seemed to be smiling; but on a closer view, it seemed not to be a smile after all. It was a queer taut set of the muscles round his mouth.

'He's a marvellous dancer,' said Marigold. 'You'd never dream he's . . .' She lowered her voice abruptly as they came near to him, and her last words were inaudible – stone something or other, it sounded like.

She cried, 'Timmy, hullo!'

He had been looking towards her without recognition, but now his face lit up faintly.

'Marigold?'

His voice had an edge of question. He put his hand out in a wooden way, straight in front of him, and she clasped it in both her own.

'Timmy darling, I meant to come and find you ages ago.

489

But I've been so whizzed about all the evening. Are you happy?'

Her voice had a softer, more caressing note than one had ever heard before. He answered with not quite convincing enthusiasm, 'Yes, rather.' He waited a moment, then said hesitatingly: 'When can I have a dance, Marigold?'

Then he waited again. His face became suddenly patient and listening. His voice was patient too, quiet, flat, rapid. He didn't look at her.

'Oh, darling! I'm so full up. Isn't it sickening?'

'That's bad luck – for me.'

Patient and cheerful.

'Timmy, I've brought Olivia Curtis to dance with you.' He turned his head slightly and sharply; out came his hand again. His eyes, upon which the full lids constantly opened and fell with a long spasmodic movement, were opaque, navy blue in colour, like those of a new-born baby.

'How d'you do?'

The smile that wasn't a smile tightened the muscles of mouth and cheek.

'Olivia's very nice with her practically black hair turned round each side of her face in a plaited bun, and a red dress.'

Had she really said that? The dream had come on again.

'I must fly, Timmy darling. I'll come back later, for sure and certain.' Brushing past Olivia, her fingers clung for a second on her arm, she whispered fiercely, *'Did you hear*? He's . . .' but again the last word, sharply muted, was lost as she fled on.

He stood without moving, his head a little bent as if he were listening to her going. He said in his pleasant flat voice, 'She's got more vitality than half a dozen ordinary people. She just leaves it in the air around her, wherever she's been.'

Invitation to the Waltz

It was quite true. It was the secret of Marigold, that one had never been able to define. She agreed, pleased, surprised. It was an unusual thing to say.

'It's a marvellous possession,' he said. 'The only gift I'd trouble a fairy godmother for. If you've got it, you can't be beaten. What's more, you make other people imagine they can't be . . .'

He smiled now, a real smile, but faint. He himself looked as if he lacked vitality. He was pale and thin, rather worn-looking. He had beautifully cut long delicate features and straight light hair growing rather far back above a high frail prominent forehead. He gave an impression of scrupulous cleanness and neatness.

'Would you care to dance?' he said. 'I'm afraid I'm apt to barge into people. The room's pretty full, isn't it?'

'Rather full.'

She looked at him, puzzled. Once again he had turned an obvious statement into a question. She looked at him, and in a sudden stab flash of realization, saw him as one isolated, remote, a figure alone in a far place. He was . . .

'However if you don't mind steering a bit. I generally manage more or less.'

He stood and waited, crooking his right arm ready to receive her. She saw that he was blind. She led him out on to the floor and they started to dance.

I'll guide you, I'll look after you. Depend on me . . . Blinded in the war? There wasn't a scar – nothing to proclaim it – only the opaque swimming irises between the heavily twitching lids; and the set of his face. His hand, holding hers, vibrated as if it had a separate, infinitely sensitive life – long fingers, exquisite nails. He'll guess what I'm like from my voice, from touching me. What will he guess? They say blind people always know, you can't deceive them.

They collided badly with another couple, who looked at him in cold surprise.

'Sorry,' he said pleasantly, 'my fault.'

He waited while they moved on. She saw the girl's face alter suddenly, not in pity, but in a look of avid curiosity. She whispered something to her partner, they both turned to stare at him. How dare they stare like that! ...

'I'm sorry,' she said. 'I never saw them. You dance so beautifully, I just forgot to steer.'

He looked a little bit pleased.

'We used to dance a lot at the place I was – St Dunstan's, you know. I don't do much in that line now. Molly's awfully keen on it. I wish she got more.'

'Is that your wife?'

'Yes, she's dancing, I think – I believe she's dancing with Rollo Spencer.'

'Oh yes, I see her.'

She saw Rollo quite close to them, dancing with a shortish person in rather a dowdy royal-blue dress – quite commonplace, quite insignificant. She had a good deal of straight brown hair, inclined to wispiness at the sides, blue eyes, some moles on her face, a weather-beaten skin without powder or make-up. There was nothing one could say about her, think about her. Olivia searched in vain for traces of spiritual intensity, renunciation, suffering, such as might fitly mark the face of one devoting, sacrificing all to a blind husband. She looked sensible, capable, her eyes clear and hard. Rollo must be dancing with her out of niceness. She glanced at her husband and his partner, but only for a minute, without apparent interest. I suppose you get used – I suppose you soon get used. ... It all depends how you let yourself think about it. Even now, already, it was getting quite easy to behave towards him as his simplicity, his utter non-assumption of the role of martyr, his rather negative, low-pitched but unforced cheerfulness demanded – to treat him as one like other men. It was as if he were tacitly demonstrating: You see, it isn't a tragedy at all. You needn't be sorry for me. ....

Invitation to the Waltz

Yet the first image persisted in the background of her mind: a figure in its essence far apart.

'The Spencers are most frightfully nice, aren't they?' he said. 'They've been most awfully decent to us.'

'Do you live near?'

'Oh yes, I'm one of their tenants. We've got that little house beyond the church – about a mile away. Do you know it? Cherry Tree Cottage it's called – and it's actually got a cherry tree too.' His voice was more lively now. He liked talking about his house. 'Lady Spencer's helped us no end – Sir John too . . . We're chicken-farmers. Thanks to them, we've worked up quite a big connection – that's the right term, isn't it? We supply all the eggs and poultry for the house too.'

'Do you like doing it?'

'Oh yes, I like it all right. There's more in chickens than you'd think.' He smiled. 'I used to think they were the most ghastly feeble animals. If anybody'd told me I'd be keeping them for a living, I'd have – well, I don't know what. As a matter of fact, I wanted to be an architect – that's what I was keen on. But if you really take up a thing you can't help getting interested – don't you think?'

'Oh yes, I quite agree.'

She searched his face – it was placid; his voice, now he was surer of his ground, equable and very young-sounding. How did one look after chickens when one was blind?

'Molly's awfully keen on it, luckily. In fact it was she who got the whole thing going. She's awfully practical and good at running things. She does most of the dirty work, really. It keeps us busy. It's all jolly scientific these days, a proper chicken farm, I can tell you.'

'Is it? How frightfully interesting.'

'Molly's always lived in the country, but I'm a London bird. I didn't think I'd like it at first, but I've got quite used to it. I must say one does feel better – don't you think? Sort of more peaceful. It's nice for the infant too,

493

to be brought up in the country. She loves animals. She's got a pet duckling that follows her everywhere.'

His smile spread clear over his face.

'Have you got a little girl?'

'Rather.'

'How old is she?'

'Getting on for two. She runs about like anything, and chatters all day. She's pretty forward, I think.'

'What's her name?'

'Elizabeth. Molly wanted Marjorie and I wanted Susan, so we split the difference with Elizabeth. It's a good name, don't you think?'

'Yes. I love the old English names.'

She was moved by his simple pride and pleasure in his possessions – his family, his farm, everything that told him he was a man with a background, a place in the world; a successful grown-up man who had by his own labours established his security. But he looked so young to be a husband and father – not more than twenty-two. Molly didn't look nearly so young. Perhaps she'd been his nurse. Probably he'd never seen her. . . . He'd never see his daughter either. One must try not to let that seem too pathetic. It was the sort of thing that brought a too-easy sob in the throat. It doesn't matter, it doesn't matter really.

'Marigold rides over to see us pretty often,' he said. 'We look forward to that.' (It was queer really that Marigold had never mentioned him. . . . But she was so secretive.) 'She'd buck anybody up, wouldn't she? She's so frightfully amusing, isn't she? Really witty. . . . Otherwise it's a quiet life. Not that I mind. I play the gramophone a lot in the evenings. I like music awfully. But I wish Molly got out more. It's dull for her.'

She plucked up courage to say timidly: 'Do you – can you find your way about – fairly well in your house?'

'Oh Lord, yes. Anywhere. Like a cat, you know. I see in the dark.' He smiled at his joke, adding mildly but

Invitation to the Waltz

emphatically, 'Oh, Molly's not tied like that – not to that extent. I can do pretty well everything for myself.'

She saw him going up and downstairs, dressing, undressing, feeding himself, patiently listening to his gramophone, changing the needle, walking over his farm, scattering grain to the hens, painstakingly independent, giving no trouble.

She murmured, 'I know – I'm sure – you're simply . . . It's so difficult to realize there's anything wrong. I hadn't an idea.'

'Oh well,' he said equably, 'it's all a question of one's point of view, isn't it? One's taught not to – well, not to think of it as a misfortune, you know.'

'When were you – how long ago . . .?'

'June 1918.' His voice was even. 'I went out from school. I only had three months of it. A sniper got me plunk behind the eyes.'

She was silent. War, a cloud on early adolescence, weighing not too darkly, long lifted. . . . A cousin in the flying corps killed, the cook's nephew gone down at Jutland, rumour of the death of neighbours' sons (that included Marigold's elder brother) and, among the village faces, about half a dozen familiar ones that had disappeared and never come back . . . and butter and sugar rations; and the lawn dug up for potatoes (the crop had failed); and knitting scratchy mittens and mufflers; and Dad being a special constable and getting bronchitis from it: that was about all that war had meant. And during that safe, that sheltered unthinking time, he had gone out to fight, and had his eyes destroyed. She saw him reel backwards, his hands on his face, crying; I'm blind . . . or coming to in hospital, not realizing, thinking it was the middle of the night. . . . Imagination stretched shudderingly towards his experience. She had a moment's dizziness, a moment's wild new conscious indignation and revolt, thinking for the first time: This was war – never, never to be forgiven or forgotten, for his sake.

I'd stay with you, I'd look after you. I'd be your eyes and show you everything. Oh – is she nice enough to you? But if it was me, I'd be too sorry, I'd upset him. She's sensible, she's matter-of-fact, she takes it for granted. How dare she. . . . She keeps his life practical and orderly, keeps him cheerful. They've got a child. So he must love her. And it doesn't matter to him that she's not young or pretty. . . . Yes, all his gratitude, all his solicitude were for her.

The band stopped.

'Thank you very much indeed,' he said. 'I'm just getting the hang of the room. It's jolly big, isn't it?'

'Yes, very big, with big mirrors in the panels, and chandeliers. It's very bright – the light, I mean.'

'I can remember photographs of this house in some paper. I remember it quite well. It's a beautiful house. A perfect specimen, but just unconventional enough to have a character of its own.'

He stood in the middle of the room, thinking about it.

She said nervously, 'What would you like to do? Shall we go and sit somewhere?'

'Rather. Anything you like . . .'

'Would you like an ice – or anything?'

'Yes, what about an ice? A drink anyway – I could do with a drink.'

He laid his fingers on the tip of her elbow, and she led him to the dining-room. He walked with a light quick step straight on his course, his touch on her arm almost imperceptible; not at all like one's idea of the shuffle and grope of a blind man. Only his head looked somehow vulnerable and wary. She felt important, self-assured, helping him, not shy or self-conscious in spite of people staring.

'Here's a beautiful armchair,' she said.

'Thanks.'

He lowered himself into it after a second's hesitation.

'Wait here, I'll get you a drink. What would you like?'

Invitation to the Waltz

'Oh, anything cool, thanks. I'm a teetotaller these days.'

Waiting at the buffet for orangeade, she watched him take out his silver case and a matchbox and light his cigarette, slowly and carefully. Then he smoothed his hair, adjusted his tie, brushed his sleeve, his shoulders. In case I've left any mark, powder, a hair or anything. He's afraid of looking slovenly, neglected, ridiculous, and not knowing it. That's why he's neater, more polished up than anybody else. He didn't smoke his cigarette, but let it burn away between his long fingers. He sat back, his head slightly bent, the muscles taut in his face, waiting.

Now he looks like a blind man.

He was very easy to talk to. She chatted to him without effort or embarrassment until the next dance began, and his wife came strolling towards them. She walked with her square shoulders hunched. The skin of her neck and arms was rather rough and red, and her legs were short, muscular, slightly bandy. She looked like a hockey-playing cross-country-striding person, in striking contrast to his pallor, his elegant narrow-hipped length.

'Hullo!' she said. Her voice was rather rough too, with a twang in it.

He stirred without lifting his face.

'Oh hullo, Molly!' He added politely to Olivia, 'Can I introduce my wife?'

She smiled, meeting Olivia's shy and eager beam. Her smile was limited, but direct and pleasant, and her eyes were nice too, a clear bright blue.

Reggie was approaching. He looked a little congested about the face. He mustn't meet Timmy.

'Goodbye,' she said, and walked away.

She heard him say after a moment: 'Has she gone?'

It was just a question. No suspicion, regret, or relief in it. No interest.

Doris Lessing
The New Man

About three miles on the track to the station a smaller overgrown road branched to the Manager's House. This house had been built by the Rich Mitchells for their manager. Then they decided to sell a third of their farm, with the house ready for its owner. It stood empty a couple of years, with sacks of grain and ox-hides in it. The case had been discussed and adjudicated on the verandas of the district: no, Rich Mitchell was not right to sell that part of his farm, which was badly watered and poorish soil, except for a hundred acres or so. At the very least he should have thrown in a couple of miles of his long vlei with the lands adjacent to it. No wonder Rich Mitchell was rich (they said); and when they met him their voices had a calculated distance: 'Sold your new farm yet, Mich?' No, he hadn't sold it, nor did he, for one year, then another. But the rich can afford to wait. (As they said on the verandas.)

The farm was bought by a Mr Rooyen who had already gone broke farming down Que Que way. The Grants went to visit, Mrs Grant in her new silk, Mr Grant grumbling because it was the busy season. The small girl did not go, she refused, she wanted to stay in the kitchen with old Tom the cookboy, where she was happy, watching him make butter.

That evening, listening with half an ear to the parents' talk, it was evident things weren't too good. Mr Rooyen hadn't a penny of his own; he had bought the farm through the Land Bank, and was working on an eight-hundred pounds loan. What it amounted to was, it was a gamble on the first season. It's all very well,' said Mr Grant, summing up with the reluctant critical note in his voice that meant he knew he would have to help Mr Rooyen, would do so, but found it all too much. And, sure enough, in the dry season the Rooyen cattle were running on Grant land and using the Grant well. But Mr Rooyen had become 'the new man in the Manager's House'.

The first season wasn't too bad, so the small girl gathered from the talk on the verandas, and Mr Rooyen might make out after all. But he was very poor. Mrs Grant, when they had too much cheese or butter, or baked, sent supplies over by the cook. In the second year Mr Grant lent Mr Rooyen two hundred pounds to tide him over. The small girl knew that the new neighbour belonged for ever to that category of people who, when parting from the Grants, would wring their hands and say in a low, half-ashamed voice, 'You've been very good to me and I'll never forget it.'

The first time she saw the new farmer, who never went anywhere, was when the Grants went into the station and gave Mr Rooyen a lift. He could not afford a car yet. He stood on the track waiting for the Grants, and behind him the road to his house was even more overgrown with bushes and grass, like a dry river-bed between the trees. He sat in the back, answering Mr Grant's questions about how things were going. She did not notice him much, or rather refused to notice him, because she definitely did not like him, although he was nothing she had not known all her life. A tallish man, dressed in bush khaki, blue eyes inflamed by the sun, he was burned – not a healthy reddish brown – but a mahogany colour, because he was never out of the sun, never stopped working. This colour in a white man, the small girl already knew, meant a desperate struggling poverty and it usually preceded going broke or getting very ill. But the reason she did not like him, or that he scared her, was the violence of

The New Man

his grievance. The hand which lay on the back of the car seat behind Mr Grant trembled slightly; his voice trembled as he spoke of Rich Mitchell, his neighbour, who had a vlei seven miles long and would neither sell nor rent him any of it. 'It isn't right,' he kept saying. 'He doesn't make use of my end. Perhaps his cattle graze there a couple of weeks in the dry season, but that's all.' All this meant that his cattle would be running with the Grants' again when the grass was low. More: that he was appealing, through Mr Grant, for justice, to the unconstituted council of farmers who settled these matters on their verandas.

That night Mr Grant said, It's all very well! a good many times. Then he rang up Mr Matthews (Glasgow Bob) from the Glenisle Farm; and Mr Paynter (Tobacco Paynter) from Bellevue; and Mr Van Doren (The Dutchman) from Blue Hills. Their farms adjoined Rich Mitchell's.

Soon after, the Grants went into the station again. At the last minute they had remembered to ring up and ask Mr Rooyen if he wanted a lift. He did. It wasn't altogether convenient, particularly for the small girl, because two-thirds of the back seat was packed to the roof with plough parts being sent into town for repair. And beside Mrs Grant on the front seat was a great parcel full of dead chickens ready for sale to the hotel. 'It's no bother,' said Mrs Grant, to Mr Rooyen, 'the child can sit on your knee.'

The trouble was that the small girl was definitely not a child. She was pretty certain she was no longer a small girl, either. For one thing, her breasts had begun to sprout, and while this caused her more embarrassment than pleasure, she handled her body in a proud gingerly way that made it impossible, as she would have done even a season before, to snuggle in on to the grown-up's lap. She got out of the car in a mood of fine proud withdrawal, not looking at Mr Rooyen as he fitted himself into the narrow space on the back seat. Then, with a clumsy fastidiousness, she perched on the very edge of his bare bony knees and supported herself with two hands on the back of the front seat. Mr Rooyen's arms were about her waist, as if she were indeed a child, and they trembled, as she had known they would – as his voice still trembled, talking about Rich Mitchell. But soon he stopped talking. The car sped forward through the heavy, red-dust-laden trees, rocking and bouncing over the dry ruts, and she was jerked back to fit against the body of Mr Rooyen, whose fierceness was that of lonely tenderness, as she knew already, though never before in her life had she met it. She longed for the ride to be over, while she sat squeezed, pressed, suffering, in the embrace of Mr Rooyen, a couple of feet behind the Grants. She ignored, so far as was possible, with politeness; was stiff with resistance; looked at the backs of her parents' heads and marvelled at their blindness. 'If you only knew what your precious Mr Rooyen was doing to your precious daughter. . . .'

When it was time to come home from the station, she shed five years and became petulant and wilful: she would sit on her mother's knee, not on Mr Rooyen's. Because now the car was stacked with groceries, and it was a choice of one knee or the other. 'Why, my dear child,' said the fond Mrs Grant, pleased at this rebirth of the charming child in her daughter. But the girl sat as stiffly on her mother's knee as she had on the man's, for she felt his eyes continually returning to her, over her mother's shoulder, in need, or in fear, or in guilt.

When the car stopped at the turning to the Manager's House, she got off her mother's knee, and would not look at Mr Rooyen. Who then did something really not allowable, not in the code, for he bent, squeezed her in his great near-black hairy arms and kissed her. Her mother laughed, gay and encouraging. Mr Grant said merely, 'Good-bye, Rooyen,' as the tall forlorn fierce man walked off to his house along the grass-river road.

The girl got into the back seat, silent. Her mother

The New Man

had let her down, had let her new breasts down by that gay social laugh. As for her father, she looked at his profile, absorbed in the business of starting the car and setting it in motion, but the profile said nothing. She said, resentful, 'Who does he think he *is*, kissing me.' And Mrs Grant said briskly, 'My dear child, why ever not?' At which Mr Grant gave his wife a quick, grave look, but remained silent. And this comforted the girl, supported her.

She thought about Mr Rooyen. Or rather, she felt him – felt the trembling of his arms, felt as if he were calling to her. One hot morning, saying she was going for a walk, she set off to his house. When she got there she was overheated and tired and needed a drink. Of course there was no one there. The house was two small rooms, side by side under corrugated iron, with a lean-to kitchen behind. In front was a narrow brick veranda with pillars. Plants stood in painted paraffin tins, and they were dry and limp. She went into the first room. It had two old leather armchairs, a sideboard with a mirror that reflected trees and blue sky and long grass from the low window, and an eating table. The second room had an iron bed and a chest-of-drawers. She looked, long and thoughtful, at the narrow bed, and her heart was full of pity because of the lonely trembling of Mr Rooyen's arms. She went into the tiny kitchen. It had an iron Carron Dover stove, where the fire was out. A wooden table had some cold meat on it with a piece of gauze over it. The meat smelled sourish. Flies buzzed. Up the legs of the table small black ants trickled. There was no servant visible. After getting herself a glass of tepid-tasting water from the filter, she walked very slowly through the house again, taking in everything, then went home.

At supper she said, casual, 'I went to see Mr Rooyen today.'

Her father looked quickly at her mother, who dropped her eyes and crumbled bread. That meant they had discussed the incident of the kiss. 'How is he?' asked Mrs Grant, casual and bright. 'He wasn't there.' Her father said nothing.

Next day she lapsed back into her private listening world. In the afternoon she read, but the book seemed childish. She wept enjoyably, alone. At supper she looked at her parents from a long way off, and knew it was a different place where she had never been before. They were smaller, definitely. She saw them clear: the rather handsome phlegmatic man at one end of the table, brown in his khaki (but not mahogany, he could afford not to spend every second of his waking hours in the sun). And at the other end a brisk, airy, efficient woman in a tailored striped dress. The girl thought: I came out of them; and shrank away in dislike from knowing how she had. She looked at these two strange people and felt Mr Rooyen's arms call to her across three miles of veld. Before she went to bed she stood for a long time gazing at the small light from his house.

Next morning she went to his house again. She wore a new dress, which her mother had made. It was a childish dress that ignored her breasts, which is why she chose it. Not that she expected to see Mr Rooyen. She wanted to see the small, brick, ant and fly-ridden house, walk through it, and come home again.

When she got there, there was not a sign of anyone. She fetched water in a half-paraffin tin from the kitchen and soaked the half-dead plants. Then she sat on the edge of the brick veranda with her feet in the hot dust. Quite soon Mr Rooyen came walking up through the trees from the lands. He saw her, but she could not make out what he thought. She said, girlish, 'I've watered your plants for you.'

'The boy's supposed to water them,' he said, sounding angry. He strode on to the veranda, into the room behind and out at the back in three great paces shouting, 'Boy! Boy!'

The New Man

A shouting went on, because the cook had gone to sleep under a tree. The girl watched the man run himself a glass of water from the filter, gulp it down, run another, gulp that. He came back to the veranda. Standing like a great black hot tower over her, he demanded, 'Does your father know you're here?'

She shook her head, primly. But she felt he was unfair. He would not have liked her father to know how his arms had trembled and pressed her in the car.

He returned to the room, and sat, knees sprawling apart, his arms limp, in one of the big ugly leather chairs. He looked at her steadily, his mouth tight. He had a thin mouth. The lips were burned and black from the sun, and the cracks in them showed white and unhealthy.

'Come here,' he said, softly. It was tentative and she chose not to hear it, remained sitting with her back to him. Over her shoulder she asked, one neighbour to another, 'Have you fixed up your vlei with Mr Mitchell yet?' He sat looking at her, his head lowered. His eyes were really ugly, she thought, red with sun-glare. He was an ugly man, she thought. For now she was wishing – not that she had not come – but that he had not come. Then she could have walked, secretly and delightfully, through the house, and gone, secretly. And tomorrow she could have come and watered his plants again. She imagined saying to him, meeting him by chance somewhere, 'Guess who was watering your plants all that time?'

'You're a pretty little girl,' he said. He was grinning. The grin had no relationship to the lonely hunger of his touch on her in the car. Nor was it a grin addressed to a pretty little girl – far from it. She looked at the grin, repudiating it for her future, and was glad that she wore this full, childish dress.

'Come and sit on my knee,' he tried again, in the way people had been saying through her childhood: come and sit on my knee. She obligingly went, like a small girl, and balanced herself on a knee that felt all bone under her.

His hands came out and gripped her thin arms. His face changed from the ugly grin to the look of lonely hunger. She was sitting upright, using her feet as braces on the floor to prevent herself being pulled into the trembling man's body. Unable to pull her, he leaned his face against her neck, so that she felt his eyelashes and eyebrows hairy on her skin, and he muttered, 'Maureen, Maureen, Maureen, my love.'

She stood up, smoothing down her silly dress. He opened his eyes, sat still, hands on his knees. His mouth was half-open, he breathed irregularly, and his eyes stared, not at her, but at the brick floor where tiny black ants trickled.

She sat herself on the chair opposite, tucking her dress well in around her legs. In the silence the roof cracked suddenly overhead from the heat. There was the sound of a car on the main road half a mile off. The car came nearer. Neither the girl nor the man moved. Their eyes met from time to time, frowning, serious, then moved away to the ants, to the window, anywhere. He still breathed fast. She was full of revulsion against his body, yet she remembered the heat of his face, the touch of his lashes on her neck, and his loneliness spoke to her through her dislike of him, so that she longed to assuage him. The car stopped outside the house. She saw, without surprise, that it was her father. She remained where she was as Mr Grant stepped out of the car, and came in, his eyes narrowed because of the glare and the heat under the iron roof. He nodded at his daughter, and said, 'How do you do, Rooyen?' There being only two chairs, the men were standing; but the girl knew what she had to do, so she went out on to the veranda, and sat on the hot rough brick, spreading her blue skirts wide so that air could come under them and cool her thighs.

Now the two men were sitting in the chairs.

'Like some tea, Mr Grant?'

'I could do with a cup.'

The New Man

Mr Rooyen shouted, 'Tea, boy!' and a shout came back from the kitchen. The girl could hear the iron stove being banged and blown into heat. It was nearly midday and she wondered what Mr Rooyen would have for lunch. That rancid beef?

She thought: if I were Maureen I wouldn't leave him alone, I'd look after him. I suppose she's some silly woman in an office in town. ... But since he loved Maureen, she became her, and heard his voice saying: Maureen, Maureen, my love. Simultaneously she held her thin brown arms into the sun and felt how they were dark dry brown, she felt the flesh melting off hard lank bones.

'I spoke to Tobacco Paynter last night on the telephone, and he said he thinks Rich Mitchell might very well be in a different frame of mind by now, he's had a couple of good seasons.'

'If a couple of good seasons could make any difference to Mr Mitchell,' came Mr Rooyen's hot, resentful voice. 'But thank you, Mr Grant. Thank you.'

'He's close,' said her father. 'Near. Canny. Careful. Those North Country people are, you know.' He laughed. Mr Rooyen laughed too, after a pause – he was a Dutchman, and had to work out the phrase 'North Country'.

'If I were you,' said Mr Grant, 'I'd get the whole of the lands on either side of the vlei under mealies the first season. Rich has never had it under cultivation, and the soil'd go sixteen bags to the acre for the first couple of seasons.'

'Yes, I've been thinking that's what I should do.'

She heard the sounds of tea being brought in.

Mr Rooyen said to her through the door, 'Like a cup?' but she shook her head. She was thinking that if she were Maureen she'd fix up the house for him. Her father's next remark was therefore no surprise to her.

'Thought of getting married, Rooyen?'

He said bitterly, 'Take a look at this house, Mr Grant.'

'Well, you could build on a couple of rooms for about thirty, I reckon. I'll lend you my building boy. And a wife'd get it all spick-and-span in no time.'

Soon the two men came out, and Mr Rooyen stood on the veranda as she and her father got into the car and drove off. She waved to him, politely, with a polite smile.

She waited for her father to say something, but although he gave her several doubtful looks, he did not. She said, 'Mr Rooyen's in love with a girl called Maureen.'

'Did he say so?'

'Yes, he did.'

'Well,' he said, talking to her, as was his habit, one grown person to another, 'I'd say it was time he got married.'

'Yes.'

'Everything all right?' he inquired, having worked out exactly the right words to use.

'Yes, thank you.'

'Good.'

That season Rich Mitchell leased a couple of miles of his big vlei to Mr Rooyen, with a promise of sale later. Tobacco Paynter's wife got a governess from England, called Miss Betty Blunt, and almost at once Mr Rooyen and she were engaged. Mrs Paynter complained that she could never keep a governess longer than a couple of months, they always got married, but she couldn't have been too angry about it, because she laid on a big wedding for them, and all the district was there. The girl was asked if she would be a bridesmaid, but she very politely refused. On the track to the station there was a new signpost pointing along a well-used road which said: 'The Big Vlei Farm C. Rooyen.'

Olivia Manning

extract from

The Spoilt City

The first book of Olivia Manning's Balkan trilogy, The Great Fortune, *introduces her two main characters, Guy and Harriet Pringle. Recently married and not yet entirely at ease with each other they are drawn closer by the dangers of their situation. It is 1940 and the 'phoney war' is coming to an end. Guy is a gregarious, impulsive man, a lecturer in English at the University of Bucharest. Harriet often feels excluded from his world and resents the demands of his many friends. Her own fears about the impending crisis are heightened by a sense of isolation.*

In the second volume of the trilogy, The Spoilt City, *from which this extract is taken, events are closing in on the pair and those they have befriended, especially Guy's half-Jewish student, Sophie, the exuberantly parasitic Prince Yakimov and young Sasha Drucker, the saddest of the three, whose father and family fortune are now both lost to him.*

Yakimov had played Pandarus in Guy's production of *Troilus and Cressida*. The play over, his triumph forgotten, he was suffering from a sense of anti climax and of grievance. Guy, who had cosseted him through it all, had now abandoned him. And what, he asked himself, had come of the hours spent at rehearsals? Nothing, nothing at all.

Walking in the Calea Victoriei, in the increasing heat of midday, his sad camel face arun with sweat, he wore a panama hat, a suit of corded silk, a pink silk shirt and a tie that was once the colour of Parma violets. His clothes were very dirty. The hat was brim-broken and yellow with age. His jacket was tattered, brown beneath the armpits, and so shrunken that it held him as in a brace.

During the winter he had felt the ridges of frozen snow through the holes in his shoes: now he felt, just as painfully, the flagstones' white candescence. Steadily edged out to the kerb by the vigour of those about him, he caught the hot draught of cars passing at his elbow. He was agitated by the clangour of trams, by the flash of windscreens, blaring of horns and shrieking of brakes – all at a time when he would ordinarily have been safe in the refuge of sleep.

He had been wakened that morning by the relentless ringing of the telephone. Though from the lie of the light he could guess it was no more than ten o'clock, apparently even Harriet was out. Damp and inert beneath a single sheet, he lay without energy to stir and waited for the ringing to stop. It did not stop. At last, tortured to full consciousness, he dragged himself up and found the call was for him. The caller was his old friend Dobbie Dobson of the Legation.

'Lovely to hear your voice,' Yakimov said. He settled down in anticipation of a pleasurable talk about their days together in *Troilus*, but Dobson, like everyone else, had put the play behind him.

'Look here, Yaki,' he said, 'about those transit visas...'

'What transit visas, dear boy?'

'You know what I'm talking about.' Dobson spoke with the edge of a good-natured man harassed beyond endurance. 'Every British subject was ordered to keep in his passport valid transit visas against the possibility of sudden evacuation. The consul's been checking up and he finds you haven't obtained any.'

'Surely, dear boy, that wasn't a serious order? There's no cause for alarm.'

'An order is an order,' said Dobson. 'I've made excuses for you, but the fact is if you don't get those visas today you'll be sent to Egypt under open arrest.'

'*Dear boy*! But I haven't a bean.'

'Charge them to me. I'll deduct the cost when your next remittance arrives.'

Before he left the flat that morning, it had occurred to Yakimov to see if he could find anything useful in it. Guy was careless with money. Yakimov had more than once picked up and kept notes which his host had pulled out with his handkerchief. He had never before actually searched for money, but now, in his condition of grievance, he felt that Guy owed him anything he could find. In the Pringles' bedroom he went through spare trousers and handbags, but came upon nothing. In the sitting-room he pulled out the drawers of sideboard and writing-desk and spent some time looking through the stubs of Guy's old cheque-books which recorded payments made into London banks on behalf of local Jews. In view of

The Spoilt City

the fact Drucker was awaiting trial on a technical charge of black-market dealing, he considered the possibility of blackmail. But the possibility was not great. Use of the black market was so general that, even now, the Jews would laugh at him.

In the small central drawer of the writing-desk he came on a sealed envelope marked 'Top Secret'. This immediately excited him. He was not the only one inclined to suspect that Guy's occupation in Bucharest was not as innocent as it seemed. Affable, sympathetic, easy to know, Guy would, in Yakimov's opinion, make an ideal agent.

The flap of the envelope, imperfectly sealed, opened as he touched it. Inside was a diagram of a section through – what? A pipe or a well. Having heard so much talk of sabotage in the English Bar, he guessed that it was an oil well. A blockage in the pipe was marked 'detonator'. Here was a simple exposition of how and where the amateur saboteur should place his gelignite.

This was a find! He resealed and replaced the empty envelope, but the plan he put into his pocket. He did not know what eventual use he might make of it, but he would have some fun showing it around the English Bar as proof of the dangerous duties being exacted from him by King and country. He felt a few moments of exhilaration. Then as he trudged off to visit the consulates the plan was forgotten, the exhilaration was no more.

The consulates, taking advantage of the times, were charging high prices. Yakimov, disgusted by the thought of money wasted on such things, obtained visas for Hungary, Bulgaria and Turkey. That left only Yugoslavia, the country that nine months before had thrown him out and impounded his car for debt. He entered the consulate with aversion, handed over his passport and was – he'd expected nothing better – kept waiting half an hour.

When the clerk returned the passport, he made a movement as though drawing a shutter between them. '*Zabranjeno*,' he said.

Yakimov had been refused a visa.

It had always been at the back of his mind that when he could borrow enough to remit the debt, he would reclaim his Hispano-Suiza. Now, he saw, they would prevent him doing so.

As he wandered down the Calea Victoriei, indignation grew in him like a nervous disturbance of the stomach. He began to brood on his car – the last gift of his dear old friend Dollie; the last souvenir – apart from his disintegrating wardrobe – of their wonderful life together. Suddenly, its loss became grief. He decided to see Dobson. But first he must console himself with a drink.

During rehearsals, to keep a hold on him, Guy had bought Yakimov drinks at the Doi Trandifuri, but Guy was a simple soul. He drank beer and *ţuica* and saw no reason why Yakimov should not do the same. Yakimov had longed for the more dashing company of the English Bar. As soon as the play was over, he returned to the bar in expectation of honour and applause. What he found there bewildered him. It was not only that his entry was ignored, but it was ignored by strangers. The place was more crowded than he had ever known it. Even the air had changed, smelling not of cigarettes, but cigars.

As he pushed his way in, he had heard German spoken on all sides. Bless my soul, German in the English Bar! He stretched his neck, trying to see Galpin or Screwby, and it came to him that he was the only Englishman in the room.

Attempting to reach the counter, he found himself elbowed back with deliberate hostility. As he breathed at a large man 'Steady, dear boy!' the other, all chest and shoulders, threw him angrily aside with '*Verfluchter Lümmell*'.

Yakimov was unnerved. He lifted a hand, trying to attract the attention of Albu, who, because of his uncompromising remoteness of manner, was reputed to be the model of an English barman. Albu had no eyes for him.

The Spoilt City

Realizing he was alone in enemy-occupied territory, Yakimov was about to take himself off when he noticed Prince Hadjimoscos at the farther end of the bar.

The Rumanian, who looked with his waxen face, his thin, fine black hair and black eyes, like a little mongoloid doll, was standing tiptoe in his soft kid shoes and lisping in German to a companion. Relieved and delighted to see a familiar face, Yakimov ran forward and seized him by the arm. 'Dear boy,' he called out, 'who *are* all these people?'

Hadjimoscos slowly turned his head, looking surprised at Yakimov's intrusion. He coldly asked; 'Is it not evident to you, *mon prince*, that I am occupied?' He turned away, only to find his German companion had taken the opportunity to desert him. He gave Yakimov an angry glance.

To placate him, Yakimov attempted humour, saying with a nervous giggle; 'So many Germans in the bar! They'll soon be demanding a plebiscite.'

'They have as much right here as you. More, in fact, for they have not betrayed us. Personally, I find them charming.'

'Oh, so do I, dear boy,' Yakimov assured him. 'Had a lot of friends in Berlin in '32,' then changing to a more interesting topic; 'Did you happen to see the play?'

'The play? You mean that charity production at the National Theatre? I'm told you looked quite ludicrous.'

'Forced into it, dear boy,' Yakimov apologized, knowing himself despised for infringing the prescripts of the idle. 'War on, you know. Had to do m'bit.'

Hadjimoscos turned down his lips. Without further comment, he moved away to find more profitable companionship. He attached himself to a German group and was invited to take a drink. Watching enviously, Yakimov wondered if, son of a Russian father and an Irish mother, he could hint that his sympathies were with the Reich. He put the thought from his mind. The British Legation had lost its power here, but not, alas, over him.

*

The English Bar was itself again. The English journalists had re-established themselves and the Germans, bored with the skirmish, were drifting back to the Minerva. The few that remained were losing their audacity.

Hadjimoscos was again willing to accept Yakimov's company, but cautiously. He would not join him in an English group – that would have been too defined an attachment in a changing world – but if Yakimov had money he would stand with him in a no man's land and help him to spend it.

Yakimov, though not resentful by nature, did occasionally feel a little sore at this behaviour. Practised scrounger though he was, he was not as practised as Hadjimoscos. When he had money, he spent it. Hadjimoscos, whether he had it or not, never spent it. With his softly insidious and clinging manner, his presence affected men like the presence of a woman. They expected nothing from him. By standing long enough, first on one foot then on the other, he remained so patiently, so insistently *there*, that those to whom he attached himself bought him drinks in order to be free to ignore him.

Yakimov, entering the bar that morning, saw Hadjimoscos with his friend Horvatz and Cici Palu, all holding empty glasses and watching out for someone to refill them.

He bought his own drink before approaching them. Seeing them eye the whisky in his hand, he began, in self-defence, to complain of the high cost of the visas he had been forced to buy. Hadjimoscos, smiling maliciously, slid forward a step and put a hand on Yakimov's arm. '*Cher prince*,' he said, 'what does it matter what you spend your money on, so long as you spend it on yourself?'

Palu gave a snigger. Horvatz remained blank. Yakimov knew, had always known, they did not want his company. They did not even want each other. They stood in a group, bored by their own aimlessness, because

The Spoilt City

no one else wanted them. To Yakimov there came the thought that he was one of them – he who had once been the centre of entertainment in a vivacious set. He attempted to be entertaining now: 'Did you hear? When the French minister, poor old boy, was recalled to Vichy France, Princess Teodorescu said to him; *"Dire adieu, c'est mourir un peu."*'

'Is it likely that the Princess of all people would be so lacking in tact?' Hadjimoscos turned his back, attempting to exclude Yakimov from the conversation as he said, 'Things are coming to a pretty pass! What do I learn at the *cordonnier* this morning? Three weeks to wait and five thousand to pay for a pair of hand-made shoes!'

'At the *tailleur*,' said Palu, 'it is the same. The price of English stuff is a scandal. And now they declare meatless days. What, I ask, is a fellow to eat?' He looked at Yakimov, for all the world as though it were the British and not the Germans who were plundering the country.

Yakimov attempted to join in. 'A little fish,' he meekly suggested, 'a little game, in season. Myself, I never say no to a slice of turkey.'

Hadjimoscos cut him short with contempt: 'Those are *entrées* only. How, without meat, can a man retain his virility?'

Discomfited, casting about in his mind for some way of gaining the attention he loved, Yakimov remembered the plan he had found that morning. He took it out. Sighing, he studied it. The conversation faltered. Aware of their interest, he lowered the paper so it was visible to all. 'What will they want me to do next?' he asked the world.

Hadjimoscos averted his glance. 'I advise you, *mon prince*,' he said, 'if you have anything to hide, now is the time to hide it.'

Knowing he could do nothing to please that morning, Yakimov put the plan away and let his attention wander. He became aware that a nearby stranger had

519

been attempting to intercept it. The stranger smiled. His shabby, tousled appearance did not give much cause for hope, but Yakimov, always amiable, went forward and held out his hand. 'Dear boy,' he said, 'where have we met before?'

The young man took his pipe out from under his big, fluffy moustache and spluttering like a syphon in which the soda level was too low, he managed to say at last, 'The name's Lush. Toby Lush. I met you once with Guy Pringle.'

'So you did,' agreed Yakimov, who had no memory of it.

'Let me get you a drink. What is it?'

'Why, whisky, dear boy. Can't stomach the native rot-gut.'

Neighing wildly at Yakimov's humour, Lush went to the bar. Yakimov, having decided his new acquaintance was 'a bit of an ass', was surprised when he was led purposefully over to one of the tables by the wall. He did not receive his glass until he had sat down and he realized something would be demanded in return for it.

After a few moments of nervous pipe-sucking, Lush said, 'I'm here for keeps this time.'

'Are you indeed? That's splendid news.'

With his elbows close to his side, his knees clenched, Lush sat as though compressed inside his baggy sports-jacket and flannels. He sucked and gasped, gasped and spluttered, then said, 'When the Russkies took over Bessarabia, I told myself: "Toby, old soul, now's the time to shift your bones." There's always the danger of staying too long in a place.'

'Where do you come from?'

'Cluj. Transylvania. I never felt safe there. I'm not sure I'm safe here.'

It occurred to Yakimov that he had heard the name Toby Lush before. Didn't the fellow turn up for a few days in the spring, having bolted from Cluj because of

The Spoilt City

some rumour of a Russian advance? Yakimov, always sympathetic towards fear, said reassuringly, 'Oh, you're all right here. Nice little backwater. The Germans are getting all they want. They won't bother us.'

'I hope you're right.' Lush's pale, bulging eyes surveyed the bar. 'Quite a few of them about though. I don't feel they like us being here.'

'It's the old story,' said Yakimov, 'infiltrate, then complain about the natives. Still, it was worse last week. I said to Albu, "Dry Martini", and he gave me three martinis.'

Squeezing his knees together, Lush swayed about, gulping with laughter. 'You're a joker,' he said. 'Have another?'

When he returned with the second whisky, Lush had sobered up, intending to speak what was on his mind. 'You're a friend of Guy Pringle, aren't you?'

Yakimov agreed. 'Very old and dear friend. You know I played Pandarus in his show?'

'Your fame reached Cluj. And you lodge with the Pringles?'

'We share a flat. Nice little place. You must come and have a meal with us.'

Lush nodded, but he wanted more than that. 'I'm looking for a job,' he said. 'Pringle runs the English Department, doesn't he? I'm going to see him, of course, but I thought perhaps you'd put in a word for me. Just say, "I met Toby Lush today. Nice bloke," something like that.' Toby gazed earnestly at Yakimov, who assured him at once; 'If I say the word, you'll get the job tomorrow.'

'If there's a job to be got.'

'These things can always be arranged.' Yakimov emptied his glass and put it down. Lush rose, but said with unexpected firmness, 'One more, then I have to drive round to the Legation. Must make my number.'

'You have a car? Wonder if you'd give me a lift?'

'With pleasure.'

521

Lush's car was an old mud-coloured Humber, high-standing and hooded like a palanquin.

'Nice little bus,' said Yakimov. Placing himself in an upright seat from which the wadding protruded, he thought of the beauties of his own Hispano-Suiza.

The Legation, a brick-built villa in a side-street, was hedged around with cars. On the dry and patchy front lawn a crowd of men – large, practical-looking men in suits of khaki drill – were standing about, each with an identical air of despondent waiting. They watched the arrival of the Humber as though it might bring them something. As he passed among them, Yakimov noted with surprise that they were speaking English. He could identify none of them.

Lush was admitted to the chancellery. Yakimov, as had happened before, was intercepted by a secretary.

'Oh, Prince Yakimov, can I help you?' she said, extruding an elderly charm. 'Mr Dobson is so busy. All the young gentlemen are busy these days, poor young things. At their age life in the service should be all parties and balls, but with this horrid war on they have to work like everyone else. I suppose it's to do with your *permit de séjour*?'

'It's a personal matter. *Ra*-ther important. I'm afraid I must see Mr Dobson.'

She clicked her tongue, but he was admitted to Dobson's presence.

Dobson, whom he had not seen since the night of the play, raised his head from his work in weary inquiry. 'Hello, how are you?'

'Rather the worse for war,' said Yakimov. Dobson gave a token smile, but his plump face, usually bland, was jaded, his eyes rimmed with pink; his whole attitude discouraging. 'We've had an exhausting week with the crisis. And now, on top of everything, the engineers have been dismissed from the oil-fields.'

'Those fellows outside?'

The Spoilt City

'Yes. They've been given eight hours to get out of the country. A special train is to take them to Constanza. Poor devils, they're hanging around in hope we can do something!'

'So sorry, dear boy.'

At the genuine sympathy in Yakimov's tone, Dobson let his pen drop and rubbed his hands over his head. 'H.E.'s been ringing around for the last two hours, but it's no good. The Rumanians are doing this to please the Germans. Some of these engineers have been here twenty years. They've all got homes, cars, dogs, cats, horses . . . I don't know what. It'll make a lot of extra work for us.'

'Dear me, yes.' Yakimov slid down to a chair and waited until he could introduce his own troubles. When Dobson paused, he ventured, 'Don't like to worry you at a time like this, but . . .'

'Money, I suppose?'

'Not altogether. You remember m'Hispano-Suiza. The Jugs are trying to prig it.' He told his story. 'Dear boy,' he pleaded, 'you can't let them do it. The Hispano's worth a packet. Why, the chassis alone cost two thousand five hundred quid. Body by Fernandez — heaven knows what Dollie paid for it. Magnificent piece of work. All I've got in the world. Get me a visa, dear boy. Lend me a few thou. I'll get the car and flog it. We'll have a bean-feast, a royal night at Cina's — champers and the lot. What d'you say?'

Dobson, listening with sombre patience, said, 'I suppose you know the Rumanians are requisitioning cars.'

'Surely not British cars?'

'No.' Dobson had to admit that the tradition of British privilege prevailed in spite of all. 'Mostly Jewish cars. The Jews are always unfortunate, but they *do* own the biggest cars. What I mean is, this isn't a good time to sell. People are unwilling to buy an expensive car that might be requisitioned.'

'But I don't really want to sell, dear boy. I love the

523

old bus. . . . She'd be useful if there were an evacuation.'

Dobson drew down his cheek and plucked at his round pink mouth. 'I'll tell you what! One of us is going to Belgrade in a week or so – probably Foxy Leverett. You've got the receipt and car key and so on? Then I'll get him to collect it and drive it back. I suppose it's in order?'

'She was in first-class order when I left her.'

'Well, we'll see what we can do,' Dobson rose, dismissing him.

Outside the Legation, the oil-men were still standing about, but the Humber had gone. As Yakimov set out to walk back through the sultry noonday, he told himself, 'No more tramping on m'poor old feet. And,' he added on reflection, 'she's worth money. I'd make a packet if I sold her.'

* * *

A week after the visit to the park café, Harriet, drawn out to the balcony by a sound of rough singing, saw a double row of marching men rounding the church immediately below her. They crossed the main square.

Processions were not uncommon in Bucharest. They were organized for all sorts of public occasions, descending in scale from grand affairs in which even the cabinet ministers were obliged to take part, to straggles of schoolchildren in the uniform of the Prince's youth movement.

The procession she saw now was different from any of the others. There was no grandeur about it, but there was a harsh air of purpose. Its leaders wore green shirts. The song was unknown to her, but she caught one word of it which was repeated again and again on a rising note: '*Capitanul, Capitanul*. . . .'

The Captain. Who the captain was she did not know.

The Spoilt City

She watched the column take a sharp turn into the Calea Victoriei, then, two by two, the marchers disappeared from sight. When they were all gone, she remained on the balcony with a sense of nothing to do but stand there.

The flat behind her was silent. Despina had gone to market. Yakimov was in bed. (She sometimes wished she could seal herself off, as he did, in sleep.) Sasha – for he was still with them despite her decree of 'one night only' – was somewhere up on the roof. (Like Yakimov, he had nowhere else to go.) Guy, of course, was busy at the University.

The 'of course' expressed a growing resignation. She had looked forward to the end of the play and the end of the term, imagining she would have his companionship and support against their growing insecurity. Instead, she saw no more of him than before. The summer school, planned as a part-time occupation, had attracted so many Jews awaiting visas to the States, he had had to organize extra classes. Now he taught and lectured even during the siesta time.

On the day the oil engineers were expelled from Ploesti, the Pringles, like other British subjects, received their first notice to quit the country. Guy was just leaving the flat when a buff slip was handed him by a *prefectura* messenger. He passed it over to Harriet. 'Take it to Dobson,' he said. 'He'll deal with it.'

He spoke casually, but Harriet was disturbed by this order to pack and go. She said, 'But supposing we have to leave in eight hours?'

'We won't have to.'

His unconcern had made the matter seem worse to her, yet he had been proved right. Dobson had had their order rescinded, and that of the other British subjects in Bucharest, but the oil engineers had had to go.

At different times during the day, Harriet had seen

525

their wives and children sitting about in cafés and restaurants. The children, becoming peevish and troublesome, had been frowned on by the Rumanians, who did not take children to cafés. The women, uprooted, looked stunned yet trustful, imagining perhaps that, in the end, it would all prove a mistake and they would return to their homes. Instead, they had had to take the train to Constanza and the boat to Istanbul.

Despite the Rumanian excuse that the expulsion had been carried out on German orders, the German Minister was reported to have said, 'Now we know how Carol would treat us if we were the losers.'

Well, the engineers, however unwillingly they may have gone, had gone to safety. Harriet could almost wish Guy and she had been forced to go with them.

While she stood on the balcony with these reflections in mind, the city shook. For an instant, it seemed to her that the balcony shelved down. She saw, or thought she saw, the cobbles before the church. In terror she put out her hand to hold on to something, but it was as though the world had become detached in space. Everything moved with her and there was nothing on which to hold. An instant – then the tremor passed.

She hurried into the room and took up her bag and gloves. She could not bear to be up here on the ninth floor. She had to feel the earth beneath her feet. When she reached the pavement, that burnt like the Sahara sand, her impulse was to touch it.

Gradually, as she crossed the square and saw the buildings intact and motionless, the familiar crowds showing no unusual alarm, she lost her sense of the tremor's supernatural strangeness. Perhaps here, in this inland town with its empty sky ablaze and the sense of the land-mass of Europe lying to the west, earthquakes were common enough. But when, in the Calea Victoriei, she came on Bella Niculescu, she cried out, forgetting the check on their relationship, 'Bella, did you feel the earthquake?'

The Spoilt City

'Didn't I just?' Bella responded as she used to respond. 'It scared me stiff. Everyone's talking about it. Someone's just said it wasn't an earthquake at all, but an explosion at Ploesti. It's started a rumour that British agents are blowing up the oil-wells. Let's hope not. Things are tricky enough for us without that.'

The first excitement of their meeting over, Bella looked disconcerted and glanced about her to see who might have witnessed it. Harriet felt she had done wrong in accosting her friend. Neither knowing what to say, they were about to make excuses and separate when they were distracted by a lusty sound of singing from the distance. Harriet recognized the refrain of '*Capitanul*'. The men in green shirts were returning.

'Who are they?' Harriet asked.

'The Iron Guard, of course. Our local fascists.'

'But I though they'd been wiped out.'

'*That's* what we were told.'

As the leaders advanced, lifting their boots and swinging their arms, Harriet saw they were the same young men she had observed in the spring, exiles returned from training in the German concentration camps. Then, shabby and ostracized, they had hung unoccupied about the street corners. Now they were marching on the crown of the road, forcing the traffic into the kerb, filling the air with their anthem, giving an impression of aggressive confidence.

Like everyone else, the two women, silenced by the uproar of '*Capitanul*', stood and watched the column pass. It was longer than it had been that morning. The leaders, well dressed and drilled, gained an awed attention, but this did not last. The middle ranks, without uniforms, were finding it difficult to keep in step, while the rear was brought up by a collection of out-of-works, no doubt converted to Guardism that very morning. Some were in rags. Shuffling, stumbling, they gave nervous side-glances and grins at the bystanders and their only contribution to the song was an occasional shout of '*Capitanul*'. This was too much for the Rumanian sense of humour. People began to comment and snigger, then to laugh outright.

'Did you ever see the like!' said Bella.

Harriet asked, 'Who is this "*capitanul*"?'

'Why, the Guardist leader – Codreanu: the one who was 'shot trying to escape', on Carol's orders, needless to say. A lot of his chums were shot with him. Some got away to Germany, but the whole movement was broken up. Who would have thought they'd have the nerve to reappear like this? Carol must be losing his grip.'

From the remarks about them, it was clear that other onlookers were thinking the same. The procession passed, the traffic crawled after, and people went on their way. From the distance the refrain of '*Capitanul*' came in spasms, then died out.

Bella was saying, 'They tried to make a hero of that Codreanu. It would take some doing. I saw him once. He looked disgusting with his dirty, greasy hair hanging round his ears. *And* he needed a shave. Oh, by the way,' she suddenly added, 'you were talking about that Drucker boy. Funny you should mention him. A day or two after, I got a letter from Nikko and he'd been hearing about him too. Apparently they only took him off to do his military service. (I bet old Drucker had been buying his exemption. Trust *them*!) Anyway, the boy's deserted and the military are on the look-out. They've had orders to find him at all costs. I suppose it's this business of the fortune being in his name. They'll make him sign the money over.'

'Supposing he refuses?'

'He wouldn't dare. Nikko says he could be shot as a deserter.'

'Rumania's not at war.'

'No, but it's a time of national emergency. The country's conscripted. Anyway, they're determined to get him. And I bet, when they do, he'll disappear for good. Oh,

The Spoilt City

well!' Bella dismissed Sasha with a gesture. 'I'm thinking of going to Sinai. I'm sick of stewing in this heat waiting for something to happen. My opinion is, nothing will happen. You should get Guy to take you to the mountains.'

'We can't get away. He's started a summer school.'

'Will he get any students at this time of the year?'

'He has quite a number.'

'Jews, I bet?'

'Yes, they are mostly Jews.'

Bella pulled down her mouth and raised her brows. 'I wouldn't encourage that, my dear. If we're going to have the Iron Guard on the rampage again, there's no knowing what will happen. They beat up the Jewish students last time. But they're not only anti-Semitic, they're anti-British.' She gave a grim, significant nod, then, when she was satisfied that she had made an impression, her face cleared. 'Must be off,' she cheerfully said. 'I've an appointment with the hairdresser.' She lifted a hand, working her fingers in farewell, and disappeared in the direction of the square.

Harriet could not move. With the crowd pushing about her, she stood chilled and confused by perils. There was the peril of Sasha under the same roof as Yakimov, a potential informer – she did not know what the punishment might be for harbouring a deserter, but she pictured Guy in one of the notorious prisons Klein had described; and there was the more immediate threat from the marching Guardists.

Her instinct was to hurry at once to Guy and urge him to close down the summer school, but she knew she must not do that. Guy would not welcome her interference. He had put her out of his production on the grounds that no man could 'do a proper job with his wife around'. She wandered on as a preliminary to action, not knowing what action to take.

When she reached the British Propaganda Bureau, she came to a stop, thinking of Inchcape, who could, if he

529

wished, put an end to the summer school. Why should she not appeal to him?

She stood for some minutes looking at the photographs of battleships and a model of the Dunkirk beaches, all of which had been in the window a month and were likely to remain, there being nothing with which to replace them.

She paused, not from fear of Inchcape but of Guy. Once before by speaking to Inchcape she had put a stop to one of Guy's activities and by doing so had brought about their first disagreement. Was she willing to bring about another?

Surely, she told herself, the important point was that her interference in the past had extricated Guy from a dangerous situation. It might do so again.

She entered the Bureau. Inchcape's secretary, knitting behind her typewriter, put up a show of uncertainty. Domnul Director might be too busy to see anyone.

'I won't keep him a moment,' Harriet said, running upstairs before the woman could ring through. She found Inchcape stretched on a sofa with the volumes of *A la Recherche du Temps Perdu* open around him. He was wearing a shirt and trousers. Seeing her, he roused himself reluctantly and put on the jacket that hung on the back of a chair.

'Hello, Mrs P.,' he said with a smile that did not hide his irritation at being disturbed.

Harriet had not been in the office since the day they had come here to view Calinescu's funeral. Then the rooms had been dilapidated and the workmen had been fitting shelves. Now everything was painted white, the shelves were filled with books and the floor close-carpeted in a delicate shade of grey-blue. On the Biedermeier desk, among other open books, lay some Reuter's sheets.

'What brings you here?' Inchcape asked.

'The Iron Guard.'

He eyed her with his irritated humour. 'You mean that collection of neurotics and nonentities who trailed

The Spoilt City

past the window just now? Don't tell me they frightened you?'

Harriet said, 'The Nazis began as a collection of neurotics and nonentities.'

'So they did!' said Inchcape, smiling as though she must be joking. 'But in Rumania fascism is just a sort of game.'

'It wasn't a game in 1937 when Jewish students were thrown out of the University windows. I'm worried about Guy. He's alone there except for the three old ladies who assist him.'

'There's Dubedat.'

'What good would Dubedat be if the Guardist broke in?'

'Except when Clarence puts in an appearance, which isn't often, I'm alone here. I don't let it worry me.'

She was about to say, 'No one notices the Propaganda Bureau,' but stopped in time and said, 'The summer school is a provocation. All the students are Jews.'

Although Inchcape retained his appearance of urbane unconcern, the lines round his mouth had tightened. He shot out his cuffs and studied his garnet cuff-links. 'I imagine Guy can look after himself,' he said.

His neat, Napoleonic face had taken on a remote expression intended to conceal annoyance. Harriet was silenced. She had come here convinced that the idea of the summer school had originated with Guy – now she saw her mistake. Inchcape was a powerful member of the organization in which Guy hoped to make a career. Though she did not dislike him – they had come to terms early on – she still felt him an unknown quantity. Now she had challenged his vanity. There was no knowing what he might not say about Guy in the reports which he sent home.

When in the past, she had been critical of Inchcape, saying, 'He's so oddly mean: he economizes on food and drink, yet spends a fortune on china or furniture in order to impress his guests,' Guy had explained that Inchcape's possessions were a shield that hid the emotional emptiness of his life. Whatever they were, they were a form of self-aggrandizement. She realized the summer school was, too.

Knowing he could not be persuaded to close it, she decided to placate him. 'I supposed it *is* important,' she said.

He glanced up, pleased, and at once his tone changed. 'It certainly is. It's a sign that we're not defeated here. Our morale is high. And we'll do better yet. I have great plans for the future . . .'

'You think we have a future?'

'Of course we have a future. No one's going to interfere with us. Rumanian policy has always been to keep a foot in both camps. As for the Germans, what do they care so long as they're getting what they want? I'm confident that we'll keep going here. Indeed, I'm so confident that I'm arranging for an old friend, Professor Lord Pinkrose, to be flown out. He's agreed to give the Cantecuzene Lecture.'

Meeting Harriet's astonished gaze, Inchcape gave a grin of satisfaction. 'This is a time to show the flag,' he said. 'The lecture usually deals with some aspect of English literature. It will remind the Rumanians that we have one of the finest literatures in the world. And it is a great social occasion. The last time, we had eight princesses in the front row.' He started to lead her towards the door. 'Of course, it calls for a lot of organization. I've got to find a hall and I'll have to book Pinkrose into an hotel. I'm not sure yet whether he'll come alone.'

'He may bring his wife?'

'Good heavens, he has no wife.' Inchcape spoke as though marriage were some ridiculous custom of primitive tribes. 'But he's not so young as he was. He may want to bring a companion.'

Inchcape opened the door and said in parting, 'My dear child, we must maintain our equilibrium. Not so easy,

The Spoilt City

I know, in this weather, when one's body seems to be melting inside one's clothes. Well, goodbye.'

He shut the door on her, and she descended to the street with a sense of nothing achieved.

Shortly before the Guardists passed the University, Sophie Oresanu had come to see Guy in his office. The office had once been Inchcape's study, and the desk at which Guy sat still held Inchcape's papers. The shelves around were full of his books.

Sophie Oresanu, perched opposite Guy on the arm of a leather chair, had joined the summer school with enthusiasm. She now said, 'I cannot work in such heat,' leaning back with an insouciance that displayed her chief beauty, her figure. She pouted her heavily darkened mouth, then sighed and pushed a forefinger into one of her full, pasty cheeks. 'At this time the city is terrible,' she said.

Guy, viewing Sophie's languishings with indifference, remembered a conversation he had overheard between two male students: '*La* Oresanu is not nice, she is *le* "cock-tease"'. 'Ah, j'adore le "*cocktease*."'

He smiled as she wriggled about on the chair-arm, flirting her rump at him. Poor girl! An orphan without a dowry, possessed of a freedom that devalued her in Rumanian eyes, she had to get herself a husband somehow. Remembering her grief when he had returned to Bucharest with a wife, he said the more indulgently, 'The other students seem to be bearing up.'

She shrugged off the other students. 'My skin is delicate. I cannot tolerate much sun.'

'Still, you're safer in the city this summer.'

'No. They say now the Russians are satisfied there will be no more troubles. Besides' – she made a disconsolate little gesture – 'I am not happy at the summer school. All the students are Jews. They are not nice to me.'

'Oh, come!' Guy laughed at her. 'You used to complain

that because you are half-Jewish, it was the Rumanians who were "not nice" to you.'

'It is true,' she agreed. 'No one is nice to me. I don't belong anywhere. I don't like Rumanian men. They live off women and despise them. They are so conceited. And the women here are such fools! They want to be despised. If the young man gives them *un coup de pied*, they do like this.' She wriggled and threw up her eyes in a parody of sensual ecstasy. 'Me, I wish to be respected. I am advanced, so I prefer Englishmen.'

Guy nodded, sympathizing with this preference. He had avoided marrying her himself, but he would have been delighted could he have married her off to a friend with a British passport. He had attempted to interest Clarence in her unfortunate situation, but Clarence had dismissed her, saying, 'She's an affected bore,' while of Clarence she said, 'How terrible to be a man so unattractive to women!'

'Besides,' she went on, 'it is expensive, Bucharest. Every quarter my allowance goes, pouf! Other summers, for an economy, I let my flat and go to a little mountain hotel. Already I would have taken myself there, but my allowance is spent.'

She paused, looking at him with a pathetic tilt of the head, expecting his usual query: 'How much do you need?'

Instead, he said, 'You'll get your allowance next month. Wait until then.'

'My doctor says my health will suffer. Would you have me die?'

He smiled his embarrassment. Harriet had forced him to recognize Sophie's wiles and now he wondered how he had ever been taken in by them. Before his marriage, he had lent Sophie what he could not afford, seeing these loans, which were never repaid, as the price of friendship. With a wife as well as parents dependent on him, he had been forced to refuse her. His refusal had kept her at bay

The Spoilt City

for the last few months and he was acutely discomforted at the prospect of having to refuse her again.

Leaning forward with one of the persuasive gestures she had effectively used in *Troilus*, she said, 'I worked hard for the play. It was nice to have such a success, but I am not strong. It exhausted me. I have lost a kilo from my weight. Perhaps you like girls that are thin, but here they say it is not pretty.'

So that was it! She wanted a return for services rendered. He looked down at his desk, having no idea, in the face of this, how to reject her claim. He could only think of Harriet, not certain whether the thought came as a protection or a threat. Anyway, he could use her as an excuse. Sophie knew she could get nothing out of Harriet.

He was beginning to recognize that Harriet was, in some ways, stronger than himself. And yet perhaps not stronger. He had a complete faith in his own morality and he would not let her override it. But she could be obdurate where he could not, and though he stood up to her, knowing if he did not he would be lost, he was influenced by her clarity of vision; unwillingly. It was probably significant that he was physically short-sighted. He could not recognize people until almost upon them. Their faces were like so many buns. Good-natured buns, he would have said, but Harriet did not agree. She saw them in detail and did not like them any the better for it.

He was troubled by her criticism of their acquaintances. He preferred to like people, knowing this fact was the basis of his influence over them. The sense of his will to like them gave them confidence: so they liked in return. He could see that Harriet's influence, given sway, could undermine his own successful formula for living and he felt bound to resist it. Yet there were occasions when he let her be obdurate for him.

While these thoughts were in his mind Sophie's chatter had come to a stop. Looking up, he found her watching him, puzzled and hurt that he let her talk on without the expected interruption.

As she concluded in a small, dispirited voice, 'And I need only perhaps fifty thousand, not any more,' she dropped all her little artifices and he saw the naïveté behind the whole performance. He had often, in the past, thought Sophie unfairly treated by circumstances. She had been forced, much too young, to face life alone with nothing but the weapons her sex provided. He thought, 'The truth is, she's not much more than a scared kid,' thankful nevertheless that he did not have fifty thousand to lend her.

He said as lightly as he could, 'Harriet looks after the family finances now. She's better at it than I am. If anyone asks me for a loan I have to refer them to her.'

Sophie's expression changed abruptly. She sat upright, affronted that he should bring Harriet in between them. She rose, about to take herself off in indignation when a sound of marching and singing distracted her. They heard the repeated refrain *'Capitanul'*.

'But that is a forbidden song,' she said.

They reached the open window in time to see the leading green shirts pass the University. Sophie caught her breath. Guy, having talked with David's informants, was less surprised than she by this resurgence of the Iron Guard. He expected an appalled outcry from her, but she said nothing until the last stragglers had passed, then merely, 'So! We shall have troubles again!'

He said, 'You must have been at the University during the pogroms of 1938?'

She nodded. 'It was terrible, of course, but I was all right. I have a good Rumanian name.'

Remembering her annoyance with him, she turned suddenly and went without another word. She apparently had not been much disturbed by the spectacle of the marching Guardists, but Guy, when he returned to his

The Spoilt City

desk, sat for some time abstracted. He had seen a threat made manifest and knew exactly what he faced.

When they had discussed the organization of the summer school, Guy had said to Inchcape, 'There's only one thing against it. It will give rise to a concentration of Jewish students. With the new anti-Semitic policy, they might be in a dangerous position.'

Inchcape had scoffed at this. 'Rumanian policy has always been anti-Semitic and all that happens is the Jews get richer and richer.'

Guy felt he could not argue further without an appearance of personal fear. Inchcape, who had retained control of the English department, wanted a summer school. His organization must do something to justify its presence here. More than that, there was his need to rival the Legation. Speaking of the British Minister, he would say, 'The old charmer's not afraid to stay, so why should I be?' If anyone pointed out that the Minister, unlike Inchcape and his men, had diplomatic protection, Inchcape would say, 'While the Legation's here, we'll be protected too.'

Guy knew that Inchcape liked him and, because of that, he liked Inchcape. He also admired him. With no great belief in his own courage, he esteemed audacious people like Inchcape and Harriet. Yet he tended to pity them. Inchcape he saw as a lonely bachelor who had nothing in life but the authority which his position gave. If a summer school made Inchcape happy, then Guy would back it to the end.

Harriet, he felt, must be protected from the distrust that had grown out of an unloved childhood. He would say to himself, 'Oh, stand between her and her fighting soul,' touched by the small, thin body that contained her spirit. And he saw her unfortunate because life, which he took easily, was to her so unnecessarily difficult.

He picked up a photograph which was propped against the inkstand on his desk. It had been taken in the Calea Victoriei: one of those small prints that had to be provided when one applied for a *permit de séjour*. In it Harriet's face – remarkable chiefly for its oval shape and the width of the eyes – was fixed in an expression of contemplative sadness. She looked ten years older than her age. Here was something so different from her usual vivacity that he said when he first saw it, 'Are you really so unhappy?' She had denied being unhappy at all.

Yet, he thought, the photograph betrayed some inner discontent. He believed it to be the discontent of the confused and the undedicated. He replaced the photograph with a sense of regret. He could help her if she would let him; but would she let him?

He remembered that when he had set about her political education, she had rebuffed him with, 'I cannot endure organized thought,' and, having taken up that position, refused to be moved from it.

Before she married, she had worked in an art gallery and been the friend of artists, mostly poor and unrecognized. He had pointed out to her that were they working in the Soviet Union they would be honoured and rewarded. She said, 'Only if they conformed.' He had argued that in every country everyone had to conform in some way or other. She said, 'But artists must remain a privileged community if they're to produce anything important. They can't just echo what they're told. They have to think for themselves. That's why totalitarian countries can't afford them.'

He had to admit that she, too, thought for herself. She would not be influenced. Feminine and intolerant though she might be in particular, she could take a wide general view of things. Coming from the narrowest, most prejudiced class, she had nevertheless declassed herself. The more the pity, then, that she had rejected the faith which gave his own life purpose. He saw her muddled and lost in anarchy and a childish mysticism.

What did she want? The question was for him the more difficult because he was content. He wanted nothing for

The Spoilt City

himself. Possession he found an embarrassment, a disloyalty to his family that had to survive on so little. While he was taking his degree, he had worked as a part-time teacher. His mother had also worked. Between them they had paid the rent and kept the family together.

He had envied no one except the men without responsibilities who had been free to go and fight in Spain. These men of the International Brigade had been his heroes. He would still recite their poetry to himself, with emotion:

> From small beginnings mighty ends:
> From calling rebel generals friends,
> From being taught at public schools
> To think the common people fools,
> Spain bleeds, and Britain wildly gambles
> To bribe the butcher in the shambles.

The marching Guardists that morning had brought to his mind the Blackshirts and their 'Monster Rally' in his home town. That was when his friend Simon had been beaten up and he had recognized the fact that one day he, too, would have to pay for his political faith.

Simon had arrived late and sat by himself. When the rest of them, sitting in a body, attempted to break up the meeting they were frog-marched into the street. Simon, left alone, had with a fanatical, almost hysterical courage, carried on the interruptions unsupported. The thugs had had him to themselves. They had dragged him out through a back door to a garage behind the hall. There he was eventually found unconscious.

At that time the stories of fascist savagery were only half believed. It was a new thing in the civilized world. The sight of Simon's injured and blackened face had appalled Guy. He told himself he knew now what lay ahead – and from that time had never doubted that his turn would come.

While he sat now at his desk, confronting his own

physical fear, his door opened. It opened with ominous slowness. He stared at it. A tousled head appeared.

With playful solemnity, Toby Lush said, 'Hello, old soul! I'm back again, you see!'

Harriet, walking home with all her fears intact, allayed them with the determination to act somehow. If she could not surmount one danger, she must tackle another. There was the situation at home — at least she need not tolerate that.

She must make it clear to Guy that they could not keep both Yakimov and Sasha. He had brought them into the flat. Now it was for him to decide which of the two should remain, and to dismiss the other.

When, however, she entered the sitting-room and found Yakimov there, awaiting his luncheon, she decided for herself. Sasha was the one who needed their help and protection. As for Yakimov, only sheer indolence kept him from fending for himself. And she was sick of the sight of him.

Her mind was made up. He must go. She would tell him so straightaway.

Yakimov, sprawled in the armchair, was drinking from a bottle of *ţuica* which Despina had brought in that morning. He moved uneasily at the sight of her and, putting a hand to the bottle, excused himself. 'Took the liberty of opening it, dear girl. Came in dropping on m'poor old feet. The heat's killing me. Why not have a snifter yourself?'

She refused, but sat down near him. Used to being ignored by her, he became flustered and his hand was unsteady as he refilled his glass.

Her idea had been to order him, there and then, to pack and go, but she did not know how to begin.

His legs were crossed and one of his narrow shoes dangled towards her. His foot shook. Through a gap between sole and upper, she could see the tips of his toes and the rags of his violet silk socks. His dilapidation reproached

The Spoilt City

her. He lay back, pretending nonchalance, but his large, flat-looking, green eyes flickered apprehensively, looking at her and away from her, so she could not speak.

He tried to make conversation, asking, 'What's on the menu today?'

She said, 'It is a meatless day. Despina bought some sort of river fish.'

He sighed. 'This morning,' he said, 'I was thinking about *blinis*. We used to get them at Korniloff's. They'd give you a heap of pancakes. You'd spread the bottom one with caviare, the next with sour cream, the next with caviare, and so on. Then you'd cut right through the lot. Ouch!' He made a noise in his throat as at a memory so delicious it was scarcely to be endured. 'I don't know why we don't get them here. Plenty of caviare. The fresh grey sort's the best, of course.' He gave her an expectant look. When she made no offer to prepare the dish, he glanced away as though excusing her inhospitality with, 'I admit there's nothing to compare with the Russian Beluga. Or Osetrova, for that matter.' He sighed again and, on a note of yearning, asked, 'Do you remember ortolans? Delicious, weren't they?'

'I don't know. Anyway, I don't believe in killing small birds.'

He looked puzzled. 'But you eat chickens! All birds are birds. What does the size matter? Surely the important thing is the taste?'

Finding this reasoning unanswerable, she glanced at the clock, causing him to say, 'The dear boy's late. Where *does* he get to these days?' His tone told Harriet that, having been dropped from Guy's scheme of things, he was feeling neglected.

She said, 'He's started a summer school at the University. I expect you miss the fun of rehearsals?'

'They were fun, of course, but the dear boy did keep us at it. And, in the end, what came of it all?'

'What could come of it? I mean, so far from home and

with a war on, you could not hope to make a career of acting?'

'A career! Never thought of such a thing.'

His surprise was such, she realized he had probably looked for no greater reward than a lifetime of free food and drink. The fact was, he had never grown up. She had thought once that Yakimov was a nebula which, under Guy's influence, had started to evolve. But Guy, having set him in motion, had abandoned him to nothingness, and now, like a child displaced by a newcomer, he scarcely knew what had happened to him.

He said, 'Was happy to help the dear boy.'

'You'd never acted before, had you?'

'Never, dear girl, never.'

'What did you do before the war? Had you a job of any sort?'

He looked slightly affronted by the question and protested, 'I had m'remittance, you know.'

She supposed he lived off a show of wealth: which was as good a confidence trick as any.

Conscious of her disapproval, he tried to improve things. 'I did do a little work now and then. I mean, when I was a bit short of the ready.'

'What sort of work?'

He shifted about under this inquiry. His foot began to shake again. 'Sold cars for a bit,' he said. 'Only the best cars, of course: Rolls-Royces, Bentleys. . . . M'own old girl's an Hispano-Suiza. Finest cars in the world. Must get her back. Give you a run in her.'

'What else did you do?'

'Sold pictures, bric-à-brac . . .'

'Really?' Harriet was interested. 'Do you know about pictures?'

'Can't say I do, dear girl. Don't claim to be a professional. Helped a chap out now and then. Had a little flat in Clarges Street. Would hang up a picture, put out a bit of bric-à-brac, pick up some well-heeled gudgeon,

The Spoilt City

indicate willingness to sell. "Your poor old Yaki's got to part with family treasure." You know the sort of thing. Not work, really. Just a little side-line.' He spoke as though describing a respected way of life, then, as his shifting eye caught hers, his whole manner suddenly disintegrated. He struggled upright in his seat and, with head hanging, gazing down into his empty glass he mumbled, 'Expecting m'remittance any day now. Don't worry. Going to pay back every penny I owe. . . .'

They were both relieved to hear Guy letting himself into the flat. He entered the room, smiling broadly as though he were bringing Harriet some delightful surprise. 'You remember Toby Lush?' he said.

'It's wonderful to see you again! Wonderful!' Toby said, gazing at Harriet, his eyes bulging with excited admiration, giving the impression that theirs was some eagerly awaited reunion.

She had met him once before and barely remembered him. She did her best to respond but had never been much impressed by him. He was in the middle twenties, heavy-boned and clumsy in movement. His features were pronounced, his skin coarse, yet his face seemed to be made of something too soft and pliable for its purpose.

Sucking at his pipe, he turned to Guy and jerked out convulsively, 'You know what she always makes me think of? Those lines of Tennyson: "She walks in beauty like the night of starless climes and something skies."'

'Byron,' said Guy.

'Oh, crumbs!' Toby clapped a hand over his eyes in exaggerated shame. 'I'm always doing it. It's not that I don't know: I don't remember.' He suddenly noticed Yakimov and crying, 'Hello, hello, hello,' he rushed forward with outstretched hand.

Harriet went into the kitchen to tell Despina there would be a guest for luncheon. When she returned, Toby, with many irrelevant guffaws, was describing the situation in the Transylvanian capital from which he had evacuated himself.

Although Cluj had been under Rumanian rule for twenty years, it was still an Hungarian city. The citizens only waited for the despised regime to end.

'It's not that they're pro-German,' he said, 'they just want the Hunks back. They shut their eyes to the fact that when the Hunks come the Huns'll follow. If you point it out, they make excuses. A woman I know, a Jewess, said, "We don't want it for ourselves, we want it for our children." They think it'll happen any day now.'

Toby was standing by the open French window, the dazzle of out-of-doors limning his ragged outline. 'I can tell you,' he said, 'the only Englishman among that lot, I had to keep my wits about me. And what do you think happened before I left? The Germans installed a Gauleiter – a Count Frederich von Flügel. "Get out while the going's good," I told myself.'

'Freddi von Flügel!' Yakimov broke in in delighted surprise. 'Why, he's an old friend of mine. A dear old friend.' He looked happily about him. 'When I get the Hispano, we might all drive to Cluj and see Freddi. I'm sure he'd do us proud.'

Toby gazed open-mouthed at Yakimov, then his shoulders shook as though giving some farcical imitation of laughter. 'You're a joker,' he said and Yakimov, though surprised, seemed gratified to be thought one.

While they were eating, Harriet asked Toby, 'Will you remain in Bucharest?'

'If I can get some teaching,' he said. 'I'm a freelancer, no organization behind me. Came out on my own, drove the old bus all the way. Bit of an adventure. The fact is, if I don't work, I don't eat. Simple as that.' He gazed at Guy, supplicant and inquiring. 'Hearing you were short-staffed, I turned up on the doorstep.'

The question of his employment had obviously been

The Spoilt City

raised already, for Guy merely nodded and said, 'I must see what Inchcape says before taking anyone on.'

Harriet looked again at Toby, considering him not so much as a teacher as a possible help in time of trouble. She had noticed his heavy brogues. He was wearing grey flannel trousers bagged at the knees and a sagging tweed jacket, much patched with leather. It was the uniform of most young English civilians and yet on him it looked like a disguise. 'The man's man!' The last time he had arrived in Bucharest, during one of the usual invasion scares, he had fled from Cluj in a panic: but she was less inclined to condemn panic since she had experienced it herself. How would he react to a sudden Guardist attack? All this pipe-sucking masculinity, this casual costume, would surely require him, when the time came, to prove himself 'a good man in a tight corner'. She looked to Guy, who was saying, 'If Inchcape agrees, I might be able to give you twenty hours a week. That should keep you going.'

Toby ducked his head gratefully, then asked, 'What about lectures?'

'I would only need you to teach.'

'I used to lecture at Cluj – Mod. Eng. Lit. I must say, I enjoy giving the odd lecture.' Toby, from behind his hair and moustache, gazed at Guy like an old sheepdog confident he would be put to use. Harriet felt sorry for him. He probably imagined, as others had done before him, that Guy was easily persuadable. The truth was, that in authority Guy could be inflexible. Even if he needed a lecturer, he would not choose one who mistook Byron for Tennyson.

'The other day,' Yakimov suddenly spoke, slowly and sadly, out of his absorption in his food, 'I was thinking, strange as it must seem, I haven't seen a banana for about a year.' He sighed at the thought.

The Pringles had grown too used to him to react to his chance observations, but Toby rocked about, laughing as though Yakimov's speech had been one of hilarious impropriety.

Yakimov modestly explained, 'Used to be very fond of bananas.'

When luncheon was over and Yakimov had retired to his room Harriet looked for Toby's departure, but when he eventually made a move Guy detained him saying, 'Stay to tea. On my way back to the University, I'll take you to the Bureau to meet Inchcape.'

Harriet went into the bedroom. Determined to incite him to act while the power to incite was in her, she called Guy in, shut the door of the sitting-room and said, 'You must speak to Yakimov. You must tell him to go.'

Mystified by the urgency of her manner and unwilling to obey, he said, 'All right, but not now.'

'Yes, *now*.' She stood between him and the door. 'Go in and see him. It's too risky having him here with Sasha around. He must go.'

'Well, if you say so.' Guy's agreement was tentative, a playing for time. He paused, then said, 'It would be better if you spoke to him.'

'You brought him here, you must get rid of him.'

'It's a difficult situation. I was glad to have him here while he was rehearsing. He worked hard and helped to make the show a success. In a way, I owe him something. I can't just tell him to go now the show's over, but it's different for you. You can be firm with him.'

'What you mean is, if there's anything unpleasant to be done, you prefer that I should do it?'

Cornered, he reacted with rare exasperation. 'Look here, darling, I have other things to worry about. Sasha is up on the roof. Yakimov's not likely to see him and probably wouldn't be interested if he did see him. So why worry? Now I must go back and talk to Toby.'

She let him go, knowing nothing more would be gained by talk. And she realized it would always be the same. If action had to be taken, she would have to be the one to

The Spoilt City

take it. That was the price to be paid for a relationship that gave her more freedom than she had bargained for. Freedom, after all, was not a basic concept of marriage. As for Guy, he did not want a private life: he chose to live publicly. She said to herself, 'He's crassly selfish' – an accusation that would have astounded his admirers.

She went over to the window and leant out. Looking down the drop of nine floors to the cobbles below, she thought of the kitten that had fallen from the balcony five months before. The scene dissolved into a marbling of blue and gold as her eyes filled with tears, and she suffered again the outrageous grief with which she had learnt of the kitten's death. It had been her kitten. It had acknowledged her. It did not bite her. She was the only one who had no fear of it. Possessed by memory of the little red-golden flame of a cat that for a few weeks had hurtled itself, a ball of fur and claws, about the flat, she wept, 'My kitten. My poor kitten,' feeling she had loved it as she could never again love anything or anybody. Guy, after all, did not permit himself to be loved in this way.

She did not return to the room until she heard Despina taking in the tea things. Toby was saying, 'But someone's certain to march in here sooner or later. I suppose the Legation'll give us proper warning?'

Guy did not know and did not seem much to care. He said, 'The important thing is not to panic. We must keep the school going.'

Toby ducked his head in vehement agreement. 'Still,' he said, 'one must keep the old weather eye open.'

Yakimov had appeared for tea in his tattered brocade dressing-gown and when Guy and Toby went off to see Inchcape there he still was, his apprehensions forgotten, comfortably eating his way through the cakes and sandwiches that were left. Well, here was her opportunity to say, 'You have been living on top of us since Easter. I've had enough of you. Please pack your bags and go.' At which Yakimov, with his most pitiful expression, would ask, 'But where can poor Yaki go?' There had been no answer to that question four months before, and there was no answer now. He had exhausted his credit in Bucharest. No one would take him in. If she wanted to get rid of him, she would have to pack his bags herself and lock him out. And if she did that, he would probably sit on the doorstep until Guy brought him back in again.

When he had emptied the plates he stretched and sighed, 'Think I'll take a bath.' He went, and she had still said nothing. Knowing herself no more capable than Guy was of throwing Yakimov out, she had thought of a different move. She would go and see Sasha. The boy probably imagined that they, like the diplomats, were outside Rumanian law. She could explain to him that by sheltering him Guy ran the same risk as anyone else. Then what would Sasha do?

The problem of their responsibility lay between desperation and desperation. The only loophole was the possibility that Sasha could think of a friend who might shelter him, perhaps a Jewish schoolfriend. Or there was his stepmother, who was claiming maintenance from the Drucker fortune. Someone surely would take him in.

She went out to the kitchen. Despina was on the fire-escape, bawling down to other servants who had a free hour or so before it was time to prepare dinner. Feeling anomalous in these regions, Harriet slipped past her and started to ascend the cast iron ladder, but Despina missed nothing. 'That's right,' she called out. 'Visit the poor boy. He's lonely up there.'

Despina had adopted Sasha. Although Despina had been told that he must not come into the flat, Harriet had several times heard them laughing together in the kitchen. Despina scoffed at her fears, saying she could pass the boy off to anyone as her relative. Sasha was settling into a routine of life here and would soon, if undisturbed, become, like Yakimov, an unmovable part of the household.

The Spoilt City

The roof, high above its neighbours, was in the full light of the lowering sun. The sun was still very warm. Heat not only poured down on to the concrete but rose from it.

A row of wooden huts, like bathing-boxes, stood against the northern parapet, numbered one for each flat. Harriet, as she reached the roof-level, could see Sasha sitting outside his hut, holding a piece of stick which he had been throwing for a dog. The dog, a rough, white mongrel, apparently lived up here.

As soon as he saw her, Sasha got to his feet while the dog remained expectant, swaying a tail like a dirty feather.

She explained her visit by saying, 'How are you managing up here? Is Despina looking after you?'

'Oh, yes.' He was eagerly reassuring, adding thanks for all that was done for him. The fact of his presence being a danger to them seemed not to have occurred to him.

While he talked she looked beyond him through the open door of the hut where he was living. The hut had no window and was ventilated by a hole in the door. On the floor was a straw pallet that Despina must have borrowed for him, a blanket, some books Guy had brought up and a stub of candle.

Before she left England she would have believed it impossible for a human being to survive through the freezing winter, the torrid summer, in a cell like this. She had discovered in Rumania that there were millions to whom such shelter would be luxury. She took a step towards it but, repelled by the interior smell and heat, came to a stop saying, 'It's very small.'

Sasha smiled as though it were his place to apologize. He had been here only a few days but he was already putting on weight. When she had seen him on the night of his reappearance, she had been repelled by his abject squalor. Now, clean, wearing a shirt and trousers Guy had given him, the edge of fear gone from his face, his hair beginning to show like a shadow over

549

his head, he was already the boy she had first met in the Drucker flat.

He was rather an ugly boy with his long nose, close-set eyes and long, drooping body, but there was an appeal about his extreme gentleness of manner, which on their first meeting had made her think of some nervous animal grown meek in captivity. Because of this, he seemed completely familiar to her.

Feeling no restraint with him, she put out her hand and said, 'Let us sit on the wall,' and, jumping up, she settled herself on the low parapet that surrounded the roof. From here she could see almost the whole extent of the city, the roofs gleaming through a heat-mist that was beginning to grow dense and golden with evening. Sasha came and leant against the wall beside her. She asked him what he passed for among the servants who slept in the other huts.

He said, 'Despina says I come from her village.'

He looked nothing like a peasant, but he might be the son of some Jewish tallyman. Anyway, no one, it seemed, took much notice of him. Despina said the kitchen quarters of Bucharest harboured thousands of deserters.

'How long had you been in Bucharest when we met you?' she asked.

'Two nights.' He told her that he had separated from his company in Czernowitz and stowed away in a freight train that brought him to the capital. On the night of his arrival, he had slept under a market stall near the station, but had been turned out soon after midnight by some beggars whose usual sleeping place it was. The next night he had tried to sleep in the park, but there had been one of the usual spy scares on. The police, in their zeal, had tramped about all night, forcing him repeatedly to move his position.

He had not known what had happened to his family. When in Bessarabia, he had written to his aunts but received no reply. When he reached Bucharest, he had

The Spoilt City

looked up at the windows of the family flat and, seeing the curtains changed, realized the Druckers were not there. In the streets he had caught sight of people he knew, but in his fear of re-arrest dared approach no one until he saw Guy.

While he talked, he glanced shyly aside at her, smiling, all the misery gone from his gaze.

She said, 'You know that your family have left Rumania?'

'Guy told me.' If he knew they had taken flight immediately, without a backward glance for him or his father, he did not seem much concerned.

She decided the time had come to mention the possibility of his finding another shelter. She said, 'Your stepmother is still here, of course. Don't you think she could help you? She might be willing to let you live with her.'

He whispered, 'Oh, no,' startled and horrified by the suggestion.

'She wouldn't hurt you, would she? She wouldn't give you away?'

'Please don't tell her anything about me.'

His tone was a complete rejection of his stepmother. So much for her. Then what about the possible friends? She said, 'You must have known a lot of people in Bucharest. Isn't there anyone who would give you a better hiding-place than this?'

He explained that, having been at an English public school, he had no friends of long standing here. She asked, what about his University acquaintances? He simply shook his head. He had known people, but not well. There seemed to be no one on whom he could impose himself now. Jews did not make friends easily. They were suspicious and cautious in this anti-Semitic society, and Sasha had been enclosed by a large family. The Druckers formed their own community, one which depended on Drucker's power for its safety. His arrest had been the signal for flight. If they had hesitated, they might all have suffered.

Watching him, wondering what they were to do with him, Harriet caught Sasha's glance and saw her questions had disturbed him. He had again the fearful, wary look of the hunted, and she knew she was no better than Guy at displacing the homeless. Indeed, she was worse for, unlike Guy, she had been resolved and had failed. When it came to a battle of human needs, her resolution did not count for much.

Glancing away from her, Sasha saw the dog, stick in mouth, patiently awaiting his attention. He put out his hand to it.

The extreme gentleness of his gesture moved her. She suddenly felt his claim on her and knew it was the claim of her lost red kitten, and of all the animals to whom she had given her love in childhood because there had been no one else who wanted it. She wondered why Yakimov had not moved her in this way. Was it because he lacked the quality of innocence?

She said to Sasha, 'There's someone living with us in the flat, a Prince Yakimov. We have to keep him for the moment, he has nowhere else to go, but I don't trust him. You must be careful. Don't let him see you.' She slid down from the wall, saying as she left him, 'This is a wretched hut. It's the best we can do for the moment. If Yakimov leaves – and I hope he will – you can have his room.'

Sasha smiled after her, his fears forgotten, content like a stray animal that, having found a resting-place, has no complaint to make.

Next morning only *Timpul* mentioned the 'trickle of riff-raff in green shirts that provoked laughter in the Calea Victoriei'. By evening this attitude had changed. Every paper reported the march with shocked disapproval, for the King had announced that were it repeated the military would be called out to fire on the marchers.

The Guardists went under cover again, but this, people said, was the result not of the King's threat but an address made to the Guardists by their chief, Horia Sima, who was newly returned from exile in Germany. He advised them to leave off their green shirts and sing *'Capitanul'* only in their hearts. The time for action was not yet come.

Their leading spirits again hung unoccupied about the streets, sombre, shabby, malevolent, awaiting the call. These men, whom it seemed only Harriet had noticed in the spring, suddenly became visible and significant to everyone, giving rise to fresh excitements and apprehensions, and renewed terror among the Jews.

Katherine Mansfield
Prelude

I

There was not an inch of room for Lottie and Kezia in the buggy. When Pat swung them on top of the luggage they wobbled; the grandmother's lap was full and Linda Burnell could not possibly have held a lump of a child on hers for any distance. Isabel, very superior, was perched beside the new handy-man on the driver's seat. Holdalls, bags and boxes were piled upon the floor. 'These are absolute necessities that I will not let out of my sight for one instant,' said Linda Burnell, her voice trembling with fatigue and excitement.

Lottie and Kezia stood on the patch of lawn just inside the gate all ready for the fray in their coats with brass anchor buttons and little round caps with battleship ribbons. Hand in hand, they stared with round solemn eyes, first at the absolute necessities and then at their mother.

'We shall simply have to leave them. That is all. We shall simply have to cast them off,' said Linda Burnell. A strange little laugh flew from her lips; she leaned back against the buttoned leather cushions and shut her eyes, her lips trembling with laughter. Happily at that moment Mrs Samuel Josephs, who had been watching the scene from behind her drawing-room blind, waddled down the garden path.

'Why nod leave the chudren with be for the afterdoon,

Brs Burnell? They could go on the dray with the storeban when he comes in the eveding. Those thigs on the path have to go, dod't they?'

'Yes, everything outside the house is supposed to go,' said Linda Burnell, and she waved a white hand at the tables and chairs standing on their heads on the front lawn. How absurd they looked! Either they ought to be the other way up, or Lottie and Kezia ought to stand on their heads, too. And she longed to say: 'Stand on your heads, children, and wait for the storeman.' It seemed to her that would be so exquisitely funny that she could not attend to Mrs Samuel Josephs.

The fat creaking body leaned across the gate, and the big jelly of a face smiled. 'Dod't you worry, Brs Burnell. Loddie and Kezia can have tea with my chudren in the dursery, and I'll see theb on the dray afterwards.'

The grandmother considered. 'Yes, it really is quite the best plan. We are very obliged to you, Mrs Samuel Josephs. Children, say "thank you" to Mrs Samuel Josephs.'

Two subdued chirrups: 'Thank you, Mrs Samuel Josephs.'

'And be good little girls, and – come closer –' they advanced, 'don't forget to tell Mrs Samuel Josephs when you want to . . .'

'No, granma.'

'Dod't worry, Brs Burnell.'

At the last moment Kezia let go Lottie's hand and darted towards the buggy.

'I want to kiss my granma goodbye again.'

But she was too late. The buggy rolled off up the road, Isabel bursting with pride, her nose turned up at all the world, Linda Burnell prostrated, and the grandmother rummaging among the very curious oddments she had had put in her black silk reticule at the last moment,

Prelude

for something to give her daughter. The buggy twinkled away in the sunlight and fine golden dust up the hill and over. Kezia bit her lip, but Lottie, carefully finding her handkerchief first, set up a wail.

'Mother! Granma!'

Mrs Samuel Josephs, like a huge warm black silk tea-cosy, enveloped her.

'It's all right, by dear. Be a brave child. You come and blay in the dursery!'

She put her arm round weeping Lottie and led her away. Kezia followed, making a face at Mrs Samuel Josephs' placket, which was undone as usual, with two long pink corset laces hanging out of it....

Lottie's weeping died down as she mounted the stairs, but the sight of her at the nursery door with swollen eyes and a blob of a nose gave great satisfaction to the S.J.'s who sat on two benches before a long table covered with American cloth and set out with immense plates of bread and dripping and two brown jugs that faintly steamed.

'Hullo! You've been crying!'

'Ooh! Your eyes have gone right in.'

'Doesn't her nose look funny.'

'You're all red-and-patchy.'

Lottie was quite a success. She felt it and swelled, smiling timidly.

'Go and sid by Zaidee, ducky,' said Mrs Samuel Josephs, 'and Kezia, you sid ad the end by Boses.'

Moses grinned and gave her a nip as she sat down; but she pretended not to notice. She did hate boys.

'Which will you have?' asked Stanley, leaning across the table very politely, and smiling at her. 'Which will you have to begin with – strawberries and cream or bread and dripping?'

'Strawberries and cream, please,' said she.

'Ah-h-h-h.' How they all laughed and beat the table with their teaspoons. Wasn't that a take-in! Wasn't it now! Didn't he fox her! Good old Stan!

'Ma! She thought it was real.'

Even Mrs Samuel Josephs, pouring out the milk and water, could not help smiling. 'You bustn't tease theb on their last day,' she wheezed.

But Kezia bit a big piece out of her bread and dripping, and then stood the piece up on her plate. With the bite out it made a dear little sort of gate. Pooh! She didn't care! A tear rolled down her cheek, but she wasn't crying. She couldn't have cried in front of those awful Samuel Josephs. She sat with her head bent, and as the tear dripped slowly down, she caught it with a neat little whisk of her tongue and ate it before any of them had seen.

II

After tea Kezia wandered back to their own house. Slowly she walked up the back steps, and through the scullery into the kitchen. Nothing was left in it but a lump of gritty yellow soap in one corner of the kitchen window-sill and a piece of flannel stained with blue bag in another. The fireplace was choked up with rubbish. She poked among it but found nothing except a hair-tidy with a heart painted on it that had belonged to the servant girl. Even that she left lying, and she trailed through the narrow passage into the drawing-room. The Venetian blind was pulled down but not drawn close. Long pencil rays of sunlight shone through and the wavy shadow of a bush outside danced on the gold lines. Now it was still, now it began to flutter again, and now it

Prelude

came almost as far as her feet. Zoom! Zoom! a bluebottle knocked against the ceiling; the carpet-tacks had little bits of red fluff sticking to them.

The dining-room window had a square of coloured glass at each corner. One was blue and one was yellow. Kezia bent down to have one more look at a blue lawn with blue arum lilies growing at the gate, and then at a yellow lawn with yellow lilies and a yellow fence. As she looked a little Chinese Lottie came out on to the lawn and began to dust the tables and chairs with a corner of her pinafore. Was that really Lottie? Kezia was not quite sure until she had looked through the ordinary window.

Upstairs in her father's and mother's room she found a pill box black and shiny outside and red in, holding a blob of cotton wool.

'I could keep a bird's egg in that,' she decided.

In the servant girl's room there was a stay-button stuck in a crack of the floor, and in another crack some beads and a long needle. She knew there was nothing in her grandmother's room; she had watched her pack. She went over to the window and leaned against it, pressing her hands to the pane.

Kezia liked to stand so before the window. She liked the feeling of the cold shining glass against her hot palms, and she liked to watch the funny white tops that came on her fingers when she pressed them hard against the pane. As she stood there, the day flickered out and dark came. With the dark crept the wind snuffling and howling. The windows of the empty house shook, a creaking came from the walls and floors, a piece of loose iron on the roof banged forlornly. Kezia was suddenly quite, quite still, with wide open eyes and knees pressed together. She was frightened. She wanted to call Lottie and to go on calling all the while she ran downstairs and out of the house. But IT was just behind her, waiting at the door, at the head of the stairs, at the bottom of the stairs, hiding in the passage, ready to dart out at the back door. But Lottie was at the back door, too.

'Kezia!' she called cheerfully. 'The storeman's here. Everything is on the dray and three horses, Kezia. Mrs Samuel Josephs has given us a big shawl to wear round us, and she says to button up your coat. She won't come out because of asthma.'

Lottie was very important.

'Now then, you kids,' called the storeman. He hooked his big thumbs under their arms and up they swung. Lottie arranged the shawl 'most beautifully' and the storeman tucked up their feet in a piece of old blanket.

'Lift up. Easy does it.'

They might have been a couple of young ponies. The storeman felt over the cords holding his load, unhooked the brakechain from the wheel, and whistling, he swung up beside them.

'Keep close to me,' said Lottie, 'because otherwise you pull the shawl away from my side, Kezia.'

But Kezia edged up to the storeman. He towered beside her big as a giant and he smelled of nuts and new wooden boxes.

III

It was the first time that Lottie and Kezia had ever been out so late. Everything looked different – the painted wooden houses far smaller than they did by day, the gardens far bigger and wilder. Bright stars speckled the sky and the moon hung over the harbour dabbling the

Prelude

waves with gold. They could see the lighthouse shining on Quarantine Island, and the green lights on the old coal hulks.

'There comes the Picton boat,' said the storeman, pointing to a little steamer all hung with bright beads.

But when they reached the top of the hill and began to go down the other side the harbour disappeared, and although they were still in the town they were quite lost. Other carts rattled past. Everybody knew the storeman.

'Night, Fred.'

'Night O,' he shouted.

Kezia liked very much to hear him. Whenever a cart appeared in the distance she looked up and waited for his voice. He was an old friend; and she and her grandmother had often been to his place to buy grapes. The storeman lived alone in a cottage that had a glasshouse against one wall built by himself. All the glasshouse was spanned and arched over with one beautiful vine. He took her brown basket from her, lined it with three large leaves, and then he felt in his belt for a little horn knife, reached up and snapped off a big blue cluster and laid it on the leaves so tenderly that Kezia held her breath to watch. He was a very big man. He wore brown velvet trousers, and he had a long brown beard. But he never wore a collar, not even on Sunday. The back of his neck was burnt bright red.

'Where are we now?' Every few minutes one of the children asked him the question.

'Why, this is Hawk Street, or Charlotte Crescent.'

'Of course it is,' Lottie pricked up her ears at the last name; she always felt that Charlotte Crescent belonged specially to her. Very few people had streets with the same name as theirs.

'Look, Kezia, there is Charlotte Crescent. Doesn't it

look different?' Now everything familiar was left behind. Now the big dray rattled into unknown country, along new roads with high clay banks on either side, up steep hills, down into busy valleys, through wide shallow rivers. Further and further. Lottie's head wagged; she drooped, she slipped half into Kezia's lap and lay there. But Kezia could not open her eyes wide enough. The wind blew and she shivered; but her cheeks and ears burned.

'Do stars ever blow about?' she asked.

'Not to notice,' said the storeman.

'We've got a nuncle and a naunt living near our new house,' said Kezia. 'They have got two children, Pip, the eldest is called, and the youngest's name is Rags. He's got a ram. He has to feed it with a nenamuel teapot and a glove top over the spout. He's going to show us. What is the difference between a ram and a sheep?'

'Well, a ram has horns and runs for you.'

Kezia considered. 'I don't want to see it frightfully,' she said. 'I hate rushing animals like dogs and parrots. I often dream that animals rush at me – even camels – and while they are rushing, their heads swell e-enormous.'

The storeman said nothing. Kezia peered up at him, screwing up her eyes. Then she put her finger out and stroked his sleeve; it felt hairy. 'Are we near?' she asked.

'Not far off, now,' answered the storeman. 'Getting tired?'

'Well, I'm not an atom bit sleepy,' said Kezia. 'But my eyes keep curling up in such a funny sort of way.' She gave a long sigh, and to stop her eyes from curling she shut them. . . . When she opened them again they were clanking through a drive that cut through the garden like whiplash, looping suddenly an island of

Prelude

green, and behind the island, but out of sight until you came upon it, was the house. It was long and low built, with a pillared veranda and balcony all the way round. The soft white bulk of it lay stretched upon the green garden like a sleeping beast. And now one and now another of the windows leaped into light. Someone was walking through the empty rooms carrying a lamp. From the window downstairs the light of a fire flickered. A strange beautiful excitement seemed to stream from the house in quivering ripples.

'Where are we?' said Lottie, sitting up. Her reefer cap was all on one side and on her cheek there was the print of an anchor button she had pressed against while sleeping. Tenderly the storeman lifted her, set her cap straight, and pulled down her crumpled clothes. She stood blinking on the lowest veranda step watching Kezia, who seemed to come flying through the air to her feet.

'Ooh!' cried Kezia, flinging up her arms. The grandmother came out of the dark hall carrying a little lamp. She was smiling.

'You found your way in the dark?' said she.

'Perfectly well.'

But Lottie staggered on the lowest veranda step like a bird fallen out of the nest. If she stood still for a moment she fell asleep; if she leaned against anything her eyes closed. She could not walk another step.

'Kezia,' said the grandmother, 'can I trust you to carry the lamp?'

'Yes, my granma.'

The old woman bent down and gave the bright breathing thing into her hands and then she caught up drunken Lottie. 'This way.'

Through a square hall filled with bales and hundreds

of parrots (but the parrots were only on the wallpaper) down a narrow passage where the parrots persisted in flying past Kezia with her lamp.

'Be very quiet,' warned the grandmother, putting down Lottie and opening the dining-room door. 'Poor little mother has got such a headache.'

Linda Burnell, in a long cane chair, with her feet on a hassock and a plaid over her knees, lay before a crackling fire. Burnell and Beryl sat at the table in the middle of the room eating a dish of fried chops and drinking tea out of a brown china teapot. Over the back of her mother's chair leaned Isabel. She had a comb in her fingers and in a gentle absorbed fashion she was combing the curls from her mother's forehead. Outside the pool of lamp and firelight the room stretched dark and bare to the hollow windows.

'Are those the children?' But Linda did not really care; she did not even open her eyes to see.

'Put down the lamp, Kezia,' said Aunt Beryl, 'or we shall have the house on fire before we are out of packing cases. More tea, Stanley?'

'Well, you might just give me five-eighths of a cup,' said Burnell, leaning across the table. 'Have another chop, Beryl. Tip-top meat, isn't it? Not too lean and not too fat.' He turned to his wife. 'You're sure you won't change your mind, Linda darling?'

'The very thought of it is enough.' She raised one eyebrow in the way she had. The grandmother brought the children bread and milk and they sat up to table, flushed and sleepy behind the wavy steam.

'I had meat for my supper,' said Isabel, still combing gently.

'I had a whole chop for my supper, the bone and all and Worcester sauce. Didn't I, Father?'

Prelude

'Oh, don't boast, Isabel,' said Aunt Beryl.

Isabel looked astounded. 'I wasn't boasting, was I, Mummy? I never thought of boasting. I thought they would like to know. I meant to tell them.'

'Very well. That's enough,' said Burnell. He pushed back his plate, took a toothpick out of his pocket and began picking his strong white teeth.

'You might see that Fred has a bite of something in the kitchen before he goes, will you, Mother?'

'Yes, Stanley.' The old woman turned to go.

'Oh, hold on half a jiffy. I suppose nobody knows where my slippers were put? I suppose I shall not be able to get at them for a month or two – what?'

'Yes,' came from Linda. 'In the top of the canvas holdall marked "urgent necessities".'

'Well, you might get them for me, will you, Mother?'

'Yes, Stanley.'

Burnell got up, stretched himself, and going over to the fire he turned his back to it and lifted up his coat tails.

'By Jove, this is a pretty pickle. Eh, Beryl?'

Beryl, sipping tea, her elbows on the table, smiled over the cup at him. She wore an unfamiliar pink pinafore; the sleeves of her blouse were rolled up to her shoulders showing her lovely freckled arms, and she had let her hair fall down her back in a long pigtail.

'How long do you think it will take to get straight – couple of weeks – eh?' he chaffed.

'Good heavens, no,' said Beryl airily. 'The worst is over already. The servant girl and I have simply slaved all day, and ever since Mother came she has worked like a horse, too. We have never sat down for a moment. We have had a day.'

Stanley scented a rebuke.

'Well, I suppose you did not expect me to rush away from the office and nail carpets – did you?'

'Certainly not,' laughed Beryl. She put down her cup and ran out of the dining-room.

'What the hell does she expect us to do?' asked Stanley. 'Sit down and fan herself with a palm-leaf fan while I have a gang of professionals to do the job? By Jove, if she can't do a hand's turn occasionally without shouting about it in return for . . .'

And he gloomed as the chops began to fight the tea in his sensitive stomach. But Linda put up a hand and dragged him down to the side of her long chair.

'This is a wretched time for you, old boy,' she said. Her cheeks were very white, but she smiled and curled her fingers into the big red hand she held. Burnell became quiet. Suddenly he began to whistle 'Pure as a lily, joyous and free' – a good sign.

'Think you're going to like it?' he asked.

'I don't want to tell you, but I think I ought to, Mother,' said Isabel. 'Kezia is drinking tea out of Aunt Beryl's cup.'

IV

They were taken off to bed by the grandmother. She went first with a candle; the stairs rang to their climbing feet. Isabel and Lottie lay in a room to themselves, Kezia curled in her grandmother's soft bed.

'Aren't there going to be any sheets, my granma?'

'No, not tonight.'

'It's tickly,' said Kezia, 'but it's like Indians.' She dragged her grandmother down to her and kissed her under the chin.

Prelude

'Come to bed soon and be my Indian brave.'

'What a silly you are,' said the old woman, tucking her in as she loved to be tucked.

'Aren't you going to leave me a candle?'

'No. Sh-h. Go to sleep.'

'Well, can I have the door left open?'

She rolled herself up into a round but she did not go to sleep. From all over the house came the sound of steps. The house itself creaked and popped. Loud whispering voices came from downstairs. Once she heard Aunt Beryl's rush of high laughter, and once she heard a loud trumpeting from Burnell blowing his nose. Outside the window hundreds of black cats with yellow eyes sat in the sky watching her – but she was not frightened. Lottie was saying to Isabel: 'I'm not going to say my prayers in bed tonight.'

'No, you can't, Lottie.' Isabel was very firm. 'God only excuses you saying your prayers in bed if you've got a temperature.' So Lottie yielded:

> 'Gentle Jesus meek anmile,
> Look pon a little chile.
> Pity me, simple Lizzie,
> Suffer me to come to thee.'

And then they lay down back to back, their little behinds just touching, and fell asleep.

Standing in a pool of moonlight Beryl Fairfield undressed herself. She was tired, but she pretended to be more tired than she really was – letting her clothes fall, pushing back with a languid gesture her warm, heavy hair.

'Oh, how tired I am – very tired.'

She shut her eyes a moment, but her lips smiled. Her breath rose and fell in her breast like two fanning wings.

The window was wide open; it was warm, and somewhere out there in the garden a young man, dark and slender, with mocking eyes, tiptoed among the bushes, and gathered the flowers into a big bouquet, and slipped under her window and held it up to her. She saw herself bending forward. He thrust his head among the bright waxy flowers, sly and laughing. 'No, no,' said Beryl. She turned from the window and dropped her nightgown over her head.

'How frightfully unreasonable Stanley is sometimes,' she thought, buttoning. And then as she lay down, there came the old thought, the cruel thought – ah, if only she had money of her own.

A young man, immensely rich, has just arrived from England. He meets her quite by chance. . . . The new governor is unmarried. . . . There is a ball at Government house. . . . Who is that exquisite creature in eau-de-nil satin? Beryl Fairfield. . . .

'The thing that pleases me,' said Stanley, leaning against the side of the bed and giving himself a good scratch on his shoulders and back before turning in, 'is that I've got the place dirt cheap, Linda. I was talking about it to little Wally Bell today and he said he simply could not understand why they had accepted my figure. You see land about here is bound to become more and more valuable . . . in about ten years' time . . . of course we shall have to go very slow and cut down expenses as fine as possible. Not asleep – are you?'

'No, dear, I've heard every word,' said Linda.

He sprang into bed, leaned over her and blew out the candle.

'Good night, Mr Business Man,' said she, and she took hold of his head by the ears and gave him a quick

Prelude

kiss. Her faint far-away voice seemed to come from a deep well.

'Good night, darling.' He slipped his arm under her neck and drew her to him.

'Yes, clasp me,' said the faint voice from the deep well.

Pat the handy-man sprawled in his little room behind the kitchen. His sponge-bag, coat and trousers hung from the door-peg like a hanged man. From the edge of the blanket his twisted toes protruded, and on the floor beside him there was an empty cane bird-cage. He looked like a comic picture.

'Honk, honk,' came from the servant girl. She had adenoids.

Last to go to bed was the grandmother.

'What. Not asleep yet?'

'No, I'm waiting for you,' said Kezia. The old woman sighed and lay down beside her. Kezia thrust her head under her grandmother's arm and gave a little squeak. But the old woman only pressed her faintly, and sighed again, took out her teeth, and put them in a glass of water beside her on the floor.

In the garden some tiny owls, perched on the branches of a lace-bark tree, called: 'More pork; more pork.' And far away in the bush there sounded a harsh rapid chatter: 'Ha-ha-ha . . . Ha-ha-ha.'

V

Dawn came sharp and chill with red clouds on a faint green sky and drops of water on every leaf and blade. A breeze blew over the garden, dropping dew and dropping

571

petals, shivered over the drenched paddocks, and was lost in the sombre bush. In the sky some tiny stars floated for a moment and then they were gone – they were dissolved like bubbles. And plain to be heard in the early quiet was the sound of the creek in the paddock running over the brown stones, running in and out of the sandy hollows, hiding under clumps of dark berry bushes, spilling into a swamp of yellow water flowers and cresses.

And then at the first beam of sun the birds began. Big cheeky birds, starlings and mynahs, whistled on the lawns, the little birds, the goldfinches and linnets and fan-tails, flicked from bough to bough. A lovely kingfisher perched on the paddock fence preening his rich beauty, and a *tui* sang his three notes and laughed and sang them again.

'How loud the birds are,' said Linda in her dream. She was walking with her father through a green paddock sprinkled with daisies. Suddenly he bent down and parted the grasses and showed her a tiny ball of fluff just at her feet. 'Oh, Papa, the darling.' She made a cup of her hands and caught the tiny bird and stroked its head with her finger. It was quite tame. But a funny thing happened. As she stroked it began to swell, it ruffled and pouched, it grew bigger and bigger and its round eyes seemed to smile knowingly at her. Now her arms were hardly wide enough to hold it and she dropped it into her apron. It had become a baby with a big naked head and a gaping bird-mouth, opening and shutting. Her father broke into a loud clattering laugh and she woke to see Burnell standing by the windows rattling the Venetian blind up to the very top.

'Hullo,' he said. 'Didn't wake you, did I? Nothing much wrong with the weather this morning.'

Prelude

He was enormously pleased. Weather like this set a final seal on his bargain. He felt, somehow, that he had bought the lovely day, too – got it chucked in dirt cheap with the house and ground. He dashed off to his bath and Linda turned over and raised herself on one elbow to see the room by daylight. All the furniture had found a place – all the old paraphernalia, as she expressed it. Even the photographs were on the mantelpiece and the medicine bottles on the shelf above the washstand. Her clothes lay across a chair – her outdoor things, a purple cape and a round hat with a plume in it. Looking at them she wished that she was going away from this house, too. And she saw herself driving away from them all in a little buggy, driving away from everybody and not even waving.

Back came Stanley girt with a towel, glowing and slapping his thighs. He pitched the wet towel on top of her hat and cape, and standing firm in the exact centre of a square of sunlight he began to do his exercises. Deep breathing, bending and squatting like a frog and shooting out his legs. He was so delighted with his firm, obedient body that he hit himself on the chest and gave a loud 'Ah'. But this amazing vigour seemed to set him worlds away from Linda. She lay on the white tumbled bed and watched him as if from the clouds.

'Oh, damn! Oh, blast!' said Stanley, who had butted into a crisp white shirt only to find that some idiot had fastened the neck-band and he was caught. He stalked over to Linda waving his arms.

'You look like a big fat turkey,' said she.

'Fat. I like that,' said Stanley. 'I haven't a square inch of fat on me. Feel that.'

'It's rock – it's iron,' mocked she.

'You'd be surprised,' said Stanley, as though this were

intensely interesting, 'at the number of chaps at the club who have got a corporation. Young chaps, you know – men of my age.' He began parting his bushy ginger hair, his blue eyes fixed and round in the glass, his knees bent, because the dressing-table was always – confound it – a bit too low for him. 'Little Wally Bell, for instance,' and he straightened, describing upon himself an enormous curve with the hairbrush. 'I must say I've a perfect horror . . .'

'My dear, don't worry. You'll never be fat. You are far too energetic.'

'Yes, yes, I suppose that's true,' said he, comforted for the hundredth time, and taking a pearl penknife out of his pocket he began to pare his nails.

'Breakfast, Stanley.' Beryl was at the door. 'Oh, Linda, Mother says you are not to get up yet.' She popped her head in at the door. She had a big piece of syringa stuck through her hair.

'Everything we left on the veranda last night is simply sopping this morning. You should see poor dear Mother wringing out the tables and the chairs. However, there is no harm done –' this with the faintest glance at Stanley.

'Have you told Pat to have the buggy round in time? It's a good six and a half miles to the office.'

'I can imagine what this early start for the office will be like,' thought Linda. 'It will be very high pressure indeed.'

'Pat, Pat.' She heard the servant girl calling. But Pat was evidently hard to find; the silly voice went baa-baaing through the garden.

Linda did not rest again until the final slam of the front door told her that Stanley was really gone.

Later she heard her children playing in the garden.

Prelude

Lottie's stolid, compact little voice cried: 'Ke-zia. Isabel.' She was always getting lost or losing people only to find them again, to her great surprise, round the next tree or the next corner. 'Oh, there you are after all.' They had been turned out after breakfast and told not to come back to the house until they were called. Isabel wheeled a neat pramload of prim dolls and Lottie was allowed for a great treat to walk beside her holding the doll's parasol over the face of the wax one.

'Where are you going to, Kezia?' asked Isabel, who longed to find some light and menial duty that Kezia might perform and so be roped in under her government.

'Oh, just away,' said Kezia. . . .

Then she did not hear them any more. What a glare there was in the room. She hated blinds pulled up to the top at any time, but in the morning it was intolerable. She turned over to the wall and idly, with one finger, she traced a poppy on the wallpaper with a leaf and a stem and a fat bursting bud. In the quiet, and under her tracing finger, the poppy seemed to come alive. She could feel the sticky, silky petals, the stem, hairy like a gooseberry skin, the rough leaf and the tight glazed bud. Things had a habit of coming alive like that. Not only large substantial things like furniture but curtains and the patterns of stuffs and the fringes of quilts and cushions. How often she had seen the tassel fringe of her quilt change into a funny procession of dancers with priests attending. . . . For there were some tassels that did not dance at all but walked stately, bent forward as if praying or chanting. How often the medicine bottles had turned into a row of little men with brown top-hats on; and the washstand jug had a way of sitting in the basin like a fat bird in a round nest.

'I dreamed about birds last night,' thought Linda. What was it? She had forgotten. But the strangest part of this coming alive of things was what they did. They listened, they seemed to swell out with some mysterious important content, and when they were full she felt that they smiled. But it was not for her, only, their sly secret smile; they were members of a secret society and they smiled among themselves. Sometimes, when she had fallen asleep in the daytime, she woke and could not lift a finger, could not even turn her eyes to left or right because THEY were there; sometimes when she went out of a room and left it empty, she knew as she clicked the door to that THEY were filling it. And there were times in the evenings when she was upstairs, perhaps, and everybody else was down, when she could hardly escape from them. Then she could not hurry, she could not hum a tune; if she tried to say ever so carelessly – 'Bother that old thimble' – THEY were not deceived. THEY knew how frightened she was; THEY saw how she turned her head away as she passed the mirror. What Linda always felt was that THEY wanted something of her, and she knew that if she gave herself up and was quiet, more than quiet, silent, motionless, something would really happen.

'It's very quiet now,' she thought. She opened her eyes wide, and she heard the silence spinning its soft endless web. How lightly she breathed; she scarcely had to breathe at all.

Yes, everything had come alive down to the minutest, tiniest particle, and she did not feel her bed, she floated, held up in the air. Only she seemed to be listening with her wide open watchful eyes, waiting for someone to come who just did not come, watching for something to happen that just did not happen.

Prelude

VI

In the kitchen at the long deal table under the two windows old Mrs Fairfield was washing the breakfast dishes. The kitchen window looked out on to a big grass patch that led down to the vegetable garden and the rhubarb beds. On one side the grass patch was bordered by the scullery and wash-house and over this white-washed lean-to there grew a knotted vine. She had noticed yesterday that a few tiny corkscrew tendrils had come right through some cracks in the scullery ceiling and all the windows of the lean-to had a thick frill of ruffled green.

'I am very fond of a grape vine,' declared Mrs Fairfield, 'but I do not think that the grapes will ripen here. It takes Australian sun.' And she remembered how Beryl when she was a baby had been picking some white grapes from the vine on the back veranda of the Tasmanian house and she had been stung on the leg by a huge red ant. She saw Beryl in a little plaid dress with red ribbon tie-ups on the shoulders screaming so dreadfully that half the street rushed in. And how the child's leg had swelled! 'T-t-t-t!' Mrs Fairfield caught her breath remembering. 'Poor child, how terrifying it was.' And she set her lips tight and went over to the stove for some more hot water. The water frothed up in the big soapy bowl with pink and blue bubbles on top of the foam. Old Mrs Fairfield's arms were bare to the elbow and stained a bright pink. She wore a grey foulard dress patterned with large purple pansies, a white linen apron and a high cap shaped like a jelly mould of white muslin. At her throat there was a silver crescent moon with five little owls seated on it, and round her neck she wore a watch-guard made of black beads.

It was hard to believe that she had not been in that kitchen for years; she was so much a part of it. She put the crocks away with a sure, precise touch, moving leisurely and ample from the stove to the dresser, looking into the pantry and the larder as though there were not an unfamiliar corner. When she had finished, everything in the kitchen had become part of a series of patterns. She stood in the middle of the room wiping her hands on a check cloth; a smile beamed on her lips; she thought it looked very nice, very satisfactory.

'Mother! Mother! Are you there?' called Beryl.

'Yes, dear. Do you want me?'

'No. I'm coming,' and Beryl rushed in, very flushed, dragging with her two big pictures.

'Mother, whatever can I do with these awful hideous Chinese paintings that Chung Wah gave Stanley when he went bankrupt? It's absurd to say that they are valuable, because they were hanging in Chung Wah's fruit shop for months before. I can't make out why Stanley wants them kept. I'm sure he thinks them just as hideous as we do, but it's because of the frames,' she said spitefully. 'I suppose he thinks the frames might fetch something some day or other.'

'Why don't you hang them in the passage?' suggested Mrs Fairfield; 'they would not be much seen there.'

'I can't. There is no room. I've hung all the photographs of his office there before and after building, and the signed photos of his business friends, and that awful enlargement of Isabel lying on the mat in her singlet.' Her angry glance swept the placid kitchen. 'I know what I'll do. I'll hang them here. I will tell Stanley they got a little damp in the moving so I have put them in here for the time being.'

She dragged a chair forward, jumped on it, took a

Prelude

hammer and a big nail out of her pinafore pocket and banged away.

'There! That is enough! Hand me the picture, Mother.'

'One moment, child.' Her mother was wiping over the carved ebony frame.

'Oh, Mother, really you need not dust them. It would take years to dust all those little holes.' And she frowned at the top of her mother's head and bit her lip with impatience. Mother's deliberate way of doing things was simply maddening. It was old age, she supposed, loftily.

At last the two pictures were hung side by side. She jumped off the chair, stowing away the little hammer.

'They don't look so bad there, do they?' said she. 'And at any rate nobody need gaze at them except Pat and the servant girl – have I got a spider's web on my face, Mother? I've been poking into that cupboard under the stairs and now something keeps tickling my nose.'

But before Mrs Fairfield had time to look Beryl had turned away. Someone tapped on the window: Linda was there, nodding and smiling. They heard the latch of the scullery door lift and she came in. She had no hat on; her hair stood upon her head in curling rings and she was wrapped up in an old cashmere shawl.

'I'm so hungry,' said Linda. 'Where can I get something to eat, Mother? This is the first time I've been in the kitchen. It says "Mother" all over; everything is in pairs.'

'I will make you some tea,' said Mrs Fairfield, spreading a clean napkin over a corner of the table, 'and Beryl can have a cup with you.'

'Beryl, do you want half my gingerbread?' Linda waved the knife at her. 'Beryl, do you like the house now that we are here?'

'Oh yes, I like the house immensely and the garden is beautiful, but it feels very far away from everything to me. I can't imagine people coming out from town to see us in that dreadful jolting bus, and I am sure there is not anyone here to come and call. Of course it does not matter to you because —'

'But there's the buggy,' said Linda. 'Pat can drive you into town whenever you like.'

That was a consolation, certainly, but there was something at the back of Beryl's mind, something she did not even put into words for herself.

'Oh, well, at any rate it won't kill us,' she said drily, putting down her empty cup and standing up and stretching. 'I am going to hang curtains.' And she ran away singing:

> 'How many thousand birds I see
> That sing aloud from every tree . . .

. . . birds I see That sing aloud from every tree . . .' But when she reached the dining-room she stopped singing, her face changed; it became gloomy and sullen.

'One may as well rot here as anywhere else,' she muttered savagely, digging the stiff brass safety-pins into the red serge curtains.

The two left in the kitchen were quiet for a little. Linda leaned her cheek on her fingers and watched her mother. She thought her mother looked wonderfully beautiful with her back to the leafy window. There was something comforting in the sight of her that Linda felt she could never do without. She needed the sweet smell of her flesh, and the soft feel of her cheeks and her arms and shoulders still softer. She loved the way her hair curled, silver at her forehead, lighter at her neck and bright brown still in the big coil under the muslin cap.

Prelude

Exquisite were her mother's hands, and the two rings she wore seemed to melt into her creamy skin. And she was always so fresh, so delicious. The old woman could bear nothing but linen next to her body and she bathed in cold water winter and summer.

'Isn't there anything for me to do?' asked Linda.

'No, darling. I wish you would go into the garden and give an eye to your children; but that I know you will not do.'

'Of course I will, but you know Isabel is much more grown up than any of us.'

'Yes, but Kezia is not,' said Mrs Fairfield.

'Oh, Kezia has been tossed by a bull hours ago,' said Linda, winding herself up in her shawl again.

But no, Kezia had seen a bull through a hole in a knot of wood in the paling that separated the tennis lawn from the paddock. But she had not liked the bull frightfully, so she had walked away back through the orchard, up the grassy slope, along the path by the lace-bark tree and so into the spread tangled garden. She did not believe that she would ever not get lost in this garden. Twice she had found her way back to the big iron gates they had driven through the night before, and then had turned to walk up the drive that led to the house, but there were so many little paths on either side. On one side they all led into a tangle of tall dark trees and strange bushes with flat velvet leaves and feathery cream flowers that buzzed with flies when you shook them – this was the frightening side, and no garden at all. The little paths here were wet and clayey with tree roots spanned across them like the marks of big fowls' feet.

But on the other side of the drive there was a high box border and the paths had box edges and all of them led into a deeper and deeper tangle of flowers. The camellias were in bloom, white and crimson and pink and white striped with flashing leaves. You could not see a leaf on the syringa bushes for the white clusters. The roses were in flower – gentlemen's button-hole roses, little white ones, but far too full of insects to hold under anyone's nose, pink monthly roses with a ring of fallen petals round the bushes, cabbage roses on thick stalks, moss roses, always in bud, pink smooth beauties opening curl on curl, red ones so dark they seemed to turn back as they fell, and a certain exquisite cream kind with a slender red stem and bright scarlet leaves.

There were clumps of fairy bells, and all kinds of geraniums, and there were little trees of verbena and bluish lavender bushes and a bed of pelargoniums with velvet eyes and leaves like moths' wings. There was a bed of nothing but mignonette and another of nothing but pansies – borders of double and single daisies and all kinds of little tufty plants she had never seen before.

The red-hot pokers were taller than she; the Japanese sunflowers grew in a tiny jungle. She sat down on one of the box borders. By pressing hard at first it made a nice seat. But how dusty it was inside! Kezia bent down to look and sneezed and rubbed her nose.

And then she found herself at the top of the rolling grassy slope that led down to the orchard. . . . She looked down at the slope a moment; then she lay down on her back, gave a squeak and rolled over and over into the thick flowery orchard grass. As she lay waiting for things to stop spinning, she decided to go up to the house and ask the servant girl for an empty matchbox. She wanted to make a surprise for the grandmother. . . . First she would put a leaf inside with a big violet lying on it, then she would put a very small white picotee, perhaps, on

Prelude

each side of the violet, and then she would sprinkle some lavender on the top, but not to cover their heads.

She often made these surprises for the grandmother, and they were always most successful.

'Do you want a match, my granny?'

'Why, yes, child, I believe a match is just what I'm looking for.'

The grandmother slowly opened the box and came upon the picture inside.

'Good gracious, child! How you astonished me!'

'I can make her one every day here,' she thought, scrambling up the grass on her slippery shoes.

But on her way back to the house she came to that island that lay in the middle of the drive, dividing the drive into two arms that met in front of the house. The island was made of grass banked up high. Nothing grew on the top except one huge plant with thick, grey-green, thorny leaves, and out of the middle there sprang up a tall stout stem. Some of the leaves of the plant were so old that they curled up in the air no longer; they turned back, they were split and broken; some of them lay flat and withered on the ground.

Whatever could it be? She had never seen anything like it before. She stood and stared. And then she saw her mother coming down the path.

'Mother, what is it?'

Linda looked up at the fat swelling plant with its cruel leaves and fleshy stem. High above them, as though becalmed in the air, and yet holding so fast to the earth it grew from, it might have had claws instead of roots. The curving leaves seemed to be hiding something; the blind stem cut into the air as if no wind could ever shake it.

'That is an aloe, Kezia,' said her mother.

'Does it ever have any flowers?'

'Yes, Kezia,' and Linda smiled down at her, and half shut her eyes. 'Once every hundred years.'

VII

On his way home from the office Stanley Burnell stopped the buggy at the Bodega, got out and bought a large bottle of oysters. At the Chinaman's shop next door he bought a pineapple in the pink of condition, and noticing a basket of fresh black cherries he told John to put him in a pound of those as well. The oysters and the pine he stowed away in the box under the front seat, but the cherries he kept in his hand.

Pat, the handy-man, leapt off the box and tucked him up again in the brown rug.

'Lift yer feet, Mr Burnell, while I give yer a fold under,' said he.

'Right! Right! First rate!' said Stanley. 'You can make straight for home now.'

Pat gave the grey mare a touch and the buggy sprang forward.

'I believe this man is a first-rate chap,' thought Stanley. He liked the look of him sitting up there in his neat brown coat and brown bowler. He liked the way Pat had tucked him in, and he liked his eyes. There was nothing servile about him – and if there was one thing he hated more than another it was servility. And he looked as if he was pleased with his job – happy and contented already.

The grey mare went very well; Burnell was impatient to be out of the town. He wanted to be home. Ah, it was splendid to live in the country – to get right out of that hole of a town once the office was closed; and this drive

Prelude

in the fresh warm air, knowing all the while that his own house was at the other end, with its garden and paddocks, its three tip-top cows and enough fowls and ducks to keep them in poultry, was splendid too.

As they left the town finally and bowled away up the deserted road his heart beat hard for joy. He rooted in the bag and began to eat the cherries, three or four at a time, chucking the stones over the side of the buggy. They were delicious, so plump and cold, without a spot or bruise on them.

Look at those two, now – black one side and white the other – perfect! A perfect little pair of Siamese twins. And he stuck them in his button-hole. . . . By Jove, he wouldn't mind giving that chap up there a handful – but no, better not. Better wait until he had been with him a bit longer.

He began to plan what he would do with his Saturday afternoons and his Sundays. He wouldn't go to the club for lunch on Saturday. No, cut away from the office as soon as possible and get them to give him a couple of slices of cold meat and half a lettuce when he got home. And then he'd get a few chaps out from town to play tennis in the afternoon. Not too many – three at most. Beryl was a good player, too. . . . He stretched out his right arm and slowly bent it, feeling the muscle. . . . A bath, a good rub-down, a cigar on the veranda after dinner. . . .

On Sunday morning they would go to church – children and all. Which reminded him that he must hire a pew, in the sun if possible and well forward so as to be out of the draught from the door. In fancy he heard himself intoning extremely well: 'When thou did overcome the *Sharp*ness of Death Though didst open the *King*dom of heaven to *all* Believers.' And he saw the neat brass-edged card on the corner of the pew – Mr Stanley Burnell and family. . . . The rest of the day he'd loaf about with Linda. . . . Now they were walking about the garden; she was on his arm, and he was explaining to her at length what he intended doing at the office the week following. He heard her saying: 'My dear, I think that is most wise. . . .' Talking things over with Linda was a wonderful help even though they were apt to drift away from the point.

Hang it all! They weren't getting along very fast. Pat had put the brake on again. Ugh! What a brute of a thing it was. He could feel it in the pit of his stomach.

A sort of panic overtook Burnell whenever he approached near home. Before he was well inside the gate he would shout to anyone within sight: 'Is everything all right?' And then he did not believe it was until he heard Linda say: 'Hullo! Are you home again?' That was the worst of living in the country – it took the deuce of a long time to get back. . . . But now they weren't far off. They were on the top of the last hill; it was a gentle slope all the way now and not more than half a mile.

Pat trailed the whip over the mare's back and he coaxed her: 'Goop now. Goop now.'

It wanted a few minutes to sunset. Everything stood motionless bathed in bright, metallic light and from the paddocks on either side there streamed the milky scent of ripe grass. The iron gates were open. They dashed through and up the drive and round the island, stopping at the exact middle of the veranda.

'Did she satisfy yer, sir?' said Pat, getting off the box and grinning at his master.

'Very well indeed, Pat,' said Stanley.

Linda came out of the glass door; her voice rang in the shadowy quiet. 'Hullo! Are you home again?'

Prelude

At the sound of her his heart beat so hard that he could hardly stop himself dashing up the steps and catching her in his arms.

'Yes, I'm home again. Is everything all right?'

Pat began to lead the buggy round to the side gate that opened into the courtyard.

'Here, half a moment,' said Burnell. 'Hand me those two parcels.' And he said to Linda, 'I've brought you back a bottle of oysters and a pineapple,' as though he had brought her back all the harvest of the earth.

They all went into the hall; Linda carried the oysters in one hand and the pineapple in the other. Burnell shut the glass door, threw his hat down, put his arms round her and strained her to him, kissing the top of her head, her ears, her lips, her eyes.

'Oh, dear! Oh, dear!' said she. 'Wait a moment. Let me put down these silly things,' and she put the bottle of oysters and the pine on a little carved chair. 'What have you got in your button-hole – cherries?' She took them out and hung them over his ear.

'Don't do that, darling. They are for you.'

So she took them off his ear again. 'You don't mind if I save them. They'd spoil my appetite for dinner. Come and see your children. They are having tea.'

The lamp was lighted on the nursery table. Mrs Fairfield was cutting and spreading bread and butter. The three little girls sat up to table wearing large bibs embroidered with their names. They wiped their mouths as their father came in ready to be kissed. The windows were open; a jar of wild flowers stood on the mantelpiece, and the lamp made a big soft bubble of light on the ceiling.

'You seem pretty snug, Mother,' said Burnell, blinking at the light. Isabel and Lottie sat one on either side of the table, Kezia at the bottom – the place at the top was empty.

'That's where my boy ought to sit,' thought Stanley. He tightened his arm round Linda's shoulder. By God, he was a perfect fool to feel as happy as this!

'We are, Stanley. We are very snug,' said Mrs Fairfield, cutting Kezia's bread into fingers.

'Like it better than town – eh, children?' asked Burnell.

'Oh, yes,' said the three little girls, and Isabel added as an afterthought: 'Thank you very much indeed, Father dear.'

'Come upstairs,' said Linda. 'I'll bring your slippers.'

But the stairs were too narrow for them to go up arm in arm. It was quite dark in the room. He heard her ring tapping on the marble mantelpiece as she felt for the matches.

'I've got some, darling. I'll light the candles.'

But instead he came up behind her and again he put his arms round her and pressed her head into his shoulder.

'I'm so confoundedly happy,' he said.

'Are you?' She turned and put her hands on his breast and looked up at him.

'I don't know what has come over me,' he protested.

It was quite dark outside now and heavy dew was falling. When Linda shut the window the cold dew touched her finger tips. Far away a dog barked. 'I believe there is going to be a moon,' she said.

At the words, and with the cold wet dew on her fingers, she felt as though the moon had risen – that she was being strangely discovered in a flood of cold light. She shivered; she came away from the window and sat down upon the box ottoman beside Stanley.

*

Prelude

In the dining-room, by the flicker of a wood fire, Beryl sat on a hassock playing the guitar. She had bathed and changed all her clothes. Now she wore a white muslin dress with black spots on it and in her hair she had pinned a black silk rose.

> 'Nature has gone to her rest, love,
> See, we are alone.
> Give me your hand to press, love,
> Lightly within my own.'

She played and sang half to herself, for she was watching herself playing and singing. The firelight gleamed on her shoes, on the ruddy belly of the guitar, and on her white fingers. . . .

'If I were outside the window and looked in and saw myself I really would be rather struck,' thought she. Still more softly she played the accompaniment – not singing now but listening.

'. . . The first time that I ever saw you, little girl – oh, you had no idea that you were not alone – you were sitting with your little feet upon a hassock, playing the guitar. God, I can never forget. . . .' Beryl flung up her head and began to sing again:

> 'Even the moon is aweary . . .'

But there came a loud bang at the door. The servant girl's crimson face popped through.

'Please, Miss Beryl, I've got to come and lay.'

'Certainly, Alice,' said Beryl, in a voice of ice. She put the guitar in a corner. Alice lunged in with a heavy black iron tray.

'Well, I have had a job with that oving,' said she. 'I can't get nothing to brown.'

'Really!' said Beryl.

589

But no, she could not stand that fool of a girl. She ran into the dark drawing-room and began walking up and down. . . . Oh, she was restless, restless. There was a mirror over the mantel. She leaned her arms along and looked at her pale shadow in it. How beautiful she looked, but there was nobody to see, nobody.

'Why must you suffer so?' said the face in the mirror. 'You were not made for suffering. . . . Smile!'

Beryl smiled, and really her smile was so adorable that she smiled again – but this time because she could not help it.

VIII

'Good morning, Mrs Jones.'

'Oh, good morning, Mrs Smith. I'm so glad to see you. Have you brought your children?'

'Yes, I've brought both my twins. I have had another baby since I saw you last, but she came so suddenly that I haven't had time to make her any clothes yet. So I left her. . . . How is your husband?'

'Oh, he is very well, thank you. At least he had an awful cold but Queen Victoria – she's my godmother, you know – sent him a case of pineapples and that cured it im-mediately. Is that your new servant?'

'Yes, her name's Gwen. I've only had her two days. Oh, Gwen, this is my friend, Mrs Smith.'

'Good morning, Mrs Smith. Dinner won't be ready for about ten minutes.'

'I don't think you ought to introduce me to the servant. I think I ought to just begin talking to her.'

'Well, she's more of a lady-help than a servant and you

Prelude

do introduce lady-helps, I know, because Mrs Samuel Josephs had one.'

'Oh, well, it doesn't matter,' said the servant carelessly, beating up a chocolate custard with half a broken clothes peg. The dinner was baking beautifully on a concrete step. She began to lay the cloth on a pink garden seat. In front of each person she put two geranium leaf plates, a pine-needle fork and a twig knife. There were three daisy heads on a laurel leaf for poached eggs, some slices of fuchsia petal cold beef, some lovely little rissoles made of earth and water and dandelion seeds, and the chocolate custard which she had decided to serve in the pawa shell she had cooked it in.

'You needn't trouble about my children,' said Mrs Smith graciously. 'If you'll just take this bottle and fill it at the tap – I mean at the dairy.'

'Oh, all right,' said Gwen, and she whispered to Mrs Jones: 'Shall I go and ask Alice for a little bit of real milk?'

But someone called from the front of the house and the luncheon party melted away, leaving the charming table, leaving the rissoles and the poached eggs to the ants and to an old snail who pushed his quivering horns over the edge of the garden seat and began to nibble a geranium plate.

'Come round to the front, children. Pip and Rags have come.'

The Trout boys were the cousins Kezia had mentioned to the storeman. They lived about a mile away in a house called Monkey Tree Cottage. Pip was tall for his age, with lank black hair and a white face, but Rags was very small and so thin that when he was undressed his shoulder blades stuck out like two little wings. They had a mongrel dog with pale blue eyes and a long tail turned up at the end who followed them everywhere; he was called Snooker. They spent half their time combing and brushing Snooker and dosing him with various awful mixtures concocted by Pip, and kept secretly by him in a broken jug covered with an old kettle lid. Even faithful little Rags was not allowed to know the full secret of these mixtures. . . . Take some carbolic tooth powder and a pinch of sulphur powdered up fine, and perhaps a bit of starch to stiffen up Snooker's coat. . . . But that was not all; Rags privately thought that the rest was gun-powder. . . . And he never was allowed to help with the mixing because of the danger. . . . 'Why, if a spot of this flew in your eye, you would be blinded for life,' Pip would say, stirring the mixture with an iron spoon. 'And there's always the chance – just the chance, mind you – of it exploding if you whack it hard enough. . . . Two spoons of this in a kerosene tin will be enough to kill thousands of fleas.' But Snooker spent all his spare time biting and snuffling, and he stank abominably.

'It's because he is such a grand fighting dog,' Pip would say. 'All fighting dogs smell.'

The Trout boys had often spent the day with the Burnells in town, but now that they lived in this fine house and boncer garden they were inclined to be very friendly. Besides, both of them liked playing with girls – Pip, because he could fox them so, and because Lottie was so easily frightened, and Rags for a shameful reason. He adored dolls. How he would look at a doll as it lay asleep, speaking in a whisper and smiling timidly, and what a treat it was to him to be allowed to hold one. . . .

'Curve your arms round her. Don't keep them stiff like that. You'll drop her,' Isabel would say sternly.

Prelude

Now they were standing on the veranda and holding back Snooker, who wanted to go into the house but wasn't allowed to because Aunt Linda hated decent dogs.

'We came over in the bus with Mum,' they said, 'and we're going to spend the afternoon with you. We brought over a batch of our gingerbread for Aunt Linda. Our Minnie made it. It's all over nuts.'

'I skinned the almonds,' said Pip. 'I just stuck my hand into a saucepan of boiling water and grabbed them out and gave them a kind of pinch and the nuts flew out of the skins, some of them as high as the ceiling. Didn't they, Rags?'

Rags nodded. 'When they make cakes at our place,' said Pip, 'we always stay in the kitchen, Rags and me, and I get the bowl and he gets the spoon and the egg-beater. Sponge cake's the best. It's all frothy stuff, then.'

He ran down the veranda steps to the lawn, planted his hands on the grass, bent forward, and just did not stand on his head.

'That lawn's all bumpy,' he said. 'You have to have a flat place for standing on your head. I can walk round the monkey tree on my head at our place. Can't I, Rags?'

'Nearly,' said Rags faintly.

'Stand on your head on the veranda. That's quite flat,' said Kezia.

'No, smarty,' said Pip. 'You have to do it on something soft. Because if you give a jerk and fall over, something in your neck goes click, and it breaks off. Dad told me.'

'Oh, do let's play something,' said Kezia.

'Very well,' said Isabel quickly, 'we'll play hospitals.

I will be the nurse and Pip can be the doctor and you and Lottie and Rags can be the sick people.'

Lottie didn't want to play that, because last time Pip had squeezed something down her throat and it hurt awfully.

'Pooh,' scoffed Pip. 'It was only the juice out of a bit of mandarin peel.'

'Well, let's play ladies,' said Isabel. 'Pip can be the father and you can be all our dear little children.'

'I hate playing ladies,' said Kezia. 'You always make us go to church hand in hand and come home and go to bed.'

Suddenly Pip took a filthy handkerchief out of his pocket. 'Snooker! Here, sir,' he called. But Snooker, as usual, tried to sneak away, his tail between his legs. Pip leapt on top of him, and pressed him between his knees.

'Keep his head firm, Rags,' he said, and he tied the handkerchief round Snooker's head with a funny knot sticking up at the top.

'Whatever is that for?' asked Lottie.

'It's to train his ears to grow more close to his head — see?' said Pip. 'All fighting dogs have ears that lie back. But Snooker's ears are a bit too soft.'

'I know,' said Kezia. 'They are always turning inside out. I hate that.'

Snooker lay down, made one feeble effort with his paw to get the handkerchief off, but finding he could not, trailed after the children, shivering with misery.

IX

Pat came swinging along; in his hand he held a little tomahawk that winked in the sun.

Prelude

'Come with me,' he said to the children, 'and I'll show you how the kings of Ireland chop the head off a duck.'

They drew back – they didn't believe him, and besides, the Trout boys had never seen Pat before.

'Come on now,' he coaxed, smiling and holding out his hand to Kezia.

'Is it a real duck's head? One from the paddock?'

'It is,' said Pat. She put her hand in his hard dry one, and he stuck the tomahawk in his belt and held out the other to Rags. He loved little children.

'I'd better keep hold of Snooker's head if there's going to be any blood about,' said Pip, 'because the sight of blood makes him awfully wild.' He ran ahead dragging Snooker by the handkerchief.

'Do you think we ought to go?' whispered Isabel. 'We haven't asked or anything. Have we?'

At the bottom of the orchard a gate was set in the paling fence. On the other side a steep bank led down to a bridge that spanned the creek, and once up the bank on the other side you were on the fringe of the paddocks. A little old stable in the first paddock had been turned into a fowl-house. The fowls had strayed far away across the paddock down to a dumping ground in a hollow, but the ducks kept close to that part of the creek that flowed under the bridge.

Tall bushes overhung the stream with red leaves and yellow flowers and clusters of blackberries. At some places the stream was wide and shallow, but at others it tumbled into deep little pools with foam at the edges and quivering bubbles. It was in these pools that the big white ducks had made themselves at home, swimming and guzzling along the weedy banks.

Up and down they swam, preening their dazzling

breasts, and other ducks with the same dazzling breasts and yellow bills swam upside down with them.

'There is the little Irish navy,' said Pat, 'and look at the old admiral there with the green neck and the grand little flag-staff on his tail.'

He pulled a handful of grain from his pocket and began to walk towards the fowl-house, lazy, his straw hat with the broken crown pulled over his eyes.

'Lid. Lid—lid—lid—lid—' he called.

'Qua. Qua—qua—qua—qua—' answered the ducks, making for land, and flapping and scrambling up the bank they streamed after him in a long waddling line. He coaxed them, pretending to throw the grain, shaking it in his hands and calling to them until they swept round him in a white ring.

From far away the fowls heard the clamour and they too came running across the paddock, their heads thrust forward, their wings spread, turning in their feet in the silly way fowls run and scolding as they came.

Then Pat scattered the grain and the greedy ducks began to gobble. Quickly he stooped, seized two, one under each arm, and strode across to the children. Their darting heads and round eyes frightened the children – all except Pip.

'Come on, sillies,' he cried, 'they can't bite. They haven't any teeth. They've only got those two little holes in their beaks for breathing through.'

'Will you hold one while I finish with the other?' asked Pat. Pip let go of Snooker. 'Won't I? Won't I? Give us one. I don't mind how much he kicks.'

He nearly sobbed with delight when Pat gave the white lump into his arms.

There was an old stump beside the door of the fowl-house. Pat grabbed the duck by the legs, laid it flat

Prelude

across the stump, and almost at the same moment down came the little tomahawk and the duck's head flew off the stump. Up the blood spurted over the white feathers and over his hand.

When the children saw the blood they were frightened no longer. They crowded round him and began to scream. Even Isabel leaped about crying: 'The blood! The blood!' Pip forgot all about his duck. He simply threw it away from him and shouted, 'I saw it. I saw it,' and jumped round the wood block.

Rags, with cheeks as white as paper, ran up to the little head, put out a finger as if he wanted to touch it, shrank back again and then again put out a finger. He was shivering all over.

Even Lottie, frightened little Lottie, began to laugh and pointed at the duck and shrieked: 'Look, Kezia, look.'

'Watch it!' shouted Pat. He put down the body and it began to waddle – with only a long spurt of blood where the head had been; it began to pad away without a sound towards the steep bank that led to the stream. . . . That was the crowning wonder.

'Do you see that? Do you see that?' yelled Pip. He ran among the little girls tugging at their pinafores.

'It's like a little engine. It's like a funny little railway engine,' squealed Isabel.

But Kezia suddenly rushed at Pat and flung her arms round his legs and butted her head as hard as she could against his knees.

'Put head back! Put head back!' she screamed.

When he stooped to move her she would not let go or take her head away. She held on as hard as she could and sobbed: 'Head back! Head back!' until it sounded like a loud strange hiccup.

'It's stopped. It's tumbled over. It's dead,' said Pip.

Pat dragged Kezia up into his arms. Her sun-bonnet had fallen back, but she would not let him look at her face. No, she pressed her face into a bone in his shoulder and clasped her arms round his neck.

The children stopped screaming as suddenly as they had begun. They stood round the dead duck. Rags was not frightened of the head any more. He knelt down and stroked it now.

'I don't think the head is quite dead yet,' he said. 'Do you think it would keep alive if I gave it something to drink?'

But Pip got very cross: 'Bah! You baby.' He whistled to Snooker and went off.

When Isabel went up to Lottie, Lottie snatched away. 'What are you always touching me for, Isabel?'

'There now,' said Pat to Kezia. 'There's the grand little girl.'

She put up her hands and touched his ears. She felt something. Slowly she raised her quivering face and looked. Pat wore little round gold ear-rings. She never knew that men wore ear-rings. She was very much surprised.

'Do they come on and off?' she asked huskily.

X

Up in the house, in the warm tidy kitchen, Alice, the servant girl, was getting the afternoon tea. She was 'dressed'. She had on a black stuff dress that smelt under the arms, a white apron like a large sheet of paper, and a lace bow pinned on to her hair with two jetty pins. Also her comfortable carpet slippers were changed for a

Prelude

pair of black leather ones that pinched her corn on her little toe something dreadful. . . .

It was warm in the kitchen. A blowfly buzzed, a fan of whity steam came out of the kettle, and the lid kept up a rattling jig as the water bubbled. The clock ticked in the warm air, slow and deliberate, like the click of an old woman's knitting needle, and sometimes – for no reason at all, for there wasn't any breeze – the blind swung out and back, tapping the window.

Alice was making watercress sandwiches. She had a lump of butter on the table, a barracouta loaf, and the cresses tumbled in a white cloth.

But propped against the butter dish there was a dirty, greasy little book, half unstitched, with curled edges, and while she mashed the butter she read:

To dream of black-beetles drawing a hearse is bad. Signifies death of one you hold near or dear, either father, husband, brother, son, or intended. If beetles crawl backwards as you watch them it means death from fire or from great height such as flight of stairs, scaffolding, etc.

Spiders. To dream of spiders creeping over you is good. Signifies large sum of money in near future. Should party be in family way an easy confinement may be expected. But care should be taken in sixth month to avoid eating of probable present of shellfish. . . .

'How many thousand birds I see.'

Oh, life. There was Miss Beryl. Alice dropped the knife and slipped the *Dream Book* under the butter dish. But she hadn't time to hide it quite, for Beryl ran into the kitchen and up to the table, and the first thing her eye lighted on were those greasy edges. Alice saw Miss Beryl's meaning little smile and the way she raised her eyebrows and screwed up her eyes as though she were not quite sure what that could be. She decided to answer if Miss Beryl should ask her: 'Nothing as belongs to you, Miss.' But she knew Miss Beryl would not ask her.

Alice was a mild creature in reality, but she had the most marvellous retorts ready for questions that she knew would never be put to her. The composing of them and the turning of them over and over in her mind comforted her just as much as if they'd been expressed. Really, they kept her alive in places where she'd been that chivvied she'd been afraid to go to bed at night with a box of matches on the chair in case she bit the tops off in her sleep, as you might say.

'Oh, Alice,' said Miss Beryl. 'There's one extra to tea, so heat a plate of yesterday's scones, please. And put on the Victoria sandwich as well as the coffee cake. And don't forget to put little doyleys under the plates – will you? You did yesterday, you know, and the tea looked so ugly and common. And, Alice, don't put that dreadful old pink and green cosy on the afternoon teapot again. That is only for the mornings. Really, I think it ought to be kept for the kitchen – it's so shabby, and quite smelly. Put on the Japanese one. You quite understand, don't you?'

Miss Beryl had finished.

'That sing aloud from every tree . . .'

she sang as she left the kitchen, very pleased with her firm handling of Alice.

Oh, Alice was wild. She wasn't one to mind being told, but there was something in the way Miss Beryl had of speaking to her that she couldn't stand. Oh, that she

Prelude

couldn't. It made her curl up inside, as you might say, and she fair trembled. But what Alice really hated Miss Beryl for was that she made her feel low. She talked to Alice in a special voice as though she wasn't quite all there; and she never lost her temper with her – never. Even when Alice dropped anything or forgot anything important Miss Beryl seemed to have expected it to happen.

'If you please, Mrs Burnell,' said an imaginary Alice, as she buttered the scones, 'I'd rather not take my orders from Miss Beryl. I may be only a common servant girl as doesn't know how to play the guitar, but . . .'

This last thrust pleased her so much that she quite recovered her temper.

'The only thing to do,' she heard, as she opened the dining-room door, 'is to cut the sleeves out entirely and just have a broad band of black velvet over the shoulders instead. . . .'

XI

The white duck did not look as if it had ever had a head when Alice placed it in front of Stanley Burnell that night. It lay, in beautifully basted resignation, on a blue dish – its legs tied together with a piece of string and a wreath of little balls of stuffing round it.

It was hard to say which of the two, Alice or the duck, looked the better basted; they were both such a rich colour and they both had the same air of gloss and strain. But Alice was fiery red and the duck a Spanish mahogany.

Burnell ran his eye along the edge of the carving knife. He prided himself very much upon his carving, upon making a first-class job of it. He hated seeing a woman carve; they were always too slow and they never seemed to care what the meat looked like afterwards. Now he did; he took a real pride in cutting delicate shaves of cold beef, little wads of mutton, just the right thickness, and in dividing a chicken or a duck with nice precision. . . .

'Is this the first of the home products?' he asked, knowing perfectly well that it was.

'Yes, the butcher did not come. We have found out that he only calls twice a week.'

But there was no need to apologize. It was a superb bird. It wasn't meat at all, but a kind of very superior jelly. 'My father would say,' said Burnell, 'this must have been one of those birds whose mother played to it in infancy upon the German flute. And the sweet strains of the dulcet instrument acted with such effect upon the infant mind . . . Have some more, Beryl? You and I are the only ones in this house with a real feeling for food. I'm perfectly willing to state, in a court of law, if necessary, that I love good food.'

Tea was served in the drawing-room, and Beryl, who for some reason had been very charming to Stanley ever since he came home, suggested a game of crib. They sat at a little table near one of the open windows. Mrs Fairfield disappeared, and Linda lay in a rocking-chair, her arms above her head, rocking to and fro.

'You don't want the light – do you, Linda?' said Beryl. She moved the tall lamp so that she sat under its soft light.

How remote they looked, those two, from where Linda sat and rocked. The green table, the polished cards, Stanley's big hands and Beryl's tiny ones, all seemed to be part of one mysterious movement. Stanley himself, big and solid, in his dark suit, took his ease, and Beryl

Prelude

tossed her bright head and pouted. Round her throat she wore an unfamiliar velvet ribbon. It changed her, somehow – altered the shape of her face – but it was charming, Linda decided. The room smelled of lilies; there were two big jars of arums in the fireplace.

'Fifteen two – fifteen four – and a pair is six and a run of three is nine,' said Stanley, so deliberately, he might have been counting sheep.

'I've nothing but two pairs,' said Beryl, exaggerating her woe because she knew how he loved winning.

The cribbage pegs were like two little people going up the road together, turning round the sharp corner, and coming down the road again. They were pursuing each other. They did not so much want to get ahead as to keep near enough to talk – to keep near, perhaps that was all.

But no, there was always one who was impatient and hopped away as the other came up, and would not listen. Perhaps the white peg was frightened of the red one, or perhaps he was cruel and would not give the red one a chance to speak. . . .

In the front of her dress Beryl wore a bunch of pansies, and once when the little pegs were side by side, she bent over and the pansies dropped out and covered them.

'What a shame,' said she, picking up the pansies. 'Just as they had a chance to fly into each other's arms.'

'Farewell, my girl,' laughed Stanley, and away the red peg hopped.

The drawing-room was long and narrow with glass doors that gave on to the veranda. It had a cream paper with a pattern of gilt roses, and the furniture, which had belonged to old Mrs Fairfield, was dark and plain. A little piano stood against the wall with yellow pleated silk let into the carved front. Above it hung an oil painting by Beryl of a large cluster of surprised-looking clematis. Each flower was the size of a small saucer, with a centre like an astonished eye fringed in black. But the room was not finished yet. Stanley had set his heart on a Chesterfield and two decent chairs. Linda liked it best as it was. . . .

Two big moths flew in through the window and round and round the circle of lamplight.

'Fly away before it is too late. Fly out again.'

Round and round they flew; they seemed to bring the silence and the moonlight in with them on their silent wings. . . .

'I've two kings,' said Stanley. 'Any good?'

'Quite good,' said Beryl.

Linda stopped rocking and got up. Stanley looked across. 'Anything the matter, darling?'

'No, nothing. I'm going to find Mother.'

She went out of the room and standing at the foot of the stairs she called, but her mother's voice answered her from the veranda.

The moon that Lottie and Kezia had seen from the storeman's wagon was full, and the house, the garden, the old woman and Linda – all were bathed in dazzling light.

'I have been looking at the aloe,' said Mrs Fairfield. 'I believe it is going to flower this year. Look at the top there. Are those buds or is it only an effect of light?'

As they stood on the steps, the high grassy bank on which the aloe rested rose up like a wave, and the aloe seemed to ride upon it like a ship with the oars lifted. Bright moonlight hung upon the lifted oars like water, and on the green wave glittered the dew.

'Do you feel it, too,' said Linda, and she spoke to her

Prelude

mother with the special voice that women use at night to each other as though they spoke in their sleep or from some hollow cave – 'Don't you feel that it is coming towards us?'

She dreamed that she was caught up out of the cold water into the ship with the lifted oars and the budding mast. Now the oars fell striking quickly, quickly. They rowed far away over the top of the garden trees, the paddocks and the dark bush beyond. Ah, she heard herself cry: 'Faster! Faster!' to those who were rowing.

How much more real this dream was than that they should go back to the house where the sleeping children lay and where Stanley and Beryl played cribbage.

'I believe those are buds,' said she. 'Let us go down into the garden, Mother. I like that aloe. I like it more than anything here. And I am sure I shall remember it long after I've forgotten all the other things.'

She put her hand on her mother's arm and they walked down the steps, round the island and on to the main drive that led to the front gates.

Looking at it from below she could see the long sharp thorns that edged the aloe leaves, and at the sight of them her heart grew hard. . . . She particularly liked the long sharp thorns. . . . Nobody would dare to come near the ship or to follow after.

'Not even my Newfoundland dog,' thought she, 'that I'm so fond of in the daytime.'

For she really was fond of him; she loved and admired and respected him tremendously. Oh, better than anyone else in the world. She knew him through and through. He was the soul of truth and decency, and for all his practical experience he was awfully simple, easily pleased and easily hurt. . . .

If only he wouldn't jump at her so, and bark so loudly,

and watch her with such eager, loving eyes. He was too strong for her; she had always hated things that rush at her, from a child. There were times when he was frightening – really frightening. When she just had not screamed at the top of her voice, 'You are killing me.' And at those times she had longed to say the most coarse, hateful things. . . .

'You know I'm very delicate. You know as well as I do that my heart is affected, and the doctor has told you I may die any moment. I have had three great lumps of children already. . . .'

Yes, yes, it was true. Linda snatched her hand from her mother's arm. For all her love and respect and admiration she hated him. And how tender he always was after times like those, how submissive, how thoughtful. He would do anything for her; he longed to serve her. . . . Linda heard herself saying in a weak voice, 'Stanley, would you light a candle?'

And she heard his joyful voice answer, 'Of course I will, my darling.' And he leapt out of bed as though he were going to leap at the moon for her.

It had never been so plain to her as it was at this moment. There were all her feelings for him, sharp and defined, one as true as the other. And there was this other, this hatred, just as real as the rest. She could have done her feelings up in little packets and given them to Stanley. She longed to hand him that last one, for a surprise. She could see his eyes as he opened that. . . .

She hugged her folded arms and began to laugh silently. How absurd life was – it was laughable, simply laughable. And why this mania of hers to keep alive at all? For it really was a mania, she thought, mocking and laughing.

'What am I guarding myself for so preciously? I shall

Prelude

go on having children and Stanley will go on making money and the children and the gardens will grow bigger and bigger, with whole fleets of aloes in them for me to choose from.'

She had been walking with her head bent, looking at nothing. Now she looked up and about her. They were standing by the red and white camellia trees. Beautiful were the rich dark leaves spangled with light and the round flowers that perch among them like red and white birds. Linda pulled a piece of verbena and crumpled it, and held her hands to her mother.

'Delicious,' said the old woman. 'Are you cold, child? Are you trembling? Yes, your hands are cold. We had better go back to the house.'

'What have you been thinking about?' said Linda. 'Tell me.'

'I haven't really been thinking of anything. I wondered as we passed the orchard what the fruit trees were like and whether we should be able to make much jam this autumn. There are splendid healthy currant bushes in the vegetable garden. I noticed them today. I should like to see those pantry shelves thoroughly well stocked with our own jam. . . .'

XII

My darling Nan,

Don't think me a piggy wig because I haven't written before. I haven't had a moment, dear, and even now I feel so exhausted that I can hardly hold a pen.

Well, the dreadful deed is done. We have actually left the giddy whirl of town, and I can't see how we shall ever go back again, for my brother-in-law has bought this house "lock, stock and barrel", to use his own words.

In a way, of course, it is an awful relief, for he has been threatening to take a place in the country ever since I've lived with them – and I must say the house and garden are awfully nice – a million times better than that awful cubby-hole in town.

But buried, my dear. Buried isn't the word.

We have got neighbours, but they are only farmers – big louts of boys who seem to be milking all day, and two dreadful females with rabbit teeth who brought us some scones when we were moving and said they would be pleased to help. But my sister who lives a mile away doesn't know a soul here, so I am sure we never shall. It's pretty certain nobody will ever come out from town to see us, because though there is a bus it's an awful old rattling thing with black leather sides that any decent person would rather die than ride in for six miles.

Such a life. It's a sad ending for poor little B. I'll get to be a most awful frump in a year or two and come and see you in a mackintosh and a sailor hat tied on with a white china silk motor veil. So pretty.

Stanley says that now we are settled – for after the most awful week of my life we really are settled – he is going to bring out a couple of men from the club on Saturday afternoons for tennis. In fact, two are promised as a great treat today. But, my dear, if you could see Stanley's men from the club ... rather fattish, the type who look frighfully indecent without waistcoats – always with toes that turn in rather – so conspicuous when you are walking about a court in white shoes. And they are pulling up their trousers every minute – don't you know – and whacking at imaginary things with their rackets.

Prelude

I used to play with them at the club last summer, and I am sure you will know the type when I tell you that after I'd been there about three times they all called me Miss Beryl. It's a dreary world. Of course Mother simply loves the place, but then I suppose when I am Mother's age I shall be content to sit in the sun and shell peas into a basin. But I'm not – not – not.

What Linda thinks about the whole affair, per usual, I haven't the slightest idea. Mysterious as ever. . . .

My dear, you know that white satin dress of mine. I have taken the sleeves out entirely, put bands of black velvet across the shoulders and two big red poppies off my dear sister's *chapeau*. It is a great success, though when I shall wear it I do not know.'

Beryl sat writing this letter at a little table in her room. In a way, of course, it was all perfectly true, but in another way it was all the greatest rubbish and she didn't believe a word of it. No, that wasn't true. She felt all those things, but she didn't really feel them like that.

It was her other self who had written that letter. It not only bored, it rather disgusted her real self.

'Flippant and silly,' said her real self. Yet she knew that she'd send it and she'd always write that kind of twaddle to Nan Pym. In fact, it was a very mild example of the kind of letter she generally wrote.

Beryl leaned her elbows on the table and read it through again. The voice of the letter seemed to come up to her from the page. It was faint already, like a voice heard over the telephone, high, gushing, with something bitter in the sound. Oh, she detested it today.

'You've always got so much animation,' said Nan Pym. 'That's why men are so keen on you.' And she had added, rather mournfully, for men were not at all keen on Nan, who was a solid kind of girl, with fat hips and a high colour – 'I can't understand how you can keep it up. But it is your nature, I suppose.'

What rot. What nonsense. It wasn't her nature at all. Good heavens, if she had ever been her real self with Nan Pym, Nannie would have jumped out of the window with surprise. . . . My dear, you know that white satin of mine. . . . Beryl slammed the letter-case to.

She jumped up and half unconsciously, half consciously she drifted over to the looking-glass.

There stood a slim girl in white – a white serge skirt, a white silk blouse, and a leather belt drawn in very tightly at her tiny waist.

Her face was heart-shaped, wide at the brows and with a pointed chin – but not too pointed. Her eyes, her eyes were perhaps her best feature; they were such a strange uncommon colour – greeny blue with little gold points in them.

She had fine black eyebrows and long lashes – so long, that when they lay on her cheeks you positively caught the light in them, someone or other had told her.

Her mouth was rather large. Too large? No, not really. Her underlip protruded a little; she had a way of sucking it in that somebody else had told her was awfully fascinating.

Her nose was her least satisfactory feature. Not that it was really ugly. But it was not half as fine as Linda's. Linda really had a perfect little nose. Hers spread rather – not badly. And in all probability she exaggerated the spreadiness of it just because it was her nose, and she was so awfully critical of herself. She pinched it with a thumb and first finger and made a little face. . . .

Lovely, lovely hair. And such a mass of it. It had the colour of fresh fallen leaves, brown and red with a glint

Prelude

of yellow. When she did it in a long plait she felt it on her backbone like a long snake. She loved to feel the weight of it dragging her head back, and she loved to feel it loose, covering her bare arms. 'Yes, my dear, there is no doubt about it, you really are a lovely little thing.'

At the words her bosom lifted; she took a long breath of delight, half closing her eyes.

But even as she looked the smile faded from her lips and eyes. Oh, God, there she was, back again, playing the same old game. False – false as ever. False as when she'd written to Nan Pym. False even when she was alone with herself, now.

What had that creature in the glass to do with her, and why was she staring? She dropped down to one side of her bed and buried her face in her arms.

'Oh,' she cried, 'I am so miserable – so frightfully miserable. I know that I'm silly and spiteful and vain; I'm always acting a part. I'm never my real self for a moment.' And plainly, plainly, she saw her false self running up and down the stairs, laughing a special trilling laugh if they had visitors, standing under the lamp if a man came to dinner, so that he should see the light on her hair, pouting and pretending to be a little girl when she was asked to play the guitar. Why? She even kept it up for Stanley's benefit. Only last night when he was reading the paper her false self had stood beside him and leaned against his shoulder on purpose. Hadn't she put her hand over his, pointing out something so that he should see how white her hand was beside his brown one.

How despicable! Despicable! Her heart was cold with rage. 'It's marvellous how you keep it up,' said she to the false self. But then it was only because she was so miserable – so miserable. If she had been happy and leading her own life, her false life would cease to be. She saw the real Beryl – a shadow ... a shadow. Faint and unsubstantial she shone. What was there of her except the radiance? And for what tiny moments she was really she. Beryl could almost remember every one of them. At those times she had felt: 'Life is rich and mysterious and good, and I am rich and mysterious and good, too.' Shall I ever be that Beryl for ever? Shall I? How can I? And was there ever a time when I did not have a false self? ... But just as she had got that far she heard the sound of little steps running along the passage; the door handle rattled. Kezia came in.

'Aunt Beryl, Mother says will you please come down? Father is home with a man and lunch is ready.'

Botheration! How she had crumpled her skirt, kneeling in that idiotic way.

'Very well, Kezia.' She went over to the dressing-table and powdered her nose.

Kezia crossed too, and unscrewed a little pot of cream and sniffed it. Under her arm she carried a very dirty calico cat.

When Aunt Beryl ran out of the room she sat the cat up on the dressing-table and stuck the top of the cream jar over its ear.

'Now look at yourself,' she said sternly.

The calico cat was so overcome by the sight that it toppled over backwards and bumped and bumped on to the floor. And the top of the cream jar flew through the air and rolled like a penny in a round on the linoleum – and did not break.

But for Kezia it had broken the moment it flew through the air, and she picked it up, hot all over, and put it back on the dressing-table.

Then she tiptoed away, far too quickly and airily. ....

Alice Munro
Miles City, Montana

Alice Munro

Miles City, Montana

My father came across the field carrying the body of the boy who had been drowned. There were several men together, returning from the search, but he was the one carrying the body. The men were muddy and exhausted, and walked with their heads down, as if they were ashamed. Even the dogs were dispirited, dripping from the cold river. When they all set out, hours before, the dogs were nervy and yelping, the men tense and determined, and there was a constrained, unspeakable excitement about the whole scene. It was understood that they might find something horrible.

The boy's name was Steve Gauley. He was eight years old. His hair and clothes were mud-coloured now and carried some bits of dead leaves, twigs and grass. He was like a heap of refuse that had been left out all winter. His face was turned in to my father's chest, but I could see a nostril, an ear, plugged up with greenish mud.

I don't think so. I don't think I really saw all this. Perhaps I saw my father carrying him, and the other men following along, and the dogs, but I would not have been allowed to get close enough to see something like mud in his nostril. I must have heard someone talking about that and imagined that I saw it. I see his face unaltered except for the mud – Steve Gauley's familiar, sharp-honed, sneaky-looking face – and it wouldn't have been like that; it would have been bloated and changed and perhaps muddied all over after so many hours in the water.

To have to bring back such news, such evidence, to a waiting family, particularly a mother, would have made searchers move heavily, but what was happening here was worse. It seemed a worse shame (to hear people talk) that there was no mother, no woman at all – no grandmother or aunt, or even a sister – to receive Steve Gauley and give him his due of grief. His father was a hired man, a drinker but not a drunk, an erratic man without being entertaining, not friendly but not exactly a troublemaker. His fatherhood seemed accidental, and the fact that the child had been left with him when the mother went away, and that they continued living together, seemed accidental. They lived in a steep-roofed, grey-shingled hillbilly sort of house that was just a bit better than a shack – the father fixed the roof and put supports under the porch, just enough and just in time – and their life was held together in a similar manner; that is, just well enough to keep the Children's Aid at bay. They didn't eat meals together or cook for each other, but there was food. Sometimes the father would give Steve money to buy food at the store, and Steve was seen to buy quite sensible things, such as pancake mix and macaroni dinner.

I had known Steve Gauley fairly well. I had not liked him more often than I had liked him. He was two years older than I was. He would hang around our place on Saturdays, scornful of whatever I was doing but unable to leave me alone. I couldn't be on the swing without him wanting to try it, and if I wouldn't give it up he came and pushed me so that I went crooked. He

Miles City, Montana

teased the dog. He got me into trouble – deliberately and maliciously, it seemed to me afterward – by daring me to do things I wouldn't have thought of on my own: digging up the potatoes to see how big they were when they were still only the size of marbles, and pushing over the stacked firewood to make a pile we could jump off. At shool, we never spoke to each other. He was solitary, though not tormented. But on Saturday mornings, when I saw his thin, self-possessed figure sliding through the cedar hedge, I knew I was in for something and he would decide what. Sometimes it was all right. We pretended we were cowboys who had to tame wild horses. We played in the pasture by the river, not far from the place where Steve drowned. We were horses and riders both, screaming and neighing and bucking and waving whips of tree branches beside a little nameless river that flows into the Saugeen in southern Ontario.

The funeral was held in our house. There was not enough room at Steve's father's place for the large crowd that was expected because of the circumstances. I have a memory of the crowded room but no picture of Steve in his coffin, or of the minister, or of wreaths of flowers. I remember that I was holding one flower, a white narcissus, which must have come from a pot somebody forced indoors, because it was too early for even the forsythia bush or the trilliums and marsh marigolds in the woods. I stood in a row of children, each of us holding a narcissus. We sang a children's hymn, which somebody played on our piano: 'When He Cometh, When He Cometh, To Make Up His Jewels.' I was wearing white ribbed stockings, which were disgustingly itchy, and wrinkled at the knees and ankles. The feeling of these stockings on my legs is mixed up with another feeling in my memory. It is hard to describe. It had to do with my parents. Adults in general but my parents in particular. My father, who had carried Steve's body from the river, and my mother, who must have done most of the arranging of this funeral. My father in his dark-blue suit and my mother in her brown velvet dress with the creamy satin collar. They stood side by side opening and closing their mouths for the hymn, and I stood removed from them, in the row of children, watching. I felt a furious and sickening disgust. Children sometimes have an access of disgust concerning adults. The size, the lumpy shapes, the bloated power. The breath, the coarseness, the hairiness, the horrid secretions. But this was more. And the accompanying anger had nothing sharp and self-respecting about it. There was no release, as when I would finally bend and pick up a stone and throw it at Steve Gauley. It could not be understood or expressed, though it died down after a while into a heaviness, then just a taste, an occasional taste – a thin, familiar misgiving.

Twenty years or so later, in 1961, my husband, Andrew, and I got a brand-new car, our first – that is, our first brand-new. It was a Morris Oxford, oyster-coloured (the dealer had some fancier name for the colour) – a big small car, with plenty of room for us and our two children. Cynthia was six and Meg three and a half.

Andrew took a picture of me standing beside the car. I was wearing white pants, a black turtleneck, and sunglasses. I lounged against the car door, canting my hips to make myself look slim

'Wonderful,' Andrew said. 'Great. You look like Jackie

Miles City, Montana

Kennedy.' All over this continent probably, dark-haired, reasonably slender young women were told, when they were stylishly dressed or getting their pictures taken, that they looked like Jackie Kennedy.

Andrew took a lot of pictures of me, and of the children, our house, our garden, our excursions and possessions. He got copies made, labelled them carefully, and sent them back to his mother and his aunt and uncle in Ontario. He got copies for me to send to my father, who also lived in Ontario, and I did so, but less regularly than he sent his. When he saw pictures he thought I had already sent lying around the house, Andrew was perplexed and annoyed. He liked to have this record go forth.

That summer, we were presenting ourselves, not pictures. We were driving back from Vancouver, where we lived, to Ontario, which we still called 'home', in our new car. Five days to get there, ten days there, five days back. For the first time, Andrew had three weeks' holiday. He worked in the legal department at B.C. Hydro.

On a Satuday morning, we loaded suitcases, two thermos bottles – one filled with coffee and one with lemonade – some fruit and sandwiches, picture books and colouring books, crayons, drawing pads, insect repellent, sweaters (in case it got cold in the mountains), and our two children into the car. Andrew locked the house, and Cynthia said ceremoniously, 'Goodbye, house.'

Meg said, 'Goodbye, house.' Then she said, 'Where will we live now?'

'It's not goodbye forever,' said Cynthia. 'We're coming back. Mother! Meg thought we weren't ever coming back!'

'I did not,' said Meg, kicking the back of my seat.

Andrew and I put on our sunglasses, and we drove away, over the Lions Gate Bridge and through the main part of Vancouver. We shed our house, the neighbourhood, the city, and – at the crossing point between Washington and British Columbia – our country. We were driving east across the United States, taking the most northerly route, and would cross into Canada again at Sarnia, Ontario. I don't know if we chose this route because the Trans-Canada Highway was not completely finished at the time or if we just wanted the feeling of driving through a foreign, a very slightly foreign, country – that extra bit of interest and adventure.

We were both in high spirits. Andrew congratulated the car several times. He said he felt so much better driving it than our old car, a 1951 Austin that slowed down dismally on the hills and had a fussy-old-lady image. So Andrew said now.

'What kind of image does this one have?' said Cynthia. She listened to us carefully and liked to try out new words such as 'image'. Usually she got them right.

'Lively,' I said. 'Slightly sporty. It's not show-off.'

'It's sensible, but it has class,' Andrew said. 'Like my image.'

Cynthia thought that over and said with a cautious pride, 'That means like you think you want to be, Daddy?'

As for me, I was happy because of the shedding. I loved taking off. In my own house, I seemed to be often looking for a place to hide – sometimes from the children but more often from the jobs to be done and the phone ringing and the sociability of the neighbourhood. I wanted to hide so that I could get busy at my real work, which was a sort of wooing of distant parts of myself. I lived in a state of siege, always losing just what I wanted to hold on to. But on trips there was no difficulty. I could be talking to Andrew, talking to the children and looking at whatever they wanted me to look at – a pig on a sign, a pony in a field, a Volkswagen on a revolving stand – and pouring lemonade into plastic cups, and all the time those bits and pieces would be flying together inside me. The essential composition would be achieved. This made me hopeful and light-hearted. It was being a watcher that did it. A watcher, not a keeper.

We turned east at Everett and climbed into the Cascades. I showed Cynthia our route on the map. First I showed her the map of the whole United States, which showed also the bottom part of Canada. Then I turned to the separate maps of each of the states we were going to pass through. Washington, Idaho, Montana, North Dakota, Minnesota, Wisconsin. I showed her the dotted line across Lake Michigan, which was the route of the ferry we would take. Then we would drive across Michigan to the bridge that linked the United States and Canada at Sarnia, Ontario. Home.

Meg wanted to see, too.

'You won't understand,' said Cynthia. But she took the road atlas into the back seat.

'Sit back,' she said to Meg. 'Sit still. I'll show you.'

I could hear her tracing the route for Meg, very accurately, just as I had done it for her. She looked up all the states' maps, knowing how to find them in alphabetical order.

'You know what that line is?' she said. 'It's the road. That line is the road we're driving on. We're going right along this line.'

Meg did not say anything.

'Mother, show me where we are right this minute,' said Cynthia.

I took the atlas and pointed out the road through the mountains, and she took it back and showed it to Meg. 'See where the road is all wiggly?' she said. 'It's wiggly because there are so many turns in it. The wiggles are the turns.' She flipped some pages and waited a moment. 'Now,' she said, 'show me where we are.' Then she called to me, 'Mother, she understands! She pointed to it! Meg understands maps!'

It seems to me now that we invented characters for our children. We had them firmly set to play their parts. Cynthia was bright and diligent, sensitive, courteous, watchful. Sometimes we teased her for being too conscientious, too eager to be what we in fact depended on her to be. Any reproach or failure, any rebuff, went terribly deep with her. She was fair-haired, fair-skinned, easily showing the effects of the sun, raw winds, pride, or humiliation. Meg was more solidly built, more reticent – not rebellious but stubborn sometimes, mysterious. Her silences seemed to us to show her strength of character, and her negatives were taken as signs of an imperturbable independence. Her hair was brown, and we cut it in straight bangs. Her eyes were a light hazel, clear and dazzling.

We were entirely pleased with these characters, enjoying the contradictions as well as the confirmations of them. We disliked the heavy, the uninventive, approach to being parents. I had a dread of turning into a certain kind of mother – the kind whose body sagged, who moved in a woolly-smelling, milky-smelling fog, solemn with trivial burdens. I believed that all the attention these mothers paid, their need to be burdened, was the cause of colic, bed-wetting, asthma. I favoured another

Miles City, Montana

approach – the mock desperation, the inflated irony of the professional mothers who wrote for magazines. In those magazine pieces, the children were splendidly self-willed, hard-edged, perverse, indomitable. So were the mothers, through their wit, indomitable. The real-life mothers I warmed to were the sort who would phone up and say, 'Is my embryo Hitler by any chance over at your house?' They cackled clear above the milky fog.

We saw a dead deer strapped across the front of a pickup truck.

'Somebody shot it,' Cynthia said. 'Hunters shoot the deer.'

'It's not hunting season yet,' Andrew said. 'They may have hit it on the road. See the sign for deer crossing?'

'I would cry if we hit one,' Cynthia said sternly.

I had made peanut-butter-and-marmalade sandwiches for the children and salmon-and-mayonnaise for us. But I had not put any lettuce in, and Andrew was disappointed.

'I didn't have any,' I said.

'Couldn't you have got some?'

'I'd have had to buy a whole head of lettuce just to get enough for sandwiches, and I decided it wasn't worth it.'

This was a lie. I had forgotten.

'They're a lot better with lettuce.'

'I didn't think it made that much difference.' After a silence, I said, 'Don't be mad.'

'I'm not mad. I like lettuce on sandwiches.'

'I just didn't think it mattered that much.'

'How would it be if I didn't bother to fill up the gas tank?'

'That's not the same thing.'

623

Alice Munro

'Sing a song,' said Cynthia. She started to sing:

> 'Five little ducks went out one day,
> Over the hills and far away.
> One little duck went
> "Quack-quack-quack."
> Four little ducks came swimming back.'

Andrew squeezed my hand and said, 'Let's not fight.'

'You're right. I should have got lettuce.'

'It doesn't matter that much.'

I wished that I could get my feelings about Andrew to come together into a serviceable and dependable feeling. I had even tried writing two lists, one of things I liked about him, one of things I disliked – in the cauldron of intimate life, things I loved and things I hated – as if I hoped by this to prove something, to come to a conclusion one way or the other. But I gave it up when I saw that all it proved was what I already knew – that I had violent contradictions. Sometimes the very sound of his footsteps seemed to me tyrannical, the set of his mouth smug and mean, his hard, straight body a barrier interposed – quite consciously, even dutifully, and with a nasty pleasure in its masculine authority – between me and whatever joy or lightness I could get in life. Then, with not much warning, he became my good friend and most essential companion. I felt the sweetness of his light bones and serious ideas, the vulnerability of his love, which I imagined to be much purer and more straightforward than my own. I could be greatly moved by an inflexibility, a harsh propriety, that at other times I scorned. I would think how humble he was, really, taking on such a ready-made role of husband, father,

Miles City, Montana

breadwinner, and how I myself in comparison was really a secret monster of egotism. Not so secret, either – not from him.

At the bottom of our fights, we served up what we thought were the ugliest truths. 'I know there is something basically selfish and basically untrustworthy about you,' Andrew once said. 'I've always known it. I also know that that is why I fell in love with you.'

'Yes,' I said, feeling sorrowful but complacent.

'I know that I'd be better off without you.'

'Yes. You would.'

'You'd be happier without me.'

'Yes.'

And finally – finally – racked and purged, we clasped hands and laughed, laughed at those two benighted people, ourselves. Their grudges, their grievances, their self-justification. We leap-frogged over them. We declared them liars. We would have wine with dinner, or decide to give a party.

I haven't seen Andrew for years, don't know if he is still thin, has gone completely grey, insists on lettuce, tells the truth, or is hearty and disappointed.

We stayed the night in Wenatchee, Washington, where it hadn't rained for weeks. We ate dinner in a restaurant built about a tree – not a sapling in a tub but a tall, sturdy cottonwood. In the early morning light, we climbed out of the irrigated valley, up dry, rocky, very steep hillsides that would seem to lead to more hills, and there on the top was a wide plateau, cut by the great Spokane and Columbia rivers. Grainland and grassland, mile after mile. There were straight roads here, and little farming towns with grain elevators. In fact, there was a sign announcing that this county we were going through, Douglas County, had the second-highest wheat yield of any county in the United States. The towns had planted shade trees. At least, I thought they had been planted, because there were no such big trees in the countryside.

All this was marvellously welcome to me. 'Why do I love it so much?' I said to Andrew. 'Is it because it isn't scenery?'

'It reminds you of home,' said Andrew. 'A bout of severe nostalgia.' But he said this kindly.

When we said 'home' and meant Ontario, we had very different places in mind. My home was a turkey farm, where my father lived as a widower, and though it was the same house my mother had lived in, had papered, painted, cleaned, furnished, it showed the effects now of neglect and of some wild sociability. A life went on in it that my mother could not have predicted or condoned. There were parties for the turkey crew, the gutters and pluckers, and sometimes one or two of the young men would be living there temporarily, inviting their own friends and having their own impromptu parties. This life, I thought, was better for my father than being lonely, and I did not disapprove, had certainly no right to disapprove. Andrew did not like to go there, naturally enough, because he was not the sort who could sit around the kitchen table with the turkey crew, telling jokes. They were intimidated by him and contemptuous of him, and it seemed to me that my father, when they were around, had to be on their side. And it wasn't only Andrew who had trouble. I could manage those jokes, but it was an effort.

I wished for the days when I was little, before we had the turkeys. We had cows, and sold the milk to the cheese factory. A turkey farm is nothing like as

Miles City, Montana

pretty as a dairy farm or a sheep farm. You can see that the turkeys are on a straight path to becoming frozen carcasses and table meat. They don't have the pretence of a life of their own, a browsing idyll, that cattle have, or pigs in the dappled orchard. Turkey barns are long, efficient buildings – tin sheds. No beams or hay or warm stables. Even the smell of guano seems thinner and more offensive than the usual smell of stable manure. No hints there of hay coils and rail fences and songbirds and the flowering hawthorn. The turkeys were all let out into one long field, which they picked clean. They didn't look like great birds there but like fluttering laundry.

Once, shortly after my mother died, and after I was married – in fact, I was packing to join Andrew in Vancouver – I was at home alone for a couple of days with my father. There was a freakishly heavy rain all night. In the early light, we saw that the turkey field was flooded. At least, the low-lying parts of it were flooded – it was like a lake with many islands. The turkeys were huddled on these islands. Turkeys are very stupid. (My father would say, 'You know a chicken? You know how stupid a chicken is? Well, a chicken is an Einstein compared with a turkey.') But they had managed to crowd to higher ground and avoid drowning. Now they might push each other off, suffocate each other, get cold and die. We couldn't wait for the water to go down. We went out in an old rowboat we had. I rowed and my father pulled the heavy, wet turkeys into the boat and we took them to the barn. It was still raining a little. The job was difficult and absurd and very uncomfortable. We were laughing. I was happy to be working with my father. I felt close to all hard, repetitive, appalling work, in which the body is finally worn out, the mind sunk (though sometimes the spirit can stay marvellously light), and

Alice Munro

I was homesick in advance for this life and this place. I thought that if Andrew could see me there in the rain, red-handed, muddy, trying to hold on to turkey legs and row the boat at the same time, he would only want to get me out of there and make me forget about it. This raw life angered him. My attachment to it angered him. I thought that I shouldn't have married him. But who else? One of the turkey crew?

And I didn't want to stay there. I might feel bad about leaving, but I would feel worse if somebody made me stay.

Andrew's mother lived in Toronto, in an apartment building looking out on Muir Park. When Andrew and his sister were both at home, his mother slept in the living room. Her husband, a doctor, had died when the children were still too young to go to school. She took a secretarial course and sold her house at Depression prices, moved to this apartment, managed to raise her children, with some help from relatives – her sister Caroline, her brother-in-law Roger. Andrew and his sister went to private schools and to camp in the summer.

'I suppose that was courtesy of the Fresh Air fund?' I said once, scornful of his claim that he had been poor. To my mind, Andrew's urban life had been sheltered and fussy. His mother came home with a headache from working all day in the noise, the harsh light of a department-store office, but it did not occur to me that hers was a hard or admirable life. I don't think she herself believed that she was admirable – only unlucky. She worried about her work in the office, her clothes, her cooking, her children. She worried most of all about what Roger and Caroline would think.

Caroline and Roger lived on the east side of the park, in a handsome stone house. Roger was a tall man with a

Miles City, Montana

bald, freckled head, a fat, firm stomach. Some operation on his throat had deprived him of his voice – he spoke in a rough whisper. But everybody paid attention. At dinner once in the stone house – where all the dining-room furniture was enormous, darkly glowing, palatial – I asked him a question. I think it had to do with Whittaker Chambers, whose story was then appearing in the *Saturday Evening Post*. The question was mild in tone, but he guessed its subversive intent and took to calling me Mrs Gromyko, referring to what he alleged to be my 'sympathies'. Perhaps he really craved an adversary, and could not find one. At that dinner, I saw Andrew's hand tremble as he lit his mother's cigarette. His Uncle Roger had paid for Andrew's education, and was on the board of directors of several companies.

'He is just an opinionated old man,' Andrew said to me later. 'What is the point of arguing with him?'

Before we left Vancouver, Andrew's mother had written, 'Roger seems quite intrigued by the idea of your buying a small car!' Her exclamation mark showed apprehension. At that time, particularly in Ontario, the choice of a small European car over a large American car could be seen as some sort of declaration – a declaration of tendencies Roger had been sniffing after all along.

'It isn't that small a car,' said Andrew huffily.

'That's not the point,' I said. 'The point is, it isn't any of his business!'

We spent the second night in Missoula. We had been told in Spokane, at a gas station, that there was a lot of repair work going on along Highway 2, and that we were in for a very hot, dusty drive, with long waits, so we turned on to the interstate and drove through Coeur d'Alene and Kellogg into Montana. After Missoula, we turned south toward Butte, but detoured to see Helena, the state capital. In the car, we played Who Am I?

Cynthia was somebody dead, and an American, and a girl. Possibly a lady. She was not in a story. She had not been seen on television. Cynthia had not read about her in a book. She was not anybody who had come to the kindergarten, or a relative of any of Cynthia's friends.

'Is she human?' said Andrew, with a sudden shrewdness.

'No! That's what you forgot to ask!'

'An animal,' I said reflectively.

'Is that a question? Sixteen questions!'

'No, it is not a question. I'm thinking. A dead animal.'

'It's the deer,' said Meg, who hadn't been playing.

'That's not fair!' said Cynthia. 'She's not playing!'

'What deer?' said Andrew.

I said, 'Yesterday.'

'The day before,' said Cynthia. 'Meg wasn't playing. Nobody got it.'

'The deer on the truck,' said Andrew.

'It was a lady deer, because it didn't have antlers, and it was an American and it was dead,' Cynthia said.

Andrew said, 'I think it's kind of morbid, being a dead deer.'

'I got it,' said Meg.

Cynthia said, 'I think I know what morbid is. It's depressing.'

Helena, an old silver-mining town, looked forlorn to us even in the morning sunlight. Then Bozeman and Billings, not forlorn in the slightest – energetic, strung-out towns, with miles of blinding tinsel fluttering over used-car lots. We got too tired and hot even to play Who Am I? These busy, prosaic cities reminded me of

Miles City, Montana

similar places in Ontario, and I thought about what was really waiting there – the great tombstone furniture of Roger and Caroline's dining-room, the dinners for which I must iron the children's dresses and warn them about forks, and then the other table a hundred miles away, the jokes of my father's crew. The pleasures I had been thinking of – looking at the countryside or drinking a Coke in an old-fashioned drugstore with fans and a high, pressed-tin ceiling – would have to be snatched in between.

'Meg's asleep,' Cynthia said. 'She's so hot. She makes me hot in the same seat with her.'

'I hope she isn't feverish,' I said, not turning around.

What are we doing this for, I thought, and the answer came – to show off. To give Andrew's mother and my father the pleasure of seeing their grandchildren. That was our duty. But beyond that we wanted to show them something. What strenuous children we were, Andrew and I, what relentless seekers of approbation. It was as if at some point we had received an unforgettable, indigestible message – that we were far from satisfactory, and that the most commonplace success in life was probably beyond us. Roger dealt out such messages, of course – that was his style – but Andrew's mother, my own mother and father couldn't have meant to do so. All they meant to tell us was 'Watch out. Get along.' My father, when I was in high school, teased me that I was getting to think I was so smart I would never find a boyfriend. He would have forgotten that in a week. I never forgot it. Andrew and I didn't forget things. We took umbrage.

'I wish there was a beach,' said Cynthia.

'There probably is one,' Andrew said. 'Right around the next curve.'

'There isn't any curve,' she said, sounding insulted. 'That's what I mean.'

'I wish there was some more lemonade.'

'I will just wave my magic wand and produce some,' I said. 'Okay, Cynthia? Would you rather have grape juice? Will I do a beach while I'm at it?'

She was silent, and soon I felt repentant. 'Maybe in the next town there might be a pool,' I said. I looked at the map. 'In Miles City. Anyway, there'll be something cool to drink.'

'How far is it?' Andrew said.

'Not so far,' I said. 'Thirty miles, about.'

'In Miles City,' said Cynthia, in the tones of an incantation, 'there is a beautiful blue swimming pool for children, and a park with lovely trees.'

Andrew said to me, 'You could have started something.'

But there was a pool. There was a park, too, though not quite the oasis of Cynthia's fantasy. Prairie trees with thin leaves – cottonwoods and poplars – worn grass, and a high wire fence around the pool. Within this fence, a wall, not yet completed, of cement blocks. There were no shouts or splashes; over the entrance I saw a sign that said the pool was closed every day from noon until two o'clock. It was then twenty-five after twelve.

Nevertheless I called out, 'Is anybody there?' I thought somebody must be around, because there was a small truck parked near the entrance. On the side of the truck were these words: 'We have Brains, to fix your Drains. (We have Roto-Rooter too.)'

A girl came out, wearing a red lifeguard's shirt over her bathing suit. 'Sorry, we're closed.'

'We were just driving through,' I said.

Miles City, Montana

'We close every day from twelve until two. It's on the sign.' She was eating a sandwich.

'I saw the sign,' I said. 'But this is the first water we've seen for so long, and the children are awfully hot, and I wondered if they could just dip in and out – just five minutes. We'd watch them.'

A boy came into sight behind her. He was wearing jeans and a T-shirt with the words 'Roto-Rooter' on it.

I was going to say that we were driving from British Columbia to Ontario, but I remembered that Canadian place names usually meant nothing to Americans. 'We're driving right across the country,' I said. 'We haven't time to wait for the pool to open. We were just hoping the children could get cooled off.'

Cynthia came running up barefoot behind me. 'Mother. Mother, where is my bathing suit?' Then she stopped, sensing the serious adult negotiations. Meg was climbing out of the car – just wakened, with her top pulled up and her shorts pulled down, showing her pink stomach.

'Is it just those two?' the girl said.

'Just the two. We'll watch them.'

'I can't let any adults in. If it's just the two, I guess I could watch them. I'm having my lunch.' She said to Cynthia, 'Do you want to come in the pool?'

'Yes, please,' said Cynthia firmly.

Meg looked at the ground.

'Just a short time, because the pool is really closed,' I said. 'We appreciate this very much,' I said to the girl.

'Well, I can eat my lunch out there, if it's just the two of them.' She looked toward the car as if she thought I might try to spring some more children on her.

When I found Cynthia's bathing suit, she took it into the changing room. She would not permit anybody, even Meg, to see her naked. I changed Meg, who stood on the front seat of the car. She had a pink cotton bathing suit with straps that crossed and buttoned. There were ruffles across the bottom.

'She *is* hot,' I said. 'But I don't think she's feverish.'

I loved helping Meg to dress or undress, because her body still had the solid unself-consciousness, the sweet indifference, something of the milky smell, of a baby's body. Cynthia's body had long ago been pared down, shaped and altered, into Cynthia. We all liked to hug Meg, press and nuzzle her. Sometimes she would scowl and beat us off, and this forthright independence, this ferocious bashfulness, simply made her more appealing, more apt to be tormented and tickled in the way of family love.

Andrew and I sat in the car with the windows open. I could hear a radio playing, and thought it must belong to the girl or her boyfriend. I was thirsty, and got out of the car to look for a concession stand, or perhaps a soft-drink machine, somewhere in the park. I was wearing shorts, and the backs of my legs were slick with sweat. I saw a drinking fountain at the other side of the park and was walking toward it in a roundabout way, keeping to the shade of the trees. No place became real till you got out of the car. Dazed with the heat, with the sun on the blistered houses, the pavement, the burned grass, I walked slowly. I paid attention to a squashed leaf, ground a Popsicle stick under the heel of my sandal, squinted at a trash can strapped to a tree. This is the way you look at the poorest details of the world resurfaced, after you've been driving for a long time – you feel their singleness and precise location and the forlorn coincidence of your being there to see them.

Where are the children?

I turned around and moved quickly, not quite running,

Miles City, Montana

to a part of the fence beyond which the cement wall was not completed. I could see some of the pool. I saw Cynthia, standing about waist-deep in the water, fluttering her hands on the surface and discreetly watching something at the end of the pool, which I could not see. I thought by her pose, her discretion, the look on her face, that she must be watching some byplay between the lifeguard and her boyfriend. I couldn't see Meg. But I thought she must be playing in the shallow water – both the shallow and deep ends of the pool were out of my sight.

'Cynthia!' I had to call twice before she knew where my voice was coming from. 'Cynthia! Where's Meg?'

It always seems to me, when I recall this scene, that Cynthia turns very gracefully toward me, then turns all around in the water – making me think of a ballerina on point – and spreads her arms in a gesture of the stage. 'Dis-ap-peared!'

Cynthia was naturally graceful, and she did take dancing lessons, so these movements may have been as I have described. She did say 'Disappeared' after looking all around the pool, but the strangely artificial style of speech and gesture, the lack of urgency, is more like my invention. The fear I felt instantly when I couldn't see Meg – even while I was telling myself she must be in the shallower water – must have made Cynthia's movements seem unbearably slow and inappropriate to me, and the tone in which she could say 'Disappeared' before the implications struck her (or was she covering, at once, some ever-ready guilt?) was heard by me as quite exquisitely, monstrously self-possessed.

I cried out for Andrew, and the lifeguard came into view. She was pointing toward the deep end of the pool, saying, 'What's that?'

There, just within my view, a cluster of pink ruffles appeared, a bouquet, beneath the surface of the water. Why would a lifeguard stop and point, why would she ask what that was, why didn't she just dive into the water and swim to it? She didn't swim; she ran all the way around the edge of the pool. But by that time Andrew was over the fence. So many things seemed not quite plausible – Cynthia's behaviour, then the lifeguard's – and now I had the impression that Andrew jumped with one bound over this fence, which seemed about seven feet high. He must have climbed it very quickly, getting a grip on the wire.

I could not jump or climb it, so I ran to the entrance, where there was a sort of lattice gate, locked. It was not very high, and I did pull myself over it. I ran through the cement corridors, through the disinfectant pool for your feet, and came out on the edge of the pool.

The drama was over.

Andrew had got to Meg first, and had pulled her out of the water. He just had to reach over and grab her, because she was swimming somehow, with her head underwater – she was moving toward the edge of the pool. He was carrying her now, and the lifeguard was trotting along behind. Cynthia had climbed out of the water and was running to meet them. The only person aloof from the situation was the boyfriend, who had stayed on the bench at the shallow end, drinking a milkshake. He smiled at me, and I thought that unfeeling of him, even though the danger was past. He may have meant it kindly. I noticed that he had not turned the radio off, just down.

Meg had not swallowed any water. She hadn't even scared herself. Her hair was plastered to her head and her eyes were wide open, golden with amazement.

Miles City, Montana

'I was getting the comb,' she said. 'I didn't know it was deep.'

Andrew said, 'She was swimming! She was swimming by herself. I saw her bathing suit in the water and then I saw her swimming.'

'She nearly drowned,' Cynthia said. 'Didn't she? Meg nearly drowned.'

'I don't know how it could have happened,' said the lifeguard. 'One moment she was there, and the next she wasn't.'

What had happened was that Meg had climbed out of the water at the shallow end and run along the edge of the pool toward the deep end. She saw a comb that somebody had dropped lying on the bottom. She crouched down and reached in to pick it up, quite deceived about the depth of the water. She went over the edge and slipped into the pool, making such a light splash that nobody heard – not the lifeguard, who was kissing her boyfriend, or Cynthia, who was watching them. That must have been the moment under the trees when I thought, Where are the children? It must have been the same moment. At that moment, Meg was slipping, surprised, into the treacherously clear blue water.

'It's okay,' I said to the lifeguard, who was nearly crying. 'She can move pretty fast.' (Though that wasn't what we usually said about Meg at all. We said she thought everything over and took her time.)

'You swam, Meg,' said Cynthia, in a congratulatory way. (She told us about the kissing later.)

'I didn't know it was deep,' Meg said. 'I didn't drown.'

We had lunch at a take-out place, eating hamburgers and fries at a picnic table not far from the highway. In my excitement, I forgot to get Meg a plain hamburger, and had to scrape off the relish and mustard with plastic spoons, then wipe the meat with a paper napkin, before she would eat it. I took advantage of the trash can there to clean out the car. Then we resumed driving east, with the car windows open in front. Cynthia and Meg fell asleep in the back seat.

Andrew and I talked quietly about what had happened. Suppose I hadn't had the impulse just at that moment to check on the children? Suppose we had gone uptown to get drinks, as we had thought of doing? How had Andrew got over the fence? Did he jump or climb? (He couldn't remember.) How had he reached Meg so quickly? And think of the lifeguard not watching. And Cynthia, taken up with the kissing. Not seeing anything else. Not seeing Meg drop over the edge.

Disappeared.

But she swam. She held her breath and came up swimming.

What a chain of lucky links.

That was all we spoke about – luck. But I was compelled to picture the opposite. At this moment, we could have been filling out forms. Meg removed from us, Meg's body being prepared for shipment. To Vancouver – where we had never noticed such a thing as a graveyard – or to Ontario? The scribbled drawings she had made this morning would still be in the back seat of the car. How could this be borne all at once, how did people bear it? The plump, sweet shoulders and hands and feet, the fine brown hair, the rather satisfied, secretive expression – all exactly the same as when she had been alive. The most ordinary tragedy. A child drowned in a swimming pool at noon on a sunny day. Things tidied up quickly. The pool opens as usual at two o'clock. The lifeguard is a bit shaken up and gets the afternoon off. She drives away with her boyfriend in the Roto-Rooter truck. The body sealed away in some kind of shipping coffin. Sedatives, phone calls, arrangements. Such a sudden vacancy, a blind sinking and shifting. Waking up groggy from the pills, thinking for a moment it wasn't true. Thinking if only we hadn't stopped, if only we hadn't taken this route, if only they hadn't let us use the pool. Probably no one would ever have known about the comb.

There's something trashy about this kind of imagining, isn't there? Something shameful. Laying your finger on the wire to get the safe shock, feeling a bit of what it's like, then pulling back. I believed that Andrew was more scrupulous than I about such things, and that at this moment he was really trying to think about something else.

When I stood apart from my parents at Steve Gauley's funeral and watched them, and had this new, unpleasant feeling about them, I thought that I was understanding something about them for the first time. It was deadly serious thing. I was understanding that they were implicated. Their big, stiff, dressed-up bodies did not stand between me and sudden death, or any kind of death. They gave consent. So it seemed. They gave consent to the death of children and to my death not by anything they said or thought but by the very fact that they had made children – they had made me. They had made me, and for that reason my death – however grieved they were, however they carried on – would seem to them anything but impossible or unnatural. This was a fact, and even then I knew they were not to blame.

But I did blame them. I charged them with effrontery, hypocrisy. On Steve Gauley's behalf, and on behalf of all children, who knew that by rights they should have sprung up free, to live a new, superior kind of life, not to be caught in the snares of vanquished grown-ups, with their sex and funerals.

Steve Gauley drowned, people said, because he was next thing to an orphan and was let run free. If he had been warned enough and given chores to do and kept in check, he wouldn't have fallen from an untrustworthy tree branch into a spring pond, a full gravel pit near the river – he wouldn't have drowned. He was neglected, he was free, so he drowned. And his father took it as an accident, such as might happen to a dog. He didn't have a good suit for the funeral, and he didn't bow his head for the prayers. But he was the only grown-up that I let off the hook. He was the only one I didn't see giving consent. He couldn't prevent anything, but he wasn't implicated in anything, either – not like the others, saying the Lord's Prayer in their unnaturally weighted voices, oozing religion and dishonour.

At Glendive, not far from the North Dakota border, we had a choice – either to continue on the interstate or head north-east, toward Williston, taking Route 16, then some secondary roads that would get us back to Highway 2.

We agreed that the interstate would be faster, and that it was important for us not to spend too much time – that is, money – on the road. Nevertheless we decided to cut back to Highway 2.

'I just like the idea of it better,' I said.

Andrew said, 'That's because it's what we planned to do in the beginning.'

'We missed seeing Kalispell and Havre. And Wolf Point. I like the name.'

'We'll see them on the way back.'

Miles City, Montana

Andrew's saying 'on the way back' was a surprising pleasure to me. Of course, I had believed that we would be coming back, with our car and our lives and our family intact, having covered all that distance, having dealt somehow with those loyalties and problems, held ourselves up for inspection in such a foolhardy way. But it was a relief to hear him say it.

'What I can't get over,' said Andrew, 'is how you got the signal. It's got to be some kind of extra sense that mothers have.'

Partly I wanted to believe that, to bask in my extra sense. Partly I wanted to warn him – to warn everybody – never to count on it.

'What I can't understand,' I said, 'is how you got over the fence.'

'Neither can I.'

So we went on, with the two in the back seat trusting us, because of no choice, and we ourselves trusting to be forgiven, in time, for everything that had first to be seen and condemned by those children: whatever was flippant, arbitrary, careless, callous – all our natural, and particular, mistakes.

Iris Murdoch

extract from

The Bell

The lay religious community at Imber Court is well-intentioned if also self-deceiving. Dora and Toby, both outsiders, are young enough to withstand the moral pressures brought to bear by their elders — Dora's husband Paul, Toby's mentor Michael. Nevertheless, the two visitors resent the roles being forced upon them by the group and their extraordinary plan to raise the medieval bell sunk in Imber lake proves most effective in re-establishing their true identities and in exposing the unconscious and somewhat predatory motives of those around them.

By the time Dora arrived back at Imber she felt considerably more subdued. She had caught a train at once, but it was a slow one. She was vastly hungry again. She was afraid of Paul's anger. She tried to keep on believing that something good had happened to her; but now it seemed that this good thing had after all nothing whatever to do with her present troubles. It had been a treat and now it was over. At any rate, Dora was tired and couldn't think any more and felt discouraged, frightened, and resentful. The village taxi took her most of the way down the drive; she would not let it come right up to the house as she wanted the fact of her return to dawn quietly on the brotherhood. She was also afraid that, unless she could first see him alone, Paul would make a public scene. She saw from a distance the lights of the Court and they looked to her hostile and censorious.

It was well after ten o'clock. As Dora approached along the last part of the drive, stepping as quietly as possible on the gravel, she saw that there were lights on in the hall and the common-room. She could not see the window of her and Paul's room, which faced the other reach of the lake. The Court loomed darkly over her, blotting out the stars; and then she heard a sound of music. She stopped. Quite clearly on the soft and quiet warm night air there came the sharp sound of a piano. Dora listened, puzzled. Surely there was no piano at Imber. Then she thought, of course, a gramophone record, the Bach recital. This was the night for it and the community must all be gathered in the common-room listening. She wondered if Paul would be there. Leaning carefully on the balustrade so as to step more lightly she glided up the steps on to the balcony.

The lights from the hall and from the modern French windows of the common-room made a brightly illuminated area in the space at the top of the steps. Dora could see the flagstones clearly revealed. The music was now very loud and it was plain that no one could have heard her approaching. Dora stood for a moment or two, well out of the beam of light, attending to the music. Yes, that was Bach all right. Dora disliked any music in which she could not participate herself by singing or dancing. Paul had given up taking her to concerts since she could not keep her feet still. She listened now with distaste to the hard patterns of sound which plucked at her emotions without satisfying them and which demanded in an arrogant way to be contemplated. Dora refused to contemplate them.

She slithered round, still well in the darkness, until she reached a place from which she could see into the common-room. She trusted that the sharp contrast of light and dark would curtain her from the observation of those within. She found, with something of a shock, that she could see in quite clearly and that by moving round she could inspect the whole room. The music had seemed to make, like a waterfall, some enormous barrier, and it was strange now to find so many people so close to her. They were, however, people under a spell; and she felt she could survey them as an enchanter surveys his victims.

The Bell

The community were gathered in a semi-circle and seated in the uncomfortable wooden-armed common-room chairs, except for Mrs Mark who was sitting on the floor cross-legged, her skirt well tucked in under her ankles. She was leaning back against the leg of her husband's chair. Mark Strafford, his hand arrested in the act of stroking his beard, was turned towards the corner where the gramophone was, and looked like someone acting Michelangelo's Moses in a charade. Next to him sat Catherine, her hands clasped, the palms moving slightly against each other. Her head was inclined forward, her eyes brooding, the heavy expanse between the lashes and the high curved eyebrows slumberously revealed. Her gipsy hair was thrust carelessly behind her ears. Dora wondered if she was really listening to the music. Toby sat in the centre, opposite to the window, curled gracefully in the chair, one long leg under him, the other hooked over the arm, a hand dangling. He looked absent-minded and rather worried. Next to him was Michael who was leaning his elbows on his knees, his face hidden in his hands, his faded yellow hair spurting through his fingers. Beside him James sat with head thrown back in shameless almost smiling enjoyment of the music. In the corner was Paul, sitting rigid and wearing that somewhat military air which his moustache sometimes gave him and which went so ill with the rest of his personality. He looked tense, concentrated, as if he were about to bark out an order.

Dora was sorry to find Paul at the recital. With any luck he might have been more easily accosted, moping upstairs; as indeed he ought to be, she reflected resentfully, with the mystery of his wife's disappearance still unsolved. Dora watched him for a while, nervously, and then returned to scanning the whole group. Seeing them all together like that she felt excluded and aggressive, and Noel's exhortations came back to her. They had a secure complacent look about them: the spiritual ruling class; and she wished suddenly that she might grow as large and fierce as a gorilla and shake the flimsy doors off their hinges, drowning the repulsive music in a savage carnivorous yell.

Dora had now watched for so long that she felt herself invisible. She moved slightly, about to withdraw, and as she did so she saw that Toby was looking straight out of the window towards her. She wasn't sure for a moment whether he had seen her and she stood quite still. Then a change in his expression, a widening and focusing of his eyes, a slight tensing of his body told her that she had been observed. Dora waited, wondering what Toby would do. To her surprise he did nothing. He sat for a moment giving her a look of intense concentration; and then he dropped his eyes again. Dora slid quietly back into the darkness. No one else in the room had noticed anything.

She stood at the far corner of the balcony dejected, apprehensive, wondering what to do. She supposed she ought to go up to their bedroom and wait for Paul; but the prospect of this gloomy vigil was so appalling that she could not bring herself to mount the stairs. She wandered down again to the terrace and began to walk slowly along the path that led to the causeway. The moon was just rising and there was enough light to see where she was going. The silhouette of the Abbey trees and the tower could be seen, as on her first night at Imber. She reached the lake which seemed to glimmer blackly, not yet fully struck by the rays of the moon.

As she looked back towards the house she was alarmed to see that there was a dark figure following her down the

The Bell

path. She felt sure it must be Paul, and her old deep fear of him suddenly made the whole night scene terrifying. She was ready to run; but she stood still, her hand at her breast, as if to take a physical shock. The figure came nearer, hurrying soundlessly along the grassy track. When it was quite near she saw it was Toby.

'Oh, Toby,' said Dora with relief. 'Hello. You came out of the music.'

'Yes,' said Toby. He seemed breathless. 'I came out before the last movement.'

'Do you like that music?' said Dora.

'Not terribly, actually,' said Toby. 'I was going to come out anyway. Then I saw you through the window.'

'Did you say I was back?' said Dora.

'No, I thought I'd better not talk between the movements. I just slipped out. They're good for another three-quarters of an hour in there,' he added.

'Ah well,' said Dora. 'It's a nice night.'

'Let's walk along a bit,' said Toby.

He seemed pleased to see her. Thank heaven somebody was. They walked along the path beside the lake opposite the Abbey walls. The moon, risen further, was spreading a golden fan across the surface of the water. Dora looked at Toby and found that he was looking at her. Dora was glad to be with Toby. She felt a natural complicity with him which convinced her of the abiding strength and wholeness of her youth. Here was one who was not concerned to enclose or judge her. The rest of them, however, she gloomily reflected, Paul in one way and the brotherhood in another, would make her play their role. A few hours ago she had felt free and she had come back to Imber of her own free will, performing a real action. Yet *they* would make of it the guilty enforced return of an escaped prisoner. Contemplating the inevitability, whose nature she scarcely understood, of *their* superiority over her, and the impossibility of ever getting even with them, Dora was beginning to regret that she had come back.

They walked on, exchanging a word or two about the moonlight, until the path entered the wood. The cavern of darkened foliage covered them, illuminated here and there by glimpses of the gilded water. Toby plunged on confidently and Dora followed, finding silence easy in his company. She had decided to let the three-quarters of an hour which Toby had said they were 'good for' elapse, and then a little more time, to allow the company to disperse to their rooms; then she could be sure of finding Paul alone.

'Why, here we are!' said Toby.

'Where?' said Dora. She came up beside him. The trees stood back from the water and the moonlight clearly showed a grassy space and a sloping stone ramp leading down into the lake.

'Oh, just a place I know,' said Toby. 'I swam here once or twice. No one comes here but me.'

'It's nice,' said Dora. She sat down on the stones at the top of the ramp. The lake seemed quite still and yet made strange liquid noises in the silence that followed. The Abbey wall with its battlement of trees could be seen on the other side, some distance away to the left. But opposite there was only the dark wood, the continuation across the water of the wood that lay behind. It seemed to Dora that the wide moonlit circle at the edge of which she sat was apprehensive, inhabited. An owl called. She looked up at Toby. She was glad she was not there alone.

Toby was standing quite near at the head of the ramp, looking down at her. Dora forgot what she was going to

The Bell

say. The darkness, the silence, and their proximity made her quite suddenly physically aware of Toby's presence. She felt a line of force between his body and hers. She wondered if at this moment he felt it too. She remembered how she had seen him naked, and she smiled. The moon revealed her smile and Toby smiled back.

'Tell me something, Toby,' said Dora.

Toby, seeming a little startled, came down the ramp and squatted beside her. The cool weedy smell of the water was in their nostrils. 'What?' he said.

'Oh, nothing in particular,' said Dora. 'Just tell me something, anything.'

Toby sat back on the stones. After a pause he said, 'I'll tell you something very strange.'

'Go on,' said Dora.

'There's a huge bell down there in the water.'

'*What?*' said Dora. She half rose, amazed, scarcely understanding him.

'Yes,' said Toby, pleased with the effect he had produced. 'Isn't it odd? I found it when I was swimming underwater. I wasn't sure at first, but I came back a second time. I'm certain it's a bell.'

'You saw it, touched it?'

'I touched it, I felt it all over. It's only half buried in the mud. It's too dark to see.'

'Had it carvings on it?' said Dora.

'Carvings?' said Toby. 'Well, it was sort of fretted and worked on the outside. But that might have been anything. Why do you ask?'

'Good God!' said Dora. She stood up. Her hand covered her mouth.

Toby got up too. He was quite alarmed. 'Why, what is it?'

'Have you told anyone else?' said Dora.

651

'No. I don't know why, but I thought I'd keep it a secret till I'd visited it once again.'

'Well, look,' said Dora, 'don't tell anyone. Let it be *our* secret now, will you?' Dora, who felt no doubts either about Toby's story or about the identity of the object, was suddenly filled with the uneasy elation of one to whom great power has been given which he does not yet know how to use. She clutched her discovery as an Arab boy might clutch a papyrus. What it was she did not know, but she was determined to sell it dear.

'All right,' said Toby, rather gratified. 'I won't utter a word. I suppose it is very odd, isn't it? I don't know why I wasn't more thrilled about it. At first I wasn't sure — and, well, a lot of other things distracted me since. Anyway, I *might* be wrong. But you seem so specially excited about it.'

'I'm sure you're not wrong,' said Dora. Then she told him the legend which Paul had told her, and which had so much seized upon her imagination, of the erring nun and the bishop's curse.

By the end of the tale Toby was as agitated as she was. 'But something like that *couldn't* be true,' he said.

'Well, no,' said Dora, 'but Paul said there's usually *some* truth in those old stories. The bell probably did get into the lake somehow, and there it is.' She pointed at the smooth surface of the water. 'If it is the medieval bell it's very important for art and history and so on. Could we pull it out?'

'We, you mean you and me?' said Toby amazed. 'We couldn't possibly. It's a huge thing, it must weigh an immense amount. And anyway, it's sunk in the mud.'

'You said only half sunk,' said Dora. 'You're an engineer. Couldn't we do it with a pulley or something?'

'We might rig up a pulley,' said Toby, 'but we haven't

The Bell

any power. At least, I suppose we might use the tractor. But what do you want to do?'

'I don't know yet,' said Dora. Her face was cupped in her hands, her eyes shining. 'Surprise everybody. Make a miracle. James said the age of miracles wasn't over.'

Toby looked dubious. 'If it's important,' he said, 'oughtn't we just to tell the others?'

'They'll know soon enough,' said Dora. 'We won't do any harm. But it would be such a marvellous surprise. Suppose – oh, well, I wonder – suppose, suppose we were to substitute the old bell for the new bell somehow, you know, when the new bell arrives next week? They're going to have the bell veiled, and unveil it at the Abbey gate. Think of the sensation when they find the medieval bell underneath the veil! Why, it would be wonderful, it would be like a real miracle, the sort of thing that makes people go on pilgrimages!'

'But it would be just a trick,' said Toby. 'And besides, the bell may be all broken and damaged. And anyway it's too difficult.'

'Nothing is too difficult,' said Dora. 'I feel this was meant for us. I should like to shake everybody up a bit. They'd get a colossal surprise – and then they'd be so pleased at having the bell, it would be like an unexpected present. Don't you think?'

'Wouldn't it be – somehow in bad taste?' said Toby.

'When something's fantastic enough and marvellous enough it can't be in bad taste,' said Dora. 'In the end, it would give everyone a lift. It would certainly give me a lift! Are you game?'

Toby began to laugh. He said, 'It's a most extraordinary idea. But I'm sure we couldn't manage it.'

'With an engineer to help me,' said Dora, 'I can do

anything.' And indeed as she stood there in the moonlight, looking at the quiet water, she felt as if by the sheer force of her will she could make the great bell rise. After all, and after her own fashion, she would fight. In this holy community she would play the witch.

* * *

'The chief requirement of the good life,' said Michael, 'is that one should have some conception of one's capacities. One must know oneself sufficiently to know what is the next thing. One must study carefully how best to use such strength as one has.'

It was Sunday, and Michael's turn to give the address. Although the idea of preaching was at this moment intensely distasteful to him, he forced himself dourly to the task, thinking it best to maintain as steadily as possible the normal pattern of his life. He spoke fluently, having thought out what he wanted to say beforehand and uttering it now without hesitations or consulting of notes. He found his present role abysmally ludicrous, but he was not at a loss for words. He stood upon the dais looking out over his tiny congregation. It was a familiar scene. Father Bob sat in the front row as usual, his hands folded, his bright bulging eyes intent upon Michael, devouring him with attention. Mark Strafford, his eyes ambiguously screwed up, sat in the second row with his wife and Catherine. Pete Topglass sat in the third row, busy polishing his spectacles on a silk handkerchief. Every now and then he peered at them and then, unsatisfied, went on polishing. He was always nervous when Michael spoke. Next to him was Patchway, who usually turned up to hear Michael, and

The Bell

who had removed his hat to reveal a bald spot which although so rarely uncovered contrived to be sunburnt. Paul and Dora were not present, having gone out for a walk looking irritable and obviously in the middle of a quarrel. Toby sat at the back, his head bowed so low in his hands that Michael could see the ruff of hair at the back of his neck.

Michael was aware now, when the knowledge was too late to do him any good, that it had been a great mistake to see Toby. The meeting, the clasp of the hands, had had an intensity, and indeed a delightfulness, which he had not foreseen – or had not cared to foresee – and which now made, with the earlier incident, something which had the weight and momentum of a story. There had been a development; there was an expectancy. Michael knew that he ought to have managed the interview with Toby differently, yet, that, being himself, he could not have done so: and since this was the case he ought to have written Toby a letter, or better still done nothing whatsoever and let the boy think of him what ill he pleased. He was ready to measure *now* how far the interview had been necessary to him in order that he might somehow refurbish Toby's conception of him, so rudely shaken by what had occurred.

The trouble was, as Michael now saw, that he had performed the action which belonged by right to a better person; and yet too, by an austere paradox, a better person would not have been in the situation that required that action. It would have been possible to conduct the meeting with Toby in an unemotional way which left the matter completely closed; it was only not possible for Michael. He remembered his prayers, and how he had taken the thing almost as a test of his faith. It was true that a person of great faith could with impunity have acted boldly: it was only that Michael was not that person. What he had failed to do was accurately to estimate his own resources, his own spiritual level: and it was indeed from his later reflections on this matter that he had, with a certain bitterness, drawn the text for his sermon. One must perform the lower act which one can manage and sustain: not the higher act which one bungles.

Michael was aware that to overestimate the importance of what was going on was itself a danger. He sighed for some robust common sense which would envisage his action as deplorable but now at least completed without disastrous consequences. He felt, rather pusillanimously, that a sturdy, even cynical, confidant could have helped him to reduce the power which the situation had over him, by seeing it in a more ordinary and less dramatic proportion. But he had no possible confidant; and he remained continually and miserably aware of one consequence which his action had had. He had completely destroyed Toby's peace of mind. He had turned the boy from an open, cheerful hard-working youth into someone anxious, secretive, and evasive. The change in Toby's conduct seemed to Michael so marked that he was surprised that no one else seemed to have noticed it.

He had also destroyed his own peace of mind. An unhealthy excitement consumed him. He worked steadily, but his work was bad. He found now that he awoke each morning with a feeling of curiosity and expectation. He could not prevent himself from continually observing Toby. Toby, on his part, avoided Michael, while being obviously extremely aware of him. Michael guessed on general grounds, and then read in the boy's behaviour, that a reaction had set in. When he had spoken with

The Bell

Toby in the nightjar alley he knew that the emotion which he had felt had received an echo: the memory of this moved him still. The sense that Toby's feelings were now ebbing, that he was perhaps deliberately hardening his heart and regarding with disgust that impulse of affection drove Michael to a sort of frenzy. He longed to speak to Toby, to question him, once more to explain; and he could not help hoping that Toby would sooner or later force such a tête-à-tête upon him. He wished that somehow he could pull out of this mess the atom of good which was in it, crystallizing out his harmless goodwill for Toby, Toby's for him. But he knew, and knew it very well, that this was impossible. In this world, it was almost certain, Toby and he could never now be friends: and hardening of the heart was perhaps indeed the best solution. He prayed constantly for Toby, but found that his prayers drifted into fantasies. He was tormented by vague physical desires and by the memory of Toby's body, warm and relaxed against his in the van; and his dreams were haunted by an ambiguous and elusive figure who was sometimes Toby and sometimes Nick.

The thought, when he let his mind dwell upon it, that Nick and Toby were together at the Lodge, added another dimension to Michael's unrest. He returned, fruitlessly, again and again, to the question of whether Nick could possibly have seen him embracing Toby. On each occasion he decided that it was impossible, but then found himself wondering afresh. Such a cloud of distress surrounded this subject that he was not sure what it was, here, that he was regretting: the damage to his own reputation, the possible damage to Nick, or something far more primitive, the loss of Nick's affection, which after all he had no reason to think he still retained and certainly no right to wish to hold.

The only result of these agitations was that it became more impossible than ever to 'do anything' about Nick himself; though he was still resolved to speak to Catherine. When his imagination, with its cursed visual agility, conjured up possible scenes at the Lodge, he was tormented by a two-way jealousy which also prevented him from reconsidering his plan, so desirable from many points of view, of moving Nick or Toby or both up to the Court. His motives, he felt, would be so evident, at any rate in the quarters which at present concerned him most, nor could he bring himself to act on such motives, even though supported by other good reasons. His only consolation was that Toby would be leaving Imber in any case in another couple of weeks; and Nick would probably leave when Catherine had entered the Abbey. It was a matter of hanging on. Afterwards he would, with God's help, set his mind in order and return to his tasks and his plans, which he was determined should not be altered by this nightmarish interlude.

Michael was continuing with his address. He went on, 'It is the positive thing that saves. Can we doubt that God requires of us that we know ourselves? Remember the parable of the talents. In each of us there are different talents, different propensities, many of them capable of good or evil use. We must endeavour to know our possibilities and use what energy we really possess in the doing of God's will. As spiritual beings, in our imperfection and also in the possibility of our perfection, we differ profoundly one from another. How different we are from each other is something which it may take a long time to find out; and certain differences may never appear at all. Each one of us has his own way of apprehending God. I am sure you will know what I mean when I say that one finds God, as it were, in certain places; one has, where

The Bell

God is concerned, a sense of direction, a sense that *here* is what is most real, most good, most true. This sense of reality and weight attaches itself to certain experiences in our lives – and for different people these experiences may be different. God speaks to us in various tongues. To this, we must be attentive.

'You will remember that last week James spoke to us about innocence. I would add this to what he so excellently said. We have been told to be, not only as harmless as doves, but also as wise as serpents. To live in innocence, or having fallen to return to the way, we need all the strength that we can muster – and to use our strength we must know where it lies. We must not, for instance, perform an act because abstractly it seems to be a good act if in fact it is so contrary to our instinctive apprehensions of spiritual reality that we cannot carry it through, that is, cannot really perform it. Each one of us apprehends a certain kind and degree of reality and from this springs our power to live as spiritual beings: and by using and enjoying what we already know we can hope to know more. Self-knowledge will lead us to avoid occasions of temptation rather than to rely on naked strength to overcome them. We must not arrogate to ourselves actions which belong to those whose spiritual vision is higher or other than ours. From this attempt, only disaster will come, and we shall find that the action which we have performed is after all not the high action which we intended, but something else.

'I would use here, again following the example of James, the image of the bell. The bell is subject to the force of gravity. The swing that takes it down must also take it up. So we too must learn to understand the mechanism of our spiritual energy, and find out where, for us, are the hiding places of our strength. This is what

I meant by saying that it is the positive thing that saves. We must work, from inside outwards, through outwards, through our strength, and by understanding and using exactly that energy which we have, acquire more. This is the wisdom of the serpent. This is the struggle, pleasing surely in the sight of God, to become more fully and deeply the person that we are; and by exploring and hallowing every corner of our being, to bring into existence that one and perfect individual which God in creating us entrusted to our care.'

Michael returned to his seat, his eyes glazed, feeling like a sleep-walker in the alarming silence which followed his words. He fell on his knees with the others and prayed the prayer for quietness of mind, which was at such moments all that he could compass. Laboriously he followed the petitions of Father Bob Joyce; and when the service was over he slipped quickly out of the Long Room and took temporary refuge in his office. He wondered how obvious it had been that he was saying the exact opposite of what James had been saying last week. This led him to reflect on how little, in all the drama of the previous days, he had dwelt upon the simple fact of having broken a rule. He recalled James's words: sodomy is not deplorable, it is forbidden. Michael knew that for himself it was just the how and why of it being deplorable that engaged his attention. He did not in fact believe that it was *just* forbidden. God had created men and women with these tendencies, and made these tendencies to run so deep that they were, in many cases, the very core of the personality. Whether in some other, and possibly better, society it could ever be morally permissible to have homosexual relations was, Michael felt, no business of his. He felt pretty sure that in any world in which he would live he would judge it,

The Bell

for various reasons, to be wrong. But this did not make him feel that he could sweep, as James did, the whole subject aside. It was complicated. For himself, God had made him so and he did not think that God had made him a monster.

It was complicated; it was *interesting*: and there was the rub. He realized that in this matter, as in many others, he was always engaged in performing what James had called the second best act: the act which goes with exploring one's personality and estimating the consequences rather than austerely following the rules. And indeed his sermon this very day had been a commendation of the second best act. But the danger here was the very danger which James had pointed out: that if one departs from a simple apprehension of certain definite commandments one may become absorbed in the excitement of a spiritual drama for its own sake.

Michael looked at his watch. He remembered now that he had arranged to see Catherine before lunch, having nerved himself at last to make the appointment. It was already time to go and find her. He knew that he must endeavour now to say something to her about Nick, to ask her to give him definite advice on how to make her brother participate more in the activities of the community. He did not look forward to raising this topic, or indeed to seeing Catherine at all, but at least it was something ordinary and patently sensible to do. He found himself hoping that Catherine might strongly advise the removal of Nick from the Lodge. He descended the stairs and glanced round the hall and put his head into the common-room.

Catherine was not to be seen; nor was she on the balcony or the terrace. Mark Strafford was sunning himself on the steps. Michael called, 'Seen Catherine anywhere?'

'She's in the stable yard with her delightful twin,' said Mark. 'Brother Nick has at last decided to mend the lorry. *Deo gratias*.'

Michael disliked this information. He was a little tempted to postpone the interview, but decided quickly that he must not do so. Catherine might be waiting for him to, as it were, release her from Nick; and since he had at last, and with such difficulty, made up his mind to talk to her about her brother he had better not let his decision become stale. It would be a relief, anyway, to get that talk over, not least because he could then feel that, to some wretchedly small degree, he had 'done something' about Nick. He set off for the stable yard.

The big gates that led on to the drive were shut. Michael noticed gloomily, and not for the first time, that they needed a coat of paint and one gate post was rotting. He entered by a little gate in the wall. The yard, one of William Kent's minor triumphs, was composed on three sides of loose boxes surmounted by a second storey lit by alternate circular and rectangular windows under a dentil cornice. It gave somewhat the impression of a small residential square. The stone-tiled roof was surmounted opposite the gates by a slender clock tower. The clock no longer went. On the right side a part of the building had been gutted by fire, and corrugated iron, contributed by Michael's grandfather, still filled the gaping holes in the lower story. The yard sloped markedly towards the lake and was divided from the drive by a high wall. Now, in the heat of the day, it was enclosed, dusty, stifling, rather dazzling in the sunshine. It reminded Michael of an arena.

The fifteen-hundredweight lorry was standing in the middle of the yard just beyond the shadow of the wall, its nose towards the lake. The bonnet was open and from underneath the vehicle a pair of feet could be seen sticking out. Nearby, regardless of the dust, Catherine Fawley was sitting on the ground. Her skirt was hitched up towards her waist and her two long legs, crossed at the ankle, were exposed almost completely to the sun. Michael was surprised to see her in this pose and surprised too that she did not, on seeing him, get up, or at least pull her skirt down. Instead she looked up at him without smiling. Michael, for the first time since he had met her, conjectured that she might positively dislike him.

Nick came edging out from underneath the lorry, his feet disappearing on one side, his head appearing on the other. He lay supine, half emerged, his head resting in the dust. He swivelled his eyes back towards Michael who, from where he was standing, saw his face upside down. He seemed to be smiling, but his inverted face looked so odd it was hard to tell.

'The big chief,' said Nick.

'Hello,' said Michael. 'Very good of you to fix the lorry. Will it be all right?'

'What drivel,' said Nick. 'It's not very good of me to fix the lorry. It's shocking of me not to have done it earlier. Why don't you say what you mean? It was only a blocked petrol feed. It should be all right now.' He continued to lie there, his strange face of a bearded demon looking up at Michael.

Michael, still conscious of Catherine's stare, fumbled for words. 'I was just looking for your sister,' he said.

'I was just talking to my sister,' said Nick. 'We were discussing our childhood. We spent our childhood together, you know.'

'Ah,' said Michael idiotically. Somehow, he could not deal with both of them, and it occurred to him that this was one of the very few occasions when he had seen them together.

'I know it's wicked to chat and reminisce,' said Nick, 'but you must forgive us two, since it's our last chance. Isn't it, Cathie?'

Catherine said nothing.

Michael mumbled, 'Well, I'll be off. I can easily see Catherine another time.'

'All shall be well and all shall be well and all manner of bloody thing shall be well,' said Nick. 'Isn't that so, Cathie?'

Michael realized he was a bit drunk. He turned to go. 'Wait a minute,' said Nick. 'You're always "off", confound you, like the bloody milk by the time it reaches me at the Lodge. If you want all manner of thing to be well there's a little service you could perform for me. Will you?'

'Certainly,' said Michael. 'What is it?'

'Just get into the lorry and put the gear lever in neutral and release the hand-brake.'

Michael, moving instinctively toward the vehicle, checked himself. 'Nick,' he said, 'don't be an imbecile, that's not funny. And do get out from under that thing. You know the slope makes it dangerous, anyway. You ought to have put the lorry sideways.'

Nick pulled himself slowly out and stood up, dusting his clothes and grinning. Seeing him now in overalls and apparently doing a job of work Michael saw how much thinner and tougher he looked than when he had arrived: handsomer too, and considerably more alert. Michael also realized that these words were the first real words which he had addressed to Nick since the day of his arrival. Nick, who had obviously angled for them, was looking pleased.

The Bell

Michael was about to utter some excuse and go when the wooden door from the drive was heard creaking open once again. They all turned. It was Toby. He stood blinking at the enclosed scene, Catherine still sitting bare-legged and Michael and Nick close to each other beside the lorry. He hesitated with the air of one interrupting an intimate talk, and then since retreat was obviously impossible, came on into the yard and closed the door. Michael's immediate thought was that Toby was looking for him. He felt as if he were blushing.

'Why, here's my understudy,' said Nick. 'You might have had a lesson. But it's all over now.' Then turning his back on Toby he said to Catherine, 'Cathie, would you mind starting her up?'

To Michael's surprise, who had never associated her with engines of any kind, Catherine got up slowly, shook out her skirts, and climbed into the lorry. Watching her he had the feeling, which he had never had before, that she was acting a part. She started the engine. Nick, peering into the bonnet, surveyed the results. They seemed satisfactory. He closed the bonnet and stood for a moment grinning at Michael. Then he said, raising his voice in the continuing din of the engine, 'I think we'll take her for a little spin to make sure she's all right. Catherine shall drive. Come along, Toby.'

Toby, who had been standing uneasily near the gate, looked startled and came forward.

'Come along, quickly,' said Nick, holding open the door of the driving cabin, 'you're coming too.'

Toby got in.

'How about you, Michael?' said Nick. 'It would be rather a squeeze, but I expect someone could sit on someone's knee.'

Michael shook his head.

'Then would you mind opening the gates for us?' said Nick. He was sitting in the middle between Toby and Catherine, his arms spread out along the back of the seat so that he embraced the boy and his sister.

As in a dream Michael went to the big wooden gates and dragged them open. Catherine let in the clutch smoothly and the lorry swept past him in a cloud of dust and disappeared into the drive. A few moments later, as he still stood exasperated and wretched in the empty yard, he saw it reappear far off on the other side of the lake, roar up towards the Lodge, and vanish on to the main road.

* * *

Toby rose from his bed and picked up his shoes. He had not undressed, and had not dared to go to sleep for fear of oversleeping. His rendezvous with Dora was for two-thirty a.m. It was now just after two. He opened the door of his room and listened. The door of Nick's room was open, but snores could be heard from within. Toby glided down the stairs and reached the outer door. A movement behind him gave him a momentary shock, but it was only Murphy who had evidently followed him downstairs. The dog snuffled against his trouser leg, looking up at him interrogatively. He patted him, half guiltily, and slipped out of the door alone, closing it firmly behind him. On this particular expedition even Murphy was not to be trusted.

This was the night when Toby and Dora were to attempt to raise the bell. Since its apparently crazy inception this plan had grown in substance and complication; and Toby, who had at first regarded it as a dream,

The Bell

had now become its business-like and enthusiastic manager. Just why Dora was so keen on something so dotty had not at first been clear to Toby. It was still not clear to him, but now he no longer troubled about anything except to please Dora: and also to overcome certain technical problems whose fascination had become evident to his mechanical mind.

On the day after his first conversation with Dora about the bell he had gone for another solitary swim. He had dived a large number of times investigating the shape and position of the object in detail. He had now no doubts, fired by Dora's certainty and confirmed by his own findings, that this was indeed *the* bell. Two colossal problems now faced him. The first was how to get the bell out of the water, and the second was how to effect the substitution of the old bell for the new which was to constitute Dora's miracle: both these tasks to be performed undiscovered and with no helper but Dora. It was a tall order.

Dora, who had clearly got no conception of how large and how heavy the bell was, seemed to think it all perfectly possible, and relied upon Toby's skill with an *insouciance* which both exasperated and melted him. Even though he knew it to be based on ignorance, her confidence infected him: he was infected too by her curious vision, her grotesque imagination of the return to life of the medieval bell. It was as if, for her, this was to be a magical act of shattering significance, a sort of rite of power and liberation; and although it was not an act which Toby could understand, or which in any other circumstance he would have had any taste for, he was prepared to catch her enthusiasm and to be, for this occasion, the sorcerer's apprentice.

It was the apprentice, however, who had to contrive

the details of the sorcery. He had discussed various plans with Dora, whose ignorance of dynamics turned out to be staggering. The fact was, after some suggestions involving cart-horses had been set aside, that the only motive power available to them which could have even a chance of doing the job was the tractor. Even then, as Toby tried to impress upon Dora, it was possible that they would be simply unable to shift the bell. The amount of muddy ooze inside it alone would double its weight; and the lower part of it might turn out to be thoroughly jammed in the thicker mud of the floor of the lake. Toby had attempted to dig the ooze away from it on his last diving expedition, but with only partial success. It was a bore that Dora could neither swim nor drive the tractor, since this meant that the bell could not be given an extra helping hand from below while it was being pulled from above.

'I'm afraid I'm perfectly useless!' said Dora, her hands about her knees, her large eyes glowing at him with submissive admiration as they sat in the wood having their final conference. Toby found her perfectly captivating.

The official plan for the new bell was as follows. It was arriving at the Court on Thursday morning. It would then be placed upon one of the iron trolleys which were sometimes used to bring logs from the wood, and it would thereon be attired with white garments and surrounded with flowers. So apparelled it would be blessed and 'baptized' by the Bishop at a little service planned to take place immediately after the latter's arrival on Thursday evening, and at which only the brotherhood would be present. The bell would spend the night of Thursday to Friday in the stable yard. On Friday morning shortly before seven o'clock, the time at which postulants were customarily admitted to the

The Bell

Abbey, the bell would be the centre of a little country festival, whose details had been lovingly designed by Mrs Mark, during which it would be danced to by the local Morris, serenaded by a recorder band from the village school, and sung in solemn procession across the causeway by the choir from the local church, who had for some time now been studying ambitious pieces in its honour, one indeed composed for the occasion by the choirmaster. The procession, whose form and order was still under dispute, would consist of the performers, the brotherhood, and any villagers who cared to attend; and as interest was rather unexpectedly running high in the village quite a number of people seemed likely to come in spite of the earliness of the hour. The great gate of the Abbey would be opened as the procession approached and as its attendants fanned out on either side of it on the opposite bank the bell would be unveiled during a final burst of song. After it had stood for a suitable interval, revealed to the general admiration, it would be wheeled into the Abbey by specially selected workmen who had a dispensation to enter the enclosure for the purpose of erecting the bell. The closing of the gates behind the bell would end the ceremony as far as the outside world was concerned.

Toby and Dora's plan was as follows. On Wednesday night they would endeavour to raise the old bell. For this purpose they would use the tractor which as good fortune would have it Toby was now being permitted sometimes to drive. The ploughing up of the pastureland had commenced, and since the beginning of the week Toby had been working on the pasture with Patchway. The evening departure of the latter usually took place with unashamed punctuality; it would be an easy matter for Toby, about whose activities at that hour nobody would be bothering, instead of putting the tractor away, to drive it into the wood near the old barn. He had already cleared the branches and larger obstacles from the path that led through the barn to the lakeside, so that the tractor could be taken right through and almost to the water's edge. There it would be left until some time after midnight when Toby and Dora would meet at the ramp.

The tractor possessed a winch and a stout steel hawser with a hook at the end, used for hauling logs. With the hawser attached to the great ring which formed part of the head of the bell Toby hoped to be able to raise the bell, first by the winch and then by towing, and drag it into the barn. He had taken the precaution of sinking some stones and gravel at the foot of the ramp in case the bell should catch on the edge of the ramp where it ended under the level of the ooze. The danger at this point, apart from the unpredictability of the bell's behaviour, was that the sound of the tractor might be heard; but Toby judged that, with the south-west wind blowing as it had now been for some time, the noise was not likely to be audible at the Court, or if heard would not be recognizable. It might pass for a car or a distant aeroplane.

The next stage of the operation was no less complex. The large iron trolley on which the new bell was to rest had, fortunately, a twin brother. It was indeed the existence of this twin which made the plan feasible at all. Once the bell was inside the barn, the steel hawser would be passed over one of the large beams and the winch used to raise it from the ground. From this position it could be lowered onto the second trolley and made fast. The trolley could then, on Thursday night, without undue difficulty, be propelled along the concrete road

The Bell

which led beside the wood, sloping slightly down in the direction of the Court. The road led directly via the market-garden to the stable yard where the wood store was; and where the new bell would be, apparelled for its trip on the morrow. Here it should be possible for the bells to change clothes. The flowers and other garnishings of the trolley would conceal any small differences of shape which a sharp eye might notice between the two twins. If the bells turned out to be of vastly different sizes this would certainly be a snag: but Toby, who had slyly discovered the dimensions of the new bell, and who had taken what measurements he could of the old, was confident that they were roughly of a size. The new bell, disrobed, would then be wheeled into one of the empty loose-boxes into which no one ever peered, and the operation would be complete. The most perilous, as opposed to difficult, part of it would be the last; but as the stable yard was a little distant from the house, and as none of the brotherhood slept on the side nearest the yard, it was to be hoped that no one would hear anything.

There was one final annoyance. The second iron trolley, which would convey the old bell, was in daily use in the packing sheds. Mrs Mark used it as a table on which she arranged her goods, before pushing it up to the back of the van for loading. If Toby were to remove it on Wednesday night its absence would be noted on Thursday. It must therefore be removed on Thursday night. A minimum of operations at the barn would, however, be left for Thursday. On Wednesday the bell would be lifted, by the hawser passing over the beam, to a point, measured by Toby, a fraction higher than the level of the trolley. A second hawser, which Toby had discovered in the store room, would then be brought into action, hooked into the bell at one end, thrown over the beam, and made fast in the fork of a nearby tree by means of a crowbar passed through the ring in which the hawser ended. The first hawser, which was attached to the tractor, could then be released and the bell left hanging. The tractor would be taken back to the ploughing very early on Thursday morning. The bell would spend Thursday hanging in the barn. Dora had collected a quantity of green boughs and creepers with which it might be disguised; but in fact discovery during that day was exceedingly unlikely. On Thursday night the trolley would be brought and passed under the bell. If Toby's measurements, including the allowance he had made for sagging in the hawser, were exact enough the two surfaces would meet without interval; if his measurements were not quite exact the trolley could be lifted a little on earth and stones, or else dug into the floor of the barn, to take the rim of the bell. The hawser would then be removed and the bell would be resting on the trolley. This ingenious arrangement made it unnecessary to have the tractor in attendance on the second night.

The mechanical details of the plan aroused in Toby a sort of ecstasy. It was all so difficult and yet so exquisitely possible and he brooded over it as over a work of art. It was also his homage to Dora and his proof to himself that he was in love. Ever since the moment in the chapel when Dora's image had so obligingly filled out that blank form of femininity towards which Toby interrogatively turned his inclinations he had been, he felt, under her domination, indeed as he almost precisely put it, under her orders. The fact that Dora was married troubled Toby very little. He had no intention of making any declaration to Dora or revealing by any word or gesture what was his state of mind. He took a proud

The Bell

satisfaction in this reticence, and felt rather like a medieval knight who sighs and suffers for a lady whom he has scarcely seen and will never possess. This conception of her remoteness made the vitality of her presence and the easy friendliness with which, in their curious enterprise, she treated him, all the more delightful. She had for him a radiance and an authority, and the freshness of the emotion which she aroused gave him a sense almost of the renewal of innocence.

Strangely co-existent with the revelation of himself which, with daily additions, Dora was unconsciously bringing about, there was a dark continuing twisted concern about Michael. Toby avoided Michael but watched him and could not keep his thoughts from him; and his feelings veered between resentment and guilt. He had a sense of having been plunged into something unclean; and at the same time a miserable awareness that he was hurting Michael. Yet how could he not? His imagination dwelt vaguely upon some momentous interview which he would have with Michael before he left Imber; and there were many moments when he was strongly tempted to go and knock on the door of Michael's office. He had little conception of what he would do or say inside, but cherished, partly with embarrassment and partly with satisfaction, the view that Michael was in need of his forgiveness, and in need more simply of a kind word. Toby had, altogether, where this matter was concerned, a strong sense of unfinished business.

He made his way cautiously along the path beside the lake. The moon had not failed them and was high in the sky and almost full and the wide glimmering scene of trees and water was attentive, significant, as if aware of a great deed which was to be done. The lake, so soon to yield up its treasure, was serene, almost inviting, and the air was warm. He walked faster now, watching out for the figure of Dora ahead of him, almost breathless with anticipation and excitement. They had agreed to meet at the barn. He knew very well that there were a hundred things which could go wrong; but he burned with confidence and with the hope of delighting Dora and with a sheer feverish desire to get at the bell.

He reached the open space by the ramp and stopped. After the soft swishing sound of his footsteps there was an eerie silence. Then Dora emerged, taking shape in the moonlight, from the path leading to the barn. He spoke her name.

'Thank God,' said Dora in a low voice. 'I've been absolutely scared stiff in this place. There were such funny noises, I kept thinking the drowned nun was after me.'

A clear sound arose quite near them suddenly in the reeds and they both jumped. It was a harsh yet sweet trilling cry which rose several notes and then died bubbling away.

'Whatever was that?' said Dora.

'The sedge warbler,' said Toby. 'The poor man's nightingale, Peter Topglass calls him. He won't bother us. Now, Dora, quickly to work.'

'I think we're perfectly mad,' said Dora. 'Why did we ever have this insane idea? Why did you encourage me?' She was half serious.

'Everything will be all right,' said Toby. Dora's flutter made him calm and decisive. He paused, breathing deeply. The sedge warbler sang again, a little farther off. The lake was brittle and motionless, the reeds and grasses moving very slightly in the warm breeze, the moon as bright as it could be. It seemed then to Toby fantastic that in a moment there would be the roar of the tractor, the breaking into the lake. He felt as an army

The Bell

commander might feel just before launching a surprise attack.

He took a few steps into the wood. The tractor was there where he had left it, just outside the barn on the lake side. It was lucky that the barn had large doors opening both ways so that it had been possible to drive the tractor straight through. He had not dared to bring it any nearer to the water for fear its polished red radiator might be visible during daylight from the causeway. He quickly took off his clothes, and dressed only in his bathing trunks approached the tractor, shining his torch on it and checking the hawser and the winch. The winch had not been in use lately, but Toby had given it a good oiling and it seemed to be perfectly sound. He unwound a good length of hawser and looped it loosely round the drum. All this while Dora was hovering about behind him. At such a moment, attached as he was to her, he envied his medieval prototype who at least did not have to deal with both his lady and his adventure at the same time. For most of the operation Dora was useless.

'Just stand by near the water, would you,' said Toby, 'and do what I tell you.' He took a deep breath. He felt himself magnificent. He started the engine of the tractor.

A shattering roar broke the expectant moonlit silence of the wood. Toby could hear Dora's exclamations of dismay. He wasted no time but jumped on to the seat of the tractor, released the clutch, and let the great thing amble slowly in reverse toward the water. He felt love for the tractor, delight and confidence in its strength. He stopped it in the space near the top of the ramp and jumped off. He put the brake well on and began to drag a large log of wood across under the wheels. Dora rushed to help. He left the engine running, judging that a distant sound which continues is less likely to attract attention than an intermittent one. Then holding the end of the hawser, with its stout hook, he began to walk down the ramp.

The water was cold and its chilly touch shocked Toby, making him aware for a moment how completely he was entranced. He gasped, but plunged on till his feet left the stones and he was swimming, holding the hook in one hand. He now knew by heart the geography of the lake floor beyond the ramp. He felt he could almost see the bell. With the rhythmical sound of the tractor in his ears he dived. The hawser was heavy and helped to take him to the bottom, and his hand immediately encountered the mouth of the bell. Trailing the hook on the lake floor, the hawser running loosely through his fingers, he began to fumble towards the other end of the bell to find its great eye. As he did so a sudden consciousness of what he was doing came over him. He made as if to open his mouth and in a moment of panic shot up to the surface letting the hawser drop below him into the mud. Gasping, restored to the now terrifying scene of the moonlit lake and the roar of the engine, he swam back to the ramp.

Dora was standing with her feet in the water. She said something inaudible to him in frantic tones. Toby ignored her and began to drag the hawser in from the bottom. It came slowly, muddily. At last he had the hook in his hand again, and breathing steadily he swam out once more and dived. He grasped the rim of the bell and pulled himself towards it. With his next clutch he had his hand on the eye, his fingers slipping into the wide hole. Clinging on to the bell with one hand he approached the large hook with the other. With a sense of desperate joy he felt the hook pass through the hole.

The Bell

Then he rose, directing himself towards the ramp, and holding the hawser as taut as possible in his hand. He scrambled out. There was not much slack, he had judged the length needed very well. He pushed Dora out of the way and mounted the tractor. He geared the engine on to the winch and let it turn at a slow pace, first taking in the slack, and ready to switch off hastily if at any moment the bell seemed likely to pull the tractor into the lake. The hawser became taut, and he could feel the direct pull beginning between the tractor and the bell.

The winch came to a standstill. The engine roared, but the power was of no avail. Thinking quickly, Toby switched the power off the winch, moved the tractor a little away from the water, letting the hawser unwind, and brought it back to the tree-trunk in a new position. He switched over again to the winch and the hawser tightened. A heaving struggle began. Although the winch did not yet begin to move, he could feel a colossal agitation at the other end of the line. This was the moment at which the hawser was most likely to break. Toby sent up a prayer. Then he saw with incredulity and wild delight that very slowly the drum was beginning to turn. A fearful dragging could be heard, or perhaps felt, in that pandemonium it was hard to say which, upon the floor of the lake. Enormous muddy bubbles were breaking the surface. The movement was continuous now. The tractor was drawing the bell somewhat jerkily but steadily towards it as the strong winch turned. Toby could feel the great arching wheels braced against the tree-trunk. Like a live thing the tractor pulled. Then a grinding sound was to be heard: the bell must have reached the stony pile at the bottom of the ramp. Holding his breath Toby kept his eyes fixed on the point at which the thin line of the hawser, silvered by the moonlight, broke the heaving surface of the water. He felt a shock, which was probably the rim of the bell passing over the bottom edge of the ramp, and almost at the same moment, and sooner than he had expected, the hook came into view. Behind it an immense bulk rose slowly from the lake.

Hardly believing his eyes, yet chill with determined concentration, Toby waited until the bell lay upon the ramp, clear of the water, stranded like a terrible fish. He switched the power off the winch, and let the hawser fall slack, making sure that the bell was lodged securely on the gentle slope. Then he jumped down and began to pull the log away from under the wheels. A pale flurry seen from the corner of his eye was Dora still trying to help. He got back on to the roaring tractor, slipped the engine back into its normal gear, and very slowly released the clutch. The tractor bucked for a moment and then the great wheels began to turn and Toby saw the foliage moving past his head. He turned back to look at the bell. The rim was scraping hard on the stone and the upper end just clearing the ground. It jolted over the head of the ramp and the rim bit into the softer surface of the earth. Gathering beneath it a pile of earth and stones it followed the tractor into the darkness of the wood. Already Toby sensed the blackness of the barn roof above him, and he steadied the tractor across the floor and out through the wide door on the opposite side. When he judged that the bell had reached the middle of the barn he stopped the tractor and switched off the engine.

An appalling almost stunning silence followed. Toby sat quite still on the seat of the tractor. Then he breathed out slowly and rubbed his hands over his face and brows. He felt rather as if he would like now to crawl away

The Bell

somewhere and go to sleep. The last few minutes had been too crammed with experience. He began to climb from his seat and was mildly surprised to find that the extreme tension of his muscles had made him stiff. He got down and leaned over to rub his leg. He was amazed to find himself naked except for the bathing trunks.

'Toby, you were marvellous!' said Dora's voice beside him. 'You're an absolute hero. Are you all right? Toby, we've succeeded!'

Toby was in no mood for transports. He sneezed, and said, 'Yes, yes, I'm O.K. Let's look at the thing now. It'll probably turn out to be an old bedstead or something.' He stumbled past the dark shape in the middle of the floor and found his torch. Then he played the light upon it.

The bell lay upon its side, the black hole of its mouth still jagged with mud. Its outer surface, much encrusted with watery growths and shell-like incrustations, was a brilliant green. It lay there, gaping and enormous, and they looked at it in silence. It was a thing from another world.

'Well, good heavens,' said Dora at last. She spoke in a low voice as if awed by the presence of the bell. She reached out cautiously and touched it. The metal was thick, rough, and curiously warm. The thing was monstrous, lying there stranded upon the floor. She said, 'I had no idea it would be so huge.'

'Is it *the* one?' said Toby. He was amazed as he looked at it to think that it had been possible to make so large and inert an object obey his will. It was weird too that a thing so brightly coloured should have come out of so dark a place. He touched it too, almost humbly.

'Bring the torch closer,' said Dora. 'Paul said there were scenes of the life of Christ.'

They bent over the bell together, playing the light closely upon the vivid uneven surface. A little way from the rim it seemed to be divided into sections. Toby clawed with his fingers in the circle of light, pulling off encrusted mud and algae. Something was appearing. 'My God,' said Toby. Eyes stared at them out of square faces and a scene of squat figures was revealed.

'It must be!' said Dora. 'But I don't recognize that. Go on scraping. How grotesque they are. Yes, there's another scene. Why, it's the nativity for sure! Do you see the ox and the ass? And there are people catching fish. And all those men at the table must be having the Last Supper. And here's the crucifixion.'

'And the resurrection,' said Toby.

'There's something written,' said Dora.

Toby turned the light on to the rim of the bell. The words, interspersed with strangely shaped crosses, stood out clearly in the green metal. After a moment he said, 'Yes, it's Latin.'

'Read it out,' said Dora.

Toby read out, '*Vox ego sum Amoris. Gabriel vocor.* "I am the voice of Love. I am called Gabriel."'

'Gabriel!' cried Dora. 'Why, that was its name! Paul told me. It *is* the bell!' She looked up at Toby from where she was kneeling near its mouth. Toby turned the torch on to her. Her hair was wet with lake water and her cheeks were smudged with mud. A dark trickle was finding its way into the bosom of her hastily buttoned dress. Her hands laid upon the bell she blinked in the light, smiling up at Toby.

'Dora!' said Toby. He dropped the torch on the ground where its curtailed arc of light continued to shine. Naked as a fish, Toby felt a miraculous strength twisting inside him. He, and he alone, had pulled the bell from the lake.

The Bell

He was a hero, he was a king. He fell upon Dora, his two hands reaching for her shoulders, his body collapsing upon hers. He heard her gasp and then relax, receiving his weight, her arms passing round his neck. Clumsily, passionately, Toby's hard lips sought her in the darkness. Struggling together they rolled into the mouth of the bell.

As they did so the clapper, moving within the dark metal hollow, struck violently against the side, and a muted boom arose and echoed away across the lake whose waters had now once again subsided to rest.

*   *   *

Michael Meade was awakened by a strange hollow booming sound which seemed to come from the direction of the lake. He lay rigid for a moment listening anxiously to the silence that succeeded the sound, and then got out of bed and went to the open window. It was a bright moonlight night and the moon, full and risen high, cast a brilliance which was almost golden on the tranquil expanse of the water. Michael rubbed his eyes, amazed at the speed of his reaction, and still wondering whether he was awake or dreaming. He stood a while watching the quiet scene. Then he turned the light on and looked at his watch which said ten past three. He felt wide awake now and anxious. He sat on the edge of his bed, tense, listening. He had again that strange sense of impending evil. He sniffed, wondering if there were in fact some nauseating smell pervading the room. He remembered that just before he woke he had been dreaming of Nick.

He was too uneasy to sleep again. The noise he had

heard – he was sure this time that he had really heard it – unnerved him. He had vague memories of stories heard in childhood of noises coming out of the sea to portend disaster. He got dressed, intending to make a tour round the house to see that everything was all right. Strange visions afflicted him of finding that the Court was on fire. He turned the light on in the corridor and walked about a bit. Everything was as usual and no one else seemed to be stirring. He went out on to the balcony and looked round him in the splendid night. He saw at once in the distance that there was a light on in the Lodge. Nick at least was up. Or Toby. He scanned the banks of the lake as far as he could see in either direction. All seemed quiet.

Then he noticed something moving, and saw that a figure was walking along the path that led from the causeway to the ferry. He was clearly revealed now, with a long shadow, the figure of a man walking purposefully. Michael felt an immediate thrill of alarm and apprehension. He watched for a moment and then hurried down the steps and across the terrace to intercept the night wanderer, whoever he might be. The man, seeing Michael coming, stopped abruptly and waited for him to come nearer. Straining his eyes in the moonlight, and almost running now, Michael approached; and then recognized the figure, with mingled disappointment and relief, as Paul Greenfield.

'Oh, it's you,' said Paul.

'Hello,' said Michael. 'Anything the matter?'

'Dora's vanished,' said Paul. 'I woke up and found her gone. Then when she didn't come back I thought I'd go and look for her.'

'Did you hear an extraordinary sound just now?' said Michael.

The Bell

'Yes,' said Paul. 'I was just falling into a gorse bush at the time. What was it?'

'I don't know,' said Michael. 'It sounded like a bell.'

'A *bell*?' said Paul.

'I see there's a light on in the Lodge,' said Michael.

'That's just where I'm going now,' said Paul. 'I thought Dora might be there. Or if she isn't, I'd be interested to know whether Master Gashe is in his bed. Have you noticed those two rushing round together like a pair of conspirators?'

Michael who had indeed on his own account noticed this said, 'No, I noticed nothing.' They began to walk towards the ferry.

'Do you mind if I come with you?' said Michael. He too felt an intense desire to know what was going on at the Lodge.

Paul seemed to have no objection. They crossed in the boat and began to hurry along the path to the avenue. The light beaconed out clearly now. They passed out of the moonlight into the darkness of the trees and felt the firm gravel of the drive underfoot.

As they neared the Lodge they saw that the door was open. The light from the living-room, through the door and the uncurtained windows, revealed the gravel, the tall grasses, the iron rails of the gate. Paul, beginning to run, reached the doorway before Michael. He pushed his way in without knocking. Michael hastened after him, looking over his shoulder.

The scene in the living-room was peaceful and indeed familiar. The usual litter of newspapers covered the floor and the table. The stove was lit and Murphy was lying stretched out beside it. Behind the table, in his usual place, sat Nick. On the table there was a bottle of whisky and a glass. There was no one else to be seen.

Paul seemed nonplussed. He said to Nick, 'Oh, good evening, Fawley.' Paul was the only person who addressed Nick in this manner. 'I was just wondering if my wife was here.'

Nick, who had shown a little surprise, Michael thought, at his own arrival, was now smiling in his characteristic grimacing manner. With his greasy curling hair and his grimy white shirt, unbuttoned, and his long legs sticking straight out under the table he looked like some minor Dickensian rake. He reached for the bottle, and raised his eyebrows, possibly to express the slightly patronizing amazement, which Michael had often felt, too, at the frankness with which Paul revealed his matrimonial difficulties.

'Good morning, Greenfield,' said Nick. 'No, she ain't here. Why should she be? Have a drink?'

Paul said irritably, 'Thank you, no, I never take whisky.'

'Michael?' said Nick.

Michael jumped at his name, and took a moment to realize what Nick meant. He shook his head.

'Is Toby upstairs?' said Paul.

Nick went on smiling at him and kept him waiting for the answer. Then he said, 'No. He ain't here either.'

'Do you mind if I look upstairs?' said Paul. He pushed through the room.

Michael, who was just beginning to realize that Paul was in fact in a frantic state, found himself left alone with Nick. He cast a glance at him without smiling. He was fairly frantic himself.

Nick smiled. 'One of the deadly sins,' he said.

'What?' said Michael.

'Jealousy,' said Nick.

The Bell

Paul's feet were heard on the stairs. He came blundering back into the living-room.

'Satisfied?' said Nick.

Paul did not reply to this, but stood in the middle of the room, his face wrinkled up with anxiety. He said to Nick.

'Do you know where he is?'

'Gashe?' said Nick. 'No. I am not Gashe's keeper.'

Paul stood irresolutely for a moment, and then turned to go. As he passed Michael he paused. 'It was odd what you said about a bell.'

'Why?' said Michael.

'Because there's a legend about this place. I meant to tell you. The sound of a bell portends a death.'

'Did you hear that strange sound a little while ago?' Michael asked Nick.

'I heard nothing,' said Nick.

Paul stumped out of the door and began walking back along the drive.

Michael stayed where he was. He felt very tired and confused. If Nick would only have stayed quiet he would like to have sat with him for a while in silence. But those were all mad thoughts.

'Have a drink?' said Nick.

'No thanks, Nick,' said Michael. He found it very hard not to look at Nick. A solemn face seemed hostile and a smiling face provocative. He cast a rather twisted smile in his direction and then looked away.

Nick got up and came towards Michael. Michael stiffened as he approached. For a moment he thought Nick was going to come right up to him and touch him. But he stopped about two feet away, still smiling. Michael looked at him fully now. He wished he could drive that smile off his face. He had a strong impulse to reach out and put his two hands on Nick's shoulders. The sound that had awakened him, the moonlight, the madness of the night, made him feel suddenly that communication between them was now permitted. His whole body was aware, almost to trembling, of the proximity of his friend. Perhaps after all this was the moment at which he should in some way remove the barrier which he had set up between them. No good had come of it. And the fact remained, as he deeply realized in this moment, for whatever it meant and whatever it was worth, that he loved Nick. Some good might yet come of that.

'Nick,' Michael began.

Speaking almost at the same time Nick said, 'Don't you want to know where Toby is?'

Michael flinched at the question. He hoped his face was without expression. He said, 'Well, where is he?'

'He's in the wood making love to Dora,' said Nick.

'How do you know?'

'I saw them.'

'I don't believe you,' said Michael. But he did believe. He added, 'Anyway, it's no business of mine.' That was foolish, since on any view of the matter it was his business.

Nick stepped back to sit in a leisurely way on the table, watching Michael and still smiling.

Michael turned and went out, banging the door behind him.

* * *

'Well, and what happened then?' said James Tayper Pace.

The Bell

It was the next morning, and James and Michael were in the greenhouse picking tomatoes. The good weather was breaking, and although the sun still shone, a strong wind, which had arisen towards dawn, was sweeping across the kitchen garden. The tall lines of runner-beans swayed dangerously and Patchway went about his work with one hand clutching his hat. Inside the greenhouse however all was quiet and the warm soil-scented air and the firm red bunches of fruit made an almost tropical peace. Today all routines were altered because of the arrival of the bell, which was due to be delivered some time during the morning. The Bishop was to make his appearance during the afternoon, and after the baptism service would partake of tea with the community, a meal which, in the form of a stand-up buffet, was being planned on a grand scale by Margaret Strafford. He would then stay the night and officiate at the more elaborate rites on the following morning.

'Nothing happened,' said Michael. 'After I met Paul I went with him to the Lodge. Toby wasn't there. We came away again and I went back to bed and Paul wandered off to do some more searching. When I saw him this morning he said that he went back to his room about three-quarters of an hour later and found Dora there. She said it was such a hot night she'd been for a walk round the lake.'

James laughed his gruff booming laugh and lined another box with newspaper. 'I'm afraid,' he said, 'that Mrs Greenfield is what is popularly called a bitch. I'm sorry to say so, but one must call things by their names. Only endless trouble comes from not doing so.'

'You say you didn't hear any noise in the night?' said Michael.

'Not a sound. But I'm so dead tired these days I sleep

like the proverbial log. The last trump wouldn't wake me. They'd have to send a special messenger!'

Michael was silent. Nimbly he fingered the glowing tomatoes, warm with the sun and firm with ripeness. The boxes were filling fast.

James went on, 'One oughtn't to laugh, of course. I can't believe anything serious happened last night. Paul is a dreadful alarmist and a chronically jealous man. All the same, we ought to keep an eye on things; and I think it's regrettable that they've gone as far as they have.'

'Yes,' said Michael.

'I'm sure Toby and Dora have done nothing but run around together like a couple of youngsters,' said James. 'Dora is just about his mental age anyway. But with a woman like that you can't be sure that there wouldn't be some gesture, some word that might upset him. After all, he's not like my young East-enders. He's been a very sheltered child. A boy's first intimations of sex are so important, don't you think? And tampering with the young's a serious matter.'

'Quite,' said Michael.

'It's a pity,' said James, 'that we seem to have made so little impression on Mrs G. I wish she'd have a talk with Mother Clare. I'm sure it'd straighten her out a bit. That girl's just a great emotional mess at present. I feel we've let Paul down rather.'

'Possibly,' said Michael.

'And you know, we're fully responsible for the boy,' said James. 'He came here, after all, as a sort of retreat, a preparation for Oxford. Of course there's nothing seriously amiss in his rampaging around with Dora in a companionable way – but I think someone ought to put in a word.'

'Who to?' said Michael.

The Bell

'To Dora, I'd say,' said James. 'Appealing to Dora's better nature may turn out to be a difficult operation. I fear that girl is a blunt instrument at the best of times – and also resembles the *jeune homme de Dijon qui n'avait aucune religion!* But even if she doesn't care about her husband's blood pressure she ought to show some respect for the boy. She should see *that* point. Suppose you gave her a little kindly admonition, Michael?'

'Not me,' said Michael.

'Well, how about Margaret?' said James. 'Margaret is such a motherly soul and Dora seems to like her – and maybe that sort of advice would come better from a woman. Why, here is Margaret!'

Michael looked up sharply. Margaret Strafford could be seen running along the concrete path towards them her full skirt flapping in the wind. Michael interpreted her portentous haste immediately and his heart sank.

Margaret threw open the door, letting in a great blast of chill air. 'Michael,' she cried, delighted with her commission, 'the Abbess wants to see you at once!'

'I say, you *are* in luck!' said James. Their two bright amiable faces looked at him enviously.

Michael washed his hands at the tap in the corner of the greenhouse and dried them on his handkerchief. 'Sorry to leave you with the job,' he said to James. 'Excuse me if I dash.'

He set off at a run down the path which led along behind the house to the lake. It was customary to run when summoned by the Abbess. As he turned to the left towards the causeway the full blast of the wind caught him. It was almost blowing a gale. Then he saw, looking across the other reach of the lake, that an enormous lorry had just emerged from the trees of the avenue and was proceeding at a slow pace along the open part of the drive. It must be the bell. He should have been interested, excited, pleased. He noted its arrival coldly and forgot it at once. He turned on to the causeway. He felt certain that the Abbess must know all about Toby. It was irrational to think this. How could she possibly have found out? Yet it was astonishing what she knew. Breathlessly, as he reached the wooden section in the centre of the causeway, he slowed down. His footsteps echoed hollow upon the wood. He had not expected this summons. He felt as if he were about to undergo some sort of spiritual violence. He felt closed, secretive, unresponsive, almost irritated.

At the corner of the parlour building Sister Ursula was waiting. She always acted watchdog to audiences with the Abbess. Her large commanding face beamed approval at Michael from some way off. She saw the summons as a sign of special grace. After all, interviews with the Abbess were coveted by all and granted only to a few.

'In the first parlour,' she said to Michael, as he passed her mumbling a salutation.

Michael burst into the narrow corridor and paused a moment to get his breath before opening the first door. The gauze panel was drawn across on his side in front of the grille and there was silence beyond. It was usual for the person summoned to arrive first. Michael pulled back the panel on his side to reveal the grille and the second gauze panel on the far side which screened the opposite parlour inside the enclosure. Then he straightened his shirt collar – he was wearing no tie – buttoned up his shirt, smoothed down his hair, and made a strenuous effort to become calm. He stood, he could not bring himself to sit down, looking at the blank face of the inner panel.

The Bell

After a minute or two during which he could feel the uncomfortable violence of his heart he heard a movement and saw a dim shadow upon the gauze. Then the panel was pulled open and he saw the tall figure of the Abbess opposite to him, and behind her another little room exactly similar to his. He genuflected in the accustomed way and waited for her to sit down. Slightly smiling she sat, and motioned him to be seated too. Michael pulled his chair well up to the grille and sat down on the edge of it sideways so that their two heads were close together.

'Well, my dear son, I'm glad to see you,' said the Abbess in the brisk voice with which she always opened an audience. 'I hope I haven't chosen the most dreadfully inconvenient time? You must be so busy today.'

'It's perfectly all right,' said Michael, 'it's a good time for me.' He smiled at her through the bars. His irritation, at least, was gone, overwhelmed by the profound affection which, mingled with respect and awe, he felt for the Abbess. Her bright, gentle, authoritative, exceedingly intelligent face, its long dry wrinkles as if marked with a fine tool, the ivory light from her wimple reflected upon it, reminiscent of some Dutch painting, reminded him of his mother, so long ago dead.

'I'm in a dreadful rush myself,' said the Abbess. 'I just felt I wanted to see you. It's been ages now, hasn't it? And there are one or two little business details. I won't keep you long.'

Michael felt relieved by this exordium. He had been afraid of being in some way hauled over the coals: and this was not the moment at which he wanted an intimate talk with the Abbess. In his present state he felt that any pressure from her would tip him over into a morass of profitless self-accusation. Taking courage from her business-like tone he said, 'I think everything's in train for tonight and tomorrow. Margaret Strafford has been doing marvels.'

'Bless her!' said the Abbess. 'We're all so excited, we can hardly wait for tomorrow morning. I believe the Bishop is arriving this afternoon? I hope I shall catch a glimpse of him before he goes. He's such a busy man. So good of him to give us his time.'

'I hope he won't think we're a lot of ineffectual muddlers,' said Michael. 'I'm afraid the procession tomorrow may be a bit wild and impromptu. There's plenty of goodwill, but not much spit and polish!'

'So much the better!' said the Abbess. 'When I was a girl I often saw religious processions in Italy and they were usually quite chaotic, even the grand ones. But it seemed to make them all the more spontaneous and alive. I'm sure the Bishop doesn't want a drill display. No, I've no doubt tomorrow will be splendid. What I really wanted to ask you about was the financial question.'

'We've drafted the appeal,' said Michael, 'and we've made a list of possible Friends of Imber. I'd be very grateful if you'd cast your eye over both documents. I thought, subject to your views, we'd send the appeal out about a fortnight from now. We can cyclostyle it ourselves at the Court.'

'That's right,' said the Abbess. 'I think, for a cause of this kind, not a printed appeal. After all, it's something quite domestic, isn't it? There are times when money calls to money, but this isn't one of them. We're only writing to our friends. I'd like to see what you've done, if you'd send it in today by Sister Ursula. We can probably add some names to the list. I wonder what sort of publicity our bell will get? That might help in some

The Bell

quarters, mightn't it? I see no harm in the world being reminded, very occasionally, that we exist!'

Michael smiled. 'I thought of that too,' he said. 'That's why I don't want the appeal delayed. We won't have any journalists present of course. Not that any have shown signs of wanting to turn up. But I've prepared a hand-out for the local press, and a shorter one for the national press. I talked the wording over with Mother Clare. And I've asked Peter to take some photographs which we might send along as well.'

'Well done,' said the Abbess. 'I just can't think how you find the time to do all the things you do do. I hope you aren't overworking. You look rather pale.'

'I'm in excellent health,' said Michael. 'There'll be a let-up in a week or two anyway. I'm sure the others are working far harder than I am. James and Margaret simply never stop.'

'I'm worried about your young friend at the Lodge,' said the Abbess.

Michael breathed in deeply. That was it after all. He could feel a hot blush spreading up into his face. He kept his eyes away from the Abbess, fixing them on one of the bars beyond her head. 'Yes?' he said.

'I know it's very difficult,' said the Abbess, 'and of course I know very little about it, but I feel he's not exactly getting what he came to Imber to get.'

'You may be right,' said Michael tonelessly, waiting for the direct attack.

'I expect it's largely his own fault,' said the Abbess, 'but he is dreadfully out of things, isn't he? And will be more so when Catherine is in with us.'

Michael realized with a shock of relief that the Abbess was speaking of Nick, not of Toby. He turned to look at her. Her eyes were sharp. 'I know,' he said. 'It's been very much on my mind. I ought to have done more about it. I'll see to it that something *is* done. I'll put someone, perhaps James, quite seriously on his tail. We'll move him up to the house and just make him join in somehow. But as you say, it's not easy. He doesn't want to work. I'm afraid he's only putting in a little time here. He'll soon be off to London.'

'He's a *mauvais sujet* to be sure,' said the Abbess, 'and that's all the more reason for us to take trouble. But a man like that does not come to a place like this for fun. Of course he came to be near Catherine. But the fact that he wants to be near her *now*, and the fact that he wants to stay in the community and not in the village, are at least suggestive. We cannot be certain that there is not some genuine grain of hope for better things. And if I may say so, the person who ought to be, as you express it, on his tail, is not James, but you.'

Michael sustained her gaze which was quizzical rather than accusing. 'I find him difficult to deal with,' he said. 'But I'll think carefully about it.' He felt an increased determination not to be frank with the Abbess.

The Abbess studied his face. 'I confess to you,' she said, 'that I feel worried and I'm not quite sure why. I feel worried about him and I feel worried about you. I wonder if there's anything you'd like to tell me?'

Michael held on to his chair. From behind her the spiritual force of the place seemed to blow upon him like a gale. It was ironical, he reflected, that when he had wanted to tell the Abbess all about it she had not let him and now when she wanted to know he would not tell her. The fact was, he wanted her advice but not her absolution; and he could not ask the one without seeming to ask the other. Not that the Abbess would be tolerant. But he shied away almost with disgust

The Bell

from the idea of revealing to her his pitiable state of confusion. The story of Nick she almost certainly knew already in outline; what she wanted was to understand his present state of mind, and that would inevitably involve the story of Toby. If he began to tell the whole tale he knew that he could not tell it, now, without an absurd degree of emotion and without indulging in that particular brand of self-pity which he had been used to mistake for penitence. Silence was cleaner, better, in such a case. Looking down he saw, laid along the ledge of the grille, quite near to him like a deliberate temptation, infinitely wrinkled and pale, her hand, which had been covered with the tears of better men than himself. If he were to reach out to that hand he was lost. He averted his eyes and said, 'I don't think so.'

The Abbess went on looking at him for a little while, while he, feeling shrivelled and small and dry, looked at the corner of the room behind her. She said, 'You are most constantly in our prayers. And your friend too. I know how much you grieve over those who are under your care: those you try to help and fail, those you cannot help. Have faith in God and remember that He will in His own way and in His own time complete what we so poorly attempt. Often we do not achieve for others the good that we intend; but we achieve something, something that goes on from our effort. Good is an overflow. Where we generously and sincerely intend it, we are engaged in a work of creation which may be mysterious even to ourselves – and because it is mysterious we may be afraid of it. But this should not make us draw back. God can always show us, if we will, a higher and a better way; and we can only learn to love by loving. Remember that all our failures are ultimately failures in love. Imperfect love must not be condemned and rejected, but made perfect. The way is always forward, never back.'

Michael, facing her now, nodded slightly. He could not trust himself to utter any words after this speech. She turned her hand over, opening the palm towards him. He took it, feeling her cool dry grip.

'Well, I've kept you too long, dear child,' said the Abbess. 'I'd like to see you again in a little while, when this hurly-burly's done. Try not to overwork, won't you?'

Michael bent over her hand. Closing his eyes he kissed it and pressed it to his cheek. Then he raised a calm face to her. He felt obscurely that by his silence he had won a spiritual victory. He felt that he merited her approval. They both rose, and as Michael bowed to her again she closed the gauze panel and was gone.

He stood a while in the silent room looking at the bars of the grille and at the blank shut door of the panel behind them. Then he closed the panel on his side. How well she knew his heart. But her exhortations seemed to him a marvel rather than a practical inspiration. He was too tarnished an instrument to do the work that needed doing. Love. He shook his head. Perhaps only those who had given up the world had the right to use that word.

Edna O'Brien

extract from

Girl With Green Eyes

Caithleen's family invoke everything from the Virgin Mary to their own questionable assumptions concerning their daughter's mental instability in an effort to break off her relationship with a married man. But the attraction between the young Irish girl and the older, cosmopolitan Eugene is only strengthened by opposition.

At tea-time a wind began to rise, and rattled the shutters. Anna rushed out to bring in napkins which she had spread on one of the thorny bushes. A galvanized bucket rolled along the cobbled yard.

I had felt afraid all day, knowing that they were bound to come – but if a mountain storm blew up, it might keep them away. By the morrow I'd be gone.

After tea we sat in the study with a map of London spread on both our knees while he marked various streets and sights for me. I was to go early next morning and he had sent a telegram to Ginger, so that she could meet me.

'We ought to lock the doors,' I said, unnerved by the rattling of shutters.

'All right,' he said, 'we'll lock everything.' And I carried the big flashlamp around while he locked the potting-shed door, the back door, and another side door. The keys had rusted in their locks and he had to tap the bolts with a block of wood to loosen them. Anna and Denis had gone backstairs to their own apartments, and we could hear dance music from their radio.

'Tell them if there's a knock, not to answer it,' I suggested.

'Nonsense,' he said, 'they never come down once they've

gone up at night. They go to bed after the nine-o'clock news.' He was very proud and did not wish to share his troubles with anyone.

'Now the hall door,' I said. We opened it for a minute and looked out at the windy night and listened to the trees groaning.

'Go away from the window, bogy man,' he said as we came in and sat on the couch in front of the study fire. The oak box was stocked with logs and he said that we were perfectly safe and that no one could harm us.

There was a shot-gun in the corner of the hall, and I thought that maybe he should get it to be on the safe side.

'Nonsense,' he said. 'You just want some melodrama. . . .'

I could hear the wind and I imagined that I heard a car driving up to the house; I heard it all the time, but it was only in my imagination. I rubbed his hair and massaged the muscles at the back of his neck, and he said that it was very nice and very comforting.

'We get on well together, you and I,' he said.

'Yes,' I said, and thought how easy it would be, if he said then, I love you, or I could love, or I'm falling in love with you, but he didn't; he just said that we got on well together.

'We only know each other a couple of months,' he said to the fire, as if he had sensed my disappointment. I knew that he believed in the slow, invisible processes of growth, the thing which had to take root first in the lonely, dark part of one, away from the light. He liked to plant trees and watch them grow; he liked our friendship to take its course; he was not ready for me.

'Do you believe in God?' I said abruptly. I don't know why I said it.

'Not when I'm sitting at my own fire. I may do when I'm driving eighty miles an hour. It varies.' I thought it a very peculiar answer, altogether.

'What things are you afraid of?' I wished that somehow he would make some deep confession to me and engross me in his fears so that I could forget my own, or that we could play I-spy-with-my-little-eye, or something.

'Just bombs,' he said, and I thought that a peculiar answer too.

'But not hell?' I said, naming my second greatest fear.

'They'll give me a job making fires in hell, I'm good at fires.' I wondered how his voice could be so calm, his face so still. Sometimes I rubbed his neck and then again I rested my arm and sat very close to him, wondering how I could live without him in London for the while – until things blew over, he said.

'The best thing you can do about hell . . .' he began, but I never heard the end of the sentence, because just then the dog barked in the yard outside. She barked steadily for a few seconds and then let out a low, warning howl that was almost human-sounding. I jumped up.

'Sssh, ssh,' he said, as I stumbled over a tray of tea-things that was on the floor. He ran across and lowered the Tilley lamp; then we waited. Nothing happened, no footsteps, no car, nothing but the wind and the beating rain. Yet, I knew they were coming and that in a moment they would knock on the door.

'Must have been a badger or a fox.' He poured me a drink from the whisky bottle on the gun bureau.

'You look as white as a sheet,' he said, sipping the whisky. Then the dog barked again, loudly and continuously, and I knew by her hysterical sounds that she was trying to leap the double doors in the back yard. We had not locked them. My whole body began to shake and tremble.

'It's them,' I said, going cold all over. We heard boots on the gravel and men talking, and suddenly great banging and tapping on the hall door. The dog continued to bark hysterically, and above the noise of banging fists and wind blowing I heard the beating of my own heart. Knuckles rapped on the window, the shutters rattled, and at the same time the stiff knocker boomed. I clutched Eugene's sleeve and prayed.

'Oh God,' I said to him.

'Open up,' a man's voice shouted.

'They'll break down the door,' I said. Five or six of them seemed to be pounding on it, all at once. I thought that my heart would burst.

'How dare they abuse my door like that,' he said as he moved towards the hall.

'Don't, don't!' I stood in his way and told him not to be mad. 'We won't answer,' I said, but I had spoken too late. One of my people had gone around the back of the house, and we heard the metallic click of the back-door latch being raised impatiently. Then the bold was drawn and I heard Anna say, 'What'n the name of God do you want at this hour of night?'

I suppose that she must have been half asleep and had tumbled down thinking that we had been locked out or that the police had come for me.

I heard the Ferret's voice speak my name. 'We've come to take that girl out of here.'

'I don't know anything about it. Wait outside,' Anna said insolently, and then he must have walked straight past her because she shouted: 'How dare you!' and the sheepdog ran up the passage from the kitchen, yelping. The others were still knocking at the front of the house.

'This is beyond endurance,' Eugene said, and as he went to open the hall door, I ran back into the study, and looked around for somewhere to hide. I crawled under the spare bed hoping that he would bring them to the sitting-room, because he did not like people in the study where he worked. I heard him say:

'I can't answer you that, I'm afraid.'

'Deliver her out,' a voice demanded.

I had to think, to recall who it was.

'Come on now.' It was Andy, my father's cousin, a cattle-dealer. I recalled strange cattle – making the noises which cows make in unfamiliar places – being driven into our front field on the evenings preceding a fair day. Then cousin Andy would come up to the house for tea, and sitting in the kitchen in his double-breasted brown suit he'd discuss the price of heifers with my father. Once he gave me a threepenny bit which was so old and worn that the King had been rubbed off.

'Where is my only child?' my father cried.

She's under the bed, she's suffocating, I said to myself, praying that I would be there only for a second, while Eugene picked up the lamp and brought them across to the sitting-room. Could I then hide in the barn – and take the torch to ward off rats!

'My only child,' my father cried again.

For two pins I'd come out and tell him a thing or two about his only child!

'Who are you looking for?' Eugene said. 'We'll confer in the other room.'

But my father had noticed the fire, and with a sinking feeling I heard them all troop into the study. Someone sat on the bed; the spring touched my back, and smelling cow-dung from his boots, I guessed that it was cousin Andy. I recognized two other voices – Jack Holland's and the Ferret's.

'Don't you think it is a little late in the day for social calls?' Eugene said.

'We want that poor, innocent girl,' cousin Andy said – he, the famed bachelor, who had spoken only to cows and bullocks all his life, bullying them along the road to country fairs. 'Hand the girl over, and by God if there's a hair astray on her, you'll pay dear for it,' he shouted, and I imagined how he looked with his miser's face and a mean little mouth framed by a red moustache. He always had to carry stomach mixture with him everywhere, and had once raised his hand to my mother because she hinted about all the free grazing he took from Dada. On that occasion my father in his one known act of chivalry said, 'If you lay a finger on my missus, I'll lay you out.'

'This is outrageous,' Eugene said.

Various matches were struck – they were settling in.

'Allow me,' Jack Holland said, proceeding to make introductions, but he was shouted down by my father.

'A divorced man. Old enough to be her father. Carrying off my little daughter.'

'To set the record straight I did not bring her here, she came,' Eugene said.

I thought, he's going to let me down, he's going to send me away with them; my mother was right, 'Weep and you weep alone.'

'You got her with dope. Everyone knows that,' my father said.

Eugene laughed. I thought how odd, and immoral, he

Girl With Green Eyes

must look to them, in his corduroy trousers and his old check shirt. I hoped that all his buttons were done up. My nose began to itch with the dust.

'You're her father?' Eugene said.

'Allow me,' Jack Holland said again, and this time he performed the introductions. I wondered if it was *he* who had betrayed me.

'Yes, I'm her father,' Dada said, in a doleful voice.

'Go on now and get the girl,' Andy shouted.

I began to tremble anew. I couldn't breathe. I would suffocate under those rusty springs. I would die while they sat there deciding my life. I would die – with Andy's dungy boots under my nose. It was ironic. My mother used to scrub the rungs of the chair after his visits to our house. I said short prayers and multiplication-tables and the irregular plural of Latin nouns – anything that I knew by heart – to distract myself. I thought of a line from *Julius Caesar* which I had once recited, wearing a red nightdress, at a school concert – 'I see thee still and on thy blade and dudgeon gouts of blood. . . .'

'Are you a Catholic?' the Ferret asked, in a policeman's voice.

'I'm not a Catholic,' Eugene answered.

'D'you go to Mass?' my father asked.

'But, my dear man –' Eugene began.

'There's no "my dear man". Cut it out. Do you go to Mass or don't you? D'you eat meat on Fridays?'

'God help Ireland,' Eugene said, and I imagined him throwing his hands up in his customary gesture of impatience.

'None of that blasphemy,' cousin Andy shouted, making a noise as he struck his fist into his palm.

'What about a drink to calm us down?' Eugene suggested, and then, sniffing, he added, 'Perhaps better not – you seem to have brought enough alcohol with you.'

I could smell their drink from under the bed now, and I guessed that they had stopped at every pub along the way to brace themselves for the occasion. Probably my father had paid for most of it.

'Well . . . a sip of port wine all round might be conducive to negotiation,' Jack Holland suggested in his soft, mannerly way.

'Could I have a drink of water – to take an aspirin?' my father said.

'Good idea. I'll join you in an aspirin,' Eugene said, and I thought for a second that things were going to be all right. Water was poured. I closed my eyes to pray, dropped my forehead on to the back of my hand, and gasped. My face was damp with cold sweat.

'I would like you to realize that your daughter is escaping from *you*. I'm not abducting her. *I'm* not forcing her – she is running away from you and your way of living . . .' Eugene began.

'What the hell is he talking about?' Andy said.

'The tragic history of our fair land,' Jack Holland exclaimed. 'Alien power sapped our will to resist.'

'They get girls with dope,' the Ferret said. 'Many an Irish girl ends up in the white-slave traffic in Piccadilly. Foreigners run it. All foreigners.'

'Where's your wife, Mister? Would you answer that?' Andy said.

'And what are you doing with my daughter?' my father asked fiercely, as if recollecting what they had come for.

'I'm not *doing* anything with her,' Eugene said, and I thought, he has shed all responsibility for me, he does not love me.

Girl With Green Eyes

'You're a foreigner,' Andy said contemptuously.

'Not at all,' Eugene said pleasantly. 'Not at all as foreign as *your* tiny, blue, Germanic eyes, my friend.'

'What are your intentions?' my father asked abruptly. And then he must have drawn the anonymous letter from his pocket, because he said, 'There's a few things here would make your hair stand on end.'

'He hasn't much hair, he's near bald,' the Ferret said.

'I haven't any *intentions*; I suppose in time I would like to marry her and have children.... Who knows?'

'Ah, the patter of little feet,' said Jack Holland idiotically, and Dada told him to shut up and stop making a fool of himself.

He doesn't really want me, I thought as I took short, quick breaths and said an Act of Contrition, thinking that I was near my end. I don't know why I stayed under there, it was stifling.

'Would you turn?' my father said, and of course Eugene did not know what he meant by that.

'Turn?' he asked, in a puzzled voice.

'Be a Catholic,' the Ferret said. And then Eugene sighed and said, 'Why don't we all have a cup of tea?' And Dada said, 'Yes, yes.'

It will go on all night and I'll be found dead under this bed, I thought as I wished more and more that I could scratch a place between my shoulder-blades which itched terribly.

When he opened the door to fetch some tea he must have found Anna listening at the keyhole, because I heard him say to her, 'Oh Anna, you're here, can you bring us a tray of tea, please?' And then he seemed to go out of the room, because suddenly they were all talking at once.

'She could have got out the back way,' my father said.

'Get tough, boy, get tough,' Andy said. 'Follow him out, you fool, before he makes a run for it.'

'Poor Brady,' the Ferret said when Dada had apparently gone out, 'that's the thanks he gets for sending that little snotty-nose to a convent and giving her a fine education.'

'She was never right, that one,' cousin Andy said, 'reading books and talking to trees. Her mother spoilt her. . . .'

'Ah, her dear mother,' said Jack Holland, and while he raved on about Mama being a lady, the other two passed remarks about the portrait of Eugene over the fire.

'Look at the nose of him — you know what he is? They'll be running this bloody country soon,' Andy said.

'God 'tis a bloody shame, ruining a girl like that,' Andy said, and I thought how baffled they'd be if they had known that I was not seduced yet, even though I had slept in his bed for two whole nights.

I heard the rattle of cups as Eugene and my father came back.

'How much money do you earn in a year?' my father asked, and I knew how they would sneer if they heard that he made poky little films about rats, and sewerage.

'I earn lots of money,' Eugene lied.

'You're old enough to be her father,' Dada said. 'You're nearly as old as myself.'

'Look,' Eugene said after a minute, 'where is all this ill-temper going to get us? Why don't you go down to the village and stay in the hotel for the night, then come up in the morning and discuss it with Caithleen. She won't be so frightened in the morning and I will try and get her to agree to seeing you.'

'Not on your bloody life,' cousin Andy said.

'We'll not go without her,' my father added threateningly, and I lost heart then and knew that there was no escape. They would find me and pull me forth. We would go out in the wind and sit in the Ferret's car and drive all night, while they abused me. If only Baba was there, she'd find a way. . . .

'She's over twenty-one, you can't force her,' Eugene said, 'not even in Ireland.'

'Can't we? We won our fight for freedom. It's our country now,' Andy said.

'We can have her put away. She's not all there,' my father said.

'Mental,' the Ferret added.

'What about that, Mister?' cousin Andy shouted. 'A very serious offence having to do with a mentally affected girl. You could get twenty years for that.'

I gritted my teeth, my head boiled – why was I such a coward as to stay under there? They'd make a goat ashamed. Tears of rage and shame ran over the back of my hand and I wanted to scream, I disown them, they're nothing to do with me, don't connect me with them, but I said nothing – just waited.

'Go and get her,' my father said. '*Now!*' And I imagined the spits that shot out of his mouth in anger.

'You heard what Mr Brady said,' cousin Andy shouted, and he must have risen from the bed because the springs lifted. I knew how ratty he must look with his small blue eyes, his red moustache, his stomach ulcer.

'Very well then,' Eugene said, 'she's in my legal care. A guest in my house. When she leaves she will do so of her own free will. Leave my house or I'll telephone for the police.' I wondered if they'd notice that there *was* no phone.

Edna O'Brien

'You heard me,' Eugene said, and I thought, oh God he'll get hit. Didn't he know how things ended – 'Man in hospital with fifty-seven penknife wounds'. I started to struggle out, to give myself up.

I heard the first smack of their fists and then they must have knocked him over because the Tilley lamp crashed and the globe broke into smithereens.

I screamed as I got out and staggered up. Flames from the wood fire gave enough light for me to see by. Eugene was on the floor, trying to struggle up and Andy and the Ferret were hitting and kicking him. Jack Holland tried to hold them back, and my father, hardly knowing what he was doing, held the back of Jack Holland's coat, saying, 'Now Jack, now Jack, God save us, now Jack – oh Jack –'

My father saw me suddenly and must have thought that I had risen up from the ground – my hair was all tossed and there was fluff and dust on me. He opened his mouth so wide that his loose dental-plate dropped on to his tongue. They were cheap teeth that he had made by a dental mechanic.

'I didn't do it, I didn't do it, Maura,' he whispered, and backed away from me clutching his teeth. Long after, I realized that he thought I was Mama risen from her grave in the Shannon lake. I must have looked like a ghost; my face daubed with tears and grey dust, my hair hanging in my eyes.

I shouted at the Ferret to stop, when the door burst open and the room lit up with a great red and yellow flash, as Anna had fired the shot-gun at the ceiling. The thunder-clap made me stagger back against the bed with my head numb and singing. I tried to stay still, waiting to die. I thought I'd been shot, but it was only the shock of the explosion in my ears. The black smoke

Girl With Green Eyes

of gunpowder entered our throats and made me cough. Jack Holland was on his knees, praying and coughing, while Andy and the Ferret were turned to the door with their hands to their ears. My father leaned over a chair gasping, and Eugene moaned on the floor and put his hand to his bleeding nose. Shattered plaster fell down all over the carpet and the white dust mixed with gun smoke. The smell was awful.

'There's another one in it, I'll blow your brains out,' Anna said. She stood at the study door, in her nightdress, holding Eugene's shot-gun. Denis stood beside her with a lighted Christmas candle.

'Out you get,' she said to them, holding the gun steadily up.

'By God, I'm getting out of this,' the Ferret said. 'These people would kill you!' I went to Eugene, who was still sitting on the floor with blood coming from his nose. I put my handkerchief to it.

'Dangerous savages,' my father said, his face white, holding his teeth in one hand. 'She might have killed us.'

'I'll blow your feet off if you don't clear out of here,' Anna said in a quivering voice.

'Get out,' Eugene said to them as he stood up. His shirt was torn. 'Get out. Go. Leave. Never come inside my gates again.'

'Have you a drop of whisky?' my father said, shakily, putting his hand to his heart.

'No,' Eugene said. 'Leave my house, immediately.'

'A pretty night's work, a pretty night's work,' Jack Holland said sadly, as they left. Anna stood to one side to let them pass and Denis opened the hall door. The last thing I saw was the Ferret's hooked iron hand being shaken back at us.

Eugene slammed the door and Denis bolted it. I collapsed on to the bed, trembling.

'That's the way to handle them,' Anna said, as she put the gun on the table.

'You saved my life,' Eugene said, and he sat on the couch and drew up the leg of his trousers. There was blood on his shin, where he had been kicked. His nose also was bleeding.

'I'm sorry, I'm sorry,' I said between sobs.

'Oh tough men, tough men,' Denis said solemnly as we heard them outside arguing, and the dog barking from the back yard.

'Get some iodine,' Eugene said. I went upstairs but couldn't find it, so Anna had to go and get it, along with a clean towel and a basin of water. He lay back on the armchair, and I opened his shoe-laces and took off his shoes.

'Wh'ist,' Denis said. We heard the car drive away.

Anna washed the cuts on Eugene's face and legs. He squirmed with pain as she swabbed on iodine.

'I shouldn't have hidden,' I said, handing him a clean handkerchief from the top drawer of his desk, where he kept them. 'Oh, I shouldn't have come here.'

Through the handkerchief he said, 'Go get yourself a drink. It will help you to stop shaking. Get me one too.'

After a while the nose-bleed stopped and he raised his head and looked at me. His upper lip had swollen.

'It was terrible,' I said.

'It was,' he said, 'ridiculous. Like this country.'

'Only for me where would we be?' Anna said.

'What about a cup of tea?' he said in a sad voice, and I knew that he would never forget what had happened and that some of their conduct had rubbed off on to me.

*

Girl With Green Eyes

We went to bed late. His shin ached and a cut over his eye throbbed a lot. It was an hour before he went to sleep. I lay for most of the night, looking at the moonlit wall, thinking. Near dawn I found him awake, and looking at me.

'I love you,' I said suddenly. I had not prepared it or anything, it just fell out of my mouth.

'Love!' he said, as if it were a meaningless word, and he moved his head on the pillow to face me. He smiled and closed his eyes, going back to sleep again. What could I do to make up? I wasn't any good in bed, never mind not being able to fire a gun. I'd go back to Baba. I cried a bit, and later got up to make some tea.

Anna was in the kitchen putting on her good shoes and silk stockings, preparing to go to Mass.

'I'm not over it yet,' she said.

'I'll never be over it,' I said, and to myself, they've ruined, and ruined, and ruined me. He'll never look at me again. I'll have to go away.

* * *

She came back from Mass, bubbling over with news.

'They think in the village that you must be a film star,' she said as she took a long hatpin out of her blue hat, removed the hat and stuck the pin through it for the next Sunday. She said that I was the topic of conversation in the three shops. My father and his friends had stopped at the hotel for drinks on the way up.

As she put the frying-pan on the range, I noticed the tracks of mice in the cold fat.

'I expect you'll be leaving today,' she said.

'I expect so.'

It was after ten so I made Eugene's tea and carried it upstairs. Standing for a moment in the doorway with the tray I felt suddenly privileged to be in his room while he slept. The hollows of his cheeks were more pronounced in sleep and his face bore a slight look of pain. He had a nice gentle mouth, his lips handsomely shaped.

I drew back the curtains.

'You'll break the curtain rings,' he said, sitting up. His startled eyes looked twice their normal size.

'Oh, hello,' he said, surprised to see me and then rubbed his lids and probably remembered everything. I put a pullover across his shoulders and knotted the two sleeves under his chin.

'Nice tea,' he said as he lay there, like a Christ, sipping tea; his head resting on the mahogany bedhead.

Anna tapped on the door and burst in, before he had time to cry halt.

'I handed in the telegram – it will go first thing in the morning,' she said. It was to his solicitor.

She told me that my black pudding, below on the range, would be dried up if I didn't go down and eat.

'Black pudding!' he groaned.

'Your nose is a nice sight,' she said to him.

'Probably broken,' he said, without a smile.

'Oh – not broken!' I said.

'Lucky I don't earn my living with my nose,' he said. 'Or make love with it.'

'Hmmmh,' Anna said as she stood in the middle of the room, hands on hips, surveying the tossed bed and my nightdress on a chair.

'All right,' he said to us both, 'trot off,' and I went but she stayed there. I listened outside the door:

Girl With Green Eyes

'I saved your life, didn't I?'

'You did. I am very grateful to you, Anna. Remind me to strike you a leather medal.'

'Will you loan me fifty pounds?' she asked. 'I want to get a sewing-machine and a few things for the baba. If I had a sewing-machine we could mend all your shirts.'

'We could?' he said, mockingly.

'Will you loan me it?'

'Why don't you say "give me fifty pounds". I know that word "loan" has no meaning here.'

'That's not a nice thing to say.' She sounded offended.

'Anna, I'll give it to you,' he said. 'A reward.'

'Good man. Keep it to yourself, not a word to Denis. If he knew I had fifty pounds he'd buy a bull or something.'

She came out of the room beaming, and I ran away, ashamed at having been caught listening.

'Tell-tale-tattle,' she said as I hurried guiltily along the carpeted passage. 'Come on, I'll race you down the stairs,' and we ran the whole way to the kitchen.

She read the Sunday papers.

'She's the image of Laura,' she said, pointing to an heiress who was reported as being in love with a barber.

'Fitter changes sex,' she read aloud. 'Mother of God, I don't understand people at all. Do they never look at themselves when they're taking their clothes off!'

She read our horoscopes – Denis's, the baby's, Eugene's, mine, and Laura's. She included Laura in everything, so that by the time she went out after lunch with Denis and the baby, I had the feeling that Laura was due back any minute. It was with this unsettling feeling that I made my first tour of the house. Eugene had gone down the fields to look at the ram pump.

There were five bedrooms. The mattresses were folded over and the wardrobes empty, except for wooden hangers. The furniture was old, dark, unmatching, and in lockers beside the beds there were chamber-pots with pink china roses on the insides of them.

In the top drawer of a linen chest I found a silver evening bag with a diary of Laura's inside. The diary had no entries, just names and telephone numbers. There was also a purple evening glove that smelt of stale but wonderful perfume. I fitted on the glove and for some reason my heart began to pound. There was nothing in any of the other drawers, just chalk marks stating the number of each drawer.

Nearing dusk I came downstairs and raised the wick of the hanging lamp which Anna had lit for me before she went out. The rabbit was on the table, as she had left it, skinned and ready to be cooked. Denis had caught it the day before.

'The dinner,' I said aloud, as I got a cookery book and looked up the index under R.

Radishes,
Ragout of Kidneys,
Raisin Bread,
Raisin Pie,
Raisin Pudding,
Rarebit,
Raspberries.

Rabbit was not mentioned. The cookery book had belonged to Laura. Her maiden name and her married name were written in strong handwriting on the fly-leaf.

Girl With Green Eyes

'The dinner,' I said, to suppress a tear, and then I remembered how Eugene had asked, earlier in the day, 'Can you cook?'

'Sort of,' I had said.

It was a total lie. I never cooked in my whole life, except the Friday Gustav and Joanna went to a solicitor's to make a will. I brought home two fish for lunch, one for Baba, one for me. Baba laid the table while I fried the fish. I knew nothing about cleaning them. I just put the grey, podgy little fish on the big frying-pan and lit the gas under it. Nothing happened for a few minutes and then the side of one fish burst.

'There's a hell of a stink out there,' Baba called from the dining-room.

'It's just the fish,' I said. Both fish had burst by then.

'It's just what?' she said, rushing into the kitchen, holding her nose.

When she saw the mess she simply took hold of the pan and ran down the garden to dump it on Gustav's compost heap.

'Phew,' she said, coming back in to the house. 'You should have been alive when they ate raw cows and bones and things. A bloody savage.' And she put the pan into the sink and ran the tap on it.

We went out to lunch to Woolworths. It was a big thrill being able to march around with a tray, helping ourselves to whatever we fancied – chips, sausages, trifle topped with custard, coffee, a little jug of cream, and lemon meringue pie.

Sitting in the big flagged kitchen I thought of Baba and cried. I missed her. I had never been alone before in my whole life, alone and dependent on my own resources. I thought with longing of all the evenings we went out together, reeking with vanilla essence and good humour. Usually we ended up in the cinema, thrilled by the darkness, and the big screen, with perhaps a choc ice to keep us going.

'Oh God,' I said, remembering Baba, my father, everyone; and I buried my face in my hands and cried, not knowing what I cried for.

Three or four times, I went around the corner of the front drive and leaned on the wet, white gate to see if there was a sign of anybody coming. Nobody came, except a policeman who cycled down the by-road, stood at the gate-lodge for a minute, relieved himself, and cycled off again. He was probably keeping an eye out for poachers.

By the time Eugene came back I had dried my eyes; and I wondered if perhaps he expected me to have left discreetly while he was out.

'I'm still here,' I said.

'I'm glad,' he said as he kissed me. It was dusk and we proceeded to light the Tilley lamps.

As we sat by the study fire he said, 'Ah you poor little lonely bud, it's not a nice honeymoon for you, is it? Think of nice things . . . sunshine, mountain rivers, fuchsia, birds flying . . .'

I lay in his arms and could think only about what would happen next. He had put a record on the wind-up gramophone, and music filled the room. Outside, rain spattered against the window, and the water had lodged on the inner ledge of the window frame. It was very quiet except for the music and the rain. His eyes were closed, as he listened to the music. Music had a strange effect on him: his face softened, his whole spirit responded to it.

'That's Mahler,' he said, just when I expected him to say, 'You can stay or you can go.'

'I like songs that have words,' I said to clarify my position. But his eyes were closed and I did not think that he heard me at all. The music still reminded me of birds, birds wheeling out of a bush and startling the mellow hush of a summer evening; crows above an old slate quarry at home, multiplied by their own shadows and by their screaming and cawing. I wondered about my father then, and felt that they would come again, that night.

'But this music has words,' Eugene said, unexpectedly. So he had heard me. 'Words of a more perfect order, this music says things about people, people's lives, progress, wars, hunger, revolution. . . . Music can express with as simple instruments as reeds, the grey bodiless pain of living.'

I thought he must be a little mad to talk like that, especially when I worried about my father coming; and feeling very apart from him, I jumped up, on the excuse that I must look at the dinner. We had put on the rabbit.

It simmered very slowly and the white meat was falling away from the bone, gradually. I thickened the gravy with cornflour but it lumped a lot. Little beads of the flour floated on the surface.

''Twill have to do, I thought, as I went away to put some more powder on my face – the steam of the dinner had reddened my cheeks. When I came back to the room he was reading.

I sat opposite him and stared up at the circle of wrecked plaster – the result of Anna's shot. I thought, when I leave here tomorrow it is this that I will remember, I will always remember it.

'I'll go tomorrow,' I said suddenly. The yellow lamplight shone on his forehead and the reflection of a vase showed in the top part of his lenses. He had put on horn-rimmed glasses.

'*Go?*' he said, raising his eyes from the paper which rested on his knee. 'Where will you go?'

'I might go to London.'

'Do you want to?'

'No.'

'Then why are you going?'

'What else can I do?'

'You can stay.'

'That wouldn't be right,' I said, pleased that it was he who suggested it, and not me.

'Why not?'

'Because it would be throwing myself at you,' I said. 'I'll go away, and then when I'm gone you can write to me, and maybe I'll come back.'

'Supposing I don't want you to go away, then what?' he asked.

'I wouldn't believe it,' I said, and he raised his eyes to the ceiling, in mild irritation. I kept thinking that he asked me to stay because he pitied me, or maybe he was lonely.

'Why do you want me to stay?' I asked.

'Because I like you. I've lived like a hermit for so long, I mean, sometimes I feel lonely.' And he stopped himself suddenly, because he saw my eyes fill with tears.

'Caithleen,' he said softly – he usually said Kate, or Katie – 'Caithleen, stay,' and he put out his hand for mine.

'I'll stay for a week or two,' I said, and he kissed me and said how pleased he was.

We closed the shutters and had dinner. The rabbit meat and potatoes were crushed in the flour-thickened sauce, and the meal tasted very nice. He said that he

Girl With Green Eyes

would buy me a marriage ring, so that Anna and the neighbours would not bother me with questions.

'We can't actually get married, I'm not divorced and there is the child,' he said as he looked away from me, towards the crooked ink on the graph paper of the barograph. I followed his gaze – the jagged ink line suggested to me the jagged lines of all our lives, and I said, to hide my disappointment:

'I don't ever intend to get married, anyhow.'

'We'll see,' he said, and laughed, and then to cheer me up he told me all about his family.

He began – 'My mother is a hypochondriac' – he seemed to have forgotten that I met her – 'and she married my father in those fortunate days when women's legs were covered in long skirts. I say fortunate because her legs are like match-sticks. They met going down Grafton Street. He was a visiting musician – tall, dark, foreign, on his way to buy a French-English dictionary – and very courteously he asked the lady if she could direct him to a bookshop. I' – he tapped his chest – 'am the product of that accidental encounter.'

I laughed and thought how odd that his mother should have charmed the stranger so quickly. He went on to tell me that his father had left them when he was about five. He remembered his father dimly as a man who came home from work with a fiddle and oranges; his mother had worked as a waitress to feed them both, and like nine-tenths of the human race he had had a hard life and an unhappy childhood.

'Your turn,' he said, making an elegant gesture in my direction.

Fragments of my childhood came to mind – eating bread and sugar on the stone step of the back kitchen, and drinking hot jelly which had been put aside to cool.

Sometimes one word can recall a whole span of life. I said, 'Mama was in America when she was young, so she had American words for everything – "apple-sauce", "sweater", "greenhorn", and "dessert".'

I thought of incidental things – of the tinker woman stealing Mama's good shoes from the back-kitchen window, and of Mama having to go to court to give evidence and later regretting it because the tinker woman got a month in jail; of the dog having fits, and of a hundred day-old chickens being killed once by a weasel. In talking of it I could see the place again, the fields green and peaceful, rolling out from the solid cut-stone house; and in summertime, meadowsweet, creamy-white along the headlands, and Hickey humming 'How can you buy Killarney' as he sat like an emperor on the rusted mowing machine, swearing to me that dried cow-dung was sold in the shops as tobacco. I watched the grease settle on the dinner plates and still I sat there talking to Eugene as I had never talked before. He was a good listener. I did not tell him about Dada drinking.

We went to bed long after midnight. He limped upstairs while I followed behind with the Tilley lamp and wondered foolishly if I were likely to drop it and set fire to the turkey-red carpet.

'So we both need a father,' he said. 'We have a common bond.'

He did not make love to me that night. We had talked too much and anyhow he was stiff from having been kicked.

'There's no hurry,' I said.

He petted my stomach and we said warm, comforting things to lull each other to sleep.

Girl With Green Eyes

*   *   *

On Monday afternoon Eugene's solicitor drove out from Dublin. We had a fire in the sitting-room as we were expecting him. He was an austere, red-haired man with red eyebrows and pale blue eyes.

'And you say these people assaulted Mr Gaillard?' he asked.

'Yes. They did.'

'Did you witness this?'

'No, I was under the bed.'

'The bed?' He raised his sandy eyebrows and looked at me with cold disapproval.

'She's getting it all garbled, she means the spare bed in my study,' Eugene explained quickly. 'She hid under it when they came, because she was afraid.'

'Yes, a bed,' I said, annoyed with both of them.

'I see,' the lawyer said coldly as he wrote something down.

'Are you married, Miss Ah. . .?'

'No,' I said, and caught Eugene smiling at me, as much as to say, You will be.

Then the solicitor asked me what was my father's Christian name and surname, and the names of the others and their proper addresses. I felt badly about being the cause of sending them solicitors' letters but Eugene said that it had to be.

'It is just routine,' the solicitor said. 'We will warn them that they cannot come here again and molest Mr Gaillard. You are quite certain that you are over twenty-one?'

'I am quite certain,' I said, adopting his language.

Then he questioned Eugene, while I sat there looping and unlooping my hanky around my finger. Eugene had made notes of the whole scene which led up to their attacking him. He was very methodical like that.

I brought tea, and fresh scones with apple jelly and cream; but even that did not cheer the solicitor up. He talked to Eugene about dupress trees.

He left shortly after four and I waved to the moving motor-car, out of habit. It was getting dark and the air was full of those soft noises that come at evening – cows lowing, the trees rustling, the hens wandering around, crowing happily, availing themselves of the last few minutes before being shut up for the night.

'Well, that's that,' Eugene said as we came back in to the room, and he felt the teapot to see if the tea had gone cold.

'They won't trouble us again,' he said, pouring a half-cup of strong tea.

'They'll trouble us always,' I said. Recounting the whole incident had saddened me again.

'They'll have to accept it,' he said; but two mornings later I had a wretched letter from my aunt.

> Dear Caithleen;
> None of us has slept a wink since, nor eaten a morsel. We are out of our minds to know what's happening to you. If you have any pity in you, write to me, and tell me what are you doing. I pray for you, night and day! You know that you always have a welcome here, when you come back. Write by return and may God and His Blessed Mother watch over you and keep you pure and safe. Your father does nothing but cry. Write to him.
>
> Your aunt Molly

'Don't answer it,' Eugene said. 'Do nothing.'

'But I can't leave them worrying like that.'

'Look,' he said, 'this sentimentality will get you nowhere; once you make a decision you must stick to it. You've got to be hard on people, you've got to be hard on yourself.'

It was early morning and we had vowed never to begin an argument before lunch. In the mornings he was usually testy, and he liked to walk alone for an hour or two before talking to me.

'It's cruel,' I said.

'Yes,' he said. 'Kicking me with hobnailed boots is cruel. If you write to them,' he warned, 'they will come here and this time I leave *You* to deal with them.' His mouth was bitter, but that did not stop me from loving him.

'All right,' I said and I went away to think about it. Out in the woods everything was damp; the trees dripped and brooded, the house brooded, the brown mountain hung above me, deep in sullen recollection. It was a lonely place.

In the end I did nothing but have a cry, and by afternoon he was in better humour.

That night, he said, 'We're going into town tomorrow.' And taking a spare wallet from a drawer, he put notes in it and gave it to me. His initials were in gold on the beige-coloured leather, and he said it had been a present from someone.

'We'll buy you a ring and one or two other things,' he said; and then as he had his back to me, hefting a big log on to the fire, I peeped into the wallet and counted the number of notes he had given me. There were twenty in all.

Next day, walking down Grafton Street in a bitter wind,

I felt as if people were going to accuse me of my sin in public.

'Bang, bang,' he said, shooting our imaginary enemies, but I was still afraid, and glad to escape into a jeweller's shop.

We bought a wide gold ring and he put it on me in the shop – 'With this expensive ring, I thee bed,' he said, and I gave a little shiver and laughed.

We bought groceries and wine and two paperback novels and some note-paper. I asked him in the bookshop if he were very rich.

'Not very,' he said. 'The money is nearly gone, but I'll get your dowry or I'll work. . . .' There was some talk about his going to South America in the spring to do a documentary film on irrigation for a chemical company. And already I worried about whether he would bring me or not.

He had a haircut in a place that was attached to a hotel. He left me in the lounge, sipping a whisky and soda, but the minute he was out of sight I gulped the drink down and fled to the cloakroom in case anyone should recognize me. I washed my hands a few times and put on more make-up and each time I washed my hands the attendant rushed over with a clean towel for me. I suppose she thought that I was mad, washing my hands so often, but it passed the time. My ring shone beautifully after washing and I could see myself in it, when I brought my hand close to my face.

I must stop biting my nails, I thought, as I pressed the cuticles back, and remembered the time when I was young and bit my nails and thought foolishly that once I became seventeen I would grow up quite suddenly and be a lady and have long painted nails and no problems.

Girl With Green Eyes

I gave the grey-haired attendant five shillings and she got very flustered and asked if I wanted change.

'It's all right,' I said. 'I got married today.' I had to say it to someone. She shook my hand and tears filled her kind eyes as she wished me a long life of happiness. I cried a bit myself, to keep her company. She was motherly; I longed to stay there and tell her the truth and have her assurances that I had done the right thing, but that would have been ridiculous, so I came away.

Fortunately I was back in the lounge, sitting in one of the armchairs, when I saw him return. Even after such a short absence as that, I thought when I saw him, how beautiful he is with his olive skin and his prominent jawbones.

'That's done,' he said as he bent down and brushed his cheek against mine. He had had a shave too.

I had put on a lot of perfume and he said how opulent I smelled. Then, as a celebration, we crossed the hall to the empty dining-room and were the first to be served with dinner that night. He ordered a half-bottle of champagne, but when the waiter brought it in a tub of ice it looked so miserable that he sent it back again and got a full bottle. I asked to be given the cork and I still have it. It is the only possession I have which I regard as mine, that cork with its round silvered top.

We touched glasses and he said, 'To us,' and I drank, hoping that I would stay young always.

That night was pleasant. His face looked young and boyish because of the haircut, and I had a new black dress, bought with the money he gave me. In certain lights and at certain moments, most women look beautiful – that light and that moment were mine, and in the wall mirror I saw myself, fleetingly beautiful.

'I could eat you,' he said, 'like an ice-cream,' and later when we were home in bed, he re-said it, as he turned to make love to me. He twisted the wedding ring round and round my finger:

'It's a bit big for you, we'll get a clip on it,' he said.

''Twill do,' I said, being lazy and feeling mellow just then from champagne and the reassurance of his voice in my ear, as he smelled the warm scent of my hair.

'That ring has to last you a long time,' he said.

'How long?'

'As long as you keep your girlish laughter.'

I noticed with momentary regret that he never used dangerous words like 'for ever and ever'.

'Knock, knock, let me in,' he said, coaxing his way gently into my body.

'I am not afraid, I am not afraid,' I said. For days he had told me to say this to myself, to persuade myself that I was not afraid. The first thrust pained, but the pain inspired me and I lay there astonished with myself, as I licked his bare shoulder.

I let out a moan but he kissed it silent and I lay quiet, caressing his buttocks with the soles of my feet. It was very strange, being part of something so odd, so comic: and then I thought of how Baba and I used to hint about this particular situation and wonder about it and be appalled by our own curiosity. I thought of Baba and Martha and my aunt and all the people who regarded me as a child and I knew that I had now passed – inescapably – into womanhood.

I felt no pleasure, just some strange satisfaction that I had done what I was born to do. My mind dwelt on foolish, incidental things. I thought to myself, so this is it; the secret I dreaded, and longed for. . . . All the

Girl With Green Eyes

perfume, and sighs, and purple brassières, and curling-pins in bed, and gin-and-it, and necklaces, had all been for this. I saw it as something comic, and beautiful. The growing excitement of his body enthralled me – like the rhythm of the sea. So did the love words that he whispered to me. Little moans and kisses; kisses and little cries that he put into my body, until at last he expired on me and washed me with his love.

Then it was quiet; such quietness; quietness and softness and the tender limp thing like a wet flower between my legs. And all the time the moon shining in on the old brown carpet. We had not bothered to draw the curtains.

He lay still, holding me in his arms; then tears slowly filled my eyes and ran down my cheeks, and I moved my face sideways so that he should not mistake the tears because he had been so happy.

'You're a ruined woman now,' he said, after some time. His voice seemed to come from a great distance, because in hearing his half-articulated words of love I had forgotten that his speaking voice was so crisp.

'Ruined!' I said, re-echoing his words with a queer thrill.

I felt different from Baba now and from every other girl I knew. I wondered if Baba had experienced this, and if she had been afraid, or if she had liked it. I thought of Mama and of how she used to blow on hot soup before she gave it to me and of the rubber bands she put inside the turn-down of my ankle-socks, to keep them from falling.

He moved over and lay on his back and I felt lonely, without the weight of his body. He lit a candle and from it he lit himself a cigarette.

'Well, a new incumbent, more responsibility, more trouble.'

'I'm sorry for coming like this, without being asked,' I said, thinking that 'incumbent' was an insulting word; I mixed it up with 'encumbrance'.

'It's all right; I wouldn't throw a nice girl like you out of my bed,' he joked, and I wondered what he really thought of me. I was not sophisticated and I couldn't talk very well nor drive a car.

'I'll try and get sophisticated,' I said. I would cut my hair, buy tight skirts and a corset.

'I don't want you sophisticated,' he said, 'I just want to give you nice babies.'

'Babies –' I nearly died when he said that and I sat up and said anxiously, 'but you said that we wouldn't have babies.'

'Not now,' he said, shocked by the sudden change in my voice. Babies terrified me – I remembered the day Baba first told me about breast feeding and I felt sick again, just as I had done that day walking across the field eating a packet of sherbet. I got sick then and hid it with dock leaves while Baba finished the sherbet.

'Don't worry,' he said, easing me back on to the bed, 'don't worry about things like that. It will come out all right in the end. Don't think about it, this is your honeymoon.'

'The bed is all tossed,' I said, in an effort to get my mind on to something simple. But we were too comfortable to get up and rearrange it. He reached to the end of the bed for his shirt and his undervest which was inside it. I helped him put it on and kissed the hollow between his shoulder-blades, recalling their apricot colour in daylight.

'Are you hungry?' I asked, when he lay down. I was wide awake and wanted to prolong the happiness of the night.

Girl With Green Eyes

'No, just sleepy,' he yawned, and lay on the side nearest to me.

'I was a good girl,' I said as he put his hand on my stomach.

'You were a marvellous girl.'

'It's not so terrible.'

'No more old chat out of you,' he said, 'go to sleep.' I could feel my stomach rising and falling gently under the weight of his hand.

'What's your diaphragm?' I asked.

'Meet you outside Jacobs at nine tomorrow night, Miss Potbelly.' He was asleep almost as he spoke, and slowly his hand slid down off my stomach.

I did not expect to sleep but somehow I did.

When I wakened the room was bright and I saw him staring at me.

'Hello,' I said, blinking because of the bright sunshine.

'Kate,' he said, 'you look so peaceful in your sleep. I've been looking at you for the past half-hour. You're like a doll.'

I moved my head over on to his pillow so that our faces were close together.

'Oh,' I said with happiness, and stretched my feet. Our toes stuck out at the end of the tossed bed. He said that we ought to have another little moment before we got up and washed ourselves; and he made love to me very quickly that time, and it did not seem so strange any more.

In the bathroom we washed together. We couldn't have a bath because the range had not been lit and the water was cold. It was freezing cold water which came from a tank up in the woods and I gasped with the cold of it, and the pleasure of it, as he dabbed a wet sponge on my body.

'Don't, don't,' I begged, but he said that it was good for the circulation.

He washed that part of himself without taking off his clothes again; he just rained the rubber tube that was fixed to the end of the cold tap on it, saying that it had had a monk's life.

'Have to make up for lost time,' he said as I dabbed it dry with a clean towel and asked, unwisely, if he loved me.

'Lucky you don't snore,' he said, 'or I'd send you back.'

'Do you love me?' I asked again.

'Ask me that in ten years' time, when I know you better,' he said as he linked me down to breakfast and told Anna that we had got married.

'That's great news,' she said, but I knew that she knew we were lying.

Kathy Page

*The
Ancient Siddanese*

Our guide steps from the shadows to greet us. He looks cool in his loose white suit and dark glasses; we, fresh from the dark-windowed hoverbug, are reeling in the desert heat.

'Ladies and gentlemen, I don't believe in false modesty so I can tell you that you're fortunate to have me as your official guide for today! Do come inside, out of this terrible heat . . .' He makes a little bow as he greets us. We eye the perspex dome behind him suspiciously: the walls of pinkish stone beneath it look squat, plain and, frankly, ugly. It all seems terribly small, set in such an unremitting expanse of space.

'I have spent twenty-three years studying these ruins,' our guide continues as we wipe our brows and sigh in the shade of the reception area. He gives the faintest of smiles, 'And I'm personally responsible for several of the discoveries which have at last made a definitive interpretation of the site possible. Furthermore, I'm one of the few people who can claim to be descended from the ancient Siddanese themselves . . .'

Sidda, I've read in the monograph, has been open to the public for over a hundred years, though even now when everyone travels so incessantly, few people arrive here, it being so remote. That's part of the attraction, I suppose. We're an odd group, about fifteen, all different in our ages, nationalities and states of health. But we're all pilgrims of a kind: the couple bent with age, the father with his two sons, the photographer, the three girls, the woman with the baby and the sun-resistant clothes she has designed herself and constantly recommends to the rest of us.

'Everything covered!' she declares proudly. 'Even the face. No need for all those chemical creams which are probably as bad for you as the sun itself.' She is an optimist, she told me on the way out: 'There's always a way.'

I suspect I am not the only one who wishes that the fat man with the peppering of dark growths creeping across his face and the backs of his hands would wear her outfit – would tuck the thin silvery veil into his collar, sit his hat back on top, slide his hands into the stretch gloves you can't even feel, and let us all forget. Not that it's easy:

'Before we move out on to the site, I must ask you to change into the soft shoes provided, and warn you about the light here. Despite the dome erected over the site to prevent wind-damage and cut out some of the glare, no one should venture outside without some kind of extra protection, particularly on their head and shoulders. The shading and air conditioning are efficient, but deceptive.'

Obediently we re-cream our faces and hands, search for hats and sunglasses in our bags. Except, that is, for Mr Melanoma, who stands defiant and tries unsuccessfully to catch the guide's eye, as if to say man to man – what a silly pointless fuss, shutting the stable door, eh? – and the veiled woman, of course, who quickly checks her baby's layers of protection, then waits – serene, I suppose, though, hidden beneath that silvery curtain, she could be weeping for all I really know.

The Ancient Siddanese

'Terrible thing to do,' someone mutters, poking me in the side, 'exposing a child like that.' I smile and shrug. I don't want to be distracted. I want to get what I came for. Our guide waits, unmoving, until we are finished.

'Despite the discomfort, what you are to see today is certainly absolutely unique and you'll all thank yourselves for having made the effort. Thank you.' He makes his bow again. 'Come over to the observation panel please.'

There is something about our guide that I like. I'm hopeful. It's a great responsibility, I think, watching how he stands, turning his head smoothly from us to the observation panel and back, telling us of the recent history of the site – as great a responsibility, if not greater, than that of the pilot who bore me safely from home to here, speeding between the sun and the too-bright sea. A careless or malicious guide can ruin a trip like this, can leave you with nightmares and a very bitter taste in your mouth.

'Let's begin with an overview –'

The party falls silent. Through the tinted pane that makes all colours seem richer than they are, lending the desert an almost damp appearance, a tempting succulence, we gaze at the pinkish stones that are Sidda. Before this one, there have been other guides here, official and unofficial, and before them of course came explorers, those first archaeologists who sought such places out, and they in turn had guides of their own. Now there is him. It is his job to make Sidda complete for us, to add something to the things we can read in books.

'Sidney Carbourne,' he begins, 'is credited with the discovery of Sidda . . .'

*

Two men, crossing the desert. Both wearing cloths draped over their heads then wrapped around their necks according to the local custom, but one of them a European: Mr Sidney Carbourne, gentleman. Behind the two men, three imported camels, heavily laden – not only with the necessities of life: tents, water, food, but also with notebooks, ink, pens and many lumps of stone.

'What is that, in the distance to the left?' Mr Carbourne asks, gesturing at a small eminence, indistinct and pinkish in the haze of heat.

'To the left, sir?' The other man does not look up; although he knows the desert better than anyone alive, he has never seen it, for he was born blind. Besides, he is old and each journey he makes tires him more. This one he thinks – almost hopes – will be his last.

'That will be the old city of Sidda,' he says. 'I don't recommend we stop: it's little more than a heap of stones.'

'Aha!' Mr Carbourne's voice is always loud, and now it is jubilant as well. Since they set out he has continually suspected his guide of laziness and of trying to cheat him: were the man's eyes not so obviously useless, seamed shut as if by tiny stitches, he would suspect him of counterfeiting his blindness itself. 'But that could be said of many sites. You people are so used to the ancient wonders of your land that you often fail to appreciate them. Let us go to Sidda. Perhaps we can camp there for the night.'

'It's a long way,' the old man says.

'Nonsense!' Mr Carbourne smiles broadly. They have been together four months now. Sometimes he relieves his irritation by making faces at the other man, secure in the knowledge that his rudeness won't be detected. He straightens his back. 'Sidda, by nightfall!' he cries.

'It is further than you think,' the old man replies

The Ancient Siddanese

quietly, 'and I need to rest.' Nonetheless, he alters direction. Mr Carbourne begins to whistle a marching song.

By the time it is dark they are perhaps halfway there.

'I presume,' Mr Carbourne says, 'you can find our way just as well in the dark?'

'Please give me some water,' the old man replies. 'Yes. Besides, we are going the right way. Our mounts will take us there.'

After many hours, through most of which Mr Carbourne has slept, something alerts him to a change and he wakes. The moon has emerged, and they are riding through a walled square. He stops, dismounts, then grabs the halter of his guide's beast.

'Wake up, you!' he shouts at the figure slumped in the saddle. 'There's work to be done! I know your game!' He waits for the figure to start and straighten, but when the camel stamps, it slips further down in the seat. The old man has died, leaving Mr Carbourne to tend the camels, tie them to a crude statue standing in the centre of the square, light a dung fire, unpack blankets and sleep alone till dawn.

When it is light he heaves the body, rigid but very light, from the camel, and carries it to the corner of the square: the death was obviously from the most natural cause of all, and not in any way his fault; the man he tells himself, is too old to have anyone waiting for his return. Then he wanders round the ruins of Sidda . . .

'Immediately,' says our guide, gesturing gracefully through the panel, 'immediately, you are struck by the central feature: a square of open ground a hundred metres across, bordered by four very thick walls roughly two metres high. Even from here you can see that these walls are in fact even thicker at their base than at the top, and that they're built from irregular but precisely interlocking pieces of pinkish stone. There is no mortar. These stones were mined, shaped and assembled here without the use of any tools other than other pieces of stone. You'll notice that this isn't strictly speaking a square at all, because the four walls do not join at the corners and show no sign of ever having done so. In the centre of the square, where the paths that pass through these openings meet, exactly where it was found, is a large statue made of similar stone but of a greenish hue.

'Beyond the confines of the square you'll notice the seemingly irregular disposition of thirty-nine circular holes surmounted with low stonework rims. I don't want anyone to try and get inside these holes – they are very deep indeed and do provide a cool resting place for several types of snake. Bear in mind that these rims were originally several metres high, but that early explorers of the site were driven to knock them down in order to make them conform to their mistaken notions about the purpose of the pits. Over there to the left of the site you can see one of the pit mouths which is in the slow process of painstaking reconstruction, and far out on the edge of the site that mound is where the stones so dishonestly removed were hidden. Many of these stones were used to construct the base for the protective dome so as to be in harmony with the site it protects and also as an experiment to calculate how long it would have taken to construct Sidda. Our low wall took a team of twenty men fifteen years to build, using the interlocking method. Sidda was not built in a day!

'Leading up to each of the square's open corners are what look like narrow roads or paths – these lead due

The Ancient Siddanese

north, south, east and west, and appear to peter out just beyond the limits of the site as defined by our dome, though it's my view that proper exploration would show them to lead straight on for very many miles. The paths are made from millions of brittle pottery shards, and amongst these have been found many which bear finely preserved examples of the letters of an ancient alphabet.

'Outside the north, south, west and east walls of the square you can see the remains of three hexagonal structures. In the southern hexagon were found the only human remains the site has yielded, and these can now be seen in the site museum. Now, let us go outside, and I'll tell you a little about the people who constructed Sidda, and the way they lived . . .'

We follow him out into the tinted dome. You can tell he is right about the sun, for though it is cooler than outside, thin shadows trail behind us and the dry walls are hot to touch. We are a unique generation, skipping as we do from shadow to shadow, our skins screened to escape the fire that once created us. A generation of greedy travellers, living in the last days and wanting to see it all, the world as onion, layer on layer going back beneath today's crisp dry skin.

Sidney Carbourne lived in a different world and saw different things. He missed the interlocking stones entirely, had not the slightest thought of alphabets. He stepped out protected only by a cotton cloth wrapped over his head. He examined the numerous circular holes in the ground: wells, he thought, now gone dry, and the reason, probably, for the city being abandoned. The hexagonal structures he judged to be fortifications. If the old man had still been with him, he would have pretended a greater interest than he felt, but, alone, he could admit that the city was indeed little more than a heap of stones piled together to form a courtyard – without ornament other than the crude statue. He was disappointed, but there was no point in staying.

It was only as he walked back to the square that he was struck by the enormous thickness of its walls and noticed also that, whereas their inner surface seemed roughly perpendicular, the outer one sloped ever so slightly inwards towards the top. He stood back, shielded his eyes and projected this angle into the sky. Suddenly the stones of Sidda leapt to life. He saw the place, as new. He stood, filled with it, a great smile carving up his sunburnt face.

In a fever of excitement he returned to unload his drawing and measuring instruments. If only he had taken the risk of bringing a whole team out! If only he had more water! If only his guide had not chosen such a moment to die! All day he worked, recording Sidda in plan, section and elevations, all to scale, on fine cartridge paper, his ink drying instantaneously in the heat. Here and there he embellished the scene with a scrubby tree, a lizard or some imaginary birds wheeling in the sky, for it was all rather plain. He drew until dark came, suddenly as it does in these latitudes, then wandered restlessly around the ruins in the dark, feeling the stones, collecting handfuls of pottery shards. It would take him two months to organise a proper expedition: he felt he would be unable to sleep until he returned.

In the morning he spent an hour with his maps and a compass. Sidda was unmarked, which gladdened his heart, but also made his way on perilous, a matter of estimating degrees and times and speeds. As a precaution, he composed a letter to his fellow enthusiast,

The Ancient Siddanese

Dr Fellows, and fixed it to his bundle of drawings and notes before packing them safely away:

... Here my esteemed friend and fellow enthusiast, and quite unexpectedly, I have at last made a real Discovery! I believe this ruined city of Sidda to be indeed the cradle of civilization, a crude thing, but of immense scientific importance. It would seem to me that the courtyard walls – so immensely thick – were meant to support some further construction, since disappeared. From the evidence of the numerous wells, one can conjecture that this land was not always so dry, not always such a perfect desert as it is now. Many years before the birth of Christ, I think it quite reasonable to assume that some kind of trees may have grown here in reasonable abundance. Hence I conclude that the structure erected above these four walls was made of timber, and that has disappeared due to the action of the voracious ants and termites found in these parts. Projecting the angle of the walls skywards (see drawing numbered 14), you will see that we have a pyramidical edifice – not one such as is found in Egypt based on the equilateral triangle, but rather one that conforms exactly to the rule of isosceles. I have sketched out the possible method of construction for such a Pyramid, using only short lengths of timber such as might have been available. It is my conviction that Sidda became subject to prolonged drought and was gradually abandoned. Some few of the inhabitants may well have taken the long route by sea to Egypt itself, and there, in the course of many years, refined their original structure.

This desert is an inhospitable place for any man

and if by any chance, mishap should befall me
on my return to the capital I wish to entrust you,
my esteemed friend, with the discovery of this
inestimable treasure. I beg of you in the name
of our long association and our common love of
science to publish my findings as well as you can,
and then make your way with all haste here to
continue my work. I have no doubt but that items
of immense value and beauty are to be found in
the sand beneath the tombs. Your affectionate
friend . . .

Not forty years ago – when the man standing before us today with a small ironic smile playing about his lips was still in the deep shade of his mother's womb – before we passed the millennium, before the shady dome was built – another guide, a short, fattish man not half so elegant, though just as perfectly spoken as ours, would have been much preoccupied with the story of Sidney Carbourne . . .

'It was only after Dr Fellows' death,' he says, 'that this letter was found, plunging his family into disgrace. His daughter was so ashamed that she committed suicide. He even passed off the drawings, which Carbourne had neglected to sign, as his own!'

There is more than a suspicion of military background about this other guide, and an angry passion about the eyes. His party, larger than ours, obey his every instruction with alacrity: eyes right, eyes left, marching forth on the sand hot as coals. Yet they are freer than us in their dress: the women, hatless, in low-cut tops and calf-length dresses or baggy shorts, the men with blazers off, short-sleeved shirts undone at the neck and stained

The Ancient Siddanese

beneath the arms. Their skins are deeply tanned, even red and flaking here and there, but they do not care. They want to soak it all up, history and sunshine alike.

'I'm afraid the early history of archaeology is full of such unscrupulousness. These were colonial times. Foreigners came with their heads full of nonsense and everyone believed them.' He laughs bitterly. Some of the party smile, but uncertainly – they are foreigners too and feel his contempt. 'Nowadays we are much more scrupulous. Carbourne's theory, though correct in some respects, is largely a fairy tale fuelled by his consuming jealousy of a friend of his who had made his reputation and fortune by means of a discovery in Egypt. It was a minor one compared to what was to come – but considered important at the time. Sidney Carbourne dreamed of addressing the Royal Society back in England, but he never did. Some say that he wasn't even the first to discover Sidda: the remains of a single human skeleton of recent origin were found buried in a shallow grave.

'Carbourne's Pyramid is clearly a ridiculous hypothesis easily disproved by a few calculations' – forceful and intense, this other guide jabs contemptuously at the glass case containing Sidney's last written words, and a piece of pink stone he collected and marked with indian ink – 'and in seeing Sidda merely as a precursor of Egyptian civilization he severely underestimated it. Nowadays' – he stands a little straighter – 'we value it as the first emergence of that ingenuity and fortitude we like to think of as an essential feature of our national character. Follow me!

'You have to imagine these surrounding lands, as Carbourne suggested, far greener than they are today. There was water in relative abundance, for beneath this sand is a thick band of rock and beneath that there were at the time underground streams. Here and there, a fault in the bed of rock allowed water to seep upwards, creating fertile patches of land. This area was particularly rich in such secret wells, and the Siddanese took a vital first step when they decided to dig down and search beneath the sand for the source of the damp. They found that as they went down the dampness increased, and that with much labour they could in the end tap the source of water itself. This was sufficient to turn them from a nomadic to a settled people. With the stones they had brought up from beneath the sand they began to build, and with the water they irrigated the land round about. By the second century of its existence Sidda had fifteen functioning wells. They can still be distinguished: the larger ones, clustered together to your left. Imagine how Sidda must have appeared to the traveller: a shimmering oasis of green on the horizon, scarcely believable in its beauty. As the land began to yield a surplus and trade developed, a class system began to emerge, with an upper tier of landowners and a lower of manual workers, employed year in year out with the cutting and carrying of stone and the transport of water. Above both of these were the four well guardians or priests, who ensured that life was lived so as to please the gods responsible for their city's good fortune. These four hexagonal towers were the priest houses. Follow me inside the courtyard!

'Imagine this sculpture in its full glory: beneath it was a powerful natural spring, forcing water upwards like a fountain. See how it's built from many stones, leaving cracks and fissures between which the water gushed out, then flowed down into the sand. If you will excuse the gesture – see how a little saliva brings out the rich green of the rock, so like the green of healthy leaves.

The Ancient Siddanese

This we think was the centre of the water ceremonies, in which celebrants approached from the four corners of the square along these paths, watched by the priests in their towers . . .' Nowadays, this guide's story would not excite us. We'd know what was to come, and we'd turn away: 'Then disaster struck –' Who wants to hear of such things? Who wants to see Mr Melanoma's face? But back then it was different, they felt quite safe, and liked to hear of catastrophe:

'One by one the fifteen wells ran dry. Twenty-four new ones were dug in an increasingly desperate search for water, making the number up to thirty-nine. If you look at the path you're standing beside, you will see many fragments of pottery. Pick one up – you hold in your hand a pattern of lines and dots in which we can read the story of the end of Sidda. The marks are arranged in units ranging from fifteen to seventy-eight, which is twice thirty-nine. Each dot is a well still functioning, each line is a dry one. Thus we have a record of the fluctuating fortunes of the city, and indeed the main work of the Institute is now to arrange them chronologically so as to piece together a history of each well. Each fragment is part of a water bowl, and these, we think, were brought before the statue of the water god, filled, and then smashed on the way back out of the square as a gesture of homage and propitiation. Please put the pieces back.

'Gather round. I can show you here – an exact replica from the last days – look: all lines. Empty, empty, empty. No water. Sidda was destroyed by the very forces of nature that had brought it into being in the first place, its inhabitants forced to take up again the harsh nomadic life of times before. Yet, naturally, we hope that one day the desert will flower again, and even now plans are afoot to bring a team of international scientists into the desert north of here in the hope of discovering underground waters. Then we could grow barley and tomatoes, avocado, watermelon, even strawberries, and you visitors would not see so many starving children begging in the street.

'Ladies and gentlemen, you will leave in ten minutes. Please ask me questions if you wish, or take a cold drink in the café by the car-park. Nowadays, I'm afraid the water comes many miles by road in glass bottles! Thank you.' He salutes them at the end, looking over the tops of their heads at his imaginary oasis, of which there is now no trace.

'Where did you learn your English?' a woman with white skin baked brown but for the thin marks of swim-suit straps would have asked.

'In Oxford.' He would have smiled. 'I have read all your literature.'

'What's your view of the dreadful bombings last week?' That would be the woman's husband, standing stiffly beside her. 'I understand several tourists were killed.'

'You must understand' – then that other guide's face would have grown dark – 'that we are struggling hard to establish ourselves as a nation in our own right, and no one is helping us. You might say we are trying to recreate, in hostile circumstances, a beautiful garden, such as once flourished here. Violence . . . such things are unpleasant, I think, but inevitable.'

'Where would you be without tourism? It's crazy, blowing people up.'

And a thin boy with very short hair would have asked, scratching at his scalp, red from the sun, 'Where did the people live? Why aren't there any houses?'

The Ancient Siddanese

'Because,' that other guide would have declared, smiling again, 'they were built of wood. And I expect you have seen the ants and termites in the grounds of your hotel? In two weeks one colony of termites can devour four tons of timber. The homes of the ancient Siddanese are nothing but dust blowing in the wind. Of course, now everything is painted with preservative.'

We can't blame these other guides – times change – nor must we forget them: they are part of the picture too.

'But,' says our guide now, and I feel as if behind those thick dark lenses he is staring straight at me, 'they were telling – if we are charitable – half-truths. Sidda is the most misunderstood archaeological site on the face of the earth. Today, I will tell you facts.

'How many people do you think occupied this site? Five hundred? A thousand? The answer is none. "City" isn't really the appropriate term for Sidda. We think of cities as bustling centres of trade, places on a crossroads where people gather and live in close proximity. Sidda was indeed a busy place, but no one lived here. It was the creation of many people who lived scattered about in the surrounding lands, but not their home.

'It was one of the fundamental beliefs of the ancient Siddanese that *individuals* should leave nothing behind them. When a house fell into disuse, such materials as could not be reused were burned and the ashes scattered to the winds. And when a person died, their body was taken to a lonely place and left unguarded on the sand so that ants and vultures could feast upon the flesh. A year later, the bones were buried, without marking, deep in the desert sand. This way, please . . .'

A trickle of sweat runs down between my shoulder-blades, and somehow sand has slipped inside my shoes:

I can feel the tiny grains pressing in. We gather quietly round our guide without him having to ask, and wait for the two old ones to catch us up, inching forward on the uneven ground.

'The only memorial allowed the dead can in fact be seen right at your feet: these countless pottery shards, which are all fragments of decorated bowls, some large, some small. The day of the bowl came after the day of the bones, and on it the dead person's relatives carried his or her drinking bowl to the city of Sidda and once within the confines of the city' – he holds up an imaginary bowl, then brings his hands suddenly down – 'smashed it on the ground. Every night the day's shards were swept into the four sunken paths, gradually filling them, until, as you can see, they are almost level with the rest of the ground.'

The pottery fragments are dry, reddish and openpored. As people shift on their feet I can hear them crunch and snap.

'But Sidda isn't simply a city of remembrance. It's also a monument. Two contradictory impulses were behind its painstaking creation: on the one hand a desire to honour the Siddanese way of life – obsession might be a better word, for it was long before they were in any danger of extinction that building commenced – and on the other the urge to hide it from other peoples' understanding and, in particular, that of those coming after them. Sidda was built to impress, but not to inform. And largely, until now, it has succeeded.' He beckons; we draw more closely round and watch him reach into his pocket.

'Consider the alphabet. Here are examples of some of the commonest symbols. They consist of collections of dots and lines, up to thirty-nine of each per unit, which can be enclosed in a circle or a rectangle and arranged

The Ancient Siddanese

either horizontally or vertically in various orders. This is not a picture alphabet, but a phonetic one. Each unit represents a sound. A rectangle or a circular enclosure implies a stressed or unstressed sound – syllable is not the correct term, for the language of Sidda was composed literally of strings of sounds, each discrete. Now, please pass these around . . .'

The piece I hold is roughly triangular, but slightly curved. The inside is smooth, and a slightly darker red. I turn it over: there they are, the ridges and the dots, carefully traced, perhaps with a twig –

'Close your eyes,' our guide says, 'and touch it lightly with your fingertips . . . Yes. Can you feel the difference between the bumps and the holes? The ridges and the lines? I think you'll find that if you run your fingernail across, it's quite easy to count them rapidly.' We do so. The sound, like the buzz of tiny crickets, is all around me and continues as he speaks.

'You understand? This is an alphabet of the blind. But not, like our braille, a second-hand thing, representing another alphabet, representing in turn a language spoken and invented by the sighted, that is, an alphabet *for* not *of* the blind. No. This alphabet represents a language created and spoken by the sightless, and the city around you was built entirely by a race of people who could not see.' I open my eyes briefly, am dazzled by the light, close them again.

'There are several theories. My colleague, Professor Nielsen, has recently published his theory that the Siddanese blinded their own offspring at birth, much as in some cultures the foreskin is automatically removed. And I believe Mossinsky has argued that the Siddanese were in fact a community of outcasts from the surrounding regions, where it is well known that many tribes expelled those with mental or physical abnormalities. The sightless, he argues, continued this custom in their own way by keeping themselves apart and developing a culture so arcane as to be impenetrable to the other groups and the tribes that had expelled them. Intriguing as both these hypotheses are, they do in the end seem over-elaborate to me. It seems far more likely that these people were, like myself, born sightless –' Everyone opens their eyes wide at this. 'Or else victims of a progressive dulling of their sight due to disease or perhaps even the fearful intensity of the desert light.' One and all we stare at our elegant guide, peer at his close-fitting glasses, so very dark. Is he really telling the truth? But we don't dare ask, and anyway, he reads our minds.

'Indeed. I find my way around this city by memory, the feel of the ground under my feet, the sense of where shadows fall – and something more than any of these – a feeling that I have always known the city of Sidda. Outside I carry a stick, but here it has never seemed necessary.

'To return to the alphabet. Whilst it has so far been impossible to decode more than a handful of words, we have learned the way in which it was written: not left to right, right to left or up and down, but starting always with the first symbol enclosed in a square centrally positioned in the available space. The next would be to the top left corner, top right corner, bottom right, bottom left; those following would be positioned between the top right of the outer top left symbol and the top left of the outer top right symbol and so on, forming a regular pattern like checks – or a honeycomb – of symbols and space. We think, for instance, that these symbols make up the word for her or his, and these make up the word

The Ancient Siddanese

for bowl. Perhaps this one is bone. Of course, we have no idea as to which sound a given letter represents. It's my view the alphabet will never be fully understood.' Mr Melanoma holds his piece of pottery out to give it back. I slip mine in my bag: it'll do no harm, I think, there are plenty more.

The thick pink walls cut off our view of the desert; the path that snaps like brittle bones beneath our feet leads straight as a die to the sculpture where Sidney Carbourne tied his camel.

'It's the only pictorial image of any kind the Siddanese left in their city,' our guide says. 'The stone is of uniform colour, but see how the texture varies' – he reaches out – 'here porous, here almost as smooth as glass, with the smoothest pieces of all used for the face and arms. Notice the intricacy of the work on the face – no less than forty pieces, carefully chosen to indicate the ears, nose and mouth. The space beneath the brows is blank – and what other reason could there be for this than that the Siddanese knew how they differed from others? This sculpture could rank alongside any of the great pieces in the world – above, I say, for consider how it was made without sight and without tools, other than perhaps another stone to knock a corner off here and there: what judgement and patience, what philosophy, must have gone into its construction!

'Around this statue, ladies and gentlemen, the Siddanese gathered to produce and appreciate their culture. They travelled many miles from their flimsy homes, going always on foot. They sang and played instruments, they told stories and riddles, and drank an intoxicant brewed from moulds cultivated inside the mouths of the thirty-nine pits beyond the square. Traces of this mould have been found on the concave surfaces of the pottery fragments we have discussed, and inside the hexagonal towers which we deduce to be public kitchens. Under the influence of this drink, they became convinced that they could read the future. They saw or guessed how their own demise would come, and how the sighted world would inevitably misunderstand their achievements. Consider these people, blind, scattered, knowing themselves to be unique in their peaceful and economical culture – proud, and justifiably so, but also vulnerable, afraid and alone. Perhaps it's not surprising that they wanted to build a city such as this, itself a riddle that could be unlocked only by the knowing touch of those, like them, free of the distraction of sight.

'Ladies and gentlemen, you have here a moving testimony as to the diversity of the human species. For almost two thousand years the Siddanese lived here, in a completely different manner from the other peoples of the world. Navigating in their inner darkness across the desert, they built a city without the use of tools; they refrained from eating meat or using animals as beasts of burden, they avoided trade and eschewed science: developing not astronomy like the Egyptians or geometry like the Greeks but their own austere metaphysics and philosophy. Whilst all the other peoples of the globe were slaves to superstition, the Siddanese pondered the problems of communication and interpretation, fitting one stone carefully on top of the next. Whilst others looked back to the origins of the gods and sought to bend nature to their will, the Siddanese felt their way forward to the future and guessed what was to come. But I like to think of them as a deeply sensual as well as a serious people, rather as I like to see myself.' He smiles at us properly for the first time.

'We are lucky, I think, that such a people lived. You

The Ancient Siddanese

may take photographs if you wish, though remember, this place is not designed to appeal to the eyes! There are various publications on sale by the entrance, and some small-scale replicas of the statue – an intriguing puzzle which you can try to assemble yourselves . . . But what I suggest is that in the few remaining minutes you close your eyes and explore Sidda by touch, for it's only in darkness that its full beauty can be appreciated.'

Nowadays, no one asks questions of a guide. It either works or it does not. He moves to wait in the shade for the next group. Gratefully, I close my eyes again and wander, arms outstretched, blundering unpractised until my fingers touch Sidda's walls. I can feel the sun's fatal heat on my back as I trace the border between one stone and the next. I slip my fingernail into the gap between. I feel how in these last hot days and years the world is full of parables, prefiguration and correspondence. Even half-truths or outright lies hide lessons and examples; and somewhere, beneath one of these dry stones, curled like a bug, is hope. I can hear other people on the path, and the cry of the veiled woman's child, but apart from that it is quiet under the dome. I press against the wall, opening myself to its roughness and accumulated warmth. I have come to my last site. I want to touch our guide, to take his hand in mine – it would be dry and warm, like old stone – with my eyes still closed.

I know that there may be yet other guides. I know that they may even come in shapes different than ours – limbless, green-skinned, minute, extra-sensory, photosynthetic, mechanic, invisible: 'We're nearing the end of our tour. Just one more thing – below is the planet earth. Mostly desert now, though once it was uniquely fertile and inhabited by many forms of life, one of which came to dominate, and, we guess, was responsible for the change. We're passing now over one of the smaller sites they occupied: you can see the form of a circle, and inside that a square, with several smaller circles scattered about. These beings left their mark, but they had no culture to speak of, and have often been compared, in their compulsion to build and multiply without thought, to the blue beetles which caused such havoc on our planet some years ago.'

'But on what evidence do we make such statements about their culture?' says one of these beings, maybe not through lips and teeth with air, but somehow, somehow. 'No one's troubled to go and look, have they?' Already it's gone, passed from view; but the shape of Sidda and the idea of those earth-beetles long ago move her, and she decides she will return one day to vindicate their name . . .

That's hope! I walk slowly beside the wall, just grazing it with my fingertips. I sense where it ends just before my fingers slip into air. I believe the blind man who waits in the shade; I must. I have closed my eyes and touched one of the wonders of the world, forgotten for a moment the terrible heat and the fearful sound of a wind blowing full of sand.

Sylvia Plath

extract from

The Bell Jar

Sylvia Plath's novel was first published under the pseudonym Victoria Lucas, which suggests that it was important for her as a writer to distance herself from the strong autobiographical elements in the book. It describes the breakdown of a nineteen-year-old college star, Esther Greenwood; her unhappy introduction to New York life and her return to her mother's home in Connecticut for the summer. Treated for depression with ECT (electric shock treatment) she finds herself drawn increasingly to the idea of suicide.

Sylvia Plath's novel was first published under the pseudonym Victoria Lucas, which suggests that it was important for her as a writer to distance herself from the strong autobiographical elements in the book. It describes the breakdown of a nineteen-year-old college star, Esther Greenwood; her unhappy introduction to New York life and her return to her mother's home in Connecticut for the summer. Treated for depression with ECT (electric shock treatment) she finds herself drawn increasingly to the idea of suicide.

'Of course his mother killed him.'

I looked at the mouth of the boy Jody had wanted me to meet. His lips were thick and pink and a baby face nestled under the silk of white-blond hair. His name was Cal, which I thought must be short for something, but I couldn't think what it would be short for, unless it was California.

'How can you be sure she killed him?' I said.

Cal was supposed to be very intelligent, and Jody had said over the phone that he was cute and I would like him. I wondered, if I'd been my old self, if I would have liked him.

It was impossible to tell.

'Well, first she says No no no, and then she says Yes.'

'But then she says No no again.'

Cal and I lay side by side on an orange and green striped towel on a mucky beach across the swamps from Lynn. Jody and Mark, the boy she was pinned to, were swimming. Cal hadn't wanted to swim, he had wanted to talk, and we were arguing about this play where a young man finds out he has a brain disease, on account of his father fooling around with unclean women, and in the end his brain, which has been softening all along, snaps completely, and his mother is debating whether to kill him or not.

I had a suspicion that my mother had called Jody and begged her to ask me out, so I wouldn't sit around in my room all day with the shades drawn. I didn't want to go at first, because I thought Jody would notice the change in me, and that anybody with half an eye would see I didn't have a brain in my head.

But all during the drive north, and then east, Jody had joked and laughed and chattered and not seemed to mind that I only said 'My' or 'Gosh' or 'You don't say'.

We browned hotdogs on the public grills at the beach, and by watching Jody and Mark and Cal very carefully I managed to cook my hotdog just the right amount of time and didn't burn it or drop it into the fire, the way I was afraid of doing. Then, when nobody was looking, I buried it in the sand.

After we ate, Jody and Mark ran down to the water hand-in-hand, and I lay back, staring into the sky, while Cal went on and on about this play.

The only reason I remembered this play was because it had a mad person in it, and everything I had ever read about mad people stuck in my mind, while everything else flew out.

'But it's the Yes that matters,' Cal said. 'It's the Yes she'll come back to in the end.'

I lifted my head and squinted out at the bright blue plate of the sea – a bright blue plate with a dirty rim. A big round grey rock, like the upper half of an egg, poked out of the water about a mile from the stony headland.

'What was she going to kill him with? I forget.'

I hadn't forgotten. I remembered perfectly well, but I wanted to hear what Cal would say.

'Morphia powders.'

The Bell Jar

'Do you suppose they have morphia powders in America?'

Cal considered a minute. Then he said, 'I wouldn't think so. They sound awfully old-fashioned.'

I rolled over on to my stomach and squinted at the view in the other direction, towards Lynn. A glassy haze rippled up from the fires in the grills and the heat on the road, and through the haze, as through a curtain of clear water, I could make out a smudgy skyline of gas tanks and factory stacks and derricks and bridges.

It looked one hell of a mess.

I rolled on to my back again and made my voice casual. 'If you were going to kill yourself, how would you do it?'

Cal seemed pleased. 'I've often thought of that. I'd blow my brains out with a gun.'

I was disappointed. It was just like a man to do it with a gun. A fat chance I had of laying my hands on a gun. And even if I did, I wouldn't have a clue as to what part of me to shoot at.

I'd already read in the papers about people who'd tried to shoot themselves, only they ended up shooting an important nerve and getting paralysed, or blasting their face off, but being saved, by surgeons and a sort of miracle, from dying outright.

The risks of a gun seemed great.

'What kind of a gun?'

'My father's shotgun. He keeps it loaded. I'd just have to walk into his study one day and,' Cal pointed a finger to his temple and made a comical, screwed-up face, 'click!' He widened his pale grey eyes and looked at me.

'Does your father happen to live near Boston?' I asked idly.

'Nope. In Clacton-on-Sea. He's English.'

Jody and Mark ran up hand-in-hand, dripping and shaking off water drops like two loving puppies. I thought there would be too many people, so I stood up and pretended to yawn.

'I guess I'll go for a swim.'

Being with Jody and Mark and Cal was beginning to weigh on my nerves, like a dull wooden block on the strings of a piano. I was afraid that at any moment my control would snap, and I would start babbling about how I couldn't read and couldn't write and how I must be just about the only person who had stayed awake for a solid month without dropping dead of exhaustion.

A smoke seemed to be going up from my nerves like the smoke from the grills and the sun-saturated road. The whole landscape – beach and headland and sea and rock – quavered in front of my eyes like a stage backcloth.

I wondered at what point in space the silly, sham blue of the sky turned black.

'You swim too, Cal.'

Jody gave Cal a playful little push.

'Ohhh,' Cal hid his face in the towel. 'It's too cold.'

I started to walk towards the water.

Somehow, in the broad, shadowless light of noon, the water looked amiable and welcoming.

I thought drowning must be the kindest way to die, and burning the worst. Some of those babies in the jars that Buddy Willard showed me had gills, he said. They went through a stage where they were just like fish.

A little, rubbishy wavelet, full of candy wrappers and orange peel and seaweed, folded over my foot.

I heard the sand thud behind me, and Cal came up.

'Let's swim to that rock out there.' I pointed at it.

'Are you crazy? That's a mile out.'

The Bell Jar

'What are you?' I said. 'Chicken?'

Cal took me by the elbow and jostled me into the water. When we were waist high, he pushed me under. I surfaced, splashing, my eyes seared with salt. Underneath, the water was green and semi-opaque as a hunk of quartz.

I started to swim, a modified dogpaddle, keeping my face towards the rock. Cal did a slow crawl. After a while he put his head up and treaded water.

'Can't make it.' He was panting heavily.

'Okay. You go back.'

I thought I would swim out until I was too tired to swim back. As I paddled on, my heartbeat boomed like a dull motor in my ears.

I am I am I am.

That morning I had tried to hang myself.

I had taken the silk cord of my mother's yellow bathrobe as soon as she left for work, and, in the amber shade of the bedroom, fashioned it into a knot that slipped up and down on itself. It took me a long time to do this, because I was poor at knots and had no idea how to make a proper one.

Then I hunted around for a place to attach the rope.

The trouble was, our house had the wrong kind of ceilings. The ceilings were low, white and smoothly plastered, without a light fixture or a wood beam in sight. I thought with longing of the house my grandmother had before she sold it to come and live with us, and then with my Aunt Libby.

My grandmother's house was built in the fine, nineteenth-century style, with lofty rooms and sturdy chandelier brackets and high closets with stout rails across them, and an attic where nobody ever went, full of trunks and parrot cages and dressmaker's dummies and overhead beams thick as a ship's timbers.

But it was an old house, and she'd sold it, and I didn't know anybody else with a house like that.

After a discouraging time of walking about with the silk cord dangling from my neck like a yellow cat's tail and finding no place to fasten it, I sat on the edge of my mother's bed and tried pulling the cord tight.

But each time I would get the cord so tight I could feel a rushing in my ears and a flush of blood in my face, my hands would weaken and let go, and I would be all right again.

Then I saw that my body had all sorts of little tricks, such as making my hands go limp at the crucial second, which would save it, time and again, whereas if I had the whole say, I would be dead in a flash.

I would simply have to ambush it with whatever sense I had left, or it would trap me in its stupid cage for fifty years without any sense at all. And when people found out my mind had gone, as they would have to, sooner or later, in spite of my mother's guarded tongue, they would persuade her to put me into an asylum where I could be cured.

Only my case was incurable.

I had bought a few paperbacks on abnormal psychology at the drug store and compared my symptoms with the symptoms in the books, and sure enough, my symptoms tallied with the most hopeless cases.

The only thing I could read, beside the scandal sheets, were these abnormal psychology books. It was as if some slim opening had been left, so I could learn all I needed to know about my case to end it in the proper way.

I wondered, after the hanging fiasco, if I shouldn't just give it up and turn myself over to the doctors, but

The Bell Jar

then I remembered Doctor Gordon and his private shock machine. Once I was locked up they could use that on me all the time.

And I thought of how my mother and brother and friends would visit me, day after day, hoping I would be better. Then their visits would slacken off, and they would give up hope. They would grow old. They would forget me.

They would be poor, too.

They would want me to have the best of care at first, so they would sink all their money in a private hospital like Doctor Gordon's. Finally, when the money was used up, I would be moved to a state hospital, with hundreds of people like me, in a big cage in the basement.

The more hopeless you were, the further away they hid you.

Cal had turned around and was swimming in.

As I watched, he dragged himself slowly out of the neck-deep sea. Against the khaki-coloured sand and the green shore wavelets, his body was bisected for a moment, like a white worm. Then it crawled completely out of the green and on to the khaki and lost itself among dozens and dozens of other worms that were wriggling or just lolling about between the sea and the sky.

I paddled my hands in the water and kicked my feet. The egg-shaped rock didn't seem to be any nearer than it had been when Cal and I had looked at it from the shore.

Then I saw it would be pointless to swim as far as the rock, because my body would take that excuse to climb out and lie in the sun, gathering strength to swim back.

The only thing to do was to drown myself then and there.

So I stopped.

I brought my hands to my breast, ducked my head, and dived, using my hands to push the water aside. The water pressed in on my eardrums and on my heart. I fanned myself down, but before I knew where I was, the water had spat me up into the sun, and the world was sparkling all about me like blue and green and yellow semi-precious stones.

I dashed the water from my eyes.

I was panting, as after a strenuous exertion, but floating, without effort.

I dived, and dived again, and each time popped up like a cork.

The grey rock mocked me, bobbing on the water easy as a lifebuoy.

I knew when I was beaten.

I turned back.

The flowers nodded like bright, knowledgeable children as I trundled them down the hall.

I felt silly in my sage-green volunteer's uniform, and superfluous, unlike the white-uniformed doctors and nurses, or even the brown-uniformed scrubwomen with their mops and their buckets of grimy water, who passed me without a word.

If I had been getting paid, no matter how little, I could at least count this a proper job, but all I got for a morning of pushing round magazines and candy and flowers was a free lunch.

My mother said the cure for thinking too much about yourself was helping somebody who was worse off than you, so Teresa had arranged for me to sign on as a volunteer at our local hospital. It was difficult to be a volunteer at this hospital, because that's what all the

Junior League women wanted to do, but luckily for me, a lot of them were away on vacation.

I had hoped they would send me to a ward with some really gruesome cases, who would see through my numb, dumb face to how I meant well, and be grateful. But the head of the volunteers, a society lady at our church, took one look at me and said, 'You're on maternity.'

So I rode the elevator up three flights to the maternity ward and reported to the head nurse. She gave me the trolley of flowers. I was supposed to put the right vases at the right beds in the right rooms.

But before I came to the door of the first room I noticed that a lot of the flowers were droopy and brown at the edges. I thought it would be discouraging for a woman who'd just had a baby to see somebody plonk down a big bouquet of dead flowers in front of her, so I steered the trolley to a wash-basin in an alcove in the hall and began to pick out all the flowers that were dead.

Then I picked out all those that were dying.

There was no waste-basket in sight, so I crumpled the flowers up and laid them in the deep white basin. The basin felt cold as a tomb. I smiled. This must be how they laid the bodies away in the hospital morgue. My gesture, in its small way, echoed the larger gesture of the doctors and nurses.

I swung the door of the first room open and walked in, dragging my trolley. A couple of nurses jumped up, and I had a confused impression of shelves and medicine cabinets.

'What do you want?' one of the nurses demanded sternly. I couldn't tell one from the other, they all looked just alike.

'I'm taking the flowers round.'

The nurse who had spoken put a hand on my shoulder

and led me out of the room, manoeuvring the trolley with her free, expert hand. She flung open the swinging doors of the room next to that one and bowed me in. Then she disappeared.

I could hear giggles in the distance till a door shut and cut them off.

There were six beds in the room, and each bed had a woman in it. The women were all sitting up and knitting or riffling through magazines or putting their hair in pincurls and chattering like parrots in a parrot house.

I had thought they would be sleeping, or lying quiet and pale, so I could tiptoe round without any trouble and match the bed numbers to the numbers inked on adhesive tape on the vases, but before I had a chance to get my bearings, a bright, jazzy blonde with a sharp, triangular face beckoned to me.

I approached her, leaving the trolley in the middle of the floor, but then she made an impatient gesture, and I saw she wanted me to bring the trolley too.

I wheeled the trolley over to her bedside with a helpful smile.

'Hey, where's my larkspur?' A large, flabby lady from across the ward raked me with an eagle eye.

The sharp-faced blonde bent over the trolley. 'Here are my yellow roses,' she said, 'but they're all mixed up with some lousy iris.'

Other voices joined the voices of the first two women. They sounded cross and loud and full of complaint.

I was opening my mouth to explain that I had thrown a bunch of dead larkspur in the sink, and that some of the vases I had weeded out looked skimpy, there were so few flowers left, so I had joined a few of the bouquets together to fill them out, when the swinging door flew open and a nurse stalked in to see what the commotion was.

'Listen, nurse, I had this big bunch of larkspur Larry brought last night.'

'She's loused up my yellow roses.'

Unbuttoning the green uniform as I ran, I stuffed it, in passing, into the washbasin with the rubbish of dead flowers. Then I took the deserted side steps down to the street two at a time, without meeting another soul.

'Which way is the graveyard?'

The Italian in the black leather jacket stopped and pointed down an alley behind the white Methodist church. I remembered the Methodist church. I had been a Methodist for the first nine years of my life, before my father died and we moved and turned Unitarian.

My mother had been a Catholic before she was a Methodist. My grandmother and my grandfather and my Aunt Libby were all still Catholics. My Aunt Libby had broken away from the Catholic Church at the same time my mother did, but then she'd fallen in love with an Italian Catholic, so she'd gone back again.

Lately I had considered going into the Catholic Church myself. I knew that Catholics thought killing yourself was an awful sin. But perhaps, if this was so, they might have a good way to persuade me out of it.

Of course, I didn't believe in life after death or the virgin birth or the Inquisition or the infallibility of that little monkey-faced Pope or anything, but I didn't have to let the priest see this, I could just concentrate on my sin, and he would help me repent.

The only trouble was, Church, even the Catholic Church, didn't take up the whole of your life. No matter how much you knelt and prayed, you still had to eat three meals a day and have a job and live in the world.

I thought I might see how long you had to be a Catholic before you became a nun, so I asked my mother, thinking she'd know the best way to go about it.

My mother had laughed at me. 'Do you think they'll take somebody like you, right off the bat? Why you've got to know all these catechisms and credos and believe in them, lock, stock and barrel. A girl with your sense!'

Still, I imagined myself going to some Boston priest – it would have to be Boston, because I didn't want any priest in my home town to know I'd thought of killing myself. Priests were terrible gossips.

I would be in black, with my dead white face, and I would throw myself at this priest's feet and say, 'O Father, help me.'

But that was before people had begun to look at me in a funny way, like those nurses in the hospital.

I was pretty sure the Catholics wouldn't take in any crazy nuns. My Aunt Libby's husband had made a joke once, about a nun that a nunnery sent to Teresa for a check-up. This nun kept hearing harp notes in her ears and a voice saying over and over, 'Alleluia!' Only she wasn't sure, on being closely questioned, whether the voice was saying Alleluia or Arizona. The nun had been born in Arizona. I think she ended up in some asylum.

I tugged my black veil down to my chin and strode in through the wrought-iron gates. I thought it odd that in all the time my father had been buried in this graveyard, none of us had ever visited him. My mother hadn't let us come to his funeral because we were only children then, and he had died in hospital, so the graveyard and even his death, had always seemed unreal to me.

I had a great yearning, lately, to pay my father back

for all the years of neglect, and start tending his grave. I had always been my father's favourite, and it seemed fitting I should take on a mourning my mother had never bothered with.

I thought that if my father hadn't died, he would have taught me all about insects, which was his speciality at the university. He would also have taught me German and Greek and Latin, which he knew, and perhaps I would be a Lutheran. My father had been a Lutheran in Wisconsin, but they were out of style in New England, so he had become a lapsed Lutheran and then, my mother said, a bitter atheist.

The graveyard disappointed me. It lay at the outskirts of the town, on low ground, like a rubbish dump, and as I walked up and down the gravel paths, I could smell the stagnant salt marshes in the distance.

The old part of the graveyard was all right, with its worn, flat stones and lichen-bitten monuments, but I soon saw my father must be buried in the modern part with dates in the 1940s.

The stones in the modern part were crude and cheap, and here and there a grave was rimmed with marble, like an oblong bath-tub full of dirt, and rusty metal containers stuck up about where the person's navel would be, full of plastic flowers.

A fine drizzle started drifting down from the grey sky, and I grew very depressed.

I couldn't find my father anywhere.

Low, shaggy clouds scudded over that part of the horizon where the sea lay, behind the marshes and the beach shanty settlements, and raindrops darkened the black mackintosh I had bought that morning. A clammy dampness sank through to my skin.

I had asked the salesgirl, 'Is it water-repellent?'

And she had said, 'No raincoat is ever water-*repellent*. It's showerproofed.'

And when I asked her what showerproofed was, she told me I had better buy an umbrella.

But I hadn't enough money for an umbrella. What with bus fare in and out of Boston and peanuts and newspapers and abnormal psychology books and trips to my old home town by the sea, my New York fund was almost exhausted.

I had decided that when there was no more money in my bank account I would do it, and that morning I'd spent the last of it on the black raincoat.

Then I saw my father's gravestone.

It was crowded right up by another gravestone, head to head, the way people are crowded in a charity ward when there isn't enough space. The stone was of a mottled pink marble, like tinned salmon, and all there was on it was my father's name and, under it, two dates, separated by a little dash.

At the foot of the stone I arranged the rainy armful of azaleas I had picked from a bush at the gateway of the graveyard. Then my legs folded under me, and I sat down in the sopping grass. I couldn't understand why I was crying so hard.

Then I remembered that I had never cried for my father's death.

My mother hadn't cried either. She had just smiled and said what a merciful thing it was for him he had died, because if he had lived he would have been crippled and an invalid for life, and he couldn't have stood that, he would rather have died than had that happen.

I laid my face to the smooth face of the marble and howled my loss into the cold salt rain.

*

The Bell Jar

I knew just how to go about it.

The minute the car tyres crunched off down the drive and the sound of the motor faded, I jumped out of bed and hurried into my white blouse and green figured skirt and black raincoat. The raincoat felt damp still, from the day before, but that would soon cease to matter.

I went downstairs and picked up a pale blue envelope from the dining-room table and scrawled on the back, in large, painstaking letters: *I am going for a long walk.*

I propped the message where my mother would see it the minute she came in.

Then I laughed.

I had forgotten the most important thing.

I ran upstairs and dragged a chair into my mother's closet. Then I climbed up and reached for the small green strongbox on the top shelf. I could have torn the metal cover off with my bare hands, the lock was so feeble, but I wanted to do things in a calm, orderly way.

I pulled out my mother's upper right-hand bureau drawer and slipped the blue jewellery box from its hiding-place under the scented Irish linen handkerchiefs. I unpinned the little key from the dark velvet. Then I unlocked the strongbox and took out the bottle of new pills. There were more than I had hoped.

There were at least fifty.

If I had waited until my mother doled them out to me, night by night, it would have taken me fifty nights to save up enough. And in fifty nights, college would have opened, and my brother would have come back from Germany, and it would be too late.

I pinned the key back in the jewellery box among the clutter of inexpensive chains and rings, put the jewellery box back in the drawer under the handkerchiefs, returned the strongbox to the closet shelf and set the chair on the rug in the exact spot I had dragged it from.

Then I went downstairs and into the kitchen. I turned on the tap and poured myself a tall glass of water. Then I took the glass of water and the bottle of pills and went down into the cellar.

A dim, undersea light filtered through the slits of the cellar windows. Behind the oil burner, a dark gap showed in the wall at about shoulder height and ran back under the breezeway, out of sight. The breezeway had been added to the house after the cellar was dug, and built out over this secret, earth-bottomed crevice.

A few old, rotting fireplace logs blocked the hole mouth. I shoved them back a bit. Then I set the glass of water and the bottle of pills side by side on the flat surface of one of the logs and started to heave myself up.

It took me a good while to heft my body into the gap, but at last, after many tries, I managed it, and crouched at the mouth of the darkness, like a troll.

The earth seemed friendly under my bare feet, but cold. I wondered how long it had been since this particular square of soil had seen the sun.

Then, one after the other, I lugged the heavy, dust-covered logs across the hole mouth. The dark felt thick as velvet. I reached for the glass and bottle, and carefully, on my knees, with bent head, crawled to the farthest wall.

Cobwebs touched my face with the softness of moths. Wrapping my black coat round me like my own sweet shadow, I unscrewed the bottle of pills and started taking them swiftly, between gulps of water, one by one by one.

At first nothing happened, but as I approached the

The Bell Jar

bottom of the bottle, red and blue lights began to flash before my eyes. The bottle slid from my fingers and I lay down.

The silence drew off, baring the pebbles and shells and all the tatty wreckage of my life. Then, at the rim of vision, it gathered itself, and in one sweeping tide, rushed me to sleep.

* * *

It was completely dark.

I felt the darkness, but nothing else, and my head rose, feeling it, like the head of a worm. Someone was moaning. Then a great, hard weight smashed against my cheek like a stone wall and the moaning stopped.

The silence surged back, smoothing itself as black water smooths to its old surface calm over a dropped stone.

A cool wind rushed by. I was being transported at enormous speed down a tunnel into the earth. Then the wind stopped. There was a rumbling, as of many voices, protesting and disagreeing in the distance. Then the voices stopped.

A chisel cracked down on my eye, and a slit of light opened, like a mouth or a wound, till the darkness clamped shut on it again. I tried to roll away from the direction of the light, but hands wrapped round my limbs like mummy bands, and I couldn't move.

I began to think I must be in an underground chamber, lit by blinding lights, and that the chamber was full of people who for some reason were holding me down.

Then the chisel struck again, and the light leapt into

my head, and through the thick, warm, furry dark, a voice cried, 'Mother!'

Air breathed and played over my face.

I felt the shape of a room around me, a big room with open windows. A pillow moulded itself under my head, and my body floated, without pressure, between thin sheets.

Then I felt warmth, like a hand on my face. I must be lying in the sun. If I opened my eyes, I would see colours and shapes bending in upon me like nurses.

I opened my eyes.

It was completely dark.

Somebody was breathing beside me.

'I can't see,' I said.

A cheery voice spoke out of the dark. 'There are lots of blind people in the world. You'll marry a nice blind man some day.'

The man with the chisel had come back.

'Why do you bother?' I said. 'It's no use.'

'You mustn't talk like that.' His fingers probed at the great, aching boss over my left eye. Then he loosened something, and a ragged gap of light appeared, like the hole in a wall. A man's head peered round the edge of it.

'Can you see me?'

'Yes.'

'Can you see anything else?'

Then I remembered. 'I can't see anything.' The gap narrowed and went dark. 'I'm blind.'

'Nonsense! Who told you that?'

'The nurse.'

The man snorted. He finished taping the bandage

The Bell Jar

back over my eye. 'You are a very lucky girl. Your sight is perfectly intact.'

'Somebody to see you.'

The nurse beamed and disappeared.

My mother came smiling round the foot of the bed. She was wearing a dress with purple cartwheels on it and she looked awful.

A big tall boy followed her. At first I couldn't make out who it was, because my eye only opened a short way, but then I saw it was my brother.

'They said you wanted to see me.'

My mother perched on the edge of the bed and laid a hand on my leg. She looked loving and reproachful, and I wanted her to go away.

'I didn't think I said anything.'

'They said you called for me.' She seemed ready to cry. Her face puckered up and quivered like a pale jelly.

'How are you?' my brother said.

I looked my mother in the eye.

'The same,' I said.

'You have a visitor.'

'I don't want a visitor.'

The nurse bustled out and whispered to somebody in the hall. Then she came back. 'He'd very much like to see you.'

I looked down at the yellow legs sticking out of the unfamiliar white silk pyjamas they had dressed me in. The skin shook flabbily when I moved, as if there wasn't a muscle in it, and it was covered with a short, thick stubble of black hair.

'Who is it?'

'Somebody you know.'

'What's his name?'
'George Bakewell.'
'I don't know any George Bakewell.'
'He says he knows you.'
Then the nurse went out, and a very familiar boy came in and said, 'Mind if I sit on the edge of your bed?'

He was wearing a white coat, and I could see a stethoscope poking out of his pocket. I thought it must be somebody I knew dressed up as a doctor.

I had meant to cover my legs if anybody came in, but now I saw it was too late, so I let them stick out, just as they were, disgusting and ugly.

'That's me,' I thought. 'That's what I am.'

'You remember me, don't you, Esther?'

I squinted at the boy's face through the crack of my good eye. The other eye hadn't opened yet, but the eye doctor said it would be all right in a few days.

The boy looked at me as if I were some exciting new zoo animal and he was about to burst out laughing.

'You remember me, don't you, Esther?' He spoke slowly, the way one speaks to a dull child. 'I'm George Bakewell. I go to your church. You dated my room-mate once at Amherst.'

I thought I placed the boy's face then. It hovered dimly at the rim of memory – the sort of face to which I would never bother to attach a name.

'What are you doing here?'

'I'm houseman at this hospital.'

How could this George Bakewell have become a doctor so suddenly? I wondered. He didn't really know me, either. He just wanted to see what a girl who was crazy enough to kill herself looked like.

The Bell Jar

I turned my face to the wall.

'Get out,' I said. 'Get the hell out and don't come back.'

'I want to see a mirror.'

The nurse hummed busily as she opened one drawer after another, stuffing the new underclothes and blouses and skirts and pyjamas my mother had bought me into the black patent leather overnight case.

'Why can't I see a mirror?'

I had been dressed in a sheath, striped grey and white, like mattress ticking, with a wide, shiny red belt, and they had propped me up in an armchair.

'Why can't I?'

'Because you better not.' The nurse shut the lid of the overnight case with a little snap.

'Why?'

'Because you don't look very pretty.'

'Oh, just let me see.'

The nurse sighed and opened the top bureau drawer. She took out a large mirror in a wooden frame that matched the wood of the bureau and handed it to me.

At first I didn't see what the trouble was. It wasn't a mirror at all, but a picture.

You couldn't tell whether the person in the picture was a man or a woman, because their hair was shaved off and sprouted in bristly chicken-feather tufts all over their head. One side of the person's face was purple, and bulged out in a shapeless way, shading to green along the edges, and then to a sallow yellow. The person's mouth was pale brown, with a rose-coloured sore at either corner.

The most startling thing about the face was its supernatural conglomeration of bright colours.

I smiled.

The mouth in the mirror cracked into a grin.

A minute after the crash another nurse ran in. She took one look at the broken mirror, and at me, standing over the blind, white pieces, and hustled the young nurse out of the room.

'Didn't I *tell* you,' I could hear her say.

'But I only . . .'

'Didn't I *tell* you!'

I listened with mild interest. Anybody could drop a mirror. I didn't see why they should get so stirred up.

The other, older nurse came back into the room. She stood there, arms folded, staring hard at me.

'Seven years' bad luck.'

'What?'

'I said,' the nurse raised her voice, as if speaking to a deaf person, '*seven years' bad luck*.'

The young nurse returned with a dustpan and brush and began to sweep up the glittery splinters.

'That's only a superstition,' I said then.

'Huh!' The second nurse addressed herself to the nurse on her hands and knees as if I wasn't there. 'At you-know-where they'll take care of *her*!'

From the back window of the ambulance I could see street after familiar street funnelling off into a summery green distance. My mother sat on one side of me, and my brother on the other.

I had pretended I didn't know why they were moving me from the hospital in my home town to a city hospital, to see what they would say.

'They want you to be in a special ward,' my mother said. 'They don't have that sort of ward at our hospital.'

The Bell Jar

'I liked it where I was.'

My mother's mouth tightened. 'You should have behaved better, then.'

'What?'

'You shouldn't have broken that mirror. Then maybe they'd have let you stay.'

But of course I knew the mirror had nothing to do with it.

I sat in bed with the covers up to my neck.

'Why can't I get up? I'm not sick.'

'Ward rounds,' the nurse said. 'You can get up after ward rounds.' She shoved the bed-curtains back and revealed a fat young Italian woman in the next bed.

The Italian woman had a mass of tight black curls, starting at her forehead, that rose in a mountainous pompadour and cascaded down her back. Whenever she moved, the huge arrangement of hair moved with her, as if made of stiff black paper.

The woman looked at me and giggled. 'Why are you here?' She didn't wait for an answer. 'I'm here on account of my French-Canadian mother-in-law.' She giggled again. 'My husband knows I can't stand her, and still he said she could come and visit us, and when she came, my tongue stuck out of my head, I couldn't stop it. They ran me into Emergency and then they put me up here,' she lowered her voice, 'along with the nuts.' Then she said, 'What's the matter with you?'

I turned her my full face, with the bulging purple and green eye. 'I tried to kill myself.'

The woman stared at me. Then, hastily, she snatched up a movie magazine from her bed-table and pretended to be reading.

The swinging door opposite my bed flew open, and a whole troop of young boys and girls in white coats came in, with an older, grey-haired man. They were all smiling with bright, artificial smiles. They grouped themselves at the foot of my bed.

'And how are you feeling this morning, Miss Greenwood?'

I tried to decide which one of them had spoken. I hate saying anything to a group of people. When I talk to a group of people I always have to single out one and talk to him, and all the while I am talking I feel the others are peering at me and taking unfair advantage. I also hate people to ask cheerfully how you are when they know you're feeling like hell and expect you to say 'Fine'.

'I feel lousy.'

'Lousy. Hmm,' somebody said, and a boy ducked his head with a little smile. Somebody else scribbled something on a clipboard. Then somebody pulled a straight, solemn face and said, 'And why do you feel lousy?'

I thought some of the boys and girls in that bright group might well be friends of Buddy Willard. They would know I knew him, and they would be curious to see me, and afterwards they would gossip about me among themselves. I wanted to be where nobody I knew could ever come.

'I can't sleep . . .'

They interrupted me. 'But the nurse says you slept last night.' I looked round the crescent of fresh, strange faces.

'I can't read.' I raised my voice. 'I can't eat.' It occurred to me I'd been eating ravenously ever since I came to.

The people in the group had turned from me and

The Bell Jar

were murmuring in low voices to each other. Finally, the grey-haired man stepped out.

'Thank you, Miss Greenwood. You will be seen by one of the staff doctors presently.'

Then the group moved on to the bed of the Italian woman.

'And how are you feeling today, Mrs . . .' somebody said, and the name sounded long and full of l's, like Mrs Tomolillo.

Mrs Tomolillo giggled. 'Oh, I'm fine, doctor. I'm just fine.' Then she lowered her voice and whispered something I couldn't hear. One or two people in the group glanced in my direction. Then somebody said, 'All right, Mrs Tomolillo,' and somebody stepped out and pulled the bed-curtain between us like a white wall.

I sat on one end of a wooden bench in the grassy square between the four brick walls of the hospital. My mother, in her purple cartwheel dress, sat at the other end. She had her head propped in her hand, index finger on her cheek, and thumb under her chin.

Mrs Tomolillo was sitting with some dark-haired, laughing Italians on the next bench down. Every time my mother moved, Mrs Tomolillo imitated her. Now Mrs Tomolillo was sitting with her index finger on her cheek and her thumb under her chin, and her head tilted wistfully to one side.

'Don't move,' I told my mother in a low voice. 'That woman's imitating you.'

My mother turned to glance round, but quick as a wink, Mrs Tomolillo dropped her fat white hands in her lap and started talking vigorously to her friends.

'Why no, she's not,' my mother said. 'She's not even paying any attention to us.'

But the minute my mother turned round to me again, Mrs Tomolillo matched the tips of her fingers together the way my mother had just done and cast a black, mocking look at me.

The lawn was white with doctors.

All the time my mother and I had been sitting there, in the narrow cone of sun that shone down between the tall brick walls, doctors had been coming up to me and introducing themselves. 'I'm Doctor Soandso, I'm Doctor Soandso.'

Some of them looked so young I knew they couldn't be proper doctors, and one of them had a queer name that sounded just like Doctor Syphilis, so I began to look out for suspicious, fake names, and sure enough, a dark-haired fellow who looked very like Doctor Gordon, except that he had black skin where Doctor Gordon's skin was white, came up and said, 'I'm Doctor Pancreas,' and shook my hand.

After introducing themselves, the doctors all stood within listening distance, only I couldn't tell my mother that they were taking down every word we said without their hearing me, so I leaned over and whispered into her ear.

My mother drew back sharply.

'Oh, Esther, I wish you would co-operate. They say you don't co-operate. They say you won't talk to any of the doctors or make anything in Occupational Therapy . . .'

'I've got to get out of here,' I told her meaningly. 'Then I'd be all right. You got me in here,' I said. 'You get me out.'

'I thought if only I could persuade my mother to get me out of the hospital I could work on her sympathies, like that boy with brain disease in the play, and convince her what was the best thing to do.

To my surprise, my mother said, 'All right, I'll try to get you out – even if only to a better place. If I try to get you out,' she laid a hand on my knee, 'promise you'll be good?'

I spun round and glared straight at Doctor Syphilis, who stood at my elbow taking notes on a tiny, almost invisible pad. 'I promise,' I said in a loud, conspicuous voice.

The negro wheeled the food cart into the patients' dining-room. The Psychiatric Ward at the hospital was very small – just two corridors in an L-shape, lined with rooms, and an alcove of beds behind the OT shop, where I was, and a little area with a table and a few seats by a window in the corner of the L, which was our lounge and dining-room.

Usually it was a shrunken old white man that brought our food, but today it was a negro. The negro was with a woman in blue stiletto heels, and she was telling him what to do. The negro kept grinning and chuckling in a silly way.

Then he carried a tray over to our table with three lidded tin tureens on it, and started banging the tureens down. The woman left the room locking the door behind her. All the time the negro was banging down the tureens and then the dinted silver and the thick, white china plates, he gawped at us with big, rolling eyes.

I could tell we were his first crazy people.

Nobody at the table made a move to take the lids off the tin tureens, and the nurse stood back to see if any of us would take the lids off before she came to do it. Usually Mrs Tomolillo had taken the lids off and dished out everybody's food like a little mother, but then they sent her home, and nobody seemed to want to take her place.

Sylvia Plath

I was starving, so I lifted the lid off the first bowl.

'That's very nice of you, Esther,' the nurse said pleasantly. 'Would you like to take some beans and pass them round to the others?'

I dished myself out a helping of green string beans and turned to pass the tureen to the enormous red-headed woman at my right. This was the first time the red-headed woman had been allowed up to the table. I had seen her once, at the very end of the L-shaped corridor, standing in front of an open door with bars on the square, inset window.

She had been yelling and laughing in a rude way and slapping her thighs at the passing doctors, and the white-jacketed attendant who took care of the people in that end of the ward was leaning against the hall radiator, laughing himself sick.

The red-headed woman snatched the tureen from me and upended it on her plate. Beans mountained up in front of her and scattered over on to her lap and on to the floor like stiff, green straws.

'Oh, Mrs Mole!' the nurse said in a sad voice. 'I think you better eat in your room today.'

And she returned most of the beans to the tureen and gave it to the person next to Mrs Mole and led Mrs Mole off. All the way down the hall to her room, Mrs Mole kept turning round and making leering faces at us, and ugly, oinking noises.

The negro had come back and was starting to collect the empty plates of people who hadn't dished out any beans yet.

'We're not done,' I told him. 'You can just wait.'

'Mah, mah!' The negro widened his eyes in mock wonder. He glanced round. The nurse had not yet returned from locking up Mrs Mole. The negro made me an

The Bell Jar

insolent bow. 'Miss Mucky-Muck,' he said under his breath.

I lifted the lid off the second tureen and uncovered a wodge of macaroni, stone-cold and stuck together in a gluey paste. The third and last tureen was chock-full of baked beans.

Now I knew perfectly well you didn't serve two kinds of beans together at a meal. Beans and carrots, or beans and peas, maybe, but never beans and beans. The negro was just trying to see how much we would take.

The nurse came back, and the negro edged off at a distance. I ate as much as I could of the baked beans. Then I rose from the table, passing round to the side where the nurse couldn't see me below the waist, and behind the negro, who was clearing the dirty plates. I drew my foot back and gave him a sharp, hard kick on the calf of the leg.

The negro leapt away with a yelp and rolled his eyes at me. 'Oh Miz, oh Miz,' he moaned, rubbing his leg. 'You shouldn't of done that, you shouldn't, you reely shouldn't.'

'That's what *you* get,' I said, and stared him in the eye.

'Don't you want to get up today?'

'No.' I huddled down more deeply in the bed and pulled the sheet up over my head. Then I lifted a corner of the sheet and peered out. The nurse was shaking down the thermometer she had just removed from my mouth.

'You *see*, it's normal.' I had looked at the thermometer before she came to collect it, the way I always did. 'You *see*, it's normal, what do you keep taking it for?'

Sylvia Plath

I wanted to tell her that if only something were wrong with my body it would be fine, I would rather have anything wrong with my body than something wrong with my head, but the idea seemed so involved and wearisome that I didn't say anything. I only burrowed down further in the bed.

Then, through the sheet, I felt a slight, annoying pressure on my leg. I peeped out. The nurse had set her tray of thermometers on my bed while she turned her back and took the pulse of the person who lay next to me, in Mrs Tomolillo's place.

A heavy naughtiness pricked through my veins, irritating and attractive as the hurt of a loose tooth. I yawned and stirred, as if about to turn over, and edged my foot under the box.

'Oh!' The nurse's cry sounded like a cry for help, and another nurse came running. 'Look what you've done!'

I poked my head out of the covers and stared over the edge of the bed. Around the overturned enamel tray, a star of thermometer shards glittered, and balls of mercury trembled like celestial dew.

'I'm sorry,' I said. 'It was an accident.'

The second nurse fixed me with a baleful eye. 'You did it on purpose. I *saw* you.'

Then she hurried off, and almost immediately two attendants came and wheeled me, bed and all, down to Mrs Mole's old room, but not before I had scooped up a ball of mercury.

Soon after they had locked the door, I could see the negro's face, a molasses-coloured moon, risen at the window grating, but I pretended not to notice.

I opened my fingers a crack, like a child with a secret and smiled at the silver globe cupped in my palm. If I dropped it, it would break into a million

The Bell Jar

little replicas of itself, and if I pushed them near each other, they would fuse, without a crack, into one whole again.

I smiled and smiled at the small silver ball.

I couldn't imagine what they had done with Mrs Mole.

Jean Rhys

extract from

Wide Sargasso Sea

Antoinette Bertha Cosway, known by her step-father's name, Mason, first appeared in Charlotte Brontë's *Jane Eyre*. She runs the Creole heiress whom Mr Rochester married on his father's instructions who was later to haunt Miss Eyre as the mad woman kept hidden in the attic of Thornfield Hall. Jean Rhys also found herself haunted by Antoinette. In *Wide Sargasso Sea*, her best novel, she invents a childhood for this tragic character, as the daughter of a Jamaican family ruined by the emancipation of the slaves.

Antoinette Bertha Cosway, known by her stepfather's name, Mason, first appeared in Charlotte Brontë's Jane Eyre. *She was the Creole heiress whom Mr Rochester married on his father's orders, and who was later to haunt Miss Eyre as the mad woman kept hidden in the attics of Thornfield Hall. Jean Rhys also found herself haunted by Antoinette. In* Wide Sargasso Sea, *her best novel, she invents a childhood for this tragic character as the daughter of a Jamaican family ruined by the emancipation of the slaves.*

They say when trouble comes close ranks, and so the white people did. But we were not in their ranks. The Jamaican ladies had never approved of my mother, 'because she pretty like pretty self' Christophine said.

She was my father's second wife, far too young for him they thought, and, worse still, a Martinique girl. When I asked her why so few people came to see us, she told me that the road from Spanish Town to Coulibri Estate where we lived was very bad and that road repairing was now a thing of the past. (My father, visitors, horses, feeling safe in bed – all belonged to the past.)

Another day I heard her talking to Mr Luttrell, our neighbour and her only friend. 'Of course they have their own misfortunes. Still waiting for this compensation the English promised when the Emancipation Act was passed. Some will wait for a long time.'

How could she know that Mr Luttrell would be the first who grew tired of waiting? One calm evening he shot his dog, swam out to sea and was gone for always. No agent came from England to look after his property – Nelson's Rest it was called – and strangers from Spanish Town rode up to gossip and discuss the tragedy.

'Live at Nelson's Rest? Not for love or money. An unlucky place.'

Mr Luttrell's house was left empty, shutters banging

in the wind. Soon the black people said it was haunted, they wouldn't go near it. And no one came near us.

I got used to a solitary life, but my mother still planned and hoped – perhaps she had to hope every time she passed a looking glass.

She still rode about every morning not caring that the black people stood about in groups to jeer at her, especially after her riding clothes grew shabby (they notice clothes, they know about money).

Then, one day, very early I saw her horse lying down under the frangipani tree. I went up to him but he was not sick, he was dead and his eyes were black with flies. I ran away and did not speak of it for I thought if I told no one it might not be true. But later that day, Godfrey found him, he had been poisoned. 'Now we are marooned,' my mother said, 'now what will become of us?'

Godfrey said, 'I can't watch the horse night and day. I too old now. When the old time go, let it go. No use to grab at it. The Lord make no distinction between black and white, black and white the same for Him. Rest yourself in peace for the righteous are not forsaken.' But she couldn't. She was young. How could she not try for all the things that had gone so suddenly, so without warning. 'You're blind when you want to be blind,' she said ferociously, 'and you're deaf when you want to be deaf. The old hypocrite,' she kept saying. 'He knew what they were going to do.' 'The devil prince of this world,' Godfrey said, 'but this world don't last so long for mortal man.'

She persuaded a Spanish Town doctor to visit my younger brother Pierre who staggered when he walked and couldn't speak distinctly. I don't know what the doctor told her or what she said to him but he never came again and after that she changed. Suddenly, not gradually. She grew thin and silent, and at last she refused to leave the house at all.

Our garden was large and beautiful as that garden in the Bible – the tree of life grew there. But it had gone wild. The paths were overgrown and a smell of dead flowers mixed with the fresh living smell. Underneath the tree ferns, tall as forest tree ferns, the light was green. Orchids flourished out of reach or for some reason not to be touched. One was snaky looking, another like an octopus with long thin brown tentacles bare of leaves hanging from a twisted root. Twice a year the octopus orchid flowered – then not an inch of tentacle showed. It was a bell-shaped mass of white, mauve, deep purples, wonderful to see. The scent was very sweet and strong. I never went near it.

All Coulibri Estate had gone wild like the garden, gone to bush. No more slavery – why should *anybody* work? This never saddened me. I did not remember the place when it was prosperous.

My mother usually walked up and down the *glacis*, a paved roofed-in terrace which ran the length of the house and sloped upwards to a clump of bamboos. Standing by the bamboos she had a clear view to the sea, but anyone passing could stare at her. They stared, sometimes they laughed. Long after the sound was far away and faint she kept her eyes shut and her hands clenched. A frown came between her black eyebrows, deep – it might have been cut with a knife. I hated this frown and once I touched her forehead trying to smooth it. But she pushed me away, not roughly but calmly, coldly, without a word, as if she had decided once and for all that I was useless to her. She wanted to sit with Pierre or walk where she pleased without being pestered, she wanted peace and quiet. I was old enough to look after myself. 'Oh, let me alone,' she would say, 'let me alone,' and after I knew that she talked aloud to herself I was a little afraid of her.

So I spent most of my time in the kitchen which was in an outbuilding some way off. Christophine slept in the little room next to it.

When evening came she sang to me if she was in the mood. I couldn't always understand her patois songs – she also came from Martinique – but she taught me the one that meant 'The little ones grow old, the children leave us, will they come back?' and the one about the cedar tree flowers which only last for a day.

The music was gay but the words were sad and her voice often quavered and broke on the high note. 'Adieu.' Not adieu as we said it, but *à dieu*, which made more sense after all. The loving man was lonely, the girl was deserted, the children never came back. Adieu.

Her songs were not like Jamaican songs, and she was not like the other women.

She was much blacker – blue-black with a thin face and straight features. She wore a black dress, heavy gold earrings and a yellow handkerchief – carefully tied with the two high points in front. No other negro woman wore black, or tied her handkerchief Martinique fashion. She had a quiet voice and a quiet laugh (when she did laugh), and though she could speak good English if she wanted to, and French as well as patois, she took care to talk as they talked. But they would have nothing to do with her and she never saw her son who worked in Spanish Town. She had only one friend – a woman called Maillotte, and Maillotte was not a Jamaican.

The girls from the bayside who sometimes helped

Wide Sargasso Sea

with the washing and cleaning were terrified of her. That, I soon discovered, was why they came at all – for she never paid them. Yet they brought presents of fruit and vegetables and after dark I often heard low voices from the kitchen.

So I asked about Christophine. Was she very old? Had she always been with us?

'She was your father's wedding present to me – one of his presents. He thought I would be pleased with a Martinique girl. I don't know how old she was when they brought her to Jamaica, quite young. I don't know how old she is now. Does it matter? Why do you pester and bother me about all these things that happened long ago? Christophine stayed with me because she wanted to stay. She had her own very good reasons you may be sure. I dare say we would have died if she'd turned against us and that would have been a better fate. To die and be forgotten and at peace. Not to know that one is abandoned, lied about, helpless. All the ones who died – who says a good word for them now?'

'Godfrey stayed too,' I said. 'And Sass.'

'They stayed,' she said angrily, 'because they wanted somewhere to sleep and something to eat. That boy Sass! When his mother pranced off and left him here – a great deal *she* cared – why he was a little skeleton. Now he's growing into a big strong boy and away he goes. We shan't see him again. Godfrey is a rascal. These new ones aren't too kind to old people and he knows it. That's why he stays. Doesn't do a thing but eat enough for a couple of horses. Pretends he's deaf. He isn't deaf – he doesn't want to hear. What a devil he is!'

'Why don't you tell him to find somewhere else to live?' I said and she laughed.

797

'He wouldn't go. He'd probably try to force us out. I've learned to let sleeping curs lie,' she said.

'Would Christophine go if you told her to?' I thought. But I didn't say it. I was afraid to say it.

It was too hot that afternoon. I could see the beads of perspiration on her upper lip and the dark circles under her eyes. I started to fan her, but she turned her head away. She might rest if I left her alone, she said.

Once I would have gone back quietly to watch her asleep on the blue sofa – once I made excuses to be near her when she brushed her hair, a soft black cloak to cover me, hide me, keep me safe.

But not any longer. Not any more.

These were all the people in my life – my mother and Pierre, Christophine, Godfrey, and Sass who had left us.

I never looked at any strange negro. They hated us. They called us white cockroaches. Let sleeping dogs lie. One day a little girl followed me singing, 'Go away white cockroach, go away, go away.' I walked fast, but she walked faster. 'White cockroach, go away, go away. Nobody want you. Go away.'

When I was safely home I sat close to the old wall at the end of the garden. It was covered with green moss soft as velvet and I never wanted to move again. Everything would be worse if I moved. Christophine found me there when it was nearly dark, and I was so stiff she had to help me to get up. She said nothing, but next morning Tia was in the kitchen with her mother Maillotte, Christophine's friend. Soon Tia was my friend and I met her nearly every morning at the turn of the road to the river.

Sometimes we left the bathing pool at midday, sometimes we stayed till late afternoon. Then Tia would light a fire (fires always lit for her, sharp stones did not hurt her bare feet, I never saw her cry). We boiled green bananas in an old iron pot and ate them with our fingers out of a calabash and after we had eaten she slept at once. I could not sleep, but I wasn't quite awake as I lay in the shade looking at the pool – deep and dark green under the trees, brown-green if it had rained, but a bright sparkling green in the sun. The water was so clear that you could see the pebbles at the bottom of the shallow part. Blue and white and striped red. Very pretty. Late or early we parted at the turn of the road. My mother never asked me where I had been or what I had done.

Christophine had given me some new pennies which I kept in the pocket of my dress. They dropped out one morning so I put them on a stone. They shone like gold in the sun and Tia stared. She had small eyes, very black, set deep in her head.

Then she bet me three of the pennies that I couldn't turn a somersault under water 'like you say you can'.

'Of course I can.'

'I never see you do it,' she said. 'Only talk.'

'Bet you all the money I can,' I said.

But after one somersault I still turned and came up choking. Tia laughed and told me that it certainly look like I drown dead that time. Then she picked up the money.

'I did do it,' I said when I could speak, but she shook her head. I hadn't done it good and besides pennies didn't buy much. Why did I look at her like that?

'Keep them then, you cheating nigger,' I said, for I was tired, and the water I had swallowed made me feel sick. 'I can get more if I want to.'

That's not what she hear, she said. She hear all we

poor like beggar. We ate salt fish – no money for fresh fish. That old house so leaky, you run with calabash to catch water when it rain. Plenty white people in Jamaica. Real white people, they got gold money. They didn't look at us, nobody see them come near us. Old time white people nothing but white nigger now, and black nigger better than white nigger.

I wrapped myself in my torn towel and sat on a stone with my back to her, shivering cold. But the sun couldn't warm me. I wanted to go home. I looked round and Tia had gone. I searched for a long time before I could believe that she had taken my dress – not my underclothes, she never wore any – but my dress, starched, ironed, clean that morning. She had left me hers and I put it on at last and walked home in the blazing sun feeling sick, hating her. I planned to get round the back of the house to the kitchen, but passing the stables I stopped to stare at three strange horses and my mother saw me and called. She was on the *glacis* with two young ladies and a gentleman. Visitors! I dragged up the steps unwillingly – I had longed for visitors once, but that was years ago.

They were very beautiful I thought and they wore such beautiful clothes that I looked away down at the flagstones and when they laughed – the gentleman laughed the loudest – I ran into the house, into my bedroom. There I stood with my back against the door and I could feel my heart all through me. I heard them talking and I heard them leave. I came out of my room and my mother was sitting on the blue sofa. She looked at me for some time before she said that I had behaved very oddly. My dress was even dirtier than usual.

'It's Tia's dress.'

'But why are you wearing Tia's dress? Tia? Which one of them is Tia?'

Wide Sargasso Sea

Christophine, who had been in the pantry listening, came at once and was told to find a clean dress for me. 'Throw away that thing. Burn it.'

Then they quarrelled.

Christophine said I had no clean dress. 'She got two dresses, wash and wear. You want clean dress to drop from heaven? Some people crazy in truth.'

'She must have another dress,' said my mother. 'Somewhere.' But Christophine told her loudly that it shameful. She run wild, she grow up worthless. And nobody care.

My mother walked over to the window. ('Marooned,' said her straight narrow back, her carefully coiled hair. 'Marooned.')

'She has an old muslin dress. Find that.'

While Christophine scrubbed my face and tied my plaits with a fresh piece of string, she told me that those were the new people at Nelson's Rest. They called themselves Luttrell, but English or not English they were not like old Mr Luttrell. 'Old Mr Luttrell spit in their face if he see how they look at you. Trouble walk into the house this day. Trouble walk in.'

The old muslin dress was found and it tore as I forced it on. She didn't notice.

No more slavery! She had to laugh! 'These new ones have Letter of the Law. Same thing. They got magistrate. They got fine. They got jail house and chain gang. They got tread machine to mash up people's feet. New ones worse than old ones – more cunning, that's all.'

All that evening my mother didn't speak to me or look at me and I thought, 'She is ashamed of me, what Tia said is true.'

I went to bed early and slept at once. I dreamed that I was walking in the forest. Not alone. Someone who hated me was with me, out of sight. I could hear heavy footsteps coming closer and though I struggled and screamed I could not move. I woke crying. The covering sheet was on the floor and my mother was looking down at me.

'Did you have a nightmare?'

'Yes, a bad dream.'

She sighed and covered me up. 'You were making such a noise. I must go to Pierre, you've frightened him.'

I lay thinking, 'I am safe. There is the corner of the bedroom door and the friendly furniture. There is the tree of life in the garden and the wall green with moss. The barrier of the cliffs and the high mountains. And the barrier of the sea. I am safe. I am safe from strangers.'

The light of the candle in Pierre's room was still there when I slept again. I woke next morning knowing that nothing would be the same. It would change and go on changing.

I don't know how she got money to buy the white muslin and the pink. Yards of muslin. She may have sold her last ring, for there was one left. I saw it in her jewel box – that, and a locket with a shamrock inside. They were mending and sewing first thing in the morning and still sewing when I went to bed. In a week she had a new dress and so had I.

The Luttrells lent her a horse, and she would ride off very early and not come back till late next day – tired out because she had been to a dance or a moonlight picnic. She was gay and laughing – younger than I had ever seen her and the house was sad when she had gone.

So I too left it and stayed away till dark. I was never long at the bathing pool, I never met Tia.

I took another road, past the old sugar works and the water-wheel that had not turned for years. I went to

Wide Sargasso Sea

parts of Coulibri that I had not seen, where there was no road, no path, no track. And if the razor grass cut my legs and arms I would think, 'It's better than people.' Black ants or red ones, tall nests swarming with white ants, rain that soaked me to the skin – once I saw a snake. All better than people.

Better. Better, better than people.

Watching the red and yellow flowers in the sun thinking of nothing, it was as if a door opened and I was somewhere else, something else. Not myself any longer.

I knew the time of day when though it is hot and blue and there are no clouds, the sky can have a very black look.

I was bridesmaid when my mother married Mr Mason in Spanish Town. Christophine curled my hair. I carried a bouquet and everything I wore was new – even my beautiful slippers. But their eyes slid away from my hating face. I had heard what all these smooth smiling people said about her when she was not listening and they did not guess I was. Hiding from them in the garden when they visited Coulibri, I listened.

'A fantastic marriage and he will regret it. Why should a very wealthy man who could take his pick of all the girls in the West Indies, and many in England too probably?' 'Why *probably*?' the other voice said. '*Certainly*.' 'Then why should he marry a widow without a penny to her name and Coulibri a wreck of a place? Emancipation troubles killed old Cosway? Nonsense – the estate was going downhill for years before that. He drank himself to death. Many's the time when – well! And all those women! She never did anything to stop him – she encouraged him. Presents and smiles for the bastards every Christmas. Old customs? Some old customs are better dead and buried. Her new husband will have to spend a pretty penny before the house is fit to live in – leaks like a sieve. And what about the stables and the coach house dark as pitch, and the servants' quarters and the six-foot snake I saw with my own eyes curled up on the privy seat last time I was here. Alarmed? I screamed. Then that horrible old man she harbours came along, doubled up with laughter. As for those two children – the boy an idiot kept out of sight and mind and the girl going the same way in my opinion – a *lowering* expression.'

'Oh I agree,' the other one said, 'but Annette is such a pretty woman. And what a dancer. Reminds me of that song "light as cotton blossom on the something breeze", or is it air? I forget.'

Yes, what a dancer – that night when they came home from their honeymoon in Trinidad and they danced on the *glacis* to no music. There was no need for music when she danced. They stopped and she leaned backwards over his arm, down till her black hair touched the flagstones – still down, down. Then up again in a flash, laughing. She made it look so easy – as if anyone could do it, and he kissed her – a long kiss. I was there that time too but they had forgotten me and soon I wasn't thinking of them. I was remembering that woman saying, 'Dance! He didn't come to the West Indies to dance – he came to make money as they all do. Some of the big estates are going cheap, and one unfortunate's loss is always a clever man's gain. No, the whole thing is a mystery. It's evidently useful to keep a Martinique obeah woman on the premises.' She meant Christophine. She said it mockingly, not meaning it, but soon other people were saying it – and meaning it.

Wide Sargasso Sea

While the repairs were being done and they were in Trinidad, Pierre and I stayed with Aunt Cora in Spanish Town.

Mr Mason did not approve of Aunt Cora, an ex-slave-owner who had escaped misery, a flier in the face of Providence.

'Why did she do nothing to help you?'

I told him that her husband was English and didn't like us and he said, 'Nonsense.'

'It isn't nonsense, they lived in England and he was angry if she wrote to us. He hated the West Indies. When he died not long ago she came home, before that what could she do? *She* wasn't rich.'

'That's her story. I don't believe it. A frivolous woman. In your mother's place I'd resent her behaviour.'

'None of you understand about us,' I thought.

Coulibri looked the same when I saw it again, although it was clean and tidy, no grass between the flagstones, no leaks. But it didn't feel the same. Sass had come back and I was glad. They can *smell* money, somebody said. Mr Mason engaged new servants – I didn't like any of them excepting Mannie the groom. It was their talk about Christophine that changed Coulibri, not the repairs or the new furniture or the strange faces. Their talk about Christophine and obeah changed it.

I knew her room so well – the pictures of the Holy Family and the prayer for a happy death. She had a bright patchwork counterpane, a broken-down press for her clothes, and my mother had given her an old rocking-chair.

Yet one day when I was waiting there I was suddenly very much afraid. The door was open to the sunlight, someone was whistling near the stables, but I was

805

afraid. I was certain that hidden in the room (behind the old black press?) there was a dead man's dried hand, white chicken feathers, a cock with its throat cut, dying slowly, slowly. Drop by drop the blood was falling into a red basin and I imagined I could hear it. No one had ever spoken to me about obeah – but I knew what I would find if I dared to look. Then Christophine came in smiling and pleased to see me. Nothing alarming ever happened and I forgot, or told myself I had forgotten.

Mr Mason would laugh if he knew how frightened I had been. He would laugh even louder than he did when my mother told him that she wished to leave Coulibri.

This began when they had been married for over a year. They always said the same things and I seldom listened to the argument now. I knew that we were hated – but to go away ... for once I agreed with my stepfather. That was not possible.

'You must have some reason,' he would say, and she would answer, 'I need a change' or 'We could visit Richard'. (Richard, Mr Mason's son by his first marriage, was at school in Barbados. He was going to England soon and we had seen very little of him.)

'An agent could look after this place. For the time being. The people here hate us. They certainly hate me.' Straight out she said that one day and it was then he laughed so heartily.

'Annette, be reasonable. You were the widow of a slave-owner, the daughter of a slave-owner, and you had been living here alone, with two children, for nearly five years when we met. Things were at their worst then. But you were never molested, never harmed.'

'How do you know that I was not harmed?' she said. 'We were so poor then,' she told him, 'we were something to laugh at. But we are not poor now,' she said.

Wide Sargasso Sea

'You are not a poor man. Do you suppose that they don't know all about your estate in Trinidad? And the Antigua property? They talk about us without stopping. They invent stories about you, and lies about me. They try to find out what we eat every day.'

'They are curious. It's natural enough. You have lived alone far too long, Annette. You imagine enmity which doesn't exist. Always one extreme or the other. Didn't you fly at me like a little wild cat when I said nigger. Not nigger, nor even negro. Black people I must say.'

'You don't like, or even recognize, the good in them,' she said, 'and you won't believe in the other side.'

'They're too damn lazy to be dangerous,' said Mr Mason. 'I know that.'

'They are more alive than you are, lazy or not, and they can be dangerous and cruel for reasons you wouldn't understand.'

'No, I don't understand,' Mr Mason always said. 'I don't understand at all.'

But she'd speak about going away again. Persistently. Angrily.

Mr Mason pulled up near the empty huts on our way home that evening. 'All gone to one of those dances,' he said. 'Young and old. How deserted the place looks.'

'We'll hear the drums if there is a dance.' I hoped he'd ride on quickly but he stayed by the huts to watch the sun go down, the sky and the sea were on fire when we left Bertrand Bay at last. From a long way off I saw the shadow of our house high up on its stone foundations. There was a smell of ferns and river water and I felt safe again, as if I was one of the righteous. (Godfrey said that we were not righteous. One day when he was drunk he told me that we were all damned and no use praying.)

807

'They've chosen a very hot night for their dance,' Mr Mason said, and Aunt Cora came on to the *glacis*. 'What dance? Where?'

'There is some festivity in the neighbourhood. The huts were abandoned. A wedding perhaps?'

'Not a wedding,' I said. 'There is never a wedding.' He frowned at me but Aunt Cora smiled.

When they had gone indoors I leaned my arms on the cool *glacis* railings and thought that I would never like him very much. I still called him 'Mr Mason' in my head. 'Goodnight white pappy,' I said one evening and he was not vexed, he laughed. In some ways it was better before he came, though he'd rescued us from poverty and misery. 'Only just in time too.' The black people did not hate us quite so much when we were poor. We were white but we had not escaped and soon we would be dead for we had no money left. What was there to hate?

Now it had started up again and worse than before, my mother knows but she can't make him believe it. I wish I could tell him that out here is not at all like English people think it is. I wish . . .

I could hear them talking and Aunt Cora's laugh. I was glad she was staying with us. And I could hear the bamboos shiver and creak though there was no wind. It had been hot and still and dry for days. The colours had gone from the sky, the light was blue and could not last long. The *glacis* was not a good place when night was coming, Christophine said. As I went indoors my mother was talking in an excited voice.

'Very well. As you refuse to consider it, *I* will go and take Pierre with me. You won't object to that, I hope?'

'You are perfectly right, Annette,' said Aunt Cora and that did surprise me. She seldom spoke when they argued.

Wide Sargasso Sea

Mr Mason also seemed surprised and not at all pleased.

'You talk so wildly,' he said. 'And you are so mistaken. Of course you can get away for a change if you wish it. I promise you.'

'You have promised that before,' she said. 'You don't keep your promises.'

He sighed. 'I feel very well here. However, we'll arrange something. Quite soon.'

'I will not stay at Coulibri any longer,' my mother said. 'It is not safe. It is not safe for Pierre.'

Aunt Cora nodded.

As it was late I ate with them instead of by myself as usual. Myra, one of the new servants, was standing by the sideboard, waiting to change the plates. We ate English food now, beef and mutton, pies and puddings.

I was glad to be like an English girl but I missed the taste of Christophine's cooking.

My stepfather talked about a plan to import labourers – coolies he called them – from the East Indies. When Myra had gone out Aunt Cora said, 'I shouldn't discuss that if I were you. Myra is listening.'

'But the people here won't work. They don't want to work. Look at this place – it's enough to break your heart.'

'Hearts have been broken,' she said. 'Be sure of that. I suppose you all know what you are doing.'

'Do you mean to say –'

'I said nothing, except that it would be wiser not to tell that woman your plans – necessary and merciful no doubt. I don't trust her.'

'Live here most of your life and know nothing about the people. It's astonishing. They are children – they wouldn't hurt a fly.'

'Unhappily children do hurt flies,' said Aunt Cora.

Myra came in again looking mournful as she always did though she smiled when she talked about hell. Everyone went to hell, she told me, you had to belong to her sect to be saved and even then – just as well not to be too sure. She had thin arms and big hands and feet and the handkerchief she wore round her head was always white. Never striped or a gay colour.

So I looked away from her at my favourite picture, 'The Miller's Daughter', a lovely English girl with brown curls and blue eyes and a dress slipping off her shoulders. Then I looked across the white tablecloth and the vase of yellow roses at Mr Mason, so sure of himself, so without a doubt English. And at my mother, so without a doubt not English, but no white nigger either. Not my mother. Never had been. Never could be. Yes, she would have died, I thought, if she had not met him. And for the first time I was grateful and liked him. There are more ways than one of being happy, better perhaps to be peaceful and contented and protected, as I feel now, peaceful for years and long years, and afterwards I may be saved whatever Myra says. (When I asked Christophine what happened when you died, she said, 'You want to know too much.') I remembered to kiss my stepfather goodnight. Once Aunt Cora had told me, 'He's very hurt because you never kiss him.'

'He does not look hurt,' I argued. 'Great mistake to go by looks,' she said, 'one way or the other.'

I went into Pierre's room which was next to mine, the last one in the house. The bamboos were outside his window. You could almost touch them. He still had a crib and he slept more and more, nearly all the time. He was so thin that I could lift him easily. Mr Mason had promised to take him to England later on, there he would be cured, made like other people. 'And how will you like that?' I thought, as I kissed him. 'How will you like being made exactly like other people?' He looked happy asleep. But that will be later on. Later on. Sleep now. It was then I heard the bamboos creak again and a sound like whispering. I forced myself to look out of the window. There was a full moon but I saw nobody, nothing but shadows.

I left a light on the chair by my bed and waited for Christophine, for I liked to see her last thing. But she did not come, and as the candle burned down, the safe peaceful feeling left me. I wished I had a big Cuban dog to lie by my bed and protect me, I wished I had not heard a noise by the bamboo clump, or that I were very young again, for then I believed in my stick. It was not a stick, but a long narrow piece of wood, with two nails sticking out at the end, a shingle, perhaps. I picked it up soon after they killed our horse and I thought I can fight with this, if the worst comes to the worst I can fight to the end though the best ones fall and that is another song. Christophine knocked the nails out, but she let me keep the shingle and I grew very fond of it, I believed that no one could harm me when it was near me, to lose it would be a great misfortune. All this was long ago, when I was still babyish and sure that everything was alive, not only the river or the rain, but chairs, looking-glasses, cups, saucers, everything.

I woke up and it was still night and my mother was there. She said, 'Get up and dress yourself, and come downstairs quickly.' She was dressed, but she had not put up her hair and one of her plaits was loose. 'Quickly,' she said again, then she went into Pierre's room, next door. I heard her speak to Myra and I heard Myra answer her. I lay there, half asleep, looking at the lighted candle on the chest of drawers, till I heard a noise as though a chair had fallen over in the little room, then I got up and dressed.

The house was on different levels. There were three steps down from my bedroom and Pierre's to the dining-room and then three steps from the dining-room to the rest of the house, which we called 'downstairs'. The folding doors of the dining-room were not shut and I could see that the big drawing-room was full of people. Mr Mason, my mother, Christophine and Mannie and Sass. Aunt Cora was sitting on the blue sofa in the corner now, wearing a black silk dress, her ringlets were carefully arranged. She looked very haughty, I thought. But Godfrey was not there, or Myra, or the cook, or any of the others.

'There is no reason to be alarmed,' my stepfather was saying as I came in. 'A handful of drunken negroes.' He opened the door leading to the *glacis* and walked out. 'What is all this,' he shouted. 'What do you want?' A horrible noise swelled up, like animals howling, but worse. We heard stones falling on to the *glacis*. He was pale when he came in again, but he tried to smile as he shut and bolted the door. 'More of them than I thought, and in a nasty mood too. They will repent in the morning. I foresee gifts of tamarinds in syrup and ginger sweets tomorrow.'

'Tomorrow will be too late,' said Aunt Cora, 'too late for ginger sweets or anything else.' My mother was not listening to either of them. She said, 'Pierre is asleep and Myra is with him, I thought it better to leave him in his own room, away from this horrible noise. I don't know. Perhaps.' She was twisting her hands together, her wedding ring fell off and rolled into a corner near the steps. My stepfather and Mannie both stooped for it, then Mannie straightened up and said, 'Oh, my God, they get at the back, they set fire to the back of the house.' He pointed to my bedroom door which I had shut after me, and smoke was rolling out from underneath.

I did not see my mother move she was so quick. She opened the door of my room and then again I did not see her, nothing but smoke. Mannie ran after her, so did Mr Mason but more slowly. Aunt Cora put her arms round me. She said, 'Don't be afraid, you are quite safe. We are all quite safe.' Just for a moment I shut my eyes and rested my head against her shoulder. She smelled of vanilla, I remember. Then there was another smell, of burned hair, and I looked and my mother was in the room carrying Pierre. It was her loose hair that had burned and was smelling like that.

I thought, Pierre is dead. He looked dead. He was white and he did not make a sound, but his head hung back over her arm as if he had no life at all and his eyes were rolled up so that you only saw the whites. My stepfather said, 'Annette, you are hurt – your hands . . .' But she did not even look at him. 'His crib was on fire,' she said to Aunt Cora. 'The little room is on fire and Myra was not there. She has gone. She was not there.'

'That does not surprise me at all,' said Aunt Cora. She laid Pierre on the sofa, bent over him, then lifted up her skirt, stepped out of her white petticoat and began to tear it into strips.

'She left him, she ran away and left him alone to die,' said my mother, still whispering. So it was all the more dreadful when she began to scream abuse at Mr Mason, calling him a fool, a cruel stupid fool. 'I told you,' she said, 'I told you what would happen again and again.' Her voice broke, but still she screamed, 'You would not listen, you sneered at me, you grinning hypocrite, you ought not to live either, you know so much, don't you? Why don't you go out and ask them to let you go? Say how innocent you are. Say you have always trusted them.'

I was so shocked that everything was confused. And it happened quickly. I saw Mannie and Sass staggering along with two large earthenware jars of water which were kept in the pantry. They threw the water into the bedroom and it made a black pool on the floor, but the smoke rolled over the pool. Then Christophine, who had run into my mother's bedroom for the pitcher there, came back and spoke to my aunt. 'It seems they have fired the other side of the house,' said Aunt Cora. 'They must have climbed that tree outside. This place is going to burn like tinder and there is nothing we can do to stop it. The sooner we get out the better.'

Mannie said to the boy, 'You frightened?' Sass shook his head. 'Then come on,' said Mannie. 'Out of my way,' he said and pushed Mr Mason aside. Narrow wooden stairs led down from the pantry to the outbuildings, the kitchen, the servants' rooms, the stables. That was where they were going. 'Take the child,' Aunt Cora told Christophine, 'and come.'

It was very hot on the *glacis* too, they roared as we came out, then there was another roar behind us. I had not seen any flames, only smoke and sparks, but now I saw tall flames shooting up to the sky, for the bamboos had caught. There were some tree ferns near, green and damp, one of those was smouldering too.

'Come quickly,' said Aunt Cora, and she went first, holding my hand. Christophine followed, carrying Pierre, and they were quite silent as we went down the *glacis* steps. But when I looked round for my mother I saw

Wide Sargasso Sea

that Mr Mason, his face crimson with heat, seemed to be dragging her along and she was holding back, struggling. I heard him say, 'It's impossible, too late now.'

'Wants her jewel case?' Aunt Cora said.

'Jewel case? Nothing so sensible,' bawled Mr Mason. 'She wanted to go back for her damned parrot. I won't allow it.' She did not answer, only fought him silently, twisting like a cat and showing her teeth.

Our parrot was called Coco, a green parrot. He didn't talk very well, he could say *Qui est là? Qui est là?* and answer himself *Ché Coco, Ché Coco*. After Mr Mason clipped his wings he grew very bad tempered, and though he would sit quietly on my mother's shoulder, he darted at everyone who came near her and pecked their feet.

'Annette,' said Aunt Cora. 'They are laughing at you, do not allow them to laugh at you.' She stopped fighting then and he half supported, half pulled her after us, cursing loudly.

Still they were quiet and there were so many of them I could hardly see any grass or trees. There must have been many of the bay people but I recognized no one. They all looked the same, it was the same face repeated over and over, eyes gleaming, mouth half open to shout. We were past the mounting stone when they saw Mannie driving the carriage round the corner. Sass followed, riding one horse and leading another. There was a ladies' saddle on the one he was leading.

Somebody yelled, 'But look the black Englishman! Look the white niggers!' and then they were all yelling. 'Look the white niggers! Look the damn white niggers!' A stone just missed Mannie's head, he cursed back at them and they cleared away from the rearing, frightened horses. 'Come on, for God's sake,' said Mr Mason. 'Get to the carriage, get to the horses.' But we could

815

not move for they pressed too close round us. Some of them were laughing and waving sticks, some of the ones at the back were carrying flambeaux and it was light as day. Aunt Cora held my hand very tightly and her lips moved but I could not hear because of the noise. And I was afraid, because I knew that the ones who laughed would be the worst. I shut my eyes and waited. Mr Mason stopped swearing and began to pray in a loud pious voice. The prayer ended, 'May Almighty God defend us.' And God who is indeed mysterious, who had made no sign when they burned Pierre as he slept – not a clap of thunder, not a flash of lightning – mysterious God heard Mr Mason at once and answered him. The yells stopped.

I opened my eyes, everybody was looking up and pointing at Coco on the *glacis* railings with his feathers alight. He made an effort to fly down but his clipped wings failed him and he fell screeching. He was all on fire.

I began to cry. 'Don't look,' said Aunt Cora. 'Don't look.' She stooped and put her arms round me and I hid my face, but I could feel that they were not so near. I heard someone say something about bad luck and remembered that it was very unlucky to kill a parrot, or even to see a parrot die. They began to go then, quickly, silently, and those that were left drew aside and watched us as we trailed across the grass. They were not laughing any more.

'Get to the carriage, get to the carriage,' said Mr Mason. 'Hurry!' He went first, holding my mother's arm, then Christophine carrying Pierre, and Aunt Cora was last, still with my hand in hers. None of us looked back.

Mannie had stopped the horses at the bend of the cobblestone road and as we got closer we heard him

Wide Sargasso Sea

shout, 'What all you are, eh? Brute beasts?' He was speaking to a group of men and a few women who were standing round the carriage. A coloured man with a machete in his hand was holding the bridle. I did not see Sass or the other two horses. 'Get in,' said Mr Mason. 'Take no notice of him, get in.' The man with the machete said no. We would go to police and tell a lot of damn lies. A woman said to let us go. All this an accident and they had plenty witness. 'Myra she witness for us.'

'Shut your mouth,' the man said. 'You mash centipede, mash it, leave one little piece and it grow again . . . What you think police believe, eh? You, or the white nigger?'

Mr Mason stared at him. He seemed not frightened, but too astounded to speak. Mannie took up the carriage whip but one of the blacker men wrenched it out of his hand, snapped it over his knee and threw it away. 'Run away, black Englishman, like the boy run. Hide in the bushes. It's better for you.' It was Aunt Cora who stepped forward and said, 'The little boy is very badly hurt. He will die if we cannot get help for him.'

The man said, 'So black and white, they burn the same, eh?'

'They do,' she said. 'Here and hereafter, as you will find out. Very shortly.'

He let the bridle go and thrust his face close to hers. He'd throw her on the fire, he said, if she put bad luck on him. Old white jumby, he called her. But she did not move an inch, she looked straight into his eyes and threatened him with eternal fire in a calm voice. 'And never a drop of sangoree to cool your burning tongue,' she said. He cursed her again but he backed away. 'Now get in,' said Mr Mason. 'You, Christophine, get in with the child.' Christophine got in. 'Now you,' he said to my mother. But she had turned and was looking back at the house and when he put his hand on her arm, she screamed.

One woman said she only come to see what happen. Another woman began to cry. The man with the cutlass said, 'You cry for her – when she ever cry for you? Tell me that.'

But now I turned too. The house was burning, the yellow-red sky was like sunset and I knew that I would never see Coulibri again. Nothing would be left, the golden ferns and the silver ferns, the orchids, the ginger lilies and the roses, the rocking-chairs and the blue sofa, the jasmine and the honeysuckle, and the picture of the Miller's Daughter. When they had finished, there would be nothing left but blackened walls and the mounting stone. That was always left. That could not be stolen or burned.

Then, not so far off, I saw Tia and her mother and I ran to her, for she was all that was left of my life as it had been. We had eaten the same food, slept side by side, bathed in the same river. As I ran, I thought, I will live with Tia and I will be like her. Not to leave Coulibri. Not to go. Not. When I was close I saw the jagged stone in her hand but I did not see her throw it. I did not feel it either, only something wet, running down my face. I looked at her and I saw her face crumple up as she began to cry. We stared at each other, blood on my face, tears on hers. It was as if I saw myself. Like in a looking-glass.

Françoise Sagan

extract from

Bonjour Tristesse

Cécile, holidaying with her widowed father, has long been accustomed to sharing his affections with a string of girlfriends and is unperturbed when the latest of these, Elsa, arrives at the villa. Although Cécile has inherited her father's charm she is too young to understand the deeper manipulations binding men and women. Her feelings towards Anne, who appears to be supplanting Elsa, reflect her own reservations concerning love.

Anne was extraordinarily kind to Elsa during the following days. In spite of the numerous silly remarks that punctuated Elsa's conversation, she never gave vent to any of those cutting phrases which were her speciality, and which would have covered the poor girl with ridicule. I was most surprised, and began to admire Anne's forbearance and generosity without realizing how subtle she was; for my father, who would soon have tired of such cruel tactics, was now filled with gratitude towards her. He used his appreciation as a pretext for drawing her, so to speak, into the family circle; by implying all the time that I was partly her responsibility, and altogether behaving towards her as if she were a second mother to me. But I noticed that his every look and gesture betrayed a secret desire for her. Whenever I caught a similar gleam in Cyril's eye, it left me undecided whether to egg him on or to run away. On that point I must have been more easily influenced than Anne, for her attitude to my father expressed such indifference and calm friendliness that I was reassured. I began to believe that I had been mistaken the first day. I did not notice that this unconcern of hers was just what provoked my father. And then there were her silences, apparently so artless and full of fine feeling, and such a contrast to Elsa's incessant chatter, that it was like light and shade. Poor Elsa! She had really no suspicions whatsoever, and although still suffering from the effects of the sun, remained her usual talkative and exuberant self.

A day came, however, when she must have intercepted a look of my father's and drawn her own conclusions from it. Before lunch I saw her whispering into his ear. For a moment he seemed rather put out, but then he nodded and smiled. After coffee Elsa walked over to the door, turned round, and striking a languorous, film-star pose, said in an affected voice, 'Are you coming, Raymond?'

My father got up and followed her, muttering something about the benefits of the siesta. Anne had not moved, her cigarette was smouldering between her fingers. I felt I ought to say something:

'People say that a siesta is restful, but I think it is the opposite . . .'

I stopped short, conscious that my words were equivocal.

'That's enough,' said Anne dryly.

There was nothing equivocal about her tone. She had of course found my remark in bad taste, but when I looked at her I saw that her face was deliberately calm and composed. It made me feel that perhaps at that moment she was passionately jealous of Elsa. While I was wondering how I could console her, a cynical idea occurred to me. Cynicism always enchanted me by producing a delicious feeling of self-assurance and of being in league with myself. I could not keep it back.

'I imagine that with Elsa's sunburn that kind of siesta can't be very exciting for either of them.'

I would have done better to say nothing.

'I detest that kind of remark. At your age it's not only stupid, but deplorable.'

Bonjour Tristesse

I suddenly felt angry:

'I only said it as a joke, you know. I'm sure they are really quite happy.'

She turned to me with an outraged expression, and I at once apologized. She closed her eyes and began to speak in a low, patient voice.

'Your idea of love is rather primitive. It is not a series of sensations, independent of each other. . . .'

I realized how every time I had fallen in love it had been like that: a sudden emotion, roused by a face, a gesture or a kiss, which I remembered only as incoherent moments of excitement. 'It is something different,' said Anne. 'There are such things as lasting affection, sweetness, a sense of loss . . . but I suppose you wouldn't understand.'

She made an evasive gesture and took up a newspaper. If only she had been angry instead of showing that resigned indifference to my emotional irresponsibility! All the same I felt she was right: that I was governed by my instincts like an animal, swayed this way and that by other people, that I was shallow and weak. I despised myself, and it was a horribly painful sensation, all the more since I was not used to self-criticism. I went up to my room in a daze. Lying in bed on my lukewarm sheet I thought of Anne's words: 'It is something different, it's a sense of loss.' Had I ever missed anyone?

The next fortnight is rather vague in my memory because I deliberately shut my eyes to any threat to our security, but the rest of the holiday stands out all the more clearly because of the role I chose to play in it.

To go back to those first three weeks, three happy weeks after all: when exactly did my father begin to treat Anne with a new familiarity? Was it the day he reproached her for her indifference, while pretending to laugh at it? Or the time he grimly compared her subtlety with Elsa's semi-imbecility? My peace of mind was based on the stupid idea that they had known each other for fifteen years, and that if they had been going to fall in love, they would have done so earlier. And I thought also that if it had to happen, the affair would last at the most three months, and Anne would be left with her memories and perhaps a slight feeling of humiliation. Yet all the time I knew in my heart that Anne was not a woman who could be lightly abandoned.

But Cyril was there, and I was fully occupied. In the evenings we often drove to Saint-Tropez and danced in various bars to the soft music of a clarinet. At those moments we felt we were madly in love, but by the next morning it was all forgotten. During the day we went sailing. My father sometimes came with us. He thought a lot of Cyril, especially since he had been allowed to beat him in a swimming race. He called Cyril 'my boy', Cyril called him 'sir', but I sometimes wondered which of the two was the adult.

One afternoon we went to tea with Cyril's mother, a quiet smiling old lady who spoke to us of her difficulties as a widow and mother. My father sympathized with her, looked gratefully at Anne, and paid innumerable compliments. I must say he never minded wasting his time! Anne looked on at the spectacle with an amiable smile, and afterwards said she thought her charming. I broke into imprecations against old ladies of that sort. They both seemed amused, which made me furious.

'Don't you realize how self-righteous she is?' I insisted. 'That she pats herself on the back because she feels she has done her duty by leading a respectable bourgeois life?'

'But it is true,' said Anne. 'She has done her duty as a wife and mother, as they say.'

'You don't understand at all,' I said. 'She brought up her child; most likely she was faithful to her husband, and so had no worries; she has led the life of millions of other women, and she's proud of it. She glorifies herself for a negative reason, and not for having accomplished anything.'

'Your ideas are fashionable, but you don't know what you are talking about,' Anne said.

She was probably right: I believed what I said at the time, but I must admit that I was only repeating what I had heard. Nevertheless my life and my father's upheld that theory, and Anne hurt my feelings by despising it. One can be just as attached to futilities as to anything else. I suddenly felt an urgent desire to undeceive her. I did not think the opportunity would occur so soon, nor that I would be able to seize it. Anyhow it was quite likely that in a month's time I might have entirely different opinions on any given subject. What more could have been expected of me?

* * *

And then one day things came to a head. In the morning my father announced that he would like to go to Cannes that evening to dance at the casino, and perhaps gamble as well. I remember how pleased Elsa was. In the familiar casino atmosphere she hoped to resume her role of a 'femme fatale', slightly obscured of late by her sunburn and our semi-isolation. Contrary to my expectation Anne did not oppose our plans; she even seemed quite pleased. As soon as dinner was over I went up to my room to put on an evening frock, the only one I possessed, by the way. It had been chosen by my father, and was made of an exotic material, probably too exotic for a girl of my age, but my father, either from inclination or habit, liked to give me a veneer of sophistication. I found him downstairs, sparkling in a new dinner jacket, and I put my arms round his neck.

'You're the best-looking man I know!'

'Except Cyril,' he answered without conviction. 'And as for you, you're the prettiest girl I know.'

'After Elsa and Anne,' I replied without believing it myself.

'Since they're not down yet, and have the cheek to keep us waiting, come and dance with your rheumaticky old father!'

Once again I felt the thrill that always preceded our evenings out together. He really had nothing of an old father about him! While dancing I inhaled the warmth of his familiar perfume, eau de cologne and tobacco. He danced slowly with half-closed eyes, a happy, irrepressible little smile, like my own, on his lips.

'You must teach me the bebop,' he said, forgetting his talk of rheumatism.

He stopped dancing to welcome Elsa with polite flattery. She came slowly down the stairs in her green dress, a conventional smile on her face, her casino smile. She had made the most of her lifeless hair and scorched skin, but the result was more meretricious than brilliant. Fortunately she seemed unaware of it.

'Are we going?'

'Anne's not here yet,' I remarked.

'Go up and see if she's ready,' said my father. 'It will be midnight before we get to Cannes.'

I ran up the stairs, getting somewhat entangled with

my skirt, and knocked at Anne's door. She called to me to come in, but I stopped on the threshold. She was wearing a grey dress, a peculiar grey, almost white, which, when it caught the light, resembled the colour of the sea at dawn. She seemed to me the personification of mature charm.

'Oh Anne, what a magnificent dress!' I said.

She smiled into the mirror as one smiles at a person one is about to leave.

'This grey is a success,' she said.

'You are a success!' I answered.

She pinched my ear, her eyes were dark blue, and I saw them light up with a smile.

'You're a dear child, even though you can be tiresome at times.'

She went out in front of me without a glance at my dress. In a way I was relieved, but all the same it was mortifying. I followed her down the stairs and I saw my father coming to meet her. He stopped at the bottom, his foot on the first step, his face raised. Elsa was looking on. I remember the scene perfectly. First of all, in front of me, Anne's golden neck and perfect shoulders, a little lower down my father's fascinated face and extended hand, and, already in the distance, Elsa's silhouette.

'Anne, you are wonderful!' said my father.

She smiled as she passed him and took her coat.

'Shall we meet there?' she asked. 'Cécile, will you come with me?'

She let me drive. At night the road appeared so beautiful that I went slowly. Anne was silent; she did not even seem to notice the blaring wireless. When my father's car passed us at a bend she remained unmoved. I felt I was out of the race, watching a performance in which I could no longer intervene.

At the casino my father saw to it that we soon lost sight of each other. I found myself at the bar with Elsa and one of her acquaintances, a half-tipsy South American. He was connected with the stage and had such a passionate love for it that even in his inebriated condition he could remain amusing. I spent an agreeable hour with him, but Elsa was bored. She knew one or two big names, but that was not her world. All of a sudden she asked me where my father was, as if I had some means of knowing. She then left us. The South American seemed put out for a moment, but another whisky set him up again. My mind was a blank. I was quite light-headed, for I had been drinking with him out of politeness. It became grotesque when he wanted to dance. I was forced to hold him up and to extricate my feet from under his, which required a lot of energy. We laughed so much that when Elsa tapped me on the shoulder and I saw her Cassandra-like expression, I almost felt like telling her to go to the devil.

'I can't find them,' she said.

She looked utterly distraught. Her powder had worn off leaving her skin shiny, her features were drawn; she was a pitiable sight. I suddenly felt very angry with my father; he was being most unkind.

'Ah, I know where they are,' I said, smiling as if I referred to something quite ordinary about which she need have no anxiety. 'I'll soon be back.'

Deprived of my support, the South American fell into Elsa's arms and seemed comfortable enough there. I reflected somewhat sadly that she was more experienced than I, and that I could not very well bear her a grudge.

The casino was big, and I went all round it twice without any success. I scanned the terrace and at last thought of the car. It took me some time to find it in the car park. They were inside. I approached from behind and saw them through the rear window. Their profiles were very close together and very serious, and looked strangely beautiful in the lamplight. They were facing each other and must have been talking in low tones, for I saw their lips move. I would have liked to go away again, but the thought of Elsa made me open the door. My father had his hand on Anne's arm, and they scarcely noticed me.

'Are you having a good time?' I asked politely.

'What is the matter?' said my father irritably. 'What are you doing here?'

'And you? Elsa has been searching for you everywhere for the past hour.'

Anne turned her head slowly and reluctantly towards me.

'We're going home. Tell her I was tired and your father drove me back. When you've had enough take my car.'

I was trembling with indignation and could hardly speak.

'Had enough? But you don't realize what you're saying, it's disgusting!'

'What is disgusting?' asked my father with astonishment.

'You take a red-haired girl to the seaside, expose her to the hot sun which she can't stand, and when her skin has all peeled you abandon her. It's altogether too simple! What on earth shall I say to Elsa?'

Anne turned to him with an air of weariness. He smiled at her, obviously not listening. My exasperation knew no bounds.

'I shall tell Elsa that my father has found someone

else to sleep with, and that she had better come back some other time. Is that right?'

My father's exclamation and Anne's slap were simultaneous. I hurriedly withdrew my head from the car-door. She had hurt me.

'Apologize at once!' said my father.

I stood motionless, with my thoughts in a whirl. Noble attitudes always occur to me too late.

'Come here,' said Anne.

She did not sound menacing, and I went closer. She put her hand against my cheek and spoke slowly and gently as if I were rather simple.

'Don't be naughty. I'm very sorry for Elsa, but you are tactful enough to arrange everything for the best. Tomorrow we'll discuss it all. Did I hurt you very much?'

'Not at all,' I said politely. Her sudden gentleness after my intemperate rage made me want to burst into tears. I watched them drive away, feeling completely deflated. My only consolation was the thought of my tactfulness.

I walked slowly back to the casino, where I found Elsa with the South American clinging to her arm.

'Anne wasn't well,' I said in an off-hand manner. 'Papa had to take her home. What about a drink?'

She looked at me without answering. I tried to find a more convincing explanation.

'She was awfully sick,' I said. 'It was ghastly, her dress is ruined.' This detail seemed to me to make my story more plausible, but Elsa began to weep quietly and sadly. I did not know what to do.

'Oh, Cécile, we were so happy!' she said, and her sobs redoubled in intensity. The South American began to cry, repeating 'We were so happy, so happy!' At that moment I heartily detested Anne and my father.

I would have done anything to stop Elsa from crying, her eye-black from running, and the South American from howling.

'Nothing is settled yet, Elsa. Come home with me now!'

'No! I'll fetch my suitcases later,' she sobbed. 'Goodbye, Cécile, we got on well together, didn't we?'

We had never talked of anything but clothes or the weather, but still it seemed to me that I was losing an old friend. I quickly turned away and ran to the car.

* * *

The following morning was wretched, probably because of the whisky I had drunk the night before. I awoke to find myself lying across my bed in the dark; my tongue heavy, my limbs unbearably damp and sticky. A single ray of sunshine filtered through the slats of the shutters and I could see a million motes dancing in it. I felt no desire to get up, nor to stay in bed. I wondered how Anne and my father would look if Elsa were to turn up that morning. I forced myself to think of them in order to be able to get out of bed without effort. At last I managed to stand up on the cool stone floor. I was giddy and aching. The mirror reflected a sad sight; I leant against it and peered at those dilated eyes and dry lips, an unknown face; mine? If I was weak and cowardly, could it be because of those lips, the particular shape of my body, these odious, arbitrary limits? And if I were limited, why had I only now become aware of it? I amused myself by detesting my reflection, hating that wolf-like face, hollow and worn by debauch. I repeated the word 'debauch' dumbly, looking into my eyes in the mirror, and suddenly I saw myself smile. What a debauch! A few unfortunate drinks, a slap in the face and some tears! I brushed my teeth and went downstairs.

My father and Anne were already on the terrace sitting beside each other in front of their breakfast tray. I sat down opposite them, muttering a vague 'good morning'. A feeling of shyness made me keep my eyes lowered, but after a time, as they remained silent I was forced to look at them. Anne appeared tired, the only sign of a night of love. They were both smiling happily, and I was very much impressed, for happiness has always seemed to me a great achievement.

'Did you sleep well?' asked my father.

'Not too badly,' I replied. 'I drank a lot of whisky last night.'

I poured out a cup of coffee, but after the first sip I quickly put it down. Their silence had a waiting quality that made me feel uneasy. I was too tired to bear it for long.

'What's the matter? You look so mysterious.'

My father lit a cigarette, making an obvious effort to seem unconcerned, and for once in her life Anne seemed embarrassed.

'I would like to ask you something,' she said at last.

'I suppose you want me to take another message to Elsa?' I said, imagining the worst.

She turned towards my father.

'Your father and I want to get married,' she said.

I stared first at her, then at my father. I half expected some sign from him, perhaps a wink, which, though I might have found it shocking, would have reassured me, but he was looking down at his hands. I said to myself 'it can't be possible!' but I already knew it was true.

'What a good idea,' I said to gain time.

Bonjour Tristesse

I could not understand how my father, who had always set himself so obstinately against marriage and its chains, could have decided on it in a single night. We were about to lose our independence. I could visualize our future family life, a life which would suddenly be given equilibrium by Anne's intelligence and refinement; the life I had envied her. We would have clever tactful friends, and quiet pleasant evenings.... I found myself despising noisy dinners, South Americans and girls like Elsa. I felt proud and superior.

'It's a very, very good idea,' I repeated, and I smiled at them.

'I knew you'd be pleased, my pet,' said my father.

He was relaxed and delighted. Anne's face, subtly changed by love, seemed gentler, making her appear more accessible than she had ever been before.

'Come here, my pet,' said my father; and holding out his hands, he drew me close to them both. I was half-kneeling in front of them, while they stroked my hair and looked at me with tender emotion. But I could not stop thinking that although my life was perhaps at that very moment changing its whole course, I was in reality nothing more than a kitten to them, an affectionate little animal. I felt them above me, united by a past and a future, by ties that I did not know and which could not hold me. But I deliberately closed my eyes and went on playing my part, laying my head on their knees and laughing. For was I not happy? Anne was all right, I had no serious fault to find with her. She would guide me, relieve me of responsibility, and be at hand whenever I might need her. She would make both my father and me into paragons of virtue.

My father got up to fetch a bottle of champagne. I felt sickened. He was happy, which was the chief thing, but I had so often seen him happy on account of a woman.

'I was rather frightened of you,' said Anne.

'Why?' I asked. Her words had given me the impression that a veto from me could have prevented their marriage.

'I was afraid of your being frightened of me,' she said laughing.

I began to laugh too, because actually I was a little scared of her. She wanted me to understand that she knew it, and that it was unnecessary.

'Does the marriage of two old people like ourselves seem ridiculous to you?'

'You're not old,' I said emphatically, as my father came dancing back with a bottle in his hand.

He sat down next to Anne and put his arm round her shoulders. She moved nearer to him and I looked away in embarrassment. She was no doubt marrying him for just that; for his laughter, for the firm reassurance of his arm, for his vitality, his warmth. At forty there could be the fear of solitude, or perhaps a last upsurge of the senses. . . . I had never thought of Anne as a woman, but as an entity. I had seen her as a self-assured, elegant and clever person, but never weak or sensual. I quite understood that my father felt proud, the self-satisfied, indifferent Anne Larsen was going to marry him. Did he love her, and if so, was he capable of loving her for long? Was there any difference between this new feeling and the affection he had shown Elsa? The sun was making my head spin, and I shut my eyes. We were all three on the terrace, full of reserves, of secret fears, and of happiness.

Elsa did not come back just then. A week flew by, seven happy, agreeable days, the only ones. We made elaborate plans for furnishing our home, and discussed time tables which my father and I took pleasure in cutting as fine as possible with the blind obstinacy of those who have never had any use for them. Did we ever believe in them for one moment? Did my father really think it possible to have lunch every day at the same place at 12.30 sharp, to have dinner at home, and not to go out afterwards? However, he gaily prepared to inter Bohemianism, and began to preach order, and to extol the joys of an elegant, organized bourgeois existence. No doubt for him, as well as for myself, all these plans were merely castles in the air.

How well I remember that week! Anne was relaxed, confident and very sweet; my father loved her. I saw them coming down in the mornings, leaning on each other, laughing gaily, with shadows under their eyes, and I swear that I should have like nothing better than that their happiness should last all their lives. In the evening we often drank our aperitif sitting on some café terrace by the sea. Everywhere we went we were taken for a happy, normal family, and I, who was used to going out alone with my father and seeing the knowing smiles, and malicious or pitying glances, was delighted to play a role more suitable to my age. They were to be married on our return to Paris.

Poor Cyril had witnessed the transformation in our midst with a certain amazement, but he was comforted by the thought that this time it would be legalized. We went out sailing together and kissed when we felt inclined, but sometimes during our embraces I thought of Anne's face as I saw it in the mornings, with its softened contours. I recalled the happy nonchalance, the languid grace that love imparted to her movements, and I envied her. One can grow tired of kissing, and no doubt if Cyril had not been so fond of me I would have become his mistress that week.

At six o'clock, on our return from the islands, Cyril would pull the boat on to the sand. We would go up the house through the pine wood in single file, pretending we were Indians, or run handicap races to warm ourselves up. He always caught me before we reached the house and would spring on me with a shout of victory, rolling me on the pine needles, pinning my arms down and kissing me. I can still remember those light, breathless kisses, and Cyril's heart beating against mine in rhythm with the soft thud of the waves on the sand. Four heart beats and four waves, and then gradually he would regain his breath and his kisses would become more urgent, the sound of the sea would grow dim and give way to the pulse in my ears.

One evening we were surprised by Anne's voice. Cyril was lying close to me in the red glow of the sunset. I can understand that Anne might have been misled by the sight of us there in our scanty bathing things. She called me sharply.

Cyril bounded to his feet, naturally somewhat ashamed. Keeping my eyes on Anne, I slowly got up in my turn. She faced Cyril, and looking right through him spoke in a quiet voice, 'I don't wish to see you again.'

He made no reply, but bent over and kissed my shoulder before departing. I felt surprised and touched, as if his gesture had been a sort of pledge. Anne was staring at me with the same grave and detached look, as though she were thinking of something else. Her manner infuriated me. If she was so deep in thought, why speak at all? I went up to her, feigning embarrassment for the sake of politeness. At last she seemed to notice me and mechanically removed a pine needle from my neck. I

Bonjour Tristesse

saw her face assume its beautiful mask of disdain, that expression of weariness and disapproval which became her so well, and which always frightened me a little.

'You should know that such diversions usually end up in a nursing home.'

She stood there looking straight at me as she spoke, and I was horribly ashamed. She was one of those women who can stand perfectly still while they talk; I always needed the support of a chair, or some object to hold like a cigarette, or the distraction of swinging one leg over the other and watching it move.

'You mustn't exaggerate,' I said with a smile. 'I was only kissing Cyril, and that won't lead me to any nursing home.'

'Please don't see him again,' she said, as if she did not believe me. 'Do not protest: you are seventeen and I feel a certain responsibility for you now. I'm not going to let you ruin your life. In any case you have work to do, and that will occupy your afternoons.'

She turned her back on me and walked towards the house in her nonchalant way. A paralysing sense of calamity kept me rooted to the spot. She had meant every word; what was the use of arguments or denials when she would receive them with the sort of indifference that was worse than contempt, as if I did not even exist, as if I were something to be squashed underfoot, and not myself, Cécile, whom she had always known. My only hope now was my father; surely he would say as usual: 'Well now, who's the boy? I suppose he's a handsome fellow, but beware, my girl!' If he did not react like this, my holidays would be ruined.

Dinner was a nightmare. Not for one moment had Anne suggested that she would not tell my father anything if I promised to work; it was not in her nature to bargain. I was pleased in one way, but also disappointed that she had deprived me of a chance to despise her. As usual she avoided a false move, and it was only when we had finished our soup that she seemed to remember the incident.

'I do wish you'd give your daughter some advice, Raymond. I found her in the wood with Cyril this evening, and they seemed to be going rather far.'

My father, poor man, tried to pass the whole thing off as a joke.

'What's that you say? What were they up to?'

'I was kissing him,' I said. 'And Anne thought . . .'

'I never thought anything at all,' she interrupted. 'But it might be a good idea for her to stop seeing him for a time and to work at her philosophy instead.'

'Poor little thing!' said my father. 'After all Cyril's a nice boy, isn't he?'

'And Cécile is a nice girl,' said Anne. 'That's why I should be heartbroken if anything should happen to her, and it seems to me inevitable that it will, if you consider what complete freedom she enjoys here, and that they are constantly together and have nothing whatever to do. Don't you agree?'

At her last words I looked up and saw that my father was very perturbed.

'You are probably right,' he said. 'After all, you ought to do some work, Cécile. You surely don't want to fail in philosophy and have to take it again?'

'What do you think I care?' I answered.

He glanced at me and then turned away. I was bewildered. I realized that procrastination can rule our lives, yet not provide us with any arguments in its defence.

'Listen,' said Anne, taking my hand across the table. 'Won't you exchange your role of a wood nymph for that of a good schoolgirl for one month? Would it be so serious?'

They both looked at me expectantly; seen in that light, the argument was simple enough. I gently withdrew my hand.

'Yes, very serious,' I said, so softly that they did not hear it, or did not want to.

The following morning I came across a phrase from Bergson:

> Whatever irrelevance one may at first find between the cause and the effects, and although a rule of guidance towards an assertion concerning the root of things may be far distant, it is always in a contact with the generative force of life that one is able to extract the power to love humanity.

I repeated the phrase, quietly at first, so as not to get agitated, then in a louder voice. I held my head in my hands and looked at the book with great attention. At last I understood it, but I felt as cold and impotent as when I had read it the first time. I could not continue. With the best will in the world I applied myself to the next lines, and suddenly something arose in me like a storm and threw me on to the bed. I thought of Cyril waiting for me down in the creek, of the swaying boat, of the pleasure of our kisses, and then I thought of Anne, but in a way that made me sit up on my bed with a fast-beating heart, telling myself that I was stupid, monstrous, nothing but a lazy, spoilt child, and had no right to have such thoughts. But all the same, in spite of myself I continued to reflect that she was dangerous, and that I must get rid of her. I thought of the lunch I had endured with clenched teeth, tortured by a feeling of resentment for which I despised and ridiculed myself. Yes, it was for this I reproached Anne: she prevented me from liking myself. I, who was so naturally meant for happiness and gaiety, had been forced by her into a world of self-criticism and guilty conscience, where, unaccustomed to introspection, I was completely lost. And what did she bring me? I took stock: she wanted my father; she had got him. She would gradually make of us the husband and step-daughter of Anne Larsen; that is to say, she would turn us into two civilized, well-behaved and happy people. For she would certainly make us happy. How easily, unstable and irresponsible as we were, we would yield to her influence, and be drawn into the attractive framework of her orderly plan of living. She was much too efficient: already my father was estranged from me. I was obsessed by his embarrassed face turning away from me at table. Tears came into my eyes at the thought of the jokes we used to have together, our gay laughter as we drove home at dawn through the empty streets of Paris. All that was over. In my turn I would be influenced, re-orientated, re-modelled by Anne. I would not even mind it, she would act with intelligence, irony and sweetness, and I would be incapable of resistance; in six months I should no longer even wish to resist.

At all costs I must take steps to regain my father and our former life. How infinitely desirable those two years suddenly appeared to me, those happy years I was so willing to renounce the other day ... the liberty to think, even to think wrongly or not at all, the freedom to choose my own life, to choose myself. I cannot say 'to be myself', for I was only soft clay, but still I could refuse to be moulded.

I realize that one might find complicated motives for

Bonjour Tristesse

this change in me, one might endow me with spectacular complexes: such as an incestuous love for my father, or a morbid passion for Anne, but I know the true reasons were the heat, Bergson, and Cyril, or at least his absence. I dwelt on this all the afternoon in a most unpleasant mood, induced by the discovery that we were entirely at Anne's mercy. I was not used to reflection, and it made me irritable. At dinner, as in the morning, I did not open my mouth. My father thought it appropriate to chaff me.

'What I like about youth is its spontaneity, its gay conversation.'

I was trembling with rage. It was true that he loved youth; and with whom could I have talked if not with him? We had discussed everything together: love, death, music. Now he himself had disarmed and abandoned me. Looking at him I thought: 'You don't love me any more, you have betrayed me!' I tried to make him understand without words how desperate I was. He seemed suddenly alarmed; perhaps he understood that the time for joking was past, and that our relationship was in danger. I saw him stiffen, and it appeared as though he were about to ask a question. Anne turned to me.

'You don't look well. I feel sorry now for making you work.'

I did not reply. I felt too disgusted that I had got myself into a state which I could no longer control. We had finished dinner. On the terrace, in the rectangle of light projected from the dining-room window, I saw Anne's long nervous hand reach out to find my father's. I thought of Cyril. I would have liked him to take me in his arms on that moonlit terrace, alive with crickets. I would have liked to be caressed, consoled, reconciled with myself. My father and Anne were silent, they had a night of love to look forward to; I had Bergson. I tried to cry, to feel sorry for myself, but in vain; it was already Anne for whom I was sorry, as if I were certain of victory.

Ntozake Shange

extract from

Sassafrass, Cypress & Indigo

Sassafrass, the eldest of three sisters, is a poet and weaver like her mother. She leaves Charleston, South Carolina and goes north to college, enjoying a bohemian life in Los Angeles and testing out her own set of values in respect of her man, her work, her evaluation of the past.

Nothing but tenor sax solos ever came out of that house. Sometimes you could hear a man and a woman arguing, but almost always some kind of music. Sassafrass and Mitch lived together in that house, sort of hidden behind untended hedges and the peeling shingles. Even though they were living in L.A., there were always some dried leaves lying all across their stoop. Sassafrass thought it was the spirits, bringing them good luck; Mitch thought it was because she didn't ever sweep. But there was still the music, and the black Great Dane, Albert, whose real name was My-Name-Is-Albert-Ayler. None of the neighbours knew the dog's full name, so Sassafrass never worried about him being stolen because he only came when someone called his whole name. Sassafrass had named him after the screenplay she had started after the album she had made, and after her lover she never met ... Albert Ayler was found in the East River. That was one of the reasons Mitch was attracted to her, because she had named her dog so irreverently after his mentor, alto-saxist Ayler. Still, Sassafrass was so full of love she couldn't call anybody anything without bringing good vibes from a whole lot of spirits to everything she touched.

Walter Cronkite's voice could be heard through the

open window next to Sassafrass' bed. She was sitting there in a long blue and red cotton skirt, crocheting another hat for Mitch. The long walls of the fallen-down, almost Victorian house were totally covered with murals of African exploits. Every time the landlady came to repair the falling plaster on the ceiling she'd look so uncomfortable; her redneck lips would get littler than a needle and her cheeks would get all stiff. Sassafrass loved watching that old peckerwood get nervous from total blackness all through the house. The old peckerwood got $100.00 a month for the whole flat, which Sassafrass and Mitch had worked on to be a permanent monument to the indelibility of black creative innovation. She glanced up from her sixty-sixth stitch to see if there was anything else to do to the house to make it the most perfect place for her and Mitch to stay in until the black revolution, or until they moved to the black artists' and craftsmen's commune starting up just outside New Orleans, and pretty near a black nationalist settlement. Sassafrass believed it was absolutely necessary to take black arts out of the white man's hands; to take black people out of the white man's hands. But here she was in Highland Park, Los Angeles, with rednecks and Chicanos, because Mitch's parole officer refused to grant permission for them to live in any black area – and because they could only afford $100.00 a month – and because they didn't have the money to buy into the artists' commune near New Orleans anyhow: almost one thousand dollars, cash. So Sassafrass looked around to see if there was something else she could make to make them feel more like loving each other and hitting sunrise with hope, instead of the groans and crabbiness that ate through them toward the end of every poor month.

There were the exasperating patchwork curtains she

had managed to get done, and macrame hangings in every doorway – one named for each of their heroes. There was the long and knotted purple jute, hanging for Malcolm, who was a king. It had bullets woven through the ends of it, and dried sand covered twigs passing in and out of the centre. 'Bullets and land of our own,' Sassafrass had said, standing on Mitch's shoulders to hang it. Then there were the ones for Fidel, Garvey, Archie Shepp, and Coltrane. In her study, Sassafrass had sequestered a sequin-and-feather hanging shaped like a vagina, for Josephine Baker, but Mitch had made her hide it because it wasn't proper for a new Afrikan woman to make things of such a sexual nature. Just as she was remembering Mitch's tirade against her feather-work, Sassafrass felt the doors open and there he was – the cosmic lover and wonder of wonders to her: Mitch.

Mitch had to stoop a little under the doorway; he was almost seven feet tall, and long-limbed like a Watusi with Ethiopian eyes that arched like rainbows, and gold ear-rings in both ears, etched real fine because they were from Mexico (antiques). His nose was slightly hooked like Nasser's, and his presence was that of one of those Olmec gods. Mitch thought of himself as a god, and he was always telling Sassafrass not to succumb to her mortality; to live like she was one of God's stars.

That particular day Mitch was wearing his blue homespun shirt Sassafrass had made with laced cuffs, and an orange coral medallion and some copper corduroy pants that sat on his thighs like he was the hottest thing in town. But this time Mitch was serious and brusque when he spoke to Sassafrass, who was trying to push her crocheting under her skirts.

'Why aren't you writing, girl? Do you think you gonna

be some kind of writer sitting up here making me hats? I got so many damn hats I have to give some away, and you sittin' here makin' me another one. Well, if I didn't know you were being so considerate because you don't wanna deal with your writing, I'd say thanks, but you makin' me stuff and hangin' all this shit around the walls in every room so you won't haveta write nothing today.'

Sassafrass was holding her lips so tight between her teeth she could barely stand the pain, and she was making moves to get up and away from Mitch's harangue when he pushed her back on the bed.

'Look, Sassafrass, I just want you to be happy with yourself. You want to write and create new images for black folks, and you're always sittin' around making things with your hands. There's nothing wrong with that, 'cept you've known how to do that all your damn life.' Mitch began to grow fierce again, and held Sassafrass briskly by the shoulder with one hand, bringing her chin and eyes straight to his gaze with the other. And Sassafrass couldn't avoid the truth: the man she loved was not happy with her charade of homebodiness, because all this weaving and crocheting and macrameing she'd been doing all her life, and Sassafrass was supposed to be a writer. Mitch forcefully held her face close to his and continued.

'Now Sassafrass, get into yourself and find out what's holding you back. You can create whole worlds, girl. I don't wanna come and see you like this any more, listening to some white man make it easy for you to stop thinking, telling you all the white folks' news, so you think that nobody doesn't know you got to pay your dues to the spirits. Sassafrass, if another person don't tell you you're a writer, you'll know it all your life. And

Sassafrass, Cypress & Indigo

you better take care of it or you'll end up some kind of wino or slut, trying to fuck it away with some punk-assed schoolteacher who can't see you a jive-assed little bitch.' Mitch slowly let Sassafrass' face come into her control, and stood all the way up so Sassafrass couldn't forget who was overwhelmingly right in any situation. He straightened his shirt in his pants, and left the room to go practise horn playing.

Sassafrass was weak from Mitch's torrent. She sat so still her old fear of actually being a catatonic came back, and scared her so much she wiggled just to make sure. Mitch didn't have to say all that even if it was true; it was ridiculous for some man to come tell her she had to create. That's the same as telling her she had to have babies, and she didn't want to have babies . . . she could hardly feed herself, and Mitch didn't feed anybody. All he did was play that old horn, and look for the nearest bar that could use an 'avant-garde free-music' sax man. 'Humph.' Sassafrass caught herself focusing in on Mitch again instead of herself, because she did want to be perfected for him, like he was perfected and creating all the time. Sassafrass was running all through herself looking for some way to get into her secrets and share, like Richard Wright had done and Zora Neale Hurston had done . . . the way The Lady gave herself, every time she sang.

> Do Nothing till You Hear from Me
> Pay No Attention to What's Said

From out of the closet came Billie, The Lady, all decked out in navy crêpe and rhinestones. She was pinning a gardenia in her hair, when Sassafrass realized what was happening.

Ntozake Shange

The Lady sighed a familiar sigh. Sassafrass tried to look as calm as possible and said, 'I sure am glad to see you – why you haven't come to visit since Mama used to put me to bed singing "God Bless The Child", and you would sit right on my pillow singing with her.' The Lady smiled sort of haughty and insisted Sassafrass listen carefully to everything she was going to say.

'It's the blues, Sassafrass, that's keepin' you from your writing, and the spirits sent me because I know all about the blues . . . that's who I am: Miss Brown's Blues . . .' The Lady was holding a pearl-studded cigarette holder that dazzled Sassafrass, who could hardly believe what she was hearing. The Lady went on and on. 'Who do you love among us, Sassafrass? Ma Rainey, Mamie Smith, Big Mama Thornton, Freddie Washington, Josephine, Carmen Miranda? Don't ya know we is all sad ladies because we got the blues, and joyful women because we got our songs? Make you a song, Sassafrass, and bring it out so high all us spirits can hold it and be in your tune. We need you, Sassafrass, we need you to sing best as you can; that's our nourishment, that's how we live. But don't you get all high and mighty, 'cause all us you love so much is hussies too, and we catch on if somebody don't do us right. So make us some poems and some stories, so we can sing a liberation song. Free us from all these blues and sorry ways.'

The Lady turned to the doorway on her right and shouted, 'Come on, y'all,' and multitudes of brown-skinned dancing girls with ostrich-feather headpieces and tap shoes started doing the cake-walk all around Sassafrass, who was trying to figure out the stitching pattern on their embroidered dresses, and trying to keep from jumping up and shaking her ass when, in unison, the elaborately beaded women started swinging their hips towards her, singing: SASSAFRASS IS WHERE IT'S AT, SASSAFRASS GOTTA HIPFUL OF LOVE, A HIPFUL OF TRUTH . . . SASSAFRASS GOTTA JOB TO DO, DUES TO PAY SO SHE COULD DANCE WITH US . . . WHOOEEE!

And all of a sudden the chorus line disintegrated into a dressing-room conversation; the women started sharing secrets about lovers, managers, and children staying with their grandmas till the tour was over . . . and Sassafrass gathered all there was that was more to her than making cloth. Just as she was about to slip out of the room, Sassafrass turned to The Lady to capture just a little more of the magic, and The Lady only murmured, 'We need you to be Sassafrass 'til you can't hardly stand it . . . 'til you can't recognize yourself, and you sing all the time.'

Sassafrass closed the door on the babbling women-visitors quickly. Mitch was coming toward her, making the room reel with the craziness of his music; like he was tearing himself all up, beating and scratching through his skin. The horn rocked gently with his body, but the sounds were devastating: pure anger and revenge. He pulled the slight instrument from his mouth and licked the reed once or twice, before he slipped his hand up Sassafrass' skirts to tickle her a little.

'You gonna make me something to eat, lovely one?' Mitch grinned a Valentino grin, horn in one hand, Sassafrass on the other. She giggled distractedly and mumbled, 'Yeah, I just wanna write down a few things before I get stuck in the kitchen.'

She rubbed her temples impatiently, because for a change Mitch wasn't on her mind. She didn't want to play; she wanted to write, and Mitch was messing around, being nasty. She caught his wrist with her thumb and index finger. 'Not now, Mitch. Not now. I wanna go do something.' Mitch released her instantly. He wasn't into taking any woman who didn't want him desperately, so Sassafrass could go. And Mitch picked up his horn and tooted the melody of Looney Tune cartoons he had to watch when he was a child at the boys' reformatory in Philadelphia: dadadadada dadadadada, and then he imitated Porky Pig saying, 't-t-t-t-that's all, folks!' He smiled to himself when Sassafrass slammed the door to the kitchen and made obviously rebellious noises with every pot she handled.

Mitch had convinced Sassafrass that everything was an art, so nothing in life could be approached lightly. Creation was inherent in everything anybody ever did right; that was one of the mottos of the house. Sassafrass had made an appliquéd banner saying just that, and hung it over the stove:

> CREATION IS
>
> EVERYTHING YOU DO
>
> MAKE SOMETHING

She sat on her personal chair to concentrate on what to create for dinner. She was busy thinking of nothing when

Sassafrass, Cypress & Indigo

she fixed on the idea of a rice casserole, sautéed spinach and mushrooms with sweet peppers, and broiled mackerel with red sauce. If she prepared this scrumptious meal there wouldn't be hardly enough food left to finish off the week, but since Mitch was into her being perfect today, she decided to make a perfect meal and let him perfect out the menu for later, because 'you can't cut no corners and be right' is what he always said. And Sassafrass set to work.

Sassafrass' Rice Casserole # 36

1½ cups medium grain brown rice
3 ounces pimentos
1 cup baby green peas
½ cup fresh walnuts

⅔ pound smoked cheddar cheese
½ cup condensed milk
Diced garlic to taste
Cayenne to taste

Cook rice as usual. In an eight-inch baking dish, layer rice, cheese, pimentos, walnuts and peas. Spread garlic and cayenne as you see fit. Pour milk around side of dish so it cushions rice against the edge. Bake in oven 20–30 minutes or until all the cheese melts and the top layer has a nice brown tinge.

Sassafrass' Favourite Spinach for Mitch # 10

1–2 bunches Japanese spinach
8 good-sized mushrooms
2 tablespoons vegetable oil (safflower oil is very light)

2 tablespoons tamari
½ teaspoon finely crushed rosemary
4 sweet hot peppers

Wash spinach carefully in cold water. Break leaves from stem with fingers – do not cut – and set spinach in colander. Wash mushrooms. Slice vertically so each slice maintains its shape. Put oil in heavy iron skillet, heat until drop of water makes it pop. Turn flame down and lay spinach evenly in pan. Spread mushrooms; sprinkle rosemary and tamari. Simmer until leaves are soft and hot. Do not overcook. Place peppers in nice design around spinach and serve quickly.

Sassafrass: The Only Way to Broil Fish: Mackerel

Clean fish thoroughly. Dip in melted butter, add salt and pepper. Cook 4–6 minutes on each side in broiler.

Red Sauce: Sassafrass' Variation Du-Wop '59

1 small can tomato sauce	1/2 cup finely chopped onion
1 cup cooking sherry or sangria	Garlic to taste
1/2 cup finely chopped parsley	Cayenne

Mix tomato sauce and wine in saucepan. Add sautéed onions, parsley and seasonings. Spread some sauce over fish while broiling; save the rest to use on plate.

While Sassafrass cooked she usually did yoga breathing exercises or belly dance pelvic contractions as she puttered around. The movements were almost accidental: tearing the spinach she'd contract on each pull from a stem and release as soon as it hit the colander. She would breathe ten quick breaths out and ten quick ones in as she crossed the kitchen from the sink to the stove. Not wanting to waste a moment, she would do *relevés* on alternate sets of ten contractions, so it would be: contract-*relevé*-release-down. This went on for as long as it took to cook dinner, and as the mackerel came out of the oven, Sassafrass was a buoyant and contented woman.

Sassafrass made her way out of the kitchen to get Mitch for dinner. She stepped into the studio to see how his art supplies were standing up against his create-every-day saga. The acrylic paints would probably last just another week before Mitch would have only ochre left; watercolours, sufficient; oils, absolutely tubes' end. Sassafrass was figuring the actual cost or barter price some new brushes would come to, when she heard calamitous booted feet traipsing through her house, and some men's voices upsetting her resting plants. She hurriedly took an overall inventory of Mitch's drawing equipment, and copped a gracious hostess attitude for the unexpected dinner guests. Otis and Howard Goodwin-Smith, two brothers from Chicago, had been in L.A. since Korea, most of their growing-up days. They tried, sometimes, to act like they were from Chi-town, but in a couple of minutes that Southern California hip-lessness would ooze from every word. Otis was a writer, which made Sassafrass uneasy, and Howard was a painter of contorted phallic symbols dipped in Afrikan mystique and loaded with latent rapist bravado. The Goodwin-Smiths from the South Side. Sassafrass held her tongue while she greeted them; she wanted to ask why they hadn't brought their white wives. She felt her eyes sneer and her mouth smile, saying, 'Too bad

Jennie and Olga couldn't make it . . . I never see them, you know.'

Otis and Howard looked over to Mitch, who was looking at Albert the dog, to make sure Sassafrass could enjoy putting the brothers on the spot. Then Albert moved over to Howard, who was kneeling on the floor trying to get a whole idea of Mitch's new mural. Albert on his haunches was almost six feet, and he got on his haunches to try to hump the chauvinist Howard. Sassafrass saw Albert rear back and slam his front paws across Howard's back, saw his dick hanging oily-like from its fur pouch, aiming for Howard's jeans-covered backside. Howard was shocked, and steady trying to get out of Albert's way. They made circles around the room, Albert chasing Howard past the aging velvet couch, the barber's seat that doubled as a chaise longue, the driftwood coffee table, and the mural lying on the floor. Round and round they went. Sassafrass glimmered, and went to get the food. Mitch started playing the Lone Ranger's theme song. Otis was rolled over laughing, and Howard finally tore off one of his sneakers to appease Albert, who always tried to make it with small men. They ate with chopsticks, in time to Ron Carter's *Uptown Conversation*.

Otis had reconnoitred the barber's seat for himself, and from his lofty perch, began, 'I brought y'all a copy of my new book, *Ebony Cunt* . . . I autographed it special, Mitch; see here . . .'

for sassafrass . . .
I know yours is good

Sassafrass' face nearly hit the floor. She glanced at Mitch to see where he was at, and he was enjoying his clout with the fellas, because he announced: 'Sassafrass got some of the best pussy west of the Rockies, man, and I don't care who knows it, 'cause it's mine!'

They all laughed raucously, except Sassafrass was glaring from her inmost marrow and wishing there was some way to get rid of male crassness once and for all time. She called herself being kind to Mitch, because he liked his friends, while she began discreetly leaving the room. But Otis called out for a thorough reading of his new work, to Mitch's accompaniment on sax and Howard's innovative percussion with a worn-down tambourine.

THE REVUE

Otis
Sassafrass, you gotta sit in this barber chair and be the queen you are, while I read this masterpiece (*teehee*) of mine for all y'all black women all over the world.

Sassafrass
Otis, I, ah, gotta get started on something, ya know.

Otis, Mitch, Howard (in unison)
Nononono . . . you gotta hear this one, babeee!

(Mitch picks Sassafrass off her feet and places her in the chair, squeezes her leg, and smiles)

Mitch
Go on, Otis. We gotta celebrate this woman of mine even if she doesn't understand why we gotta have her, every morning . . . in the evenin' when the sun go down . . .

(Mitch sings like he is Ray Charles, and shakes all around like Little Richard)

Ntozake Shange

Otis
I'ma start now. I'ma read all about it, but first I wanna say, a la Edwin Starr circa 1963:

> *extra extra reeeeeeead allll about itttttt*
> *extra extra reeeeeeead allll about itttttt*

(Howard, Mitch, and Otis do old Temptations Apollo routines around Sassafrass, who is enjoying this worship from the du-wop straddlers in spite of herself)

Howard
Aw right. Now Otis, get it on . . . we ready.

Otis
EBONY CUNT: for my mama and my grandma and all the women I rammed in Macon, Georgia, when I was visitin' my cousins at age sixteen:

The white man want you/the Indian run off with you
Spaniards created whole nations with you/black queen-silk snatch
I wander all in your wombs & make babies in the Bronx when I come/you screammmmmmm/ jesus/ my blk man ebony cunt is worth all the gold in the world/ 15 millions of your shinin' blk bodies crossed the sea to bring all that good slick pussy to me . . .

(Sassafrass stands up like a mannequin, and gazes absolutely red-faced at Otis, Mitch and Howard, all of who stare back at her, uncomprehending)

Mitch
Sassafrass, what's wrong with you? Sit down. Otis

gotta finish the book; he isn't even done with the first page . . .

Sassafrass (standing still)
Just one god-damned minute, Mitch. You gotta mother you supposedly love so much, and a daughter by a black woman who won't see you . . . and you got me all messed up, and tryin' to make you happy . . . god damn it, I don't haveta listen to this shit. I am not interested in your sick, sick, weakly rhapsodies about all the women you fucked in all your damn lives . . . I don't like it. I am not about to sit heah and listen to a bunch of no account niggahs talk about black women; me and my sisters; like we was the same bought and sold at slave auction . . . breeding heifers the white man created 'cause y'all was fascinated by some god-damn beads he brought you on the continent . . . muthafuckahs. Yeah, that's right; muthafuckahs, don't you ever sit in my house and ask me to celebrate my inherited right to be raped. Goddamn muthafuckahs. Don't you know about anythin' besides taking women off, or is that really all you good for?

(Mitch looks at Sassafrass like she was a harlot. He puts his horn away and remains silent. Otis and Howard chuckle nervously, and get ready to split)

Otis
Look now Sassafrass, I'm sorry you took it the wrong way . . .

(He smiles. All three men leave the house. On the way out, Howard pokes his head back through the bagging-screen door)

Ntozake Shange

Howard
I don't care *what* you say, Sassafrass... I *know* you got good pussy!

(They all laugh jauntily on the way to the '59 Chevy two-door sedan. Sassafrass stands still in front of the barber's chair for an indefinite time)

When she moved, she went to her looms...

> *makin cloth, bein a woman & longin*
> *to be of the earth*
> *a rooted blues*
> *some ripe berries*
> *happenin inside*
> *spirits*
> *walkin in a dirt road*
> *toes dusted & free*
> *faces movin windy*
> *brisk like*
> *dawn round*
> *gingham windows &*
> *opened eyes*
> *reelin to days*
> *ready-made*
> *nature's image*
> *i'm rejoicin*
> *with a throat deep*
> *shout & slow*
> *like a river*
> *gatherin*
> *space*

i am sassafrass/ a weaver's daughter/ from charleston/
i'm a woman makin cloth like all good women do/

860

Sassafrass, Cypress & Indigo

*the moon's daughter made cloth/ the gold array of
the sun/ the moon's daughter sat all night/ spinnin/
i have inherited fingers that change fleece to tender
garments/ i am the maker of warmth & emblems
of good spirit/ mama/ didn't ya show me how/ to
warp a loom/ to pattern stars into cotton homespun/
mama/ didn't ya name me for yr favourite natural
dye/ sassafrass/ so strong & even/ go good with deep
fertile greens/ & make tea to temper chilly evenings/
i'm a weaver with my sistahs from any earth &
fields/ we always make cloth/ love our children/
honour our men/ who protect us from our enemies/
we prepare altars & anoint candles to offer our
devotion to our guardians/ we proffer hope/ & food
to eat/ clothes to wear/ wombs to fill.*

Almost unconsciously Sassafrass had begun the laborious process of warping the four-harness table loom she had transported from Charleston. The eccentric family her family had worked for as slaves, and then as freed women weavers, had seen fit to grant Sassafrass the looms her forebears had warped and wefted thousands of times since emancipation. Sassafrass had always been proud that her mother had a craft; that all the women in her family could make something besides a baby, and shooting streams of sperm. She had grown up in a room full of spinning wheels, table and floor looms, and her mother always busy making cloth because the Fitzhugh family never wore anything but hand-woven cloth ... until they couldn't afford it any more. Sassafrass had never wanted to weave, she just couldn't help it. There was something about the feel of raw fleece and finished threads and dainty patterned pieces that was as essential to her as dancing is to

Ntozake Shange

Carmen DeLavallade, or singing to Aretha Franklin. Her mama had done it, and her mama before that; and making cloth was the only tradition Sassafrass inherited that gave her a sense of womanhood that was rich and sensuous, not tired and stingy. She thought that if Kingfish had bought Sapphire a loom, she would never have been such a bitch. She thought that the bronze Dionysius was not saving the sad frigid women of Thebes by seducing them away from their looms, but rather he was planning, under Osiris' aegis, to wipe out Europeans before they went around the world enslaving rainbow-coloured people ... because when women make cloth, they have time to think, and Theban women stopped thinking, and the town fell. So Sassafrass was certain of the necessity of her skill for the well-being of women everywhere, as well as for her own. As she passed the shuttle through the claret cotton warp, Sassafrass conjured images of women weaving from all time and all places: Toltecas spinning shimmering threads; East Indian women designing intricate patterns for Shakti, the impetus and destruction of creation; and Navajo women working on thick tapestries. She tried to compel an African woman to come join them – women, making cloth – and the spirits said, 'No. You cannot have her ... in Africa men make cloth, and women ...' Sassafrass tossed her head to the left side, and dismissed her congregation of international cloth makers while she rethreaded her shuttle. And Mitch was home ...

* * *

Hi there Sassafrass ...
How's mama's favourite dumpling? Sounds to me like

Sassafrass, Cypress & Indigo

you have indeed worked wonders on your little house. Just watch now that you don't overdo with too much colour. Houses are supposed to comfort us, as well as invigorate the senses. You don't get one by ignoring the other. There, you see, I do have a notion of aesthetics, black or not. They're Southern, and that's close enough. (smile)

The Wheeler girls came home from Vassar last week. They were a little behind you, I think. At any rate, they have gone completely African. Changed their names; wear these big old pieces of cloth... look just like mammies, to my mind. Their mother, Gertie, has refused to let them out of the house till they go round to Mrs Calhoun's and get that hair pressed. So, it's all right that you and your sisters don't come home, when I think about how you must look!

That little Shuyler boy, the one who went to Dartmouth and is now at Meharry, has wrecked two cars already, and still his father hasn't put his foot down. I can't understand loving somebody so much, you let them make you a fool, but, thank god he's no child of mine. That's that boy who kept you out all weekend when I came to visit you in New England. Don't try to act like I'm mistaken – I may not be a liberated woman, but I wasn't born yesterday. I can't see what you saw in him. For all that breeding, and the money spent on him, he acts like a natural-born hoodlum.

What else... oh, guess what? Your name is in the alumni magazine of the Callahan School. Seems like you are the only one, out of all those rich children, to go on ahead and be an artist. Don't be upset with me. I sent the information in myself, with samples of your work. It's the least I could do, after Mrs Fitzhugh sponsored you and all. I can't understand why you hated that place so ... not going to your graduation, refusing to go on to college. Oh, Sassafrass, weaving is a fine craft, but with the opportunities open to Negroes your age, I just don't know why you insist on doing everything the hard way.

I hate to say this, but it follows my thoughts about your resisting the bounties our Lord has laid before you, in order to take up with the most unfortunate among us. How could you take up with a man who wasn't raised in a proper home ... not even an orphan, just a delinquent? Even I have heard stories of the terrible conditions in the reform schools, and here my very own daughter searches far and wide, moves all the way to California, to fall in love with a man who has nothing to offer, no background, no education, no future. If you think for a minute, darling, you'll see that all the training you've had is far and away more than that boy can imagine. So what is it that you're going to learn from him? You should get down on your knees and pray for guidance. And while you're down there, thank the Lord for giving you the good sense not to compromise yourself by living in sin. You can at least still meet some more folks who are up to you, and who'll appreciate what a fine young woman you are. Truly, dear, try to get out and enjoy yourself. The race has had problems ever since we got here. You can't do anything about them by staying in your house, refusing to take part in the world you belong in.

Call cousin Loreen. I told you, her step-sons are all doctors, and mighty good-looking ... (a word to the wise).

Love,
Mama

PS You don't have to tell Mitch everything I said about him . . . if that's an open relationship, humpf. You need a closed one!!

PS You don't have to tell Mitch everything I said about him . . . if that's an open relationship, hrmpf. You need a closed one!

Elizabeth Smart

extract from

By Grand Central Station I Sat Down and Wept

A major achievement in poetic prose and a demanding, disturbing text, Elizabeth Smart's novel about the passion between a man and two women, one of them his wife, communicates its story with remarkable accessibility and candour.

I am over-run, jungled in my bed, I am infested with a menagerie of desires: my heart is eaten by a dove, a cat scrambles in the cave of my sex, hounds in my head obey a whipmaster who cries nothing but havoc as the hours test my endurance with an accumulation of tortures. Who, if I cried, would hear me among the angelic orders?

I am far, far beyond that island of days where once, it seems, I watched a flower grow, and counted the steps of the sun, and fed, if my memory serves, the smiling animal at his appointed hour. I am shot with wounds which have eyes that see a world all sorrow, always to be, panoramic and unhealable, and mouths that hang unspeakable in the sky of blood.

How can I be kind? How can I find bird-relief in the nest-building of day-to-day? Necessity supplies no velvet wing with which to escape. I am indeed and mortally pierced with the seeds of love.

Then she leans over in the pool and her damp dark hair falls like sorrow, like mercy, like the mourning-weeds of pity. Sitting nymphlike in the pool in the late afternoon her pathetic slenderness is covered over with a love as gentle as trusting as tenacious as the birds who rebuild their continually violated nests. When she clasps her hands happily at a tune she likes, it is more moving than I can bear. She is the innocent who is always the offering. She is the goddess of all things which the vigour of living destroys. Why are her arms so empty?

In the night she moans with the voice of the stream below my window, searching for the child whose touch she once felt and can never forget: the child who obeyed the laws of life better than she. But by day she obeys the voice of love as the stricken obey their god, and she walks with the light step of hope which only the naïve and the saints know. Her shoulders have always the attitude of grieving, and her thin breasts are pitiful like Virgin Shrines that have been robbed.

How can I speak to her? How can I comfort her? How can I explain to her any more than I can to the flowers that I crush with my foot when I walk in the field? He also is bent towards her in an attitude of solicitude. Can he hear his own heart while he listens for the tenderness of her sensibilities? Is there a way at all to avoid offending the lamb of god?

Under the waterfall he surprised me bathing and gave me what I could no more refuse than the earth can refuse the rain. Then he kissed me and went down to his cottage.

Absolve me, I prayed, up through the cathedral redwoods, and forgive me if this is sin. But the new moss caressed me and the water over my feet and the ferns approved me with endearments: My darling, my darling, lie down with us now for you also are earth whom nothing but love can sow.

And I lay down on the redwood needles and seemed to flow down the canyon with the thunder and confusion of the stream, in a happiness which, like birth, can afford to ignore the blood and the tearing. For nature has no time for mourning, absorbed by the turning world, and will, no matter what devastation attacks her, fulfil in underground ritual, all her proper prophecy.

Gently the woodsorrel and the dove explained the confirmation and guided my return. When I came out of the woods on to the hill, I had pine-needles in my hair for a bridal wreath, and the sea and the sky and the gold hills smiled benignly. Jupiter has been with Leda, I thought, and now nothing can avert the Trojan Wars. All legend will be born, but who will escape alive?

But what can the woodsorrel and the mourning-dove, who deal only with eternals, know of the thorny sociabilities of human living? Of how the pressure of the hours of waiting, silent and inactive, weigh upon the head with a physical force that suffocates? The simplest daily pleasantries are torture, and a samson effort is needed to avoid his glance that draws me like gravity.

For excuse, for our being together, we sit at the typewriter, pretending a necessary collaboration. He has a book to be typed, but the words I try to force out die on the air and dissolve into kisses whose chemicals are even more deadly if undelivered. My fingers cannot be martial at the touch of an instrument so much connected with him. The machine sits like a temple of love among the papers we never finish, and if I awake at night and see it outlined in the dark, I am electrified with memories of dangerous propinquity.

The frustrations of past postponement can no longer be restrained. They hang ripe to burst with the birth of any moment. The typewriter is guilty with love and flowery with shame, and to me it speaks so loudly I fear it will communicate its indecency to casual visitors.

How stationary life has become, and the hours impossibly elongated. When we sit on the gold grass of the cliff, the sun between us insists on a solution for which we search in vain, but whose urgency we feel unbearably. I never was in love with death before, nor felt grateful because the rocks below could promise certain death. But now the idea of dying violently becomes an act wrapped in attractive melancholy, and displayed with every blandishment. For there is no beauty in denying love, except perhaps by death, and towards love what way is there?

To deny love, and deceive it meanly by pretending that what is unconsummated remains eternal, or that love sublimated reaches highest to heavenly love, is repulsive, as the hypocrite's face is repulsive when placed too near the truth. Farther off from the centre of the world, of all worlds, I might be better fooled, but can I see the light of a match while burning in the arms of the sun?

No, my advocates, my angels with sadist eyes, this is the beginning of my life, or the end. So I lean affirmation across the café table, and surrender my fifty years away with an easy smile. But the surety of my love is not dismayed by any eventuality which prudence or pity can conjure up, and in the end all that we can do is to sit at the table over which our hands cross, listening to tunes from the wurlitzer, with love huge and simple between us, and nothing more to be said.

So hourly, at the slightest noise, I start, I stand ready to feel the roof cave in on my head, the thunder of God's punishment announcing the limit of his endurance.

She walks lightly, like the child whose dancing feet will touch off gigantic explosives. She knows nothing, but like autumn birds feels foreboding in the air. Her movements are nervous, there are draughts in every room, but less wise than the birds whom small signs send on three-thousand-mile flights, she only looks vaguely out to the Pacific, finding it strange that heaven has, after all, no Californian shore.

I have learned to smoke because I need something to hold on to. I dare not be without a cigarette in my hand. If I should be looking the other way when the hour of doom is struck, how shall I avoid being turned into stone unless I can remember something to do which will lead me back to the simplicity and safety of daily living?

IT is coming. The magnet of its imminent finger draws each hair of my body, the shudder of its approach disintegrates kisses, loses wishes on the disjointed air. The wet hands of the castor-tree at night brush me and I shriek, thinking that at last I am caught up with. The clouds move across the sky heavy and tubular. They gather and I am terror-struck to see them form a long black rainbow out of the mountain and disappear across the sea. The Thing is at hand. There is nothing to do but crouch and receive God's wrath.

Amy Tan

extract from

The Joy Luck Club

Sitting at what was once her mother's place at the mah-jong table, Jing-Mei Woo becomes an essential member of the Joy Luck Club, a gathering of four mothers and their first-generation Chinese-American daughters. By telling each other true stories, both groups of women come to terms with a rich and sometimes puzzling cultural heritage. One of the most moving of these accounts is the extract here, entitled 'Half and Half', related by Rose Hsu Jordan.

Sitting at what was once her mother's place at the mah-jong table, Jing-Mei Woo becomes an essential member of the Joy Luck Club, a gathering of four mothers and their first-generation Chinese-American daughters. By telling each other true stories, both groups of women come to terms with a rich and sometimes puzzling cultural heritage. One of the most moving of these accounts is the extract here, entitled 'Half and Half', related by Rose Hsu Jordan.

As proof of her faith, my mother used to carry a small leatherette Bible when she went to the First Chinese Baptist Church every Sunday. But later, after my mother lost her faith in God, that leatherette Bible wound up wedged under a too-short table leg, a way for her to correct the imbalances of life. It's been there for over twenty years.

My mother pretends that Bible isn't there. Whenever anyone asks her what it's doing there, she says, a little too loudly, 'Oh, this? I forgot.' But I know she sees it. My mother is not the best housekeeper in the world, and after all these years that Bible is still clean white.

Tonight I'm watching my mother sweep under the same kitchen table, something she does every night after dinner. She gently pokes her broom around the table leg propped up by the Bible. I watch her, sweep after sweep, waiting for the right moment to tell her about Ted and me, that we're getting divorced. When I tell her, I know she's going to say, 'This cannot be.'

And when I say that it is certainly true, that our marriage is over, I know what else she will say: 'Then you must save it.'

And even though I know it's hopeless – there's

absolutely nothing left to save – I'm afraid if I tell her that, she'll still persuade me to try.

I think it's ironic that my mother wants me to fight the divorce. Seventeen years ago she was chagrined when I started dating Ted. My older sisters had dated only Chinese boys from church before getting married.

Ted and I met in a politics of ecology class when he leaned over and offered to pay me two dollars for the last week's notes. I refused the money and accepted a cup of coffee instead. This was during my second semester at UC Berkeley, where I had enrolled as a liberal arts major and later changed to fine arts. Ted was in his third year in pre-med, his choice, he told me, ever since he dissected a fetal pig in the sixth grade.

I have to admit that what I initially found attractive in Ted were precisely the things that made him different from my brothers and the Chinese boys I had dated: his brashness; the assuredness in which he asked for things and expected to get them; his opinionated manner; his angular face and lanky body; the thickness of his arms; the fact that his parents immigrated from Tarrytown, New York, not Tientsin, China.

My mother must have noticed these same differences after Ted picked me up one evening at my parents' house. When I returned home, my mother was still up, watching television.

'He is American,' warned my mother, as if I had been too blind to notice. A *waigoren*.'

'I'm American too,' I said. 'And it's not as if I'm going to marry him or something.'

Mrs Jordan also had a few words to say. Ted had casually invited me to a family picnic, the annual clan

The Joy Luck Club

reunion held by the polo fields in Golden Gate Park. Although we had dated only a few times in the last month – and certainly had never slept together, since both of us lived at home – Ted introduced me to all his relatives as his girlfriend, which, until then, I didn't know I was.

Later, when Ted and his father went off to play volleyball with the others, his mother took my hand, and we started walking along the grass, away from the crowd. She squeezed my palm warmly but never seemed to look at me.

'I'm so glad to meet you *finally*,' Mrs Jordan said. I wanted to tell her I wasn't really Ted's girlfriend, but she went on, 'I think it's nice that you and Ted are having such a lot of fun together. So I hope you won't misunderstand what I have to say.'

And then she spoke quietly about Ted's future, his need to concentrate on his medical studies, why it would be years before he could even think about marriage. She assured me she had nothing whatsoever against minorities; she and her husband, who owned a chain of office-supply stores, personally knew many fine people who were Oriental, Spanish, and even black. But Ted was going to be in one of those professions where he would be judged by a different standard, by patients and other doctors who might not be as understanding as the Jordans were. She said it was so unfortunate the way the rest of the world was, how unpopular the Vietnam War was.

'Mrs Jordan, I am not Vietnamese,' I said softly, even though I was on the verge of shouting. 'And I have no intention of marrying your son.'

When Ted drove me home that day, I told him I couldn't see him any more. When he asked me why,

I shrugged. When he pressed me, I told him what his mother had said, verbatim, without comment.

'And you're just going to sit there! Let my mother decide what's right?' he shouted, as if I were a co-conspirator who had turned traitor. I was touched that Ted was so upset.

'What should we do?' I asked, and I had a pained feeling I thought was the beginning of love.

In those early months, we clung to each other with a rather silly desperation, because, in spite of anything my mother or Mrs Jordan could say, there was nothing that really prevented us from seeing one another. With imagined tragedy hovering over us, we became inseparable, two halves creating the whole: yin and yang. I was victim to his hero. I was always in danger and he was always rescuing me. I would fall and he would lift me up. It was exhilarating and draining. The emotional effect of saving and being saved was addicting to both of us. And that, as much as anything we ever did in bed, was how we made love to each other: conjoined where my weaknesses needed protection.

'What should we do?' I continued to ask him. And within a year of our first meeting we were living together. The month before Ted started medical school at UCSF we were married in the Episcopal church, and Mrs Jordan sat in the front pew, crying as was expected of the groom's mother. When Ted finished his residency in dermatology, we bought a run-down three-storey Victorian with a large garden in Ashbury Heights. Ted helped me set up a studio downstairs so I could take in work as a freelance production assistant for graphic artists.

Over the years, Ted decided where we went on vacation. He decided what new furniture we should buy. He decided we should wait until we moved into a better

The Joy Luck Club

neighbourhood before having children. We used to discuss some of these matters, but we both knew the question would boil down to my saying, 'Ted, you decide.' After a while, there were no more discussions. Ted simply decided. And I never thought of objecting. I preferred to ignore the world around me, obsessing only over what was in front of me: my T-square, my X-acto knife, my blue pencil.

But last year Ted's feelings about what he called 'decision and responsibility' changed. A new patient had come to him asking what she could do about the spidery veins on her cheeks. And when he told her he could suck the red veins out and make her beautiful again, she believed him. But instead, he accidentally sucked a nerve out, and the left side of her smile fell down and she sued him.

After he lost the malpractice lawsuit – his first, and a big shock to him I now realize – he started pushing me to make decisons. Did I think we should buy an American car or a Japanese car? Should we change from whole-life to term insurance? What did I think about that candidate who supported the contras? What about a family?

I thought about things, the pros and the cons. But in the end I would be so confused, because I never believed there was ever any one right answer, yet there were many wrong ones. So whenever I said, 'You decide,' or 'I don't care,' or 'Either way is fine with me,' Ted would say in his impatient voice, 'No *you* decide. You can't have it both ways, none of the responsibility, none of the blame.'

I could feel things changing between us. A protective veil had been lifted and Ted now started pushing me about everything. He asked me to decide on the most trivial matters, as if he were baiting me. Italian food or Thai. One appetizer or two. Which appetizer. Credit card or cash. Visa or MasterCard.

Last month, when he was leaving for a two-day dermatology course in Los Angeles, he asked if I wanted to come along and then quickly, before I could say anything, he added, 'Never mind, I'd rather go alone.'

'More time to study,' I agreed.

'No, because you can never make up your mind about anything,' he said.

And I protested, 'But it's only with things that aren't important.'

'Nothing is important to you, then,' he said in a tone of disgust.

'Ted, if you want me to go, I'll go.'

And it was as if something snapped in him. 'How the hell did we ever get married? Did you just say "I do" because the minister said "repeat after me"? What would you have done with your life if I had never married you? Did it ever occur to you?'

This was such a big leap in logic, between what I said and what he said, that I thought we were like two people standing apart on separate mountain peaks, recklessly leaning forward to throw stones at one another, unaware of the dangerous chasm that separated us.

But now I realize Ted knew what he was saying all along. He wanted to show me the rift. Because later that evening he called from Los Angeles and said he wanted a divorce.

Ever since Ted's been gone, I've been thinking, Even if I had expected it, even if I had known what I was going to do with my life, it still would have knocked the wind out of me.

When something that violent hits you, you can't help

but lose your balance and fall. And after you pick yourself up, you realize you can't trust anybody to save you – not your husband, not your mother, not God. So what can you do to stop yourself from tilting and falling all over again?

My mother believed in God's will for many years. It was as if she had turned on a celestial faucet and goodness kept pouring out. She said it was faith that kept all these good things coming our way, only I thought she said 'fate', because she couldn't pronounce that 'th' sound in 'faith'.

And later, I discovered that maybe it was fate all along, that faith was just an illusion that somehow you're in control. I found out the most *I* could have was hope, and with that I was not denying any possibility, good or bad. I was just saying, If there is a choice, dear God or whatever you are, here's where the odds should be placed.

I remember the day I started thinking this, it was such a revelation to me. It was the day my mother lost her faith in God. She found that things of unquestioned certainty could never be trusted again.

We had gone to the beach, to a secluded spot south of the city near Devil's Slide. My father had read in *Sunset* magazine that this was a good place to catch ocean perch. And although my father was not a fisherman but a pharmacist's assistant who had once been a doctor in China, he believed in his *nengkan*, his ability to do anything he put his mind to. My mother believed she had *nengkan* to cook anything my father had a mind to catch. It was this belief in their *nengkan* that had brought my parents to America. It had enabled them to have seven children and buy a house in the Sunset district with very little money. It had given them the confidence to believe their luck would never run out, that God was on their side, that the house gods had only benevolent things to report and our ancestors were pleased, that lifetime warranties meant our lucky streak would never break, that all the elements were in balance, the right amount of wind and water.

So there we were, the nine of us: my father, my mother, my two sisters, four brothers, and myself, so confident as we walked along our first beach. We marched in single file across the cool grey sand, from oldest to youngest. I was in the middle, fourteen years old. We would have made quite a sight, if anyone else had been watching, nine pairs of bare feet trudging, nine pairs of shoes in hand, nine black-haired heads turned toward the water to watch the waves tumbling in.

The wind was whipping the cotton trousers around my legs and I looked for some place where the sand wouldn't kick into my eyes. I saw we were standing in the hollow of a cove. It was like a giant bowl, cracked in half, the other half washed out to sea. My mother walked toward the right, where the beach was clean, and we all followed. On this side, the wall of the cove curved around and protected the beach from both the rough surf and the wind. And along this wall, in its shadow, was a reef ledge that started at the edge of the beach and continued out past the cove where the waters became rough. It seemed as though a person could walk out to sea on this reef, although it looked very rocky and slippery. On the other side of the cove, the wall was more jagged, eaten away by the water. It was pitted with crevices, so when the waves crashed against the wall, the water spewed out of these holes like white gulleys.

Thinking back, I remember that this beach cove was

The Joy Luck Club

a terrible place, full of wet shadows that chilled us and invisible specks that flew into our eyes and made it hard for us to see the dangers. We were all blind with the newness of this experience: a Chinese family trying to act like a typical American family at the beach.

My mother spread out an old striped bedspread, which flapped in the wind until nine pairs of shoes weighed it down. My father assembled his long bamboo fishing pole, a pole he had made with his own two hands, remembering its design from his childhood in China. And we children sat huddled shoulder to shoulder on the blanket, reaching into the grocery sack full of bologna sandwiches, which we hungrily ate salted with sand from our fingers.

Then my father stood up and admired his fishing pole, its grace, its strength. Satisfied, he picked up his shoes and walked to the edge of the beach and then on to the reef to the point just before it was wet. My two older sisters, Janice and Ruth, jumped up from the blanket and slapped their thighs to get the sand off. Then they slapped each other's back and raced off down the beach shrieking. I was about to get up and chase them, but my mother nodded toward my four brothers and reminded me: '*Dangsying tamende shenti*,' which means 'Take care of them,' or literally, 'Watch out for their bodies.' These bodies were the anchors of my life: Matthew, Mark, Luke and Bing. I fell back on to the sand, groaning as my throat grew tight, as I made the same lament: 'Why?' Why did *I* have to care for them?

And she gave me the same answer: '*Yiding*.'

I must. Because they were my brothers. My sisters had once taken care of me. How else could I learn responsibility? How else could I appreciate what my parents had done for me?

Matthew, Mark and Luke were twelve, ten and nine, old enough to keep themselves loudly amused. They had already buried Luke in a shallow grave of sand so that only his head stuck out. Now they were starting to pat together the outlines of a sand-castle wall on top of him.

But Bing was only four, easily excitable and easily bored and irritable. He didn't want to play with the other brothers because they had pushed him off to the side, admonishing him, 'No, Bing, you'll just wreck it.'

So Bing wandered down the beach, walking stiffly like an ousted emperor, picking up shards of rock and chunks of driftwood and flinging them with all his might into the surf. I trailed behind, imagining tidal waves and wondering what I would do if one appeared. I called to Bing every now and then, 'Don't go too close to the water. You'll get your feet wet.' And I thought how much I seemed like my mother, always worried beyond reason inside, but at the same time talking about the danger as if it were less than it really was. The worry surrounded me, like the wall of the cove, and it made me feel everything had been considered and was now safe.

My mother had a superstition, in fact, that children were predisposed to certain dangers on certain days, all depending on their Chinese birthdate. It was explained in a little Chinese book called *The Twenty-Six Malignant Gates*. There, on each page, was an illustration of some terrible danger that awaited young innocent children. In the corners was a description written in Chinese, and since I couldn't read the characters, I could only see what the picture meant.

The same little boy appeared in each picture: climbing a broken tree limb, standing by a falling gate, slipping in a wooden tub, being carried away by a snapping dog,

The Joy Luck Club

fleeing from a bolt of lightning. And in each of these pictures stood a man who looked as if he were wearing a lizard costume. He had a big crease in his forehead, or maybe it was actually that he had two round horns. In one picture, the lizard man was standing on a curved bridge, laughing as he watched the little boy falling forward over the bridge rail, his slippered feet already in the air.

It would have been enough to think that even one of these dangers could befall a child. And even though the birthdates corresponded to only one danger, my mother worried about them all. This was because she couldn't figure out how the Chinese dates, based on the lunar calendar, translated into American dates. So by taking them all into account, she had absolute faith she could prevent every one of them.

The sun had shifted and moved over the other side of the cove wall. Everything had settled into place. My mother was busy keeping sand from blowing on to the blanket, then shaking sand out of shoes, and tacking corners of blankets back down again with the now clean shoes. My father was still standing at the end of the reef, patiently casting out, waiting for *nengkan* to manifest itself as a fish. I could see small figures farther down on the beach, and I could tell they were my sisters by their two dark heads and yellow pants. My brothers' shrieks were mixed with those of seagulls. Bing had found an empty soda bottle and was using this to dig sand next to the dark cove wall. And I sat on the sand, just where the shadows ended and the sunny part began.

Bing was pounding the soda bottle against the rock, so I called to him, 'Don't dig so hard. You'll bust a hole in the wall and fall all the way to China.' And I laughed when he looked at me as though he thought what I said was true. He stood up and started walking toward the water. He put one foot tentatively on the reef, and I warned him, 'Bing.'

'I'm gonna see Daddy,' he protested.

'Stay close to the wall, then, away from the water,' I said. 'Stay away from the mean fish.'

And I watched as he inched his way along the reef, his back hugging the bumpy cove wall. I still see him, so clearly that I almost feel I can make him stay there for ever.

I see him standing by the wall, safe, calling to my father, who looks over his shoulder toward Bing. How glad I am that my father is going to watch him for a while! Bing starts to walk over and then something tugs on my father's line and he's reeling as fast as he can.

Shouts erupt. Someone has thrown sand in Luke's face and he's jumped out of his sand grave and thrown himself on top of Mark, thrashing and kicking. My mother shouts for me to stop them. And right after I pull Luke off Mark, I look up and see Bing walking alone to the edge of the reef. In the confusion of the fight, nobody notices. I am the only one who sees what Bing is doing.

Bing walks one, two, three steps. His little body is moving so quickly, as if he spotted something wonderful by the water's edge. And I think, *He's going to fall in*. I'm expecting it. And just as I think this, his feet are already in the air, in a moment of balance, before he splashes into the sea and disappears without leaving so much as a ripple in the water.

I sank to my knees watching that spot where he disappeared, not moving, not saying anything. I couldn't

The Joy Luck Club

make sense of it. I was thinking, Should I run to the water and try to pull him out? Should I shout to my father? Can I rise on my legs fast enough? Can I take it all back and forbid Bing from joining my father on the ledge?

And then my sisters were back, and one of them said, 'Where's Bing?' There was silence for a few seconds and then shouts and sand flying as everyone rushed past me toward the water's edge. I stood there unable to move as my sisters looked by the cove wall, as my brothers scrambled to see what lay behind pieces of driftwood. My mother and father were trying to part the waves with their hands.

We were there for many hours. I remember the search boats and the sunset when dusk came. I had never seen a sunset like that: a bright orange flame touching the water's edge and then fanning out, warming the sea. When it became dark, the boats turned their yellow orbs on and bounced up and down on the dark shiny water.

As I look back, it seems unnatural to think about the colours of the sunset and boats at a time like that. But we all had strange thoughts. My father was calculating minutes, estimating the temperature of the water, readjusting his estimate of when Bing fell. My sisters were calling, 'Bing! Bing!' as if he were hiding in some bushes high above the beach cliffs. My brothers sat in the car, quietly reading comic books. And when the boats turned off their yellow orbs, my mother went for a swim. She had never swum a stroke in her life, but her faith in her own *nengkan* convinced her that what these Americans couldn't do, she could. She could find Bing.

And when the rescue people finally pulled her out of the water, she still had her *nengkan* intact. Her hair, her clothes, they were all heavy with the cold water, but she stood quietly, calm and regal as a mermaid queen who had just arrived out of the sea. The police called off the search, put us all in our car, and sent us home to grieve.

I had expected to be beaten to death, by my father, by my mother, by my sisters and brothers. I knew it was my fault. I hadn't watched him closely enough, and yet I saw him. But as we sat in the dark living room, I heard them, one by one whispering their regrets.

'I was selfish to want to go fishing,' said my father.

'We shouldn't have gone for a walk,' said Janice, while Ruth blew her nose yet another time.

'Why'd you have to throw sand in my face?' moaned Luke. 'Why'd you have to make me start a fight?'

And my mother quietly admitted to me, 'I told you to stop their fight. I told you to take your eyes off him.'

If I had had any time at all to feel a sense of relief, it would have quickly evaporated, because my mother also said, 'So now I am telling you, we must go and find him, quickly, tomorrow morning.' And everybody's eyes looked down. But I saw it as my punishment: to go out with my mother, back to the beach, to help her find Bing's body.

Nothing prepared me for what my mother did the next day. When I woke up, it was still dark and she was already dressed. On the kitchen table was a thermos, a teacup, the white leatherette Bible, and the car keys.

'Is Daddy ready?' I asked.

'Daddy's not coming,' she said.

'Then how will we get there? Who will drive us?'

She picked up the keys and I followed her out the door to the car. I wondered the whole time as we drove

The Joy Luck Club

to the beach how she had learned to drive overnight. She used no map. She drove smoothly ahead, turning down Geary, then the Great Highway, signalling at all the right times, getting on the Coast Highway and easily winding the car around the sharp curves that often led inexperienced drivers off and over the cliffs.

When we arrived at the beach, she walked immediately down the dirt path and over to the end of the reef ledge, where I had seen Bing disappear. She held in her hand the white Bible. And looking out over the water, she called to God, her small voice carried up by the gulls to heaven. It began with 'Dear God' and ended with 'Amen' and in between she spoke in Chinese.

'I have always believed in your blessings,' she praised God in that same tone she used for exaggerated Chinese compliments. 'We knew they would come. We did not question them. Your decisions were our decisions. You rewarded us for our faith.

'In return we have always tried to show our deepest respect. We went to your house. We brought you money. We sang your songs. You gave us more blessings. And now we have misplaced one of them. We were careless. This is true. We had so many good things, we couldn't keep them in our mind all the time.

'So maybe you hid him from us to teach us a lesson, to be more careful with your gifts in the future. I have learned this. I have put it in my memory. And now I have come to take Bing back.'

I listened quietly as my mother said these words, horrified. And I began to cry when she added, 'Forgive us for his bad manners. My daughter, this one standing here, will be sure to teach him better lessons of obedience before he visits you again.'

After her prayer, her faith was so great that she saw

him, three times, waving to her from just beyond the first wave. *'Nale!'* – There! And she would stand straight as a sentinel, until three times her eyesight failed her and Bing turned into a dark spot of churning seaweed.

My mother did not let her chin fall down. She walked back to the beach and put the Bible down. She picked up the thermos and teacup and walked to the water's edge. Then she told me that the night before she had reached back into her life, back when she was a girl in China, and this is what she had found.

'I remember a boy who lost his hand in a firecracker accident,' she said. 'I saw the shreds of this boy's arm, his tears, and then I heard his mother's claim that he would grow back another hand, better than the last. This mother said she would pay back an ancestral debt ten times over. She would use a water treatment to soothe the wrath of Chu Jung, the three-eyed god of fire. And true enough, the next week this boy was riding a bicycle, both hands steering a straight course past my astonished eyes!'

And then my mother became very quiet. She spoke again in a thoughtful, respectful manner.

'An ancestor of ours once stole water from a sacred well. Now the water is trying to steal back. We must sweeten the temper of the Coiling Dragon who lives in the sea. And then we must make him loosen his coils from Bing by giving him another treasure he can hide.'

My mother poured out tea sweetened with sugar into the teacup, and threw this into the sea. And then she opened her fist. In her palm was a ring of watery blue sapphire, a gift from her mother, who had died many years before. This ring, she told me, drew coveting stares from women and made them inattentive to the children they guarded so jealously. This would make the

Coiling Dragon forgetful of Bing. She threw the ring into the water.

But even with this, Bing did not appear right away. For an hour or so, all we saw was seaweed drifting by. And then I saw her clasp her hands to her chest, and she said in a wondrous voice, 'See, it's because we were watching the wrong direction.' And I too saw Bing trudging wearily at the far end of the beach, his shoes hanging in his hand, his dark head bent over in exhaustion. I could feel what my mother felt. The hunger in our hearts was instantly filled. And then the two of us, before we could even get to our feet, saw him light a cigarette, grow tall, and become a stranger.

'Ma, let's go,' I said as softly as possible.

'He's there,' she said firmly. She pointed to the jagged wall across the water. 'I see him. He is in a cave, sitting on a little step above the water. He is hungry and a little cold, but he has learned now not to complain too much.'

And then she stood up and started walking across the sandy beach as though it were a solid paved path, and I was trying to follow behind, struggling and stumbling in the soft mounds. She marched up the steep path to where the car was parked, and she wasn't even breathing hard as she pulled a large inner tube from the trunk. To this lifesaver, she tied the fishing line from my father's bamboo pole. She walked back and threw the tube into the sea, holding on to the pole.

'This will go where Bing is. I will bring him back,' she said fiercely. I had never heard so much *nengkan* in my mother's voice.

The tube followed her mind. It drifted out, toward the other side of the cove where it was caught by stronger waves. The line became taut and she strained to hold on tight. But the line snapped and then spiralled into the water.

We both climbed toward the end of the reef to watch. The tube had now reached the other side of the cove. A big wave smashed it into the wall. The bloated tube leapt up and then it was sucked in, under the wall and into a cavern. It popped out. Over and over again, it disappeared, emerged, glistening black, faithfully reporting it had seen Bing and was going back to try to pluck him from the cave. Over and over again, it dove and popped back up again, empty but still hopeful. And then, after a dozen or so times, it was sucked into the dark recess, and when it came out, it was torn and lifeless.

At that moment, and not until that moment, did she give up. My mother had a look on her face that I'll never forget. It was one of complete despair and horror, for losing Bing, for being so foolish as to think she could use faith to change fate. And it made me angry – so blindingly angry – that everything had failed us.

I know now that I had never expected to find Bing, just as I know now I will never find a way to save my marriage. My mother tells me, though, that I should still try.

'What's the point?' I say. 'There's no hope. There's no reason to keep trying.'

'Because you must,' she says. 'This is not hope. Not reason. This is your fate. This is your life, what you must do.'

'So what can I do?'

And my mother says, 'You must think for yourself, what you must do. If someone tells you, then you are not trying.' And then she walks out of the kitchen to let me think about this.

The Joy Luck Club

I think about Bing, how I knew he was in danger, how I let it happen. I think about my marriage, how I had seen the signs, really I had. But I just let it happen. And I think now that fate is shaped half by expectation, half by inattention. But somehow, when you lose something you love, faith takes over. You have to pay attention to what you lost. You have to undo the expectation.

My mother, she still pays attention to it. That Bible under the table, I know she sees it. I remember seeing her write in it before she wedged it under.

I lift the table and slide the Bible out. I put the Bible on the table, flipping quickly through the pages, because I know it's there. On the page before the New Testament begins, there's a section called 'Deaths', and that's where she wrote 'Bing Hsu' lightly, in erasable pencil.

Alice Walker
Everyday Use
for your grandmama

I will wait for her in the yard that Maggie and I made so clean and wavy yesterday afternoon. A yard like this is more comfortable than most people know. It is not just a yard. It is like an extended living-room. When the hard clay is swept clean as a floor and the fine sand around the edges lined with tiny, irregular grooves, anyone can come and sit and look up into the elm tree and wait for the breezes that never come inside the house.

Maggie will be nervous until after her sister goes: she will stand hopelessly in corners, homely and ashamed of the burn scars down her arms and legs, eyeing her sister with a mixture of envy and awe. She thinks her sister has held life always in the palm of one hand, that 'no' is a word the world never learned to say to her.

You've no doubt seen those TV shows where the child who has 'made it' is confronted, as a surprise, by her own mother and father, tottering in weakly from backstage. (A pleasant surprise, of course: what would they do if parent and child came on the show only to curse out and insult each other?) On TV mother and child embrace and smile into each other's faces. Sometimes the mother and father weep, the child wraps them in her arms and leans across the table to tell how she would not have made it without their help. I have seen these programmes.

Sometimes I dream a dream in which Dee and I are suddenly brought together on a TV programme of this sort. Out of a dark and soft-seated limousine I am ushered into a bright room filled with many people. There I meet a smiling, grey, sporty man like Johnny Carson who shakes my hand and tells me what a fine girl I have. Then we are on the stage and Dee is embracing me with tears in her eyes. She pins on my dress a large orchid, even though she has told me once that she thinks orchids are tacky flowers.

In real life I am a large, big-boned woman with rough, man-working hands. In the winter I wear flannel nightgowns to bed and overalls during the day. I can kill and clean a hog as mercilessly as a man. My fat keeps me hot in zero weather. I can work outside all day, breaking ice to get water for washing; I can eat pork liver cooked over the open fire minutes after it comes steaming from the hog. One winter I knocked a bull calf straight in the brain between the eyes with a sledge hammer and had the meat hung up to chill before nightfall. But of course all this does not show on television. I am the way my daughter would want me to be: a hundred pounds lighter, my skin like an uncooked barley pancake. My hair glistens in the hot bright lights. Johnny Carson has much to do to keep up with my quick and witty tongue.

But that is a mistake. I know even before I wake up. Who ever knew a Johnson with a quick tongue? Who can even imagine me looking a strange white man in the eye? It seems to me I have talked to them always with one foot raised in flight, with my head turned in whichever way is farthest from them. Dee, though. She would always look anyone in the eye. Hesitation was no part of her nature.

*

Everyday Use

'How do I look, Mama?' Maggie says, showing just enough of her thin body enveloped in pink skirt and red blouse for me to know she's there, almost hidden by the door.

'Come out into the yard,' I say.

Have you ever seen a lame animal, perhaps a dog run over by some careless person rich enough to own a car, sidle up to someone who is ignorant enough to be kind to him? That is the way my Maggie walks. She has been like this, chin on chest, eyes on ground, feet in shuffle, ever since the fire that burned the other house to the ground.

Dee is lighter than Maggie, with nicer hair and a fuller figure. She's a woman now, though sometimes I forget. How long ago was it that the other house burned? Ten, twelve years? Sometimes I can still hear the flames and feel Maggie's arms sticking to me, her hair smoking and her dress falling off her in little black papery flakes. Her eyes seemed stretched open, blazed open by the flames reflected in them. And Dee. I see her standing off under the sweet gum tree she used to dig gum out of; a look of concentration on her face as she watched the last dingy grey board of the house fall in toward the red-hot brick chimney. Why don't you do a dance around the ashes? I'd wanted to ask her. She had hated the house that much.

I used to think she hated Maggie, too. But that was before we raised the money, the church and me, to send her to Augusta to school. She used to read to us without pity; forcing words, lies, other folks' habits, whole lives upon us two, sitting trapped and ignorant underneath her voice. She washed us in a river of make-believe, burned us with a lot of knowledge we didn't necessarily need to know. Pressed us to her with the serious way she read, to shove us away at just the moment, like dimwits, we seemed about to understand.

Dee wanted nice things. A yellow organdie dress to wear to her graduation from high school; black pumps to match a green suit she'd made from an old suit somebody gave me. She was determined to stare down any disaster in her efforts. Her eyelids would not flicker for minutes at a time. Often I fought off the temptation to shake her. At sixteen she had a style of her own: and knew what style was.

I never had an education myself. After second grade the school was closed down. Don't ask me why: in 1927 coloured asked fewer questions than they do now. Sometimes Maggie reads to me. She stumbles along good-naturedly but can't see well. She knows she is not bright. Like good looks and money, quickness passed her by. She will marry John Thomas (who has mossy teeth in an earnest face) and then I'll be free to sit here and I guess just sing church songs to myself. Although I never was a good singer. Never could carry a tune. I was always better at a man's job. I used to love to milk till I was hooked in the side in '49. Cows are soothing and slow and don't bother you, unless you try to milk them the wrong way.

I have deliberately turned my back on the house. It is three rooms, just like the one that burned, except the roof is tin; they don't make shingle roofs any more. There are no real windows, just some holes cut in the sides, like the portholes in a ship, but not round and not square, with rawhide holding the shutters up on the outside. This house is in a pasture, too, like the other one. No doubt when Dee sees it she will want to tear it down.

Everyday Use

She wrote me once that no matter where we 'choose' to live, she will manage to come see us. But she will never bring her friends. Maggie and I thought about this and Maggie asked me, 'Mama, when did Dee ever *have* any friends?'

She had a few. Furtive boys in pink shirts hanging about on wash-day after school. Nervous girls who never laughed. Impressed with her they worshipped the well-turned phrase, the cute shape, the scalding humour that erupted like bubbles in lye. She read to them.

When she was courting Jimmy T she didn't have much time to pay to us, but turned all her fault-finding power on him. He *flew* to marry a cheap city girl from a family of ignorant flashy people. She hardly had time to recompose herself.

When she comes I will meet – but there they are!

Maggie attempts to make a dash for the house, in her shuffling way, but I stay her with my hand. 'Come back here,' I say. And she stops and tries to dig a well in the sand with her toe.

It is hard to see them clearly through the strong sun. But even the first glimpse of leg out of the car tells me it is Dee. Her feet were always neat-looking, as if God himself had shaped them with a certain style. From the other side of the car comes a short, stocky man. Hair is all over his head a foot long and hanging from his chin like a kinky mule tail. I hear Maggie suck in her breath. 'Uhnnnh' is what it sounds like. Like when you see the wriggling end of a snake just in front of your foot on the road. 'Uhnnnh.'

Dee next. A dress down to the ground, in this hot weather. A dress so loud it hurts my eyes. There are yellows and oranges enough to throw back the light of the sun. I feel my whole face warming from the heat waves it throws out. Ear-rings gold, too, and hanging down to her shoulders. Bracelets dangling and making noises when she moves her arm up to shake the folds of the dress out of her armpits. The dress is loose and flows, and as she walks close, I like it. I hear Maggie go 'Uhnnnh' again. It is her sister's hair. It stands straight up like the wool on a sheep. It is black as night and around the edges are two long pigtails that rope about like small lizards disappearing behind her ears.

'Wa-su-zo-Tean-o!' she says, coming on in that gliding way the dress makes her move. The short stocky fellow with the hair to his navel is all grinning and he follows up with 'Asalamalakim, my mother and sister!' He moves to hug Maggie but she falls back, right up against the back of my chair. I feel her trembling there and when I look up I see the perspiration falling off her chin.

'Don't get up,' says Dee. Since I am stout it takes something of a push. You can see me trying to move a second or two before I make it. She turns, showing white heels through her sandals, and goes back to the car. Out she peeks next with a Polaroid. She stoops down quickly and lines up picture after picture of me sitting there in front of the house with Maggie cowering behind me. She never takes a shot without making sure the house is included. When a cow comes nibbling around the edge of the yard she snaps it and me and Maggie *and* the house. Then she puts the Polaroid in the back seat of the car, and comes up and kisses me on the forehead.

Meanwhile Asalamalakim is going through motions with Maggie's hand. Maggie's hand is as limp as a fish, and probably as cold, despite the sweat, and she keeps trying to pull it back. It looks like Asalamalakim wants

Everyday Use

to shake hands but wants to do it fancy. Or maybe he don't know how people shake hands. Anyhow, he soon gives up on Maggie.

'Well,' I say. 'Dee.'

'No, Mama,' she says. 'Not "Dee," Wangero Leewanika Kemanjo!'

'What happened to "Dee"?' I wanted to know.

'She's dead,' Wangero said. 'I couldn't bear it any longer, being named after the people who oppress me.'

'You know as well as me you was named after your aunt Dicie,' I said. Dicie is my sister. She named Dee. We called her 'Big Dee' after Dee was born.

'But who was *she* named after?' asked Wangero.

'I guess after Grandma Dee,' I said.

'And who was she named after?' asked Wangero.

'Her mother,' I said, and saw Wangero was getting tired. 'That's about as far back as I can trace it,' I said. Though, in fact, I probably could have carried it back beyond the Civil War through the branches.

'Well,' said Asalamalakim, 'there you are.'

'Uhnnnh,' I heard Maggie say.

'There I was not,' I said, 'before "Dicie" cropped up in our family, so why should I try to trace it that far back?'

He just stood there grinning, looking down on me like somebody inspecting a Model A car. Every once in a while he and Wangero sent eye signals over my head.

'How do you pronounce this name?' I asked.

'You don't have to call me by it if you don't want to,' said Wangero.

'Why shouldn't I?' I asked. 'If that's what you want us to call you, we'll call you.'

'I know it might sound awkward at first,' said Wangero.

905

'I'll get used to it,' I said. 'Ream it out again.'

Well, soon we got the name out of the way. Asalamalakim had a name twice as long and three times as hard. After I tripped over it two or three times he told me to just call him Hakim-a-barber. I wanted to ask him was he a barber, but I didn't really think he was, so I didn't ask.

'You must belong to those beef-cattle peoples down the road,' I said. They said 'Asalamalakim' when they met you, too, but they didn't shake hands. Always too busy: feeding the cattle, fixing the fences, putting up salt-lick shelters, throwing down hay. When the white folks poisoned some of the herd the men stayed up all night with rifles in their hands. I walked a mile and a half just to see the sight.

Hakim-a-barber said, 'I accept some of their doctrines, but farming and raising cattle is not my style.' (They didn't tell me, and I didn't ask, whether Wangero (Dee) had really gone and married him.)

We sat down to eat and right away he said he didn't eat collards and pork was unclean. Wangero, though, went on through the chitlins and corn bread, the greens and everything else. She talked a blue streak over the sweet potatoes. Everything delighted her. Even the fact that we still used the benches her daddy made for the table when we couldn't afford to buy chairs.

'Oh, Mama!' she cried. Then turned to Hakim-a-barber. 'I never knew how lovely these benches are. You can feel the rump prints,' she said, running her hands underneath her and along the bench. Then she gave a sigh and her hand closed over Grandma Dee's butter dish. 'That's it!' she said. 'I knew there was something I wanted to ask you if I could have.' She jumped up from the table and went over in the corner

Everyday Use

where the churn stood, the milk in it clabber by now. She looked at the churn and looked at it.

'This churn top is what I need,' she said. 'Didn't Uncle Buddy whittle it out of a tree you all used to have?'

'Yes,' I said.

'Uh huh,' she said happily. 'And I want the dasher, too.'

'Uncle Buddy whittle that, too?' asked the barber.

Dee (Wangero) looked up at me.

'Aunt Dee's first husband whittled the dash,' said Maggie so low you almost couldn't hear her. 'His name was Henry, but they called him Stash.'

'Maggie's brain is like an elephant's,' Wangero said, laughing. 'I can use the churn top as a centrepiece for the alcove table,' she said, sliding a plate over the churn, 'and I'll think of something artistic to do with the dasher.'

When she finished wrapping the dasher the handle stuck out. I took it for a moment in my hands. You didn't even have to look close to see where hands pushing the dasher up and down to make butter had left a kind of sink in the wood. In fact, there were a lot of small sinks; you could see where thumbs and fingers had sunk into the wood. It was beautiful light yellow wood, from a tree that grew in the yard where Big Dee and Stash had lived.

After dinner Dee (Wangero) went to the trunk at the foot of my bed and started rifling through it. Maggie hung back in the kitchen over the dishpan. Out came Wangero with two quilts. They had been pieced by Grandma Dee and then Big Dee and me had hung them on the quilt frames on the front porch and quilted them. One was in the Lone Star pattern. The other was Walk Around the Mountain. In both of them were scraps

Alice Walker

of dresses Grandma Dee had worn fifty and more years ago. Bits and pieces of Grandpa Jarrell's Paisley shirts. And one teeny faded blue piece, about the size of a penny matchbox, that was from Great Grandpa Ezra's uniform that he wore in the Civil War.

'Mama,' Wangero said sweet as a bird. 'Can I have these old quilts?'

I heard something fall in the kitchen, and a minute later the kitchen door slammed.

'Why don't you take one or two of the others?' I asked. 'These old things was just done by me and Big Dee from some tops your grandma pieced before she died.'

'No,' said Wangero. 'I don't want those. They are stitched around the borders by machine.'

'That'll make them last better,' I said.

'That's not the point,' said Wangero. 'These are all pieces of dresses Grandma used to wear. She did all this stitching by hand. Imagine!' She held the quilts securely in her arms, stroking them.

'Some of the pieces, like those lavender ones, come from old clothes her mother handed down to her,' I said, moving up to touch the quilts. Dee (Wangero) moved back just enough so that I couldn't reach the quilts. They already belonged to her.

'Imagine!' she breathed again, clutching them closely to her bosom.

'The truth is,' I said, 'I promised to give them quilts to Maggie, for when she marries John Thomas.'

She gasped like a bee had stung her.

'Maggie can't appreciate these quilts!' she said. 'She'd probably be backward enough to put them to everyday use.'

'I reckon she would,' I said. 'God knows I been saving 'em for long enough with nobody using 'em. I hope she

Everyday Use

will!' I didn't want to bring up how I had offered Dee (Wangero) a quilt when she went away to college. Then she had told me they were old-fashioned, out of style.

'But they're *priceless*!' she was saying now, furiously; for she has a temper. 'Maggie would put them on the bed and in five years they'd be in rags. Less than that!'

'She can always make some more,' I said. 'Maggie knows how to quilt.'

Dee (Wangero) looked at me with hatred. 'You just will not understand. The point is these quilts, *these* quilts!'

'Well,' I said, stumped. 'What would *you* do with them?'

'Hang them,' she said. As if that was the only thing you *could* do with quilts.

Maggie by now was standing in the door. I could almost hear the sound her feet made as they scraped over each other.

'She can have them, Mama,' she said, like somebody used to never winning anything, or having anything reserved for her. 'I can 'member Grandma Dee without the quilts.'

I looked at her hard. She had filled her bottom lip with checkerberry snuff and it gave her face a kind of dopey, hangdog look. It was Grandma Dee and Big Dee who taught her how to quilt herself. She stood there with her scarred hands hidden in the folds of her skirt. She looked at her sister with something like fear but she wasn't mad at her. This was Maggie's portion. This was the way she knew God to work.

When I looked at her like that something hit me in the top of my head and ran down to the soles of my feet. Just like when I'm in church and the spirit of God touches me and I get happy and shout. I did something I never had done before: hugged Maggie to me, then dragged her on into the room, snatched the quilts out of Miss Wangero's hands and dumped them into Maggie's lap. Maggie just sat there on my bed with her mouth open.

'Take one or two of the others,' I said to Dee.

But she turned without a word and went out to Hakim-a-barber.

'You just don't understand,' she said, as Maggie and I came out to the car.

'What don't I understand?' I wanted to know.

'Your heritage,' she said. And then she turned to Maggie, kissed her, and said, 'You ought to try to make something of yourself, too, Maggie. It's really a new day for us. But from the way you and Mama still live you'd never know it.'

She put on some sunglasses that hid everything above the tip of her nose and her chin.

Maggie smiled; maybe at the sunglasses. But a real smile, not scared. After we watched the car dust settle I asked Maggie to bring me a dip of snuff. And then the two of us sat there just enjoying, until it was time to go in the house and go to bed.

Fay Weldon

extract from

The Hearts and Lives of Men

The sixties are in full swing when Clifford, young whizz-kid director of Leonardo's, the art house that isn't Sotheby's or Christie's, meets Helen, lovely daughter of the eccentric painter John Lally.

FAMILY RELATIONS

Clifford and Helen were, fortunately, innocently asleep, when John Lally burst in upon them. They lay exhausted on a rumpled bed, a hairy limb here, a smooth one there, her head on his chest, hardly comfortable to outside eyes; to lovers, real lovers, that is, perfectly comfortable, just not to those who know they'll presently have to get up and steal away before the embarrassing time for breakfast arrives. Real lovers sleep soundly, knowing that when they wake nothing has to end, but will simply continue. The conviction suffuses their sleep: they smile as they slumber. The sound of splintering wood entered their dreams and was converted there, in Helen's case, to the sound of a fluffy chicken emerging from an egg she had in the palm of her hand, and in Clifford's case, to the sound of his skis as he swept masterfully and unerringly down snowy mountain slopes. The sight of his sleeping smiling daughter, his smiling sleeping enemy, who had stolen his last treasure, inflamed John Lally the more. He roared. Clifford frowned in his sleep: chasms yawned beneath him. Helen stirred and woke. The cosy cheeping of the newborn chick had turned into a wail. She sat up. She saw her father and pulled the sheet above her breasts. Bruise marks had yet to develop.

'How did you know I was here?' she asked: it was the question of a born conspirator who feels no guilt but whose plans have gone awry. He did not deign to reply, but I will tell you.

By one of those mischances which dog the fates of lovers, Clifford's departure with Helen from the Bosch party had been the subject of a small item in a gossip column, and this had been taken up by one Harry Stephens, a *habitué* of the Appletree Pub in Lower Appleby. Now Harry had a cousin in Sotheby's, where Helen had her part-time job, restoring earthenware, and had enquired further, and thus word had got back to deepest Gloucestershire that Helen Lally had vanished into Clifford Wexford's house, and had not emerged since.

'Quite a daughter you've got there!' said Harry Stephens. John Lally was not popular in the neighbourhood. Lower Appleby forgave his eccentricity, his debts, his neglected orchard, but not the way he, a foreigner, drank cider in the pub and not shorts, and the way he treated his wife. Otherwise the subject of his daughter would not have been brought up, but tactfully ignored. As it was, John Lally finished up his cider, got in his battered Volkswagen – its top speed 25 m.p.h. – and made the journey to London through the night, through the dawn, not so much to rescue his daughter but fix Clifford Wexford once and for all as the villain he was.

'Whore!' cried John Lally now, tugging Helen out of bed, because she was nearest.

'Oh really, Dad,' she said, slipping out from under his grasp, on her feet, readjusting her slip, and then to the waking, startled Clifford, 'I'm sorry, it's my father.' She had caught her mother's habit of apologizing. She was never to lose it. Except that where her mother used the phrase, pathetically, in the hope of diverting torrents of abuse, Helen used it as a kind of bored reproach to the

The Hearts and Lives of Men

fates, with a wry lift of a delicate eyebrow. Clifford sat up, startled.

John Lally looked around the bedroom walls, at the paintings which were the sum of five years or so of his life and work: a rotten fig on a branch, a rainbow distorted by a toad, a line of washing in a cavern's mouth – I know they sound dreadful but, reader, they are not: they hang today in the world's most distinguished galleries, and no one blenches when they pass: the colours are so strong, sharp and layered, it is as if one reality is pasted on top of a whole series of others – and then at his daughter, who was half-laughing, half-crying, embarrassed, excited and angry all at once: and at Clifford's strong, naked body, with the fuzz of fair, almost white hair, along his bronzed arms and legs (Clifford and Angie had recently been on holiday, to Brazil where they had stayed at an art-collector's palace: a place of marble floors and gold-leafed taps and so on, and Tintorettos on the walls and hot, hot bleaching sun) and back to the rumpled, heated bed.

It was no doubt purity of heart and sheer self-righteousness which gave John Lally the strength of ten. He lifted Clifford Wexford, young puppy or hope of the Art World, depending on how you saw it, by a naked arm and a bare leg, and effortlessly, as if the younger man were a rag doll, raised him on high. Helen shrieked. The doll came to life just in time and with his free leg directed a sharp kick at John Lally's crotch, getting him just where it hurt most. John Lally shrieked in his turn; the cat – who had spent a warm but restless night on the end of the foam rubber bed – finally gave up and stalked off just in time, for Clifford Wexford came tumbling down just where a second ago he had been curled, as John Lally simply let him go. Clifford was no sooner down than up, hooked a young and flexible foot behind John Lally's stiff ankle and tugged it so that his beloved's father fell face down on the floor, hitting his face and making his nose bleed. Clifford, broad-shouldered, sinewy, young, stood proud and naked over his defeated foe. (He was no more ashamed of his body than Helen was. Though just as Helen felt more comfortable clothed in front of her father, no doubt, had his mother been present, Clifford would quickly have pulled on at least his underpants.)

'Your father really is a bore,' said Clifford to Helen. John Lally lay face down on the floor, his eyes open and burning into the Kelim rug. It was striped in dull oranges and muted reds; colours and pattern which were later to emerge in one of his most well known paintings – *The Scourging of St Ida*. (Painters, like writers, have the knack of putting the most distressing and extreme events to artistic good purpose.) In these days, rugs such as the one then flung so casually over Clifford's polished wood attic floor are rare and cost thousands of pounds at Liberty's. Then they could be bought for a fiver or so at any junk shop. Clifford, of course, with his knowing eye to the future, had already managed to pick up a dozen or so very fine specimens.

John Lally was not sure which was worse: the pain or the humiliation. As the former decreased, the latter intensified. His eyes watered: his nose bled: his groin ached. His fingers tingled. He had been painting obsessively for twenty-eight years, and so far as he could see to no commercial or practical purpose. Canvases stacked his studio, his garage. The only person who seemed to understand their merit was Clifford Wexford. Worse, and the artist had to acknowledge it, this blond young puppy of a man, with his meretricious view of the world,

The Hearts and Lives of Men

his easy way with women, money, society, knew exactly how to foster his talent by an encouraging word here, a moral slap there: a lift of an eyebrow as, on his periodic visits, he leafed through the stacked canvases in the Lally attic, garage, garden shed. 'Yes, that's interesting. No, no, good try but didn't quite come off, did it – Ah, yes –' and young Wexford would pick out the very ones the painter knew to be his best work and so most expected the world to disdain, and by now hoped it would disdain, the better for him to disdain and despise the world – and took them off. And a fiver or so would change hands – just enough to replace paints and brushes, though hardly enough to restock the kitchen cupboard, but that was Evelyn's problem – and they'd be whisked away and a cheque from Leonardo's would come through the letter-box every now and then, unexpected and unasked for. John Lally was torn, he was in conflict: he raged, he burned: he bled: so many passions, thought John Lally, face down, bleeding and weeping into the Kelim rug, might do me some real physical damage – that is to say, paralyse my painting hand. He calmed himself. He stopped writhing and groaning and lay still.

'Now you've stopped making a fool of yourself,' said Clifford, 'you'd better get up and get out before I lose my temper and kick you to death.'

John Lally continued to lie still. Clifford stirred his prostrate body with a casual foot.

'Don't,' said Helen.

'I'll do what I want,' said Clifford. 'Look what he's done to my door!' And he drew back his foot as if to deliver a hefty kick. He was angry, and not just because of his splintered wood, or having his privacy thus invaded, or Helen insulted, but because he realized at that moment that he actually envied and was jealous of John Lally, who could paint like an angel. And that to paint like an angel was the only thing in the world Clifford Wexford wanted. And because Clifford couldn't, everything else seemed unimportant – money, ambition, the quest for status – mere substitutes, second best. He wanted to kick John Lally to death and that was the truth of it.

'Please not,' said Helen. 'He's a bit mad. He can't help himself.'

John Lally looked up at his daughter and decided he didn't like her one bit. She was a patronizing bitch, spoilt by Evelyn, ruined by the world; she was shoddy goods, untalented, spoiled. He clambered to his feet.

'Little bitch,' he said, 'as if I cared whose bed you were in.' He was up just in time. Clifford delivered the kick and missed.

'Do what you want,' John Lally said to Helen. 'Just don't ever come near me or your mother again.'

And that, reader, was how Helen and Clifford met and how Helen gave up her family on Clifford's account.

Helen did not doubt but that presently she and Clifford would marry. They were made for each other. They were two halves of the one whole. They could tell, if only from the way their limbs seemed to fuse together, as if finding at last their natural home. Well, that's how love at first sight takes people. For good or bad, that's that.

LOOKING BACK

Clifford was proud and pleased to have discovered Helen just as she was satisfied and gratified to have found him. He looked back with amazement at his life pre-Helen:

the casual sexual encounters, his general don't-ring-me, I'll-ring-you amorous behaviour (and of course he seldom did, finding his attention and interest not fully engaged), the more decorous but still abortive marital skirmishing with a long list of more-or-less suitable girls, the frequent and ultimately tedious outings with the wrong person to the right restaurants and clubs. How had he put up with it? Why? I am sorry to say that Clifford, looking back, did not consider how many women he had wounded emotionally or socially, or both: he recalled only his own desolation and boredom.

And as for Helen, it was as if until now her life had been lived in shadow. Ah, but now! An unthought of sun illuminated her days, and sent its warm residual glow through her nights. Her eyes shone; how easily her colour came and went: she shook her head and her brown curls tossed about, as if even they were suffused with extra life. She went to her tiny workshop at Sotheby's, just sometimes, returning always not to her own little flat but to Clifford's home and bed. She was paid by the hour – poorly, but the very casualness of the job suited her. She sang as she worked; her speciality was the piecing together of early earthenware (most restorers prefer the hard sharp edges and colours of ceramics. Helen loved the challenging, tricky, melting, flaky softness of early country jugs and mugs). She forgot friends and suitors: she left her flatmate to pay the rent, and answer questions. She could not believe any more that money mattered, or reputation, or the continuing goodwill of friends. She was in love. They were in love. Clifford was rich. Clifford would protect her. Bother the detail. Bother her father's rage, her mother's distress: her employers' raised eyebrows as they totted up the hours she worked each week, and reckoned again the cost of the workshop space she took up. Clifford was all the family, the friends, she would ever need: he was the roof over her head, the cloth on her back, the sun in her sky.

Well, love can't heal everything, can it. Sometimes I see it just as a kind of ointment, which people apply to their wounded egos. True healing has to come from within: a matter of a patient, slow plod towards self-understanding, of gritting the teeth and enduring boredom and irritation, and smiling at milkmen and paying the rent, and wiping the children's faces and not showing hurt, or exhaustion, or impatience – but Helen would have none of that, reader. She was young, she was beautiful, the world was her oyster. She knew it. She let love sweep her away and swallow her up – and all she did was raise her pretty white hands to heaven and say 'I can't help it! This thing is greater than me!'

A KNIFE IN THE BACK

Clifford arrived at Leonardo's on the morning of his encounter with John Lally with a bruised fist and in a bad temper.

His first appointment that day was with Harry Blast, the ungallant young TV interviewer who had managed not to escort Angie Wellbrook home on the night of the Bosch party. It was Harry's first interview: it was to be inserted as an end piece to a programme called 'Monitor'. Harry was nervous and vulnerable. Clifford knew it.

The interview was set up in Sir Larry Patt's grand panelled office, overlooking the Thames. The BBC's cameras were large and unwieldy. The floor was a network of cables. Sir Larry Patt was as nervous as Harry Blast. Clifford was too warm from Helen's bed and his victory over the poor ruined hulk of an artist to be in the least unsure of himself. It was the first time before the cameras too but no one would ever have known it. It was, in fact, this particular interview which set Clifford on his own particular spot-lit path to art stardom. Clifford Wexford says this – Wex says that – quote the great CW and you'd be in business; if you were brave enough to ask him, that is; risk the slow put-down or the fast take-up, you could never be sure which: the quick glance of the bright blue eyes which would sum you up as okay and worth the hearing out, or dismiss you as one of the world's little people. He had the kind of even features that television cameras love – and a clear quick intelligence which cut through cant and pretension, while yet not being free of it himself – on the contrary.

'Well, now,' said Harry Blast, the interviewer, bluntly, when the cameras had stopped admiring the Jacobean panelling, County Hall across the river and the Gainsborough on the wall above the wide Georgian fireplace, and got down to business as he'd clearly prepared his question beforehand. 'It has been suggested that perhaps the Arts Council – by which of course we mean the unfortunate tax payer – has stood rather too high a proportion of the cost of the Bosch exhibition, and Leonardo's claimed rather too much of the profit. What do you say to this, Mr Wexford?'

'You mean *you* are suggesting it,' said Clifford. 'Why don't you just come out with it? Leonardo's are milking the taxpayer . . .'

'Well –' said Harry Blast, flustered, his large nose growing pinker and pinker as it did when he was stressed. A good thing colour television was yet to come, or his career might never have got under way. Stress is part of the media man's life!

'And how are we to judge these things?' asked Clifford. 'How are we to quantify, when it comes to matters of art, where profit lies? If Leonardo's brings art to an art-starved public, and governmental bodies have failed to do so, then surely we deserve, if not exactly reward, just a little encouragement? You saw those queues down the street. I hope you bothered to point your cameras. I tell you, the people of this country have been starved of beauty for too long.'

And of course it just so happened that Harry Blast had neglected to film the queues. Clifford knew it.

'As to the exact proportion of the Arts Council grant to Leonardo's funding, I think it's a matter of matching funds. Isn't that so, Sir Larry? He's king of finances round here.'

And the cameras turned, at Clifford's behest, to Sir Larry Patt, who of course didn't know without looking it up, and mumbled words to this effect instead of proclaiming ignorance loudly and clearly to the world, as he would have been better advised to do. Sir Larry had no television presence at all: his face was too old and the marks of self-indulgence written too large upon it, in the form of sloppy jowls and self-satisfied mouth. He, too, had had an upsetting morning. He had been woken by an early-morning call from Madame Bouser in Amsterdam.

'What kind of country is England?' she had demanded. 'Are you so lost to civilization that a husband can be seduced under his wife's very nose, and the husband of the woman who does it take no notice at all?'

'Madam,' said Sir Larry Patt. 'I have no idea what

The Hearts and Lives of Men

you're talking about.' Nor had he. Finding his wife unattractive, it did not occur to him that other men might be attracted to her. Sir Larry belonged to a class and generation which viewed women askance; he had married one as like a boy as possible (which Clifford had once pointed out to Rowena, making her cry). He was not an unimaginative man – just one made uneasy by emotion, who reserved his rapture for art, rather than love; for paintings, rather than sex. And this, in itself, was surely a reason for self-congratulation: coming as he did from a background which prided itself on its philistinism; surely he had shown self-determination enough. He knew he had good reason to be smug. The instrument had gone dead suddenly and fortunately, as if it had been wrested out of Madame Bouser's hand. He was not surprised. She was hysterical. Women so often were. He went into Rowena's bedroom and found her sleeping peacefully, in her flat-chested way, and did not disturb her, in case she became the same. He did not feel at his best. The fact became obvious to Harry Blast that Sir Larry belonged to the past. He had to, since Clifford belonged to the future, and television believes in polarities. Good, bad, old, new, left, right, funny, tragic, Patt on the way out, Wexford on the way in. And so the interview was the beginning of Sir Larry Patt's downfall; the top of a long gentle slope down, and Clifford it was who quite wilfully, that day, nudged him on to it. Sir Larry didn't even notice. Clifford looked into a future and saw that it contained the possibility of dynasty. To make Helen his queen he would have to be King. That meant he must rule over Leonardo's, and Leonardo's itself would have to grow and change, become one of those intricate complexes of power of which the modern world was fast becoming composed. He would have to do it by stealth, by playing politics, by behaving as kings and emperors always had: by demanding loyalty, and extracting fealty, allowing no one too close to him, by playing one favourite off against another, by keeping to himself the power of life and death and using it (or hiring and firing, the modern equivalent), by giving unexpected favours, meting out unexpected punishments, by letting his smile mean munificence, his frown hardship. He would become Wexford of Leonardo's. He, the ne'er-do-well, the anxious, striving, restless son of a powerful father, would cease to be an outsider, would cease to be the moon revolving around the sun, but become the sun itself. For Helen's sake he would turn the world inside out.

He sighed and stretched; how powerful he felt! Harry Blast's cameras caught the sigh and the stretch and made the still that made the programme, and was every picture editor's favourite thereafter, whenever they ran a story on wheelings and dealings in the Art World. There was just something about it: some feeling, I dare say, of the Act of Accession – that moment which is supposed to be so important, when the Archbishop actually places the crown upon the new monarch's head – that was caught by Harry Blast's cameras, unawares.

MOTHER AND DAUGHTER

And while Clifford Wexford considered his future, and regularized, professionalized, and indeed sanctified what had so far been only a vague ambition, the girl of his dreams, Helen Lally, sat with her mother and sipped

The Hearts and Lives of Men

herbal tea at Cranks, the new health food restaurant in Carnaby Street. Cranks was the prototype of a million others which were, over the next twenty-five years, to spring up all over the world. Whole food and herbal tea = spiritual and physical health. It was a very new notion at the time and Evelyn sipped her comfrey tea with some suspicion. (Comfrey is now not taken internally, for fear it may be carcinogenic, but only used in external application, so her instinct may have been right.)

'It will comfort you, Mother,' said Helen, hopefully. Evelyn clearly needed comforting. Her eyes were red-rimmed and puffy. She looked plain, desperate and old: not a good combination. On his return from 5 Coffee Place, John Lally had reaffirmed to his wife that her daughter Helen was no longer welcome in Applecore Cottage, that the only possible explanation for the girl's behaviour was that she was no child of his, and had locked himself in the garage. There within, presumably, he now painted furiously. Evelyn set food and drink on the window-sill from time to time: the food would be taken – the window raised quickly then banged shut – but the drink, rather pointedly, left. Home-made wine was stored in the garage so supposedly this was all he required. Black rage seemed to seep out under the garage door. 'It isn't fair,' said Evelyn to her daughter, as if she were the child and not the mother. 'It just isn't fair!'

Nor of course was it. She who had done so much for her husband, dedicated her whole life to him, thus to be treated!

'I try not to let you know how upset I get,' she said, 'but you're a grown girl now, and I suppose this is life.'

'Only if you let it be,' said Helen, secure in the knowledge of her new-found love, and that she for one meant to live happily ever after.

'If only you'd been more tactful about it,' said her mother, as near a reproach as she had ever uttered. 'You have no idea how to manage your father.'

'Well,' said Helen, 'I'm sorry. I suppose it is all my fault. But he keeps shutting himself in. Usually it's the attic: now it's the garage. I don't know why you get so upset about it. It's nothing unusual. If you didn't get so upset, he mightn't do it.'

She was trying to be serious but only managed, to her mother, to sound frivolous. She couldn't help it. She loved Clifford Wexford. So what if her father angered himself to death and her mother grieved herself to an untimely end; she, Helen, loved Clifford Wexford, and youth, energy, future, common sense, and good cheer were on her side, and that was that.

Evelyn presently composed herself and properly admired the unusual stripped pine, country-style of the restaurant, and agreed with her daughter that things had been going on like this for twenty-five years. She expected they'd go on like this for quite a while. Helen was quite right. There was no need to worry and all she had to do was pull herself together. 'Good heavens,' said Evelyn, pulling herself together, 'your hair *is* looking lovely. So curly!'

And Helen, who could afford to be kind, was, and did not instantly try to smooth her hair around her ears, but shook her head so it fluffed out just as her mother liked it. Helen liked to wear her hair straight, flat, silky and smooth long before such a thing was fashionable. Love seemed to be on Evelyn's side in this respect at least, thickening and curling her daughter's hair.

The Hearts and Lives of Men

'I'm in love,' Helen said. 'I expect that's it.'

Evelyn looked at her, puzzled. How had life at Applecore Cottage created such naivety?

'Well,' she said presently, 'don't rush into anything just because life at home was so horrible.'

'Oh, Mum, it was never exactly horrible,' protested Helen, though sometimes it truly had been. Applecore Cottage was quaint and charming, but her father's frequent black moods did indeed float like a noxious gas under doors and through cracks, no matter that he shut himself away, both for his family's sake (to protect them from him) and for his (to protect him from their female philistinism and general treachery) and her mother's eyes had been too often red-rimmed, thus somehow dimming the lustre of the copper pans which hung so prettily in the kitchen, throwing back the light from latticed windows; at such times Helen had longed, longed just to get away. Yet at other times they'd been a close family, sharing thought, feeling, aspirations; the two women intensely loyal to John Lally's genius, gladly putting up with hardship and penury on that account, understanding that the painter's temperament was as difficult for him to endure as it was for them. But then Helen had gone – off to Art School, and a mysterious life in London, and Evelyn had to take the full undiluted force, not of her husband's attention, for he gave her little, but of his circling, angry energy, and began to understand that though he would survive, and his paintings too, she, Evelyn, might very well not. She felt far older and more tired than she should. What was more, she understood only too well that if John Lally had to choose between his art and her, he would undoubtedly choose his art. If he loved her, she once told Helen in an uncharacteristic burst of anger, it was as a man with a

Fay Weldon

wooden leg loved that leg. He couldn't do without it, but wished he could.

Now she smiled sweetly at Helen, and patted her daughter's small firm white hand with her large loose one and said, 'It's nice of you to say so.'

'You always did your best,' said Helen, and then, panicky – 'Why are you talking as if we're saying goodbye?'

'Because if you're with Clifford Wexford,' said Evelyn, 'it is, more or less.'

'He shouldn't have burst in on us the way he did. I'm sorry Clifford hit him but he was provoked.'

'It all goes deeper than that,' said Evelyn.

'He'll get over it,' said Helen.

'No,' said her mother. 'You do have to choose.' It occurred to Helen then that with Clifford for a lover, what did she want with a father.

'Why don't you just leave home, Mum,' she said, 'and let Dad get on with his genius on his own? Don't you see it's absurd. Living with a man who locks himself in and has to have his food from a plate left on a garage window-sill.'

'But, darling,' said Evelyn, 'he's *painting*!' And Helen knew it was no use, and, in any case, hardly wanted it to be. It's one thing to suggest to your parents that they part – and many do – quite horrific if they actually act upon that suggestion.

'It's probably best,' said Evelyn to her own daughter, 'if you just stay out of the way for a while,' and Helen was more than ever glad she had Clifford, for a feeling of hurt and terror welled up inside her and had to be subdued. It looked for a moment as if her own mother was abandoning her. But of course that was nonsense. They shared a particularly novel wholewheat and honey biscuit, which Evelyn quite liked, and shared the bill, and once outside, smiled and kissed and went their separate ways, Evelyn no longer with a child, Helen no longer with a mother.

PROTECTIVE CUSTODY

'Good Lord,' said Clifford, when Helen reported the conversation to him that night, 'whatever you do, don't encourage your mother to leave home!'

They were having supper in bed, trying not to get the black sheets sticky with taramasalata, whipped up by Clifford from cod's roe, lemon juice and cream, and cheaper than buying it already made up. Not even love could induce Clifford to abandon his habits of economy – some called it parsimony but why not use the kinder word? Clifford insisted on living well, and also took pleasure in never spending a penny more than he had to in so doing.

'Why not, Clifford?'

Sometimes Clifford confused Helen, just as he confused Angie, but Helen had the quickness and sense to ask for guidance. And unlike Angie, not being stubborn, she was a quick learner. How pretty she looked this evening; enchanting! All thin soft arms and plump naked shoulders, her cream silk slip barely covering a swelling breast – cautiously nibbling, with little, even teeth, the edges of her Bath Oliver, careful not to spill the taramasalata, made by Clifford perhaps just a fraction too liquid.

'Because your mother is your father's inspiration,' said Clifford, 'and though that's hard luck on your mother, sacrifices must be made in the cause of art.

Fay Weldon

Art is more important than the individual: even than the painter who creates it: your father would be the first to acknowledge that, monster though he is. Moreover, a painter needs his gestalt – the peculiar combination of circumstances which enables him to express his particular vision of the universe. Your father's gestalt, more's the pity, includes Applecore Cottage, your mother, quarrels with neighbours, paranoia about the art world in general and me in particular. It also until now has included you. You've been snatched away. That's shock enough. It's driven him into the garage: with any luck we'll see a change of style when he emerges. Let's just hope that the new is more saleable than the old.'

He carefully removed Helen's Bath Oliver, put it to one side and kissed her salty mouth.

'I suppose,' said Helen, 'you didn't move me in here with you just to make my father's paintings easier to sell?' and he laughed, but there was a little pause before he did, as if he himself almost wondered. Truly successful people often act by an instinct which works to their advantage: they don't have to plot, or scheme. They just follow their noses, and life itself bows down before them. Clifford loved Helen. Of course he did. Nevertheless, John Lally's daughter! Part of a gestalt which needed a shock, a shove, a shaking up –

But they forgot these matters soon enough, and Clifford also forgot to say that Angie Wellbrook's father had called him from Johannesburg during the week.

'I thought I should warn you,' boomed the sad, powerful voice. 'My daughter's on the war-path.'

'What about?' Clifford had been light and cool.

'God knows. She doesn't like the Old Masters. She says the future lies with Moderns. She says Leonardo's is throwing its money away. What did you do? Stand

The Hearts and Lives of Men

her up? No, don't tell me. I don't want to know. Just remember that, though I'm a major shareholder, she acts for me in the UK and there's no controlling her. She's a shrewd girl though a pain in the arse.'

Clifford thanked him and promised to send him the excellent reviews of the Bosch exhibition and press reports of the unprecedented queues outside it, assured him that his investment was well protected, and that the furtherance and support of contemporary art was becoming increasingly part of Leonardo's provenance – in other words that Angie was out on a precarious limb. Then he rang Angie and asked her out to lunch. He forgot to tell Helen about this too. But he left her languid on the bed in such a sensuous swoon he knew well enough she'd be only just recovering when he came back that evening.

Angie and Clifford went to Claridges. Mini-skirts were just coming in. Angie turned up wearing a beige trousersuit in fine, supple suede, and asked to be shown to Clifford's table. She'd spent the morning in the beauty parlour but the hand of the girl who inserted her false eyelashes had slipped and one of Angie's eyes was red, so she had to wear dark glasses, the wearing of which other than on ski slopes she knew Clifford despised. It made her cross.

'I'm so sorry,' said the Head Waiter, rashly, 'but it is not our policy to allow ladies in trousers into the Grand Restaurant.'

'Really?' enquired Angie, dangerously, made even crosser.

'If you will allow me to take you to the Luncheon Bar –'

'No,' said Angie. 'You just take the trousers.'

And there and then she undid them, stepped out of them, handed them to the Head Waiter, and went on in, mini-skirted, to join Clifford. A pity, Clifford thought, Angie's legs were not better. They quite spoiled the gesture. All the same, he was impressed. So were many of the lunchers. Angie received a round of applause as she sat down.

'I know I'm a bastard,' Clifford said, over quails' eggs, 'I know I let you down, I know I'm a cad and a bounder, but the fact is, I've fallen in love.' And he raised his clear blue eyes to hers, and finding them covered by dark glasses, straightaway removed them.

'One of your eyes is red,' he remarked. 'Quite horrid!' Somehow the gesture, the touch, the remark, made her believe that in love with someone else he might be, but matters between him and her were not finished. She was right.

'So where does that leave us?' she asked, one hand now covering the erring eye, scraping a little fattening mayonnaise from her egg with the knife in the other. He thought that if anything she was too skinny. In his bed she'd kept herself well covered with the black sheet and with good reason. (Thinness, in those days, was not as fashionable as now. A pattern of ribs beneath the skin was seen as unsightly.) Helen, perfectly at ease in her body, could cheerfully expose any part, in any position. Yet Angie's very reticences had their charm.

'Friends,' he said.

'You mean,' she said, 'you don't want my father taking his millions out of Leonardo's.'

'How well you know me,' he said, and laughed, looking directly at her with his bright knowledgeable eyes, and this time he moved her shielding hand, and her heart turned over, but what was the use?

'They'll be my millions eventually,' said Angie. 'And

The Hearts and Lives of Men

leaving you and me right out of it, I don't like seeing them in Leonardo's. Art's a high-risk business.'

'Not any more,' said Clifford Wexford, 'not now I'm in charge.'

'But, Clifford, you're not.'

'I will be,' said Clifford.

She believed him. A crowd of photographers and reporters now clustered at Claridges' door. Word had got round. They wanted a glimpse of Angie's legs or, failing that, of the King of the Waiters discomposed: staff barred their way. The general uproar impressed Clifford. Publicity always did.

Angie was not ungratified, either. Well, she thought, Clifford will wear out Helen soon enough. Helen can't command the press, as I can. Helen, the frame-maker's daughter. Just another pretty face! Penniless, powerless, without place in the world except by courtesy of Clifford. He'd soon get bored. Angie decided to forgive Clifford and be content just to hate Helen. Should she say something scathing, unforgettable, about her rival? No. Clifford was too shrewd. He'd see through it. She'd go the other way instead.

'She's a sweet, pretty girl,' she said, 'and just what you need. Though you'll have to sharpen up her dress sense a little. She really shouldn't go round looking so humble. But I give up. I give in. I'll be yours and Helen's friend. And the crits of the Bosch exhibition were really impressive, Clifford. I may have been wrong. I'll give Dad a call and reassure him.'

Clifford stood, moved round to where Angie sat, lifted her dull-complexioned face with its poor eye, and kissed her firmly on her lips. It was her reward. It was not enough, but something. She would claim what she deserved, what she had been promised, when the time was ripe. There was, she supposed, no hurry. She would wait, decades if she had to.

While Angie lunched with Clifford, Evelyn was on the phone to Helen.

'Oh, Mum,' said Helen, gratefully. 'I thought you'd given up on me!'

'Well, I thought you'd better know just how upset your father is,' her mother said. 'He's left the garage, and now he's up in the attic, cutting up his old canvasses with the garden shears. *Fox Plus Chicken Pieces* is in shreds. He threw a section of *Beached Whale With Vultures* downstairs. He's going to be so upset when he calms down and finds out what he's done. He was on the whale painting for two years, Helen. You remember? All through your "A" levels.'

'I think you should go next door, Mum, and wait till he calms down.'

'They're getting so sick of me next door.'

'Of course they're not, Mum.'

'It is so important for your father not to be upset.'

'Mum, don't you see, I am the excuse for his upset, not the reason for his upset.'

'No, Helen, I'm afraid I can't see it that way.'

At three-fifteen Helen rang, crying, through to Leonardo's and left a message for Clifford to call home urgently. But he did not arrive back in the office until five o'clock. How he had been spending his time between two and five, reader, I am not going to divulge in detail. He had not meant such a thing to happen. Let us just say Angie kept a suite at Claridges for her convenience when shopping in Bond Street – her house in Belgravia seeming to her too far from the heart of things, and her actions too closely observed by the butler and other staff – and that opportunity is, if not all, at least four-fifths of

The Hearts and Lives of Men

illicit and unexpected sexual congress. And Clifford felt he ought to make amends and, to his credit, was amused and more impressed by the newshounds at her heels than he ever had been by her father's millions. Besides, he was so newly in love with Helen the emotion had not had time to affect a deep-rooted habit of life – that is to say, of taking his pleasures when and as he usefully found them.

Be all that as it may, come five-thirty, Clifford reacted strongly and instantly not so much to Helen's tears as to her account of her father's behaviour. *Fox Plus Chicken Pieces* was a minor and flawed piece but *Beached Whale With Vultures*, though unlikeable on account of its subject matter – rotting flesh, stretched in glistening strands across an almost ethereal canvas – was a fine major work and Clifford was not having it under attack. His lawyers were round at Judge Percibar's within the hour – the eloquent Percibar a lifelong friend of Otto Wexford, Clifford's father – and an injunction taken out restraining John Lally from damaging what turned out to be Leonardo's property, inasmuch as, or so they claimed, the artist benefited by a retainer from that august institution. And by the next morning, after a police car and a Leonardo's van had turned up at the cottage, seven John Lally canvases had been transferred to Leonardo's vaults, plus the shreds, recovered from the garden, of *Fox Plus Chicken Pieces*, and catalogued thus:

1 *Beached Whale With Vultures* – damaged
2 *Massacre of the Turtles* – in fine condition
3 *St Peter and Cripple at Heaven's Gate* – scratched
4 *The Feast of Eyes* – stained (coffee?)
5 *Kitten with Hand* – stained (bird droppings?)
6 *Dead Flowerpiece* (in fine condition)

Fay Weldon

7 *Landscape of Bones* (slashed)
8 *Fox Plus Chicken Pieces* (remnant)

The removal was done while John Lally slept off the effect of shock, overwork, temper and home-made wine. Evelyn tried to wake him as the Leonardo's team tramped up and down the steep narrow stairs to the attic, manoeuvring the wide canvasses with some difficulty, but there was no waking him. She left a note and went to neighbours.

Reader, if you know even an amateur painter, or if you daub or dabble yourself, you will understand how any painter worth his salt hates to be parted from his paintings, in just the same way as a mother hates to be parted from her children. This leaves the painter in a terrible fix. If he doesn't sell not only does he not eat, but he paints himself out of house and home: there is the enormous simple practical matter of *space*: where are the paintings to be kept? Yet if he does sell, and so makes room, it is like having a chunk of living flesh torn away. And it is so agitating. What kind of home is the work going to? Will it be safe? Was it bought because it was truly appreciated, or merely because it matched the wallpaper? Not, of course, that John Lally had many worries on the latter score. There was never any question of a Lally canvas *blending*. He is what is called a gallery painter, fit for display on large bare walls and respectful viewing in public places, where little cries of shock and awe and distaste can be quickly sopped up by the warm, gently circulating, stuffy mausoleum air. (And what kind of fate, raged John Lally, is that for a painting? *Kitten with Hand* – the fingers with claws, the paw with nails – had for a time been hoisted into the air between two pine trees in the garden of

The Hearts and Lives of Men

Applecore Cottage, the better for the birds of the air to admire it, mere earth-swarming humans being so lacking in the capacity for proper appreciation.) And as for the small private galleries, run as they are by undiscriminating rogues who will take as much as fifty per cent commission, these are the shit-holes of the Art World. Go to any opening, and see the phoneys and the poseurs gawping and gaping and very publicly writing out their cheques. On the whole John Lally preferred simply to give paintings away to friends. Then at least he could control who owned them, on whose wall they hung. Friends? What friends? For as quickly as his occasional charm won them, his paranoia and temper would drive them away. There were few enough about qualified to be Lally recipients. This was why, driven to fever pitch by the impossibility of solving the problem, or so John Lally saw it, he had consented to accept a retainer from Leonardo's. And Leonardo's (that is to say, Clifford Wexford) had done him other favours: taken a few canvasses off his hands; had the broken-down garage rebuilt, damp-coursed and air-conditioned so that other paintings could be safely stacked and stored. They had let window lights into the attic roof the better to illuminate his work with good natural north light. If John Lally chose to paint in the garage and store in the attic no great harm would be done. But if John Lally took shears to his canvasses, Leonardo's would step in to claim what turned out, thanks to the Wexford small print, to be Leonardo's property.

And John Lally had, in a way, trusted Clifford, while yet hating and despising him, because in spite of everything Clifford had some sort of proper response to his work and he'd felt sure that whatever else befell, he would at least never do what some collectors did –

put the paintings in a bank vault somewhere for safe keeping. This being to the painter the same as rendering him blind and deaf.

And now Clifford had done exactly this. And not, John Lally was convinced, when he roused himself from his stupor, and found the paintings gone, simply in order to preserve the canvasses – they had survived many such a storm before and even as he shredded *Fox Plus Chicken Pieces* he was working out a new improved version in his head – but to be revenged. John Lally the impoverished artist, breaking down, splintering Clifford Wexford's bedroom door, bursting in upon him – no, it was not forgotten, let alone forgiven! No. This was why eight fine paintings were now immured in Leonardo's vault, while Clifford smiled and said lightly, 'It's for John Lally's own good,' and stretched his white daughter yet again upon the black satanic sheets. It was the artist's punishment.

It was fifteen days before Evelyn dared to creep back into Applecore Cottage and start washing up and sweeping up again, and three months before life returned to anything resembling normal. John Lally then got on with *The Rape by the Sabine Women* in which he depicted the latter as insatiable harpies. A silly idea, but well executed: he painted it on the wall of the hen-house, on the grounds that it could then hardly end up in Leonardo's vaults. Rather, wind and rain would presently obscure the painting altogether.

LITTLE NELL'S INHERITANCE

For six weeks now little Nell snuggled tenderly and safely in Helen's womb. She had inherited at least a

The Hearts and Lives of Men

degree of her maternal grandfather's artistic talent, but not, you will be relieved to hear, his temper or his neuroses: she had all and more of her maternal grandmother's sweetness, but not her tendency to the acute masochism which so often goes with it. She had her father's energy and wit and not his, well, sneakiness. She was all set up to have her mother's looks: but, unlike her mother, to feel it below her dignity to lie. All this, of course, was simply the luck of the draw: and not just Nell's luck but ours as well – all of us who were to encounter her in later life. But our Nell had another quality too – her capacity to attract towards her the most untoward, even dangerous events, and the most disagreeable people. Perhaps it was in her stars: an event proneness inherited from Clifford's father Otto – his early life, too, was lived in hazard – or perhaps it was, as my own mother would have it, that where you have angels, you have demons too. Evil circles good, as if trying to contain it: good being the powerful, moving, active force: evil the nagging, restraining one. Well, you must make up your own mind as you read Nell's story. This is a Christmas tale, and Christmas is a time for believing in good, rather than bad: for seeing the latter, not the former, on the winning side.

As for Helen, she suspected that perhaps Nell, or someone, had come into existence, inasmuch as she suffered from a faint dizziness which affected her whenever she stood too suddenly, and because her breasts were so swollen and sore she could scarcely forget they were there – which most women do, most of the time, unless and until they're pregnant. These symptoms, mind you, or so she told herself, might be due to love, and nothing more. The fact was that Helen didn't want to be pregnant. Not yet. There was far too much to be done, seen, explored, thought about in the world which so suddenly and newly included Clifford.

And how could she, Helen, scarcely yet herself properly in the world, bring someone else along into it? And how could Clifford love her if she was pregnant; that is to say sick, swollen, tearful – as her mother had been during her last disastrous pregnancy, only five years back. That baby had miscarried, horribly and bloodily late in the pregnancy, and Helen had been horribly sorry and bloodily relieved when it happened, and confused by her own conflicting emotions. And John Lally had sat and held her mother's hand, with a tenderness she had never seen before, and she had found herself jealous – and planned there and then to leave home after 'A' levels and go to Art College, and Get Out, Get Out –

Well now, what it added up to was that Helen now just wanted to forget the past and love Clifford and prepare for a glittering future and *not* be pregnant. Because Clifford had asked her to marry him. Or had he asked her? Or just somehow said, some time in the middle of one of their lively, enchanted nights, part sticky, part silky, part velvet black, part glowing lamp-light, 'I must tell my parents about all this. They'll want some kind of marriage ceremony, they're like that,' and so, casually, the matter had been settled. Since the bride's parents were so clearly incapable of arranging anything, it would be left to the bridegroom's. Besides, the latter's income exceeded the former's by a ratio of 100 to 1, or thereabouts.

'Perhaps we should just be married quietly,' Helen said to Otto's wife, Cynthia, when the whens and hows of the wedding were discussed. Clifford had taken her down to the family home in Sussex to introduce her for the first time and say they were to be married

The Hearts and Lives of Men

all on the one day. Impetuous lad! The house was Georgian and stood in twelve acres. Dannemore Court, reader. Its gardens are opened to the public once a year. Perhaps you know it. The place is famous for its azaleas.

'Why a quiet wedding?' asked Cynthia. 'There is nothing to be ashamed of. Or is there?' Cynthia was sixty, looked forty and acted thirty. She was small, dark, elegant, vivacious and un-English, for all her tweeds.

'Oh no,' said Helen, although she had risen in the night twice to go to the bathroom, and in those days, before the pill was in common use, the symptoms of pregnancy were all too well known to every young woman. And being pregnant, and unmarried, was in most circles still something to be ashamed of.

'So let's make all the fuss we possibly can of such an important occasion,' said Cynthia, 'and as for who pays – poofey! All that etiquette is so stuffy and boring, don't you think?'

That was in the big drawing-room after lunch. Cynthia was arranging spring flowers in a bowl: they were fresh from the garden, and of amazing variety. She seemed to Helen more concerned over their welfare than that of her son.

But later Cynthia did say to Clifford, 'Darling, are you sure you know what you're doing? You've never been married before, and she's so young, and it's all so sudden.'

'I know what I'm doing,' said Clifford, gratified by her concern. It was seldom shown. His mother was always busy, looking after his father's needs, or flowers in vases, or making mysterious phone calls, and dressing up and rushing off. His father would smile fondly after her; what pleased his wife pleased him. There seemed no room for Clifford, either as a child or now he was grown, between them. They made no space for him. They squeezed him out.

'In my experience of men,' said Cynthia (and Clifford thought sadly, yes, that's quite considerable) 'when a man says he knows what he's doing it means he doesn't.'

'She's John Lally's daughter,' said Clifford. 'He's one of the greatest painters this country has. If not the greatest.'

'Well I've never heard of him,' said Cynthia, on whose walls were a minor Manet and a nice collection of Constable sketches. Otto Wexford was a director of The Distillers' Company: the days of the Wexford poverty were a long time ago.

'You will,' said Clifford, 'one day. If I have anything to do with it.'

'Darling,' said Cynthia, 'painters are great because they have a great talent, not because you or Leonardo's make them so. You are not God.'

Clifford just raised his eyebrows and said, 'No? I mean to run Leonardo's, and in the Art World that makes me God.'

'Well,' said Cynthia, 'I can't help feeling someone like Angie Wellbrook, with a couple of goldmines behind her —'

'Six —' said Clifford.

'— would have been a less, shall we say, surprising choice. Not that your Helen isn't very sweet.'

It was agreed they were to be married on Midsummer's Day, in the village church (Norman, plus lych-gate) and have the reception in a big marquee on the lawn, for all the world as if the Wexfords were landed gentry.

The Hearts and Lives of Men

Which of course they were not. Otto Wexford, builder, had fled with his Jewish wife Cynthia from Denmark to London in 1941, with their young son. By the end of the war – which Cynthia spent in a munitions factory, wearing a headscarf, and Clifford running wild as an evacuee in Somerset – Otto was a Major in the Intelligence Forces and a man with many influential friends. Whether or not he actually left the Secret Service was never made clear to his family but, be that as it may, he had risen briskly through the world of post-war finance and property development, and was now a man of wealth, power and discernment, and kept a Rolls-Royce as well as horses in the stable block of his Georgian country house, and his wife rode to hounds and had affairs with the neighbouring gentry. All the same, they never quite 'belonged'. Perhaps it was just that their eyes were too bright: they were too lively: they read novels: they said surprising things. Call to tea, and you might find the stable-hand sitting in the drawing-room, chatting, as bold as brass. No one refused the wedding invitation, all the same. The Wexfords were liked, though cautiously: young Clifford Wexford was already a name: too flashy for his own good but entertaining, and the champagne would be plentiful, and the food good, though un-English.

'Mother,' said Clifford to Cynthia, on the Sunday morning, 'what does Father say about my marrying Helen?' For Otto had said very little at all. Clifford waited for approval or disapproval, but none came. Otto was friendly, courteous and concerned, but as if Clifford was the child of close friends, rather than his own and only son.

'Why should he say anything? You're old enough to know your own mind.'

Fay Weldon

'Does he find her attractive?' It was the wrong question. He was not sure why he asked it. Only with his father was Clifford so much at a loss.

'Darling, I am the wrong person to ask,' was all she replied, and he felt he had offended her as well. Though she was cheerful and flighty and charming enough all day, heaven knows: Otto went hunting: Cynthia stayed home especially to be nice to Helen.

'This house is like a backdrop,' Clifford complained to Helen on the Sunday night. They were not leaving until the Monday morning. They had been put in separate bedrooms, but on the same corridor, so naturally, and as was expected, Clifford had made his way to Helen's room.

'It isn't real. It isn't home. It is a cover. You know my father's a spy?'

'So you've told me,' but Helen found it hard to believe.

'Well, what do you make of him? Do you find him attractive?'

'He's your father. I don't think of him like that. He's old.'

'Very well then. Does he find you attractive?'

'How would I know?'

'Women always know things like that.'

'No they don't.'

They quarrelled about it, and Clifford returned to his own room, without making love to her. He did not, in any case, like his mother's expectation that he would, putting them in separate rooms, but near. He felt insulted by her, and irritated by Helen.

But early in the morning Helen crept into his room: she was laughing and teasing, unimpressed by his bad moods, as she usually was in the first flush of their relationship – and he forgot he was angry. He thought

The Hearts and Lives of Men

Helen would make up for what his parents had never given him – a feeling of ease and closeness, of not talking behind his back, conspiring against him. When he and Helen had children he would make sure of a proper space for them, between the pair of them. Meanwhile, close together in their white-sheeted bed, in the master bedroom, Cynthia and Otto talked.

'You should take more interest in him,' said Cynthia. 'He feels your lack of interest.'

'I wish he'd stop fidgeting: he's always fidgeting,' said Otto, who moved slowly, serenely and powerfully through life.

'He was born like that,' said Cynthia. So he had been, nine months to the day after his parents' meeting, as if protesting at the suddenness and strangeness of it all. His mother barely seventeen, wild cast-off daughter of a wealthy banking family: his father, already at twenty running his own small firm of builders. Otto had been up a ladder, replacing glass in a conservatory, and had looked down at Cynthia, looking up, and that had been that: neither of them had expected the baby, nor the pursuing vengeance of Cynthia's family: snatching contracts from under Otto's nose; condemning them to poverty and a perpetual moving on: nor would it have altered their behaviour had they known. And no one expected the overwhelming vengeance of the German occupation, the deportation and murder of the Jews: Cynthia's family got to America; Cynthia and Otto went underground, joined the Resistance, Clifford handed from household to household the while: until all three were shipped to England, the better for Otto to function. The habit of secrecy was never lost for either of them. Cynthia's love affairs were all to do with it: Otto knew it and put up with it. They were no insult to him: merely the addict's passion for intrigue. He got his fixes with MI5: but where could she get hers?

'I wish he'd find himself a more solid occupation,' said Otto. 'A picture dealer! Art is not for profiteering.'

'He had a hard childhood,' said Cynthia. 'He feels the need to survive, and to survive he has to scheme. It is our example: it is what we did, you and I, and he watched us.'

'But he is the child of peace,' said Otto. 'And we were the children of war. Why is it that the products of peace are always so ignoble?'

'Ignoble!'

'He has no moral concern, no political principle; he is eaten up by self-interest.'

'Oh dear,' said Cynthia, but she did not argue. 'Well,' she said, 'I hope this one makes him happy. Do you find her attractive?'

'I see what he sees in her,' said Otto cautiously. 'But she'll lead him a dance.'

'She's soft and natural, not like me. She'll make a good mother. I look forward to grandchildren. We may do better with the next generation.'

'We've waited long enough,' said Otto.

'I just hope he settles down.'

'He's too fidgety to settle down,' said Otto, serenely, and they both slept.

Helen wept a little when she returned to Clifford's home, Clifford's bed.

'What's the matter?' he asked.

'I just wish my parents were coming to my wedding,' she said, 'that's all.' But in her heart she was glad. Her father would only make some kind of scene: her mother turn up in the old blue ribbed cotton dress, her eyes red-rimmed from the previous night's row. No. Better forget

The Hearts and Lives of Men

them. If only now she weren't beginning to feel sick in the mornings. There still might well be reasons – the change in routine, the nights of wild love-making, the many dinners out – and she so accustomed to frugal student's fare, or the pork, beans and cider-if-you're-lucky routine of the Lally household – but it was beginning to seem unlikely. No quick pregnancy tests in those days: no vacuum abortions on the side. Just, for the former, a toad which got injected with your urine and laid eggs and died forty-eight hours later if you *were* pregnant, and laid eggs and survived if you weren't, and for the latter an illegal operation which you, like the toad, had to be lucky, or very rich, to survive.

But of course the mere fact of worrying could so upset your cycle you never knew where you were. Oh, reader, what days! But at least then the penalty for untoward sex was a new life and not, as it can be now, a disagreeable and disgraceful death.

Another month and Helen could not disguise from herself the fact that she was in fact and in truth pregnant, and that she didn't want to be, and that she didn't want Clifford to know, let alone his parents, and that to go to doctors (two were required) for a legal abortion would require more lies about how more damaging to her health and sanity pregnancy would be than she – so sane and healthy – could sustain, and that she couldn't tell her friends because she couldn't trust them not to gossip, and her father would kill her if he knew and her mother simply commit suicide – round and round the thoughts flew in Helen's head, and there was no one she could turn to for help and advice, until she thought of Angie.

Now, reader, you may think this is no more than Helen deserved, to turn for help to a woman who bore her nothing but malice, however good – and she was *very* good – at disguising it Angie had so far been: giving little dinners for the handsome young couple, chatting away to Helen on the phone, recommending hairdressers and so on – but I do beg you to feel as forgiving as you can about Helen and this initial rejecting of her newly conceived child, our beloved Nell.

Helen was young and this was her first child. She had no idea, as established mothers have, of what she would be throwing away, losing along with the bathwater. It is easier for the childless woman to contemplate the termination of a pregnancy, than for those who already have children. So, please, continue to bear with Helen. Forgive her. She will learn better, with the years, I promise you.

GOING TO ANGIE FOR HELP

Helen rose out of her snowy white bed one morning, holding her pale, smooth stomach, which was in inner turmoil, and telephoned Angie.

'Angie,' she said, 'please come round. I have to talk to someone.'

Angie came round. Angie walked up the stairs and into the bedroom where she had spent four memorable if actually rather unsatisfactory nights with Clifford, in all their eleven months together: well, not exactly together, but in the promise of – eventually – together, or so she had assumed.

'So, what's the matter?' Angie asked, and noticed, for Helen was feeling too ill to so much as fasten her brown silk nightie properly, that Helen's white, full breasts were fuller than ever, almost too full, and felt for once rather proud of the chic discretion of her own, and quite

The Hearts and Lives of Men

confident that, if she managed this right, Clifford would eventually be hers.

Helen didn't reply. Helen flung herself back upon the fur bedspread and lay crumpled and dishevelled but still beautiful, and wept instead of speaking.

'It can only be one thing,' said Angie. 'You're pregnant. You don't want to be. And you don't dare tell Clifford.'

Helen did not attempt to deny it. Angie was wearing red hot-pants, and Helen did not even have the spirit to marvel at Angie's nerve, considering her legs, in so doing. Presently words formed out of tears.

'I can't have a baby,' wept Helen. 'Not now. I'm too young. I wouldn't know what to do with one.'

'What any sensible person does with babies,' said Angie, 'is hand them over to nannies.'

And this, of course, in the world in which Angie moved, was just what mothers did. But for all that Helen was only twenty-two and (as we have seen) as selfish and irresponsible as any other pretty, wilful girl of her age, she at least knew better than Angie in this respect. She knew that the handing over of a baby would be no easy matter. A baby draws love out of its mother, like a Christmas streamer out of a box, and the necessities occasioned by that love can change the mother's life altogether: make her as desperate, savage and impulsive as any wild animal.

'Please help me, Angie,' said Helen. 'I can't have the baby. Only I don't know where to go and anyway abortions cost money and I don't have any.'

Nor had she, poor girl. Clifford was not the kind of man to put money in a woman's bank account and not ask for proof of where every penny had gone, not even if that woman was his legitimate fiancée. Clifford might eat at the best restaurants, where it was useful to be seen, and might sleep between the finest, most expensive cotton sheets, because he liked to be comfortable, but he kept very careful accounts. So this had to be done without Clifford's knowing. What a fix Helen was in! Just consider the times. Only twenty years ago, and a pregnant girl, unmarried, was very much on her own: no Pregnancy Advice Centres then; no payments from the State, just trouble whichever way she turned. Helen's best friend, Lily, at seventeen, had an apparently successful abortion but after two days had been rushed to hospital with septicaemia. She'd hovered between life and death for some six hours, and Helen sat on one side of the bed and a policeman sat on the other, and he was waiting to charge Lily for procuring an illegal abortion operation. Lily died, and so was spared the punishment. Probably two years inside, the policeman said, and no more than she deserved. 'Think of the poor baby!' he said. Poor little Lily, was all Helen could think. Now how frightened she found herself: frightened to have the baby, frightened not to.

Angie thought fast. She was wearing fashionable hot-pants but did not (as we know) have the best legs in the world. They were podgy around the knees, and gnarled about the ankles; and as for her face, well, the thick make-up the times required was unkind and the hot South African sun had toughened her skin, and somehow greyed it, and she had a thick, fleshy nose. Only her eyes were large, green and beautiful. Helen, curled up on the bed, tearful and unhappy, soft, pale, female, tugging at her brown silk nightie (suddenly too small) in the attempt to make it cover her properly, and altogether too beautiful, inspired in Angie a great desire for revenge. It is really not fair that some women

The Hearts and Lives of Men

should have the luck of looks, and others not. You must agree.

'Darling Helen,' said Angie. 'Of course I'll help you! I know an address. An excellent clinic. Simply everyone goes there. Very safe, very quiet, very discreet. The de Waldo Clinic. I'll lend you the money. It just has to be done. Clifford wouldn't want you pregnant at his wedding. Everyone would think he'd married you because he had to! And it's going to be a white wedding too, isn't it, and simply everyone looks at waists.'

Simply everyone, simply everyone! Enough to frighten anyone.

Angie booked Helen into the de Waldo Clinic that very afternoon. Helen had the misfortune – rather expected by Angie – of being put into the care of a certain Dr Runcorn, a small, plump, fiftyish doctor with pebble glasses through which he stared at Helen's most private parts, while his stubby fingers moved lingeringly (or so it seemed to Helen) over her defenceless breasts and body. What could the poor girl do about it? Nothing. For in handing herself over to the de Waldo Clinic it seemed that Helen had surrendered dignity, privacy and honour: she felt she had no right to brush Dr Runcorn's hand away. She deserved no better than its tacky assault. Was she not doing away with Clifford's baby without his knowing? Was she not outside the law? Whichever way she looked, there was guilt, and Dr Runcorn's water-glinting eyes.

'We don't want to leave the little intruder in there any longer than we have to,' said Dr Runcorn, in his wheezy, nasal voice. 'At ten tomorrow we'll set about getting you back to normal! A shame for a girl as pretty as you to waste a single day of her youth.'

The little intruder! Well, he wasn't so far out. That's

Fay Weldon

what Nell felt like, to Helen. But the phrase still made her squirm. She said nothing. She knew well enough that she depended on Dr Runcorn's goodwill as well as on his greed. No matter how much he charged, his clinic was always full. If he 'did you' tomorrow, rather than in four weeks' time, you were, quite simply, in luck. For the first time in her life Helen truly understood necessity, truly suffered, and held her tongue.

'Next time you go to a party,' said Dr Runcorn, 'remember me and don't get up to mischief. You've been a very naughty girl. You'll stay in the clinic tonight, so we can keep an eye on you.'

And a very terrible night it was. Helen was never to forget it. The thick yellowy carpets, the pale green wash-basin, the TV and radio headphones did nothing to disguise the nature of the place she was in. As well train roses up the abattoir wall! And she had to call Clifford, and tell another lie.

It was six o'clock: Clifford was at Leonardo's, negotiating the purchase of an anonymous painting of the Florentine School with a delegation from the Uffizi Gallery. Clifford had a shrewd notion the painting was a Botticelli: he was banking on it, paying over the odds to obtain it, but not too much in case they looked too hard at what they were selling. Just sometimes the Italians, accustomed as they were to a sheer superfluity of cultural richness, did miss something wonderful and extraordinary beneath their very noses. Clifford's blue eyes were bluer than ever: he tossed back the wedge of his thick fair hair so it glinted – he had grown his hair long, as was the fashion then amongst the sophisticated young, and was not thirty-five still young? He wore jeans and a casual shirt. The Italians, portly and in their fifties, displayed their cultural and worldly achievement with formal suits, gold rings and ruby cuff-links. But they were at a disadvantage. They were confused. Clifford meant to confuse them. What was this young man, who belonged so much to the present, doing within these solid elderly marble portals? It unbalanced the Italians' judgement. Why was Clifford Wexford of all people foraging back into the past? What did he mean by it? Did he know more than they, or less? Was he offering too much: were they asking too little? Where were they? Perhaps life was not serious and difficult after all? Perhaps the plums went to the frivolous? The telephone rang. Clifford answered it. The men from the Uffizi clustered together and conferred, recognizing a reprieve when they heard one.

'Darling,' said Helen brightly, 'I know you hate being disturbed in the office, but I won't be at Coffee Place when you get back tonight. My mum rang to say I was allowed home. So I'm going to stay at Applecore Cottage for a couple of nights. She says she might even come to the wedding!'

'Take garlic and a crucifix,' said Clifford. 'And ward your father off!'

Helen laughed lightly and said, 'Don't be such a goose!' and rang off. The men from the Uffizi raised their price a full thousand pounds. Clifford sighed.

The phone rang again. This time it was Angie. Since such considerable millions of her father's money were invested in Leonardo's the switchboard put through her call. This privilege was accorded only to Helen, Angie and Clifford's stockbroker; the last played a chancy game of instant decisions and played it very well, but sometimes needed a quick yes or no.

'Clifford,' said Angie, 'it's me, and I want to have breakfast with you tomorrow.'

'Breakfast, Angie! These days,' he said, trying to keep the Uffizi mesmerized with his smile, and hoping Angie would get off the line quickly, 'I have breakfast with Helen. You know that.'

'Tomorrow morning you won't,' said Angie, 'because she won't be there.'

'How do you know that?' He sensed danger. 'She's gone to visit her mother. Hasn't she?'

'No she hasn't,' said Angie flatly, and would elaborate no further and Clifford agreed to meet the next morning at 8 a.m. for breakfast at Coffee Place. The early hour did not, as he had hoped, discourage her. He'd suggested Claridges but she said he might need to scream and shout a bit so he'd be better off at home. Then she rang off. The men from the Uffizi pushed up the price a further five hundred and would not be deflected and by now Clifford had lost his nerve. He reckoned the two phone calls had cost him fifteen hundred pounds. When the Italians had gone, smiling, Clifford, unsmiling, made a quick phone call to Johnnie, his father's stable-man and chauffeur – a man who'd been with Otto in the war, and still had 00 rating – and asked him to visit the Lally household and investigate. Johnnie reported back at midnight. Helen was not in the house. There was only a middle-aged woman, crying into the washing up, and a man in the garage painting what looked like a gigantic wasp stinging a naked girl.

RESCUE!

Clifford spent as bad a night as did Helen; one that he was never to forget. Into the great bubbling cauldron of distress we call jealousy goes dollop after dollop of every

The Hearts and Lives of Men

humiliation we have ever endured, every insecurity suffered, every loss we have known and feared; in goes our sense of doubt, futility; in goes the prescience of decay, death, finality. And floating to the top, like scum on jam, the knowledge that all is lost, in particular the hope that some day, somehow, we can properly love and trust and be properly loved and trusted in our turn. Plop! into Clifford's cauldron went the fear that he had only ever been admired and envied, and never truly liked, not even by his parents. Plop! the knowledge that he would never be the man his father was; that his mother saw him as some kind of curiosity. Plop! the memory of a call-girl who'd laughed at him, despising him more than he despised her, and plop! and plop! again, other occasions he had been impotent, and embarrassed; not to mention school, where he'd been fidgety, weedy, skinny, short when others had been tall – he didn't start growing until he was sixteen – and the hundred daily humiliations of childhood. Poor Clifford; both too tough and too sensitive for his own good! How these ingredients stirred and boiled and moiled into a great solid tarry wedge of distress, sealed by the shuddering conviction that Helen was in someone else's arms as he lay unsleeping in their bed: that Helen's lips were pressed beneath the searching mouth of someone younger, fiercer, kinder, yet more virile – no, Clifford was never to forget that night; nor, I'm afraid, was he ever properly to trust Helen again, so potent was the trouble brewed by Angie.

At eight o'clock the doorbell went. Unshaven, distracted, drugged by his own imaginings, affected by a woman as he had never thought possible, Clifford opened the door to Angie. 'What do you know?' he asked. 'Where is she? Where is Helen?'

Still Angie wouldn't tell him. She walked up the

stairs and took her clothes off, and lay down upon the bed, rather quickly covering herself with the sheet, and waited.

'For old times' sake,' she said. 'And for my father's millions. He'll need some consoling about the Botticelli, if it is one. I keep telling you, money is in Modern Art, not in Old Masters.'

'It's in both,' he said.

Now what Angie said was persuasive. And she was, to Clifford, familiar territory, and he was distracted beyond belief and anyway Angie was *there*. (I think we have to forgive him, yet again.) Clifford joined her on the bed, tried to pretend it was Helen there beneath him, and almost succeeded, and then on top of him and totally failed. He knew the moment it was over that he regretted it. Men do seem to regret these things even more easily than do women.

'Where is Helen?' he asked, as soon as he was able.

'She's in the de Waldo Clinic,' said Angie, 'having an abortion. The operation is booked for ten this morning.'

It was by that time 8.45. Clifford dressed, in haste.

'But why didn't she tell me?' he asked. 'The little fool!'

'Clifford,' said Angie, languorously from the bed, 'I can only suppose because it isn't your baby.'

That slowed him down. Angie knew well enough that if you have just deceived your one true love, as Clifford had just done, you are all the more ready to believe you are yourself deceived.

'You're so trusting, Clifford,' added Angie, to Clifford's back, and it was a pity for her that she did, for Clifford caught a glimpse of Angie in the big wall-mirror, gold mounted and mercury based, three hundred years old, in which a thousand women must have stared, and

The Hearts and Lives of Men

it somehow cast back a strange reflection of Angie. As if indeed she was the wickedest woman who had ever looked into it. Angie's eyes glinted with what Clifford suddenly perceived was malice, and he realized, too late to save his honour, but at least in time to save Nell, what Angie was up to. He finished tying his tie.

Clifford said not another word to Angie: he left her lying on the fur rug on the bed, where she had no right to be – it was after all Helen's place – and was at the de Waldo Clinic by 9.15 and it was fortunate there was at least some time to spare, for the reception staff were obstructive and the operation had been brought forward by half an hour. Dr Runcorn, I have a terrible feeling, could not wait to get his hands on Helen's baby and destroy it from within. Abortion is sometimes necessary, sometimes not, always sad. It is to the woman as war is to the man – a living sacrifice in a cause justified or not justified, as the observer may decide. It is the making of hard decisions – that this one must die that that one can live in honour and decency and comfort. Women have no leaders, of course: a woman's conscience must be her General; there are no stirring songs to make the task of killing easier, no victory marches and medals handed around afterwards, merely a sense of loss. And just as in war there are ghouls, vampires, profiteers and grave robbers as well as brave and noble men, so there are wicked men, as well as good, in abortion clinics and Dr Runcorn was an evil man.

Clifford pushed aside a Jamaican nurse and two Scottish ward orderlies, all three fed up with wages in the public sector and so gone into private health care, or so they told their friends, and since no one would tell him where Helen was, stalked along the shiny, pale corridors of the Clinic, throwing open doors as he went, doing without help. Startled, unhappy women, sitting up neatly in bed in frilly or fluffy bedjackets, looked up at him in sudden hope, as if perhaps here at last was their saviour, their knight in shining armour, he who was to come if all was to be explained, made happy and well. But of course it was not so: he was Helen's, not theirs.

Clifford found Helen on a trolley in the theatre annexe, white-gowned, head turbanned; a nurse bent over her; Helen was unconscious, ready to go into the theatre. Clifford tussled with the nurse for possession of the trolley.

'This woman is to go back to the ward at once,' he said, 'or by God I'll have the police in!' And he pinched her fingers nastily in the trolley's steering mechanism. The nurse yelled. Helen did not stir. Dr Runcorn emerged to see what the matter was.

'Caught red-handed!' said Clifford, bitterly, and indeed Dr Runcorn was. He had just disposed of twins, rather late on in a pregnancy, and a very messy matter it had been. But Dr Runcorn prided himself on his record for twins – not out of his clinic those frequent cases where one twin has been aborted, the other gone on, unobserved by everyone but a bewildered mother, to full term. No, if there was a twin, Dr Runcorn would weed it out.

'This young lady is about to have an exploratory examination of her abdomen,' he said, 'of her own free will. And since you are not married to her, you have no legal rights in the matter.'

At this Clifford simply hit him, and quite right too. Just occasionally violence can be seen to be justified. In his life Clifford was to hit three men. The first was Helen's father, who tried to prize him apart from Helen, the second was Dr Runcorn, who was trying to deprive him of Helen's baby, and the third we have not come to yet, but that was to do with Helen too. This is the effect some women have on some men.

Dr Runcorn fell to the ground and got up with his nose bloodied. I am sorry to say none of his staff assisted him. He was not liked.

'Very well,' he said wearily, 'I will call a private ambulance. On your own head be it.'

And as the ambulance doors closed he remarked to Clifford, 'You're wasting your time on this one. These girls are nothing but sluts. I don't do what I do for money. I do it to spare the babies a hellish future, and to save the human race from genetic pollution.'

Dr Runcorn's puffy face was puffier still from Clifford's blow, and his fingers were like red garden slugs; he seemed, all of a sudden, to want Clifford's approval, as the defeated so often do of the victor, but such was not of course forthcoming. Clifford merely despised Dr Runcorn the more thoroughly for his hypocrisy, and a little of that despising rubbed off, alas, on Helen, as if – quite leaving aside the purpose of her visit to the de Waldo Clinic – the mere stepping inside so awful and vulgar a place had been enough to taint her, and permanently.

The ambulance men carried the still unconscious Helen up the stairs of the Goodge Street house, and laid her on the bed, suggested Clifford called a doctor, and departed. (The de Waldo Clinic was later to send a bill, which Clifford declined to pay.) Clifford sat beside Helen, and watched, and waited and thought. He didn't call a doctor. He reckoned she'd be all right. She breathed easily. Anaesthesia had passed into sleep. Her forehead was damp, and her pretty hair curled and clung in dark tendrils which framed her face. Fine veins in her white temples showed blue: thick eyelashes fringed pale translucent cheeks: her eyebrows made a delicate yet confident arch. Most faces need animation to make them beautiful: Helen's was flawless even in tranquillity; as near the perfection of a painting as Clifford was ever likely to find. His anger, his outrage, failed. This rare creature was the mother of his child. Clifford knew that Angie's insinuations were absurd, by virtue of the sheer intensity of the feelings that welled up in him when he considered how narrow his baby's escape had been. This had been the first act of rescue. He did not doubt but that there would be others. He could see all too clearly that Helen was capable of deceit and folly, and lack of judgement, and worst of all, lack of taste. His child, brushed so near, so early, to the appalling Dr Runcorn! And as Helen grew older these qualities would become more apparent. The baby must be protected. 'I'll look after you,' he said aloud. 'Don't worry.' Absurdly sentimental! But I think he meant Nell, not Helen.

Clifford should have been at Leonardo's that afternoon. The Hieronymus Bosch Exhibition was to be extended a further three months. There was a great deal to be done, if the maximum publicity for the Gallery, the maximum advantage for himself, was to be gained. But still Clifford did not leave Helen's side. He let his fingers stray over her forehead. He had wanted her from the moment he saw her: so that no one else could have her and because she was John Lally's daughter, and because that in the end would open more doors to him than Angie's millions ever would – but he had not known until the torments of the previous night just how much he loved her, and in the loving exposed himself to danger. For what woman was ever faithful? His mother Cynthia had betrayed his father Otto half a dozen times a year, and always had. Why should Helen, why should any woman, be different? But now there was the child – and in that child Clifford focused all emotional aspiration, all trust in human goodness, quite bypassing poor Helen, who had been trying to save Clifford as well as herself.

Helen stirred, and woke, and seeing Clifford, smiled. He smiled back.

'It's all right,' he said. 'You still have the baby. But why didn't you tell me?'

'I was frightened,' she said simply. And then she added, abandoning herself to his care, 'You'll just have to look after everything. I don't think I'm fit.'

Clifford, conscious of simply everyone and thickening waists, rang his parents and said no church wedding, after all. He'd rather make it the Caxton Hall.

'But that's only a trumped up registry office,' complained Cynthia.

'Everyone who's anyone gets married there,' he said. 'And this is a modern marriage. God need not be present.'

'Or only his substitute here on earth,' said Cynthia.

Clifford laughed and did not deny it. And at least he'd said 'everyone' and not 'simply everyone'.

LEAPING INTO THE FUTURE

The wedding between Clifford Wexford and Helen Lally took place on Midsummer's Day, 1965. Helen wore a cream slipper satin dress, trimmed with Belgian lace, and everyone said she should have been a model, she was so exquisite. (In fact Helen was altogether too robust in her early twenties to be anything of the sort. It was only later, when trouble, love and general upset had fined her down that she was able thus to earn a living.)

Fay Weldon

Clifford and Helen made a spectacular pair; his leonine hair shone, and her brown hair curled, and everyone who was anyone was at the wedding: everyone, that is to say, except the bride's father, John Lally. The bride's mother, Evelyn, sat at the back wearing the same old blue ribbed dress she had worn at the party where Clifford and Helen first met and fell in love. She had defied her husband to attend the ceremony. It would mean a week of not-speaking, possibly more. She did not care.

Simon Harvey, the New York writer, was Clifford's best man. Clifford had known him from way back: had met him in a pub, lent him his first typewriter. Now he had to lend him the fare over, but a friend's a friend, and though Clifford's acquaintances were many, his friends were few. Simon wrote funny novels, on homosexual themes, too early for their popularity. (The word 'gay' was only just finding its feet: to be homosexual a deathly earnest, whispered matter.) Presently he would be a millionaire, of course.

'What do you think of her?' Clifford asked.

'If you have to marry a woman,' Simon said, 'she's the best you could do.' Nor did he lose the ring, and he made an affectionate speech; it was worth the air fare, which Clifford knew he would never get back.

Helen's Uncle Phil, Evelyn's brother, gave her away. He was a car salesman; middle-aged, red-faced and noisy, but all the younger men she knew had at one time or other been her lovers, or nearly been, and that seemed even less suitable – even though they would not have said and Clifford would not have known. She wanted her marriage to start without lies. Clifford didn't seem to mind Uncle Phillip, strangely, just said it was useful to have someone in the car trade in the family, and set up a deal at once – a Mercedes for his MG, now he was about to be a married man. And when it came to it Helen was glad her Uncle Phillip was there – the guests being so weighted on the Wexford family and friend side, light on the Lally's. Helen had friends enough, but like many very pretty girls, felt she got on better with men than women, and suffered a little, feeling women didn't like her.

No one (who was anyone) except Clifford knew that Helen was more than three months pregnant on her wedding day – oh, and Angie of course, but she had not been sent an invitation and had returned to Johannesburg to lick her wounds. (Though Angie meant to have Clifford in the end and no amount of 'I will's' and 'I do's' to someone else would daunt her permanently.) It was a wonderful day in any number of ways. Sir Larry Patt came up to Clifford at the reception and said, 'Clifford, I give up. You are the new world. I am the old. I am resigning. You are to be managing director of Leonardo's. The Board decided yesterday. You are much too young, and I told them so, but they didn't agree. So now it's over to you, lad.'

Clifford's happiness was complete. Never would there be such a day as this again! Helen slipped her little white hand in his and squeezed it, and he did not squeeze hers in return, but said, 'How's the baby?' and she said 'Hush!' and had no idea at all that he no longer totally accepted her, but judged her, and thought the squeeze childish and vulgar.

Lady Rowena looked boyish in a grey tunic dress, white frilly blouse and cravat, and fluttered her false eyelashes (everyone was wearing them) at one of Cynthia Wexford's cousins from Minneapolis, and made a rapid assignation with him beneath his wife's nose. Cynthia

Fay Weldon

noticed and sighed. She should never have invited the cousins over: she should have stuck to her principles and kept no contact at all with the family which had so insulted and abused her in her youth. Bad enough that these things ran in the blood. Her father had loved her dearly one day, spurned her totally the next. She had been instrumental in getting the family out of Denmark; had risked torture, life itself, to do it; he had thanked her coldly, but not smiled at her. He would not forgive. She tried not to think of him. Clifford looked like her father: had stared at her with childish eyes as blue as his grandfather's. That was the trouble. She hoped he would be happy, that Helen would do for him what she could not, that is to say, love him. But perhaps he hadn't noticed. She'd always behaved as if she loved him, or thought she had.

Otto and Cynthia went home in their Rolls-Royce. Johnnie drove. He kept a loaded revolver in the glove box, for old times' sake. Cynthia thought Otto was a little subdued.

'What's the matter?' she asked. 'I'm sure if anyone can make Clifford happy, Helen can. Mind you, as a baby he was never exactly content. She'll have her work cut out.'

'All that worries me,' said Otto gloomily, 'is what he'll do for an encore. Head of Leonardo's at his age! It'll go to his head.'

'Too late,' said Cynthia. 'He already thinks he's God.'

Clifford and Helen spent the night in the Ritz, where the double beds are the best and softest and prettiest in London.

'What did your parents give us for a wedding present?' asked Clifford, and Helen wished he hadn't asked. He

The Hearts and Lives of Men

seemed in an odd mood, both elated and yet somehow restless.

'A toaster,' she said.

'You'd think your father would have given us one of his paintings,' said Clifford. Since Clifford already had a dozen small Lallys on his walls, bought for a song, and eight major paintings in Leonardo's vaults, where no one could see them, Helen didn't think so at all. But she was twenty-two and a nobody, and Clifford was thirty-five, and very much somebody, so she didn't say so. After the episode of the de Waldo clinic, she had become less able to laugh at him, tease him out of his moods, enchant him. She took him, in fact, too seriously for his own good, let alone hers. She had been in the wrong: she was her mother's daughter as well as her father's and it showed.

She had other things to worry about, besides. She lay in bed and worried about them. Clifford had bought a house in Primrose Hill, in the then unfashionable North West London, near the Zoo, to be their marital home. He'd sold Coffee Place for £2,500 and bought the Chalcot Square house for £6,000, judging that presently it would be worth a great deal more. (He was quite right. That very house changed hands recently for half a million pounds.) Clifford hadn't put the property into joint ownership. He didn't see why he should. This, after all, was the sixties, and a man's property was a man's property, and a man's wife serviced it, and was supposed to feel grateful for the privilege. Could she run it properly? She was so young. She knew she was untidy. She had given up her work at Sotheby's, and started going to Cordon Bleu cookery lessons, but even so! Clifford had said, and she could see that he was right, that she would need all her time and energy to run the house, and entertain his friends and colleagues, who, as he himself pointed out, were getting grander and greater all the time. Would there be enough time, enough energy, with a baby on the way? And when would she tell people about the baby? It was embarrassing. Nevertheless, she was full of hope, as befitted a girl on her wedding night. She hoped, for example, Clifford's friends, colleagues and clients would not think her to be an inefficient, stupid child. She hoped that Clifford would not, either. She hoped she would be able to cope with a baby: she hoped she would not yearn for her freedom and her friends, or miss her mother and father too much; she hoped in fact she had done the right thing. Yet what choice had she ever had? You met someone, and that was that.

Clifford kissed her, and his mouth was hot and heavy, and he embraced her, and his arms were lean and strong. It had been a long day; a wedding day; a hundred hands had been shaken; a hundred good wishes received; if she was anxious it was because she was tired. But how strange, that along with the physical reassurances of love, keeping pace, marking step, like some little brother determined to be taken seriously, anxiety came too, and a fear for the future, the sense that life flowed like waves towards the shore, for ever dispersed before they quite arrive; and worse, that the higher the crest, the lower the trough must be, so that even happiness is something to be feared.

In the middle of the night, the pretty gold enamelled telephone on the bedside table rang. Helen answered it. Clifford always slept heavily, never for long, but soundly, his blond head heavy against the pillow, his hand tucked against his cheek, like a child. Helen thought, even as she picked up the receiver, quickly, so he was not disturbed, how wonderful to know so private a thing about so remarkable a man. The call came from Angie in Johannesburg. She was asking how the wedding had been, apologizing for her absence.

'But you weren't even *invited*,' Helen longed to say, but didn't. Could Angie speak to Clifford, Angie asked, and congratulate him on being made managing director of Leonardo's? After all, it was her father who had arranged it.

'It's two in the morning, Angie,' said Helen, as reproachfully as she dared. 'Clifford's asleep.'

'And he sleeps so heavily!' said Angie. 'I know only too well. Try pinching his bum. That usually works. Does he have his hand tucked under his cheek, like a child? Ah, the thought of it. Lucky old you!'

'How do you know?' asked Helen.

'The way so many of us know, darling.'

'When?' asked Helen, bleakly. 'Where?'

'Who, me? Long long in the past, darling, for Clifford. At least a couple of months. Not since your abortive night in the Clinic. That was at Coffee Place. Though before that, of course, many times, many places. But you know all that. Do just wake him. Don't be a jealous little goose. If I'm not jealous, and I'm not, why should you be?'

Helen put the phone down and wept, but quietly and silently, so that Clifford didn't hear, and wake. Then, as a practical gesture, she took the phone off the hook, so Angie couldn't ring back. Outrage and distress would get her nowhere; she knew that. She must calm herself as quickly as she could, and somehow start constructing a new vision of herself, and Clifford, and her marriage.

Fay Weldon

FIRST DAYS

It was remarkable, once the wedding was over, how Helen's waist thickened: two days later and the wedding dress would not fasten; a week, and she could not pull it over her bosom without the seams threatening to give.

'Extraordinary,' said Clifford, who kept asking her to try on the dress, as if to take the measure of her pregnancy by eye. 'I suppose now you feel you can relax. Well, you can't. There's a lot to be done.'

And so indeed there was. The house in Primrose Hill had to be turned from a rooming-house to a dwelling fit for a Wexford, his new burgeoning wife, and to receive the friends he meant to have, and since Clifford was always busy, Helen would have to do it. And so she did. He was solicitous of her pregnancy, but would not allow her to be ill. If she bent retching over the basin in the morning, he would clap his hands briskly and say 'enough!' and by some magic it would be. He required no consultation about paper, paint or furniture, other than the walls should be fit to hang paintings upon, and the furniture be antique, not new, since new had no resale value. He seemed to approve of what she did, or at least he did not say he did not. At weekends he played tennis, and she watched, and admired and clapped. He liked her applause. But then he liked anyone's applause. She understood that.

'You are not very *sportif*,' he complained. She supposed that Angie, perhaps, had been, and others.

On the surface, things went well. Days were sunny and active, the baby kicked; the nights awkward and less wild, but reassuring. Presently acquaintances of Clifford's put in a cautious appearance at the house and, finding his new young wife not as silly as they had feared, stayed around and became friends; her friends came, looked, drifted away, finding her in some way lost to them. How could they, young, poor, mildly bohemian, without ambition, be at ease with Clifford Wexford who required more than mere humanity as a recommendation? How, when it came to it, could she? She saw she must be more Wexford wife, less daughter of Applecore Cottage. She learned to do without the chatter and closeness of her friends, the agreeable warmth of their concern; when they drifted off she did not tug them back. They were nice people: they would have come, Clifford or not. Reader, the truth was, she was weighty, and heavy, and began to lumber – you know how women will in late pregnancy – and the baby pressed upon the sciatic nerve, but she gritted her teeth, and set her smile to fair against weariness and complaint, for Clifford's sake. She would be everything to Clifford. He would never look at another woman again. And at the same time she knew it was no use. She had lost him: though how or why she was not sure.

A TIME OF HAPPINESS

Baby Nell was born on Christmas Day, 1965, in the Middlesex Hospital. Now Christmas is not a good time to have a baby. The nursing staff drink too much sherry and spend their time singing carols; the young doctors kiss them under the mistletoe; senior surgeons dress up as Father Christmas. Helen gave birth to Nell unattended, in a private ward, where she lay alone. Had she been in the ordinary public ward at least one of the other patients would have been there to help; as it was, her red light glowed in Sister's Room hour after hour and no one noticed. It was not yet the fashion for fathers to be present at the birth of their baby, and Clifford, in any case, would have shuddered at the very possibility. As it was, he and Helen had been asked to a Christmas Eve dinner by the eminent painter David Firkin, who was thinking of moving from the Beaux Arts Gallery to Leonardo's, and Clifford did not wish to forgo the invitation. It seemed important. Helen had her first tentative pain in the taxi on the way to the Firkin studio. She did not, of course, want to be a nuisance.

'I don't suppose it's anything,' she said. 'Probably only indigestion. Tell you what, you drop me off at the hospital and they'll have a look at me and send me home and I'll come on to David's in a taxi.'

Clifford took Helen at her word and dropped her off at the hospital, and went on to the dinner alone. Helen did not follow.

'Even if she was in labour,' said David Firkin, 'which I doubt, first babies take for ever so there's no need to worry. It's an entirely natural process. Now don't be a bore and keep calling the hospital.' David Firkin hated children, and was proud of it. Helen was a fine, healthy girl, all the guests said; no need to worry; and no one started counting back on their fingers as to how many months it was since the marriage – or at least, no one that Clifford noticed.

As it was, Helen was indeed a fine, healthy girl, if frightened, and Nell was a fine, healthy baby, and arrived safely, if on her own, at 3.10 a.m. Nell's sun had left Sagittarius and was just into Capricorn, making her both lively and effective; she had the moon in Aquarius rising, which made her kind, charming, generous and good; Venus stood strong in mid-heaven, in its own house, Libra, and that made her full of desires, and

The Hearts and Lives of Men

capable of giving and receiving love. But Mercury was too close to Mars, and Neptune was in opposition to both, and her sun opposed her moon, and so Nell was to be prone to strange events through her life, and to great misfortunes, alternating with great good fortune. Saturn in conjunction with the sun, and powerful, and also opposed in the twelfth house, suggested that prisons and institutions would loom large in her life: there would be times when she would look out at the world from behind bars. Or that's one way of looking at it all. It will do. How better are we to account for the event that fate, and not our natures, cause?

A nurse, shame-faced, came hurrying in on hearing Nell's first cry, and when the baby, washed and wrapped, was finally placed in Helen's arms, Helen fell in love: not as she had fallen in love with Clifford, all erotic excitement and apprehension mixed, but powerfully, steadily, and permanently. When Clifford was wrested from the after-dinner brandy and crackers (Harrods Xmas Best) and came to her bedside at four in the morning, she showed him the baby, almost fearfully, leaning over the crib, pulling back the blanket from the small face. She still never knew quite what Clifford was going to like, or dislike, approve or condemn. She had become shy of him, almost timorous. She did not know what the matter was. She hoped the arrival of Nell would make things better. She did not, you will notice, think of her own pain, or resent Clifford's abandonment of her at such a time; just of how best to please him. In those first few pregnant months of her marriage, she was, as I say, more like her mother than at any other time of her life.

'A girl!' he said, and for a moment Helen thought he meant to disapprove, but he looked at his daughter and smiled, and said, 'Don't frown, sweetheart: everything's going to be okay,' and Helen could have sworn the baby stopped frowning at once and smiled back, although the nurses said that was impossible: babies did not smile for six weeks. (All nurses say this, and all mothers know otherwise.)

He picked the baby up.

'Careful,' said Helen, but there was no need. Clifford was accustomed to handling objects of great value. And there and then he felt, to his surprise, and acutely, both the pain and pleasure of fatherhood – the piercing anxious needle in the heart which is the drive to protect, the warm reassuring glow which is the conviction of immortality, the recognition of privilege, the knowledge that it is more than just a child you hold in your arms, but the whole future of the world, as it works through you. More, he felt absurdly grateful to Helen for having the baby, making the feeling possible. For the first time since he had rescued her from the de Waldo clinic, he kissed her with ungrudging love. He had forgiven her, in fact, and Helen glowed in his forgiveness.

'All be well,' she shut her eyes and said, quoting something she had read, but not quite sure what – and all will be well, and all manner of things will be well,' and Clifford did not even snub her by asking for the source of the quotation. And so it was, very well indeed, for a time.

Until she was nearly a year old, then, Nell lived in the cocoon of happiness created by her parents. Leonardo's flourished under Clifford Wexford's guidance – an interesting Rembrandt was acquired, a few tedious Dutch masters sold, the putative Botticelli labelled and hung as such, to the Uffizi's astonishment, and in the new contemporary section, the price of a David Firkin, now required to paint no more than two paintings a year, lest he spoil his own market, soared to five figures. Helen lost a whole stone and worshipped Clifford and baby Nell in turns. It is even pleasanter – if more difficult – to love, than to be loved. When both happen at once, what higher joy can there be?

A TIDAL WAVE OF TROUBLE

Reader, a marriage that is rapidly put together can rapidly unravel: like a hand-knitted jumper, which if you snip just one strand and pull, and go on pulling, comes to nothing at all. Just a pile of wrinkled junk. Or put it another way: you think you're living in a palace but actually it's just a house of cards. Disturb one card and the whole lot falls and flattens and is nothing. When Nell was ten months old, the Wexford marriage fell in ruins about the poor child's ears: phut, phut, phut – one nasty event falling fast upon another quicker than you can imagine.

This is how it happened.

The Conrans gave a November 5th firework party. Remember? Terence, who started Habitat? And Shirley, later of *Superwoman* and *Lace*? Everyone who was anyone was there, and that included the Wexfords.

Helen left Nell behind with the Nanny: she didn't want the child frightened by bangs and crashes. She went ahead of Clifford, who was coming straight from Leonardo's. She wore an embroidered leather coat and boots with many tassels, and looked slim, vulnerable, very pretty and tender, and somehow amazed, and slightly stunned, as young women recently married to active men do tend to look: that is to say, very attractive to other men, making them behave like stags

Fay Weldon

in the rutting season, all locked mighty antlers and 'I'll have what's yours, by God and nature that I will!' If she'd worn her old blue duffle it mightn't have happened.

Clifford arrived later than Helen expected. She felt sulky. Leonardo's took up too much of his time and attention. Sausages crackled and hot potatoes went splut! in cinders; rockets rippled and fountains of light poured skyward, and cries of amazement and delight drifted on a light wind over Camden Town gardens, along with the bonfire smoke. There was a lot of rum in the hot toddy. If there had been less none of it might have happened.

Helen looked through a veil of smoke and saw Clifford approaching. She forgave him: she began to smile. But who was that by his side? Angie? Helen's smile faded. Surely not. Angie, last heard of, had been in South Africa. But yes, that's who it was. Fur coated, fur hatted, high leather booted, mini-skirted, showing the bare stretch of stockinged thigh fashionable at the time; Angie, smirking at Helen, even while Angie most affectionately squeezed Clifford's hand. Helen blinked and Angie was gone. Worse still. What was she hiding? What collusion was this? Helen had kept Angie's wedding-night phone call to herself: biting pain and insult back, forgetting it, putting it out of her mind. Or that's what she thought she'd done. If only she had, and not just thought she had, none of it might have happened.

Clifford took Helen's arm, comfortingly uxorious. Helen shook it petulantly free – never what a woman should do to a man of high self regard. But she'd had four hot toddies, waiting for Clifford, and was less sober than she knew. If only she'd let him hold her arm. But no!

'That was Angie, you came with Angie, you've been with Angie.'

The Hearts and Lives of Men

'It was, I did, I have,' said Clifford coolly.

'I thought she was in South Africa.'

'She's over here helping me set up the Contemporary Section. If you took any interest at all in Leonardo's, you'd know.'

Unfair! Wasn't Helen going to daily courses in the History of Art, in order to catch up? Wasn't she, at twenty-three, running a house and servants, and entertaining, and looking after a small child as well? Wasn't she neglected by her husband for Leonardo's sake? Helen slapped Clifford's face (if only she hadn't) and Angie stepped out of the bonfire smoke, and smiled again at Helen, a little victorious smile, which Clifford didn't see. (No suggesting Angie could have behaved other than how she did. No sirree!)

'You're completely mad,' said Clifford to Helen, 'insanely jealous,' and left the party forthwith with Angie. (Oh, oh, oh!) Well, he was cross. No man likes to be hit in public, or accused of infidelity, without reason. And there certainly was no recent reason. Angie was biding her time: her relationship with Clifford had of late indeed been bounded by Leonardo's new Contemporary Section: Clifford had all but forgotten it had ever been anything else, or would he have brought Angie to the party? (If only he hadn't! It is to Clifford's credit that he, like Helen and unlike Angie, was capable of moral choice.)

Clifford took Angie back to her house in Belgravia and went straight home to Primrose Hill and listened to music and waited for Helen to come home. He decided to forgive her.

He waited until morning, and still she did not come. Then she rang to say she was at Applecore Cottage: her mother was ill. She put the phone down fast. Clifford

Fay Weldon

had heard that one before – he sent Johnnie to check. Of course Helen was not at Applecore Cottage. How could she be? Her father still barred her from his door. The very folly of the lie compounded her offence.

And where had Helen been last night? Well, I'll tell you. After Clifford had left the party with Angie on his arm, Helen, many hot toddies later, left it on the arm of a certain Laurence Durrance, script writer, and husband of little Anne-Marie Durrance, neighbour and close friend. (After this particular choice of action, there was no going back. No more if onlys. Flop, flop, flop, flop – down came the house of cards.)

Anne-Marie, four foot ten inches and six stone of *jolie-laide* energy, stayed behind to weep and wail and tell *everyone*, very excitedly, that Helen Wexford and her husband had left the party together. Not content with that, she wrung a confession out of Laurence the very next morning. (I took her to my office. On the sofa. Very uncomfortable. You know all those books and papers. I was terribly drunk. Someone had spiked the hot toddy. She seemed so upset. *She* seemed so upset! *Anne-Marie*. Just one of those things. Sorry, sorry, sorry.) And, having heard all that, and before Helen returned from wherever (staying with a girlfriend, actually, trying to compose herself, so great was her guilt), Anne-Marie went round and told Clifford where Helen had been the night before, with many unnecessary and untrue embellishments.

So when Helen did come home, Clifford was unforgiving in the most permanent kind of way. Indeed, Johnnie was just finishing changing the locks. Helen was on the doorstep in the keen November wind: her husband and baby on the other side of a locked door, in the warm.

'Let me in, let me in,' cried Helen, but he didn't. Even

though Nell set up a sympathetic wail, his heart stayed hardened. An unfaithful wife was no wife of his. She was worse than a stranger to him: she was an enemy.

So Helen had to go to a solicitor, didn't she, and Clifford was already seeing his – he wasted no time. Anne-Marie had barely finished her tale than he was on the phone – and a very powerful and expensive solicitor he was and not only that, Anne-Marie thereupon decided to take the opportunity of divorcing Laurence and citing Helen, and by Christmas not only one but two marriages had been destroyed. And the cocoon of warmth and love in which Nell lived had been unwound, faster than the eye could see let alone the mind comprehend it seemed to Helen, and words of hate, despair and spite filled the air around Nell's infant head, and when she smiled no one returned her smile, and Clifford was divorcing Helen, citing Laurence, and claiming custody of their little daughter.

You may not know about the custom of 'citing'. In the old days, when the institution of marriage was a stronger and more permanent thing than it is now, it was seen to need outside intervention to push asunder any married couple. A marriage didn't just 'irretrievably break up' as a result of internal forces. Someone came along and *did* something, usually sexual. That someone was known as 'the third party'. Sheets would be inspected for evidence, photographs taken through keyholes by private detectives, and the third party cited by the aggrieved spouse and get his (her) name in the papers. It was all perfectly horrid; and even if neither spouse was sincerely aggrieved, but simply wanted to part, the motions of sheets and keyholes would have to be gone through. Mind you, every cloud has a silver lining; a whole race of girls grew up who would inhabit seaside hotels and provide required evidence, and who earned a good and frequently easy living, sitting up all night drinking cups of coffee and embracing only when the light through the keyhole suddenly went dark.

The only other mildly glittery lining to this particular cloud was that Helen made a kind of peace with her father – any enemy of Clifford was a friend of his, albeit his own daughter (*alleged* daughter: he would not give Evelyn the comfort of ceasing to disown Helen as his flesh and blood) – and was allowed back into the little back bedroom of Applecore Cottage to weep her shame and anguish away, there where the familiar robin sat on the apple tree branch, just outside her bedroom window, red-breasted, head on one side, clucking and chirruping at her distress, promising her better times to come.

LIES, ALL LIES!

There are some babies whom nobody fights over. If they are plain, or dull, or miserable or mopey, divorced and erring mothers are allowed to keep them and toil for them through the years. But what a charmer Nell was! Everyone wanted her: both parents, both sets of grandparents. Nell had a bright clear skin and a bright clear smile, and hardly ever cried, and if she did was quickly pacified. She was a hard and dedicated worker – and no one has to work harder than babies – when it came to developing her skills: learning to touch, to grasp, to sit, to crawl, to stand, to utter the first few words. She was brave, brilliant and spirited – a prize worth having, rather than a burden just about worth the bother of bearing. And how they fought over her.

'She isn't fit to be a mother,' said Clifford to Van

The Hearts and Lives of Men

Erson, his freckled, ferocious solicitor. 'She tried to abort the child. She never wanted it.'

'He only wants her to get back at me,' wept Helen to Edwin Druse, her gentle hippie adviser. 'Please make him stop all this. I love him so much. Just that one stupid time, that silly party, I'd had too much to drink, I was only getting back at him for Angie. I can't bear to lose Nell too. I can't. Please help me!'

Edwin Druse put out a gentle hand to soothe his distraught client. He thought she was too young to cope. He thought Clifford was a very negative kind of person indeed. She needed looking after. He thought perhaps he, Edwin Druse, would be the best person to do the looking after. He could convert her to vegetarianism, and she would no longer be prey to such despair. In fact he thought he and she could get on very well indeed if only Clifford and little Nell were out of the way. Edwin Druse was not perhaps the best legal representative Helen could have chosen, in the circumstances. However, there it was.

Add to that the fact that Clifford wanted Nell, and was in the habit of getting what he wanted, and you will see that in the struggle for her custody he had everything on his side. Money, power, clever barristers, outraged virtue — and his parents Otto and Cynthia behind him, to back him up with extra dollops of the same.

'Sweetness alone is not enough,' said Cynthia of Helen. 'There must be some sense and discretion too.'

'A man can put up with many things from a wife,' said Otto, 'but not being made a fool of in public.'

And Helen had nothing, except loveliness, and helplessness and mother-love, and Edwin Druse's conscience, to put in the scales. And it was not enough.

Clifford divorced Helen for adultery, and there was no

way she could deny the fact: what is more, Anne-Marie actually stood up there on the stand and testified, as she had done in her own divorce, 'and I came home unexpectedly and found my husband Laurence in the bed with Helen. Yes, it was the marital bed. Yes, the pair of them were naked.' Lies all lies! Helen did not even try to counter-claim that Clifford had committed adultery with Angie Wellbrook – she did not want to bring him into public calumny, and Edwin Druse did not attempt to persuade her so to do. Helen was all too ready to believe she had lost Clifford through her own fault. Even while she hated him, she loved him; and the same could be said of him, for her. But his pride was hurt: he would not forgive, and she would not hurt him further. And so he came out of the divorce the innocent, and she the guilty party, and it was in all the papers for the space of a whole week. I am sorry to say that Clifford Wexford was never averse to the publicity. He thought it would be good for business and so it was.

Angie's father rang from Johannesburg and boomed down the line, 'Glad to see you're rid of that no-good wife of yours. It'll cheer Angie up no end!' Which of course it did. That, and the amazing success of David Firkin's paintings, which now hung on the trendiest walls in the land.

'See,' said Angie. 'All that Old Master junk is out, out, out.'

At the custody proceedings, a month later, Helen was to wish she had fought harder. Clifford brought up various matters to prove her unsuitability as a mother; not just her initial attempt to abort Nell, which she had expected, but her father's insanity – a man who cut up his own paintings with the garden shears could hardly be called sane – which she might have inherited, and

The Hearts and Lives of Men

Helen's own tendency to gross sexual immorality. Moreover, Helen was practically an alcoholic – had she not attempted to justify her sinning with the co-respondent, Durrance, on the grounds that she'd had too much to drink? No, Nell's mother was vain, feckless, hopeless, criminal. Moreover, Helen had no money: Clifford had. How did she mean to support a child? Had she not given up even her meagre part-time job at the drop of a hat? Work? Helen? You're joking!

Whichever way the poor girl turned, Clifford faced her, accusing, and so convincing she almost believed him herself. And what could she say against him? That he wanted Nell only to punish her? That all he would do would be to hand little Nell over to the care of a nanny; that he was too busy to be a proper father to the child; that her, Helen's, heart would break if her baby was taken away from her? Edwin Druse was not persuasive. And so Helen was branded in the eyes of the world, a second time, as a drunken trollop, and that was that. Clifford won the custody proceedings.

'Custody, Care and Control,' said the Judge. Clifford looked across the courtroom at Helen, and for the first time since the proceedings had begun actually met her eyes.

'Clifford!' she whispered, as a wife might whisper her husband's name on his deathbed, and he heard, in spite of the babel all around, and responded in his heart. Rage and spite subsided, and he wished that somehow he could put the clock back, and he, she and Nell could be together again. He waited for Helen outside the court. He wanted just to talk to her, to touch her. She had been punished enough. But Angie came out before Helen, dressed in the miniest of mini leather skirts, and no one looked at her legs, just at the gold and diamond

Fay Weldon

brooch she wore, worth at least a quarter of a million pounds sterling, and tucked her arm into his, and said, 'Well, that's an excellent outcome! You have the baby and you don't have Helen. Laurence wasn't the only one, you know,' and Clifford's moment of weakness passed.

What happened to Laurence, you ask? Anne-Marie his wife forgave him – though she never forgave Helen – and they remarried a couple of years later. Some people are just unbearably frivolous. But by her one act of indiscretion Helen had lost husband, home and lover – which happens more often than I care to think – not to mention a child, and a friend, and a reputation too. And when Baby Nell took her first steps her mother was not there to see.

Edith Wharton
Pomegranate Seed

I

Charlotte Ashby paused on her doorstep. Dark had ascended on the brilliancy of the March afternoon, and the grinding rasping street life of the city was at its highest. She turned her back on it, standing for a moment in the old-fashioned, marble-flagged vestibule before she inserted her key in the lock. The sash curtains drawn across the panes of the inner door softened the light within to a warm blur through which no details showed. It was the hour when, in the first months of her marriage to Kenneth Ashby, she had most liked to return to that quiet house in a street long since deserted by business and fashion. The contrast between the soulless roar of New York, its devouring blaze of lights, the oppression of its congested traffic, congested houses, lives, minds and this veiled sanctuary she called home, always stirred her profoundly. In the very heart of the hurricane she had found her tiny islet – or thought she had. And now, in the last months, everything was changed, and she always wavered on the doorstep and had to force herself to enter.

While she stood there she called up the scene within: the hall hung with old prints, the ladderlike stairs, and on the left her husband's long shabby library, full of books and pipes and worn armchairs inviting to meditation. How she had loved that room! Then, upstairs, her own drawing-room, in which, since the death of Kenneth's first wife, neither furniture nor hangings had been changed, because there had never been money enough, but which Charlotte had made her own by moving furniture about and adding more books, another lamp, a table for the new reviews. Even on the occasion of her only visit to the first Mrs Ashby – a distant, self-centred woman, whom she had known very slightly – she had looked about her with an innocent envy, feeling it to be exactly the drawing-room she would have liked for herself; and now for more than a year it had been hers to deal with as she chose – the room to which she hastened back at dusk on winter days, where she sat reading by the fire, or answering notes at the pleasant roomy desk, or going over her stepchildren's copy books, till she heard her husband's step.

Sometimes friends dropped in; sometimes – oftener – she was alone; and she liked that best, since it was another way of being with Kenneth, thinking over what he had said when they parted in the morning, imagining what he would say when he sprang up the stairs, found her by herself and caught her to him.

Now, instead of this, she thought of one thing only – the letter she might or might not find on the hall table. Until she had made sure whether or not it was there, her mind had no room for anything else. The letter was always the same – a square greyish envelope with 'Kenneth Ashby, Esquire' written on it in bold but faint characters. From the first it had struck Charlotte as peculiar that anyone who wrote such a firm hand should trace the letters so lightly; the address was always written as though there were not enough ink in the pen, or the writer's wrist were too weak to bear upon it. Another curious thing was that, in spite of its

Pomegranate Seed

masculine curves, the writing was so visibly feminine. Some hands are sexless, some masculine, at first glance; the writing on the grey envelope, for all its strength and assurance, was without doubt a woman's. The envelope never bore anything but the recipient's name; no stamp, no address. The letter was presumably delivered by hand – but by whose? No doubt it was slipped into the letter-box, whence the parlour maid, when she closed the shutters and lit the lights, probably extracted it. At any rate, it was always in the evening, after dark, that Charlotte saw it lying there. She thought of the letter in the singular, as 'it', because, though there had been several since her marriage – seven, to be exact – they were so alike in appearance that they had become merged in one another in her mind, become one letter, become 'it'.

The first had come the day after their return from their honeymoon – a journey prolonged to the West Indies, from which they had returned to New York after an absence of more than two months. Re-entering the house with her husband, late on that first evening – they had dined at his mother's – she had seen, alone on the hall table, the grey envelope. Her eye fell on it before Kenneth's, and her first thought was: 'Why, I've seen that writing before,' but where she could not recall. The memory was just definite enough for her to identify the script whenever it looked up at her faintly from the same pale envelope; but on that first day she would have thought no more of the letter if, when her husband's glance lit on it, she had not chanced to be looking at him. It all happened in a flash – his seeing the letter, putting out his hand for it, raising it to his short-sighted eyes to decipher the faint writing, and then abruptly withdrawing the arm he had slipped through Charlotte's,

987

and moving away to the hanging light, his back turned to her. She had waited – waited for a sound, an exclamation; waited for him to open the letter; but he had slipped it into his pocket without a word and followed her into the library. And there they had sat down by the fire and lit their cigarettes, and he had remained silent, his head thrown back broodingly against the armchair, his eyes fixed on the hearth, and presently had passed his hand over his forehead and said: 'Wasn't it unusually hot at my mother's tonight? I've got a splitting head. Mind if I take myself off to bed?'

That was the first time. Since then Charlotte had never been present when he had received the letter. It usually came before he got home from his office, and she had to go upstairs and leave it lying there. But even if she had not seen it, she would have known it had come by the change in his face when he joined her – which, on those evenings, he seldom did before they met for dinner. Evidently, whatever the letter contained, he wanted to be by himself to deal with it; and when he reappeared he looked years older, looked emptied of life and courage, and hardly conscious of her presence. Sometimes he was silent for the rest of the evening; and if he spoke, it was usually to hint some criticism of her household arrangements, suggest some change in the domestic administration, to ask, a little nervously, if she didn't think Joyce's nursery governess was rather young and flighty, or if she herself always saw to it that Peter – whose throat was delicate – was properly wrapped up when he went to school. At such times Charlotte would remember the friendly warnings she had received when she became engaged to Kenneth Ashby: 'Marrying a heartbroken widower! Isn't that rather risky? You know Elsie Ashby absolutely dominated him'; and how she had jokingly replied: 'He may be glad of a little liberty for a change.' And in this respect she had been right. She had needed no one to tell her, during the first months, that her husband was perfectly happy with her. When they came back from their protracted honeymoon the same friends said: 'What have you done to Kenneth? He looks twenty years younger'; and this time she answered with careless joy: 'I suppose I've got him out of his groove.'

But what she noticed after the grey letters began to come was not so much his nervous tentative fault-finding – which always seemed to be uttered against his will – as the look in his eyes when he joined her after receiving one of the letters. The look was not unloving, not even indifferent; it was the look of a man who has been so far away from ordinary events that when he returns to familiar things they seem strange. She minded that more than the fault-finding.

Though she had been sure from the first that the handwriting on the grey envelope was a woman's, it was long before she associated the mysterious letters with any sentimental secret. She was too sure of her husband's love, too confident of filling his life, for such an idea to occur to her. It seemed far more likely that the letters – which certainly did not appear to cause him any sentimental pleasure – were addressed to the busy lawyer than to the private person. Probably they were from some tiresome client – women, he had often told her, were nearly always tiresome as clients – who did not want her letters opened by his secretary and therefore had them carried to his house. Yes; but in that case the unknown female must be unusually troublesome, judging from the effect her letters produced. Then again, though his professional discretion was exemplary, it was odd that he had never uttered an impatient comment, never remarked to Charlotte, in a moment of expansion, that there was a nuisance of a woman who kept badgering him about a case that had gone against her. He had made more than one semi-confidence of the kind – of course without giving names or details; but concerning this mysterious correspondent his lips were sealed.

There was another possibility: what is euphemistically called an 'old entanglement'. Charlotte Ashby was a sophisticated woman. She had few illusions about the intricacies of the human heart; she knew that there were often old entanglements. But when she had married Kenneth Ashby, her friends, instead of hinting at such a possibility, had said: 'You've got your work cut out for you. Marrying a Don Juan is a sinecure to it. Kenneth's never looked at another woman since he first saw Elsie Corder. During all the years of their marriage he was more like an unhappy lover than a comfortably contented husband. He'll never let you move an armchair or change the place of a lamp; and whatever you venture to do, he'll mentally compare with what Elsie would have done in your place.'

Except for an occasional nervous mistrust as to her ability to manage the children – a mistrust gradually dispelled by her good humour and the children's obvious fondness for her – none of these forebodings had come true. The desolate widower, of whom his nearest friends said that only his absorbing professional interests had kept him from suicide after his first wife's death, had fallen in love, two years later, with Charlotte Gorse, and after an impetuous wooing had married her and carried her off on a tropical honeymoon. And ever since he had been as tender and loverlike as during those first radiant weeks. Before asking her to marry him he had spoken

Pomegranate Seed

to her frankly of his great love for his first wife and his despair after her sudden death; but even then he had assumed no stricken attitude, or implied that life offered no possibility of renewal. He had been perfectly simple and natural, and had confessed to Charlotte that from the beginning he had hoped the future held new gifts for him. And when, after their marriage, they returned to the house where his twelve years with his first wife had been spent, he had told Charlotte at once that he was sorry he couldn't afford to do the place over for her, but that he knew every woman had her own views about furniture and all sorts of household arrangements a man would never notice, and had begged her to make any changes she saw fit without bothering to consult him. As a result, she made as few as possible; but this way of beginning their new life in the old setting was so frank and unembarrassed that it put her immediately at her ease, and she was almost sorry to find that the portrait of Elsie Ashby, which used to hang over the desk in his library, had been transferred in their absence to the children's nursery. Knowing herself to be the indirect cause of this banishment, she spoke of it to her husband; but he answered: 'Oh, I thought they ought to grow up with her looking down on them.' The answer moved Charlotte, and satisfied her; and as time went by she had to confess that she felt more at home in her house, more at ease and in confidence with her husband, since that long coldly beautiful face on the library wall no longer followed her with guarded eyes. It was as if Kenneth's love had penetrated to the secret she hardly acknowledged to her own heart – her passionate need to feel herself the sovereign even of his past.

With all this stored-up happiness to sustain her, it was curious that she had lately found herself yielding to a nervous apprehension. But there the apprehension was; and on this particular afternoon – perhaps because she was more tired than usual, or because of the trouble of finding a new cook or, for some other ridiculously trivial reason, moral or physical – she found herself unable to react against the feeling. Latchkey in hand, she looked back down the silent street to the whirl and illumination of the great thoroughfare beyond, and up at the sky already aflare with the city's nocturnal life. 'Outside there,' she thought, 'skyscrapers, advertisements, telephones, wireless, aeroplanes, movies, motors, and all the rest of the twentieth century; and on the other side of the door something I can't explain, can't relate to them. Something as old as the world, as mysterious as life ... Nonsense! What am I worrying about? There hasn't been a letter for three months now – not since the day we came back from the country after Christmas ... Queer that they always seem to come after our holidays! ... Why should I imagine there's going to be one tonight!'

No reason why, but that was the worst of it – one of the worst! – that there were days when she would stand there cold and shivering with the premonition of something inexplicable, intolerable, to be faced on the other side of the curtained panes; and when she opened the door and went in, there would be nothing; and on other days when she felt the same premonitory chill, it was justified by the sight of the grey envelope. So that ever since the last had come she had taken to feeling cold and premonitory every evening, because she never opened the door without thinking the letter might be there.

Well, she'd had enough of it; that was certain. She couldn't go on like that. If her husband turned white and had a headache on the days when the letter came, he seemed to recover afterward; but she couldn't. With her the strain had become chronic, and the reason was not far to seek. Her husband knew from whom the letter came and what was in it; he was prepared beforehand for whatever he had to deal with, and master of the situation, however bad; whereas she was shut out in the dark with her conjectures.

'I can't stand it! I can't stand it another day!' she exclaimed aloud, as she put her key in the lock. She turned the key and went in; and there, on the table, lay the letter.

II

She was almost glad of the sight. It seemed to justify everything, to put a seal of definiteness on the whole blurred business. A letter for her husband; a letter from a woman – no doubt another vulgar case of 'old entanglement'. What a fool she had been ever to doubt it, to rack her brains for less obvious explanations! She took up the envelope with a steady contemptuous hand, looked closely at the faint letters, held it against the light and just discerned the outline of the folded sheet within. She knew that now she would have no peace till she found out what was written on that sheet.

Her husband had not come in; he seldom got back from his office before half-past six or seven, and it was not yet six. She would have time to take the letter up to the drawing-room, hold it over the tea-kettle which at that hour always simmered by the fire in expectation of her return, solve the mystery and replace the letter where she had found it. No one would be the wiser, and her gnawing uncertainty would be over. The alternative, of course, was to question her husband; but to do that seemed even more difficult. She weighed the letter between thumb and finger, looked at it again under the light, started up the stairs with the envelope – and came down again and laid it on the table.

'No, I evidently can't,' she said, disappointed.

What should she do, then? She couldn't go up alone to that warm welcoming room, pour out her tea, look over her correspondence, glance at a book or review – not with that letter lying below and the knowledge that in a little while her husband would come in, open it and turn into the library alone, as he always did on the days when the grey envelope came.

Suddenly she decided. She would wait in the library and see for herself; see what happened between him and the letter when they thought themselves unobserved. She wondered the idea had never occurred to her before. By leaving the door ajar, and sitting in the corner behind it, she could watch him unseen . . . Well, then, she would watch him! She drew a chair into the corner, sat down, her eyes on the crack, and waited.

As far as she could remember, it was the first time she had ever tried to surprise another person's secret, but she was conscious of no compunction. She simply felt as if she were fighting her way through a stifling fog that she must at all costs get out of.

At length she heard Kenneth's latchkey and jumped up. The impulse to rush out and meet him had nearly made her forget why she was there; but she remembered in time and sat down again. From her post she covered the whole range of his movements – saw him enter the hall, draw the key from the door and take off his hat and overcoat. Then he turned to throw his gloves on the hall

Pomegranate Seed

table, and at that moment he saw the envelope. The light was full on his face, and what Charlotte first noted there was a look of surprise. Evidently he had not expected the letter – had not thought of the possibility of its being there that day. But though he had not expected it, now that he saw it he knew well enough what it contained. He did not open it immediately, but stood motionless, the colour slowly ebbing from his face. Apparently he could not make up his mind to touch it; but at length he put out his hand, opened the envelope, and moved with it to the light. In doing so he turned his back on Charlotte, and she saw only his bent head and slightly stooping shoulders. Apparently all the writing was on one page, for he did not turn the sheet but continued to stare at it for so long that he must have re-read it a dozen times – or so it seemed to the woman breathlessly watching him. At length she saw him move; he raised the letter still closer to his eyes, as though he had not fully deciphered it. Then he lowered his head, and she saw his lips touch the sheet.

'Kenneth!' she exclaimed, and went out into the hall.

The letter clutched in his hand, her husband turned and looked at her. 'Where were you?' he said, in a low bewildered voice, like a man waked out of his sleep.

'In the library, waiting for you.' She tried to steady her voice: 'What's the matter! What's in that letter? You look ghastly.'

Her agitation seemed to calm him, and he instantly put the envelope into his pocket with a slight laugh. 'Ghastly? I'm sorry. I've had a hard day in the office – one or two complicated cases. I look dog-tired, I suppose.'

'You didn't look tired when you came in. It was only when you opened that letter –'

He had followed her into the library, and they stood gazing at each other. Charlotte noticed how quickly he had regained his self-control; his profession had trained him to rapid mastery of face and voice. She saw at once that she would be at a disadvantage in any attempt to surprise his secret, but at the same moment she lost all desire to manoeuvre, to trick him into betraying anything he wanted to conceal. Her wish was still to penetrate the mystery, but only that she might help him to bear the burden it implied. 'Even if it *is* another woman,' she thought.

'Kenneth,' she said, her heart beating excitedly, 'I waited here on purpose to see you come in. I wanted to watch you while you opened that letter.'

His face, which had paled, turned to dark red; then it paled again. 'That letter? Why especially that letter?'

'Because I've noticed that whenever one of those letters comes it seems to have such a strange effect on you.'

A line of anger she had never seen before came out between his eyes, and she said to herself: 'The upper part of his face is too narrow; this is the first time I ever noticed it.'

She heard him continue, in the cool and faintly ironic tone of the prosecuting lawyer making a point: 'Ah; so you're in the habit of watching people open their letters when they don't know you're there?'

'Not in the habit. I never did such a thing before. But I had to find out what she writes to you, at regular intervals, in those grey envelopes.'

He weighed this for a moment; then: 'The intervals have not been regular,' he said.

'Oh, I dare say you've kept a better account of the dates than I have,' she retorted, her magnanimity vanishing at his tone. 'All I know is that every time that woman writes to you –'

'Why do you assume it's a woman?'

'It's a woman's writing. Do you deny it?'

He smiled. 'No, I don't deny it. I asked only because the writing is generally supposed to look more like a man's.'

Charlotte passed this over impatiently. 'And this woman – what does she write to you about?'

Again he seemed to consider a moment. 'About business.'

'Legal business?'

'In a way, yes. Business in general.'

'You look after her affairs for her?'

'Yes.'

'You've looked after them for a long time?'

'Yes. A very long time.'

'Kenneth, dearest, won't you tell me who she is?'

'No. I can't.' He paused, and brought out, as if with a certain hesitation: 'Professional secrecy.'

The blood rushed from Charlotte's heart to her temples. 'Don't say that – don't!'

'Why not?'

'Because I saw you kiss the letter.'

The effect of the words was so disconcerting that she instantly repented having spoken them. Her husband, who had submitted to her cross-questioning with a sort of contemptuous composure, as though he were humouring an unreasonable child, turned on her a face of terror and distress. For a minute he seemed unable to speak; then, collecting himself with an effort, he stammered out; 'The writing is very faint; you must have seen me holding the letter close to my eyes to try to decipher it.'

'No. I saw you kissing it.' He was silent. 'Didn't I see you kissing it?'

He sank back into indifference. 'Perhaps.'

'Kenneth! You stand there and say that – to me?'

'What possible difference can it make to you? The letter is on business, as I told you. Do you suppose I'd lie about it? The writer is a very old friend whom I haven't seen for a long time.'

'Men don't kiss business letters, even from women who are very old friends, unless they have been their lovers, and still regret them.'

He shrugged his shoulders slightly and turned away, as if he considered the discussion at an end and were faintly disgusted at the turn it had taken.

'Kenneth!' Charlotte moved toward him and caught hold of his arm.

He paused with a look of weariness and laid his hand over hers. 'Won't you believe me?' he asked gently.

'How can I? I've watched these letters come to you – for months now they've been coming. Ever since we came back from the West Indies – one of them greeted me the very day we arrived. And after each one of them I see their mysterious effect on you, I see you disturbed, unhappy, as if someone were trying to estrange you from me.'

'No, dear; not that. Never!'

She drew back and looked at him with passionate entreaty. 'Well, then, prove it to me, darling. It's so easy!'

He forced a smile. 'It's not easy to prove anything to a woman who's once taken an idea into her head.'

'You've only got to show me the letter.'

His hand slipped from hers and he drew back and shook his head.

Pomegranate Seed

'You won't?'

'I can't.'

'Then the woman who wrote it is your mistress.'

'No, dear. No.'

'Not now, perhaps. I suppose she's trying to get you back, and you're struggling, out of pity for me. My poor Kenneth!'

'I swear to you she never was my mistress.'

Charlotte felt the tears rushing to her eyes. 'Ah, that's worse, then – that's hopeless! The prudent ones are the kind that keep their hold on a man. We all know that.' She lifted her hands and hid her face in them.

Her husband remained silent; he offered neither consolation nor denial, and at length, wiping away her tears, she raised her eyes almost timidly to his.

'Kenneth, think! We've been married such a short time. Imagine what you're making me suffer. You say you can't show me this letter. You refuse even to explain it.'

'I've told you the letter is on business. I will swear to that too.'

'A man will swear to anything to screen a woman. If you want me to believe you, at least tell me her name. If you'll do that, I promise you I won't ask to see the letter.'

There was a long interval of suspense, during which she felt her heart beating against her ribs in quick admonitory knocks, as if warning her of the danger she was incurring.

'I can't,' he said at length.

'Not even her name?'

'No.'

'You can't tell me anything more?'

'No.'

Again a pause; this time they seemed both to have reached the end of their arguments and to be helplessly facing each other across a baffling waste of incomprehension.

Charlotte stood breathing rapidly, her hands against her breast. She felt as if she had run a hard race and missed the goal. She had meant to move her husband and had succeeded only in irritating him; and this error of reckoning seemed to change him into a stranger, a mysterious incomprehensible being whom no argument or entreaty of hers could reach. The curious thing was that she was aware in him of no hostility or even impatience, but only of a remoteness, an inaccessibility, far more difficult to overcome. She felt herself excluded, ignored, blotted out of his life. But after a moment or two, looking at him more calmly, she saw that he was suffering as much as she was. His distant guarded face was drawn with pain; the coming of the grey envelope, though it always cast a shadow, had never marked him as deeply as this discussion with his wife.

Charlotte took heart; perhaps, after all, she had not spent her last shaft. She drew nearer and once more laid her hand on his arm. 'Poor Kenneth! If you knew how sorry I am for you –'

She thought he winced slightly at this expression of sympathy, but he took her hand and pressed it.

'I can think of nothing worse than to be incapable of loving long,' she continued; 'to feel the beauty of a great love and to be too unstable to bear its burden.'

He turned on her a look of wistful reproach. 'Oh, don't say that of me. Unstable!'

She felt herself at last on the right tack, and her voice trembled with excitement as she went on: 'Then what

Pomegranate Seed

about me and this other woman? Haven't you already forgotten Elsie twice within a year?'

She seldom pronounced his first wife's name; it did not come naturally to her tongue. She flung it out now as if she were flinging some dangerous explosive into the open space between them, and drew back a step, waiting to hear the mine go off.

Her husband did not move; his expression grew sadder, but showed no resentment. 'I have never forgotten Elsie,' he said.

Charlotte could not repress a faint laugh. 'Then, you poor dear, between the three of us –'

'There are not –' he began; and then broke off and put his hand to his forehead.

'Not what?'

'I'm sorry. I don't believe I know what I'm saying. I've got a blinding headache.' He looked wan and furrowed enough for the statement to be true, but she was exasperated by his evasion.

'Ah, yes; the grey-envelope headache!'

She saw the surprise in his eyes. 'I'd forgotten how closely I've been watched,' he said coldly. 'If you'll excuse me, I think I'll go up and try an hour in the dark, to see if I can get rid of this neuralgia.'

She wavered; then she said, with desperate resolution; 'I'm sorry your head aches. But before you go I want to say that sooner or later this question must be settled between us. Someone is trying to separate us, and I don't care what it costs me to find out who it is.' She looked him steadily in the eyes. 'If it costs me your love, I don't care! If I can't have your confidence I don't want anything from you.'

He still looked at her wistfully. 'Give me time.'

'Time for what? It's only a word to say.'

'Time to show you that you haven't lost my love or my confidence.'

'Well, I'm waiting.'

He turned toward the door, and then glanced back hesitatingly. 'Oh, do wait, my love,' he said, and went out of the room.

She heard his tired step on the stairs and the closing of his bedroom door above. Then she dropped into a chair and buried her face in her folded arms. Her first movement was one of compunction; she seemed to herself to have been hard, unhuman, unimaginative. 'Think of telling him that I didn't care if my insistence cost me his love! The lying rubbish!' She started up to follow him and unsay the meaningless words. But she was checked by a reflection. He had had his way, after all; he had eluded all attacks on his secret, and now he was shut up alone in his room, reading that other woman's letter.

III

She was still reflecting on this when the surprised parlour-maid came in and found her. No, Charlotte said, she wasn't going to dress for dinner; Mr Ashby didn't want to dine. He was very tired and had gone up to his room to rest; later she would have something brought on a tray to the drawing-room. She mounted the stairs to her bedroom. Her dinner dress was lying on the bed, and at the sight the quiet routine of her daily life took hold of her and she began to feel as if the strange talk she had just had with her husband must have taken place in another world, between two beings who were not Charlotte Gorse and Kenneth Ashby, but phantoms projected by her fevered imagination. She recalled the

Pomegranate Seed

year since her marriage – her husband's constant devotion; his persistent, almost too insistent tenderness; the feeling he had given her at times of being too eagerly dependent on her, too searchingly close to her, as if there were not air enough between her soul and his. It seemed preposterous, as she recalled all this, that a few moments ago she should have been accusing him of an intrigue with another woman! But, then, what –

Again she was moved by the impulse to go up to him, beg his pardon and try to laugh away the misunderstanding. But she was restrained by the fear of forcing herself upon his privacy. He was troubled and unhappy, oppressed by some grief or fear; and he had shown her that he wanted to fight out his battle alone. It would be wiser, as well as more generous, to respect his wish. Only, how strange, how unbearable, to be there, in the next room to his, and feel herself at the other end of the world! In her nervous agitation she almost regretted not having had the courage to open the letter and put it back on the hall table before he came in. At least she would have known what his secret was, and the bogey might have been laid. For she was beginning now to think of the mystery as something conscious, malevolent: a secret persecution before which he quailed, yet from which he could not free himself. Once or twice in his evasive eyes she thought she had detected a desire for help, an impulse of confession, instantly restrained and suppressed. It was as if he felt she could have helped him if she had known, and yet had been unable to tell her!

There flashed through her mind the idea of going to his mother. She was very fond of old Mrs Ashby, a firm-fleshed clear-eyed old lady, with an astringent bluntness of speech which responded to the forthright and simple in Charlotte's own nature. There had been a tacit bond between them ever since the day when Mrs Ashby senior, coming to lunch for the first time with her new daughter-in-law, had been received by Charlotte downstairs in the library, and glancing up at the empty wall above her son's desk, had remarked laconically: 'Elsie gone, eh?' adding, at Charlotte's murmured explanation, 'Nonsense. Don't have her back. Two's company.' Charlotte, at this reading of her thoughts, could hardly refrain from exchanging a smile of complicity with her mother-in-law; and it seemed to her now that Mrs Ashby's almost uncanny directness might pierce to the core of this new mystery. But here again she hesitated, for the idea almost suggested a betrayal. What right had she to call in any one, even so close a relation, to surprise a secret which her husband was trying to keep from her? 'Perhaps, by and by, he'll talk to his mother of his own accord,' she thought, and then ended, 'but what does it matter? He and I must settle it between us.'

She was still brooding over the problem when there was a knock on the door and her husband came in. He was dressed for dinner and seemed surprised to see her sitting there, with her evening dress lying unheeded on the bed.

'Aren't you coming down?'

'I thought you were not well and had gone to bed,' she faltered.

He forced a smile. 'I'm not particularly well, but we'd better go down.' His face, though still drawn, looked calmer than when he had fled upstairs an hour earlier.

'There it is; he knows what's in the letter and has fought his battle out again, whatever it is,' she reflected, 'while I'm still in darkness.' She rang and gave a hurried order that dinner should be served as soon as possible –

just a short meal, whatever could be got ready quickly, as both she and Mr Ashby were rather tired and not very hungry.

Dinner was announced, and they sat down to it. At first neither seemed able to find a word to say; then Ashby began to make conversation with an assumption of ease that was more oppressive than his silence. 'How tired he is! How terribly over-tired!' Charlotte said to herself, pursuing her own thoughts while he rambled on about municipal politics, aviation, an exhibition of modern French painting, the health of an old aunt and the installing of the automatic telephone. 'Good heavens, how tired he is!'

When they dined alone they usually went into the library after dinner, and Charlotte curled herself up on the divan with her knitting while he settled down in his armchair under the lamp and lit a pipe. But this evening, by tacit agreement, they avoided the room in which their strange talk had taken place, and went up to Charlotte's drawing-room.

They sat down near the fire, and Charlotte said; 'Your pipe?' after he had put down his hardly tasted coffee.

He shook his head. 'No, not tonight.'

'You must go to bed early; you look terribly tired. I'm sure they overwork you at the office.'

'I suppose we all overwork at times.'

She rose and stood before him with sudden resolution. 'Well, I'm not going to have you use up your strength slaving in that way. It's absurd. I can see you're ill.' She bent over him and laid her hand on his forehead. 'My poor old Kenneth. Prepare to be taken away soon on a long holiday.'

He looked up at her, startled. 'A holiday?'

'Certainly. Didn't you know I was going to carry you

off at Easter? We're going to start in a fortnight on a month's voyage to somewhere or other. On any one of the big cruising steamers.' She paused and bent closer, touching his forehead with her lips. 'I'm tired, too, Kenneth.'

He seemed to pay no heed to her last words, but sat, his hands on his knees, his head drawn back a little from her caress, and looked up at her with a stare of apprehension. 'Again? My dear, we can't; I can't possibly go away.'

'I don't know why you say "again", Kenneth; we haven't taken a real holiday this year.'

'At Christmas we spent a week with the children in the country.'

'Yes, but this time I mean away from the children, from servants, from the house. From everything that's familiar and fatiguing. Your mother will love to have Joyce and Peter with her.'

He frowned and slowly shook his head. 'No, dear; I can't leave them with my mother.'

'Why, Kenneth, how absurd! She adores them. You didn't hesitate to leave them with her for over two months when we went to the West Indies.'

He drew a deep breath and stood up uneasily. 'That was different.'

'Different? Why?'

'I mean, at that time I didn't realize –' He broke off as if to choose his words and then went on, 'My mother adores the children, as you say. But she isn't always very judicious. Grandmothers always spoil children. And she sometimes talks before them without thinking.' He turned to his wife with an almost pitiful gesture of entreaty. 'Don't ask me to, dear.'

Charlotte mused. It was true that the elder Mrs Ashby

had a fearless tongue, but she was the last woman in the world to say or hint anything before her grandchildren at which the most scrupulous parent could take offence. Charlotte looked at her husband in perplexity.

'I don't understand.'

He continued to turn on her the same troubled and entreating gaze. 'Don't try to,' he muttered.

'Not try to?'

'Not now – not yet.' He put up his hands and pressed them against his temples. 'Can't you see that there's no use in insisting? I can't go away, no matter how much I might want to.'

Charlotte still scrutinized him gravely. 'The question is, *do* you want to?'

He returned her gaze for a moment; then his lips began to tremble, and he said, hardly above his breath, 'I want – anything you want.'

'And yet –'

'Don't ask me. I can't leave – I can't!'

'You mean that you can't go away out of reach of those letters!'

Her husband had been standing before her in an uneasy half-hesitating attitude; now he turned abruptly away and walked once or twice up and down the length of the room, his head bent, his eyes fixed on the carpet.

Charlotte felt her resentfulness rising with her fears. 'It's that,' she persisted. 'Why not admit it? You can't live without them.'

He continued his troubled pacing of the room; then he stopped short, dropped into a chair and covered his face with his hands. From the shaking of his shoulders, Charlotte saw that he was weeping. She had never seen a man cry, except her father after her mother's death, when she was a little girl; and she remembered still how the sight had frightened her. She was frightened now; she felt that her husband was being dragged away from her into some mysterious bondage, and that she must use up her last atom of strength in the struggle for his freedom, and for hers.

'Kenneth – Kenneth!' she pleaded, kneeling down beside him. 'Won't you listen to me? Won't you try to see what I'm suffering? I'm not unreasonable, darling; really not. I don't suppose I should ever have noticed the letters if it hadn't been for their effect on you. It's not my way to pry into other people's affairs; and even if the effect had been different – yes, yes; listen to me – if I'd seen that the letters made you happy, that you were watching eagerly for them, counting the days between their coming, that you wanted them, that they gave you something I haven't known how to give – why, Kenneth, I don't say I shouldn't have suffered from that, too; but it would have been in a different way, and I should have had the courage to hide what I felt, and the hope that some day you'd come to feel about me as you did about the writer of the letters. But what I can't bear is to see how you dread them, how they make you suffer, and yet how you can't live without them and won't go away lest you should miss one during your absence. Or perhaps,' she added, her voice breaking into a cry of accusation – 'perhaps it's because she's actually forbidden you to leave. Kenneth, you must answer me! Is that the reason? Is it because she's forbidden you that you won't go away with me?'

She continued to kneel at his side, and raising her hands, she drew his gently down. She was ashamed of her persistence, ashamed of uncovering that baffled disordered face, yet resolved that no such scruples should arrest her. His eyes were lowered, the muscles of his face quivered; she was making him suffer even more than she suffered herself. Yet this no longer restrained her.

'Kenneth, is it that? She won't let us go away together?'

Still he did not speak or turn his eyes to her; and a sense of defeat swept over her. After all, she thought, the struggle was a losing one. 'You needn't answer. I see I'm right,' she said.

Suddenly, as she rose, he turned and drew her down again. His hands caught hers and pressed them so tightly that she felt her rings cutting into her flesh. There was something frightened, convulsive in his hold; it was the clutch of a man who felt himself slipping over a precipice. He was staring up at her now as if salvation lay in the face she bent above him. 'Of course we'll go away together. We'll go wherever you want,' he said in a low confused voice; and putting his arm about her, he drew her close and pressed his lips on hers.

IV

Charlotte had said to herself: 'I shall sleep tonight,' but instead she sat before her fire into the small hours, listening for any sound that came from her husband's room. But he, at any rate, seemed to be resting after the tumult of the evening. Once or twice she stole to the door and in the faint light that came in from the street through his open window she saw him stretched out in heavy sleep – the sleep of weakness and exhaustion. 'He's ill,' she thought – 'he's undoubtedly ill. And it's not overwork; it's this mysterious persecution.'

She drew a breath of relief. She had fought through the weary fight and the victory was hers – at least for the moment. If only they could have started at once – started for anywhere! She knew it would be useless to ask him to leave before the holidays; and meanwhile the secret influence – as to which she was still so completely in the dark – would continue to work against her, and she would have to renew the struggle day after day till they started on their journey. But after that everything would be different. If once she could get her husband away under other skies, and all to herself, she never doubted her power to release him from the evil spell he was under. Lulled to quiet by the thought, she too slept at last.

When she woke, it was long past her usual hour, and she sat up in bed surprised and vexed at having overslept herself. She always liked to be down to share her husband's breakfast by the library fire; but a glance at the clock made it clear that he must have started long since for his office. To make sure, she jumped out of bed and went into his room; but it was empty. No doubt he had looked in on her before leaving, seen that she still slept, and gone downstairs without disturbing her; and their relations were sufficiently loverlike for her to regret having missed their morning hour.

She rang and asked if Mr Ashby had already gone. Yes, nearly an hour ago, the maid said. He had given orders that Mrs Ashby should not be waked and that the children should not come to her till she sent for them ... Yes, he had gone up to the nursery himself to give the order. All this sounded usual enough; and Charlotte hardly knew why she asked, 'And did Mr Ashby leave no other message?'

Yes, the maid said, he did; she was so sorry she'd forgotten. He'd told her, just as he was leaving, to say to Mrs Ashby that he was going to see about

Pomegranate Seed

their passages, and would she please be ready to sail tomorrow?

Charlotte echoed the woman's 'Tomorrow,' and sat staring at her incredulously. 'Tomorrow – you're sure he said to sail tomorrow?'

'Oh, ever so sure, ma'am. I don't know how I could have forgotten to mention it.'

'Well, it doesn't matter. Draw my bath, please.' Charlotte sprang up, dashed through her dressing, and caught herself singing at her image in the glass as she sat brushing her hair. It made her feel young again to have scored such a victory. The other woman vanished to a speck on the horizon, as this one, who ruled the foreground, smiled back at the reflection of her lips and eyes. He loved her, then – he loved her as passionately as ever. He had divined what she had suffered, had understood that their happiness depended on their getting away at once, and finding each other again after yesterday's desperate groping in the fog. The nature of the influence that had come between them did not much matter to Charlotte now; she had faced the phantom and dispelled it. 'Courage – that's the secret! If only people who are in love weren't always so afraid of risking their happiness by looking it in the eyes.' As she brushed back her light abundant hair it waved electrically above her head, like the palms of victory. Ah, well, some women knew how to manage men, and some didn't – and only the fair – she gaily paraphrased – deserve the brave! Certainly she was looking very pretty.

The morning danced along like a cockleshell on a bright sea – such a sea as they would soon be speeding over. She ordered a particularly good dinner, saw the children off to their classes, had her trunks brought down, consulted with the maid about getting out summer clothes – for of course they would be heading for heat and sunshine – and wondered if she oughtn't to take Kenneth's flannel suits out of camphor. 'But how absurd,' she reflected, 'that I don't yet know where we're going!' She looked at the clock, saw that it was close on noon, and decided to call him up at his office. There was a slight delay; then she heard his secretary's voice saying that Mr Ashby had looked in for a moment early, and left again almost immediately ... Oh, very well; Charlotte would ring up later. How soon was he likely to be back? The secretary answered that she couldn't tell; all they knew in the office was that when he left he had said he was in a hurry because he had to go out of town.

Out of town! Charlotte hung up the receiver and sat blankly gazing into new darkness. Why had he gone out of town? And where had he gone? And of all days, why should he have chosen the eve of their suddenly planned departure? She felt a faint shiver of apprehension. Of course he had gone to see that woman – no doubt to get her permission to leave. He was as completely in bondage as that; and Charlotte had been fatuous enough to see the palms of victory on her forehead. She burst into a laugh and, walking across the room, sat down again before her mirror. What a different face she saw! The smile on her pale lips seemed to mock the rosy vision of the other Charlotte. But gradually her colour crept back. After all, she had a right to claim the victory, since her husband was doing what she wanted, not what the other woman exacted of him. It was natural enough, in view of his abrupt decision to leave the next day, that he should have arrangements to make, business matters to wind up; it was not even necessary to suppose that his mysterious trip was a visit to the writer of the letters.

Pomegranate Seed

He might simply have gone to see a client who lived out of town. Of course they would not tell Charlotte at the office; the secretary had hesitated before imparting even such meagre information as the fact of Mr Ashby's absence. Meanwhile she would go on with her joyful preparations, content to learn later in the day to what particular island of the blest she was to be carried.

The hours wore on, rather were swept forward on a rush of eager preparations. At last the entrance of the maid who came to draw the curtains roused Charlotte from her labours, and she saw to her surprise that the clock marked five. And she did not yet know where they were going the next day! She rang up her husband's office and was told that Mr Ashby had not been there since the early morning. She asked for his partner, but the partner could add nothing to her information, for he himself, his suburban train having been behind time, had reached the office after Ashby had come and gone. Charlotte stood perplexed; then she decided to telephone to her mother-in-law. Of course Kenneth, on the eve of a month's absence, must have gone to see his mother. The mere fact that the children – in spite of his vague objections – would certainly have to be left with old Mrs Ashby, made it obvious that he would have all sorts of matters to decide with her. At another time Charlotte might have felt a little hurt at being excluded from their conference, but nothing mattered now but that she had won the day, that her husband was still hers and not another woman's. Gaily she called up Mrs Ashby, heard her friendly voice, and began, 'Well, did Kenneth's news surprise you? What do you think of our elopement?'

Almost instantly, before Mrs Ashby could answer, Charlotte knew what her reply would be. Mrs Ashby had not seen her son, she had had no word from him and did not know what her daughter-in-law meant. Charlotte stood silent in the intensity of her surprise. 'But then, where *has* he been?' she thought. Then, recovering herself, she explained their sudden decision to Mrs Ashby, and in doing so, gradually regained her own self-confidence, her conviction that nothing could ever again come between Kenneth and herself. Mrs Ashby took the news calmly and approvingly. She, too, had thought that Kenneth looked worried and overtired, and she agreed with her daughter-in-law that in such cases change was the surest remedy. 'I'm always so glad when he gets away. Elsie hated travelling; she was always finding pretexts to prevent his going anywhere. With you, thank goodness, it's different.' Nor was Mrs Ashby surprised at his not having had time to let her know of his departure. He must have been in a rush from the moment the decision was taken; but no doubt he'd drop in before dinner. Five minutes' talk was really all they needed. 'I hope you'll gradually cure Kenneth of his mania for going over and over a question that could be settled in a dozen words. He never used to be like that, and if he carried the habit into his professional work he'd soon lose all his clients . . . Yes, do come in for a minute, dear, if you have time; no doubt he'll turn up while you're here.' The tonic ring of Mrs Ashby's voice echoed on reassuringly in the silent room while Charlotte continued her preparations.

Toward seven the telephone rang, and she darted to it. Now she would know! But it was only from the conscientious secretary, to say that Mr Ashby hadn't been back, or sent any word, and before the office closed she thought she ought to let Mrs Ashby know. 'Oh, that's all right. Thanks a lot!' Charlotte called out cheerfully, and hung up the receiver with a trembling hand. But perhaps by

Pomegranate Seed

this time, she reflected, he was at his mother's. She shut her drawers and cupboards, put on her hat and coat and called up to the nursery that she was going out for a minute to see the children's grandmother.

Mrs Ashby lived nearby, and during her brief walk through the cold spring dusk Charlotte imagined that every advancing figure was her husband's. But she did not meet him on the way, and when she entered the house she found her mother-in-law alone. Kenneth had neither telephoned nor come. Old Mrs Ashby sat by her bright fire, her knitting needles flashing steadily through her active old hands, and her mere bodily presence gave reassurance to Charlotte. Yes, it was certainly odd that Kenneth had gone off for the whole day without letting any of them know; but, after all, it was to be expected. A busy lawyer held so many threads in his hands that any sudden change of plan would oblige him to make all sorts of unforeseen arrangements and adjustments. He might have gone to see some client in the suburbs and been detained there; his mother remembered his telling her that he had charge of the legal business of a queer old recluse somewhere in New Jersey, who was immensely rich but too mean to have a telephone. Very likely Kenneth had been stranded there.

But Charlotte felt her nervousness gaining on her. When Mrs Ashby asked her at what hour they were sailing the next day and she had to say she didn't know – that Kenneth had simply sent her word he was going to take their passages – the uttering of the words again brought home to her the strangeness of the situation. Even Mrs Ashby conceded that it was odd; but she immediately added that it only showed what a rush he was in.

'But, Mother, it's nearly eight o'clock! He must realize that I've got to know when we're starting tomorrow.'

'Oh, the boat probably doesn't sail till evening. Sometimes they have to wait till midnight for the tide. Kenneth's probably counting on that. After all, he has a level head.'

Charlotte stood up. 'It's not that. Something has happened to him.'

Mrs Ashby took off her spectacles and rolled up her knitting. 'If you begin to let yourself imagine things —'

'Aren't you in the least anxious?'

'I never am till I have to be. I wish you'd ring for dinner, my dear. You'll stay and dine? He's sure to drop in here on his way home.'

Charlotte called up her own house. No, the maid said, Mr Ashby hadn't come in and hadn't telephoned. She would tell him as soon as he came that Mrs Ashby was dining at his mother's. Charlotte followed her mother-in-law into the dining-room and sat with parched throat before her empty plate, while Mrs Ashby dealt calmly and efficiently with a short but carefully prepared repast. 'You'd better eat something, child, or you'll be as bad as Kenneth ... Yes, a little more asparagus, please, Jane.'

She insisted on Charlotte's drinking a glass of sherry and nibbling a bit of toast; then they returned to the drawing-room, where the fire had been made up, and the cushions in Mrs Ashby's armchair shaken out and smoothed. How safe and familiar it all looked; and out there, somewhere in the uncertainty and mystery of the night, lurked the answer to the two women's conjectures, like an indistinguishable figure prowling on the threshold.

Pomegranate Seed

At last Charlotte got up and said, 'I'd better go back. At this hour Kenneth will certainly go straight home.'

Mrs Ashby smiled indulgently. 'It's not very late, my dear. It doesn't take two sparrows long to dine.'

'It's after nine.' Charlotte bent down to kiss her. 'The fact is, I can't keep still.'

Mrs Ashby pushed aside her work and rested her two hands on the arms of her chair. 'I'm going with you,' she said, helping herself up.

Charlotte protested that it was too late, that it was not necessary, that she would call up as soon as Kenneth came in, but Mrs Ashby had already rung for her maid. She was slightly lame, and stood resting on her stick while her wraps were brought. 'If Mr Kenneth turns up, tell him he'll find me at his own house,' she instructed the maid as the two women got into the taxi which had been summoned. During the short drive Charlotte gave thanks that she was not returning home alone. There was something warm and substantial in the mere fact of Mrs Ashby's nearness, something that corresponded with the clearness of her eyes and the texture of her fresh firm complexion. As the taxi drew up she laid her hand encouragingly on Charlotte's. 'You'll see; there'll be a message.'

The door opened at Charlotte's ring and the two entered. Charlotte's heart beat excitedly; the stimulus of her mother-in-law's confidence was beginning to flow through her veins.

'You'll see – you'll see,' Mrs Ashby repeated.

The maid who opened the door said no, Mr Ashby had not come in, and there had been no message from him.

'You're sure the telephone's not out of order?' his mother suggested; and the maid said, well, it certainly wasn't half an hour ago; but she'd just go and ring up to make sure. She disappeared, and Charlotte turned to take off her hat and cloak. As she did so her eyes lit on the hall table, and there lay a grey envelope, her husband's name faintly traced on it. 'Oh!' she cried out, suddenly aware that for the first time in months she had entered her house without wondering if one of the grey letters would be there.

'What is it, my dear?' Mrs Ashby asked with a glance of surprise.

Charlotte did not answer. She took up the envelope and stood staring at it as if she could force her gaze to penetrate to what was within. Then an idea occurred to her. She turned and held out the envelope to her mother-in-law.

'Do you know that writing?' she asked.

Mrs Ashby took the letter. She had to feel with her other hand for her eyeglasses, and when she had adjusted them she lifted the envelope to the light. 'Why!' she exclaimed; and then stopped. Charlotte noticed that the letter shook in her usually firm hand. 'But this is addressed to Kenneth,' Mrs Ashby said at length, in a low voice. Her tone seemed to imply that she felt her daughter-in-law's question to be slightly indiscreet.

'Yes, but no matter,' Charlotte spoke with sudden decision. 'I want to know – do you know the writing?'

Mrs Ashby handed back the letter. 'No,' she said distinctly.

The two women had turned into the library. Charlotte switched on the electric light and shut the door. She still held the envelope in her hand.

'I'm going to open it,' she announced.

She caught her mother-in-law's startled glance. 'But, dearest – a letter not addressed to you? My dear, you can't!'

Pomegranate Seed

'As if I cared about that – now!' She continued to look intently at Mrs Ashby. 'This letter may tell me where Kenneth is.'

Mrs Ashby's glossy bloom was effaced by a quick pallor; her firm cheeks seemed to shrink and wither. 'Why should it? What makes you believe – It can't possibly –'

Charlotte held her eyes steadily on that altered face. 'Ah, then you *do* know the writing?' she flashed back.

'Know the writing? How should I? With all my son's correspondents ... What I do know is –' Mrs Ashby broke off and looked at her daughter-in-law entreatingly, almost timidly.

Charlotte caught her by the wrist. 'Mother! What do you know? Tell me! You must!'

'That I don't believe any good ever came of a woman's opening her husband's letters behind his back.'

The words sounded to Charlotte's irritated ears as flat as a phrase culled from a book of moral axioms. She laughed impatiently and dropped her mother-in-law's wrist. 'Is that all? No good can come of this letter, opened or unopened. I know that well enough. But whatever ill comes, I mean to find out what's in it.' Her hands had been trembling as they held the envelope, but now they grew firm, and her voice also. She still gazed intently at Mrs Ashby. 'This is the ninth letter addressed in the same hand that has come for Kenneth since we've been married. Always these same grey envelopes. I've kept count of them because after each one he has been like a man who has had some dreadful shock. It takes him hours to shake off their effect. I've told him so. I've told him I must know from whom they come, because I can see they're killing him. He won't answer my questions; he says he can't tell me anything about the letters; but last night he promised to go away with me – to get away from them.'

Mrs Ashby, with shaking steps, had gone to one of the armchairs and sat down in it, her head drooping forward on her breast. 'Ah,' she murmured.

'So now you understand –'

'Did he tell you it was to get away from them?'

'He said, to get away – to get away. He was sobbing so that he could hardly speak. But I told him I knew that was why.'

'And what did he say?'

'He took me in his arms and said he'd go wherever I wanted.'

'Ah, thank God!' said Mrs Ashby. There was a silence, during which she continued to sit with bowed head, and eyes averted from her daughter-in-law. At last she looked up and spoke. 'Are you sure there have been as many as nine?'

'Perfectly. This is the ninth. I've kept count.'

'And he has absolutely refused to explain?'

'Absolutely.'

Mrs Ashby spoke through pale contracted lips. 'When did they begin to come? Do you remember?'

Charlotte laughed again. 'Remember? The first one came the night we got back from our honeymoon.'

'All that time?' Mrs Ashby lifted her head and spoke with sudden energy. 'Then – Yes, open it.'

The words were so unexpected that Charlotte felt the blood in her temples, and her hands began to tremble again. She tried to slip her finger under the flap of the envelope, but it was so tightly stuck that she had to hunt on her husband's writing table for his ivory letter-opener. As she pushed about the familiar objects his own hands had so lately touched, they sent through her the

Pomegranate Seed

icy chill emanating from the little personal effects of someone newly dead. In the deep silence of the room the tearing of the paper as she slit the envelope sounded like a human cry. She drew out the sheet and carried it to the lamp.

'Well?' Mrs Ashby asked below her breath.

Charlotte did not move or answer. She was bending over the page with wrinkled brows, holding it nearer and nearer to the light. Her sight must be blurred, or else dazzled by the reflection of the lamplight on the smooth surface of the paper, for, strain her eyes as she would, she could discern only a few faint strokes, so faint and faltering as to be nearly undecipherable.

'I can't make it out,' she said.

'What do you mean, dear?'

'The writing's too indistinct . . . Wait.'

She went back to the table and, sitting down close to Kenneth's reading lamp, slipped the letter under a magnifying glass. All this time she was aware that her mother-in-law was watching her intently.

'Well?' Mrs Ashby breathed.

'Well, it's no clearer. I can't read it.'

'You mean the paper is an absolute blank?'

'No, not quite. There is writing on it. I can make out something like "mine" – oh, and "come". It might be "come".'

Mrs Ashby stood up abruptly. Her face was even paler than before. She advanced to the table and, resting her two hands on it, drew a deep breath. 'Let me see,' she said, as if forcing herself to a hateful effort.

Charlotte felt the contagion of her whiteness. 'She knows,' she thought. She pushed the letter across the table. Her mother-in-law lowered her head over it in silence, but without touching it with her pale wrinkled hands.

Charlotte stood watching her as she herself, when she had tried to read the letter, had been watched by Mrs Ashby. The latter fumbled for her glasses, held them to her eyes, and bent still closer to the outspread page, in order, as it seemed, to avoid touching it. The light of the lamp fell directly on her old face, and Charlotte reflected what depths of the unknown may lurk under the clearest and most candid lineaments. She had never seen her mother-in-law's features express any but simple and sound emotions – cordiality, amusement, a kindly sympathy; now and again a flash of wholesome anger. Now they seemed to wear a look of fear and hatred, of incredulous dismay and almost cringing defiance. It was as if the spirits warring within her had distorted her face to their own likeness. At length she raised her head. 'I can't – I can't,' she said in a voice of childish distress.

'You can't make it out either?'

She shook her head, and Charlotte saw two tears roll down her cheeks.

'Familiar as the writing is to you?' Charlotte insisted with twitching lips.

Mrs Ashby did not take up the challenge. 'I can make out nothing – nothing.'

'But you do know the writing?'

Mrs Ashby lifted her head timidly; her anxious eyes stole with a glance of apprehension around the quiet familiar room. 'How can I tell? I was startled at first . . .'

'Startled by the resemblance?'

'Well. I thought –'

'You'd better say it out, Mother! You knew at once it was *her* writing?'

'Oh, wait, my dear – wait.'

'Wait for what?'

Mrs Ashby looked up; her eyes, travelling slowly past Charlotte, were lifted to the blank wall behind her son's writing table.

Charlotte, following the glance, burst into a shrill laugh of accusation. 'I needn't wait any longer! You've answered me now! You're looking straight at the wall where her picture used to hang!'

Mrs Ashby lifted her hand with a murmur of warning. 'Sh-h.'

'Oh, you needn't imagine that anything can ever frighten me again!' Charlotte cried.

Her mother-in-law still leaned against the table. Her lips moved plaintively. 'But we're going mad – we're both going mad. We both know such things are impossible.'

Her daughter-in-law looked at her with a pitying stare. 'I've known for a long time now that everything was possible.'

'Even this?'

'Yes, exactly this.'

'But this letter – after all, there's nothing in this letter –'

'Perhaps there would be to him. How can I tell? I remember his saying to me once that if you were used to a handwriting the faintest stroke of it became legible. Now I see what he meant. He *was* used to it.'

'But the few strokes that I can make out are so pale. No one could possibly read that letter.'

Charlotte laughed again. 'I suppose everything's pale about a ghost,' she said stridently.

'Oh, my child – my child – don't say it!'

'Why shouldn't I say it, when even the bare walls cry it out? What difference does it make if her letters are illegible to you and me? If even you can see her face on that blank wall, why shouldn't he read her writing on this blank paper? Don't you see that she's everywhere in this house, and the closer to him because to everyone else she's become invisible?' Charlotte dropped into a chair and covered her face with her hands. A turmoil of sobbing shook her from head to foot. At length a touch on her shoulder made her look up, and she saw her mother-in-law bending over her. Mrs Ashby's face seemed to have grown still smaller and more wasted, but it had resumed its usual quiet look. Through all her tossing anguish, Charlotte felt the impact of that resolute spirit.

'Tomorrow – tomorrow. You'll see. There'll be some explanation tomorrow.'

Charlotte cut her short. 'An explanation? Who's going to give it, I wonder?'

Mrs Ashby drew back and straightened herself heroically. 'Kenneth himself will,' she cried out in a strong voice. Charlotte said nothing, and the old woman went on; 'But meanwhile we must act; we must notify the police. Now, without a moment's delay. We must do everything – everything.'

Charlotte stood up slowly and stiffly; her joints felt as cramped as an old woman's. 'Exactly as if we thought it could do any good to do anything?'

Resolutely Mrs Ashby cried: 'Yes!' and Charlotte went up to the telephone and unhooked the receiver.

Jeanette Winterson

extract from

Sexing the Cherry

Jordan, the Dog Woman's baby son, is a voyager, apprentice and companion to the naturalist John Tradescant. On one of his journeys he meets a miller who advises him to learn the story of the Twelve Dancing Princesses, especially since the girls are still living just down the road and willingly tell their own tales.

Jordan, the Dog Woman's foster son, is a voyager, apprentice and companion to the naturalist John Tradescant. On one of his journeys he meets a miller who advises him to hear the story of the Twelve Dancing Princesses, especially since the girls are still living just down the road and willingly tell their own tale.

I banged on the door and heard a voice behind me asking my name.

'My name is Jordan,' I said, though not knowing to whom. 'Down here.'

There was a well by the door with a frayed rope and a rusty bucket.

'Are you looking for me?'

I explained to the head now poking over the edge of the well that I had come to pay my respects to the Twelve Dancing Princesses.

'You can start here then,' said the head. 'I am the eldest.'

Timidly, for I have a fear of confined spaces, I swung over the edge and climbed down a wooden ladder. I found myself in a circular room, well furnished, with a silver jug coming to the boil with fresh coffee.

'I've brought you some herrings,' I said, awkwardly.

At the word 'herring' there was a sound of great delight and a hand came over my shoulder and took the whole parcel.

'Please excuse her,' said the princess. 'She is a mermaid.'

Already the mermaid, who was very beautiful but without fine graces, was gobbling the fish, dropping them back into her throat the way you or I would an oyster.

'It is the penalty of love,' sighed the princess, and began at once to tell me the story of her life.

We all slept in the same room, my sisters and I, and that room was narrower than a new river and longer than the beard of the prophet.

So you see exactly the kind of quarters we had.

We slept in white beds with white sheets and the moon shone through the window and made white shadows on the floor.

From this room, every night, we flew to a silver city where no one ate or drank. The occupation of the people was to dance. We wore out our dresses and slippers dancing, but because we were always sound asleep when our father came to wake us in the morning it was impossible to fathom where we had been or how.

You know that eventually a clever prince caught us flying through the window. We had given him a sleeping draught but he only pretended to drink it. He had eleven brothers and we were all given in marriage, one to each brother, and as it says lived happily ever after. We did, but not with our husbands.

I have always enjoyed swimming, and it was in deep waters one day that I came to a coral cave and saw a mermaid combing her hair. I fell in love with her at once, and after a few months of illicit meetings, my husband complaining all the time that I stank of fish, I ran away and began housekeeping with her in perfect salty bliss.

For some years I did not hear from my sisters, and then, by a strange eventuality, I discovered that we had all, in one way or another, parted from the glorious princes and were living scattered, according to our tastes.

We bought this house and we share it. You will find my sisters as you walk about. As you can see, I live in the well.

'That's my last husband painted on the wall,' said the second princess, 'looking as though he were alive.'

She took me through her glass house showing me curiosities: the still-born foetus of the infamous Pope Joan who had so successfully posed as a Man of God until giving birth in the Easter parade. She had the tablets of stone on which Moses had received the Ten Commandments. The writing was blurred but it was easy to make out the gouged lines of the finger of God.

'I collect religious items.'

She had not minded her husband much more than any wife does until he had tried to stop her hobby.

'He built a bonfire and burned the body of a saint. The saint was very old and wrapped in cloth. I liked him about the house; he added something.'

After that she had wrapped her own husband in cloth and gone on wrapping the stale bandages round and round until she reached his nose. She had a moment's regret, and continued.

'He walked in beauty,' she said.

'His eyes were brown marshes, his lashes were like willow trees. His eyebrows shot together made a dam between his forehead and his face. His cheeks were steep and sheer, his mouth was a volcano. His breath was like a dragon's and his heart was torn from a bull. The sinews in his neck were white columns leading to the bolts of his collar-bone. I can still trace the cavity of his throat. His chest was a strongbox, his ribs were made of brass, they shone through his skin when the sun was out. His shoulder-blades were mountain ranges, his spine a cobbled road. His belly was filled with jewels and his cock woke at dawn. Fields of wheat still remind me of his hair, and when I see a hand whose fingers are longer than its palm I think it might be him come to touch me again.

'But he never touched me. It was a boy he loved. I pierced them with a single arrow where they lay.

'I still think it was poetic.'

My husband married me so that his liaisons with other women, being forbidden, would be more exciting. Danger was an aphrodisiac to him: he wanted nothing easy or gentle. His way was to cause whirlwinds. I was warned, we always are, by well-wishers or malcontents, but I chose to take no interest in gossip. My husband was handsome and clever. What did it matter if he needed a certain kind of outlet, so long as he loved me? I wanted to love him; I was determined to be happy with him. I had not been happy before.

At first I hardly minded his weeks away. I did not realize that part of his sport was to make me mad. Only then, when he had hurt me, could he fully enjoy the other beds he visited.

I soon discovered that the women he preferred were the inmates of a lunatic asylum. With them he arranged mock marriages in deserted barns. They wore a shroud as their wedding dress and carried a bunch of carrots as a bouquet. He had them straight after on a pig-trough altar. Most were virgins. He like to come home to me smelling of their blood.

Does the body hate itself so much that it seeks release at any cost?

I didn't kill him. I left him to walk the battlements of

Sexing the Cherry

his ruined kingdom; his body was raddled with disease. The same winter he was found dead in the snow.

Why could he not turn his life towards me, as trees though troubled by the wind yet continue in the path of the sun?

You may have heard of Rapunzel.

Against the wishes of her family, who can best be described by their passion for collecting miniature dolls, she went to live in a tower with an older woman.

Her family were so incensed by her refusal to marry the prince next door that they vilified the couple, calling one a witch and the other a little girl. Not content with names, they ceaselessly tried to break into the tower, so much so that the happy pair had to seal up any entrance that was not on a level with the sky. The lover got in by climbing up Rapunzel's hair, and Rapunzel got in by nailing a wig to the floor and shinning up the tresses flung out of the window. Both of them could have used a ladder, but they were in love.

One day the prince, who had always liked to borrow his mother's frocks, dressed up as Rapunzel's lover and dragged himself into the tower. Once inside he tied her up and waited for the wicked witch to arrive. The moment she leaped through the window, bringing their dinner for the evening, the prince hit her over the head and threw her out again. Then he carried Rapunzel down the rope he had brought with him and forced her to watch while he blinded her broken lover in a field of thorns.

After that they lived happily ever after, of course.

As for me, my body healed, though my eyes never did, and eventually I was found by my sisters, who had come in their various ways to live on this estate.

My own husband?

Oh well, the first time I kissed him he turned into a frog.

There he is, just by your foot. His name's Anton.

On New Year's Day, walking through the deep lanes slatted with light, I saw my husband on horseback, wearing his pink coat. He held his hunting horn to his lips and stood in the stirrups. The hunt rode off; soon they were only as big as holly berries hidden in the green.

I walked on, away from the path, through bushes and brambles, frightening partridges and threading a route between the patient cattle whose hooves in the mud were braceleted with beads of water. My boots were thick with mud. Every step was harder and harder to take. Soon I was lifting my feet as you would to climb a ladder. I was angry and sweating. I wanted to get home but I couldn't hurry. I had to get home to fetch the punch into the great hall and fire it with bright blue flames.

Coming with much difficulty to the top of a hill I looked across the widening valley and saw where the snow still patched the fields like sheets left out to dry. I love the thorn hedges and the trees bare overnight as though some child had stubbornly collected all the leaves, refusing to leave even one for a rival.

I saw my own house, its chimneys smoking, its windows orange.

Another year.

Then a stag and five deer came out of the wood and across the fields in front of my eyes. The fields were fenced and the stag jumped over, turning his head to bring the others. Just for a second he remained in the air, but in that second of flight I remembered my past,

Sexing the Cherry

when I had been free to fly, long ago, before this gracious landing and a houseful of things.

He disappeared into the dark and I turned my back on the house. The last thing I heard was the sound of the hunt clattering into the courtyard.

I never wanted anyone but her. I wanted to run my finger from the cleft in her chin down the slope of her breasts and across the level plains of her stomach to where I knew she would be wet. I wanted to turn her over and ski the flats of my hands down the slope of her back. I wanted to pioneer the secret passage of her arse.

When she lay down I massaged her feet with mint oil and cut her toenails with silver scissors. I coiled her hair into living snakes and polished her teeth with my saliva.

I pierced her ears and filled them with diamonds. I dropped belladonna into her eyes.

When she was sick I wiped her fever with my own towels and when she cried I kept her tears in a Ming vase.

There was no separation between us. We rose in the morning and slept at night as twins do. We had four arms and four legs, and in the afternoons, when we read in the cool orchard, we did so sitting back to back.

I liked to feel the snake of her spine.

We kissed often, our mouths filling up with tongue and teeth and spit and blood when I bit her lower lip, and with my hands I held her against my hip bone.

We made love often, especially in the afternoons with the blinds half pulled and the cold flag floor against our bodies.

For eighteen years we lived alone in a windy castle and saw no one but each other. Then someone found us and then it was too late.

The man I had married was a woman. They came to burn her. I killed her with a single blow to the head before they reached the gates, and fled that place, and am come here now.

I still have a coil of her hair.

We had been married a few years when a man came to the door selling brushes. My husband was at work so I let the man into our kitchen and gave him something to eat. I asked him to show me his bag and he spread out, as you would imagine, a layer of polishing clothes, a pile of round soaps, combs for the hair, combs for the beard of a billy goat, ordinary household things. I bought one or two useful pieces, then I asked him what he had in his other bag, the one he hadn't opened.

'What was it you wanted?' he asked.

'Poison . . .'

'Yes, for the rats.'

'No, for my husband.'

He seemed unsurprised by my intention to murder and opened the other bag. I looked inside. It was full of little jars and sealed bags.

'Is your husband a big man?'

'Very. He is very, very fat. He is the fattest man in the village. He has always been fat. He has eleven brothers, all of whom are as slender as spring corn. Every day he eats one cow followed by one pig.'

'You are right to kill him,' said the man. 'Put this in his milk at bedtime.'

Bedtime came and I stirred my husband's vat of milk and put in the powder as directed. My husband came crashing over to the stove and gulped the milk in one draught. As soon as he had finished he began to swell up. He swelled out of the house, cracking the roof, and within a few moments had exploded. Out of his belly came a herd of cattle and a fleet of pigs, all blinking in the light and covered in milk.

He had always complained about his digestion.

I rounded them up and set off to find my sisters. I prefer farming to cookery.

He called me Jess because that is the name of the hood which restrains the falcon.

I was his falcon. I hung on his arm and fed at his hand.

He said my nose was sharp and cruel and that my eyes had madness in them. He said I would tear him to pieces if he dealt softly with me.

At night, if he was away, he had me chained to our bed. It was a long chain, long enough for me to use the chamber pot or to stand at the window and wait for the late owls. I love to hear the owls. I love to see the sudden glide of wings spread out for prey, and then the dip and the noise like a lover in pain.

He used the chain when we went riding together. I had a horse as strong as his, and he'd whip the horse from behind and send it charging through the trees, and he'd follow, half a head behind, pulling on the chain and asking me how I liked my ride.

His game was to have me sit astride him when we made love and hold me tight in the small of my back. He said he had to have me above him, in case I picked his eyes out in the faltering candlelight.

I was none of these things, but I became them.

At night, in June I think, I flew off his wrist and tore

his liver from his body, and bit my chain in pieces and left him on the bed with his eyes open.

He looked surprised, I don't know why. As your lover describes you, so you are.

When my husband had an affair with someone else I watched his eyes glaze over when we ate dinner together and I heard him singing to himself without me, and when he tended the garden it was not for me.

He was courteous and polite; he enjoyed being at home, but in the fantasy of his home I was not the one who sat opposite him and laughed at his jokes. He didn't want to change anything; he liked his life. The only thing he wanted to change was me.

It would have been better if he had hated me, or if he had abused me, or if he had packed his new suitcases and left.

As it was he continued to put his arm round me and talk about building a new wall to replace the rotten fence that divided our garden from his vegetable patch. I knew he would never leave our house. He had worked for it.

Day by day I felt myself disappearing. For my husband I was no longer a reality, I was one of the things around him. I was the fence which needed to be replaced. I watched myself in the mirror and saw that I was no longer vivid and exciting. I was worn and grey like an old sweater you can't throw out but won't put on.

He admitted he was in love with her, but he said he loved me.

Translated, that means, I want everything. Translated, that means, I don't want to hurt you yet. Translated, that means, I don't know what to do, give me time.

Why, why should I give you time? What time are

Sexing the Cherry

you giving me? I am in a cell waiting to be called for execution.

I loved him and I was in love with him. I didn't use language to make a war-zone of my heart.

'You're so simple and good,' he said, brushing the hair from my face.

He meant, Your emotions are not complex like mine. My dilemma is poetic.

But there was no dilemma. He no longer wanted me, but he wanted our life.

Eventually, when he had been away with her for a few days and returned restless and conciliatory, I decided not to wait in my cell any longer. I went to where he was sleeping in another room and I asked him to leave. Very patiently he asked me to remember that the house was his home, that he couldn't be expected to make himself homeless because he was in love.

'Medea did,' I said, 'and Romeo and Juliet, and Cressida, and Ruth in the Bible.'

He asked me to shut up. He wasn't a hero.

'Then why should I be a heroine?'

He didn't answer, he plucked at the blanket.

I considered my choices.

I could stay and be unhappy and humiliated.

I could leave and be unhappy and dignified.

I could beg him to touch me again.

I could live in hope and die of bitterness.

I took some things and left. It wasn't easy, it was my home too.

I hear he's replaced the back fence.

As soon as we were married my husband took me to his family home, far from anyone I knew. He promised me a companion and a library but asked me never to interrupt

1037

him during the day. I saw him at night for a few hours, over our dinner, though he never ate much. Nor did he seem anxious to decorate my bed with his body.

I asked him what he did during the day and he said he exercised his mind over the problems of Creation. I realized this could take some time and resigned myself to forgetting the rules of normal life.

One night, as we were eating a pigeon I had shot, my husband stood up and said, 'There is a black tower where wild beasts live. The tower has no windows and no doors. No one may enter or leave. At the top of the tower is a cage whose bars are made of bone. From this cage a trapped spirit peeps at the sun. The tower is my body, the cage is my skull, the spirit singing to comfort itself is me. But I am not comforted, I am alone. Kill me.'

I did as he asked. I smashed his skull with a silver candlestick and I heard a hissing noise like damp wood on the fire. I opened the doors and dragged his body into the air, and in the air he flew away.

I still see him sometimes, but only in the distance.

Their stories ended, the twelve dancing princesses invited me to spend the night as their guest.

'Someone is missing,' I said. 'There are only eleven of you and I have only heard eleven stories. Where is your sister?'

They looked at one another, then the eldest said, 'Our youngest sister is not here. She never came to live with us. On her wedding day to the prince who had discovered our secret, she flew from the altar like a bird from a snare and walked a tightrope between the steeple of the church and the mast of a ship weighing anchor in the bay.

'She was, of all of us, the best dancer, the one who

Sexing the Cherry

made her body into shapes we could not follow. She did it for pleasure, but there was something more for her; she did it because any other life would have been a lie. She didn't burn in secret with a passion she could not express; she shone.

'We have not seen her for years and years, not since that day when we were dressed in red with our black hair unbraided. She must be old now, she must be stiff. Her body can only be a memory. The body she has will not be the body she had.'

'Do you remember,' said another sister, 'how light she was? She was so light that she could climb down a rope, cut it and tie it again in mid-air without plunging to her death. The winds supported her.'

'What was her name?'

'Fortunata.'

Virginia Woolf

extract from

To The Lighthouse

The first part of Virginia Woolf's major novel, To The Lighthouse, introduces the Ramsay family and their guests holidaying by the sea as they do each summer. In prose as bold as it is sensitive, the characters of husband and wife and their children are clearly established in the reader's mind – so that the sense of loss which comes with the passing of time in the novel, bringing as it does the death of Mrs Ramsay of her daughter in pregnancy, of her son in the First World War, may come close to being as deeply felt a grief as it undoubtedly must have been for Virginia Woolf herself, looking back to her own childhood and to the deaths of her mother and brother. Lily Briscoe, Mrs Ramsay's loving antagonist in that she is dedicated to her painting rather than to a man in marriage, surprises to celebrate the people she has known and to reassert the triumph of art.

The first part of Virginia Woolf's major work, To The Lighthouse, *introduces the Ramsay family and their guests holidaying by the sea as they do each summer. In prose as bold as it is sensitive, the characters of husband and wife and their children are clearly established in the reader's mind — so that the sense of loss which comes with the passing of time in the novel, bringing as it does the death of Mrs Ramsay, of her daughter in pregnancy, of her son in the First World War, may come close to being as deeply felt a grief as it undoubtedly must have been for Virginia Woolf herself, looking back to her own childhood and to the deaths of her mother and brother. Lily Briscoe, Mrs Ramsay's loving antagonist in that she is dedicated to her painting rather than to a man in marriage, survives to celebrate the people she has known and to reassert the triumph of art.*

III

The Lighthouse

I

What does it mean then, what can it all mean? Lily Briscoe asked herself, wondering whether, since she had been left alone, it behoved her to go to the kitchen to fetch another cup of coffee or wait here. What does it mean? – a catchword that was, caught up from some book, fitting her thought loosely, for she could not, this first morning with the Ramsays, contract her feelings, could only make a phrase resound to cover the blankness of her mind until these vapours had shrunk. For really, what did she feel, come back after all these years and Mrs Ramsay dead? Nothing, nothing – nothing that she could express at all.

She had come late last night when it was all mysterious, dark. Now she was awake, at her old place at the breakfast table, but alone. It was very early too, not yet eight. There was this expedition – they were going to the Lighthouse, Mr Ramsay, Cam and James. They should have gone already – they had to catch the tide or something. And Cam was not ready and James was not ready and Nancy had forgotten to order the sandwiches and Mr Ramsay had lost his temper and banged out of the room.

'What's the use of going now?' he had stormed.

Nancy had vanished. There he was, marching up and down the terrace in a rage. One seemed to hear doors slamming and voices calling all over the house. Now Nancy burst in, and asked, looking round the room, in a queer half dazed, half desperate way, 'What does one send to the Lighthouse?' as if she were forcing herself to do what she despaired of ever being able to do.

What does one send to the Lighthouse indeed! At any other time Lily could have suggested reasonably tea, tobacco, newspapers. But this morning everything seemed so extraordinarily queer that a question like Nancy's – What does one send to the Lighthouse? – opened doors in one's mind that went banging and swinging to and fro and made one keep asking, in a stupefied gape, What does one send? What does one do? Why is one sitting here after all?

Sitting alone (for Nancy went out again) among the clean cups at the long table she felt cut off from other people, and able only to go on watching, asking, wondering. The house, the place, the morning, all seemed strangers to her. She had no attachment here, she felt, no relations with it, anything might happen, and whatever did happen, a step outside, a voice calling ('It's not in the cupboard; it's on the landing,' someone cried), was a question, as if the link that usually bound things together had been cut, and they floated up here, down there, off, anyhow. How aimless it was, how chaotic, how unreal it was, she thought, looking at her empty coffee cup. Mrs Ramsay dead; Andrew killed; Prue dead too – repeat it as she might, it roused no feeling in her. And we all get together in a house like this on a morning like this, she said, looking out of the window – it was a beautiful still day.

To The Lighthouse

Suddenly Mr Ramsay raised his head as he passed and looked straight at her, with his distraught wild gaze which was yet so penetrating, as if he saw you, for one second, for the first time, for ever; and she pretended to drink out of her empty coffee cup so as to escape him – to escape his demand on her, to put aside a moment longer that imperious need. And he shook his head at her, and strode on ('Alone' she heard him say, 'Perished' she heard him say) and like everything else this strange morning the words became symbols, wrote themselves all over the grey-green walls. If only she could put them together, she felt, write them out in some sentence, then she would have got at the truth of things. Old Mr Carmichael came padding softly in, fetched his coffee, took his cup and made off to sit in the sun. The extraordinary unreality was frightening; but it was also exciting. Going to the Lighthouse. But what does one send to the Lighthouse? Perished. Alone. The grey-green light on the wall opposite. The empty places. Such were some of the parts, but how bring them together? she asked. As if any interruption would break the frail shape she was building on the table she turned her back to the window lest Mr Ramsay should see her. She must escape somehow, be alone somewhere. Suddenly she remembered. When she had sat there last ten years ago there had been a little sprig or leaf pattern on the table-cloth, which she had looked at in a moment of revelation. There had been a problem about a foreground of a picture. Move the tree to the middle, she had said. She had never finished that picture. It had been knocking about in her mind all these years. She would paint that picture now. Where were her paints, she wondered? Her paints, yes. She had left them in the hall last night. She would start at once. She got up quickly, before Mr Ramsay turned.

She fetched herself a chair. She pitched her easel with her precise old maidish movements on the edge of the lawn, not too close to Mr Carmichael, but close enough for his protection. Yes, it must have been precisely here that she had stood ten years ago. There was the wall; the hedge; the tree. The question was of some relation between those masses. She had borne it in her mind all these years. It seemed as if the solution had come to her: she knew now what she wanted to do.

But with Mr Ramsay bearing down on her, she could do nothing. Every time he approached – he was walking up and down the terrace – ruin approached, chaos approached. She could not paint. She stooped, she turned; she took up this rag; she squeezed that tube. But all she did was to ward him off a moment. He made it impossible for her to do anything. For if she gave him the least chance, if he saw her disengaged a moment, looking his way a moment, he would be on her, saying, as he had said last night, 'You find us much changed.' Last night he had got up and stopped before her, and said that. Dumb and staring though they had all sat, the six children whom they used to call after the Kings and Queens of England – the Red, the Fair, the Wicked, the Ruthless – she felt how they raged under it. Kind old Mrs Beckwith said something sensible. But it was a house full of unrelated passions – she had felt that all the evening. And on top of this chaos Mr Ramsay got up, pressed her hand, and said: 'You will find us much changed,' and none of them had moved or had spoken; but had sat there as if they were forced to let him say it. Only James (certainly the Sullen) scowled at the lamp; and Cam screwed her handkerchief round her finger.

To The Lighthouse

Then he reminded them that they were going to the Lighthouse tomorrow. They must be ready, in the hall, on the stroke of half-past seven. Then, with his hand on the door, he stopped; he turned upon them. Did they not want to go? he demanded. Had they dared say No (he had some reason for wanting it) he would have flung himself tragically backwards into the bitter waters of despair. Such a gift he had for gesture. He looked like a king in exile. Doggedly James said yes. Cam stumbled more wretchedly. Yes, oh yes, they'd both be ready, they said. And it struck her, this was tragedy – not palls, dust, and the shroud; but children coerced, their spirits subdued. James was sixteen, Cam seventeen, perhaps. She had looked round for someone who was not there, for Mrs Ramsay, presumably. But there was only kind Mrs Beckwith turning over her sketches under the lamp. Then, being tired, her mind still rising and falling with the sea, the taste and smell that places have after long absence possessing her, the candles wavering in her eyes, she had lost herself and gone under. It was a wonderful night, starlit; the waves sounded as they went upstairs; the moon surprised them, enormous, pale, as they passed the staircase window. She had slept at once.

She set her clean canvas firmly upon the easel, as a barrier, frail, but she hoped sufficiently substantial to ward off Mr Ramsay and his exactingness. She did her best to look, when his back was turned, at her picture; that line there, that mass there. But it was out of the question. Let him be fifty feet away, let him not even speak to you, let him not even see you, he permeated, he prevailed he imposed himself. He changed everything. She could not see the colour; she could not see the lines; even with his back turned to her, she could only think,

But he'll be down on me in a moment, demanding – something she felt she could not give him. She rejected one brush; she chose another. When would those children come? When would they all be off? she fidgeted. That man, she thought, her anger rising in her, never gave; that man took. She, on the other hand, would be forced to give. Mrs Ramsay had given. Giving, giving, giving, she had died – and had left all this. Really, she was angry with Mrs Ramsay. With the brush slightly trembling in her fingers she looked at the hedge, the step, the wall. It was all Mrs Ramsay's doing. She was dead. Here was Lily, at forty-four, wasting her time, unable to do a thing, standing there, playing at painting, playing at the one thing one did not play at, and it was all Mrs Ramsay's fault. She was dead. The step where she used to sit was empty. She was dead.

But why repeat this over and over again? Why be always trying to bring up some feeling she had not got? There was a kind of blasphemy in it. It was all dry: all withered: all spent. They ought not to have asked her; she ought not to have come. One can't waste one's time at forty-four, she thought. She hated playing at painting. A brush, the one dependable thing in a world of strife, ruin, chaos – that one should not play with, knowingly even: she detested it. But he made her. You shan't touch your canvas, he seemed to say, bearing down on her, till you've given me what I want of you. Here he was, close upon her again, greedy, distraught. Well, thought Lily in despair, letting her right hand fall at her side, it would be simpler then to have it over. Surely she could imitate from recollection the glow, the rhapsody, the self-surrender she had seen on so many women's faces (on Mrs Ramsay's, for instance) when on some occasion like this they blazed up – she could remember the look

To The Lighthouse

on Mrs Ramsay's face – into a rapture of sympathy, of delight in the reward they had, which, though the reason of it escaped her, evidently conferred on them the most supreme bliss of which human nature was capable. Here he was, stopped by her side. She would give him what she could.

2

She seemed to have shrivelled slightly, he thought. She looked a little skimpy, wispy; but not unattractive. He liked her. There had been some talk of her marrying William Bankes once, but nothing had come of it. His wife had been fond of her. He had been a little out of temper too at breakfast. And then, and then – this was one of those moments when an enormous need urged him, without being conscious what it was, to approach any woman, to force them, he did not care how, his need was so great, to give him what he wanted: sympathy.

Was anybody looking after her? he said. Had she everything she wanted?

'Oh, thanks, everything,' said Lily Briscoe nervously. No; she could not do it. She ought to have floated off instantly upon some wave of sympathetic expansion: the pressure on her was tremendous. But she remained stuck. There was an awful pause. They both looked at the sea. Why, thought Mr Ramsay, should she look at the sea when I am here? She hoped it would be calm enough for them to land at the Lighthouse, she said. The Lighthouse! The Lighthouse! What's that got to do with it? he thought impatiently. Instantly, with the force of some primeval gust (for really he could not restrain himself any longer), there issued from him such a groan that any other woman in the whole world would have done something, said something – all except myself, thought Lily, girding at herself bitterly, who am not a woman, but a peevish, ill-tempered, dried-up old maid presumably.

Mr Ramsay sighed to the full. He waited. Was she not going to say anything? Did she not see what he wanted from her? Then he said he had a particular reason for wanting to go to the Lighthouse. His wife used to send the men things. There was a poor boy with a tuberculous hip, the lightkeeper's son. He sighed profoundly. He sighed significantly. All Lily wished was that this enormous flood of grief, this insatiable hunger for sympathy, this demand that she should surrender herself up to him entirely, and even so he had sorrows enough to keep her supplied for ever, should leave her, should be diverted (she kept looking at the house, hoping for an interruption) before it swept her down in its flow.

'Such expeditions,' said Mr Ramsay, scraping the ground with his toe, 'are very painful.' Still Lily said nothing. (She is a stock, she is a stone, he said to himself.) 'They are very exhausting,' he said, looking, with a sickly look that nauseated her (he was acting, she felt, this great man was dramatizing himself), at his beautiful hands. It was horrible, it was indecent. Would they never come, she asked, for she could not sustain this enormous weight of sorrow, support these heavy draperies of grief (he had assumed a pose of extreme decrepitude; he even tottered a little as he stood there) a moment longer.

Still she could say nothing; the whole horizon seemed swept bare of objects to talk about; could only feel, amazedly, as Mr Ramsay stood there, how his gaze seemed to fall dolefully over the sunny grass and discolour it, and cast over the rubicund, drowsy, entirely contented figure of Mr Carmichael, reading a French novel on a deck-chair, a veil of crape, as if such an existence, flaunting its prosperity in a world of woe, were enough to provoke the most dismal thoughts of all. Look at him, he seemed to be saying, look at me; and indeed, all the time he was feeling, Think of me, think of me. Ah, could that bulk only be wafted alongside of them, Lily wished; had she only pitched her easel a yard or two closer to him; a man, any man, would staunch this effusion, would stop these lamentations. A woman, she had provoked this horror; a woman, she should have known how to deal with it. It was immensely to her discredit, sexually, to stand there dumb. One said – what did one say? – Oh, Mr Ramsay! Dear Mr Ramsay! That was what that kind old lady who sketched, Mrs Beckwith, would have said instantly, and rightly. But no. They stood there, isolated from the rest of the world. His immense self-pity, his demand for sympathy poured and spread itself in pools at her feet, and all she did, miserable sinner that she was, was to draw her skirts a little closer round her ankles, lest she should get wet. In complete silence she stood there, grasping her paint brush.

Heaven could never be sufficiently praised! She heard sounds in the house. James and Cam must be coming. But Mr Ramsay, as if he knew that his time ran short, exerted upon her solitary figure the immense pressure of his concentrated woe; his age; his frailty; his desolation; when suddenly, tossing his head impatiently, in his annoyance – for, after all, what woman could resist him? – he noticed that his boot-laces were untied. Remarkable boots they were too, Lily thought, looking down at them: sculptured; colossal; like everything that Mr Ramsay wore, from his frayed tie to his half-buttoned waistcoat, his own indisputably. She could see them walking to his room of their own accord, expressive in his absence of pathos, surliness, ill-temper, charm.

'What beautiful boots!' she exclaimed. She was ashamed of herself. To praise his boots when he asked her to solace his soul; when he had shown her his bleeding hands, his lacerated heart, and asked her to pity them, then to say, cheerfully, 'Ah, but what beautiful boots you wear!' deserved, she knew, and she looked up expecting to get it, in one of his sudden roars of ill-temper, complete annihilation.

Instead, Mr Ramsay smiled. His pall, his draperies, his infirmities fell from him. Ah yes, he said, holding his foot up for her to look at, they were first-rate boots. There was only one man in England who could make boots like that. Boots are among the chief curses of mankind, he said. 'Bootmakers make it their business,' he exclaimed, 'to cripple and torture the human foot.' They are also the most obstinate and perverse of mankind. It had taken him the best part of his youth to get boots made as they should be made. He would have her observe (he lifted his right foot and then his left) that she had never seen boots made quite that shape before. They were made of the finest leather in the world, also. Most leather was mere brown paper and cardboard. He looked complacently at his foot, still held in the air. They had reached, she felt, a sunny island where peace dwelt, sanity reigned and the sun for ever shone, the blessed island of good boots. Her heart warmed to him. 'Now let me see if you can tie a knot,' he said. He poohpoohed her feeble system. He showed her his own invention. Once you tied it, it never came undone. Three times he knotted her shoe; three times he unknotted it.

To The Lighthouse

Why, at this completely inappropriate moment, when he was stooping over her shoe, should she be so tormented with sympathy for him that, as she stooped too, the blood rushed to her face, and, thinking of her callousness (she had called him a play-actor) she felt her eyes swell and tingle with tears? Thus occupied he seemed to her a figure of infinite pathos. He tied knots. He bought boots. There was no helping Mr Ramsay on the journey he was going. But now just as she wished to say something, could have said something, perhaps, here they were – Cam and James. They appeared on the terrace. They came, lagging, side by side, a serious, melancholy couple.

But why was it like *that* that they came? She could not help feeling annoyed with them; they might have come more cheerfully; they might have given him what, now that they were off, she would not have the chance of giving him. For she felt a sudden emptiness; a frustration. Her feeling had come too late; there it was ready; but he no longer needed it. He had become a very distinguished, elderly man, who had no need of her whatsoever. She felt snubbed. He slung a knapsack round his shoulders. He shared out the parcels – there were a number of them, ill tied, in brown paper. He sent Cam for a cloak. He had all the appearance of a leader making ready for an expedition. Then, wheeling about, he led the way with his firm military tread, in those wonderful boots, carrying brown paper parcels, down the path, his children following him. They looked, she thought, as if fate had devoted them to some stern enterprise, and they went to it, still young enough to be drawn acquiescent in their father's wake, obediently, but with a pallor in their eyes which made her feel that they suffered something beyond their years in silence.

So they passed the edge of the lawn, and it seemed to Lily that she watched a procession go, drawn on by some stress of common feeling which made it, faltering and flagging as it was, a little company bound together and strangely impressive to her. Politely, but very distantly, Mr Ramsay raised his hand and saluted her as they passed.

But what a face, she thought, immediately finding the sympathy which she had not been asked to give troubling her for expression. What had made it like that? Thinking, night after night, she supposed – about the reality of kitchen tables, she added, remembering the symbol which in her vagueness as to what Mr Ramsay did think about Andrew had given her. (He had been killed by the splinter of a shell instantly, she bethought her.) The kitchen table was something visionary, austere; something bare, hard, not ornamental. There was no colour to it; it was all edges and angles; it was uncompromisingly plain. But Mr Ramsay kept always his eyes fixed upon it, never allowed himself to be distracted or deluded, until his face became worn too and ascetic and partook of this unornamented beauty which so deeply impressed her. Then, she recalled (standing where he had left her, holding her brush), worries had fretted it – not so nobly. He must have had his doubts about that table, she supposed; whether the table was a real table; whether it was worth the time he gave to it; whether he was able after all to find it. He had had doubts, she felt, or he would have asked less of people. That was what they talked about late at night sometimes, she suspected; and then next day Mrs Ramsay looked tired, and Lily flew into a rage with him over some absurd little thing. But now he had nobody to talk to about that table, or his boots, or his knots; and

To The Lighthouse

he was like a lion seeking whom he could devour, and his face had that touch of desperation, of exaggeration in it which alarmed her, and made her pull her skirts about her. And then, she recalled, there was that sudden revivification, that sudden flare (when she praised his boots), that sudden recovery of vitality and interest in ordinary human things, which too passed and changed (for he was always changing, and hid nothing) into that other final phase which was new to her and had, she owned, made herself ashamed of her own irritability, when it seemed as if he had shed worries and ambitions, and the hope of sympathy and the desire for praise, had entered some other region, was drawn on, as if by curiosity, in dumb colloquy, whether with himself or another, at the head of that little procession out of one's range. An extraordinary face! The gate banged.

3

So they're gone, she thought, sighing with relief and disappointment. Her sympathy seemed to fly back in her face, like a bramble sprung. She felt curiously divided, as if one part of her were drawn out there – it was a still day, hazy; the Lighthouse looked this morning at an immense distance; the other had fixed itself doggedly, solidly, here on the lawn. She saw her canvas as if it had floated up and placed itself white and uncompromising directly before her. It seemed to rebuke her with its cold stare for all his hurry and agitation; this folly and waste of emotion; it drastically recalled her and spread through her mind first a peace, as her disorderly sensations (he had gone and she had been so sorry for him and she had said nothing) trooped off the field;

and then, emptiness. She looked blankly at the canvas, with its uncompromising white stare; from the canvas to the garden. There was something (she stood screwing up her little Chinese eyes in her small puckered face) something she remembered in the relations of those lines cutting across, slicing down, and in the mass of the hedge with its green cave of blues and browns, which had stayed in her mind; which had tied a knot in her mind so that at odds and ends of time, involuntarily, as she walked along the Brompton Road, as she brushed her hair, she found herself painting that picture, passing her eye over it, and untying the knot in imagination. But there was all the difference in the world between this planning airily away from the canvas, and actually taking her brush and making the first mark.

She had taken the wrong brush in her agitation at Mr Ramsay's presence, and her easel, rammed into the earth so nervously, was at the wrong angle. And now that she had put that right, and in so doing had subdued the impertinences and irrelevances that plucked her attention and made her remember how she was such and such a person, had such and such relations to people, she took her hand and raised her brush. For a moment it stayed trembling in a painful but exciting ecstasy in the air. Where to begin? – that was the question; at what point to make the first mark? One line placed on the canvas committed her to innumerable risks, to frequent and irrevocable decisions. All that in idea seemed simple became in practice immediately complex; as the waves shape themselves symmetrically from the cliff top, but to the swimmer among them are divided by steep gulfs, and foaming crests. Still the risk must be run; the mark made.

With a curious physical sensation, as if she were urged

To The Lighthouse

forward and at the same time must hold herself back, she made her first quick decisive stroke. The brush descended. It flickered brown over the white canvas; it left a running mark. A second time she did it – a third time. And so pausing and so flickering, she attained a dancing rhythmical movement, as if the pauses were one part of the rhythm and the strokes another, and all were related; and so, lightly and swiftly pausing, striking, she scored her canvas with brown running nervous lines which had no sooner settled there than they enclosed (she felt it looming out at her) a space. Down in the hollow of one wave she saw the next wave towering higher and higher above her. For what could be more formidable than that space? Here she was again, she thought, stepping back to look at it, drawn out of gossip, out of living, out of community with people into the presence of this formidable ancient enemy of hers – this other thing, this truth, this reality, which suddenly laid hands on her, emerged stark at the back of appearances and commanded her attention. She was half unwilling, half reluctant. Why always be drawn out and haled away? Why not left in peace, to talk to Mr Carmichael on the lawn? It was an exacting form of intercourse anyhow. Other worshipful objects were content with worship; men, women, God, all let one kneel prostrate; but this form, were it only the shape of a white lampshade looming on a wicker table, roused one to perpetual combat, challenged one to a fight in which one was bound to be worsted. Always (it was in her nature, or in her sex, she did not know which) before she exchanged the fluidity of life for the concentration of painting she had a few moments of nakedness when she seemed like an unborn soul, a soul reft of body, hesitating on some windy pinnacle and exposed without protection to all the blasts of doubt. Why then did she do it? She looked at the canvas, lightly scored with running lines. It would be hung in the servants' bedrooms. It would be rolled up and stuffed under a sofa. What was the good of doing it then, and she heard some voice saying she couldn't paint, saying she couldn't create, as if she were caught up in one of those habitual currents which after a certain time forms experience in the mind, so that one repeats words without being aware any longer who originally spoke them.

Can't paint, can't write, she murmured monotonously, anxiously considering what her plan of attack should be. For the mass loomed before her; it protruded; she felt it pressing on her eyeballs. Then, as if some juice necessary for the lubrication of her faculties were spontaneously squirted, she began precariously dipping among the blues and umbers, moving her brush hither and thither, but it was now heavier and went slower, as if it had fallen in with some rhythm which was dictated to her (she kept looking at the hedge, at the canvas) by what she saw, so that while her hand quivered with life, this rhythm was strong enough to bear her along with it on its current. Certainly she was losing consciousness of outer things. And as she lost consciousness of outer things, and her name and her personality and her appearance, and whether Mr Carmichael was there or not, her mind kept throwing up from its depths, scenes, and names, and sayings, and memories and ideas, like a fountain spurting over that glaring, hideously difficult white space, while she modelled it with greens and blues.

Charles Tansley used to say that, she remembered, women can't paint, can't write. Coming up behind her he had stood close beside her, a thing she hated, as

To The Lighthouse

she painted here on this very spot. 'Shag tobacco,' he said, 'fivepence an ounce,' parading his poverty, his principles. (But the war had drawn the sting of her femininity. Poor devils, one thought, poor devils of both sexes, getting into such messes.) He was always carrying a book about under his arm – a purple book. He 'worked'. He sat, she remembered, working in a blaze of sun. At dinner he would sit right in the middle of the view. And then, she reflected, there was that scene on the beach. One must remember that. It was a windy morning. They had all gone to the beach. Mrs Ramsay sat and wrote letters by a rock. She wrote and wrote. 'Oh,' she said, looking up at last at something floating in the sea, 'is it a lobster pot? Is it an upturned boat?' She was so short-sighted that she could not see, and then Charles Tansley became as nice as he could possibly be. He began playing ducks and drakes. They chose little flat black stones and sent them skipping over the waves. Every now and then Mrs Ramsay looked up over her spectacles and laughed at them. What they said she could not remember, but only she and Charles throwing stones and getting on very well all of a sudden and Mrs Ramsay watching them. She was highly conscious of that. Mrs Ramsay, she thought, stepping back and screwing up her eyes. (It must have altered the design a good deal when she was sitting on the step with James. There must have been a shadow.) Mrs Ramsay. When she thought of herself and Charles throwing ducks and drakes and of the whole scene on the beach, it seemed to depend somehow upon Mrs Ramsay sitting under the rock, with a pad on her knee, writing letters. (She wrote innumerable letters, and sometimes the wind took them and she and Charles just saved a page from the sea.) But what a power was in the human soul! she thought. That woman sitting there, writing under the rock, resolved everything into simplicity; made these angers, irritations, fall off like old rags; she brought together this and that and then this, and so made out of that miserable silliness and spite (she and Charles squabbling, sparring, had been silly and spiteful) something – this scene on the beach for example, this moment of friendship and liking – which survived, after all these years, complete, so that she dipped into it to refashion her memory of him, and it stayed in the mind almost like a work of art.

'Like a work of art,' she repeated, looking from her canvas to the drawing-room steps and back again. She must rest for a moment. And, resting, looking from one to the other vaguely, the old question which traversed the sky of the soul perpetually, the vast, the general question which was apt to particularize itself at such moments as these, when she released faculties that had been on the strain, stood over her, paused over her, darkened over her. What is the meaning of life? That was all – a simple question; one that tended to close in on one with years. The great revelation had never come. The great revelation perhaps never did come. Instead there were little daily miracles, illuminations, matches struck unexpectedly in the dark; here was one. This, that, and the other; herself and Charles Tansley and the breaking wave; Mrs Ramsay bringing them together; Mrs Ramsay saying 'Life stand still here'; Mrs Ramsay making of the moment something permanent (as in another sphere Lily herself tried to make of the moment something permanent) – this was of the nature of a revelation. In the midst of chaos there was shape; this eternal passing and flowing (she looked at the clouds going and the leaves shaking) was struck into stability. Life stand still here, Mrs Ramsay said.

To The Lighthouse

'Mrs Ramsay! Mrs Ramsay!' she repeated. She owed this revelation to her.

All was silence. Nobody seemed yet to be stirring in the house. She looked at it there sleeping in the early sunlight with its windows green and blue with the reflected leaves. The faint thought she was thinking of Mrs Ramsay seemed in consonance with this quiet house; this smoke; this fine early morning air. Faint and unreal, it was amazingly pure and exciting. She hoped nobody would open the window or come out of the house, but that she might be left alone to go on thinking, to go on painting. She turned to her canvas. But impelled by some curiosity, driven by the discomfort of the sympathy which she held undischarged, she walked a pace or so to the end of the lawn to see whether, down there on the beach, she could see that little company setting sail. Down there among the little boats which floated, some with their sails furled, some slowly, for it was very calm, moving away, there was one rather apart from the others. The sail was even now being hoisted. She decided that there in that very distant and entirely silent little boat Mr Ramsay was sitting with Cam and James. Now they had got the sail up; now after a little flagging and hesitation the sails filled and, shrouded in profound silence, she watched the boat take its way with deliberation past the other boats out to sea.

4

The sails flapped over their heads. The water chuckled and slapped the sides of the boat, which drowsed motionless in the sun. Now and then the sails rippled with a little breeze in them, but the ripple ran over them and ceased. The boat made no motion at all. Mr Ramsay sat in the middle of the boat. He would be impatient in a moment, James thought, and Cam thought, looking at their father, who sat in the middle of the boat between them (James steered; Cam sat alone in the bow) with his legs tightly curled. He hated hanging about. Sure enough, after fidgeting a second or two, he said something sharp to Macalister's boy, who got out his oars and began to row. But their father, they knew, would never be content until they were flying along. He would keep looking for a breeze, fidgeting, saying things under his breath, which Macalister and Macalister's boy would overhear, and they would both be made horribly uncomfortable. He had made them come. He had forced them to come. In their anger they hoped that the breeze would never rise, that he might be thwarted in every possible way, since he had forced them to come against their wills.

All the way down to the beach they had lagged behind together, though he bade them 'Walk up, walk up,' without speaking. Their heads were bent down, their heads were pressed down by some remorseless gale. Speak to him they could not. They must come; they must follow. They must walk behind him carrying brown-paper parcels. But they vowed, in silence, as they walked, to stand by each other and carry out the great compact – to resist tyranny to the death. So there they would sit, one at one end of the boat, one at the other, in silence. They would say nothing, only look at him now and then where he sat with his legs twisted, frowning and fidgeting, and pishing and pshawing and muttering things to himself, and waiting impatiently for a breeze. And they hoped it would be calm. They hoped he would be thwarted. They hoped the whole expedition would fail, and they would have to put back, with their parcels, to the beach.

But now, when Macalister's boy had rowed a little way out, the sails slowly swung round, the boat quickened itself, flattened itself, and shot off. Instantly, as if some great strain had been relieved, Mr Ramsay uncurled his legs, took out his tobacco pouch, handed it with a little grunt to Macalister, and felt, they knew, for all they suffered, perfectly content. Now they would sail on for hours like this, and Mr Ramsay would ask old Macalister a question – about the great storm last winter probably – and old Macalister would answer it, and they would puff their pipes together, and Macalister would take a tarry rope in his fingers, tying or untying some knot, and the boy would fish, and never say a word to any one. James would be forced to keep his eye all the time on the sail. For if he forgot, then the sail puckered, and shivered, and the boat slackened, and Mr Ramsay would say sharply, 'Look out! Look out!' and old Macalister would turn slowly on his seat. So they heard Mr Ramsay asking some question about the great storm at Christmas. 'She comes driving round the point,' old Macalister said, describing the great storm last Christmas, when ten ships had been driven into the bay for shelter, and he had seen 'one there, one there, one there' (he pointed slowly round the bay. Mr Ramsay followed him, turning his head). He had seen three men clinging to the mast. Then she was gone. 'And at last we shoved her off,' he went on (but in their anger and their silence they only caught a word here and there, sitting at opposite ends of the boat, united by their compact to fight tyranny to the death). At last they had shoved her off, they had launched the lifeboat, and they had got her out past the point – Macalister told the story;

and though they only caught a word here and there, they were conscious all the time of their father – how he leant forward, how he brought his voice into tune with Macalister's voice; how, puffing at his pipe, and looking there and there where Macalister pointed, he relished the thought of the storm and the dark night and the fishermen striving there. He liked that men should labour and sweat on the windy beach at night, pitting muscle and brain against the waves and the wind; he liked men to work like that, and women to keep house, and sit beside sleeping children indoors, while men were drowned, out there in a storm. So James could tell, so Cam could tell (they looked at him, they looked at each other), from his toss and his vigilance and the ring in his voice, and the little tinge of Scottish accent which came into his voice, making him seem like a peasant himself, as he questioned Macalister about the eleven ships that had been driven into the bay in a storm. Three had sunk.

He looked proudly where Macalister pointed; and Cam thought, feeling proud of him without knowing quite why, had he been there he would have launched the lifeboat, he would have reached the wreck, Cam thought. He was so brave, he was so adventurous, Cam thought. But she remembered. There was the compact; to resist tyranny to the death. Their grievance weighed them down. They had been forced; they had been bidden. He had borne them down once more with his gloom and his authority, making them do his bidding, on this fine morning, come, because he wished it, carrying these parcels, to the Lighthouse; take part in those rites he went through for his own pleasure in memory of dead people, which they hated, so that they lagged after him, and all the pleasure of the day was spoilt.

To The Lighthouse

Yes, the breeze was freshening. The boat was leaning, the water was sliced sharply and fell away in green cascades, in bubbles, in cataracts. Cam looked down into the foam, into the sea with all its treasure in it, and its speed hypnotized her, and the tie between her and James sagged a little. It slackened a little. She began to think, How fast it goes. Where are we going? and the movement hypnotized her, while James, with his eye fixed on the sail and on the horizon, steered grimly. But he began to think as he steered that he might escape; he might be quit of it all. They might land somewhere; and be free then. Both of them, looking at each other for a moment, had a sense of escape and exaltation, what with the speed and the change. But the breeze bred in Mr Ramsay too the same excitement, and, as old Macalister turned to fling his line overboard, he cried aloud, 'We perished,' and then again, 'each alone.' And then with his usual spasm of repentance or shyness, pulled himself up, and waved his hand towards the shore.

'See the little house,' he said pointing, wishing Cam to look. She raised herself reluctantly and looked. But which was it? She could no longer make out, there on the hillside, which was their house. All looked distant and peaceful and strange. The shore seemed refined, far away, unreal. Already the little distance they had sailed had put them far from it and given it the changed look, the composed look, of something receding in which one has no longer any part. Which was their house? She could not see it.

'But I beneath a rougher sea,' Mr Ramsay murmured. He had found the house and so seeing it, he had also seen himself there; he had seen himself walking on the terrace, alone. He was walking up and down between the urns; and he seemed to himself very old, and bowed. Sitting in the boat he bowed, he crouched himself, acting instantly his part – the part of a desolate man, widowed, bereft; and so called up before him in hosts people sympathizing with him; staged for himself as he sat in the boat, a little drama; which required of him decrepitude and exhaustion and sorrow (he raised his hands and looked at the thinness of them, to confirm his dream) and then there was given him in abundance women's sympathy, and he imagined how they would soothe him and sympathize with him, and so getting in his dream some reflection of the exquisite pleasure women's sympathy was to him, he sighed and said gently and mournfully,

> But I beneath a rougher sea
> Was whelmed in deeper gulfs than he,

so that the mournful words were heard quite clearly by them all. Cam half started on her seat. It shocked her – it outraged her. The movement roused her father; and he shuddered, and broke off, exclaiming: 'Look! Look!' so urgently that James also turned his head to look over his shoulder at the island. They all looked. They looked at the island.

But Cam could see nothing. She was thinking how all those paths and the lawn, thick and knotted with the lives they had lived there, were gone: were rubbed out; were past; were unreal, and now this was real; the boat and the sail with its patch; Macalister with his ear-rings; the noise of the waves – all this was real. Thinking this, she was murmuring to herself 'We perished, each alone', for her father's words broke and broke again in her mind, when her father, seeing her gazing so vaguely, began to tease her. Didn't she know the points of the compass? he asked. Didn't she know the North from the South? Did she really think they lived right out there? And he pointed again, and showed her where their house was, there, by those trees. He wished she would try to be more accurate, he said: 'Tell me – which is East, which is West?' he said, half laughing at her, half scolding her, for he could not understand the state of mind of anyone, not absolutely imbecile, who did not know the points of the compass. Yet she did not know. And seeing her gazing, with her vague, now rather frightened, eyes fixed where no house was Mr Ramsay forgot his dream; how he walked up and down between the urns on the terrace; how the arms were stretched out to him. He thought, women are always like that; the vagueness of their minds is hopeless; it was a thing he had never been able to understand; but so it was. It had been so with her – his wife. They could not keep anything clearly fixed in their minds. But he had been wrong to be angry with her; moreover, did he not rather like this vagueness in women? It was part of their extraordinary charm. I will make her smile at me, he thought. She looks frightened. She was so silent. He clutched his fingers, and determined that his voice and his face and all the quick expressive gestures which had been at his command making people pity him and praise him all these years should subdue themselves. He would make her smile at him. He would find some simple easy thing to say to her. But what? For, wrapped up in his work as he was, he forgot the sort of thing one said. There was a puppy. They had a puppy. Who was looking after the puppy today? he asked. Yes, thought James pitilessly, seeing his sister's head against the sail, now she will give way. I shall be left to fight the tyrant alone. The compact would be left to him to carry out. Cam would never resist tyranny to the death, he thought grimly, watching her face, sad, sulky, yielding. And as sometimes happens when a cloud falls on a green hillside and gravity descends and there among all the surrounding hills is gloom and sorrow, and it seems as if the hills themselves must ponder the fate of the clouded, the darkened, either in pity, or maliciously rejoicing in her dismay: so Cam now felt herself overcast, as she sat there among calm, resolute people and wondered how to answer her father about the puppy; how to resist his entreaty – forgive me, care for me; while James the lawgiver, with the tablet of eternal wisdom laid open on his knee (his hand on the tiller had become symbolical to her), said, Resist him. Fight him. He said so rightly; justly. For they must fight tyranny to the death, she thought. Of all human qualities she reverenced justice most. Her brother was most god-like, her father most suppliant. And to which did she yield, she thought, sitting between them, gazing at the shore whose points were all unknown to her, and thinking how the lawn and the terrace and the house were smoothed away now and peace dwelt there.

'Jasper,' she said sullenly. He'd look after the puppy.

And what was she going to call him? her father persisted. He had had a dog when he was a little boy, called Frisk. She'll give way, James thought, as he watched a look come upon her face, a look he remembered. They look down, he thought, at their knitting or something. Then suddenly they look up. There was a flash of blue, he remembered, and then somebody sitting with him laughed, surrendered, and he was very angry. It must have been his mother, he thought, sitting on a low chair, with his father standing over her. He began to search among the infinite series of impressions which time had laid down, leaf upon leaf,

To The Lighthouse

fold upon fold softly, incessantly upon his brain; among scents, sounds; voices, harsh, hollow, sweet; and lights passing, and brooms tapping; and the wash and hush of the sea, how a man had marched up and down and stopped dead, upright, over them. Meanwhile, he noticed, Cam dabbled her fingers in the water, and stared at the shore and said nothing. No, she won't give way, he thought; she's different, he thought. Well, if Cam would not answer him, he would not bother her, Mr Ramsay decided, feeling in his pocket for a book. But she would answer him; she wished, passionately, to move some obstacle that lay upon her tongue and to say, Oh yes, Frisk. I'll call him Frisk. She wanted even to say, Was that the dog that found its way over the moor alone? But try as she might, she could think of nothing to say like that, fierce and loyal to the compact, yet passing on to her father, unsuspected by James, a private token of the love she felt for him. For she thought, dabbling her hand (and now Macalister's boy had caught a mackerel, and it lay kicking on the floor, with blood on its gills) for she thought, looking at James who kept his eyes dispassionately on the sail, or glanced now and then for a second at the horizon, you're not exposed to it, to this pressure and division of feeling, this extraordinary temptation. Her father was feeling in his pockets; in another second, he would have found his book. For no one attracted her more; his hands were beautiful to her and his feet, and his voice, and his words, and his haste, and his temper, and his oddity, and his passion, and his saying straight out before every one, we perish, each alone, and his remoteness. (He had opened his book.) But what remained intolerable, she thought, sitting upright, and watching Macalister's boy tug the hook out of the gills of another fish, was that crass blindness and tyranny of his which had poisoned her childhood and raised bitter storms, so that even now she woke in the night trembling with rage and remembered some command of his; some insolence: 'Do this', 'Do that'; his dominance: his 'Submit to me'.

So she said nothing, but looked doggedly and sadly at the shore, wrapped in its mantle of peace; as if the people there had fallen asleep, she thought; were free like smoke, were free to come and go like ghosts. They have no suffering there, she thought.

5

Yes, that is their boat, Lily Briscoe decided, standing on the edge of the lawn. It was the boat with greyish-brown sails, which she saw now flatten itself upon the water and shoot off across the bay. There he sits, she thought, and the children are quite silent still. And she could not reach him either. The sympathy she had not given him weighed her down. It made it difficult for her to paint.

She had always found him difficult. She had never been able to praise him to his face, she remembered. And that reduced their relationship to something neutral, without that element of sex in it which made his manner to Minta so gallant, almost gay. He would pick a flower for her, lend her his books. But could he believe that Minta read them? She dragged them about the garden, sticking in leaves to mark the place.

'D'you remember, Mr Carmichael?' she was inclined to ask, looking at the old man. But he had pulled his hat half over his forehead; he was asleep, or he was dreaming, or he was lying there catching words, she supposed.

'D'you remember?' she felt inclined to ask him as she passed him, thinking again of Mrs Ramsay on the beach; the cask bobbing up and down; and the pages flying. Why, after all these years, had that survived, ringed round, lit up, visible to the last detail, with all before it blank and all after it blank, for miles and miles?

'Is it a boat? Is it a cork?' she would say, Lily repeated, turning back, reluctantly again, to her canvas. Heaven be praised for it, the problem of space remained, she thought, taking up her brush again. It glared at her. The whole mass of the picture was poised upon that weight. Beautiful and bright it should be on the surface, feathery and evanescent, one colour melting into another like the colours on a butterfly's wing; but beneath the fabric must be clamped together with bolts of iron. It was to be a thing you could ruffle with your breath; and a thing you could not dislodge with a team of horses. And she began to lay on a red, a grey, and she began to model her way into the hollow there. At the same time, she seemed to be sitting beside Mrs Ramsay on the beach.

'Is it a boat? Is it a cask?' Mrs Ramsay said. And she began hunting round for her spectacles. And she sat, having found them, silent, looking out to sea. And Lily, painting steadily, felt as if a door had opened, and one went in and stood gazing silently about in a high cathedral-like place, very dark, very solemn. Shouts came from a world far away. Steamers vanished in stalks of smoke on the horizon. Charles threw stones and sent them skipping.

Mrs Ramsay sat silent. She was glad, Lily thought, to rest in silence, uncommunicative; to rest in the extreme obscurity of human relationships. Who knows what we are, what we feel? Who knows even at the moment of intimacy, This is knowledge? Aren't things spoilt then, Mrs Ramsay may have asked (it seemed to have happened so often, this silence by her side) by saying them? Aren't we more expressive thus? The moment at least seemed extraordinarily fertile. She rammed a little hole in the sand and covered it up, by way of burying in it the perfection of the moment. It was like a drop of silver in which one dipped and illumined the darkness of the past.

Lily stepped back to get her canvas – so – into perspective. It was an odd road to be walking, this of painting. Out and out one went, further and further, until at last one seemed to be on a narrow plank, perfectly alone, over the sea. And as she dipped into the blue paint, she dipped too into the past there. Now Mrs Ramsay got up, she remembered. It was time to go back to the house – time for luncheon. And they all walked up from the beach together, she walking behind with William Bankes, and there was Minta in front of them with a hole in her stocking. How that little round hole of pink heel seemed to flaunt itself before them! How William Bankes deplored it, without, so far as she could remember, saying anything about it! It meant to him the annihilation of womanhood, and dirt and disorder, and servants leaving and beds not made at mid-day – all the things he most abhorred. He had a way of shuddering and spreading his fingers out as if to cover an unsightly object, which he did now – holding his hand in front of him. And Minta walked on ahead, and presumably Paul met her and she went off with Paul in the garden.

The Rayleys, thought Lily Briscoe, squeezing her tube of green paint. She collected her impressions of the Rayleys. Their lives appeared to her in a series of scenes; one, on the staircase at dawn. Paul had come in and gone to bed early; Minta was late. There was Minta,

To The Lighthouse

wreathed, tinted, garish on the stairs about three o'clock in the morning. Paul came out in his pyjamas carrying a poker in case of burglars. Minta was eating a sandwich, standing halfway up by a window, in the cadaverous early morning light, and the carpet had a hole in it. But what did they say? Lily asked herself, as if by looking she could hear them. Something violent. Minta went on eating her sandwich, annoyingly, while he spoke. He spoke indignant, jealous words, abusing her, in a mutter so as not to wake the children, the two little boys. He was withered, drawn; she flamboyant, careless. For things had worked loose after the first year or so; the marriage had turned out rather badly.

And this, Lily thought, taking the green paint on her brush, this making up scenes about them, is what we call 'knowing' people, 'thinking' of them, 'being fond' of them! Not a word of it was true; she had made it up; but it was what she knew them by all the same. She went on tunnelling her way into her picture, into the past.

Another time, Paul said he 'played chess in coffee-houses'. She had built up a whole structure of imagination on that saying too. She remembered how, as he said it, she thought how he rang up the servant, and she said 'Mrs Rayley's out, sir', and he decided that he would not come home either. She saw him sitting in the corner of some lugubrious place where the smoke attached itself to the red plush seats, and the waitresses got to know you, playing chess with a little man who was in the tea trade and lived at Surbiton, but that was all Paul knew about him. And then Minta was out when he came home and then there was that scene on the stairs, when he got the poker in case of burglars (no doubt to frighten her too) and spoke so bitterly, saying she had ruined his life. At any rate when she went down to see them at a cottage near Rickmansworth, things were horribly strained. Paul took her down the garden to look at the Belgian hares which he bred, and Minta followed them, singing, and put her bare arm on his shoulder, lest he should tell her anything.

Minta was bored by hares, Lily thought. But Minta never gave herself away. She never said things like that about playing chess in coffee-houses. She was far too conscious, far too wary. But to go on with their story – they had got through the dangerous stage by now. She had been staying with them last summer some time and the car broke down and Minta had to hand him his tools. He sat on the road mending the car, and it was the way she gave him the tools – business-like, straightforward, friendly – that proved it was all right now. They were 'in love' no longer; no, he had taken up with another woman, a serious woman, with her hair in a plait and a case in her hand (Minta had described her gratefully, almost admiringly), who went to meetings and shared Paul's views (they had got more and more pronounced) about the taxation of land values and a capital levy. Far from breaking up the marriage, that alliance had righted it. They were excellent friends, obviously, as he sat on the road and she handed him his tools.

So that was the story of the Rayleys, Lily smiled. She imagined herself telling it to Mrs Ramsay, who would be full of curiosity to know what had become of the Rayleys. She would feel a little triumphant, telling Mrs Ramsay that the marriage had not been a success.

But the dead, thought Lily, encountering some obstacle in her design which made her pause and ponder, stepping back a foot or so, Oh the dead! she murmured, one pitied them, one brushed them aside, one had even a little contempt for them. They are at our mercy.

To The Lighthouse

Mrs Ramsay has faded and gone, she thought. We can override her wishes, improve away her limited, old-fashioned ideas. She recedes further and further from us. Mockingly she seemed to see her there at the end of the corridor of years saying, of all incongruous things, 'Marry, marry!' (sitting very upright early in the morning with the birds beginning to cheep in the garden outside). And one would have to say to her, It has all gone against your wishes. They're happy like that; I'm happy like this. Life has changed completely. At that all her being, even her beauty, became for a moment, dusty and out of date. For a moment Lily, standing there, with the sun hot on her back, summing up the Rayleys, triumphed over Mrs Ramsay, who would never know how Paul went to coffee-houses and had a mistress; how he sat on the ground and Minta handed him his tools; how she stood here painting, had never married, not even William Bankes.

Mrs Ramsay had planned it. Perhaps, had she lived, she would have compelled it. Already that summer he was 'the kindest of men'. He was 'the first scientist of his age, my husband says'. He was also 'poor William – it makes me so unhappy, when I go to see him, to find nothing nice in his house – no one to arrange the flowers'. So they were sent for walks together, and she was told, with that faint touch of irony that made Mrs Ramsay slip through one's fingers, that she had a scientific mind; she liked flowers; she was so exact. What was this mania of hers for marriage? Lily wondered, stepping to and fro from her easel.

(Suddenly, as suddenly as a star slides in the sky, a reddish light seemed to burn in her mind, covering Paul Rayley, issuing from him. It rose like a fire sent up in token of some celebration by savages on a distant beach. She heard the roar and the crackle. The whole sea for miles round ran red and gold. Some winy smell mixed with it and intoxicated her, for she felt again her own headlong desire to throw herself off the cliff and be drowned looking for a pearl brooch on a beach. And the roar and the crackle repelled her with fear and disgust, as if while she saw its splendour and power she saw too how it fed on the treasure of the house, greedily, disgustingly, and she loathed it. But for a sight, for a glory it surpassed everything in her experience, and burnt year after year like a signal fire on a desert island at the edge of the sea, and one had only to say 'in love' and instantly, as happened now, up rose Paul's fire again. And it sank and she said to herself, laughing, 'The Rayleys'; how Paul went to coffee-houses and played chess.)

She had only escaped by the skin of her teeth though, she thought. She had been looking at the table-cloth, and it had flashed upon her that she would move the tree to the middle, and need never marry anybody, and she had felt an enormous exultation. She had felt, now she could stand up to Mrs Ramsay – a tribute to the astonishing power that Mrs Ramsay had over one. Do this, she said, and one did it. Even her shadow at the window with James was full of authority. She remembered how William Bankes had been shocked by her neglect of the significance of mother and son. Did she not admire their beauty? he said. But William, she remembered, had listened to her with his wise child's eyes when she explained how it was not irreverence: how a light there needed a shadow there and so on. She did not intend to disparage a subject which, they agreed, Raphael had treated divinely. She was not cynical. Quite the contrary. Thanks to his scientific mind he

To The Lighthouse

understood – a proof of disinterested intelligence which had pleased her and comforted her enormously. One could talk of painting then seriously to a man. Indeed, his friendship had been one of the pleasures of her life. She loved William Bankes.

They went to Hampton Court and he always left her, like the perfect gentleman he was, plenty of time to wash her hands, while he strolled by the river. That was typical of their relationship. Many things were left unsaid. Then they strolled through the courtyards, and admired, summer after summer, the proportions and the flowers, and he would tell her things, about perspective, about architecture, as they walked, and he would stop to look at a tree, or the view over the lake, and admire a child (it was his great grief – he had no daughter) in the vague aloof way that was natural to a man who spent so much time in laboratories that the world when he came out seemed to dazzle him, so that he walked slowly, lifted his hand to screen his eyes and paused, with his head thrown back, merely to breathe the air. Then he would tell her how his housekeeper was on her holiday; he must buy a new carpet for the staircase. Perhaps she would go with him to buy a new carpet for the staircase. And once something led him to talk about the Ramsays and he had said how when he first saw her she had been wearing a grey hat; she was not more than nineteen or twenty. She was astonishingly beautiful. There he stood looking down the avenue at Hampton Court, as if he could see her there among the fountains.

She looked now at the drawing-room step. She saw, through William's eyes, the shape of a woman, peaceful and silent, with downcast eyes. She sat musing, pondering (she was in grey that day, Lily thought). Her eyes were bent. She would never lift them. Yes, thought

Lily, looking intently, I must have seen her look like that, but not in grey; nor so still, nor so young, nor so peaceful. The figure came readily enough. She was astonishingly beautiful, William said. But beauty was not everything. Beauty had this penalty – it came too readily, came too completely. It stilled life – froze it. One forgot the little agitations; the flush, the pallor, some queer distortion, some light or shadow, which made the face unrecognizable for a moment and yet added a quality one saw for ever after. It was simpler to smooth that all out under the cover of beauty. But what was the look she had, Lily wondered, when she clapped her deer-stalker's hat on her head, or ran across the grass, or scolded Kennedy, the gardener? Who could tell her? Who could help her?

Against her will she had come to the surface, and found herself half out of the picture, looking, a little dazedly, as if at unreal things, at Mr Carmichael. He lay on his chair with his hands clasped above his paunch not reading, or sleeping, but basking like a creature gorged with existence. His book had fallen on to the grass.

She wanted to go straight up to him and say, 'Mr Carmichael!' Then he would look up benevolently as always, from his smoky vague green eyes. But one only woke people if one knew what one wanted to say to them. And she wanted to say not one thing, but everything. Little words that broke up the thought and dismembered it said nothing. 'About life, about death; about Mrs Ramsay' – no, she thought, one could say nothing to nobody. The urgency of the moment always missed its mark. Words fluttered sideways and struck the object inches too low. Then one gave it up; then the idea sunk back again; then one became like most middle-aged

To The Lighthouse

people, cautious, furtive, with wrinkles between the eyes and a look of perpetual apprehension. For how could one express in words these emotions of the body? express that emptiness there? (She was looking at the drawing-room steps; they looked extraordinarily empty). It was one's body feeling, not one's mind. The physical sensations that went with the bare look of the steps had become suddenly extremely unpleasant. To want and not to have, sent all up her body a hardness, a hollowness, a strain. And then to want and not to have – to want and want – how that wrung the heart, and wrung it again and again! Oh Mrs Ramsay! she called out silently, to that essence which sat by the boat, that abstract one made of her, that woman in grey, as if to abuse her for having gone, and then having gone, come back again. It had seemed so safe, thinking of her. Ghost, air, nothingness, a thing you could play with easily and safely at any time of day or night, she had been that, and then suddenly she put her hand out and wrung the heart thus. Suddenly, the empty drawing-room steps, the frill of the chair inside, the puppy tumbling on the terrace, the whole wave and whisper of the garden became like curves and arabesques flourishing round a centre of complete emptiness.

'What does it mean? How do you explain it all?' she wanted to say, turning to Mr Carmichael again. For the whole world seemed to have dissolved in this early morning hour into a pool of thought, a deep basin of reality, and one could almost fancy that had Mr Carmichael spoken, a little tear would have rent the surface of the pool. And then? Something would emerge. A hand would be shoved up, a blade would be flashed. It was nonsense of course.

A curious notion came to her that he did after all hear

the things she could not say. He was an inscrutable old man, with the yellow stain on his beard, and his poetry, and his puzzles, sailing serenely through a world which satisfied all his wants, so that she thought he had only to put down his hand where he lay on the lawn to fish up anything he wanted. She looked at her picture. That would have been his answer, presumably – how 'you' and 'I' and 'she' pass and vanish; nothing stays; all changes; but not words, not paint. Yet it would be hung in the attics, she thought; it would be rolled up and flung under a sofa; yet even so, even of a picture like that, it was true. One might say, even of this scrawl, not of that actual picture, perhaps, but of what it attempted, that it 'remained for ever' she was going to say, or, for the words spoken sounded even to herself, too boastful, to hint, wordlessly; when, looking at the picture, she was surprised to find that she could not see it. Her eyes were full of a hot liquid (she did not think of tears at first) which, without disturbing the firmness of her lips, made the air thick, rolled down her cheeks. She had perfect control of herself – Oh yes! – in every other way. Was she crying then for Mrs Ramsay, without being aware of any unhappiness? She addressed old Mr Carmichael again. What was it then? What did it mean? Could things thrust their hands up and grip one; could the blade cut; the fist grasp? Was there no safety? No learning by heart of the ways of the world? No guide, no shelter, but all was miracle, and leaping from the pinnacle of a tower into the air? Could it be, even for elderly people, that this was life? – startling, unexpected, unknown? For one moment she felt that if they both got up, here, now on the lawn, and demanded an explanation, why was it so short, why was it so inexplicable, said it with violence, as two fully equipped

To The Lighthouse

human beings from whom nothing should be hid might speak, then, beauty would roll itself up; the space would fill; those empty flourishes would form into shape; if they shouted loud enough Mrs Ramsay would return. 'Mrs Ramsay!' she said aloud, 'Mrs Ramsay!' The tears ran down her face.

6

[Macalister's boy took one of the fish and cut a square out of its side to bait his hook with. The mutilated body (it was alive still) was thrown back into the sea.]

7

'Mrs Ramsay!' Lily cried, 'Mrs Ramsay!' But nothing happened. The pain increased. That anguish could reduce one to such a pitch of imbecility, she thought! Anyhow the old man had not heard her. He remained benignant, calm – if one chose to think it, sublime. Heaven be praised, no one had heard her cry that ignominious cry, stop pain, stop! She had not obviously taken leave of her senses. No one had seen her step off her strip of board into the waters of annihilation. She remained a skimpy old maid, holding a paint-brush on the lawn.

And now slowly the pain of the want, and the bitter anger (to be called back, just as she thought she would never feel sorrow for Mrs Ramsay again. Had she missed her among the coffee cups at breakfast? not in the least) lessened; and of their anguish left, as antidote, a relief that was balm in itself, and also, but more mysteriously, a sense of someone there, of Mrs Ramsay, relieved for a moment of the weight that the world had put on her, staying lightly by her side and then (for this was Mrs Ramsay in all her beauty) raising to her forehead a wreath of white flowers with which she went. Lily squeezed her tubes again. She attacked that problem of the hedge. It was strange how clearly she saw her, stepping with her usual quickness across fields among whose folds, purplish and soft, among whose flowers, hyacinths or lilies, she vanished. It was some trick of the painter's eye. For days after she had heard of her death she had seen her thus, putting her wreath to her forehead and going unquestioningly with her companion, a shadow, across the fields. The sight, the phrase, had its power to console. Wherever she happened to be, painting, here, in the country or in London, the vision would come to her, and her eyes, half closing, sought something to base her vision on. She looked down the railway carriage, the omnibus; took a line from shoulder or cheek; looked at the windows opposite; at Piccadilly, lamp-strung in the evening. All had been part of the fields of death. But always something – it might be a face, a voice, a paper boy crying *Standard*, *News* – thrust through, snubbed her, waked her, required and got in the end an effort of attention, so that the vision must be perpetually remade. Now again, moved as she was by some instinctive need of distance and blue, she looked at the bay beneath her, making hillocks of the blue bars of the waves, and stony fields of the purpler spaces. Again she was roused as usual by something incongruous. There was a brown spot in the middle of the bay. It was a boat. Yes, she realized that after a second. But whose boat? Mr Ramsay's boat, she replied. Mr Ramsay; the man who had marched past her, with his hand raised, aloof, at the head of a procession, in

To The Lighthouse

his beautiful boots, asking her for sympathy, which she had refused. The boat was now halfway across the bay.

So fine was the morning except for a streak of wind here and there that the sea and sky looked all one fabric, as if sails were stuck high up in the sky, or the clouds had dropped down into the sea. A steamer far out at sea had drawn in the air a great scroll of smoke which stayed there curving and circling decoratively, as if the air were a fine gauze which held things and kept them softly in its mesh, only gently swaying them this way and that. And as happens sometimes when the weather is very fine, the cliffs looked as if they were conscious of the ships, and the ships looked as if they were conscious of the cliffs, as if they signalled to each other some secret message of their own. For sometimes quite close to the shore, the Lighthouse looked this morning in the haze an enormous distance away.

'Where are they now?' Lily thought, looking out to sea. Where was he, that very old man who had gone past her silently, holding a brown paper parcel under his arm? The boat was in the middle of the bay.

8

They don't feel a thing there, Cam thought, looking at the shore, which, rising and falling, became steadily more distant and more peaceful. Her hand cut a trail in the sea, as her mind made the green swirls and streaks into patterns and, numbed and shrouded, wandered in imagination in that underworld of waters where the pearls stuck in clusters to white sprays, where in the green light a change came over one's entire mind and one's body shone half transparent enveloped in a green cloak.

Then the eddy slackened round her hand. The rush of the water ceased; the world became full of little creaking and squeaking sounds. One heard the waves breaking and flapping against the side of the boat as if they were anchored in harbour. Everything became very close to one. For the sail, upon which James had his eyes fixed until it had become to him like a person whom he knew, sagged entirely; there they came to a stop, flapping about waiting for a breeze, in the hot sun, miles from shore, miles from the Lighthouse. Everything in the whole world seemed to stand still. The Lighthouse became immovable, and the line of the distant shore became fixed. The sun grew hotter and everybody seemed to come very close together and to feel each other's presence, which they had almost forgotten. Macalister's fishing line went plumb down into the sea. But Mr Ramsay went on reading with his legs curled under him.

He was reading a little shiny book with covers mottled like a plover's egg. Now and again, as they hung about in that horrid calm, he turned a page. And James felt that each page was turned with a peculiar gesture aimed at him: now assertively, now commandingly; now with the intention of making people pity him; and all the time, as his father read and turned one after another of those little pages, James kept dreading the moment when he would look up and speak sharply to him about something or other. Why were they lagging about here? he would demand, or something quite unreasonable like that. And if he does, James thought, then I shall take a knife and strike him to the heart.

To The Lighthouse

He had always kept this old symbol of taking a knife and striking his father to the heart. Only now, as he grew older, and sat staring at his father in an impotent rage, it was not him, that old man reading, whom he wanted to kill, but it was the thing that descended on him – without his knowing it perhaps: that fierce sudden black-winged harpy, with its talons and its beak all cold and hard, that struck and struck at you (he could feel the beak on his bare legs, where it had struck when he was a child) and then made off, and there he was again, an old man, very sad, reading his book. That he would kill, that he would strike to the heart. Whatever he did – (and he might do anything, he felt, looking at the Lighthouse and the distant shore) whether he was in a business, in a bank, a barrister, a man at the head of some enterprise, that he would fight, that he would track down and stamp out – tyranny, despotism, he called it – making people do what they did not want to do, cutting off their right to speak. How could any of them say, But I won't, when he said, Come to the Lighthouse. Do this. Fetch me that. The black wings spread, and the hard beak tore. And then next moment, there he sat reading his book; and he might look up – one never knew – quite reasonably. He might talk to the Macalisters. He might be pressing a sovereign into some frozen old woman's hand in the street, James thought; he might be shouting out at some fisherman's sports; he might be waving his arms in the air with excitement. Or he might sit at the head of the table dead silent from one end of dinner to the other. Yes, thought James, while the boat slapped and dawdled there in the hot sun; there was a waste of snow and rock very lonely and austere; and there he had come to feel, quite often lately, when his father said something which surprised the others, were two pairs of footprints only; his own and his father's. They alone knew each other. What then was this terror, this hatred? Turning back among the many leaves which the past had folded in him, peering into the heart of that forest where light and shade so chequer each other that all shape is distorted, and one blunders, now with the sun in one's eyes, now with a dark shadow, he sought an image to cool and detach and round off his feeling in a concrete shape. Suppose then that as a child sitting helpless in a perambulator, or on someone's knee, he had seen a waggon crush ignorantly and innocently, someone's foot? Suppose he had seen the foot first, in the grass, smooth, and whole; then the wheel; and the same foot, purple, crushed. But the wheel was innocent. So now, when his father came striding down the passage knocking them up early in the morning to go to the Lighthouse down it came over his foot, over Cam's foot, over anybody's foot. One sat and watched it.

But whose foot was he thinking of, and in what garden did all this happen? For one had settings for these scenes; trees that grew there; flowers; a certain light; a few figures. Everything tended to set itself in a garden where there was none of this gloom and none of this throwing of hands about; people spoke in an ordinary tone of voice. They went in and out all day long. There was an old woman gossiping in the kitchen; and the blinds were sucked in and out by the breeze; all was blowing, all was growing; and over all those plates and bowls and tall brandishing red and yellow flowers a very thin yellow veil would be drawn, like a vine leaf, at night. Things became stiller and darker at night. But the leaf-like veil was so fine that lights lifted it, voices crinkled it; he could see through it a figure stooping, hear, coming close, going away, some dress rustling, some chain tinkling.

It was in this world that the wheel went over the person's foot. Something, he remembered, stayed and darkened over him; would not move; something flourished up in the air, something arid and sharp descended even there, like a blade, a scimitar, smiting through the leaves and flowers even of that happy world and making them shrivel and fall.

'It will rain,' he remembered his father saying. 'You won't be able to go to the Lighthouse.'

The Lighthouse was then a silvery, misty-looking tower with a yellow eye that opened suddenly and softly in the evening. Now –

James looked at the Lighthouse. He could see the white-washed rocks; the tower, stark and straight; he could see that it was barred with black and white; he could see windows in it; he could even see washing spread on the rocks to dry. So that was the Lighthouse, was it?

No, the other was also the Lighthouse. For nothing was simply one thing. The other was the Lighthouse too. It was sometimes hardly to be seen across the bay. In the evening one looked up and saw the eye opening and shutting and the light seemed to reach them in that airy sunny garden where they sat.

But he pulled himself up. Whenever he said 'they' or 'a person', and then began hearing the rustle of someone coming, the tinkle of someone going, he became extremely sensitive to the presence of whoever might be in the room. It was his father now. The strain became acute. For in one moment if there was no breeze, his father would slap the covers of his book together, and say: 'What's happening now? What are we dawdling about here for, eh?' as, once before he had brought his blade down among them on the terrace and she had gone stiff all over, and if there had been an axe handy, a knife, or anything with a sharp point he would have seized it and struck his father through the heart. His mother had gone still all over, and then, her arm slackening, so that he felt she listened to him no longer, she had risen somehow and gone away and left him there, impotent, ridiculous, sitting on the floor grasping a pair of scissors.

Not a breath of wind blew. The water chuckled and gurgled in the bottom of the boat where three or four mackerel beat their tails up and down in a pool of water not deep enough to cover them. At any moment Mr Ramsay (James scarcely dared look at him) might rouse himself, shut his book, and say something sharp; but for the moment he was reading, so that James stealthily, as if he were stealing downstairs on bare feet, afraid of waking a watch-dog by a creaking board, went on thinking what was she like, where did she go that day? He began following her from room to room and at last they came to a room where in a blue light, as if the reflection came from many china dishes, she talked to somebody; he listened to her talking. She talked to a servant, saying simply whatever came into her head. 'We shall need a big dish tonight. Where is it – the blue dish?' She alone spoke the truth; to her alone could he speak it. That was the source of her everlasting attraction for him, perhaps; she was a person to whom one could say what came into one's head. But all the time he thought of her, he was conscious of his father following his thought, shadowing it, making it shiver and falter.

At last he ceased to think; there he sat with his hand

on the tiller in the sun, staring at the Lighthouse, powerless to move, powerless to flick off these grains of misery which settled on his mind one after another. A rope seemed to bind him there, and his father had knotted it and he could only escape by taking a knife and plunging it.... But at that moment the sail swung slowly round, filled slowly out, the boat seemed to shake herself, and then to move off half conscious in her sleep, and then she woke and shot through the waves. The relief was extraordinary. They all seemed to fall away from each other again and to be at their ease and the fishing-lines slanted taut across the side of the boat. But his father did not rouse himself. He only raised his right hand mysteriously high in the air, and let it fall upon his knee again as if he were conducting some secret symphony.

9

[The sea without a stain on it, thought Lily Briscoe, still standing and looking out over the bay. The sea is stretched like silk across the bay. Distance had an extraordinary power; they had been swallowed up in it, she felt, they were gone for ever, they had become part of the nature of things. It was so calm; it was so quiet. The steamer itself had vanished, but the great scroll of smoke still hung in the air and drooped like a flag mournfully in valediction.]

10

It was like that then, the island, thought Cam, once more drawing her fingers through the waves. She had never seen it from out at sea before. It lay like that on the sea, did it, with a dent in the middle and two sharp crags, and the sea swept in there, and spread away for miles and miles on either side of the island. It was very small; shaped something like a leaf stood on end. So we took a little boat, she thought, beginning to tell herself a story of adventure about escaping from a sinking ship. But with the sea streaming through her fingers, a spray of seaweed vanishing behind them, she did not want to tell herself seriously a story; it was the sense of adventure and escape that she wanted, for she was thinking, as the boat sailed on, how her father's anger about the points of the compass, James's obstinacy about the compact, and her own anguish, all had slipped, all had passed, all had streamed away. What then came next? Where were they going? From her hand, ice cold, held deep in the sea, there spurted up a fountain of joy at the change, at the escape, at the adventure (that she should be alive, that she should be there). And the drops falling from this sudden and unthinking fountain of joy fell here and there on the dark, the slumbrous shapes in her mind; shapes of a world not realized but turning in their darkness, catching here and there, a spark of light; Greece, Rome, Constantinople. Small as it was, and shaped something like a leaf stood on end with the gold sprinkled waters flowing in and about it, it had, she supposed, a place in the universe – even that little island? The old gentlemen in the study she thought could have told her. Sometimes she strayed in from the garden purposely to catch them at it. There they were (it might be Mr Carmichael or Mr Bankes, very old, very stiff) sitting opposite each other in their low armchairs. They were crackling in front of them the pages of *The Times*, when she came in from the

To The Lighthouse

garden, all in a muddle, about something someone had said about Christ; a mammoth had been dug up in a London street; what was the great Napoleon like? Then they took all this with their clean hands (they wore grey-coloured clothes; they smelt of heather) and they brushed the scraps together, turning the paper, crossing their knees, and said something now and then very brief. In a kind of trance she would take a book from the shelf and stand there, watching her father write, so equally, so neatly from one side of the page to another, with a little cough now and then, or something said briefly to the other old gentleman opposite. And she thought, standing there with her book open, here one could let whatever one thought expand like a leaf in water; and if it did well here, among the old gentlemen smoking and *The Times* crackling, then it was right. And watching her father as he wrote in his study, she thought (now sitting in the boat) he was most lovable, he was most wise; he was not vain nor a tyrant. Indeed, if he saw she was there, reading a book, he would ask her, as gently as any one could, Was there nothing he could give her?

Lest this should be wrong, she looked at him reading the little book with the shiny cover mottled like a plover's egg. No; it was right. Look at him now, she wanted to say aloud to James. (But James had his eye on the sail.) He is a sarcastic brute, James would say. He brings the talk round to himself and his books, James would say. He is intolerably egotistical. Worst of all, he is a tyrant. But look! she said, looking at him. Look at him now. She looked at him reading the little book with his legs curled; the little book whose yellowish pages she knew, without knowing what was written on them. It was small; it was closely printed;

on the fly-leaf, she knew, he had written that he had spent fifteen francs on dinner; the wine had been so much; he had given so much to the waiter; all was added up neatly at the bottom of the page. But what might be written in the book which had rounded its edges off in his pocket, she did not know. What he thought they none of them knew. But he was absorbed in it, so that when he looked up, as he did now for an instant, it was not to see anything; it was to pin down some thought more exactly. That done, his mind flew back again and he plunged into his reading. He read, she thought, as if he were guiding something, or wheedling a large flock of sheep, or pushing his way up and up a single narrow path; and sometimes he went fast and straight, and broke his way through the thicket, and sometimes it seemed a branch struck at him, a bramble blinded him, but he was not going to let himself be beaten by that; on he went, tossing over page after page. And she went on telling herself a story about escaping from a sinking ship, for she was safe, while he sat there; safe, as she felt herself when she crept in from the garden, and took a book down, and the old gentleman, lowering the paper suddenly, said something very brief over the top of it about the character of Napoleon.

She gazed back over the sea, at the island. But the leaf was losing its sharpness. It was very small; it was very distant. The sea was more important now than the shore. Waves were all round them, tossing and sinking, with a log wallowing down one wave; a gull riding on another. About here, she thought, dabbling her fingers in the water, a ship had sunk, and she murmured, dreamily, half asleep, how we perished, each alone.

To The Lighthouse

11

So much depends then, thought Lily Briscoe, looking at the sea which had scarcely a stain on it, which was so soft that the sails and the clouds seemed set in its blue, so much depends, she thought, upon distance: whether people are near us or far from us; for her feeling for Mr Ramsay changed as he sailed further and further across the bay. It seemed to be elongated, stretched out; he seemed to become more and more remote. He and his children seemed to be swallowed up in that blue, that distance; but here, on the lawn, close at hand, Mr Carmichael suddenly grunted. She laughed. He clawed his book up from the grass. He settled into his chair again puffing and blowing like some sea monster. That was different altogether, because he was so near. And now again all was quiet. They must be out of bed by this time, she supposed, looking at the house, but nothing appeared there. But then, she remembered, they had always made off directly a meal was over, on business of their own. It was all in keeping with this silence, this emptiness, and the unreality of the early morning hour. It was a way things had sometimes, she thought, lingering for a moment and looking at the long glittering windows and the plume of blue smoke: they became unreal. So coming back from a journey, or after an illness, before habits had spun themselves across the surface, one felt that same unreality, which was so startling; felt something emerge. Life was most vivid then. One could be at one's ease. Mercifully one need not say, very briskly, crossing the lawn to greet old Mrs Beckwith, who would be coming out to find a corner to sit in, 'Oh good-morning, Mrs Beckwith! What a lovely day! Are you going to be so bold as to sit in the

Virginia Woolf

sun? Jasper's hidden the chairs. Do let me find you one!' and all the rest of the usual chatter. One need not speak at all. One glided, one shook one's sails (there was a good deal of movement in the bay, boats were starting off) between things, beyond things. Empty it was not, but full to the brim. She seemed to be standing up to the lips in some substance, to move and float and sink in it, yes, for these waters were unfathomably deep. Into them had spilled so many lives. The Ramsays'; the children's; and all sorts of waifs and strays of things besides. A washerwoman with her basket; a rook; a red-hot poker; the purples and grey-greens of flowers: some common feeling which held the whole together.

It was some such feeling of completeness perhaps which, ten years ago, standing almost where she stood now, had made her say that she must be in love with the place. Love had a thousand shapes. There might be lovers whose gift it was to choose out the elements of things and place them together and so, giving them a wholeness not theirs in life, make of some scene, or meeting of people (all now gone and separate), one of those globed compacted things over which thought lingers, and love plays.

Her eyes rested on the brown speck of Mr Ramsay's sailing boat. They would be at the Lighthouse by lunch time she supposed. But the wind had freshened, and, as the sky changed slightly and the sea changed slightly and the boats altered their positions, the view, which a moment before had seemed miraculously fixed, was now unsatisfactory. The wind had blown the trail of smoke about; there was something displeasing about the placing of the ships.

The disproportion there seemed to upset some harmony in her own mind. She felt an obscure distress.

To The Lighthouse

It was confirmed when she turned to her picture. She had been wasting her morning. For whatever reason she could not achieve that razor edge of balance between two opposite forces; Mr Ramsay and the picture; which was necessary. There was something perhaps wrong with the design? Was it, she wondered, that the line of the wall wanted breaking, was it that the mass of the trees was too heavy? She smiled ironically; for had she not thought, when she began, that she had solved her problem?

What was the problem then? She must try to get hold of something that evaded her. It evaded her when she thought of Mrs Ramsay; it evaded her now when she thought of her picture. Phrases came. Visions came. Beautiful pictures. Beautiful phrases. But what she wished to get hold of was that very jar on the nerves, the thing itself before it has been made anything. Get that and start afresh; get that and start afresh; she said desperately, pitching herself firmly again before her easel. It was a miserable machine, an inefficient machine, she thought, the human apparatus for painting or for feeling; it always broke down at the critical moment; heroically, one must force it on. She stared, frowning. There was the hedge, sure enough. But one got nothing by soliciting urgently. One got only a glare in the eye from looking at the line of the wall, or from thinking – she wore a grey hat. She was astonishingly beautiful. Let it come, she thought, if it will come. For there are moments when one can neither think nor feel. And if one can neither think nor feel, she thought, where is one?

Here on the grass, on the ground, she thought, sitting down, and examining with her brush a little colony of plantains. For the lawn was very rough. Here sitting on

Virginia Woolf

the world, she thought, for she could not shake herself free from the sense that everything this morning was happening for the first time, perhaps for the last time, as a traveller, even though he is half asleep, knows, looking out of the train window, that he must look now, for he will never see that town, or that mule-cart, or that woman at work in the fields, again. The lawn was the world; they were up here together, on this exalted station, she thought, looking at old Mr Carmichael, who seemed (though they had not said a word all this time) to share her thoughts. And she would never see him again perhaps. He was growing old. Also, she remembered, smiling at the slipper that dangled from his foot, he was growing famous. People said that his poetry was 'so beautiful'. They went and published things he had written forty years ago. There was a famous man now called Carmichael, she smiled, thinking how many shapes one person might wear, how he was that in the newspapers, but here the same as he had always been. He looked the same – greyer, rather. Yes, he looked the same, but somebody had said, she recalled, that when he had heard of Andrew Ramsay's death (he was killed in a second by a shell; he should have been a great mathematician) Mr Carmichael had 'lost all interest in life'. What did it mean – that? she wondered. Had he marched through Trafalgar Square grasping a big stick? Had he turned pages over and over, without reading them, sitting in his room in St John's Wood alone? She did not know what he had done, when he heard that Andrew was killed, but she felt it in him all the same. They only mumbled at each other on staircases; they looked up at the sky and said it will be fine or it won't be fine. But this was one way of knowing people, she thought: to know the outline, not the detail, to sit in one's garden and look at the slopes of a hill running purple down into the distant heather. She knew him in that way. She knew that he had changed somehow. She had never read a line of his poetry. She thought that she knew how it went though, slowly and sonorously. It was seasoned and mellow. It was about the desert and the camel. It was about the palm tree and the sunset. It was extremely impersonal; it said something about death; it said very little about love. There was an aloofness about him. He wanted very little of other people. Had he not always lurched rather awkwardly past the drawing-room window with some newspaper under his arm, trying to avoid Mrs Ramsay whom for some reason he did not much like? On that account, of course, she would always try to make him stop. He would bow to her. He would halt unwillingly and bow profoundly. Annoyed that he did not want anything of her, Mrs Ramsay would ask him (Lily could hear her) wouldn't he like a coat, a rug, a newspaper? No, he wanted nothing. (Here he bowed.) There was some quality in her which he did not much like. It was perhaps her masterfulness, her positiveness, something matter-of-fact in her. She was so direct.

(A noise drew her attention to the drawing-room window – the squeak of a hinge. The light breeze was toying with the window.)

There must have been people who disliked her very much, Lily thought (Yes; she realized that the drawing-room step was empty, but it had no effect on her whatever. She did not want Mrs Ramsay now) – People who thought her too sure, too drastic. Also her beauty offended people probably. How monotonous, they would say, and the same always! They preferred another type – the dark, the vivacious. Then she was weak with her husband. She let him make those scenes. Then she was reserved. Nobody knew exactly what had happened to her. And (to go back to Mr Carmichael and his dislike) one could not imagine Mrs Ramsay standing painting, lying reading, a whole morning on the lawn. It was unthinkable. Without saying a word, the only token of her errand a basket on her arm, she went off to the town, to the poor, to sit in some stuffy little bedroom. Often and often Lily had seen her go silently in the midst of some game, some discussion, with her basket on her arm, very upright. She had noted her return. She had thought, half laughing (she was so methodical with the tea cups) half moved (her beauty took one's breath away), eyes that are closing in pain have looked on you. You have been with them there.

And then Mrs Ramsay would be annoyed because somebody was late, or the butter not fresh, or the teapot chipped. And all the time she was saying that the butter was not fresh one would be thinking of Greek temples, and how beauty had been with them there. She never talked of it – she went, punctually, directly. It was her instinct to go, an instinct like the swallows for the south, the artichokes for the sun, turning her infallibly to the human race, making her nest in its heart. And this, like all instincts, was a little distressing to people who did not share it; to Mr Carmichael perhaps, to herself certainly. Some notion was in both of them about the ineffectiveness of action, the supremacy of thought. Her going was a reproach to them, gave a different twist to the world, so that they were led to protest, seeing their own prepossessions disappear, and clutch at them vanishing. Charles Tansley did that too: it was part of the reason why one disliked him. He upset the proportions of one's world. And what had happened to him, she wondered, idly stirring the plantains with her

To The Lighthouse

brush. He had got his fellowship. He had married; he lived at Golder's Green.

She had gone one day into a Hall and heard him speaking during the war. He was denouncing something: he was condemning somebody. He was preaching brotherly love. And all she felt was how could he love his kind who did not know one picture from another, who had stood behind her smoking shag ('fivepence an ounce, Miss Briscoe') and making it his business to tell her women can't write, women can't paint, not so much that he believed it, as that for some odd reason he wished it? There he was, lean and red and raucous, preaching love from a platform (there were ants crawling about among the plantains which she disturbed with her brush – red, energetic ants, rather like Charles Tansley). She had looked at him ironically from her seat in the half-empty hall, pumping love into that chilly space, and suddenly, there was the old cask or whatever it was bobbing up and down among the waves and Mrs Ramsay looking for her spectacle case among the pebbles. 'Oh dear! What a nuisance! Lost again. Don't bother, Mr Tansley. I lose thousands every summer,' at which he pressed his chin back against his collar, as if afraid to sanction such exaggeration, but could stand it in her whom he liked, and smiled very charmingly. He must have confided in her on one of those long expeditions when people got separated and walked back alone. He was educating his little sister, Mrs Ramsay had told her. It was immensely to his credit. Her own idea of him was grotesque, Lily knew well, stirring the plantains with her brush. Half one's notions of other people were, after all, grotesque. They served private purposes of one's own. He did for her instead of a whipping-boy. She found herself flagellating his lean flanks when she was out of temper.

If she wanted to be serious about him she had to help herself to Mrs Ramsay's sayings, to look at him through her eyes.

She raised a little mountain for the ants to climb over. She reduced them to a frenzy of indecision by this interference in their cosmogony. Some ran this way, others that.

One wanted fifty pairs of eyes to see with, she reflected. Fifty pairs of eyes were not enough to get round that one woman with, she thought. Among them, must be one that was stone blind to her beauty. One wanted most some secret sense, fine as air, with which to steal through keyholes and surround her where she sat knitting, talking, sitting silent in the window alone; which took to itself and treasured up like the air which held the smoke of the steamer, her thoughts, her imaginations, her desires. What did the hedge mean to her, what did the garden mean to her, what did it mean to her when a wave broke? (Lily looked up, as she had seen Mrs Ramsay look up; she too heard a wave falling on the beach.) And then what stirred and trembled in her mind when the children cried, 'How's that? How's that?' cricketing? She would stop knitting for a second. She would look intent. Then she would lapse again, and suddenly Mr Ramsay stopped dead in his pacing in front of her, and some curious shock passed through her and seemed to rock her in profound agitation on its breast when stopping there he stood over her, and looked down at her. Lily could see him.

He stretched out his hand and raised her from her chair. It seemed somehow as if he had done it before; as if he had once bent in the same way and raised her from a boat which, lying a few inches off some island, had required that the ladies should thus be helped on shore by the gentlemen. An old-fashioned scene that was, which required, very nearly, crinolines and peg-top trousers. Letting herself be helped by him, Mrs Ramsay had thought (Lily supposed) the time has come now; Yes, she would say it now. Yes, she would marry him. And she stepped slowly, quietly on shore. Probably she said one word only, letting her hand rest still in his. I will marry you, she might have said, with her hand in his; but no more. Time after time the same thrill had passed between them – obviously it had, Lily thought, smoothing a way for her ants. She was not inventing; she was only trying to smooth out something she had been given years ago folded up; something she had seen. For in the rough and tumble of daily life, with all those children about, all those visitors, one had constantly a sense of repetition – of one thing falling where another had fallen, and so setting up an echo which chimed in the air and made it full of vibrations.

But it would be a mistake, she thought, thinking how they walked off together, she in her green shawl, he with his tie flying, arm in arm, past the greenhouse, to simplify their relationship. It was no monotony of bliss – she with her impulses and quicknesses; he with his shudders and glooms. Oh no. The bedroom door would slam violently early in the morning. He would start from the table in a temper. He would whizz his plate through the window. Then all through the house there would be a sense of doors slamming and blinds fluttering as if a gusty wind were blowing and people scudded about trying in a hasty way to fasten hatches and make things shipshape. She had met Paul Rayley like that one day on the stairs. They had laughed and laughed, like a couple of children, all because Mr Ramsay, finding an earwig in his milk at breakfast, had sent the whole thing flying through the air on to the terrace outside. 'An earwig,' Prue murmured, awestruck, 'in his milk.' Other people might find centipedes. But he had built round him such a fence of sanctity, and occupied the space with such a demeanour of majesty that an earwig in his milk was a monster.

But it tired Mrs Ramsay, it cowed her a little – the plates whizzing and the doors slamming. And there would fall between them sometimes long rigid silences, when, in a state of mind which annoyed Lily in her, half plaintive, half resentful, she seemed unable to surmount the tempest calmly, or to laugh as they laughed, but in her weariness perhaps concealed something. She brooded and sat silent. After a time he would hang stealthily about the places where she was – roaming under the window where she sat writing letters or talking, for she would take care to be busy when he passed, and evade him, and pretend not to see him. Then he would turn smooth as silk, affable, urbane, and try to win her so. Still she would hold off, and now she would assert for a brief season some of those prides and airs the due of her beauty which she was generally utterly without; would turn her head; would look so, over her shoulder, always with some Minta, Paul, or William Bankes at her side. At length, standing outside the group the very figure of a famished wolfhound (Lily got up off the grass and stood looking at the steps, at the window, where she had seen him), he would say her name, once only, for all the world like a wolf barking in the snow, but still she held back; and he would say it once more, and this time something in the tone would rouse her, and she would go to him, leaving them all of a sudden, and they would walk off together among the pear trees, the cabbages, and the raspberry beds. They would have it out together. But with what attitudes and with what words? Such a dignity was theirs in this relationship that, turning away, she and Paul and Minta would hide their curiosity and their discomfort, and begin picking flowers, throwing balls, chattering, until it was time for dinner, and there they were, he at one end of the table, she at the other, as usual.

'Why don't some of you take up botany? . . . With all those legs and arms why doesn't one of you . . .?' So they would talk as usual, laughing, among the children. All would be as usual, save only for some quiver, as of a blade in the air, which came and went between them as if the usual sight of the children sitting round their soup plates had freshened itself in their eyes after that hour among the pears and the cabbages. Especially, Lily thought, Mrs Ramsay would glance at Prue. She sat in the middle between brothers and sisters, always so occupied, it seemed, seeing that nothing went wrong that she scarcely spoke herself. How Prue must have blamed herself for that earwig in the milk! How white she had gone when Mr Ramsay threw his plate through the window! How she drooped under those long silences between them! Anyhow, her mother now would seem to be making it up to her; assuring her that everything was well; promising her that one of these days that same happiness would be hers. She had enjoyed it for less than a year, however.

She had let the flowers fall from her basket, Lily thought, screwing up her eyes and standing back as if to look at her picture, which she was not touching, however, with all her faculties in a trance, frozen over superficially but moving underneath with extreme speed.

She let her flowers fall from her basket, scattered and tumbled them on to the grass and, reluctantly and hesitatingly, but without question or complaint – had she not the faculty of obedience to perfection? – went too. Down fields, across valleys, white, flower-strewn – that was how she would have painted it. The hills were austere. It was rocky; it was steep. The waves sounded hoarse on the stones beneath. They went, the three of them together, Mrs Ramsay walking rather fast in front, as if she expected to meet some one round the corner.

Suddenly the window at which she was looking was whitened by some light stuff behind it. At last then somebody had come into the drawing-room; somebody was sitting in the chair. For Heaven's sake, she prayed, let them sit still there and not come floundering out to talk to her. Mercifully, whoever it was stayed still inside; had settled by some stroke of luck so as to throw an odd-shaped triangular shadow over the step. It altered the composition of the picture a little. It was interesting. It might be useful. Her mood was coming back to her. One must keep on looking without for a second relaxing the intensity of emotion, the determination not to be put off, not to be bamboozled. One must hold the scene – so – in a vice and let nothing come in and spoil it. One wanted, she thought, dipping her brush deliberately, to be on a level with ordinary experience, to feel simply that's a chair, that's a table, and yet at the same time, it's a miracle, it's an ecstasy. The problem might be solved after all. Ah, but what had happened? Some wave of white went over the window pane. The air must have stirred some flounce in the room. Her heart leapt at her and seized her and tortured her.

'Mrs Ramsay! Mrs Ramsay! she cried, feeling the old horror come back – to want and want and not to have. Could she inflict that still? And then, quietly, as if she refrained, that too became part of ordinary

To The Lighthouse

experience, was on a level with the chair, with the table. Mrs Ramsay – it was part of her perfect goodness to Lily – sat there quite simply, in the chair, flicked her needles to and fro, knitted her reddish-brown stocking, cast her shadow on the step. There she sat.

And as if she had something she must share, yet could hardly leave her easel, so full her mind was of what she was thinking, of what she was seeing, Lily went past Mr Carmichael holding her brush to the edge of the lawn. Where was that boat now? Mr Ramsay? She wanted him.

12

Mr Ramsay had almost done reading. One hand hovered over the page as if to be in readiness to turn it the very instant he had finished it. He sat there bareheaded with the wind blowing his hair about, extraordinarily exposed to everything. He looked very old. He looked, James thought, getting his head now against the Lighthouse, now against the waste of waters running away into the open, like some old stone lying on the sand; he looked as if he had become physically what was always at the back of both of their minds – that loneliness which was for both of them the truth about things.

He was reading very quickly, as if he were eager to get to the end. Indeed they were very close to the Lighthouse now. There it loomed up, stark and straight, glaring white and black, and one could see the waves breaking in white splinters like smashed glass upon the rocks. One could see lines and creases in the rocks. One could see the windows clearly; a dab of white on one of them, and a little tuft of green on the rock.

A man had come out and looked at them through a glass and gone in again. So it was like that, James thought, the Lighthouse one had seen across the bay all these years; it was a stark tower on a bare rock. It satisfied him. It confirmed some obscure feeling of his about his own character. The old ladies, he thought, thinking of the garden at home, went dragging their chairs about on the lawn. Old Mrs Beckwith, for example, was always saying how nice it was and how sweet it was and how they ought to be so proud and they ought to be so happy, but as a matter of fact James thought, looking at the Lighthouse stood there on its rock, it's like that. He looked at his father reading fiercely with his legs curled tight. They shared that knowledge. 'We are driving before a gale – we must sink,' he began saying to himself, half aloud exactly as his father said it.

Nobody seemed to have spoken for an age. Cam was tired of looking at the sea. Little bits of black cork had floated past; the fish were dead in the bottom of the boat. Still her father read, and James looked at him and she looked at him, and they vowed that they would fight tyranny to the death, and he went on reading quite unconscious of what they thought. It was thus that he escaped, she thought. Yes, with his great forehead and his great nose, holding his little mottled book firmly in front of him, he escaped. You might try to lay hands on him, but then like a bird, he spread his wings, he floated off to settle out of your reach somewhere far away on some desolate stump. She gazed at the immense expanse of the sea. The island had grown so small that it scarcely looked like a leaf any longer. It looked like the top of a rock which some big wave would cover. Yet in its frailty were all those paths, those terraces,

To The Lighthouse

those bedrooms – all those innumerable things. But as, just before sleep, things simplify themselves so that only one of all the myriad details has power to assert itself, so, she felt, looking drowsily at the island, all those paths and terraces and bedrooms were fading and disappearing, and nothing was left but a pale blue censer swinging rhythmically this way and that across her mind. It was a hanging garden; it was a valley, full of birds, and flowers, and antelopes. . . . She was falling asleep.

'Come now,' said Mr Ramsay, suddenly shutting his book.

Come where? To what extraordinary adventure? She woke with a start. To land somewhere, to climb somewhere? Where was he leading them? For after his immense silence the words startled them. But it was absurd. He was hungry, he said. It was time for lunch. Besides, look, he said. There's the Lighthouse. 'We're almost there.'

'He's doing very well,' said Macalister, praising James. 'He's keeping her very steady.'

But his father never praised him, James thought grimly.

Mr Ramsay opened the parcel and shared out the sandwiches among them. Now he was happy, eating bread and cheese with these fishermen. He would have liked to live in a cottage and lounge about in the harbour spitting with the other old men, James thought, watching him slice his cheese into thin yellow sheets with his penknife.

This is right, this is it, Cam kept feeling, as she peeled her hard-boiled egg. Now she felt as she did in the study when the old men were reading *The Times*. Now I can go on thinking whatever I like, and I shan't fall over a precipice or be drowned, for there he is, keeping his eye on me, she thought.

At the same time they were sailing so fast along by the rocks that it was very exciting – it seemed as if they were doing two things at once; they were eating their lunch here in the sun and they were also making for safety in a great storm after a shipwreck. Would the water last? Would the provisions last? she asked herself, telling herself a story but knowing at the same time what was the truth.

They would soon be out of it, Mr Ramsay was saying to old Macalister; but their children would see some strange things. Macalister said he was seventy-five last March; Mr Ramsay was seventy-one. Macalister said he had never seen a doctor; he had never lost a tooth. And that's the way I'd like my children to live – Cam was sure that her father was thinking that, for he stopped her throwing a sandwich into the sea and told her, as if he were thinking of the fishermen and how they live, that if she did not want it she should put it back in the parcel. She should not waste it. He said it so wisely, as if he knew so well all the things that happened in the world, that she put it back at once, and then he gave her, from his own parcel, a gingerbread nut, as if he were a great Spanish gentleman, she thought, handing a flower to a lady at a window (so courteous his manner was). But he was shabby, and simple, eating bread and cheese; and yet he was leading them on a great expedition where, for all she knew, they would be drowned.

'That was where she sunk,' said Macalister's boy suddenly.

'Three men were drowned where we are now,' said the old man. He had seen them clinging to the mast

To The Lighthouse

himself. And Mr Ramsay taking a look at the spot was about, James and Cam were afraid, to burst out:

But I beneath a rougher sea,

and if he did, they could not bear it; they would shriek aloud; they could not endure another explosion of the passion that boiled in him; but to their surprise all he said was 'Ah' as if he thought to himself, But why make a fuss about that? Naturally men are drowned in a storm, but it is a perfectly straightforward affair, and the depths of the sea (he sprinkled the crumbs from his sandwich paper over them) are only water after all. Then having lighted his pipe he took out his watch. He looked at it attentively; he made, perhaps, some mathematical calculation. At last he said, triumphantly: 'Well done!' James had steered them like a born sailor.

There! Cam thought, addressing herself silently to James. You've got it at last. For she knew that this was what James had been wanting, and she knew that now he had got it he was so pleased that he would not look at her or at his father or at any one. There he sat with his hand on the tiller sitting bolt upright, looking rather sulky and frowning slightly. He was so pleased that he was not going to let anybody take away a grain of his pleasure. His father had praised him. They must think that he was perfectly indifferent. But you've got it now, Cam thought.

They had tacked, and they were sailing swiftly, buoyantly on long rocking waves which handed them on from one to another with an extraordinary lilt and exhilaration beside the reef. On the left a row of rocks showed brown through the water which thinned and became greener and on one, a higher rock, a wave incessantly broke and spurted a little column of drops which fell down in a shower. One could hear the slap of the water and the patter of falling drops and a kind of hushing and hissing sound from the waves rolling and gambolling and slapping the rocks as if they were wild creatures who were perfectly free and tossed and tumbled and sported like this for ever.

Now they could see two men on the Lighthouse, watching them and making ready to meet them.

Mr Ramsay buttoned his coat, and turned up his trousers. He took the large, badly packed, brown paper parcel which Nancy had got ready and sat with it on his knee. Thus in complete readiness to land he sat looking back at the island. With his long-sighted eyes perhaps he could see the dwindled leaf-like shape standing on end on a plate of gold quite clearly. What could he see? Cam wondered. It was all a blur to her. What was he thinking now? she wondered. What was it he sought, so fixedly, so intently, so silently? They watched him, both of them, sitting bare-headed with his parcel on his knee staring and staring at the frail blue shape which seemed like the vapour of something that had burnt itself away. What do you want? they both wanted to ask. They both wanted to say, Ask us anything and we will give it you. But he did not ask them anything. He sat and looked at the island and he might be thinking, We perished, each alone, or he might be thinking, I have reached it. I have found it, but he said nothing.

Then he put on his hat.

'Bring those parcels,' he said, nodding his head at the things Nancy had done up for them to take to the Lighthouse. 'The parcels for the Lighthouse men,' he said. He rose and stood in the bow of the boat, very straight and tall, for all the world, James thought, as if he were saying, 'There is no God,' and Cam thought, as if he were leaping into space, and they both rose to follow him as he sprang, lightly like a young man, holding his parcel, on to the rock.

13

'He must have reached it,' said Lily Briscoe aloud, feeling suddenly completely tired out. For the Lighthouse had become almost invisible, had melted away into a blue haze, and the effort of looking at it and the effort of thinking of him landing there, which both seemed to be one and the same effort, had stretched her body and mind to the utmost. Ah, but she was relieved. Whatever she had wanted to give him, when he left her that morning, she had given him at last.

'He has landed,' she said aloud. 'It is finished.' Then, surging up, puffing slightly, old Mr Carmichael stood beside her, looking like an old pagan God, shaggy, with weeds in his hair and the trident (it was only a French novel) in his hand. He stood by her on the edge of the lawn, swaying a little in his bulk, and said, shading his eyes with his hand: 'They will have landed,' and she felt that she had been right. They had not needed to speak. They had been thinking the same things and he had answered her without her asking him anything. He stood there spreading his hands over all the weakness and suffering of mankind; she thought he was surveying, tolerantly, compassionately, their final destiny. Now he has crowned the occasion, she thought, when his hand slowly fell, as if she had seen him let fall from his great height a wreath of violets and asphodels which, fluttering slowly, lay at length upon the earth.

Quickly, as if she were recalled by something over

Virginia Woolf

there, she turned to her canvas. There it was – her picture. Yes, with all its green and blues, its lines running up and across, its attempt at something. It would be hung in the attics, she thought; it would be destroyed. But what did that matter? she asked herself, taking up her brush again. She looked at the steps; they were empty; she looked at her canvas; it was blurred. With a sudden intensity, as if she saw it clear for a second, she drew a line there, in the centre. It was done; it was finished. Yes, she thought, laying down her brush in extreme fatigue, I have had my vision.

Biographical Notes

Judy Cooke, *Editor of this anthology*
was born in Wiltshire in 1938 and educated at King's College, University of London. She lectured in modern literature in the Extra-Mural Department, University of London and in the USA and became Head of the English Department at Richmond College, Surrey. In 1981 she founded *The Fiction Magazine* which she edited until its demise in 1987, when she published a collection of stories, essays and poems by its contributors, *The Best of the Fiction Magazine*. She is now a freelance editor and is working on a paperback series for the British Council; co-edited with Malcolm Bradbury, the first issue of *New Writing* was launched in Spring 1992. She writes critical articles, reviews fiction regularly for the *Guardian* and has published short stories and a novel, *New Road*.

Atwood, Margaret 1939–
Canadian poet, novelist and short story writer. Born in Ottawa and educated at the University of Toronto and at Radcliffe College. She has been writer in residence at several universities in Canada and the United States. Her first volume of poetry, *Circle Game*, was published in 1966, followed by collections which include *Selected Poems* (1976) and *Interlunar* (1983). Her novels include *The Edible Woman* (1969), *Surfacing* (1972), *Lady Oracle* (1976), *Life Before Man* (1979) *Bodily Harm* (1981), *The Handmaid's Tale* (1985) and *Cat's Eye* (1989).

Bowen, Elizabeth 1899–1973
Anglo-Irish novelist and short story writer. Born in Dublin, she spent much of her childhood at the family home in County Cork, which she inherited in 1930 and described in *Bowen's Court* (1942). Her first collection of stories, *Encounters*, was published in 1923; her *Collected Stories* in 1980. Novels include *The Hotel* (1927), *The Death of*

Biographical Notes

the Heart (1938), *The Heat of the Day* (1949) and *Eva Trout* (1969).

Brookner, Anita 1928–
Born in London, she trained as an art historian and taught at the Courtauld Institute, where she was reader in the History of Art at the University of London. In 1988 she left the Courtauld to concentrate on writing fiction. Her novels include *Family and Friends* (1985), *Hotel du Lac* (1984), *Look At Me* (1983), *A Start In Life* (1981), *The Latecomers* (1988) and *Lewis Percy* (1989). She is also the author of *Watteau, the Genius of the Future*, *Greuze* and *Jacques-Louis David*.

Carter, Angela 1940–
Novelist, short story writer and journalist. Born in London, she was educated at Bristol University, spent two years living in Japan and from 1976–78 was Fellow in Creative Writing at Sheffield University. Her first novel, *Shadow Dance*, was published in 1965. Other novels include *The Magic Toyshop* (1967), *Heroes and Villains* (1969), *The Infernal Desires of Dr Hoffman* (1972) and *Nights at the Circus* (1984). Her short story collections include *The Bloody Chamber* (1979) and *Black Venus* (1985).

Colette (Sidonie Gabrielle) 1873–1954
French novelist and short story writer who had early success as a music hall artist. Among her best known works are *Chéri* (1920), *La Maison de Claudine* (1922), *Le Kepi* (1943) and *Gigi* (1943). *Gigi* was turned into a successful musical by Alan Jay Lerner and Frederick Loewe.

Desai, Anita 1937–
Novelist and short story writer. Born in India of a Bengali father and German mother and educated in Delhi, she now lives in Bombay. Her work includes *Fire on the Mountain* (1977), a collection of short stories, and the novels *Games of Twilight* (1978), *Clear Light of Day* (1980), *In Custody* (1984) and *Baumgartner's Bombay* (1988).

Drabble, Margaret 1939–
Novelist and biographer. Born in Sheffield, she was educated at the Mount School, York, and at Newnham College,

Biographical Notes

Cambridge. Her novels include *A Summer Birdcage* (1963), *The Garrick Year* (1964), *The Millstone* (1965), *The Ice Age* (1977), *The Radiant Way* (1987) and *A Natural Curiosity* (1989). She has also written studies of Wordsworth and Arnold Bennett and is now working on a biography of Angus Wilson.

Du Maurier, Dame Daphne 1907–90
Novelist and short story writer, born in London and educated in Paris. She later lived in the West Country which provided the background to many of her novels, including *Rebecca* (1938) and *Frenchman's Creek* (1941). Adaptations of her work for film include *Rebecca* and two short stories, both thrillers, *The Birds* and *Don't Look Now*.

Duras, Marguerite 1914–
French novelist born in Indo-China. At eighteen she came to Paris where she studied mathematics, law and political science. Her novels include *La Vie Tranquille* (1944), *Le Marin Gibraltar* (1952), *Hiroshima Mon Amour* (1961), *L'Amante Anglaise* (1967) and *The Lover* (1985).

Emecheta, Buchi 1944–
Nigerian novelist. Born in Lagos, she moved to London in 1962. Her first two novels, *In The Ditch* (1972) and *Second Class Citizen* (1974), were published together as *Adah's Story* in 1983. Her later novels, several set in West Africa, include *The Bride Price* (1976) and *The Rape of Shavi* (1983). She has also written for children and for television.

Fairbairns, Zoë 1948–
Novelist and short story writer. Born in Kent, she studied history at the University of St Andrews. Her novels include *Benefits* (1979), *Here Today*, which won the 1985 Fawcett Book prize, and *Daddy's Girls* (1991). She has also contributed to a range of short story collections including *Tales I Tell My Mother* and *The Seven Deadly Sins*.

Gordimer, Nadine 1923–
South African short story writer and novelist, born in Springs, Transvaal. Her collections of stories include *Face To Face* (1949), *The Soft Voice of the Serpent* (1952), *A Soldier's Embrace* (1980) and *Something Out There* (1984).

Biographical Notes

Among her novels are *A Guest of Honour* (1970), *The Conservationist* (1974), *Burger's Daughter* (1979) and *July's People* (1981).

Hammick, Georgina 1939–
Short story writer. Born in Hampshire, she was educated at boarding schools in England and Kenya and at the Académie Julian in Paris. Her first book, *People for Lunch*, a widely acclaimed collection of short stories, was published in 1987.

Highsmith, Patricia 1921–
American novelist and short story writer, educated at Barnard College and Columbia University, New York. Her crime novel *The Talented Mr Ripley* (1956) was the first in a series of books featuring her anti-hero Ripley, including *Ripley Underground* (1971) and *Ripley's Game* (1974). Other works include *Strangers on a Train* (1950), *Little Tales of Misogyny* (1977), *Edith's Diary* (1977) and *Tales of Natural and Unnatural Catastrophes* (1987).

Jhabvala, Ruth Prawer 1927–
Novelist, short story writer and screenwriter. Born in Germany of Polish parents, she arrived in London a refugee. Resident in India from 1951, she moved to New York in 1975. Her novels include *Esmond in India* (1958), *Heat and Dust* (1975), *In Search of Love and Beauty* (1983). Her collection of stories, *How I Became a Holy Mother*, was published in 1976. As a screenwriter she has been associated with the films of Ismail Merchant and James Ivory. Her screen credits include *Shakespeare Wallah*, *The Bostonians* and *Room with a View*.

Lehmann, Rosamond 1901–90
Born in Buckinghamshire and educated privately and at Girton College, Cambridge. Her first novel, *Dusty Answer*, was a *succès de scandale*. Other novels include *Invitation to the Waltz* (1932) and its sequel *The Weather in the Streets* (1936); *The Ballad and the Source* (1944) and *The Echoing Grove* (1953). *The Swan in the Evening: Fragments of an Inner Life* (1967) is a short autobiographical account of her reactions to her daughter's sudden death and her own subsequent conversion to spiritualism.

Biographical Notes

Lessing, Doris 1917–
Novelist and short story writer. Born to English parents in Persia, she grew up on a farm in Southern Rhodesia and worked at various jobs until in 1949 she arrived in England, bringing with her the manuscript of her first book. This was the novel *The Grass Is Singing*, which was published in 1950, followed by her first collection of short stories, *This Was the Old Chief's Country* (1951). Novels include the Martha Quest sequence, collectively titled *The Children of Violence* and consisting of *Martha Quest (1959)*, *A Proper Marriage* (1954), *A Ripple From the Storm*, (1958), *Landlocked* (1965) and *The Four-Gated City* (1969). *The Golden Notebook* (1962) is one of her major works, exploring new territories in narrative. Lessing's later work includes *Briefing for a Descent into Hell* (1972) and five novels in her space fiction series, 'Canopus In Argos'. She returned to realistic narrative in two novels published under the pseudonym of Jane Somers, *The Diary of a Good Neighbour* (1983) and *If The Old Could* (1984). The novels *The Good Terrorist* and *The Fifth Child* were published in 1985 and 1988 respectively.

Manning, Olivia 1908–80
Born into a naval family, her early life was spent in Portsmouth. Her first novel, *The Wind Changes*, was published in 1937. During the war she travelled to Bucharest, Greece, Egypt and Jerusalem, and these experiences form the background to *The Balkan Trilogy*: *The Great Fortune* (1960), *The Spoilt City* (1962), *Friends and Heroes* (1965). This was followed by *The Levant Trilogy*: *The Danger Tree* (1977), *The Battle Lost and Won* (1978) and *The Sum of Things* (1980). Her collections of short stories are *Growing Up* (1948) and *A Romantic Hero* (1966).

Mansfield, Katherine 1888–1923
Born in Wellington, New Zealand, she was educated at Queen's College, London, before returning to New Zealand to study music. She came back to live in London in 1908 although her search for a cure for tuberculosis took her frequently to Europe. In the handful of work published before her early death she established herself as one of the great practitioners of the modern short story. Short stories published in her lifetime were *In A German Pension* (1911),

Biographical Notes

Prelude (1918), *Bliss and Other Stories* (1920) and *The Garden Party and Other Stories* (1922). *The Dove's Nest and Other Stories* (1923), as well as letters and journals, was published posthumously.

Munro, Alice 1931–
Short story writer and novelist. Born in Ontario, she was educated at the University of Western Ontario. Her first book of stories, *Dance of the Happy Shades*, was published in 1968 and was followed by further volumes of short stories including *Something I've Been Meaning To Tell You* (1974), *The Moons of Jupiter* (1982) and most recently *Friends of My Youth* (1990), as well as the novel *Lives of Girls and Women* (1971).

Murdoch, Dame Iris 1919–
Novelist and philosopher. Born in Dublin of Anglo-Irish parents, she was educated at Badminton School and at Somerville College, Oxford. She worked for some time in the Civil Service, then lectured in philosophy at Oxford and at the Royal College of Art in London. Her work includes studies in philosophy, plays, poetry and fiction. Her first novel was *Under the Net* (1954) and the most celebrated books of her prolific career include *A Severed Head* (1961), dramatized in 1963 by J.B. Priestley, *The Black Prince* (1973), *The Sacred and Profane Love Machine* (1974), *The Sea, The Sea* (1978), which won the Booker Prize, *The Philosopher's Pupil* (1983) and *The Book and The Brotherhood* (1987).

O'Brien, Edna 1932–
Irish novelist and short story writer. Born in County Clare, she was educated at a convent school and studied pharmacy in Dublin. *The Country Girls*, her first novel, was published in 1960, part of a trilogy, which continued with *Girl With Green Eyes* (first published as *The Lonely Girl*, 1962) and *Girls in Their Married Bliss* (1963). Subsequent novels include *August Is a Wicked Month* (1965), and short story collections include *The Love Object* (1968), *A Scandalous Woman and Other Stories* (1974) and *Mrs Reinhardt and Other Stories* (1978).

1118

Biographical Notes

Page, Kathy 1958–
Novelist and short story writer. She lives in Norwich and divides her time between her own writing and working as a writer in the community. Her novels are *Back in the First Person* (1986), *The Unborn Dream of Clara Riley* (1987) and *Island Paradise* (1989). Her collection of short stories, *As in Music*, was published in 1991.

Plath, Sylvia 1932–63
Poet and novelist. Born in Boston, she was educated at Smith College and won a Fulbright Scholarship to Newnham College, Cambridge. One book of poems, *The Colossus and Other Poems* (1960) was published before her suicide. Posthumous volumes include *Ariel* (1963), her best-known collection, *Crossing the Water* and *Winter Trees* (both 1971). Her novel *The Bell Jar* was published in 1963.

Rhys, Jean 1894–1979
Novelist and short story writer. Born in Dominica, she came to England in 1907, briefly attended the Academy of Dramatic Art, then worked as a chorus girl and film extra. She lived for many years in Paris. Novels include *Voyage in The Dark* (1934), *Good Morning Midnight* (1939) and the book for which she is best known, published late in her career, *Wide Sargasso Sea* (1966). Her collections of short stories include *Sleep It Off, Lady* (1976); an unfinished autobiography *Smile Please* was published in 1979.

Sagan, Françoise 1935–
French novelist, educated in Paris. She achieved early success with *Bonjour Tristesse* (1954). Other works include *Un Certain Sourire* (1956), *Dans Un Mois Dans Un An* (Eng: *Those Without Shadows*, 1957) and *Les Merveilleux Nuages* (1961).

Shange, Ntozake 1948–
American writer. Best known for her widely celebrated and performed choreopoem *'for colored girls who have considered suicide when the rainbow is enuf'*, she has published two novels, *Sassafrass, Cypress & Indigo* (1982) and *Betsey Brown* (1985) as well as plays and several collections of poetry.

Biographical Notes

Smart, Elizabeth 1913–86
Poet, journalist and novelist. Born of wealthy Canadian parents, she travelled widely in her teens and worked in New York, Mexico and California before moving to England where she spent much of her adult life. Her long liaison with the poet George Barker inspired her best-known novel, *By Grand Central Station I Sat Down and Wept* (1945). Other published work includes collections of poetry and a second short novel, *The Assumption of the Rogues and Rascals* (1978).

Tan, Amy 1952–
Novelist. Born in Oakland, California, two and a half years after her parents emigrated from China to the USA. Her first novel, *The Joy Luck Club*, was published in 1989.

Walker, Alice 1944–
American novelist, short story writer and poet. Born in Eatonton, Georgia, she was the youngest of eight children of a poor sharecropper family. Her first novel, *The Third Life of Grange Copeland*, was published in 1970 (UK 1985); other novels include *The Color Purple*, which won the 1983 Pulitzer Price for Fiction and was subsequently filmed, and *In the Temple of My Familiar* (1989). Short story collections include *In Love and Trouble* (1984) and *You Can't Keep a Good Woman Down* (1982). Her poetry collections *Revolutionary Petunias* (1973; UK 1988) and *Horses Make a Landscape Look More Beautiful* (1985). She now lives in San Francisco.

Weldon, Fay 1933–
Novelist, dramatist and television screenwriter. Born in Worcester, she grew up in New Zealand and studied at the University of St Andrews. She worked as an advertising copywriter for some time. Her novels include *Praxis* (1978), *Puffball* (1980), *The Life and Loves of a She-Devil* (1983), which was adapted for television and also turned into a feature film, *The President's Child* (1982) and *The Hearts and Lives of Men* (1987).

Winterson, Jeanette 1959–
Novelist. Born in Lancashire, she was educated at the University of Oxford. Her first novel, *Oranges Are Not the*

Biographical Notes

Only Fruit, won the Whitbread First Novel Award in 1985 and was adapted for television. Other novels include *The Passion* (1987) and *Sexing the Cherry* (1989).

Wharton, Edith 1862–1937
American novelist and short story writer. Born into a wealthy New York family, she was educated privately and travelled widely, eventually settling in France. Her novels include *The House of Mirth* (1905), *Ethan Frome* (1911) and the novella *Age of Innocence* (1920) which won the Pulitzer Prize (making her the first woman to receive this honour). She was appointed a Chevalier of the Legion of Honour in 1916 for her wartime relief work. In addition to a prolific career as a novelist, she wrote eleven collections of short stories, travel books and an autobiography *A Backward Glance* (1934).

Woolf, Virginia 1882–1941
Novelist and essayist. She was educated privately, spending much time in the company of her brother and his Cambridge undergraduate friends. After her father's death in 1904 she moved to 46 Garden Square, Bloomsbury – the house which became a meeting place for the writers, philosophers and painters who came to be known as the Bloomsbury Group. In 1912 she married Leonard Woolf and completed her first novel *The Voyage Out*, although her second nervous breakdown delayed its publication until 1915. In 1917 she and her husband founded the Hogarth Press which published Katherine Mansfield, T.S. Eliot, James Joyce and many of the major innovative writers of the day, as well as Woolf's own work. One of the most original novelists of her time, she was also a literary critic, essayist and journalist of distinction. *A Room Of One's Own* (1929) is a classic of feminism. Her best known critical essays were published in *The Common Reader* anthologies (1925 and 1932). She was also a prolific letter-writer and diarist. Her novels include *Jacob's Room* (1922), *Mrs Dalloway* (1925), *To The Lighthouse* (1927) and *The Waves* (1931). *Between the Acts* (1941) is a highly experimental piece of work. It was shortly after finishing it and when oppressed by the fears experienced in the war that she drowned herself near her home at Rodmell, Sussex.